# BLEEDING ROSE

## KYLA SHINDER

*For all the readers who feel emotions deeply and think that means there's something wrong with them. That's your superpower right there. Don't ever let anyone tell you otherwise.*

*P.S. if you have experienced abuse of any kind from a parent, what happened to you was not your fault. Every child deserves a shield in the battle of life.*

# TRIGGER WARNINGS

Depression, child abuse (discussed but not shown on page), self-harm (not shown on page), discussion of suicidal ideation, violence, sexual content

ACADEMIC SECTOR
FACUL
DELMART
VARMIN SECTOR
CERE
THE CANTERNA THICKET

HOUSING
HERCULEA SECTOR
ACADEMY
METEORO SECTOR
SECTOR

# PRONUNCIATION GUIDE

**Names of characters:**
**Noella Rose:** No-el-la Roh-z
**Kellen Kilic:** Kel-en Kil-i-ch
**Laya Ates:** Lay-uh At-ee-z
**Jarion Ates:** Jare-ee-on At-ee-z
**Josefyn Yilanci:** Joe-sah-Feen Yil-an-see
**Akio Takeshi:** A-key-o Tah-ke-sh-ee
**Miya Kilic:** My-ah Kil-i-ch
**Ciaran Ates:** Key-are-an At-ee-z
**Rylee Hart:** Ry-lee Heart
**Mason Hart:** May-son Heart
**Oliviana Bryan:** Olive-ee-ana Bry-uhn
**Daniel Madix:** Dan-Yuhl Mad-ix
**Eyal Drury:** Eh-yal Drew-ur-ee
**Valerie Dyer:** Val-er-ee Die-er
**Aros Cavalian:** Aa-r-oh-s Ka-val-ee-an
**Edar Lantarian:** Eh-dar Lan-tar-ee-an
**Bryara Cavalian:** Bree-ara Ka-val-ee-an
**Jamila Finely:** Jah-mill-la Fin-eh-lee
**Connor Paight:** Con-nor Pie-t

**Names of places:**
**Cavale:** Kah-va-le
**Delmarth:** Del-mar-th
**Avatia:** Ah-va-tee-ah
**Yorkdill:** York-dill
**Varminia:** Var-me-nee-ah
**Sleka:** S-leh-k-ah
**Lavalden:** Lah-val-den

**Types of Primordials and key terms**
**Primordial:** Pry-mor-dee-al
**Herculea:** Her-q-lee-ah
**Meteoro:** Me-tee-or-o
**Cerebri:** Ser-ee-bri
**Varmin:** V-ah-r-min
**Cavalisha:** Kah-val-ee-sha

CHAPTER I

# ELLA

WHEN THE PENDANT around Ella's neck vibrated, she shut her eyes to mentally prepare herself to face whatever ~~creature~~ *student* was having a panic attack today. Yesterday, she'd narrowly avoided the claws of a Varmin when the student in crisis shifted into their gryphon form and nearly scratched out her eyes. The escape from injury then was one of sheer luck, not due to any assistance she got from her coworkers. Two staff members had stood idly in the corner and watched the ordeal transpire, offering her no support during or after the fact. The day before last, she almost lost her head when a Cerebri student sent a pair of scissors soaring through the air with nothing but their mind in the middle of a rage spiral, having lost control of their faculties due to a fellow student accidentally bumping into them. It finally stopped feeling like a shock every time she had a Primordial's fang or power held up to her throat and started becoming something she expected, something she could plan for. Ella breathed deeply to calm her heart rate, then dragged herself away from her desk and headed to the elevator.

She had now spent a full month as Delmarth Academy's sole school counselor and the only human in the entire realm of Cavale. The fact that Ella could say she was beginning to adjust to this environment of teetering on the brink of death every time she interacted with a student was both emboldening and depressing.

She passed Fiona Davis in the hall and raised a hand to wave at the Meteoro instructor. Fiona squinted her eyes at Ella, then lifted her hand and spread out her fingers, sending a tumultuous gale of wind into Ella's stomach that thrust her against the wall. The flurry of wind made it difficult for Ella's lungs to expand and contract properly, a gasp tumbling off her tongue as her knees smashed into the ground.

"Dare to look at me again, and I'll force-feed the wind down your throat, earthborn," Fiona hissed, stealing the elevator Ella was about to call for herself. Ella watched the doors close, finally regaining the ability to engulf a breath that didn't burn her throat or chest once the wind-bender was gone. She pulled her body forward, using the wall to reassemble herself in a standing position. She knew the drill. *Get back on your feet quickly and don't let anyone see you sweat.*

This wasn't the first time in the last month she'd been thrown into a wall by a teacher or student.

Ella pressed the call button for the elevator and rubbed the side of her neck where it throbbed, impacted by her collision with the wall. The pendant resting between her collarbones began aggressively shaking against her clavicle. Whoever was calling her down was growing impatient for her to appear.

"I'm going as fast as I possibly can," she muttered to herself, pinching the bridge of her nose to delay a migraine from sundering her forehead. She noticed that the stone pendant was now tinted purple, which meant a Varmin student was in need. If it was a Cerebri student, it would be silver. For Meteoro, the stone would turn green, and for Herculea, red. She wished the enchanted stone could alert her as to which teacher was calling her down, but she knew if she asked Headmistress Dyer for any alterations in the amulet, she'd be met with no sympathy and in the end, no result.

In the short time she'd spent in Cavale, it was clear that the Primordials as a species valued physical strength over feeling, achievement over preserving one's mental well-being. Emotional needs weren't just secondary to all else—they were considered nuisances that weren't allowed to have life breathed into them and needed to be extinguished in order to make way for more power. This is exactly why Headmistress Dyer decided to seek out a human to hire as Delmarth's school counselor, a position that never existed before Ella. Ella hadn't been told exactly what happened last year, but the little tidbit of information she had been given was that a Meteoro student, a fire-bender, burned themselves intentionally and passed away, which caused an *understandable* surge of panic for the parents and called into question the school's ability to care for their students. Delmarth would have swept the incident under the rug and found a way to placate the parents' concerns if the incident hadn't alerted the Cavalian Gods themselves. The Gods sent an envoy on their behalf to Delmarth to force the school administration to actually deal with the matter.

Headmistress Dyer determined that the answer to this dilemma was to create a position within the school dedicated to the protection of student well-being, in an academic, physical, and social-emotional sense. Since the way of the Primordials goes against that concept, she decided to cross dimensions into the Earthly Plane and hire a human school counselor to take on the burden: Noella Rose.

Ella had no idea, when she was first hired to work with Delmarth's entire student body, from Kindergarten through twelfth grade, that she would be forced to move to a completely different *dimension* and spend every day fighting for her life amongst the students and faculty. She signed the contract under false pretenses, at the time believing she was agreeing to work for a normal boarding school in upstate New York. She'd even toured what she thought was the campus with Headmistress Dyer prior to accepting the offer.

Unbeknownst to her then, the campus she visited and faculty members she met that day weren't real. They were just a brilliantly crafted illusion, created by one of their Cerebri instructors, to get her to sign the contract, which binded her—*literally* binded her, through magic she didn't understand—to a year in Cavale.

*A year.*

Really, ten months. She just had to make it to June. This had become her mantra, the reminder that this hell she'd stumbled into wasn't permanent. She only needed to endure getting her face nearly melted off or being thrown into walls for nine more months, and then, she'd be back home in her small apartment in New York and could pretend her time in Cavale was but a ghastly nightmare.

Finally, the elevator doors opened once more. She hurried inside and stabbed her finger into the lobby button, leaning her shoulder against the wall. When the elevator closed, she found a wilting, watery reflection of herself displayed on the metal doors. Her long, honey-hued waves spilled down her chest in a chaotic rivulet of blonde tresses, crimped from the braid they'd spent the night woven into. The maroon shade of her turtleneck complimented the golden hue of her thick mane and brought a semblance of warmth to her cheeks, to a face that otherwise appeared sunken and bruised from both physical and emotional exhaustion. The grey of her irises seemed to seep out past her eyes and saturate the entirety of her flesh, causing all her features to droop. She used her fingers to smooth the skin under her eyes, pulling the sagging flesh up so she could fix her expression, so she could paint a mirage of composure over her facial features to blend in with the Primordials, a mask to protect against further attack. A mask that hadn't worked once in the last four weeks, but she was determined to maintain it, determined to make that mask melt into her face and become real.

When the elevator finally landed at the lobby, Ella froze between the now-open doors.

Kellen Kilic, head of the Varmin department, stood perched against the glass wall across the way, arms twisted over his chest. Something about Kellen's face made Ella's intestines squeeze together, revolting against one another to create a sensation internally that resembled chafing. The Varmin instructor was so disgustingly beautiful, in a rugged, harsh way that felt like an invasion on the eyes. He must have come from outside; beads of rainwater dripped down his neck from his short, curly black hair and gleaned on his sheared beard, just a ghost of scruff limning the edges of his chiseled jawline. The water smeared darker spots on his white button-down shirt, which clung to his burly physique, hugging every tantalizingly defined muscle like the cloth was thanking his figure for allowing it the honor of being close to him. His burnished, ebony brown flesh blended into scales up the column of his neck on either side, a hint of the dragon that lived within him.

Ella forced her gaze up from his chest to his eyes, to the emerald green irises that were frowning at her.

"*You* called me?" she spluttered, not attempting to conceal her surprise. While none of her Primordial coworkers were adjusting well to the fact that Headmistress Dyer hired a human from the Earthly Plane, Kellen Kilic won the prize as the most putrid in an inconceivably rotten bunch. The worst part of Ella's days consisted of some interaction with Kellen, whether that be from having insults flung at her back in passing, or worse, the kind that ended with her crashing into a wall. "Did you actually need me for something, or did you just call me down here to fuck with me?"

Kellen offered no response. The dragon-shifter just kept glaring at her as though he was willing his gaze to turn incendiary, so he could heave that fire across her body and corrode her existence with just a flick of his eyes.

"If you don't tell me in the next five seconds why you called me down here, I'm going back upstairs," she snarled, her patience thinning.

"Follow me," was all he eventually said, shoving through the exit doors. Ella huffed, then traipsed after him.

Delmarth Academy's campus was split into six sections: the Cerebri sector, the Meteoro sector, the Herculea sector, the Varmin sector, the academic sector, and the faculty housing. They'd placed Ella's office in one of the academic sector buildings, which bordered the Varmin quarter. It was no longer raining, but Ella could feel the threat of a storm still echo through the ether. The dry air fell back as if sucked up in a vacuum, leaving the atmosphere warm and laced in a weak calm.

She swallowed a breath that smelled like petrichor and tasted sweet, then asked Kellen, "Who's the student?"

"Connor Paight," he answered, his response clipped.

"What happened? Is he okay—"

"You hear that? That grating noise?" Ella whipped her head around, searching for whatever sound he was referring to.

"No? What noise?"

"The sound of your voice. It's insufferable." He pressed his index finger to his lips, shushing her.

Ella scowled. "You're not nearly as clever as you think you are, Kilic."

"Lucky for me, your opinion means nothing, earthborn."

She wished the insult could just roll off her back. With the students and most of the faculty, she didn't take anything they said too personally, but with Kellen, she found his treatment of her harder to shake off.

The Varmin sector came into view. The carefully trimmed grass delineating the grounds of the academic sector blended out into an unpaved road, the asphalt torn apart by claw marks and footprints of various sizes and shapes, belonging to diverse ~~creatures~~ Varmin species. She needed to stop referring to them in her head as creatures—that phrasing was considered offensive in Cavale, and if anyone heard her call a Varmin a *creature* rather than a shifter, they'd skin her alive and happily endure a life-sentence in the Cavalian Gods' version of hell, Terminus. Ella followed Kellen past the steel buildings, comprised of imperishable metal to ensure that no species of Varmin could obliterate the configuration from the outside or inside. They headed towards the Canterna Thicket, a deciduous forest decorated with outgrown roots, wildflowers, and fallen leaves that crunched beneath Ella's loafers.

Finally, Kellen came to a halt.

"You want to know why I called for you?" he asked, then pointed up at the sky. "See for yourself."

Ella's eyes followed the path of his finger.

A mammoth dragon cleaved through the clouds, tossing its head back and bellowing a cry that sounded strangled and pained. It continued writhing in agony, each thrash of its ginormous body lacerating a cloud in the process, sending the mist scattering into the trees. The dragon's neck swung to the side, its back arching before plumes of fire came seething out of its mouth. Flames tangled with the clouds to create a maelstrom of sparks and vapor, amalgamating with that same aggrieved scream.

"Is that Connor?!" Ella's heart dropped into her stomach. Her head spun back to Kellen. "Is he hurt? What's happening to him?"

Strangely, Kellen smirked at her.

"He's having a panic attack," Kellen replied, the cadence of his voice reminiscent of saccharine wine, the kind you get drunk off of too easily because its taste convinces you it isn't alcoholic.

Ella's jaw fell open. "Are you shitting me?" He shook his head.

She peeked back over at Connor, observing with horror as the dragon vomited fire over the trees.

"Go comfort him," Kellen ordered, waving his hand in Connor's direction.

"You're joking." He cocked his head.

"It's your job, Ms. Rose."

"If I go over there, he will eat me alive!"

"One can only hope." Ella drew her head back and scoffed.

"You're disgusting," she roared. "Have fun dealing with this yourself. I'm heading back to my office." Kellen seized her forearm before she completed any steps towards the academic sector.

"Stop," he insisted, giving her wrist a squeeze that she felt reverberate down to her toes, which curled up in her shoes to end the tingle. "Look, in spite of my poorly timed *joke*, I did call you for your help. If I go over there, I'm just going to make it worse, and I really would like to help him."

Ella raised her eyes to examine his face, searching for any indications that the dragon-shifter couldn't be trusted. She considered herself to be a good judge of character, hence how she ended up in this role and why she remained cautious around every new person she met in Cavale. When she read in Kellen's eyes his sincere desire to support his student, visible in the way the emerald hue softened in a moment of unbridled vulnerability, the kind she rarely saw in Cavale, she knew she could trust him enough to stay.

"What happens if I go over there and he mistakes me for food?"

The corner of Kellen's mouth tugged upward. "Then I'll tell everyone you died a gallant death, earthborn."

"I fucking hate you," she hissed.

"Trust me, sweetheart, the feeling is absolutely mutual. And make no mistake, if I wasn't desperate and didn't think there was a minute chance you could help him, I never would've called you."

"Oh, I believe it." Ella shook his hand off her, then began heading over to Connor. Kellen grabbed her arm again, stopping her from stalking off. "What now?!" she yelled, and damn, it felt good to yell.

"How do you plan to get up there to talk to him, smartass?" She opened her mouth, then closed it.

"Not sure. I'm open to suggestions."

A gargantuan shadow the size and bulk of Connor bathed them in darkness as Connor began his descent towards the forest grounds, the shadow twitching along with his every spasm. Ella stumbled backward and toppled right into Kellen, who'd taken the time to fold his arms across his chest and straighten his posture to the highest height, a signal that he would be of no help to her.

"If you caused this, you should leave," she warned him.

"If I *caused* this?" he repeated through a snarl.

"If you're responsible for upsetting Connor, then seeing your face right now is only going to make him more agitated. You may know this world better than I do, but panic attacks are my realm of expertise. I know what I'm doing. *Back. Up.*" She shoved him away by placing her hand on his chest.

He was so stunned by her daring to touch him that he actually staggered back.

Connor alit sloppily on the ground, hurtling into a tree and landing on his left leg, worrying Ella that he might've hurt himself in his dismount. He threw himself back with a deafening roar, the vigor of his movement slashing through the tree behind him, prompting an assemblage of shredded, charred yellow leaves to volley down around them from the interlocking branches.

"Connor?" Ella called out to him as she approached. "Connor, it's Ms. Rose. The school counselor."

Anguished, ruby eyes swung to her within Connor's thorny, narrow skull. She halted a moment in case the sight of her distressed him further, following his cues through the eye contact they now shared. She took a tentative step forward, testing him, watching for any indication that she shouldn't approach.

When she found none, she splayed her fingers out on his wing, angular in shape with bone structures clearly visible through the thin layer of skin, each ending in curved, yet blunt tips. In case those were poisonous, she'd steer clear, but she otherwise felt no fear being so close to him. Her instinct was to caress him, as though he were her dog, Freya, first with her palm, then with the backs of her fingers, flipping her hand back and forth so he could experience different textures on his wing.

"Connor, I want you to breathe for me, okay? Inhale for four seconds, then exhale for six. Can you do that for me?"

Connor's red eyes fluttered shut, his features creasing and contorting in a way that suggested he was experiencing pain somewhere in his body before she heard the dragon suck in a large gulp of air. She counted the seconds out loud for him. At the number four, Connor choked out a raucous exhale that broadcasted like a discordant clap of thunder, a flurry of sparks slipping off his tongue along with the gasp. Thankfully, the sparks weren't nearly as potent as the fire he retched in the sky, so they didn't singe anything in the forest. Connor continued his paced breathing, all while Ella kept stroking his wing, counting the seconds aloud for him. Finally, Ella felt the wing under her hand begin to shrink, Connor's dragon form melting back beneath his Varmin flesh.

When the massive dragon dispersed and Connor had successfully shifted from his Varmin form back into his human form, she found a thirteen-year-old boy curled up in a ball in the soil.

"Hey there, buddy," she cooed, dropping to her knees in the soil to join him. She paid no attention to the fact he was naked, focusing on his face. "You want to tell me what happened that upset you so much?"

"I…I…I have a test next…and I…and I…I'm…I don't want to do it," he stammered, his whole body convulsing. "Please, don't make me do it. Don't make me, Ms. Rose."

"You're feeling nervous about your test?" He nodded. "What class is the test in?"

"History of the Gods with Mr. Kilic. He's so mean." *Can't argue with that,* she thought to herself.

"What have you done in the past to prepare for a test?" His tiny brows pulled together in thought.

"I…I study."

"Did you study for this test?"

"I did." His voice sounded so small compared to the earsplitting roar he released in dragon form. "I'm just…I'm scared."

"I hear you, buddy. Tests are scary, but unfortunately, sometimes we have to do scary things."

"What…what if I fail? I can't fail, Ms. Rose. I can't fail." Her heart melted in her chest at his eyes watering.

"Have you ever failed a test before?"

"No. But what if I fail this one?"

"What will you do if that happens?" The blue of his irises transformed into red, the pupil narrowing into the slit of a dragon's eye. Before he fully shifted back into a dragon, she said, "Connor, breathe with me. Inhale for four, exhale for six. Okay?" Connor gulped down a mouthful of oxygen, trapping it in his chest for four seconds, then exhaled for six. When she was once more gazing into his human-appearing eyes, she asked, "Do you get nervous before all your tests, or is it just this one in particular?"

"All tests," he answered, twisting his fingers in the soil to avoid looking at her.

"You've managed to take all those other tests despite feeling nervous. What did you do then to calm yourself down?"

"I…I don't know." Connor hugged his knees to his chest, dropping his chin between his legs.

"What would help you right now?"

"Not having to take the test?" A twinkle of humor played in his eyes. Ella smiled at him.

"Sorry, bud, but I can't promise that. What's something I *can* do that would help you?" He shrugged his little shoulders.

"Do…do you have anything that I could…squeeze?"

"Absolutely!" Ella exclaimed. Nothing thrilled her more than a tangible solution. "Like a stress ball?"

"I don't know what that is." Connor frowned.

"That's okay. I have one in my office. Why don't you head to class…maybe grab some clothes from your locker first…and I'll bring the stress ball to you so you have it when you take your test. Would that help?"

Connor nodded. "Will I be allowed to hold it during the test?"

"Of course you can. I'll tell Mr. Kilic so he doesn't take it away from you."

"You promise you'll bring it to me?"

"I promise." Connor's shoulders unwound, his body relaxing. "Would it help if you and I started meeting once a week to talk about your anxiety? They can be short check-ins. I just want you to know that you have support here."

"Yeah…I'd like that." Tears pricked her eyes. This was the first student who agreed to begin counseling with her and was receptive to her help, the first time she felt like she'd actually been able to do her job the way she was trained to. Connor flashed a tiny smile. "Thanks, Ms. Rose."

"Of course. Go on to class. I'll meet you there in ten minutes." Ella offered Connor her hand, yanking him to his feet.

Connor rushed right past Kellen on his way out of the forest, keeping his eyes down on his bare feet.

When Connor cleared the trees, Kellen marched over to Ella. "What did you say to him?" he snapped.

"What, no thank you?" He continued glaring at her. "I'm going to get Connor a stress ball. He wants to hold it during his test."

"He can't," Kellen declined.

"Why the hell not?"

"If I let him have something to hold during the test, then everyone will want to hold something."

"You can't just let him have it under the table to hold? Is it really that big of a deal?"

"Do you want to see a classroom of thirteen-year-old Primordials be told they *can't* do something that someone else is doing? Cause if that happens, I'm calling *you*." Ella rolled her eyes.

"Fine. If that happens, then call me, but unless you want Connor to shift back into a dragon and spit fire all over your classroom, I'm getting him a stress ball, and you're going to let him hold it during his test."

Kellen trailed his eyes across her face like her features were an equation that didn't make sense.

"Tell me everything Connor said to you," he ordered.

"I can't tell you that," she refused. "Our sessions are confidential."

"That wasn't a session. I called you down here to speak to him."

"Connor asked for us to begin counseling together. I will not disclose what we spoke about." Kellen took three large steps towards her, only stopping when his shadow gobbled her whole.

"Your little human rules don't apply here, Ms. Rose. Tell me what he said."

"*NO.* I won't." Ella tipped her chin up. "You'll have to pry it from my brain with your little powers. Oh, wait! You can't! Because killing a human is *against the law,* unless you want to spend an eternity in Terminus. Yeah, that's right. I read the laws." Steam came out of Kellen's nose.

"I fucking hate you," he growled.

"Trust me, sweetheart," she mocked in a low voice to impersonate him. "The feeling is absolutely mutual."

Ella spun around and sauntered back towards the academic sector, her blonde hair slapping his chest when she turned. She knew she'd pay for that later, but right now, she felt pretty fucking good about herself.

## CHAPTER 2
# KELLEN

KELLEN SETTLED into the swivel chair behind his desk, stacking his feet on top of the table, and announced, "You may begin the exam," resting the back of his head against his clasped hands.

He watched with faint amusement as the fifteen Primordials in his class read the first question on the exam and collectively dropped their jaws when they realized he didn't play around. He knew at least half the class hadn't read a single chapter he'd assigned since the beginning of the year, apparent in their lack of participation and incorrect answers on their homework assignments. Kellen liked the sound of his own voice, but not when their unreadiness and absence of respect forced him to lecture for forty-five minutes about myths he'd read a thousand times before and truthfully couldn't care less about. This provoked him to pull a fast one on the little miscreants—he gave them *one day's* notice of an exam covering the first ten chapters in *Chronicles of the Cavalian Gods*.

Was that slightly callous of him? He had no fucks to give. That would teach them to slack off in his class.

*Why did I agree to teach History of the Gods?* he thought to himself at least twice a day. He hadn't volunteered for it. His contract only obligated him to run the Varmin department, a title he relished where he got to reap the benefits of power over his colleagues and essentially meant he was responsible for discipline, which was his specialty. The parts of this job he enjoyed the most came from working individually with the Varmin, particularly the dragon-shifters, and teaching them how to shift between their various forms while controlling the unique features that came along with their breed. Teaching History of the Gods offered him nothing but a piercing headache.

Everyone had been shocked when Kellen Kilic—top of his class at Delmarth Academy, which meant he had his pick of the litter in terms of whatever job he wanted—chose teaching to be his vocation after graduation. He'd been offered a position within the King of the Gods's personal cadre as a serjeant, fighting alongside the Cavalian army against the empire of Lantari in a war that had existed for thousands of years, one Kellen had spent the majority of his formative years dreaming of participating in. In the end, Kellen turned the offer down to attend Nosrerry University, majoring in education. He knew being trussed to a classroom, molding the minds of the youth, wasn't in keeping with his personality and skill level. He'd chosen teaching for two vital reasons.

The first: it allowed him to be in close proximity to his twin younger siblings when he began teaching at twenty-one and they started Kindergarten at Delmarth the same year. The second?

It pissed his mother off to no fucking end, the Kilic name tarnished by Kellen refusing the King of the Gods's offer of employment. That brought him more pleasure than being a legion-naire in Aros Cavalian's brigade—even if sometimes he caught himself fantasizing about what could have been, had he prioritized his talent over petty revenge. This happened most frequently while he taught History of the Gods.

Kellen swept his eyes over the classroom, verifying that every-one's focus was latched onto their own pages. He caught Anastasia Branwen pretending to yank her ginger ringlets into a ponytail, but was really stretching to the right of her to see over Elora Dagny's shoulder to read off her paper.

"Branwen," he barked, the entire class flinching at the vehe-mence of his growl. "To the front of the room, now." Anastasia exchanged a panicked look with one of her friends, then reluctantly released the tendrils still gathered between her fingers and slid out of her chair to stand in front of Kellen's desk.

"Yes, Mr. Kilic?"

"Grab your test and give it back to me."

"G-Give it back to you?" she stuttered, her lashes smacking her eyebrows from the fast pace at which they fluttered.

"Don't make me repeat myself." Anastasia recoiled.

She sidled back to her desk, her shoulders caved in as she glided the test across her desk, then handed the paper to Kellen. He paused a moment for dramatic effect, feeding his own twisted pleasure, before he crushed the paper in his fist, right in her face. Anastasia stumbled back with a gasp.

"You will stand at my desk for the remainder of the forty-five minutes," he ordered, giving her back the crumpled ball of paper. "As a warning for the rest of the class of what happens when you attempt to cheat in my class."

"Sir—"

"You will receive a zero on this exam. Now stand against the wall, facing the room." Tears slipped down her cheeks in unrestrained streams. Kellen schooled his face into a mask of disdain, even if there was a small part of his scarred heart that chipped off at her humiliation. There was no room for that sensitivity in Cavale. She'd be eaten alive if she cried like this in front of any other instructor, a fact she wouldn't appreciate right now, but one day, looking back at this moment and how she got off with nothing but verbal condemnation, she'd understand. The sooner she learned that, the better off she'd be. "What did I say about making me repeat myself? *Now,* Branwen."

Anastasia flattened herself against the wall, tucking her chin between her collarbones and dropping her eyes to the floor. Threads of tears dangled down from her eyelashes and splattered dark spots on her white sneakers. The entire class's focus stayed fixed on her, over where she stood trembling.

"Did I say you could look away from your tests?" he snapped, thirteen pairs of eyes returning to their papers. His gaze arrested over Connor Paight, who had yet to take a look at the test, his eyes remaining pasted to the door.

He was waiting for *her.*

*Noella Rose.* Just her name polluting Kellen's thoughts made the inside of his mouth taste disgusting.

He'd fought Headmistress Dyer tooth and nail when she announced to the faculty that she was hiring a *human* from the Earthly Plane to be their school counselor. Yes, Kellen agreed that what happened last year with Tifani Robinson was horrible. Yes, he agreed that the school needed to find some way to address the situation rather than just conciliate the parents with a memorial in her honor and then have everyone return to their regularly scheduled lives as usual immediately after. He could even concede that having someone at the school to defend the mental well-being of the students was a decent idea, though he didn't entirely understand how practical that would be, given the extreme nature of Primordials and their devotion to triumph at any cost. Hiring someone from the Earthly Plane, however, was a disaster waiting to strike, and that's exactly what Noella Rose had been—a disaster cunningly disguised in a beautiful package, designed to trick you into forgetting that it's poisonous.

Humans didn't belong in Cavale. They were too fragile, too weak-minded, too riddled with useless, pathetic emotions. Kellen possessed no tolerance for anyone who couldn't match his wit…but that's what bothered him most about Noella. She *did* match him. Every interaction they'd had thus far, he tried to push her to the point of eruption, just to prove to himself that she didn't have the stomach to survive here, to shatter the illusion of what she worked tirelessly to present to the world.

Every single time, against all odds, she equaled that challenge and never rewarded him with the submission he craved. Instead of pushing *her,* it just pushed *him*—deeper into the spiral he'd plummeted into since the day she arrived in Cavale.

The classroom door cracked open before Noella Rose's head slipped through the unoccupied space. A golden halo of long blonde hair dripped down the wall behind her like a torrent of spilled honey. Her eyes, a fusion derived from the sea and sky, rims of cerulean surrounding the pupil before bleeding into a storm cloud of grey, drifted over the room in search of Connor, eventually locating him. She passed him what looked like a red ball, mouthing something to him that Kellen couldn't place, but prompted a blush to bloom across the young boy's cheeks as he thanked her quietly and turned to begin his test. She was about to pull her head from the room before her eyes cinched with Kellen's.

The dragon within him stirred, scraping against the interior of his flesh, beseeching to rip through the human casing and be released from confinement. His teeth ached with the desire to lengthen into fangs. Fire singed the walls of his throat. He almost lunged across the desk to grab his leather briefcase and stuff the strap down his throat to keep the fire from leaking out onto the table.

Her gaze flickered between Kellen and the silent puddle Anastasia had turned into.

"What's going on in here?" Noella asked, the entire class shifting their heads to look back at her.

"Eyes on your papers," Kellen growled, the children dipping their gazes. He leaned back in his chair and jerked his head in Anastasia's direction. "I caught her attempting to cheat on the test, so I'm making an example of her."

"An *example?*" Noella repeated with quiet horror. "By making her stand in front of the class?"

"For the next forty minutes, yes." *Try and fight me, little earthborn. Let me prove you don't belong here.*

Her freckles danced like constellations across the bridge of her nose as it wrinkled at Kellen.

"What's your name, love?" Noella entreated Anastasia, completely disregarding Kellen's existence. Rageful heat barraged his cheeks and rushed up to the tips of his ears, plumes of steam fanning from his flared nostrils, the dragon in him clawing at his ribcage in desperation to be unfettered.

"A-A-Anastasia," Anastasia spluttered, hiccupping on a sob.

"Anastasia, come with me so we can talk," Noella offered her as a lifeline, beckoning to the young Primordial.

Noella Rose could call him the nastiest names and Kellen wouldn't bat an eye, but pretend as though he wasn't there, as if he hadn't given a directive, and address the students in that sickeningly

sweet, soothing voice of hers to try to embarrass *him,* in *his* classroom, in *his* school?

No way. Not going to happen.

Kellen threw his leg out to block Anastasia from stepping
forward, should she feel tempted to do so.

"She stays right here," he hissed, narrowing a glower drenched
in hatred over Noella. "Your presence isn't needed here, Ms. Rose.
You may leave now."

"I'm inclined to disagree," she fired back, sticking her chin out
mulishly, "since you appear to think it's acceptable to use humiliation as a tactic in teaching students the difference between right and
wrong."

"You have a problem with the way we teach at Delmarth? Go
run home to the Earthly Plane. I'm sure they'd welcome you back
there with open arms, none of which you will receive here."

*Come on. Back down, Ms. Rose. You can't beat me.*

"You have a problem with me being here, Kilic?" Her lips wilted
in a scornful frown, running her index finger down her cheek like
she was tracing a tear track. "Go cry a river to someone who
cares."

Should they have been arguing like this in front of the students?
No.

But decorum was so far from Kellen's mind, lost to the screen of
red blearing his vision, the shackles around his dragon growing
feebler and looser by the minute. He hadn't struggled to contain his
Varmin form like this since he was in middle school, when his
dragon first emerged. He could taste the flames threatening to shoot
up his throat and gush out his mouth. She needed to leave, not just
because she was a pain in his fucking ass, but because if she didn't,
he was afraid he would devour this room in wildfire and burn the
whole building, possibly the entire Varmin sector, to the ground.

Noella seemed to come to her senses, realizing that their back
and forth wasn't an appropriate exhibition for the students to bear
witness to. She *finally* backed off, though Kellen would have
preferred her to keep driving the quarrel forward until she forfeited
a genuine surrender to him.

"Anastasia?" Noella called, the thirteen-year-old lifting her chin to look at Noella. "Come find me after class."

Noella's grey eyes veered to Kellen, and in her thoughts, with the Cerebri abilities he'd inherited from his father—frankly the only gift he'd ever given Kellen that was worth keeping—Kellen heard her tell herself, *let the pissing contest go, Ella, and leave. He's not worth your time or energy.*

*I'm going to make you wish you were dead, Noella Rose,* he thought to himself as she spitefully half-closed the door, leaving it part-way open to force him to get out of his chair and shut it himself. *And I'm going to enjoy every second of it.*

# CHAPTER 3
# ELLA

Ella spent half the morning working on lesson plans for the elementary school teachers that she knew would just be tossed in the trash and waiting for her amulet to vibrate with a message from Kellen that she was needed in his class. When she watched time crawl forward and the forty-five minute period concluded, not having heard about any issues with Connor and the stress ball, she let her lips curl up in a smug smile, not that anyone was there in her office to witness it.

Soon after, she received a message through the amulet that her assistance was required in the Herculea sector.

Where the Varmin quarter embraced industrial, impenetrable steel as their primary foundation, the Herculea sector possessed a more antiquated design to the configuration of the buildings, fashioned from gleaming white limestone, displaying little to no abrasions on the walls or asphalt, as opposed to the claw marks marring the Varmin grounds. The heavens began shedding tears on her journey across campus, mourning the world below, drowning the earth in vigorous streaks of rain. By the time Ella arrived at Herculea's senior building, the strands of her blonde hair not protected by her jacket hood resembled tangled seaweed, both in appearance and texture.

She elbowed the door open, slipping inside. The number of the classroom she was being called to remained scrawled on top of her pendant. Luckily for Ella, this was a room she'd already been to in the last month, so finding it didn't take as long as when she was summoned somewhere new, which was next to impossible when no one ever helped or directed her. The moment she stepped into the training room, she knew why she'd been called.

Oken Bennet had Skylar Wolfe pinned against the wall, her frail, lanky legs kicking at the air. Her fingers stretched towards his fist in vain, but the strength-wielder wouldn't loosen his grip around her, crushing her slender windpipe. Ella's eyes swung to the two Herculea instructors standing three feet away, silently begging the only adults in the room with enough strength to actually intervene and do something.

The instructors just waved their hands toward the students, leaving this as her problem once again.

Ella knew why they really called her here, the primary reason any instructor at Delmarth summoned her to their classes. It had nothing to do with them believing she was capable of helping these kids. They hoped Oken would turn his wrath on her and kill her. The Primordial instructors wanted her gone so badly that they'd let their own students finish her off themselves, even if it sentenced them to a life in Terminus for killing a human. *Children,* fucking *children,* being used as pawns, being thought of as collateral damage in their mission to exterminate her, because her erasure from their world mattered so much more than these children's lives. Ella couldn't understand how their hatred for her, someone they didn't even know, outweighed the need to protect their students, how anyone could be so selfish.

"Oken," she shouted, marching across the room. Oken and Ella were well acquainted at this point—this was the third time this week she'd been summoned to Herculea because Oken wielded his strength against another student. "Oken, let Skye go right now." The seventeen-year-old boy was so lost within his rage spiral that he couldn't even hear her. She'd been taught in grad school to never approach within hand-and-foot striking distance a student exhibiting aggression, but if she didn't do *something*, the last of Skye's oxygen was going to shrivel up.

So, she made a split-second decision to grab Oken's wrist. It had been the wrong decision.

Oken released Skye, but only to grip Ella's forearm in exchange, mincing her bone into crumbled shards beneath her skin. Ella sunk her teeth into her bottom lip, entombing a scream inside her throat. She watched from her peripheral vision Skye crumble to the ground, spluttering wheezes, her trembling fingers embracing her inflamed throat. *Now* the two instructors rushed over to console Skye, the female instructor using her healing abilities to nurse away the imprint of Oken's fingers from Skye's neck.

"Oken," Ella gasped, his name sounding guttural through the tears she worked to subdue. She curled her fingers around his forearm with her free hand, then pulled him towards her so she could wrap her arms around him, gripping him with all her strength, which compared to the strength-wielder was next to nothing. She kept her head close to his body, enclosing them in a protective bubble of interwoven limbs. At first, he writhed in her hold, his grip on her arm fortifying to the point where she feared he would sever her hand from her wrist if he squeezed any harder.

"Let me go!" he screamed, swinging his knee forward. Ella dodged the strike before his knee made contact with her stomach.

She pleaded, "Oken, remember what we talked about yesterday? I want you to count to ten for me. Okay?"

She squeezed him harder, unsure if he could even feel it.

Oken dropped his forehead onto her shoulder, smearing perspire onto her turtleneck. Every frenzied breath he spewed bathed her whole body in flaming hot air, but no matter how strangulating the closeness was, no matter the excruciating pain in her arm that nearly clouted her to her knees, she wouldn't separate herself until she knew he'd regulated himself into a calmer state.

Though he didn't listen to her, he'd already begun tiring himself out. His breaths started to slow, less rapid and frantic, his body unwinding from the clenched shell she'd been hugging moments ago.

Finally, his fingers slipped off her.

"Good," she whispered, taking her arm off him. "Good. That's good, Oken." A single tear escaped her restraint, trickling down her cheek. She quickly smudged it away before any of the instructors or students could see. She stole a peek down at her broken arm, verifying that it was still there, that he hadn't succeeded in disuniting her hand from her wrist. He hadn't, though the limb looked mangled in a way that made Ella's stomach twist into a knot and the inside of her mouth taste like bile. Somehow, her voice stayed tender, none of her pain seeping through. "Now, can you tell me what happened?"

"We were forming a line to do boulder presses, and Skye cut me. My last name starts with B, so I'm always first in line. I told her to move, and she wouldn't, so I grabbed her." No emotion appeared to fuel his words. He spoke in a detached manner that Ella sensed was a farce, his anger prominent in the heat emanating off him in waves. The goal she'd set for herself with Oken was to help him make the connection between his actions and his thoughts, then to his emotions, so he could use that self-awareness to stop himself from attacking others and find healthier ways of managing his anger.

"What were you thinking at the time?" Oken grimaced.

"What was I *thinking?*" he repeated, his cheeks stained red from a violent flush. "That I needed her to move so I could be in the front! She wasn't supposed to be there. We always go in alphabetical order. She should've been in the back of the line."

"It bothered you that she was breaking the protocol," Ella extrapolated. Oken's lashes fluttered.

"Yeah. I guess." Oken's eyes dropped down to his sneakers.

"Who do you think was affected by what just happened?" Oken raised his head to look at her.

"Um…Skye?"

"In what way do you think Skye was affected?" His brows pulled together.

"Um…because I hurt her." His shoulders sank, the weight of that truth pressing down over him.

"Who else do you think was affected?" Oken cocked his head.

"Who *else?* I don't know."

"What about your classmates? How do you think they were affected by what just happened?"

"Um…I guess they could've been scared?" *Good,* Ella thought to herself. *Good. He's starting to get it.*

"Who else was affected by what happened?"

"I have no fucking idea, Ms. Rose." Ella pointed at her arm.

"What about me?" Oken's eyes fell, absorbing the damage he'd done to her arm for the first time.

"Oh shit," he stammered, scratching the back of his neck.

"Yeah," she mumbled, cradling her broken arm against her chest. "Oh shit." Oken's brown eyes glazed over with tears. "What do you think you need to do to make things right with Skye and your classmates? Or with me?"

"Tell them…tell them I'm sorry."

"Good. That's good, Oken." *I'm going to pass out from the pain if I don't get this treated.* "Why don't you go do that?"

Oken loitered there a moment, then said, "I'm sorry, Ms. Rose."

"You're forgiven, Oken." Her vision grew more hazy by the second, bleared with black dots, like smears of ink spilled over her eyesight. "Now go apologize to your class. We'll talk about this more later."

As Oken scampered off to apologize to Skye, Ella gathered the pendant around her neck in her fist and squeezed her eyes shut, calling out to Headmistress Dyer with the last shred of strength she possessed.

*Heal me,* she begged the Headmistress.

It took a few seconds before filaments of silver shot out from the pendant, snaking down her shoulder to envelop her injured forearm, dousing the shattered bone in a chilled cloud that sent a shiver down her spine. When the smoke cleared and the silver strings retreated into the pendant, her bone had returned to its former glory, no discomfort echoing in her limbs. The amount of times a day she requested to be healed should have alerted the Headmistress that something needed to change here.

Now that her arm was mended, she marched over to the two

Herculea instructors, snapping, "What the hell were you thinking, letting him strangle her like that! Why didn't you do anything?"

"We did something," the female hissed, narrowing her gold eyes in a scowl. "We called *you.*"

"And what if he'd killed her? What would you have done then?"

"We wouldn't have let it get that far," the male insisted, squaring his shoulders so his shadow loomed over her.

"Well, next time this happens, call me *after* you separate the students." The male instructor's hand came barreling towards Ella's face before it crashed into her cheek, the blow pulsating down to her knees, which buckled from the force. She lost control of her balance and tumbled to the floor, landing roughly on her wrist, the one that had *just* been healed by Headmistress Dyer. She was fairly certain he'd fractured her cheekbone, from the agony that lanced through her jaw when she tried to move it.

"You have no grounds to bark orders at us, earthborn." The female spat—actually *spat*—on Ella. "We don't take commands from human scum." And just like that, the two instructors left her to address their class.

Ella cupped the side of her face, still stinging from the assault. She angled her head down so no one could see her bottom lip quivering, so no one could see her eyes brim over with tears, deluging down her cheeks in unchecked stripes.

*Get on your fucking feet, Ella,* she snarled in her head, yanking herself up.

She somehow found the strength to lift one foot after the other, against all odds making it to the door. Safe inside the hallway, she sluiced the tears from her cheeks with her fingers, then squeezed the pendant to contact Headmistress Dyer. Once her cheek and wrist were healed, she began making her way back to the academic sector. As she passed through the lobby, she glanced up at the clock.

"How is it only noon?!" she groaned.

Just as she entered her office, Ella's stomach hissed at her as a reminder that she'd forgotten to eat breakfast. She scanned her desk for any food she happened to have left there, coming up empty handed. It must have slipped her mind this morning to grab something from the teacher's lounge for lunch, as she usually did before the school day officially started, when no one else occupied these halls, so she wouldn't have to interact with a single soul. This meant she'd need to enter the teacher's lounge.

During lunchtime.

When nearly the entire faculty—apart from the unlucky teachers scheduled to surveil the students in the cafeteria—would be gathered in the lounge. A scream threatened to rip Ella's throat apart.

*You've survived worse,* she coached herself on her way there. *Just run in there, grab a sandwich or something small, and run out. Don't linger longer than necessary. Remember. You've survived worse.*

Relief swamped her when she found only a small cluster of teachers congregated in the teacher's lounge, huddled together in a jumble of whispers. The period ended at twelve-twenty, so she had three minutes to grab her lunch and escape before more teachers arrived. Someone within the group, the second her foot cleared over the threshold, began inhaling the air in an overdramatized manner, overstating the act of inhaling so the sound was unavoidable from all corners of the room.

"You smell that?" the male instructor, one Ella hadn't yet been introduced to, asked his fellow coworkers. "It smells…*nasty.* Disgusting. Like a *mutt.* Like…an earthborn." Three pairs of eyes found their way to Ella.

*Fuck. Here we go again.*

"I just want to get some lunch," she tried to reason as the three instructors began advancing towards her, their progression intentionally slow and glaringly calculated. "I'll grab something and go, I promise."

"Not so fast," Oliviana Bryan, a Meteoro instructor with earth-bending abilities, crooned. She twisted her fingers, inked in tattoos that resembled vines, mirroring the vines that came germinating from the floorboards now and wrapped themselves around Ella's ankles, snaring her in a trap.

The male instructor, who Ella quickly learned was a Herculea speed-wielder when he blinked over to her in less than a second, seized her throat in his fist and forced her back against the wall.

*Again? Really? What is it with Primordials and walls?* "You're not wanted here," he growled in her face.

"Trust me, I know," she answered, which prompted the instructor's grip around her throat to tauten, his fingernails digging into her trachea. A month ago, she would have feared for her life, but now armed with the knowledge that none of them would dare kill her since they'd be sentenced to Terminus if they did, she no longer allowed fear to soil her decisions. They just wanted to scare her, and a bully trying to intimidate her with a venomous bark but no bite was something she could tolerate. "If you just let me down so I can grab some food, I won't be in your hair anymore."

"Except you *will,* because your presence will continue to stain my world."

"An unfortunate circumstance that neither one of us can control." The male instructor gasped, as if he hadn't considered that Ella wouldn't just lay here and take this treatment without any pushback.

"You hear that, Oliviana?" he laughed with malice. "The mutt thinks she's tough."

"The human thinks she's got teeth? How cute," Oliviana taunted. The earth-bender swung her wine-red hair over her shoulder, then leaned in to bring her lips right up to Ella's ear. "Where you've got teeth, little earthborn, I've got *fangs.*"

She nipped at Ella's earlobe. Ella's head jerked back on instinct, but the Herculea instructor tunneled his fingers into her jaw, refusing to allow her an inch of space to separate herself from Oliviana.

"Please," she heard herself implore, but didn't even feel her lips form the word.

"You want food, princess?" Daniel Madix, head of the Cerebri department, sneered from behind them. He raised his hand, steering his index finger towards the fridge, and directed his abilities forward, using his psychokinesis to open the fridge door and pluck what looked like a smoothie from the shelf. "Eat *this*, mutt."

He sent it hurdling towards Ella.

Her eyes squeezed shut so none of the frozen drink decided to make a home in her eye sockets. The pulverized ice and mashed fruit crashed into Ella's face and exploded between her brows, drenching her cheeks in freezing liquid. The concoction, as it slipped down her chin, nestled between the locks of her hair, coloring the blonde strands purple. Finally, the Herculea instructor released her throat, letting her slide down the wall and disintegrate on the floor like a ragged sheet of paper.

The three instructors abandoned her there in her pond, their cruel laughter ricocheting behind them.

Ella's tongue darted out to lick the smoothie on her cheek. *Raspberry and blueberry. My favorite.*

*At least it wasn't horse shit like last week,* she thought to herself before scrambling to her feet. She sprinted across the lounge, grabbed the last smoothie from off the shelf in the fridge, and bolted back to her office.

**CHAPTER 4**

# ELLA

*To do list:*
*• Check in first thing tomorrow with Connor Paight about how his test went, then discuss a time that works for him to begin counseling*
*○ Need to get access to his schedule to know where he'll be first period*
*○ REMINDER: ask Headmistress Dyer for the twentieth time for the password to the database so I can start accessing transcripts and schedules on my own*
*• Do a classroom observation of Oken Bennet—I want to see what his triggers are*
*○ Get his schedule to find a time to meet for counseling*
*○ Get him to come—even if he says no, GET HIM TO COME*
*○ Would love to have a conversation with his parents to see if his anger is an issue at home, but I need the password to the database to access his emergency contact info*
*• Check in with Skylar Wolfe and see if she needs a session to process what happened with Oken*
*• Check in with Anastasia Branwen—she never came to find me after class*
*• See if I can take a self-defense class in Cavale? Maybe off campus, since no one here will want to teach me*
*○ Find out if there are buses or trains that could take me off campus—let's be real, no one is driving me anywhere*

At three o'clock on the dot, Ella closed her brown leather notebook, tucking it safely inside her desk drawer, and grabbed her coat and briefcase, locking her office behind her and heading for the faculty housing.

Ella's apartment was located on the first floor, possibly the only kindness she'd been granted in Cavale—well, she would have considered it a benevolent gesture on Headmistress Dyer's part, if her apartment wasn't directly across the hall from Kellen Kilic. She tiptoed through the hallway to her apartment complex, careful not to release any loud noises that would alert Kellen, if he was in his apartment, that she was there, before she unlocked her door and rushed inside, bolting it shut behind her.

"Freya?" Ella called out. "I'm home!"

Entering the loft, she heard the tiny pitter-patters of her five-year-old Cavachon puppy. Ella stumbled upon Freya when she was twenty-one-years-old, living in Essex at the time during her semester of study abroad. Though Ella couldn't compute the numbers for sure, she was fairly certain Freya had only been three months when she found her, separated from her mother and a sopping, trembling mess in the rain.

From the day they met until now, the two of them had never spent a single day apart. In Ella's interview to work at Delmarth, her one condition for moving onto their campus was that she had to be allowed to bring her dog. If she didn't have Freya with her, Ella wasn't sure she'd have made it through that initial month in Cavale.

Freya came barreling around the corner and leapt into Ella's arms.

"Hi, my love!" Ella cooed, kissing the crown of her head. Freya was apricot colored, her fur a light brown with some sprinkles of white scattered throughout, her ears a tanner color at the tips. Her breed was a mix of a Caviler King Charles Spaniel and a Bichon, with more attributes of a Caviler, but a smile that was copied and pasted off a Bichon. She had big, expressive black eyes that were always filled with so much adoration and joy. Ella's favorite little quirk about Freya was the shape of her back—she sort of had a hump, and when she walked, it looked like she was wiggling, or what Ella called *spider walking*.

She licked all over Ella's face, her typical greeting, but quickly froze, pulling her head back.

"You're tasting the smoothie I had thrown in my face," Ella told her. Freya wrinkled her nose in a manner that communicated she didn't like the taste, then squirmed in Ella's arms, her way of signaling it was time to be put down. "Alright, alright. There you go." Ella set Freya on her feet.

In the five years they'd spent attached at the hip, Ella learned to converse and read Freya better than she'd ever known how to read a single human. Freya peeked up, asking with her eyes *where's my dinner?*

"You think I didn't bring you anything from the cafeteria? That I'd randomly decide to starve you *now?*"

Freya narrowed her eyes, flicking them to her bowl. She wasn't in the mood to banter, it seemed.

Ella frowned. "You're no fun."

Ella retrieved, from the plastic bag she'd lugged home in her briefcase, two meat patties she swiped from a burger when she snuck inside the kitchen around one o'clock, as she'd done every day since she finished the bag of dry food she'd packed in her suitcase. Ella had spent Freya's first five years refusing to give her any human food, but with no way for her to order any dog food from the Earthly Plane, she had to get creative in order to feed her girl. Ella placed the patties in a bowl on the floor, then poured water into Freya's metal dish. The moment Ella was no longer hovering over her dinner, Freya scampered across the carpet and shoved her face inside the meat.

Ella plopped down on their grey couch, unfurling her legs out on the wooden coffee table, and observed as Freya devoured her dinner, her thin tail slapping against the floorboard. Ella loved Freya's coiling tail—when it whipped from side to side, it looked like a windshield wiper.

When she finished eating, her chin damp from the water she'd lapped up, she flashed Ella a wet grin and vaulted onto the couch, resting her chin on Ella's chest. When she found Freya alone in that deserted alley in Essex, only five pounds at the time, she'd crawled into Ella's arms and rested her chin on Ella's sternum, peeking up at her with guileless eyes that could thaw even the emptiest, coldest of souls. Five years later, she'd grown to be fourteen pounds of pure sweetness and underrated feistiness—and she still loved lying on top of Ella this way over any other.

On the arm of the couch, Ella's phone began vibrating with an incoming call from her big sister.

"Fuck," she hissed under her breath, then reluctantly answered the call, bringing her phone to her ear. "Rylee?"

"Thank fuck. When you didn't answer right away, I thought you might be in the bottom of a ditch."

Ella choked out a bitter laugh. "That's not entirely implausible anymore."

"Don't joke like that. The thought of someone hurting you makes me absolutely murderous. The fact that I have to exist in New York knowing these things are happening to you in a different fucking *dimension* where I can't come give those jackasses a piece of my mind makes my skin feel so itchy around my bones that I wish I could crawl out of it." Ella's face split apart from a smile at her sister's hyperbole. "Are you okay, though? How did today go? Any better than yesterday?"

Headmistress Dyer never told Ella she couldn't share Cavale's existence with anyone from the Earthly Plane, so she'd never even attempted to hide anything from Rylee, not that she ever would have been able to successfully. Rylee, in her special, inimitable way, knew the second she heard Ella's voice that first day that something horrible had transpired. She believed her immediately, even without any proof.

Ella rested the back of her head against the wall.

"I had my arm broken once by a student, my cheekbone broken by a teacher, and got thrown into a wall twice. They really love to throw me into walls. Oh, and I also had a smoothie thrown in my face. *But* in some good news, I finally got a student to agree to begin counseling with me! Not the strength-wielder, yet. He's the one who broke my arm, but I do think I'm beginning to get through to him, which is progress. The kid who agreed to counseling is a middle school aged Varmin. It was the first time since I've been here that I finally got to do my actual job. I can't tell you how good that felt, Ry."

"Oh, Ella," Rylee sighed, her voice ensnared by a distressed sob.

"Stop it," Ella begged, squeezing her eyes shut so they weren't tempted to succumb to any tears. "It doesn't help me to sit here and listen to you cry about what's happening to me. I need these phone calls to be light."

"I'm sorry. I can't help it." Rylee sniffled on the other end, then pulled herself together. "Was it that same teacher who's been giving you a hard time?"

"They all give me a hard time. Kilic, you mean? I saw him twice today, with the Varmin kid. He didn't do anything too bad."

"Who broke your cheekbone?"

"A Herculea instructor."

"Remind me again what Herculea means?" Ella smiled.

"The Herculeans are the Primordials that possess strength-based powers, or abilities like super speed or flying or healing injury. They're known as wielders."

"But they don't turn into creatures?"

"No. Those are the Varmin. They're shifters. We're not supposed to say creatures. It's apparently offensive."

"Oh. Sorry," Rylee whispered, which made Ella chuckle. "Which are the ones that can do things with their minds?"

"The Cerebri. They manipulate matter, which is why they're called manipulators."

"And what's the last one?"

"Meteoro. Benders of the elements, fire, water, earth and wind." Rylee whistled through her teeth.

"I'd find it all fascinating if they weren't such assholes to my little sister."

"Yeah. Me too." Ella lay her cheek inside her palm, leaning her elbow on the arm of the couch. "I'll get through the next nine months. *We'll* get through it. We've survived worse, Ry."

"Stop saying that, Noella. Just because we've been through shit in the past doesn't excuse what's happening to you in the present. I know you use that phrasing to help yourself cope, but don't do that shit with me. What's happening to you is awful, and it's okay to sit here with me right now and admit that."

*I can't,* Ella wanted to weep, wanted to dissolve into tears, dissolve inside the comfort of her phone so she could find a way to travel back to her sister. She knew if she let herself surrender to the sob that now permanently dwelt within her throat, waiting for her to breathe life into it, she'd never be able to stop crying, never be able to walk out that door and face this world she'd been trapped in.

"Yes. It's awful. I'm miserable. Does it make you feel better to hear me say that?"

"Of course not. I just don't want you to bottle up what you're feeling. You're the queen of telling others to feel their emotions, to not let their feelings become something they fear. Don't let the way of the Primordials trick you into thinking the way you exist is wrong. Just because you've been through shit before doesn't mean you deserve to be going through shit now. Just because a feeling is familiar doesn't make it comfortable." Ella stuffed her fist inside her mouth to imprison a scream, biting down on her fingers.

When she felt certain it wouldn't leak out, she coughed up an artificial laugh for her sister's benefit.

"Maybe you should be the school counselor."

"They couldn't pay me all the money in the world to do that job." This time, Ella's laugh was genuine.

"You're right. Stick to being an attorney. You're good at that."

"I appreciate the bode of confidence, dear sister." Ella's chest warmed.

"How's Mason?" she asked, crushed by an unbearable longing to be with her sister and brother-in-law, to have *people* again, to have anything other than crushing silence be her only suitable companion.

"Mason is good. He misses you. We both do."

"I miss you too, Ry." *Every second of every single day, I miss you.* "I have to go. I need to walk Freya."

"Okay, my honey. Please, call me if you need anything. Anything at all. I love you so much."

"I love you more." She hung up the phone, dashing away a tear.

As far as Ella was concerned, Rylee raised her. Ella's father left them when she was five. What few memories she possessed of her mother now—who she referred to as Annalise when asked about her because the title of mom, in her heart, belonged to Rylee—were splintered and unclear. The older she got, the more those memories floated together and blurred, like the plumes of smoke frothing from the end of her mother's cigarette buds. All she was left with was the residue of feeling attached to the memories, the pain, the loneliness, the anguish. Sometimes Ella fantasized about what it would be like to still have her around, but it would only last for a moment before her brain intervened to permeate her eyes with images from when she was still alive.

That's all it took for the fantasy to dissolve as quickly as it formed.

Ella turned to look at Freya, who hadn't moved off her chest. "Want to go for a walk?" she asked in a falsetto, high-pitched voice, feigning excitement for the sake of her dog. Freya catapulted herself off Ella's lap and ran right to the door.

Ella and Freya's walks remained localized to the academic sector after hours, since any other quarter on campus wasn't safe. They walked in a comfortable silence, Freya plastered to her side, her leash twisted around Ella's hand. The pavement, in all its stunning decrepitude, looked as if someone had taken a sledgehammer to it, diligently hitting every cement rectangle with enough force to make a network of cracks, many of them now colonized by weeds. Ella dropped the leash, letting Freya go off on her own. She leapt through the trees that lined the path, emerging with a stick in her mouth.

"Really?" Ella shut her eyes and huffed out a sigh.

She saw the rest of her evening play out. She'd throw the branch, and it would leave brown flecks on her hands in its wake. She'd end up wiping them off on her slacks, which would result in needing to do laundry earlier than planned because she wouldn't be able to stand knowing her favorite pair of work pants were out of commission for the rest of the week. Depending on where it landed, Freya would return with dirt all over her fur and twigs tangled in her hair, and they'd end the night with Ella having to bathe her and both of them being miserable.

While Ella consciously knew all of this, she could never refuse Freya when she flashed her that beseeching, ingenuous big-eyed look.

Ella surrendered and curled her fingers around the other side of the stick that wasn't between Freya's teeth. When her arm wheeled back, Freya prematurely sprinted forward, having thought Ella already threw it. Ella decided to amuse herself and paused, holding still until Freya stopped several feet away from her, looking back with confusion. Only then did Ella hurl the stick.

While small for a cavachon, Freya had power in those tiny legs. Her eyes sparkled as she soared down the path to retrieve what was pitched, though she wasn't quite fast enough to catch it midair. After she collected the stick, Freya galloped back to where Ella stood, dropping the branch at her feet.

"Oh no," Ella refused with a shake of her head. "Once was enough. Do you want to end up in another bath tonight?"

Freya's big black eyes lifted to the heavens, as if she was considering whether one more game of fetch was worth a third bath this week. She decided it was and pushed the stick closer to Ella with her paw.

"Alright. As long as you know what this means." She wound her arm back, tossing the branch again.

Thank all the Gods in existence for dogs.

Once they returned home from their walk, Ella bathed Freya in the bathtub, then stripped off her soiled turtleneck and tossed it in the laundry bin, along with her slacks, bra, and socks. As she dressed in her bathing suit and hunted through the drawers for a dress to throw on, Freya found her way into her crate, situating herself in a half-moon shape in the bed, resting her cheek along the metal bars.

"Mommy's going to go, but she'll be home later," she told Freya, as she always did when she left her alone. "I love you." She blew

Freya three kisses, adding one for good luck, and grabbed her keys.

———

Ella yanked open the door to Delmarth's Sports Center and scuttled down the stairs to the pool, a towel and goggles in toe. The bathing suit she put on had been provided by the school, a navy blue one-piece with a tiny silver crown emblazoned on the left breast. The black dress she picked was made from supple cotton that trickled down to her ankles, appropriate for an educator to be wearing around students, should she run into any in the pool. Ella took a moment to absorb her surroundings as the most gargantuan pool she'd ever laid eyes upon unfurled before her, surrounded by polished panes of glass. The smudges of purple and pink and blue composing the sunset reflected across the surface of the water in a bleary mirror image. Dappled light spilled down onto the rivulets in clean lines through the open sunroof, kaleidoscopic wonder drenching the room in variegated color. Ella was the only person in there, so no one bore witness to the way her jaw tumbled open and nearly dislocated in awe at the grandeur of the landscape.

There was no lifeguard currently in the room, nor was there a patrolling station where one might sit. This wasn't really a surprise after observing the way of the Primordials over the last several weeks and how little they valued safety above skill. It was just further reinforcement of their urgent need for someone to be the spokesperson for mental well-being over physical capability.

Which would have to be her, because no one else here seemed up for the task.

Ella kicked off her shoes, laying her sandals and towel down on one of the cushioned lounge chairs positioned beside the pool before removing her dress. She secured her goggles over her eyes, then made her way down the steps into the pool. The water was slightly chilled, but she'd swam in pools with much colder tempera-tures and didn't mind it. She dunked her head underwater, admiring the interior design through her goggles. The walls were smothered in blue mosaics, each square glossed over in a varnish that made them glimmer when the light refracted off the tiles. The pool itself was deeper than its external appearance suggested, starting at four feet at the shallow end and finishing off at twenty feet at the deep end. She gripped the edge of the pool, positioning her feet in place against the wall, then pushed off and swept her arms out to propel herself forward, engaging her core in the process.

She kept her head above water through her breaststroke, which she knew wasn't the correct way to do it, but it made her feel safer despite the fact there was no one else in the room besides her. Ella made it to the deep end, flattening herself against the wall so she could pull her upper body out of the water, her legs remaining submerged below. She stacked her arms on top of one another on the floor, resting her cheek over the pile of limbs. In Cavale, the air tasted immaculate and uncontaminated, the wind bestowing fresh kisses onto her damp cheeks, cool beads of water saturating her flesh. The tendrils of her hair that were still underwater were doused in the late evening sun filtering down through the sunroof, emphasizing the amber undertones in the honey-golden strands. She lingered only a moment more by the edge of the pool before repositioning her feet so they were splayed on the wall and leaping out to swim back toward the shallow end.

Ten minutes passed of deliciously swimming laps back and forth without any interruption before the doors to the pool swung open. From her peripheral vision, Ella tracked where a small band of men headed over to the lounge chairs, plopping down on the one directly next to where her clothes and towel were. At first, she thought they were students and didn't think much of them. It wasn't until she finished her lap, when she could really concentrate on the group, that she realized one of the men was Kellen Kilic, along with two other department heads, Daniel Madix of the Cerebri department, and Lukas Foster of the Herculea department.

Daniel and Lukas were exchanging friendly barbs, sharing raucous laughter, but Kellen's emerald eyes were settled firmly on Ella, his index finger sliding back and forth over his bottom lip as he stared at her.

38

She glanced over at the clock. She'd wanted to complete her full forty minutes, but perhaps it would be wiser of her to leave now, before engaging in whatever back and forth she could see brewing in Kellen's intense gaze.

*No, Ella.*

If she left now, she would be handing him the power on a silver platter, tossing in her dignity as an appetizer to the main course of her conviction. Rylee would call her a coward for even *considering* leaving. She'd tell Ella to grow a pair and stop allowing the opinion of others to spoil her joy. Her swim time was integral to her sanity, and she wasn't about to let three assholes disturb her peace after enduring an excruciating four weeks where so much of her autonomy had been robbed from her.

Ella dove beneath the water, moving her chest, core, hips, and legs in a wave like a caterpillar to glide smoother along the current. Somehow, Kellen's vehement scrutiny burned even underwater.

"Looking good, Ms. Rose!" Lukas called out just as she broke through the surface after finishing her lap. She combed her hair back with her fingers, shoving the dripping tendrils behind her ears and out of her face, a deliberate move to show the jibing idiots she wasn't hiding from them.

"Would be better if you were wearing nothing at all," Daniel chimed in.

"Yeah, take it off, earthborn!" Lukas whooped, Daniel whistling through his teeth. "Show us your birthday suit!"

Kellen said absolutely nothing, not in support of his friends, or in defense of Ella. He just kept glaring at the back of her head like he was hoping the ferocity of his scowl would demolish her existence, wipe her off the face of Cavale, this human stain on his untarnished Primordial world.

"Let's see how fast the guppy can swim," she heard Kellen tell his friends before she dipped down beneath the water to push up off the wall, doing her best to ignore the frisson of fear that coursed down her spine at the threat. The sound of crackling behind her had Ella whirling around.

The mosaic tiles began crumbling, putrefying into dust, before a massive fish resembling a whale, but possessed talons instead of fins and razor-sharp yellow teeth leaking out from the sides of its mouth, crashed through the wall and lunged for her. Ella's scream was comprised of soundless bubbles, rising to the shore in their clustered way. She didn't have time to process what was happening as she kicked her feet faster and tore her way through the waves, terrified tears gathering in the lens of her goggles, blurring her vision, chlorine water toppling down her throat, clogging her esophagus.

She broke through the surface, spluttering a petrified wheeze and a mouthful of pool water before wheeling her arms forward to try, somehow, to outswim this monstrosity. The creature nipped at her ankles, and the tip of a fang, glazed in a disconcerting green slime that she would bet her life on being lethal, nearly grazed her calf. She yanked her knees towards her chest just in time before the behemoth could sink its teeth into her leg, her arms screaming in agony at being trundled at a speed they weren't accustomed to moving at.

Daniel and Lukas were seemingly cheering for her from the sidelines, but her attention wasn't on them—her peripheral focus landed on Kellen, whose irises were now eclipsed by a screen of silver as he watched the scene before him, brows furrowed and jaw clenched taut in concentration.

The creature bit a chunk out of the air, missing its target of Ella's arm when she swerved to the right. Her goggles were filled to the brim with tears, making the path ahead unfocused and watery, but through the fog, she could map out where the wall was just a few feet away, even if the image was muddled and the waves encasing them grew more rampant. She stretched out her hand, her fingers razing through the water with urgency to reach the end of the pool. She felt something slippery coil itself around her wrist, becoming as cinched as a manacle once it was fully surrounding her forearm. Then, she was tugged backward away from the safety of the wall, right into the clutches of the beast. Ella cried out, writhing in vain to try and rip her arm out of whatever strange, seaweed-esque fin had snaked out of the behemoth and was currently strangulating her wrist.

Ella swung her other hand forward, clawing at the webbed shackle digging into her wrist while continuing to kick her feet so she stayed afloat. She grated at her own flesh in the process, drawing red welts down her forearm. The creature staggered back, bellowing a strangled cry in surprise at her actions, thrashing its cumbersome body and angering the eddying water more. Ella continued to abrade it with her nails until the fin finally slipped off her. She sprung forward the moment she was free and charged for the shallow end, all the oxygen trapped in her chest torrenting out through her relieved gasp.

The second her hand touched the wall, everything calmed. The purling waves fell flat, and the roaring wind hushed. Ella spun around, searching the water for the creature, but it was gone. The wall on the opposing side of the pool, where the creature had emerged from, was now completely intact.

Daniel and Lukas headed for the exit now that the show was over, her dress and towel departing with them. They left discussing what they would eat for dinner, as if Ella hadn't almost *died* and they hadn't just sat there bearing witness to it. Kellen remained, standing over Ella at the end of the pool.

"I'm impressed," he praised, folding his burly arms. "I thought you were a guppy, but you may turn out to be a shark."

"WHAT THE HELL WAS THAT?!" she shrieked at the top of her lungs, ripping her goggles off.

Kellen sunk down, taking his sweet time lowering to the ground, so his face was leveled with hers.

Then, he spat, "You don't belong here, Rose. I'm not going to let your kind invade our world and infect our children with your skewed way of living. I'd rather finish my days in Terminus than work side by side with a disgusting earthborn who didn't earn her place in Cavale."

"You're forgetting the fact that I wasn't given a choice here," she snarled, somehow subduing the emergent tears long enough to speak her piece. "I thought I was coming to work at a normal school on the Earthly Plane. I didn't ask to enter your world, Kilic. Before four weeks ago, I didn't even know it existed. I don't want to be here just as much as you don't want me here. I was tricked into signing a contract that binds me to this place for the rest of the school year, so unfortunately for both of us, it looks like we'll just have to suck it up." Kellen shook his head in refusal.

"You're not lasting the school year," he avowed, then turned on his heel and stormed out of the room.

Ella sunk back in the water, her restraint crumbling as she loosed a scream that didn't even sound human, wrenching at the tendrils of her hair so hard that she felt the pain echo through her scalp. She'd been banking on the hope that the Primordial instructors wouldn't dare try to murder her if it meant they spent an eternity in Terminus, but if some of them would gladly take the punishment, what protection did she have then? What Rylee said earlier rang through her ears.

*Just because you've been through shit before doesn't mean you deserve to be going through shit now.*

*Fuck this,* she finally decided, climbing out of the pool. *Fuck this. I'm done.*

Ella stomped all the way to Headmistress Dyer's office, her wrath keeping her warm despite not having her dress or towel, and barged in without bothering to announce her presence. The Headmistress was sprawled out on her opulent, red couch, her wiry legs draped across her glass coffee table, smothered in a white blanket. When Ella rushed in, Headmistress Dyer jolted awake from her apparent nap, her glasses tumbling off her nose and crashing to the ground.

"I want to go home. I want to go home. I want to go home!" Ella screamed at the top of her lungs.

"Whoa, whoa!" Headmistress Dyer sprung to her feet, her frizzy mane of untamed brunette curls whipping her cheeks from the hasty movement. Her hands outstretched towards Ella. "What happened?"

"One of your teachers just tried to drown me in the fucking pool!"

A perplexed expression took occupancy of Headmistress Dyer's facial features. "Blaze?"

"No!" Ella cried in horror. "It was Mr. Kilic! How many of your instructors do shit like this?!"

"Just the one," Headmistress Dyer assured. "Those kinds of

ploys are usually Blaze's specialty. Kellen's never done something of this caliber before. You must've done something to piss him off." Ella couldn't believe how cavalier she was being about the fact that one of her staff members tried to *drown* her, or the way she was insinuating Ella was to blame for Kellen sending a sea monster after her.

"If your instructors don't care about being given a life sentence in Terminus for killing me, then what protection do I have here? What guarantees can you give me that I won't be killed?"

"You have that amulet around your neck. I will always heal you when you ask me to."

"And if I'm not in a state where I can even ask you to heal me? What *then?!*" Ella threaded her fingers in her hair and tugged on the strands. The frustration of feeling like she was talking to a brick wall ached through her core. "I can't work here. I can't work in a place where I don't feel safe."

"I think you're being a tad bit dramatic, Noella."

"*Dramatic?*" Ella repeated, sounding out the word slowly in case she misheard, giving Headmistress Dyer a chance to correct her inanity.

"Our teachers pull these kinds of pranks on each other all the time, especially at the start of the fall term. It's tradition. If anything, you should feel flattered that you were included in the custom."

Ella blinked at her, disgusted by how she first called what happened to her a *prank*, and the suggestion she should be grateful for being roped into their twisted idea of diversion, as if that made her one of them.

"Except when your teachers pull these pranks on each other, they have powers that help them combat what's being done to them. So when a Varmin, for example, infiltrates their mind and makes them think a freaking *sea monster* is chasing after them, which by the way, I thought only a Cerebri could do, they have abilities that can make it a fair fight. Right?" At that, Headmistress Dyer's lips knit shut. No argument was raised in opposition. "It's not just this. It's every fucking day I've been here. I've been broken apart and put back together far too many times to count. It has to stop!"

"I'm sorry this has clearly caused you so much distress," Headmistress Dyer offered, changing her tune—a wise decision, since Ella was on the cusp of lunging at her. "I really feel for you, Ella. What can we do to make this better?"

"Let me go home!" she shrieked.

"That's not going to happen. Think of something else I can give you." Ella wracked her brain for an answer.

All that came to mind was, "Diet Coke."

"Diet Coke?" Headmistress Dyer repeated in surprise.

"Since I can't go home, I would like a magic cup that refills itself with Diet Coke every time I finish it. And the Diet Coke never goes flat. And a fridge in my office that will make whatever food I want for me, so I don't have to go into the teacher's lounge again."

"Done," Headmistress Dyer promised. The two stared awkwardly at each other for a moment before Headmistress Dyer added, "Is that all?"

"For now. If I think of anything else, I'll tell you." Ella began her trek to the exit, but halted right in front of the door, spinning around to face Headmistress Dyer. "I'd like to say something else, if I actually have any rights to do so." Headmistress Dyer cocked her head at Ella's boldness but said nothing to prevent her from continuing. "You hired me to do a job, which I've been unable to accomplish since the moment I got here. I have absolutely no creative liberty to form my own curriculum, even though you promised me I would when I agreed to work here. You still haven't given me the password to the main database, so I can't access student transcripts and schedules. Teachers aren't even letting me inside their classrooms, let alone talking to me about their students or allowing me to offer support. They only call for me in the hopes that whatever child who's having a panic attack will kill me themselves. Not to mention, several of your teachers have tried to *kill* me, while the others have been telling the student body not to come see me because I'm human scum. I can't even begin to form relationships with the students I want to counsel because no one trusts me. I've been trained to work with all types of people, no matter their race, ethnicity, cultural background, or, in this case, species. I could actually make a difference here, but no one will let me. And I can't leave here and go work for a school where I'll actually be able to help because you tricked me into signing a magical contract that's bound me to this school for a year. I beg you, Headmistress Dyer. *Please.* Either help me so I can be able to actually do my job, or please, for the love of all the Gods in existence, let me go somewhere where I'll actually be appreciated for what I can do."

And with that, Ella marched out of the office and slammed the door behind her.

## CHAPTER 5

# KELLEN

KELLEN KNEW he was living in a rut of experiencing the same day every day, but he didn't entirely mind when he had a female easing up and down his cock.

Today's willing subject—Oliviana Bryan, the Meteoro instructor. She hovered above him, straddling his torso, her emaciated thighs squeezing his hips in a way that felt like metal pipes were digging into his sides. Wine-red tendrils spilled down her sternum to shroud her bare chest. Though the two of them had been fucking in secret since they returned to Delmarth in September, they were not exclusive—they weren't even friends as far as Kellen was concerned. Kellen didn't subscribe to the concept of friendship, or forming any deep connections with those who didn't share the same blood as him. There were people he'd learned how to tolerate for the sake of enduring the day, but they were considered a means to an end, temporary padding to be shed when it no longer suited him. He didn't think of this as cruel. He never pretended to give more than he could. He possessed a certain amount of spoons to give out, and he reserved all of them for his siblings.

Anyone who knew him, who *really* knew him, understood that. It wasn't his fault if Oliviana pretended to forget.

Oliviana tossed her head back with a strident moan, threading her fingers in her hair, and grinded her pelvis over his cock. Kellen felt nothing. Usually, he experienced at least a miniscule wave of pleasure, but today, he was so distracted, his mind so far away that it wasn't even in the room, that he held no connection to his cock or the current moment. When she spoke to him, he almost didn't hear her.

"Tell me again what you did." She'd asked this three times already.

"I manipulated her mind and sent the illusion of a sea monster after her."

"Was she scared?" Her moans grew more breathy and louder, saturating the floors and walls.

"She looked scared." Yet, she also didn't. Kellen remembered how Noella had scratched the sea monster's tentacle when it wrapped around her wrist, how she'd managed to escape every potential onslaught with the vigor of her speed, a beautiful look of determination swallowing her facial features when she slapped her hand against the wall and sent the illusion scattering. Kellen hadn't stopped the illusion himself—he'd planned to maintain the beast for longer to fuck with her more, but the moment her hand touched the wall, he'd lost control over the illusion, as though his own ability was stripped away from him. He hadn't stopped thinking about that since he left her in the pool.

What was it about Noella Rose that weakened not only his control over his Varmin form, but his ability to sustain an illusion?

"Did she cry?" Oliviana panted, her eyes closed as she pictured Noella, not even paying attention to Kellen.

"Yes, she did."

"Oh, Gods. Yes." *Fuck, this is so unattractive.* The second he gave voice to it in his head, his cock went flaccid. "What just happened?" Oliviana spluttered at the loss of her impending orgasm.

"This is supposed to be fun," he grumbled.

"*I* was having fun," she argued, her thin brows pulling together as her face scrunched up in a scowl.

"Yeah, getting off on hearing how I tortured Ms. Rose. Not the most flattering of looks for you, Oli."

"Don't try and tell me you didn't find pleasure in seeing her like that, because I won't believe you, Kell."

"Fair." He could admit that. He wasn't *that* shitty of a person. "But retelling the story of how I made a woman cry a million times so *you* can orgasm isn't fun for me. It's really fucking irritating."

"Correction. How you made a *human* cry. She doesn't even deserve the title of woman." Kellen's patience for Oliviana's trivial drama had thinned to the point of rupture, reaching its limit. He curled his fingers around her waist and guided her off him, pushing her back so he could rise from the couch.

"I think you should go," he told her, reaching for his sweatpants.

"You're kicking me out? Why?"

"Because I'm finding this conversation to be the antithesis of arousing, so I'd rather just crash for the night than struggle to maintain it."

"Gods, you're such a dick," Oliviana hissed before she gathered her jeans from off the floor.

The two raised their heads when they heard a velvety, feminine voice, muffled by the door.

"Let's do our abridged-long walk tonight. Mommy's had a rough day," Noella Rose announced to an invisible figure in the hallway.

"Is she talking to herself?' Oliviana snickered.

"She's talking to her gremlin," Kellen murmured. Oliviana cocked her head.

"Her *what?*"

"Her dog. She has a dog here with her." Kellen had yet to meet Noella's Earthly Plane pet, but the scent of the creature littered every surface of their apartment complex, the noxious odor tending to curse him with a piercing headache every time he encountered it. When he inhaled that wet, grass-like stench, he wished to trade his heightened sense of smell for any other power in Cavale.

"An Earthly Plane *mutt?*" Oliviana pretended to puke over Kellen's couch. "Why the fuck would Headmistress Dyer permit that *thing* to enter our realm, in addition to the wretched human?"

"Do I look like Headmistress Dyer? Ask her your fucking self." Kellen knew he was being an ass, but he couldn't muster the fucks he needed to give in order to stop his behavior. Oliviana didn't seem to hear, or if she did, she acted as though she didn't. She finally finished buttoning her blouse.

"Same time tomorrow?" she asked with a half-moon smile. Kellen sighed.

This was his biggest issue with Oliviana. He could treat her like shit, he could give her the cold shoulder or throw the cruelest insults at her in the hopes she got the message, but none of it registered.

She always came back. And that was so…boring. Dreadfully boring.

He needed fire. He needed someone who could match his energy, someone who wouldn't take his bullshit, who could put him in his place. If he asked Oliviana to jump, she'd ask how high and where. There was no mystery, no spontaneity. He knew exactly how she would react to any situation. He could recite every conversation they would ever have before they even happened.

But on the other end of that rope lay having nothing but his hand to pleasure himself with while the hum of Noella Rose in the apartment across the hall rung through his ears. That sounded like the epitome of Terminus to him.

So he tossed at her a non-committal, "Sure," then watched her scuttle out the front door, hating himself a tiny bit more.

Kellen fell back onto his couch, then reached into his sweatpants pocket and dialed his brother's number.

"Hey, Kell," Jarion answered after the first ring, his prepubescent voice adorably squeaky on the other end.

"Hey, Jare. Is Laya with you?"

"Duh!" His little sister, Laya, screeched from what sounded like across the room from Jarion.

Kellen's lips settled into an adoring smile, feeling more content in the company of their voices then he'd felt all day. His heart belonged solely to those two twelve-year-olds. There wasn't room for anything or anyone else. Every time he wondered if he'd made the right choice refusing Aros Cavalian's offer of employment, he heard their voices and looked at their sweet faces and was reminded why it mattered for him to be here to help care for his siblings, why he'd chosen correctly.

"Hi, my loves." *My whole fucking world. My favorite people.* "Fill me in on your days."

"Fine," Jarion forced out in a less-than-convincing tone. Kellen crunched his fingers into a fist.

"You've been saying that a lot lately," Kellen noted, not attempting to mask his concern. "You sure you're okay, Jare?"

"Yeah. Everything's fine. Got nothing to report on." *Yeah fucking right. I can smell bullshit a mile away.*

"Have either of you started to feel your Varmin forms emerge?"

At age twelve, on the precipice of puberty, a Varmin's shifter-form began surfacing. The process of a shifter-form developing was an uncomfortable and at times painful experience—especially for the dragon-shifters who taste fire in their throats for the first time—hence the imperative need to master control over their forms once they fully emerged. Kellen had been keeping a close eye on Jarion and Laya over the summer, but hadn't detected any indication that their forms were imminent…apart from the strange change in Jarion's mood the last few weeks, though that could very well be due to typical adolescence and have nothing to do with his dragon.

"I was eating yogurt yesterday and thought I tasted some smoke," Laya told him. Kellen sat up.

"Really? Tell me what it tasted like."

"Disgusting." She gagged into the phone. He heard her hair shake along with her embellished shudder. "I almost vomited."

"Yeah, it doesn't taste good," he validated. "That never gets better."

"So wonderful that I have *that* to look forward to for the rest of my life." Kellen knew she was rolling her eyes without having to look at her.

"Did your throat burn at all, or was it just a hint of the flavor of smoke?"

"No burn. Just a hint. But it's entirely possible the yogurt just didn't taste good. The food at Delmarth *sucks*. I'm always on the brink of hurling here." Kellen couldn't help but laugh at his little sister's hyperbole.

"Jare? Any signs of your dragon?"

"Nope. You don't need to keep asking every five minutes."

Kellen sighed at the brusque response. *Talk to me, Jare. Please.* "Did you see Oliviana tonight?" Jarion enquired, the suggestion of a smile seeping through his voice as he successfully changed the subject off him and dumped it onto Kellen.

"Briefly. Wasn't feeling it, so I called you guys."

"How lovely that we were your second choice," Laya quipped, her giggle drenching his ears.

"You are *never* my second choice, Eulaylia Ates. The two of you are my firsts and my only."

"Yeah, yeah. I know." Laya's voice softened with reverence.

"Kell, you're never feeling Oliviana," Jarion said, bringing the discussion back to Oliviana for some fucking reason. "Why do you keep seeing her? You don't even like her."

"Don't answer that," Laya rushed, adding, "If you answer with some shitty response of only caring about the body in front of you and not the person, I'll be forced to hate you. And I happen to love you quite a bit, so please, don't remind me that you're part of the less superior gender."

"Hey! I'm a man," Jarion reminded her. Kellen heard silence for a moment, so he assumed Laya was looking her brother up and down, stretching the moment out for dramatic effect.

"Exactly," she said after thirty seconds of quiet.

"I should really stop cursing in front of you," Kellen laughed. "What a potty mouth you've developed, Laylie."

"You should not be surprised, dear brother, considering Mother told me your first word was *fuck.*"

The mention of their mother swathed a blanket of uncomfortable silence over the three siblings.

"Have you heard anything from her since the beginning of school?" Jarion asked in a subdued voice.

"Not a word," Kellen answered, only a half-truth. He hadn't heard from her *directly* since she attempted to storm onto campus and remove Jarion and Laya from Delmarth when she learned they'd hired a human on the faculty. Kellen had been alerted by security of her presence on campus, so he hid Jarion and Laya until she was formally removed. He didn't tell his siblings that he regularly checked up on her, once a day flying off campus to stalk her whereabouts in Cavale and verify she was keeping her distance, as court ordered. He didn't tell them that last week, he'd seen her at a lawyer's office, where he overheard her discussing a plan to have Kellen replaced as Jarion and Laya's sole guardian, on the basis of him simply allowing them to be *near* a human.

Which wasn't entirely a useless argument, should a judge take interest and decide to reopen the custody agreement.

He didn't want to worry them—so instead of tell them the truth of what he'd learned, he worked tirelessly to eliminate the real issue: the disgusting human living across the hall from him.

If she was gone, so would the threat of losing his siblings to his mother.

"I don't want either of you to waste any amount of time stressing about her," Kellen told them. "That's time you need to devote to your studies and preparing your bodies for your shifter-forms to emerge. Let me deal with her, alright? That's my job. Your only job is to be twelve-year-olds."

"That's a pretty big job for you to take on," Jarion spat with scorn.

"Well, it's a good thing I'm more than capable of meeting the challenge, little brother," Kellen replied, equaling Jarion's hostile tone.

"We're very lucky to have you," Laya interrupted. Kellen could hear in her voice that she didn't understand Jarion's attitude. "I'm going to run to the restroom. I'll speak to you tomorrow, Kellings."

"I love you, Laylie. I'll speak to you tomorrow." When he heard the door shut behind her, he focused on Jarion. "Jarion, what the fuck is going on with you? You're not acting like yourself."

"Am I not entitled to some privacy, Kellen? You ask me every single fucking day about my dragon. I'm stressed enough as it is about the emergence. I don't need any added pressure from you."

"I don't mean to pressure you, Jare," Kellen insisted, softening his tone. "Please, don't mistake my interest or questions as pressure. I went through exactly what you're about to go through. I know firsthand how tough it can be, and I did it alone. I don't want either of you to endure that. If I can offer any wisdom or advice to make the transition easier, that's all I want. I love you, and I want to help.

52

That's *all*, okay?" Silence swelled between them. Kellen huffed, struggling to put a damper on his own irritation at Jarion's lack of response. "Why didn't you tell me you were stressed about your dragon form emerging?"

"We don't talk about that shit, Kell. I honestly didn't think you would care." Kellen's cheeks boiled, that heat rushing up to consume the tips of his ears. If there was one thing he couldn't tolerate, it was anyone suggesting he didn't care for the twins, when his entire fucking life since he was sixteen was dedicated to them, after the Gods decided to bless him with the two best people ever created for little siblings. Still, he tried not to let that resentment creep into his answer.

"In what universe would I not care about that, Jarion? You must be mistaking me for someone else's brother."

"Because everything comes so fucking easy for you, Kell!" Kellen doubled back at Jarion's strangled cry. "For you and for Laya. Laya gets excited every time her back hurts because she's hoping it means her wings will appear. I don't feel that way. You don't know what it's like for me, living in the shadow of the greatest dragon-shifter of our generation, the Primordial the King of the Gods personally wanted for his cadre. Forgive me for thinking you couldn't handle anything that's not perfect." For the first time in possibly his whole life, Kellen didn't know what to say.

"Jare—"

"I don't want to talk about this anymore." And just like that, the phone line went dead on the other end.

Kellen chucked his phone into the couch cushion, then buried his face in his hands, bellowing a silent scream between his fingers. Kellen wanted to reach inside his phone, pull his brother out, and slap the side of his head, then bury Jarion in his arms and tell him the truth—*nothing* came easily to Kellen. *Nothing* about Kellen could ever be considered perfect. His heart was a mangled, smushed thing, covered in seething rot, touched by the same trauma that drew scrapes along his own siblings' hearts. His ability to feel anything but anger decayed more and more with each passing day.

His brother and sister would never understand the hardships he'd faced, the pain he carried with him from watching the two most important people in his life suffer from horrific abuse at the hands of their parents before he finally intervened and saved them. They would never know how that experience maimed him, and that was how it should be. Kellen didn't want Jarion or Laya to know.

He just wanted them to be happy.

# CHAPTER 6
# ELLA

Ella awoke the next morning to two emails from Headmistress Dyer waiting in her inbox.

The first contained the password to the main database, the subject line *I heard you.* The second was a mass email to the whole student faculty, the subject reading **MANDATORY staff meeting first period in the teacher's lounge.**

When she read the capitalization on the word *mandatory,* she knew this meeting would be about her.

Ella kept herself contained in the corner of the room as faculty members began spilling into the teacher's lounge, populating the blue couches, breezing right past her due to her hood being pulled all the way over her head, concealing her blonde hair. She watched Oliviana and Daniel amble over to the windowsill and not even bat an eye in her direction, the hood protecting her from attracting unwanted attention. The only person in the room not fooled by her cover was Kellen—the moment he stepped over the threshold, his eyes pasted to her in a way that led her to believe he'd found her through her scent amidst the sea of bodies. The only thing she didn't understand was why he seemed to be searching for it, since no other Varmin with similarly heightened senses of smell appeared to be looking to flush her out.

She'd woken up that morning with a new outlook on her current circumstance. She'd worked so hard to create this illusion of resilience, to try to stand up to the Primordials, all while conflating danger with fear. When things turned physical, she allowed her fear to prevent her from upholding that mask. Last night, when she asserted herself with Headmistress Dyer, no fear in the underbelly of her actions, she seemed to have acquired real results. She decided to try something new, to truly meet their opposition with her own unique rendition, to stop trying to fit herself neatly inside the box they wanted to shove her into and instead try to authentically embody what the Primordials claimed strength was to them. If what they valued most in Cavale was one's capability to put themselves first above all else, then why shouldn't she adopt the same mindset?

Beneath the protection of her jacket, she found the confidence to meet Kellen's stare head-on, her defiant smile lost in the shadow of her hood. Ella sensed he could still see it inspite of the obscurity, his top lip curling up in a snarl.

*If I disgust you so much, then look away,* she taunted him with a cock of her head.

The way his lashes fluttered and his head jerked back made her wonder if he'd actually heard her. He sniffed the air, his posture adjusting against the window before she heard his voice fill her ears and mind.

*I count the moments until I can memorize what you look like expelling your last breath, Ms. Rose. I may cum to that image for the rest of my life.*

Ella yanked her hood down, wanting her expression of horror and fury to be unavoidable. Kellen offered her in return two soft dimples celebrating their victory in the center of his cheeks, having provoked Ella to expose herself to the room. Oliviana lunged off the couch she'd been occupying and made a beeline for Ella, the earth-bender's red hair a blur of cherry stained tendrils sullying the ether.

Vines sprouted from the floorboards with Oliviana's impending arrival, diving towards Ella and coiling around her throat. The boughs shunted her so hard into the wall that Ella heard something crack, though she wasn't sure at first if it was her back that cracked or the wall behind her.

"Is that the best you can do?" Ella laughed, though her skull and spine throbbed from the collision. "I'm getting really tired of being thrown into walls. Come up with something original for a change."

"You want my worst, little earthborn? You've got it," Oliviana threatened with a smile outlined by malice.

"Let her go, Ms. Bryan," Headmistress Dyer ordered when she stepped into the room.

The vines slipped off Ella's neck, dropping her to the ground. Oliviana's nostrils flared at Ella before she stomped back to the windowsill, dodging the hands Daniel extended for her and choosing instead to seek comfort in Kellen, leaning her head on his shoulder. Kellen didn't so much as twitch in acknowledgement of her presence—his eyes remained pinned on Ella, his absorption completely consumed by her.

"What a wonderful introduction that was into what this meeting is about," Headmistress Dyer quipped on her quest to the front of the room, stepping behind the podium that faced the entire faculty. "Ms. Rose, why don't you come join me up here?"

*Oh, fuck.*

Ella pulled herself upright, lifting her chin as she strolled to the front of the room to stand at Headmistress Dyer's side. Sixty-three pairs of eyes stalked after her, their hatred humidifying the air. Once Ella flanked her, Headmistress Dyer addressed the room.

"It's been brought to my attention that there have been numerous attacks made against Ms. Rose since the school year commenced, both verbal and physical, resulting in several broken limbs and a near-death experience of almost drowning. That ends today. I understand you may have certain opinions about Ms. Rose being hired, but those opinions should be directed at *me*, not her. You may share your concerns with me, but you will no longer be allowed to take your frustrations out on Ms. Rose. I've spoken with the Cavalian Gods' envoy, and they've decided that anyone who lays a hand on Ms. Rose that she didn't want there will be sentenced to three days in Terminus. If you continue to harass Ms. Rose, more severe punishment will be deemed appropriate, such as a permanent stay in Terminus." Headmistress Dyer's eyes swept over the room to locate Oliviana. "Ms. Bryan, you will be spending

three days in Terminus for strangling Ms. Rose, effective immediately.”

*Holy shit,* Ella almost gasped aloud.

*That* certainly fragmented the room into a frenzy. As a figure
cloaked from head to toe in silver, titanium armor came marching
into the lounge, Oliviana rose to her feet, screeching at the top of
her lungs.

“This is bullshit!” she screamed, just as the envoy reached her
and seized her arm, yanking her towards the door. “You’re
punishing *me* in defense of a *human?* This goes against everything the
Gods stand for!” Her eyes found Ella’s, and right before she was
ripped from the room, she roared, “Mark my words, I will skin you
alive with my bare hands, earthborn!”

Daniel Madix began shouting nonsense, his voice drowned out
by the multitude of faculty making their displeasure known, both
verbally and with unbecoming hand gestures. The only person in
the room who sat there in a chilling silence, no emotion readable on
his face, was Kellen.

*You know what this means, Ms. Rose?* he asked her, his voice inundating her ears above all the shouting.

*What?* she asked back through whatever connection he had with
her mind, her eyes locked with his.

*They’ll hate you more now than they did before. She’s turned the act of
slaughtering you into a game, a challenge of discretion. She’s done you no favors
here, earthborn.* Ella’s stomach churned.

She couldn’t decipher if he meant that to be a warning or a
threat.

“You will do well to remember that Ms. Rose, as a human,
would not have been permitted to enter our lands had the Gods not
sanctioned it themselves,” Headmistress Dyer continued, speaking
over the upheaval. “*They* want her here. So she will stay. Now, I’d
like to give the floor to Ms. Rose so she can explain to you what she
needs from all of you to be able to do her job.” Headmistress Dyer
stepped to the side, turning to Ella and gesticulating to the podium.

*Don’t let them see you sweat,* she thought to herself. From the corner
of her eye, she watched Kellen’s lips twitch in acknowledgement of

58

what he heard in her thoughts. She took Headmistress Dyer's place at the podium.

"Hello, everyone," she greeted the room, keeping her voice steady despite her nerves and the myriad of deadly glowers being shot at her. She flattened her hands on the podium so no one could see them tremble. "I'd like to take this time to clarify what a school counselor actually is. I'm here to provide academic, career, and social-emotional support to all students. I'm not trying to poison the minds of the youth against you or debunk any of the traditions in Cavale. I'm here to be a force of good for the students and ensure that nothing like what happened to Tifani Robinson happens again. While I work to adjust how I approach this job based on the customs of Cavale, I'd like to be extended the same courtesy. That means, if a student wishes to speak with me, please don't make it impossible for them to do so. Please don't position them against me or tell them they can't trust me. If I ask to do a classroom observation of a student, please don't shut me out of your classroom. If I ask for a student's grades, please don't blow me off. I'm not here to make your lives harder. I'm actually here to make your lives *easier*, should you allow me the chance to do so. You don't have to like me, but I implore you to accept that I'm not going anywhere. All I ask is that you respect my place here, so we can find a way to work with one another to help our students and coexist until the end of the school year."

Kellen was right.

All she felt staring back at her was the intensification of their hatred for her, not the reduction of it.

"Thank you, Ms. Rose." Headmistress Dyer nodded, her signal for Ella to step away from the podium. "Meeting adjourned." Before anyone moved, she added, "I hope to see all of you still here by our next staff meeting. I'll be fucking furious if I have to call in more substitutes for anyone being sentenced to Terminus." With that final threat looming in the air, she strutted out of the teacher's lounge.

The minute Headmistress Dyer's tightly wound ringlets disappeared behind the door, Daniel stormed across the room, plumages of rage simmering in his wake, and raised his hand like he was about to smack Ella down. Ella stumbled back, but before his fist made contact with her face, Kellen hurtled in front of her and grabbed Daniel's wrist, wrenching his arm down in a sliding arch to push him away.

"What the fuck, Kell?" Daniel growled, clasping his now dislocated shoulder.

"Did you not hear Dyer?" Kellen snapped. "One wrong move against her, and you'll be tossed into Terminus."

"She's a fucking nark! She got Oliviana banished!"

"Doesn't fucking matter. She's not worth marring your personal record too."

Daniel yanked his fingers through the blonde wisps of hair dripping over his forehead, shoving them off his face. His eyes swung to Ella, his nose wrinkling with disgust before he retreated from the room.

Ella turned to Kellen, bringing her intertwined fingers to her chest. "Thank—"

"Don't think I did that for *you*, earthborn," he hissed, her hands lowering to her sides. "I did that to save my colleague from making a rash decision that could cost him his career. I don't give a flying fuck what happens to you. I would gladly step aside and watch any other instructor damn themselves to Terminus for killing you. Just not one of my people."

Kellen expected to garner a much more enraged, or even hurt, response from her. Ella only granted him a blink of her eyes and a tiny smirk, wanting to elicit the reaction from him he'd been trying to provoke in her.

"What's wrong with your face?" he snapped, fidgeting like the sight of her smile made him uncomfortable in his skin.

"It's a smile. Ever heard of one?"

"Stop that. It's weird. What about what I just said is smile worthy?"

"You're not as scary as you think you are," she answered, holding back a laugh at how a blush blitzed his cheeks up to his ears, his confusion over her strange attitude almost tangible in the ether.

60

"What the fuck is your problem?" he sneered at her, her grin growing wider.

"What's my problem? *You* are," she answered, her smile falling away. She inclined closer and declared, her voice whetted by a coldness she'd never heard herself produce before, "You're standing in my way."

She stepped around Kellen and headed for the door, his eyes sketching lines down her back.

"Pretending you're one of us now?" he shouted at her, her feet coming to a halt at the threshold. She spun around to look at him. "It won't work. Your words may sound like they belong to a Primordial, but they reek of human desperation. You don't fit in here, Rose, and you never will."

"What makes you think I want to fit in, Kilic?" She tossed her ponytail over her shoulder, then blew him a kiss with her middle finger.

---

Mid-afternoon, just as Ella retrieved a salad from her newly-minted enchanted fridge and sat down to eat her lunch, her amulet glowed purple, her presence requested in the Varmin quarter.

*Please be anyone but Kilic,* she prayed to the Gods, then rose from her desk and grabbed her coat.

The yellow and crimson leaves dotting the curvilinear trees overhead descended upon her into the unseen cushion of air. As the petals fell, they rested as one mosaic tile after another along the dirt path she followed. Within the Varmin sector, the grounds were split between the student housing and the hundreds of large steel domes dedicated to each of the different beings the Varmin could shift into. The interior of the domes consisted of large, vacant space for the Varmin to practice shifting and/or flying, the size of the dome contingent on the magnitude of the species. Ella pulled open the door to one of the more miniature domes, belonging to the serpent-shifters.

Inside, she encountered a class in session, a throng of freshman practicing shifting between their serpent forms and their human skin.

Waiting by the entrance stood a dazzling female, with long, cascading violet-shaded hair and bright, lavender hued eyes to match. Ella found her appearance inviting despite her strong bone structure and the upturned shape of her eyes, the serration making it understandable for anyone to find the Varmin female intimidating, should they only glance fleetingly at her and not look close enough to detect her softness. Her head turned to the door when Ella's presence made the metal squeak.

A luminous smile spread across the bottom half of her face in greeting, the first smile Ella had been granted since arriving in Cavale.

"We haven't had a chance to meet!" the woman greeted. "I'm Josefyn Yilanci, lead serpent-shifter instructor."

"I'm Ella." When Josefyn extended her hand to Ella, a sob chafed the walls of Ella's throat. It had been weeks since she'd been offered any form of civility that she didn't remember how much kindness feels like a hug when you've been denied comfort for so long. "You called me down?"

"I did! I'm concerned about a student and I wonder if you might be able to help." Josefyn swung her focus back to the shifting Varmin, calling out to one of the males, "Jasper! You need to bring your hands together when you stretch your arms over your head." She emulated the movement for him, stacking one hand over the other in a graceful arch above her skull. "Make sure you engage your core and don't let your back stiffen. If you shift without assembling into the proper form, you could break your spine." Josefyn sighed, swiveling back to Ella. "Sorry about that."

"Don't be sorry." *She really called me for help.* Ella forced her lips not to slide into a smile, settling into counselor mode. "Who's the student?"

"Jamila Finley. She's a sophomore."

"Tell me what's been going on with her."

"Jamie is a serpent-shifter, but she also possesses Cerebri abilities. She can sense emotions in others. She's always been an incredibly sweet, empathetic kid. Always attending to the needs of others, always top of her class. But since returning to Delmarth this year, she's been acting different. Colder. More closed off. Less caring and attentive. She's not performing well in her classes. She's withdrawn significantly from her peers."

"Do you have any idea if anything changed for her over the summer? Anything about her family?"

"As far as I know, she comes from a loving home, which is more rare than you'd think in Cavale. Possibly something happened over the summer, but do you think that could cause such a drastic change in personality? At her age?"

"It's absolutely possible, depending on the severity of the incident. It could also indicate something deeper, something more emotional happening under the surface." Ella twisted her arms across her chest. "How does she present when you speak to her? Is she maintaining her hygiene? Does she seem more tired than usual?"

"She's well-kept. Always clean. I don't know if I'd say she seems more tired. Just less present."

"When you speak to her, do you get the sense that she seems, for lack of a better word, emotionless?"

"Yes!" Josefyn replied emphatically. "Yes, exactly. What do you think is going on?"

"I'll have to meet her before I can know for sure, but there are some possibilities for what you're describing." Ella hunkered down on one of the benches lining the wall of the dome. "Vicarious trauma, and compassion fatigue. Vicarious trauma is usually an occupational challenge for people who work in fields where they're required to listen to other people's hardships and trauma on a daily basis. Not learning to properly separate their experiences from your own can lead to an emotional and physical exhaustion. It sounds like Jamie may be experiencing a version of this. Maybe it's not that her personality has changed, but that she's emotionally drained and detaching herself from feeling in general. Or it's none of that, and something changed for her over the summer that she's struggling to cope with."

Josefyn's lavender eyes studied Ella prudently, like she was trying to cleave a hole through Ella's being and steal a peek at her soul. "Don't take this as rude, but what would you be able to do for Jamie?"

"Be someone she can open up to about whatever is troubling her. If she's experiencing compassion fatigue, I can work with her to develop skills to teach her to separate her own emotions from others. If there's something else she's struggling with, we can adapt our goals to whatever will help her come back to herself, or help her figure out who she wants to be, if she's experiencing some semblance of an identity crisis, which is common at her age." Ella rested the back of her head on the wall. "Do you think she'd be open to speaking to me?"

"I wouldn't be surprised if she isn't. You should hear what the instructors say about you."

"Trust me, I've heard plenty to last a lifetime. And I can work with hesitant. All I've been given at Delmarth is hesitant, and I've managed so far." Josefyn's full lips carved a serpentine smile. "What period do you see her?"

"Ninth period. End of the day."

"Okay. On Monday, I'm going to stop by and do a classroom observation of her. I'd like to see the behavior you're describing and get a sense of the gravity, as well as see how she interacts with her peers. Then, I'll introduce myself to her. For the next week or so, I'll attend each of your classes and make my face one she recognizes. Once she's used to me, I'll pull her aside and tell her we spoke, then offer to begin counseling with her. I'll leave it to her if she wants to meet with me or not."

"I run the class with Austin Armstrong, another serpent-shifter instructor. He won't be pleased if you join our class."

"I could give two fucks what he thinks," Ella burst out. "I won't be there with the intention to piss him off with my existence. I'll be there to watch over a student in need, and if he has a problem with that, he can go cry about it somewhere else." Josefyn's grin stretched up to her ears.

"I knew I was going to like you," she declared.

"You did?" Ella spluttered. "Why?"

"I tend to gravitate towards misfits, and I think it's fair to declare you the most supreme oddity in Cavale."

Ella choked on a laugh. "I think that's fair to say."

"Not to mention, you've been quite literally torn and ripped apart, if what Headmistress Dyer said this morning is true. You're still here, fighting to do your job, fighting to help these kids. That makes you the only person in this school worth my time or compassion." Ella's eyes burned at the corners.

"You have no idea how much I needed to hear that," Ella whispered tearfully. "Thank you, Josefyn."

"Please, call me Jo." Josefyn chewed on her nail bud, then said, "Tonight me and a Cerebri instructor named Akio were planning on heading off campus to grab some drinks. You should come."

"Really?" Ella's heart nudged against her ribcage from how it swelled with hope. Tiny prickles of doubt blemished the surface of that hope, though, blazing holes in the configuration. *Why is she being so nice to me?*

Did Josefyn have an angle? Was this a trap where Ella would be inevitably humiliated, or a ploy to get her off campus, away from the Cavalian Gods' envoy, so the Primordials could finish her off without a watchful eye stalking their every move?

"Would Akio mind if I tagged along?" she asked, some of her qualms leaking into her tone of voice.

"Doesn't matter if he minds or not. I want you there." Ella smiled for possibly the first time since she'd been in Cavale.

She wanted so badly to not be alone at Delmarth anymore that she chose to abandon her worries about Josefyn's sincerity for a later date, possibly an unwise decision, but one she felt was integral to her sanity.

"I'd love to come," she answered with a simper, receiving a wide grin from Josefyn in return.

"Amazing! What dormitory are you in?"

"Hall three. Room one-D."

"I'll collect you around seven. Dress nice." Josefyn swung her violet hair over her shoulder, then darted back to the shifting Varmin, shouting out commands for the students to follow.

Ella exited the dome, covered her mouth with her hand, and squealed into her fingers. Maybe this was the speck of light at the end of a vast, dark tunnel, planning to mature into a powerful luster that could swallow the darkness whole. A newfound determination settled in her bones, a promise that she'd not only survive the next nine months, but claim some enjoyment for herself in the crevices.

# CHAPTER 7
# ELLA

ONCE ELLA RETURNED to her office, she finally had a moment to access the official Delmarth database with her newly bestowed password. Through the laptop provided to her by the school, she searched *Connor Paight* in the system, examining his schedule to find a time for them to meet.

Headmistress Dyer told her on day one that she wasn't permitted to pull students during their Power Practice times, which occurred eighth and ninth period when the Meteoros, Varmin, Cerebri, and Herculeans trained their unique abilities to master control over their powers and bodies. She'd need to pull him from an academic class, which didn't thrill her, but she had limited options to choose from. They didn't seem to award students any free periods in Cavale, and she didn't want to rip anyone away from their lunch period. Because Connor was a Varmin, she needed to consult the head of the Varmin department before she made any alterations to his schedule.

She found Kellen's information through the database, copying his phone number, then typed out a message, sliding her plush leather chair back against the wall to give her legs enough room to splay over her desk.

**ELLA:** *Kilic. It's Ms. Rose. I'll be pulling Connor from sixth period*

*Liberal Studies on Tuesdays for counseling. Thought I'd give you the courtesy of a warning before I adjust his schedule.*

Ella lifted her enchanted mug of Diet Coke, crafted from crystal with a diamond pattern wrapped around the walls and handle, to her lips just as her phone vibrated with a response from Kellen.

**KILIC:** *1) How the fuck did you get my number? 2) Absolutely not.*

Ella squeezed her hand into a fist and huffed. She set her mug down, collecting her phone to reply.

**ELLA:** *1) I'm resourceful. 2) Students repeat the same schedule every day. He's in Liberal Studies for two periods in a row. If he misses one of the two periods for one day a week, I don't think it will kill him.*

**KILIC:** *One of those periods is Literature, and the other is History of the Gods. He will not be pulled from either.*

**ELLA:** *Then what else do you suggest I do?*

**KILIC:** *Fuck off.*

"What a fucking dick," Ella grumbled, stopping herself before she hurled her phone at the wall.

**ELLA:** *Why do you have to be so fucking difficult?*

**KILIC:** *Why are you still talking to me?*

**ELLA:** *It's either this or I pull him from Power Practice. Your choice, Kilic.*

**KILIC:** *You will NOT pull him from Power Practice, Rose. That is absolutely out of the question.*

**ELLA:** *Then I'll be changing his schedule to say he has counseling with me on Tuesdays during sixth period. Done. No further discussion is needed.*

**KILIC:** *I despise you.* Ella grinned to herself, her fingers flying across the screen in their haste to type a response.

**ELLA:** *Always a displeasure doing business with you, Mr. Kilic. You can now lose my number.*

She hit send, then tucked her phone in the front pocket of her briefcase and reached for her jacket, heading out for the day.

***

"Freya? I have a surprise for you!"

Freya scampered to the door, leaping up to lean on Ella's legs and stretching her front paws out to reach Ella's knee. Ella stroked the top of Freya's head, letting her lick at her fingers, then rifled through her briefcase. "You know how I asked Headmistress Dyer for a fridge that can make any food I want? Well, guess what it made for me today?" She yanked out a bag of dog food, shaking it in the air. "Ta-da!"

The smile vanished from Freya's face, replaced with a frown that accompanied a raspy whimper.

"Oh, come on!" Ella cried, setting the bag down on the kitchen counter. "Don't whimper. I know you like the meat patties, but this is good too!" Freya didn't even bother to acknowledge the clear lie.

She turned her back on Ella and ran to the couch.

"I didn't realize I raised a snob," Ella muttered, just as Ella's phone buzzed from inside her briefcase.

It vibrated between her fingers with an incoming video call from Rylee. Ella rejoiced in being able to see Rylee on her screen, in all her stunning splendor, her chestnut brown hair cropped to her shoulders, blow-dried straight, and tapering off where her neck collided with her shoulders.

"Ells!" Rylee squealed in greeting. "Tell me how today went."

"Today was actually the best day I've had here."

"*Really?!*" Rylee's grey eyes, identical to Ella's and the only feature from their mother the girls shared, sparkled. "That is the best news I've heard in *so* long! Tell me everything." Ella plopped down on the couch. Freya rested her squished face into Ella's lap, unable to help herself from being close to Ella inspite of her annoyance.

"To tell you about today, I have to first tell you about last night. Kilic almost drowned me in the pool."

"*WHAT?!*" Rylee dropped her phone in horror, so Ella was forced to stare up at the chipped paint peeling off Rylee's ceiling before her sister reappeared on the screen. "Are you okay?"

"I'm fine. But I was so angry that I stormed to Headmistress Dyer's office and told her that if she didn't do something to stop these attacks, I wanted to be let go and sent back to the Earthly Plane."

"Good for you, Ella! It's about fucking time. How did she react?"

"She called an emergency staff meeting today with the whole faculty and told us she'd spoken with the Cavalian Gods' envoy. Anyone who lays their hand on me again will be sentenced to three days in Terminus."

"Hallefuckinglujah!" Ella laughed while she watched Rylee set her phone down on the table and spin around her couch, twirling her fists in the air as an accessory to her raucous cheering.

"You're a terrible dancer," Ella giggled when Rylee returned to the sofa.

"Can we just take a moment to appreciate this massive win? You stood up for yourself, and you actually got results. This is *huge*. Can you let yourself do that, Ella? Can you let yourself be proud? I know I am."

Ella's smile grew heavy with longing, her desire to be with her sister aching through her core.

"I love you, Ry."

"I love *you*, Ells. And I'm so proud of you." Freya nudged Ella's hand with her snout, so Ella unfurled her fingers for Freya to lick.

"I got invited by a serpent-shifter instructor to go for drinks tonight with her and her friend."

"Ella! That's amazing! Who invited you?"

"Her name's Josefyn. I don't know if I should go, though." Rylee's scowl pierced her flesh through time and space, as though she were standing over Ella right now and not separated by the membrane of an interdimensional void.

"Yes, you should *absolutely* go!"

"What if she invited me just to get me off campus and kill me?" Rylee paused, deliberating this.

"Did your gut tell you that when speaking to her?"

"Well, no." Ella frowned. "She seemed genuine, but it's hard for me to trust in that, knowing all the different ways those feelings could be manipulated by the Primordials to trick me into a false sense of security."

"Forget trusting in her. Trust in yourself. If your instincts didn't scream *danger* when around her, then try to listen to them. Go tonight with your senses on overdrive, be ready to bolt if you need to, but you should still go." Rylee objected the moment Ella's lips divided, "No buts. You need people, Ells. You can't survive the next nine months with just Freya."

"Freya's good company, though." Ella scratched the top of Freya's head.

"She is, but she's not enough. If there's a chance for you to make some real connections here, you need to take that leap. I'm thrilled you're finally growing your voice and getting more comfortable advocating for yourself with the Primordials, but it wouldn't hurt to have someone else in your corner, sticking up for you too. Take the chance that this Josefyn can be a warrior for you while you get comfortable being a warrior for yourself." Ella wasn't fast enough this time to quell tears.

"Stop saying profound shit that makes me miss you even more," she mewled. "It's cruel."

Rylee's smile appeared wistful. "I cry about how much I miss you once a day, so it's only fitting."

"Wicked. You're wicked. Why do I even love you?" Tears painted stripes down Rylee's cheeks. Ella couldn't tolerate bearing witness to her sister's despondence, not when she couldn't easily make the trip over to her and comfort Rylee herself. "Want to help me figure out what to wear?"

"Is that even a question? Go get options!"

Rylee and Ella spent a total of thirty minutes sifting through her closet for something suitable to wear. They settled on a sleeveless red corset top with a sweetheart neckline tucked into black jeans that flared out at the ends and frayed along the hem, garnished with her favorite cropped black leather jacket. She paired the ensemble with silver teardrop earrings and her black ankle boots that were actually rain boots but possessed a pointed tip that made them modish enough to pass for evening wear. After an hour spent fiddling with her hair, whipping it in different directions and fashioning it in diverse shapes, she settled on leaving it loose over her shoulders, the golden tendrils torrenting down her chest to her mid-sternum. She then spent another fifteen minutes deciding if she should tuck the front strands of hair behind her ears, or allow them to frame her cheeks. She played with a combination of both, the right side pulled back and the left side unshackled, for five extra minutes, contemplating how long it would take to shave her whole head.

Before Ella gave in to the temptation and went looking for a pair of scissors, the door quivered from a fist pounding against the other side, followed by a feminine voice calling out, "Ella? You there?"

It was loud enough that it awoke Freya, who never had a good reaction to being unexpectedly roused from a nap. She let out a ferocious—well, her version of ferocious—bark, glowering at the door.

"Freya, quiet," Ella ordered, running to the door and yanking it open.

"Look at you!" Josefyn cried, doubling back in the hall so she could survey Ella from top to bottom.

"Wow," Ella spluttered, drinking in the immaculate ringlets of Josefyn's violet, silky strands and the silhouette of her long-sleeved black mini dress, embellished in sequins with a tie fastening at the waist. Messily applied eyeliner smirched Josefyn's waterline, not detracting but rather enhancing the soft lavender hue of her irises, while her lips were coated in red gloss, enriching the white of her teeth. "You look beautiful, Josefyn."

"Thank you! So do yo—" Josefyn's sentence was trampled by a gasp. "Is that a *dog?*" Ella spun around to look back at Freya.

She'd taken up occupancy of the doorway to their bedroom, guarding the entrance by laying down on her belly and splaying her legs out behind her splooting, widening her stance so no one could cross over her.

"Her name's Freya," Ella told Josefyn, cocking her head at Freya's strange behavior.

"I've never seen an Earthly Plane dog before." Josefyn scuttled deeper into the apartment. Ella closed the door behind her. "We have Varmin who can shift into dogs, but they don't look like this. They're less…fluffy." Josefyn sunk to her knees, proffering her palm outstretched to Freya.

Freya sniffed at the air, assessing Josefyn's scent for any reason to be cautious before she pulled herself up and dashed over to meet

Josefyn where she was still on her knees. Freya dug her nose into Josefyn's palm to further her examination.

When Ella watched Freya's tongue dart out to lick Josefyn's fingers, she relaxed, Josefyn having passed Freya's test.

"She's so sweet!" Josefyn giggled, stroking the top of Freya's head.

"Don't let her lick your face or she'll try to stick her tongue down your throat," Ella warned.

"She's a forward girl, isn't she? We love a confident queen." Ella laughed on her way to the kitchen to prepare Freya's dinner. "How old is she?"

"She's five. I found her in an alley by herself when she was three months old. She'd been separated from her mother and was living on the street. We haven't spent a day apart from each other since."

"She's lucky you found her." Ella's chest warmed.

"*I'm* lucky I found her. She's the best friend I could ever ask for." Ella broke her gaze from Josefyn and Freya before she dissolved into tears, measuring a full portion of dry dog food for Freya.

"How's she been adjusting to being in Cavale?"

"Way better than expected. Freya makes things very easy. She travels well and doesn't complain. She's not the brightest bulb in the shed, so I wouldn't be surprised if she has no idea we're not in New York anymore." Josefyn chuckled, though it was unclear if the laughter was induced by Ella's joke or by Freya leaping up to place her paws on Josefyn's shoulders in her mission to lick the gloss off Josefyn's lips. "My sister and I always joke around that Freya is the definition of lights on, nobody's home. I think she's just happy to be included in whatever it is I'm doing."

"She's such an angel, Ella." Josefyn managed to detach Freya from her face and create enough distance between them for her to rise off the floor. "You ready to go? Akio is waiting for us outside."

"One second." Ella set the bowl of dog food down on the ground beside Freya's water dish. "Dinner, my love." Freya glanced down at the bowl, then shoved it towards Ella with her paw. "Seriously?" Ella groaned. "I don't have any meat patties for you, so for today, just eat this. Please? For me?"

Freya exhaled a huff, then allowed Ella to lightly guide the bowl back over to her with her foot.

"*Now*, I'm ready," Ella declared, Josefyn snickering under her breath. She turned to grab her keys and blew Freya a kiss out the door, though Freya was too deeply submerged in her dinner to notice. "What can you tell me about Akio?" Ella asked, scurrying to keep up with Josefyn.

"He's a Cerebri instructor. He's alright, I suppose." Her words were honed by a silent laugh, comicality wrapped around the statement in a way that left Ella both confused and sensing that she was only jesting. "You'll love him," Josefyn assured when she noticed Ella's expression, sounding certain.

Josefyn held the door for Ella, her face illuminating like a cloudless dawn at the male they found leaning against a neighboring tree, his face eclipsed at first by the shadow raining down from the canopy of leaves. When he stepped out of the obscurity, Ella took in the gorgeous specimen, with ink black, borderline blue hair draped across his forehead like tassels at the end of a blanket, single-lidded eyes, and a jawline so cleanly chiseled that it looked more like a serrated knife than a bone attached to a person's face. Handsome, strong features, the face of a soldier.

"Mr. Takeshi," Josefyn greeted in a solemn voice, though in the underbelly of her words lay humor and a hint of coquetry.

"Ms. Yilanci." Akio's brown eyes devoured Josefyn's physique, consuming the length of her legs down to the red heels her feet were squeezed into. Akio smoothed the lapels of his blazer, fixing the collar of the maroon button down that lay beneath the jacket before closing the distance between them, his fingers gripping her waist to yank her into him. He leaned down to nuzzle the crook of her neck and pressed a kiss to the edge of her jaw. "You never cease to take my breath away, wife of mine."

"*Wife?*" Ella spluttered, which prompted Akio to rip his face out of Josefyn's throat to regard her.

"Surprise!" Josefyn squealed, beaming.

"You must be Ella." Akio released Josefyn to extend his hand. "I've been eager to meet you officially. I've heard a lot about you."

"Any of it good?" she quipped, slipping her hand into his. Akio released a braying laugh, squeezing her hand in a way that precipitated a blast of heat to sweep across Ella's cheeks, circulating down to her chest. She hoped the heat wasn't discernable through the sheath of her flesh.

"Not at all," he bantered, though she wouldn't be surprised to learn he wasn't joking. He dropped her hand to drape his arm around Josefyn's shoulders, threading his fingers through hers.

"Shall we go?" Josefyn asked the group, her nose tracing the column of Akio's neck.

"Come on, little earthborn," Akio beckoned as he and Josefyn began their trek to the parking lot. For the first time since she'd been in Cavale, that name, usually lobbed at her as a derogatory insult, sounded almost like a compliment, a smile attaching itself to the bottom half of Ella's face.

Ella rode in the back of Akio's black car that resembled a Volkswagen beetle, which Akio told her he named *Ace* after Josefyn's nickname for him. Ella barely spoke during that car ride into the city of Sleka, content to listen to the intimate banter pass between Akio and Josefyn while she gazed out the window, sketching invisible lines to connect the beads of rainwater gathered over the glass. Ella watched how the yellowed light from the streetlamps played in the droplets, shattering through the deluge in solitary drops. The tires unleashed a monotonous hiss over the rain-washed highway, the sound gaining velocity with the more distance they put between them and Delmarth Academy.

Ella learned on the drive to The Dow that Akio and Josefyn met when they were students at Delmarth. They grew up together and had been best friends for years before either of them considered dipping their toes in the realm of romance. In the end, it was Akio who made the first move to crawl over that friendship line, breathing life into the feelings Josefyn had been harboring secretly for years.

"That was before we learned we were Cavalisha," Josefyn mused, her fingers caressing the hair at the nape of Akio's neck.

"Cavalisha?" Ella repeated. "What's that?"

"A Cavalisha is a destined mate," Akio explained, his thumb drawing patterns along the inside of Josefyn's thigh. "It's the strongest bond you can share with another, the other half of your soul, predetermined by the Gods themselves. Time and space cannot separate you. Despite all circumstances, you will inevitably be drawn together, an unavoidable collision of hearts and minds, designed to be each other's beginning and end." Ella pulled her leather jacket tighter around her shoulders to subdue a shudder.

"How do you know someone is your Cavalisha?"

"The bond clicks into place the first time you say *I love you*. It feels like a sucker punch to the heart that forces the axis of your life to shift, making your being forever orbit around your other half, not the sun."

"That sounds painful," Ella muttered, her fingers clawing at her chest, trying to reach where her heart lay throbbing.

"Isn't love always painful, though, in a sense?" Josefyn argued, her words delivered like a soft embrace.

Ella had to admit, from her own experience—not romantic love, which she'd never had the pleasure of experiencing thus far, but from burdened familial love— Josefyn's point was valid. She'd learned from her mother that pain was an unavoidable accessory to loving someone, whether that pain arose from their absence or their presence, a necklace with thorns that could never be taken off.

"A Cavalisha is both your greatest strength and your greatest weakness," Akio continued. "Strength in the sense that through accepting that bond, your powers intensify. Weakness in the sense that when one of you is injured, you're both injured. When one of you perishes, you both perish."

"How does one accept the mating bond?"

"There's a ritual that's performed as an offering to Mara Cavalian, the Goddess of Love. It involves proving to Mara that your love is pure enough to deserve a permanent joining of hearts."

"Primordials are guaranteed a Cavalisha, but many reject the mating bond and never make an offering to Mara," Josefyn added, her thigh angling closer to Akio's hand. "While the idea of a power proliferation is attractive, possessing a Cavalisha in public places a target on your back. It's your heart walking outside your body, vulnerable for all to strike at. Which is why no one at Delmarth knows about me and Akio. To the outside world, he's Mr. Takeshi, and I'm Ms. Yilanci."

"No one knows you're mated?" The two shook their heads. "But you're telling *me*," Ella whispered.

"We're telling *you*," Josefyn confirmed, turning in her seat to meet Ella's eye. Her warm smile swore, *I know you're hesitant, and you have every right to be, but you can trust our kindness.*

"I won't tell a soul," Ella vowed, touched by the faith they'd placed in her.

"We know," Akio said, then jibed, "Besides, no one would believe you anyway." Three unique forms of laughter wove themselves together along the wind, drowning the car in sweet music.

Akio parked Ace in the lot by the pub, then circled around the car to open the doors for both Josefyn and Ella. Ella sauntered into The Dow behind Akio and Josefyn, the mated pair splintering apart from one another once they entered the thronged space. Crimson clay bricks and white, clean marble slabs amalgamated to create the outer structure of The Dow. The inside comprised of rounded, stone beams supporting the upper floor with torches attached to them, dangling heat and illumination from the rafters. Booths bordered the perimeter of the tavern in a complete circle against the walls, with a large U-shaped bar positioned in the center of the massive expanse, where patrons populated the grounds around the bar to claim space on the dancefloor. Josefyn elected to link her arm through Ella's to prevent herself from giving into temptation and draping herself across her husband. The women followed Akio into the heart of the establishment as he searched for an empty booth, the air thick with the scent of ale and roasted meat.

"Grab that booth," Akio directed Josefyn, pointing to the vacant cubicle on the far right side of the tavern, bordering the winding staircase that united the ground floor and the upper level. "Rakira good, Jo?"

"Perfect," she purred, then led Ella over to the booth.

"What's rakira?" Ella asked as she situated on the bench across the table from Josefyn, shaking her jacket off and folding it on the leather cushion.

"It's a type of liquor. It's the only thing Akio drinks. It has a sort of malty flavor with vanilla notes."

"Oh! Like scotch." Josefyn cocked her head.

"What's scotch?"

"It's an alcohol from the Earthly Plane. It's my brother-in-law's favorite. Mason always reserves his Friday evenings to lock himself in his office and enjoy a glass of scotch. He says it makes him feel fancy."

"Sounds like my kind of man," Akio said when he returned, presenting them with three glasses of amber liquid with rich red-gold tones, the liquid the same hue as the mahogany table when the ambient light peppered over the surface. "Raise your glasses, ladies," Akio requested, gliding into the spot next to Ella rather than flanking his wife—most likely to avoid the lure of touching her in public.

"What're we celebrating?" Ella asked, accepting her glass of rakira.

"We're celebrating *you*, Ms. Rose. It's not every day we welcome a new face into our little circle. You're part of the in-crowd now." Ella simpered, her cheeks burning along with the corners of her eyes.

"To our new friend," Josefyn cheered, the three of them clinking their glasses together before sampling the liquor. It tasted as though the ingredients of a campfire, firewood and kindling, had been deliquesced and coalesced into a liquid. The smoke flavor scorched Ella's throat and made her splutter a nasty cough. Akio patted her back, laughing, "Take it easy, champ. This stuff is strong even for a Primordial. I can't imagine how your human body will stomach it."

"No big gulps," Josefyn advised. "Just small sips. If it's too strong, we can get you something else."

"I'm good with this. Thank you, though." Ella wanted to prove to them, but mostly to herself, that she could keep up, that she wasn't backing down from their customs or ways of being.

"I remember my first rakira," Akio sighed dreamily.

"You nearly died, Ace," Josefyn reminded him, then clarified for Ella, "The jackass, at *fifteen* years old, mind you, thought he was tough enough to down three glasses of rakira in ten seconds. It knocked him out five minutes later. I had to drive his comatose body back to campus, in a fucking *blizzard,* so he could get his stomach pumped."

"You know that's why I only drink rakira, right?" Akio said, gazing heatedly at Josefyn. "Because it reminds me of the night you saved my life, the night I knew I loved you." Josefyn's eyes were two congealed orbs of pure love. Two halves of Ella battled for dominance of her head and heart, one half swept up in awe of the almost tangible passion the two of them shared, the other wishing to distance herself from what felt like a moment she was intruding on by sitting there. "So, Ella." Akio knit his fingers together on the table. "How the fuck did you end up in Cavale?"

"I don't even know where to begin," she laughed, her index finger tracing the mouth of her glass. She sat up straighter, then explained, "I graduated grad school in May, but I'd been looking for a job long before that, since February. I wasn't having luck finding anything in New York and wasn't looking anywhere else, because ironically, at the time, I had no wish to leave the city. In June, I received an email from Headmistress Dyer stating that Delmarth had been searching for a permanent school counseling position and my resume was passed to them."

"Who gave them your resume?" Akio asked.

"I have no idea. Headmistress Dyer never said."

"How did they find your resume from a different dimension?" Josefyn questioned, chewing on her straw.

"I don't know. I also found it strange they sent that email to my personal email, not my school email. My older sister told me it was a scam, so I almost didn't attend my interview. We researched the school, though unbeknown to me, the website we looked at and the campus I ended up touring with Headmistress Dyer was an illusion created by one of the Cerebri instructors here."

"That sounds like something Daniel Madix would do," Akio grumbled under his breath before imbibing more of his rakira. Ella didn't have to ask for verification that Akio disliked his department head.

"Or Kellen Kilic," Josefyn argued. "I know he doesn't broadcast it, but Kellen is also an image-manipulator."

"What does an image-manipulator do?" Ella asked, intrigued by the mention of Kellen.

"They can create illusions in people's minds to make them see whatever they want them to see." *Like making me believe a sea monster was going to attack me,* Ella thought to herself, a piece of the unsolved puzzle clicking into place. "They can also access people's thoughts, or communicate non-verbally into people's minds."

"How can Kellen be an image-manipulator if he's *also* a Varmin?"

"His father was a Cerebri," Akio answered. Ella clocked how Akio said *was* but decided not to further delve into the matter. "It's not common, but sometimes Primordials can take on powers from both parents. Usually, only one, even if their parents are mixed. They're known as dual-bred."

"Dual-breeders tend to not advertise their second ability and choose one to favor in public," Josefyn added. "Primordials are inherently ravenous for power. Anyone with unfair advantages is seen as a threat to the Gods. Those in the past who have exhibited an imbalanced surplus in powers have been sent to Terminus."

"Over something they can't control?" Ella spluttered in horror.

"Over something that could make the Gods look weak in comparison," Josefyn offered as a counterargument.

"That is so unfair." Ella shook her head. "I understand the Gods sending someone to Terminus over committing a crime, but sending someone to eternal damnation for something they were born with, just to make themselves feel better about their own insecurities? That's pathetic."

While Josefyn snorted into her palm, Akio cautioned Ella in a low voice, "I'd be careful what you say about the Gods. They hear everything, and they forget nothing."

"I don't care," she dismissed with a shrug of her shoulders. "They're not *my* Gods, so they can't punish me."

Josefyn's eyes swung to Akio. "See why I like her?"

"I do," he confirmed, his brown eyes scrutinizing Ella's facial features. "Seemingly quiet and sweet, but that good-natured mask is covering a shitload of fire underneath. She's like a clone of you."

"I take that as a compliment," the women said in unison, then stared at each other with enlarged eyes and squealed.

"Instant best friend," Josefyn declared, squeezing Ella's hand.

"Back to what we were discussing before," Ella said, sipping her rakira carefully. With each mouthful, she grew more accustomed to the taste. "I don't think it was Daniel or Kellen who created that illusion. If either of them had participated in bringing me to Cavale, they wouldn't be so angry that I'm here and wouldn't be trying so hard to get rid of me. I'm not sure who did it, but whoever did knew the reaction bringing a human here would garner and did it anyway."

"I bet it was all Headmistress Dyer," Josefyn guessed. "She may be a Herculea with healer abilities, but I wouldn't be surprised if she has some Cerebri in her blood too. The way she commands a room leads me to believe she has some heightened gifts in swaying others to do her bidding. I've speculated about it for a while, not that she would ever corroborate it. If she *is* an action-manipulator, and it *was* Daniel or Kellen who helped her bring you here, they might not have even known what they were doing when making that website and campus illusion. They might not even hold memories from it."

"My wife is so smart," Akio marveled, sinking his cheek against his palm as he stared lovingly across the table at her. Josefyn blew him a kiss, and he pretended to catch it in his hand and smack it on his lips.

"I have a question." Josefyn adorably raised her hand. Ella giggled before waving her fingers to grant Jo permission to speak. "So you told us how you got the job, but how did you actually *get* to Cavale?"

"*Great* question," Akio prided. Ella presented them with an impish smile, then brushed her hair out of her face.

"Headmistress Dyer sent a car to pick me up and take me to where I believed Delmarth was located, which was upstate New York in Albany. The driver's name was Marlon—"

"Marlon!" Josefyn and Akio cheered. Josefyn framed her cheeks with her hands. "Awe, he's the best security officer. He's been at Delmarth since Akio and I were in Kindergarten. He's the sweetest!"

"The *sweetest?*" Ella repeated. "From the second I got in the car, he had a raging attitude with me. When I asked bluntly, 'You don't want to be driving me, do you?' he replied, 'I would rather be anywhere in the realms than sitting in this car with you, Ms. Rose. I would've taken a life sentence in Terminus with a smile than be forced to enter the Earthly Plane and consort with the likes of *you.*"

"That's just because you're human," Akio said with a flick of his hand, as though that excused the disrespect. Ella had been enjoying herself immensely so far, so she decided to let that subtle insult slide.

"Of course, I had no idea what the fuck he was talking about. I thought he may have been on something."

Ella shut her eyes, brought back to that exact moment.

*The Hudson River unfolded to her right as they charged down the West Side Highway towards Delmarth. The white lace waves in the waterway purged in congruence with the rhythm set by the wind, which wafted into the backseat through the open window and blew her hair off her flushed cheeks. Freya sat contentedly in Ella's lap and licked her fingers. Out of nowhere, a perturbing crackling sound, as if an apparatus within the car was breaking down, drowned the totality of the car. The noise progressively amplified until it bore a resemblance to nails being dragged down a chalkboard.*

*Ella felt like her ears were bleeding.*

*"Excuse me?" she called out, cupping her hands over her ears to protect them from the racket. "Marlon? I think something's wrong with the car."*

*"Nothing's wrong with the car," Marlon spat back.*

*"Don't you hear that noise? I think the car might be breaking down."*

*"What noise?" This was the first time he actually bothered to look back at her, even if it lasted a mere two seconds.*

*"That noise. It sounds like the car is breaking down."*

*"You're the only one who hears anything." All Ella could do was blink, because what was she supposed to say to that?*

*"That doesn't mean there isn't something wrong with the car." Panic leached into her voice. "Can you please stop to check the car?"*

*"No. Then we'll be late for school."*

*"But if something's wrong with the car and it breaks down, then we'll have no way of getting to school." Ella received no response. Her heart leapt up into her throat. His silence, coupled with that grating, intensifying sound, caused the hair on her arms to rise. "Marlon? Can you please pull the car over?"*

*"You're not getting out of this car, Noella." The assertion echoed like a brash rumble of thunder.*

*Ella reached for the door handle and was immediately met with the click of the car being locked from all sides, her open window sealing shut. When she tried to roll it down, the button was no longer functional.*

*She couldn't breathe.*

*Ella checked the car's license plate before she got into the vehicle to verify it matched the one Headmistress Dyer emailed her over the weekend, but the feeling that maybe she'd gotten into the wrong car itched around her bones. Marlon never mentioned Delmarth when he collected her. He'd just said he was taking her to school, which she immediately assumed was Delmarth, so she thought she was safe.*

*Rylee lecturing her in high school to always ask her Uber drivers who they were meant to pick up, so she could confirm they were there for* her, *played on a loop in Ella's head, about fifteen minutes too late.*

*"What institution are you from?" Ella demanded, not even bothering to mask her concern.*

*"You humans are so slow," Marlon muttered under his breath, then snapped, "I'm taking you to Delmarth, Noella. Now shut the fuck up so I can concentrate, or we'll miss our exit." That answer didn't settle her.*

*"Don't talk to me like that," Ella snarled, gripping Freya so tightly that her knuckles were white and Freya fidgeted. "Tell me what's going on, or I swear to God, I will jump out of this car while it's still mo—"*

*All of a sudden, they swerved off the road.*

*Marlon jerked the car to the right, launching them through the air and over the railing, the car soaring towards the Hudson River. Ella was sent lurching forward, her seatbelt saving her from being hurled over Marlon's shoulder and launched at the window. She folded herself around Freya to protect the dog from injury, Freya whimpering within the depths of Ella's arms. The car descended towards the river, rear-ending with the water, the collision followed by an explosion of foaming waves spewing out from beneath them as the car sunk beneath the surface of the river.*

*"By all means, Ms. Rose," Marlon drawled with a smile. "Jump out of the car. It'll make my day."*

*"WHAT THE FUCK?!"* Ella screamed at the top of her lungs.

*"If you ask me any questions right now, I will not answer. Headmistress Dyer will answer all your questions when we get to Delmarth."*

*"NUH-HUH! NO WAY!"* Ella just kept thinking, on a torturous loop, this is how I die, this is how I die, this is how I die. I somehow always knew I would die by drowning. *"Take me home NOW."*

*"No. And please try to refrain from shrieking for the remainder of our drive. My ears would really appreciate it."*

*"You—"* Marlon proceeded to drag his pinched fingers over his lips, mimicking the motion of zipping something shut, then tossed an invisible key over his shoulder before turning back around.

*The car landed on a bed of sand, covered from all sides by bedrock, cobbles, mussel shells, old oyster reefs, and debris dumped by people, a revolting amount of it. Marlon just started driving again, as if they were cruising on the highway rather than at the bottom of a fucking river. Ella rocked back and forth in the backseat, hugging Freya tightly to her chest with one hand while rubbing her temples with the other to keep a migraine at bay, though she was losing the battle against the stabbing headache, three seconds away from fragmenting into a full blown panic attack.*

*Suddenly, a resplendent door appeared in the sand, gargantuan in size and gold-plated, limned with seaweed. The gate parted when it sensed their car approaching, revealing on the other side a verdant path, dressed in evergreens and multicolored florae. When they drove over the threshold, the gateway sealed shut behind them, the river and New York disappearing through it. They now sat in a luxuriant meadow, a sky entirely divergent from the one they just left behind suspended above them, streaked with pink clouds that emulated billows of cotton candy.*

*Ella's jaw dropped open.*

*She couldn't stop blinking, waiting for that one magic blink to disband the image and fracture the fantasy.*

*"This isn't real,"* she tried to convince herself. *She buried her face in her hands, failing to temper her wheezes.* *"You're still asleep. You missed your alarm. You're going to wake up in your bed, and all of this will have just been a bad dream."* *Marlon snorted in front of her. Ella almost heard his eyes roll.*

*"So human,"* he sneered, shaking his head.

*"Where the fuck are we?!"* Marlon exhaled an irritated breath, but surprisingly answered the question.

*"Welcome to Cavale, Ms. Rose."*

"Headmistress Dyer was waiting in the meadow," Ella told Josefyn and Akio, the two of them hanging onto her every word. Ella's eyes were locked over her glass of rakira. "Marlon left me in the car to go speak to her. I knew they were talking about me because they kept looking back at me."

*Ella watched them through the foggy glass, reading their lips and making out what they were saying.*

*"How is she?" Headmistress Dyer asked Marlon.*

*"She freaked out in the car. She's got a mouth on her, that one. You don't pay me enough for this shit, Valerie." Headmistress Dyer narrowed her eyes, then shook her head at him. "How will you explain it all to her?"*

*"I'll do what I should've done from the start," she replied, her gaze meeting Ella's through the window, catching her observing them behind the protection of Freya's head. Then, Headmistress Dyer said, this time directed at Ella, who she now knew was listening, "I'll be honest."*

"Headmistress Dyer told me to come out and join them. She said it would be okay. So I got out of the car."

"Then what happened?" Josefyn asked. Ella raised her head to cinch her eyes with Josefyn's.

"I ran for my fucking life," Ella replied. Josefyn's lips spread into a gargantuan smile, as though she'd predicted that outcome. "I was so scared and confused. I didn't know what to do, so with Freya in my arms, I booked it through the meadow. Headmistress Dyer sent Marlon after me. I obviously didn't know then that he was a Herculea speed-wielder. He didn't even have to run. He just teleported in front of me and blocked my path. He then dragged me back to Headmistress Dyer, who finally explained how the contract she tricked me into signing bound me to Delmarth for the rest of the school year, so I couldn't leave Cavale. Then she and Marlon drove me to campus."

"Did she ever apologize? For tricking you?" A lump clogged Ella's throat.

"No. She didn't." Akio rested his hand on her shoulder, while Josefyn reached across the table to grab Ella's hand.

"If no one's said it to you yet, let it come from us." Akio squeezed Ella's shoulder. "I'm sorry you were forced here against your will. No one should ever have to endure having their ability to choose stripped away from them." A scream mingled with a sob in Ella's throat, but rather than let the violent combination leak out, she tendered to Akio a teary-eyed smile and set her hand on top of his on her shoulder.

"Between the two of us, Ella, we *promise* you that no one will fuck with you again," Josefyn swore. "We've got you. We'll get you through the next nine months."

"I can't tell you how much I needed this," Ella murmured. "How much I needed people." One tear escaped her restraint.

"You have people now," Akio affirmed. "You're not alone." Ella inhaled a breath, tasting relief and comfort and companionship on her tongue. The hefty weight on her chest she carried in solitude was a portion less heavy, now that she had two people with her willing to help support the load. Akio glanced down at the table, then blustered a laugh. "We forgot to order food with our drinks."

"That was dumb of us," Josefyn giggled, her sobriety slipping farther and farther away from her lavender gaze, replaced by a glimmer of drunkenness.

"Let me go get us some food." Akio slid out of the booth, crossing the tavern to reach the U-shaped bar.

"He has such a fuckable ass," Josefyn sighed, prompting Ella to snort on a giggle. "I mean it. I want to bite it."

"You're so drunk," Ella snickered, dabbing tears from her eyes.

"So are you," Josefyn chortled before the smile vanished from her face and she sat up straight. "*Shit.*"

"What? What's wrong?" Josefyn gulped.

"Look who just walked in." Ella spun around, her gaze sweeping over the room before landing on the entrance.

Where she watched Kellen Kilic cross over the threshold.

## CHAPTER 8

# KELLEN

ALL KELLEN WANTED WAS to enjoy a glass of rakira in peace.

He frequented The Dow at least once a week, a necessity for his well-being to separate from Delmarth campus's claustrophobic nature. Daniel was spiraling due to Oliviana's sentencing and had begged Kellen for a night out to take his mind off the girl who would never reciprocate his feelings. He'd initially blown Daniel off to spend his evening grading the History of the Gods exam, which more than half the class *failed*. Kellen *really* needed to get out of his fucking head and let off steam, and not in the company of others like Daniel, but in the comfort of solitude.

Before making the flight over to The Dow, he first went to check on his siblings.

The twins were at dinner with a few of their friends in the dining hall on campus. Kellen could locate them in a blackout easily through scent and familial adoration. He found Laya first, her long black hair tangled in a disheveled bun atop her head, her dark brown skin glowing while she commanded the conversation. Her radiant smile signaled that despite the hell she'd been through, she found light in the crevices of darkness. Right beside her was Jarion, his scrawny, lanky limbs barely fitting under the metal table, his black curls hidden beneath a red beanie—one of Kellen's beanies, he noted with a smirk.

That smirk faded, however, as he watched his brother's shoulders cave in, folding in on himself so no one at the table could read the sadness outlined in his lightless green eyes. He hid even from Laya, whose eyes kept swinging over to him every few seconds to verify he hadn't walked off.

Kellen *never* used his Cerebri abilities to infiltrate his siblings' thoughts, but just this once, he felt he had no choice. If Jarion wouldn't tell him what was going on with him, he needed to find another way to help his brother. Reading his thoughts seemed like the only plausible solution at the time.

When Kellen concentrated over Jarion, what filled his brain wasn't coherent thoughts—it was *agony*, such an astonishing, staggering amount of it that Kellen nearly crumbled to the ground. The pain was localized in Jarion's upper back over his shoulder blades, the sensation on both sides vibrating like knives poking the interior of his flesh.

Kellen knew this pain intimately. He felt it daily, though he'd grown accustomed to the feeling so it no longer debilitated or shocked him. Jarion's wings were pleading to be released. What Kellen didn't understand was why it seemed Jarion was refusing to unfetter them, keeping this anguish contained within.

Kellen wanted to go to him. Comfort him. Beg Jarion to release his wings so he wouldn't be hurting so much. But when Laya spun her head to the side and located Kellen by the entrance of the cafeteria, she simply shook her head at him, her lips flattened in a grim line. Kellen heeded the warning and stalked out of the cafeteria.

The second he stepped outside, he stretched out his wings, feeling in that moment, after experiencing Jarion's discomfort, that if he didn't release them, he would burst. He kept the rest of his dragon at bay so he wouldn't lose his clothes by fully shifting and took off for the clouds, flapping his wings brutally to gain momentum on his journey to his hometown of Yorkdill. He shielded himself within a billow of mist while he hovered above his childhood home, peeking through the myriad of windows to check if his mother was there. He found her in her bedroom, a teal blue robe draped across emaciated shoulders, long silver threads of hair dripping down her chest and leaking onto the binder she grasped between her hands.

One look at Miya Kilic Ates, and you'd never know the evil that lurked within, tainting her soul in black smears. Her appearance was a devious, well-crafted deception. Kellen didn't necessarily blame Cavalian law enforcement for having a difficult time believing her involvement in the torture of Jarion and Laya, given what used to be her stunning reputation in Cavale amongst the community of Varmin dragon-shifters. Once the evidence was laid out for them, none could deny the truth of her participation, even if it had been the twins' father, Ciaran, who'd done the most physical damage. Miya used her connections within the system to receive a reduced sentence for her crimes, weaving a story that painted herself a victim as much as the twins had been. Somewhere, in the depths of Kellen's hatred for her, he actually believed some of that was true.

It wasn't enough for him to forgive her, though, especially as she continued to try and separate him from the twins, searching for any excuse to reopen the custody agreement and reclaim her parental rights.

Miya, as if sensing his presence somewhere in the ether, shut her binder and stuffed it under her pillow before scampering to the window to peer into the night. By the time she reached the window, Kellen was already gone.

Five minutes later, he'd flown to the city of Sleka and landed in front of The Dow, trudging inside.

Two seconds.

That's all it took for him to feel Noella Rose—not just smell her, but *feel* her—inside the tavern.

Her eyes locked on him the moment he crossed over the entrance.

The clothing Kellen usually saw Noella wear was conservative, modest, and did nothing for her figure—high neckline sweaters, colors that didn't flatter her skin tone and washed her out (unless it was that maroon turtleneck she wore the other day, or the aqua blue blouse from the second week of school) and loose trousers, typically the same black pair of pants and her loafers. What adorned her physique now was shockingly different from what he expected to see on her. The vibrant, red corset top accentuated her full chest and cinched her waist to create an hourglass shape with her curves. He could really *see* her figure in this outfit, every delicious bend and roll, and the way her waistline blended into wide hips and thick thighs. Her hair, a voluminous stream of blonde ripples, torrented down her chest to her waistline.

It was easy to ignore her beauty during the week when it was obscured by her work uniform and draining personality. With all those defenses down, nothing to conceal her splendor from him, the truth of what she was felt so far away. Kellen couldn't remember why he wasted so much time despising her. A beauty such as hers not only knocked the wind out of him, but stole the wind and refused to return it, so he was permanently forced to exist without air in his lungs.

*What the fuck is wrong with you? She's a human. Get it together, Kellen.*

Kellen ripped his eyes off Noella, shattering the trance, and noticed her table mate. Josefyn Yilanci was one of the Primordials in his grade at Delmarth. She possessed an aura of goodness about her that made it impossible not to like her. He could have seen himself becoming friends with Josefyn, had he made any effort with her when they were teenagers. Now he was technically her boss as the Varmin department head, and she dissolved into a shuddering mess every time he spoke to her.

That ship had clearly sailed.

Noella's grey gaze scrutinized Kellen fleetingly, as though he wasn't worth a closer or longer inspection, before she flipped her blonde hair over her shoulder and disregarded his presence, focusing back on Josefyn.

*Fuck no.*

He would not let her dismiss him so effortlessly, not when she looked like *that* and every Primordial in this room had taken notice of the allure she exuded with her smile. While his mind screamed *you hate her, Kellen, you hate her,* his heart and his dick didn't receive the message. Against his better judgment, he found his feet moving in her direction, making a beeline for her table.

"I see you made yourself a little friend," he said in greeting, scraping his eyes across Noella's face.

"Sucks for you that your ploy to make me a social pariah didn't work," Noella slurred with an intoxicated grin.

Kellen peeked down at her empty cup and wondered if this had been her first glass of rakira. For her first time drinking Primordial liquor, it shouldn't have been rakira. She should have started with something far more benign like emirbon, or something fruity with syrup to dilute the alcohol. Her human tolerance wouldn't be able to stomach something so strong. Did she eat before she drank?

*Wait. Why the fuck do I care?*

"That's alright," Kellen sneered despite his plunging thoughts. "I expect you'll find a way to screw it up. Or Ms. Yilanci will come to her senses and realize that associating herself with human scum is not only social, but career assassination."

"Maybe we should let *Ms. Yilanci* pick her own friends and stay out of it, Kilic," Noella snarled at Kellen.

"I like the sound of that," Josefyn murmured, avoiding the glare Kellen fired at her by sipping her drink.

"How's Oliviana holding up?" Noella tipped her chin upward at the flash of fury that sparked in his flushed cheeks. "Does she get visitors in Terminus?" Kellen swiped his tongue over his top row of teeth.

"If I were you," he hissed, leaning in so close to her that his lips almost nuzzled her cheek, "I wouldn't speak so glibly about Oliviana's sentencing. There are enough people in Cavale who would love to see your head on a spike, myself included." Noella pulled her face back slowly.

His lips dragged along her jaw. Neither of them had anticipated the interaction between his mouth and her skin due to the close proximity and the unhurried pace at which she drew away from him. Kellen hissed out a sharp breath between clenched teeth, his lips burning from the residue of her warmth, while Noella's breath stuttered, revealing that she wasn't completely unaffected by him.

"Thanks for the pep talk," she said once she regained her equi-

librium, decorating her face in that tough, Primordial mask that
Kellen didn't admit aloud was almost believable. "But I think I've
reached my quota on small-dick insecurity." Kellen grabbed her
arm before she could shove past him.

Inclining his head so his eyes were level with hers, incensed
green meeting tenacious grey, he growled, "Not that you'll ever have
the pleasure to find out, but my dick is anything but small,
sweetheart."

Noella's eyes thinned into slits.

"If your behavior is any indicator of your size, I can only
assume you're hung like my pinky finger. I would get more pleasure
from stuffing a tootsie roll up my ass than whatever you could
possibly offer me."

Josefyn spat out a mouthful of rakira, spluttering up the amber
liquid into her napkin through an inebriated cackle. Kellen was so
shocked by Noella's crudeness that he almost laughed—*almost.*

"I don't know what a tootsie roll is," he said, a smile tugging at
the corners of his mouth. "Please, Ms. Rose, describe to me what
you meant in extensive detail. I'd like to keep the image in my
spank-bank."

"Oh, to go along with the image of me dying? You're a sick
bastard." She weakly attempted to yank her arm away from him,
but he only held her tighter.

"Is this a game to you?" he roared. "What, you can dish it out,
but you can't handle it thrown back at you?"

"*No,*" she answered sharply, trying to rip her arm out from
between his fingers. "This is not a game to me. I'm trying to survive
here, Kilic. Same as you, same as everyone else. And you know
what? I have every right to be here right now as you do." He opened
his mouth to argue, but his retort plummeted to a painful death
when she yelled, "I DO! I heard Headmistress Dyer today, and I
believed her. If the Gods didn't want me here, I wouldn't be here.
Yet, I am. I have every right to stand in this bar and enjoy myself as
you do. And I'm going to exercise that right, right now."

No matter how hard she tried, she couldn't wiggle her forearm
out of his grip. No matter how hard *he* tried, he couldn't let go of
her arm, even as he sent orders down to his fingers to release her.

*Let me go, Kilic,* she demanded, speaking right into his brain.

*I would if I could,* he answered without thinking, revealing far more than he'd meant to. He didn't understand it, but standing before her right now, even under the spotlight of her hatred, was the closest feeling he got to being around his siblings, to feeling completely unencumbered and stripped bare and seen.

"Is he bothering you, Ella?" a male voice asked from behind them.

Kellen turned his head to find Akio Takeshi standing there with a basket of fried potatoes, smothered in melted, bubbling cheese. Kellen never had an issue with Akio when they were classmates or when they became colleagues, not until right this second, when the sound of his voice interrupted the way Noella had been gazing at him, for the first time with the absence of loathing and instead with something akin to interest. Her eyes tore off him to regard the creel of food in Akio's hands.

She gave the potatoes a look of pure veneration that Kellen dreamt he'd see displayed on her face.

His mind deviated to picturing what Akio's head would look like disunited from his neck.

"Yes, he is," Noella replied, taking advantage of Kellen's focus being diverted and rescuing her arm from his entrapment. She backed up against the wall to create distance between herself and Kellen.

His fingers ached from the loss of her touch. They stung so much that he needed to tuck them into his trouser pockets so he wouldn't give into the urge to leap across the bench and drag her back to him.

*What the fuck is wrong with me?*

"Don't worry. I'm leaving," Kellen snapped, grinding his teeth together to delay his fangs from lengthening. "I have no interest in hanging around the disgusting earthborn, or the Primordials who've chosen to lower their standards to associate with her." *Why does it feel like I'm lying?*

"Go frighten some fish, Kilic," Noella snarled, then beckoned for Akio to reclaim his spot next to her, bestowing onto him a luminous smile that Kellen knew she'd never present to him.

"Ella, you're my fucking hero," Josefyn gushed. Noella clinked her empty glass with Josefyn's.

This was too much for him to bear.

He couldn't handle seeing her accepted by *his* people, acclimating to *his* world, a world where she didn't belong. She acted as though she had better control over this realm than any of the Primordials who were born and raised here, her performance so convincing that he wondered if it was maybe not a performance at all.

*Leave,* Kellen ordered himself as he backed away from their table and watched Akio slide onto the bench next to her. *Leave The Dow and go back to campus.* Instead, his feet took him to the U-shaped bar.

He ordered himself a glass of rakira and plopped down on a stool.

Kellen remained *painfully* aware of where Noella Rose drifted through the tavern, the sound of her laughter skittering beneath his flesh, enveloping itself around his bones. When she stumbled to the bar to order herself another drink, he felt her. When she glided through the crowd with Josefyn and Akio to claim her place on the dancefloor, he felt her. He was acutely aware of every single time her body brushed up against another, his muscles smarting from how tightly wound he clenched them, knowing that if he let himself slacken, he'd lunge out of his stool and body slam anyone who touched her. He didn't understand it, but it took everything in him to stop himself from going back over there and picking another fight with her, just to be in her presence a little while longer.

In his peripheral vision, he caught a glimpse of a vortex of blonde hair twirling within her tiny spot on the dancefloor. He couldn't count on two hands the number of dreams he'd had where that same blonde hair was snarled in his fist, and not because he was smashing her skull into the floor like he so desperately wanted to do right now, just for the way she invaded his thoughts.

She set her hand on Josefyn's shoulder to steady herself and threw her head back, her blonde hair trickling down her spine to graze her mouthwateringly perfect ass before she laughed up at the ceiling.

Gods, her fucking *laugh.*

He wanted to tear into his flesh, gather the vestiges of her laughter twinging through his core, and toss them on the floor so he could crush them with his boot, so he could demolish every piece of her she'd planted inside him the last four weeks. His life had become overwhelmed by her. She flooded the grounds of Delmarth, her name practically intertwined with the wind from the amount he constantly heard it throughout the day. He couldn't escape her, and he wanted to, so fucking badly.

He couldn't even escape her in his apartment—she lived across the hall.

One night. He wanted *one night* to drink himself to oblivion and forget about her existence, and he couldn't even be granted that. It felt like she'd been brought to Cavale not to be a school counselor for Delmarth, not to help their students, but to be his own personal Terminus.

*LEAVE,* he commanded himself. *Stop torturing yourself by being near her. Leave.*

Someway, somehow, he mustered the strength he needed to rise from the stool and head to the door.

———

Kellen flew for hours around Cavale, spanning the complete length of the realm back and forth with no specific destination in mind. It was all he could do to stop himself from either returning to The Dow to pick another fight with Noella, or stop himself from confronting Jarion. Neither urge would benefit him, only bring more agony and conflict, so he chose to remain in the sky, where he felt safe from the plunging descent of his thoughts. When he finally returned to campus, the sun was hidden well behind the moon. Stars leaked across the canvas like sugar spilled over black marble, the galaxy flickering and swirling around him. After he landed, Kellen's wings melted back underneath the casing of his skin as he slid his phone out of his back pocket and sent a message to Laya.

**Kellen:** *I need a favor.* She answered back in less than a minute.

**Laylie:** *I shall grant you said favor depending on the severity and what I could get out of it.*

Kellen chuckled as he typed back. **Kellen:** *Being a good sister isn't enough of a reward for you?*

**Laylie:** *You had to ruin my fun. What's the favor?*

**Kellen:** *I need you to report to me what you notice about Jarion. If he complains of any pain, if he tells you anything about his dragon emerging, you need to tell me.* Kellen chewed a hangnail dangling off his thumb on his way to the faculty housing, staring intensely at his phone for a response.

**Laylie:** *I don't feel comfortable betraying his trust, Kell (not that he's told me anything. Any time I ask, he shuts me down).*

**Kellen:** *I know you're worried about him, Laylie. I am too. Between the two of us, we have to help him. Please. Don't do this for me. Do it for Jare.*

Kellen elbowed open the front door to the faculty housing, his phone vibrating between his fingers.

**Laylie:** *FINE. But if I get caught, I'm dumping all the blame on you.*

**Kellen:** *That's what big brothers are for, my love. Thank you, Laya. I really appreciate this.*

He came to a halt in the hallway.

Contorted into what looked like a smashed pretzel on the floor, Noella Rose leaned her cheek against the door of *his* apartment. Her lashes painted streaked shadows over her cheeks, her forehead crinkling in a manner that suggested there was pain echoing beneath the surface. She looked frighteningly pale and on the verge of passing out. Kellen wasn't allotted time to remember who she was and why he hated her—the phone tumbled out from between his fingers before he sprinted the rest of the span of the hallway, falling to his knees in front of her. His hands surrounded her cheeks, brushing her hair back so nothing was concealing her features from him, and lifted her face out from where it crashed into the carpet, saving her skull from colliding with the wall.

"That's a first," she muttered to herself, sounding strangely pleased. "Usually you throw me *into* walls."

"What the fuck happened, Rose?" He was surprised by the panic he felt strangle his words, how each question that came out sounded more frantic and hoarse. "Are you hurt? Did someone hurt you?"

"I shan't find me keys," she slurred, then spluttered a gale of intoxicated giggles that could have been classified as adorable, if Kellen wasn't so anxious and consumed with examining her body for injuries.

"Where are Josefyn and Akio?"

"They…they dropped me off h…ho…hours ago." She hiccupped, her nose scrunching up like she tasted something nasty in her mouth. "I think I fell asleep."

"They just left you here?" They left a human who'd experienced her first dalliance with rakira *alone?*

"I told them to go. I…I'm fine." She tried to swat him away, but he grabbed her hand before it swung in his eye.

"Yeah. So fine that you're sitting in front of *my* door." Noella lifted her head, dragging her eyes down the length of his door.

"Oh," she chortled, slapping her forehead and snorting, some spit dribbling down her chin.

*Don't find this cute.*

Kellen sunk his teeth into his bottom lip to keep from laughing with her. "Where was the last place you saw your keys?"

"My pocket."

"Pants pocket or jacket pocket?"

"Jacket. I think." Kellen didn't ask for permission before his hands dove into the pockets of her leather jacket. "Whoa!" she squealed when she felt his fingers against her hips through the sheath. Kellen tried to ignore the way her curves fit perfectly in his hands, then noticed when her foot jerked dangerously close to his crotch that she was missing a shoe. "At least buy a girl dinner first."

"Imagine if your keys were in your jeans pocket, sweetheart. This would be a very different conversation."

"Don't call me sweetheart," she groaned. "It makes me forget that I hate you." Kellen froze a moment too long, taken off guard by that unexpected revelation, then resumed his search, locating something metal and small in the depth of her left pocket, hidden within the folds of the excess material.

"Got it," he announced, dangling the keys in front of her nose before snatching them away. "Where's your other shoe?"

"My other—?" Noella peeked down at her feet, her lips wilting into a pout. "Oh no! Those were my favorite boots!"

"If you start crying," Kellen warned, "I will leave you here. Give me your hands."

"They're actually rain boots," she rambled while Kellen tugged on her arms and pulled her into a standing position. She stumbled into his chest, her chin resting on his shoulder before her little fingers fisted a handful of his button down, wrinkling the fabric. For the life of him, he didn't understand why he not only couldn't, but didn't *want* to shove her away. "Because of the pointed toe, they can masquerade as regular boots." She flexed the one boot she still possessed to show him what she meant.

"Why do they need to masquerade as regular boots? Does it fucking matter?"

"You asking that question shows you don't understand fashion." Kellen clicked his tongue, supporting her with one arm. "That is further reinforced by the fact that I've only ever seen you wear the same outfit. Do you own more clothing, or is this button down and these slacks the only items in your closet?"

"Says the girl who wears colors that don't compliment her skin tone and clothes two sizes too big."

Noella pulled her face back.

"I don't know what I'm more shocked by. The fact that you called me a *girl* and not a disgusting human, or the fact that you just admitted you've paid attention to what clothing I wear."

"You admitted it first."

"That I notice what you wear? It's hard not to when it's the same thing every day and it fits your body *perfectly,* like it was made for you." She continued babbling, a floodgate open, not even conscious of what she was saying. "Seriously, Kilic. You have a terrible personality, but *damn* do you have a ridiculously attractive body and face. How is that fair? Why can't you be as ugly on the outside as you are on the inside? It makes things very confusing." Kellen fought a smirk, completely ignoring her meaningless insults to focus on the hidden message woven through them.

"How much time do you spend thinking about my face and body, Rose?"

"About the same amount of time you spend seeking me out just to start a fight," she fired back with an arched brow, rendering him speechless from how spot-on she was. She leaned in so close that he could taste the rakira on her breath. "Tell me something, Kilic. When you walk into a room, do you purposefully search for my scent in a crowd?" Kellen didn't dignify her with a response.

He elected instead to shepherd her towards her own door, stabbing her key into the lock and twisting it for her.

"Wait, Kilic, stop." Kellen paused the process of opening her door. "I'm confused," she stammered.

"What are you confused about, Rose?"

"Why you're helping me." *Me too, earthborn.* "You hate me, yet you're helping me to my door. It's because I look hot, isn't it?" Noella fragmented into snickers, while Kellen's thoughts escalated into a frenzy.

*Yes. No. Fuck. I really am that terrible of a person.*

"Despite what you think of me, Ms. Rose, and my past actions towards you, I'm not *that* horrible. Besides, if I didn't help, you would've given up looking for your keys and slept out here, and I would've hit you with my door in the morning when I tried to leave my apartment. Just trying to avoid spending three nights in Terminus for accidentally hurting you." Noella stared at him silently for so long that he wondered if there was something on his cheek. He almost touched his face just to check.

"So it's *not* because I look hot?" The corners of Kellen's mouth capitulated and lifted in unison with her playful smile.

"Don't flatter yourself, Ms. Rose," he jested, though from her answering laugh, he knew she didn't believe that.

Kellen finally pushed her front door open. Noella buried her face in the crook of his neck with a moan, shielding her eyes from the brightness she expected to encounter when they walked inside, then allowed him to guide her by his arm around her waist into her apartment. Instantly, they were met by a furry, four-legged creature with creamy beige fur and massive, bright black eyes, flashing a *huge* smile at them the moment they stepped inside. Kellen didn't know dogs were capable of producing smiles that looked like *actual* smiles. He found nothing cute about it. It was fucking terrifying.

Yes, Delmarth Academy's Varmin department head, who could shift into a twenty thousand pound dragon and whom the King of the Gods wanted for himself as a serjeant, was afraid of the tiny little dog with the goofy grin. If Noella wasn't using him as a crutch to stand, Kellen would have gotten the fuck out of there.

"Freya!" Noella squealed as the gremlin leapt onto Noella's legs and began licking her fingers aggressively. "Freya, this is Mr. Kilic. Don't be fooled by his kind gesture. We don't like him." Noella must have felt Kellen shudder, or heard his sharp intake of breath when the creature leaned forward to sniff him, because she turned to him with a grin that outdid the dog's. "Kilic, are you afraid of the little dog?"

"Fuck no," he stuttered, refusing to make eye contact with the thing.

The creature shifted its focus onto Kellen, burrowing its snout in his knee. He tried to gently knock it away, but gentle was not in his vocabulary. It expunged a great amount of effort for him to temper the movement when what he really wanted to do was smack it. The fluffball refused to get the message and began to lick the back of his hand.

"She likes you," Noella observed with a hint of bemusement, then drawled, "I can't imagine why."

*I don't like you,* Kellen spoke into the creature's head, withdrawing his hand. *Go away.* A high-pitched, sugary voice filled his ears.

*You took care of her. So I like YOU,* the thing protested.

*I've hurt her more than I've helped her, gremlin.*

*And I know that wasn't your first choice.* Kellen furrowed his brows at the dog, who continued to present a sunny smile externally.

*What do you mean, that wasn't my first choice?* The line of communication between them went silent as the creature nudged his wrist with its snout, forcing his hand to turn over so it could nuzzle the top of its head inside his palm. *Answer me, you monster. What do you mean that wasn't my first choice?*

"I don't feel so good," Noella muttered, her lips twisting in an odd shape as her cheeks lost their healthy blush. Kellen escorted her to the couch, draping her across the cushions before he crossed the room to the kitchen and grabbed the metal trash bin, positioning it beside her on the ground next to the sofa. The dog jumped onto the couch and adjusted its shape so it could fit against Noella's body, resting its chin on her hip. Noella lifted her hand to fondle its head, rotating onto her back.

"If you feel sick, don't lie on your back," Kellen snapped, grabbing her shoulders and rolling her so she lay on her side.

*See?* The gremlin's voice returned to his ears. *Your first choice.*

*You're wrong. I hate her,* he asserted, shoving those words down his throat, forcing them to seep into his heart, to the weakest part of his being that refused to remember she was despicable, an abomination, a disgusting blemish tarnishing his world—

"My head hurts," Noella mumbled through a groan, pressing the heel of her hand to her forehead, covering her eyes with her forearm to block out the overhead light.

She represented everything he'd been taught to abhor, and yet in that moment, Kellen would have slayed all the particles of light in that room contributing to her pain, would have shredded them apart with his bare hands, if only to compensate for his touch not being enough to heal her.

*You need to leave,* he told himself. *You need to walk out that door and never turn back.*

"Alright. I've fulfilled my duty of safely delivering you to your doorstep. You've used up all my kindness. I'm going now."

Kellen began his trek to the exit, but before his fingers could stretch towards the door handle, Noella squeaked, "Kilic?"

He spun around automatically, with no control over his actions. "Yes, Rose?" he groused.

"Why do you hate me?" Her voice sounded so small, so fragile, so unlike her usual tenacity. "I get that your kind doesn't respect my kind, that you think humans are weak. But is that the *only* reason you despise me?" A thousand possible responses, all equally true, fluttered around his mind.

*I despise you because you're everywhere. I can't escape you in the waking hours or in slumber. You've taken over my thoughts, my dreams, my every breath. You represent everything we've been taught not to value, yet you're the strongest person I've encountered in all my twenty-eight years of life. I despise the fact that I respect you, that you're good with the students and you know it too. I despise the way you meet every challenge I pose and dominate every argument, that you're the only worthy adversary I've ever faced. I despise the fact that you're right—I do seek out disputes with you just to steal more of your time for myself, because fighting with you has become the best part of my day. I despise your presence in my land because it's putting my guardianship over my siblings in jeopardy. I despise how if I let my walls down with you, I know you will be the only person in Cavale who would not only try to understand me, but would probably succeed. It terrifies me how easy it would be to yield to you, how easy it was for you to take command of me tonight, how easy it would be for me to fall into you. You are drowning me, Noella Rose, and no matter how hard I try to stop it, I'm fucking letting you.*

"That's one of them," he answered elusively, swallowing a thick breath. "And a million other reasons I can't tell you."

Noella frowned. "Why not?"

"Because they'll make you *not* hate me, and it's better for us both if you do." Kellen loathed the way she was looking at him now, with a sweet softness he didn't deserve. He allowed himself one touch— his fingers danced over her temple, brushing tendrils of blonde hair out of her eyes. Her pupils eclipsed the grey of her irises as she followed his hand movement. "In fact, it's better if you don't remember this at all."

Kellen splayed his fingers over her forehead.

He gathered every memory of the last thirty minutes since he found her in the hallway and vacuumed it into his hand by pulling his fingers together and pilfering the images from her brain. When his fingers disengaged from her forehead, Noella's eyes sealed shut, a breathy yawn loosing from her parted lips as she slipped into a deep slumber. Kellen headed to the door, but stopped when he felt two beady eyes pierce his cheek, forcing him to twist around and meet the expectant stare of Noella's dog.

The creature gave him a condescending look down its nose with what he interpreted as an amused smile.

Somehow, he knew it had heard everything he'd said about Noella in his thoughts.

*Don't tell anyone,* he found himself pleading, which was fucking ridiculous since the dog couldn't talk to anyone but him. Right as his fingers enveloped the door handle, he heard the gremlin's voice in his head.

*There's a fine line between love and hate.*

*Fuck off,* he snarled, then stormed out of Noella's apartment.

## CHAPTER 9

# ELLA

A MESSAGE from Akio was waiting for Ella when she powered her phone back on the next day.

**Akio:** *Thought you'd want to know that your other boot is in my car. If you'd like to retrieve it, come join us for breakfast. There are waffles here with your name on it. Jo will leave the door unlocked for you.*

Ella spent that entire weekend with Josefyn and Akio. The three of them came together for every meal. They joined her on all her walks with Freya. They talked for hours on end without pause. By the conclusion of the weekend, Ella wasn't sure she'd ever laughed that hard in her entire life, her abdomen still aching from the residue of pure happiness. Throughout her hike to the academic sector on Monday morning, she replayed the memories from that weekend on a relentless loop, reexperiencing the comradery she'd found with Jo and Akio while unable to wipe the smile from her face.

The images grew foggy whenever she strained to remember how she returned home the night of The Dow. The camera roll in her head from that night finished off when Josefyn and Akio dropped her off at her dormitory. She'd woken up the next morning on her couch, Freya licking her cheek, and her trash bin next to her, unsure how she made it inside her apartment when what she last remembered was being unable to find her keys. Whatever the truth was of how she managed to get through the door appeared in her brain like a picture blotted with black ink, obstructed and impossible to see through. She treasured the carousel of moments from the last few days that she could remember, which gave her a glimmer of hope that she may be able to survive in Cavale after all.

Ella's smile washed away when she stepped into her office and discovered that Kellen Kilic had commandeered her space.

She froze at the threshold, her fingers garroting the door handle as she watched the Varmin department head splay his feet out on her desk. The same desk she'd spent an hour on Friday before she left for the weekend scrubbing with disinfectant after a seven-year-old songbird-shifter vomited maggots—she *wished* she were kidding—all over the mahogany surface, having mistaken her office for the nurse's station. She cocked her head at Kellen when it took him a whole minute to look up from the notebook he was perusing and notice her standing there.

"Rose," he tossed at her over his shoulder in his clipped version of a greeting, then threw in for good measure, "Your zipper is down." Her eyes and fingers dropped down to her slacks on instinct, discovering them fully zipped. Kellen's grin revealed a soft dimple in the center of his cheek.

She set her hands on her hips. "Kilic? What's wrong with this picture?"

Kellen's eyes swept over the room, scanning the desk, then drifted to the floor, where his brows lifted in recognition.

"Ah," he exclaimed, dipping to the ground to pluck a discarded gum wrapper from off the carpet, tossing it in the nearby trash. "There we go."

"No!" she cried, slamming the door shut. "What're you doing in my office when I'm not in here?"

"I needed quiet. Isn't this supposed to be a *safe zone?*" He spoke those last two words between air quotes and with derision as he pointed to the sign she'd hung up on the wall that read *this is a safe space for you to be who you are.*

"If you don't respect the safe zone, then you don't get to benefit from the safe zone," she hissed.

"You better work on your comebacks if you intend to survive the school year." Ella's eye twitched.

"You have your own classroom," she reminded him. "*With* your own office."

"The Varmin student council took over my classroom for their meeting. I told them to go somewhere else, but they said all the other classrooms were full."

Ella scoffed, "Oh, so it's a problem when other people lay claim to *your* space, but it's totally fine for you to take over mine?"

"Yes." He didn't hesitate. There was nothing sweet about the smile that unfurled over his lips.

"You are unbelievable," she grumbled, dropping her briefcase on the couch and shedding her coat. When she looked further, she realized that Kellen had *her* notebook within his grasp, the one where she kept all her notes about her interactions with students. She stretched across the desk and snatched it from between his fingers. "This is confidential," she asserted, hugging the book to her chest.

"That's your favorite word, isn't it?" he sneered.

"Ever heard of privacy? The children are entitled to it, and so am I."

"You are entitled to nothing in Cavale, Ms. Rose. You need to stop clinging to your arbitrary human laws. They mean nothing here."

"I don't care if they mean nothing *here*. They mean something to *me.*" Kellen opened his mouth to respond, but then his gaze fell onto her sweater. Ella typically wore to work colors and shapes that wouldn't bring too much notice to her, but today, she'd had the urge to step outside of her comfort zone, choosing a fuchsia sweater with a straight neckline that was more fitted then what she would normally grab. "Are you even listening to me, or just staring at my chest?" she snapped.

"Purple," he whispered to himself, as though he were tucking away important information in his brain.

"What was that?"

"Nothing." He cleared his throat before resting the back of his head against the wall behind him. "Oliviana is back today,"

Kellen reminded her, folding his fingers together over his stomach.

"I know," Ella mumbled to herself, setting her notebook on the desk to avoid his eyes.

"Are you scared she'll return with a vengeance, earthborn? Maybe she enjoyed her visit to Terminus and wants to make it permanent."

Ella glanced at Kellen, unable to read if he was messing with her or actually trying to warn her.

"Has that ever happened before?" she asked quietly.

"No, Oliviana would be the first. She's a masochist. I would know from personal experience."

"What, from having sex with her?" Ella scoffed, her volume rising along with her irritation.

He slanted his head to the side. "Does the idea of me having sex with her bother you, Rose?"

"You wish. You're just so predictable. *Of course* you're fucking her. And I already *know* you're about to tell me it's not serious, because you don't *do* serious, right? That's not your *thing?*" His silence spoke volumes. "You know what? Good for you, Kilic. Go be a depraved cliché somewhere else. This is *my* office for the next nine months, and I'd really like to have it back now."

Kellen didn't move a muscle. He kept grinning at her, his absurd, impish smile burrowing painfully under her skin.

"What're you doing?" she growled.

"It's called a smile, sweetheart. Ever heard of one?" Ella recognized her own words.

"You do realize that copying is the sincerest form of flattery, so by you quoting me back to me, you're basically admitting you think I'm a genius." Kellen just rolled his eyes. Ella finally reached her limit and clapped her hands. "Alright. Playtime's over. Get out of my chair, Kilic. Some of us have *actual* work to do."

Kellen finally released her chair from detention and allowed her to reclaim it. He started walking to the door, but suddenly came to an abrupt halt in the middle of the room and spun right back around.

"Oh, I almost forgot! I have something for you." He reached

into his trouser pocket and produced a tiny block of taffy wrapped in white packaging that had the words *Tootsie Roll* emblazoned over it. He placed the tootsie roll right on her keyboard, over the letter *K*. "For you to stuff up your ass," he drawled as his final words, swaggering to the door.

"I HATE YOU!" she screamed, chucking the taffy at the back of his head. It tumbled onto her carpet as he closed the door behind him.

Since Kellen left her office that morning, Ella felt the hefty weight of dread surround her shoulders as she waited for her unavoidable confrontation with Oliviana. Fear stalked after her when she was summoned to the Herculea sector to, once again, deal with Oken and his rage, though she escaped this encounter with no broken bones. It nestled deep within her bones every time her amulet vibrated and she checked to make sure she wasn't being summoned to the Meteoro sector. She eventually grew so anxious, the pit in her stomach swelling to the point of near rupture, that she messaged Akio and Josefyn.

**Ella:** *Have either of you seen Oliviana Bryan today?*

Ella chewed her thumbnail, realizing she'd nearly gnawed the nail down to the nub, then withdrew her hand from her mouth, opting instead to curl her fingers around her Diet Coke mug to distract from the urge to nibble.

Josefyn and Akio's answers disbanded the pit in her chest, releasing her lungs from imprisonment.

**Akio:** *Not here today. The wind-bender classroom borders the Cerebri sector, so if she was here, I would've seen her.*

**Josefyn:** *I heard she called in "sick" and Headmistress Dyer is PISSED. Maybe the Gods will smile upon you and she'll be fired?*

**Ella:** *One can only hope. The Gods seem to like me quite a bit.*

**Akio:** *You know the saying. If you want to make the Gods laugh, tell them your plans and wait for them to scream FUCK YOU in your face.*

**Ella:** *No offense, but your Gods don't sound very nice.*

**Akio:** *Fuck, whatever about the nature of Primordials gave that away? (I hope you can hear my loving sarcasm).*

**Ella:** *You ruined the joke by explaining it, Kio.*

**Josefyn:** *Sorry, my love, but I have to agree with Ella.*

**Akio:** *Wow. Betrayed by my wife and friend. However will I recover from this blow to my confidence?*

**Josefyn:** *I'll make it up to you tonight in the bedroom ;) Are you coming to Power Practice today to observe Jamie, El? She just got here.*

**Ella:** *On my way there now. Don't let your co-teacher lock me out.*

**Josefyn:** *Wouldn't dream of it.*

"Hey," Ella called out to Josefyn as she edged her way inside the serpent-shifter dome. Josefyn sat perched on the bench against the wall, violet hair woven in an intricate fishtail design. Two loose curls wiggled free from the braid and framed her gaunt cheeks. "I have a present for you."

Ella tossed Kellen's tootsie roll to Josefyn.

Jo caught the candy with one hand, unfurling her fingers to observe the tiny object balanced in her palm.

Once she read the writing on the wrapper and realized what this was, she cackled, "*This* is the size of a tootsie roll? You compared his shaft to *this?*" Josefyn whistled through her teeth. "You're a savage, El."

"Kilic left this on my desk this morning, after breaking into my office, and told me to stuff it up my ass."

"Seriously?" Jo snorted. "This war of wills between the two of you sure is entertaining to watch."

"Not so enjoyable to live, but I'm glad we're giving you a nice show."

Ella sat next to Josefyn on the bench. Josefyn held the small candy up to her face, hugging it with her thumb and index finger before examining the way it rolled between her fingers.

"How did he even get one of these? Aren't they Earthly Plane candies?"

"He must've known somehow that the fridge in my office can make any food I want, which tells me he's been inside my office when I'm not there more times than I'm aware of." The thought made her stomach churn. "The fridge was a gift from Headmistress Dyer so I wouldn't have to go into the teacher's lounge anymore. I was getting pummeled every time I went there."

"I'm sorry. That's so sad." Jo sniffed the tootsie roll. "I feel weird putting this in my mouth now."

"Give it to Akio without the wrapper. Tell him what it is after he's already eaten it." Jo dissolved into gales of laughter.

"You're a genius. Where have you been all my life?"

"In another dimension," Ella bantered, her eyes sweeping over the twelve pairs of students engaging in combat exercises. The sixteen-year-old Primordials each wielded wooden swords with padded hilts as they emulated what Mr. Armstrong was displaying at the front of the room with a dummy.

"Stand in a sloped position with bent knees," Mr. Armstrong shouted to the students, arching his knees to show what they needed to imitate. "This is the only time you'll be encouraged to make yourselves small. It aids you to present yourself as a smaller target, especially at the start of a clash. Underestimation will be your friend in battle. Preserve your strength for later."

"It's combat day, I see," Ella muttered to herself.

"We switch off every day for Power Practice," Josefyn explained. "One day, combat training. The next day, power training. I teach power training, while Mr. Armstrong teaches combat."

"And they're training to fight in the war against Lantari?" Josefyn nodded. "Why is Cavale at war with Lantari?"

"It's a long story that we don't have enough time to get fully in depth with, but I'll try to give you the cliff-note version now." Jo shifted her body to face Ella. "The Lantarians are a species known as Sireres."

"What are Sireres?" Ella had meant to make a trip to Delmarth's library and research the story behind the war between Cavale and Lantari, but the demands of her job had kept her from putting the plan into action.

"The Sireres are basically Primordials, but their powers are derived from a different God, so their abilities are somewhat different from ours, though not drastically. They also have a different grouping system. Sireres who can shift into beings in

Lantari aren't called Varmin. They're called Sirerebrates. The war isn't actually between the Primordials and the Sireres. It's between Aros Cavalian, our Godly king, and Edar Lantarian, their Godly king. Edar used to be considered a Cavalian God before he broke away from Cavale and created his own empire, renaming the Primordials there as Sireres and turning them against Aros. We have no reason to hate one another apart from the fact that our allegiances are to our Gods." Ella sensed a volume of sorrow in the underbelly of Josefyn's explanation.

"Why do Aros and Edar hate each other?"

"The answer to that question changes depending on who you ask and depending on who supports which God. There are Primordials who back Edar, just like there are Sireres who back Aros. The Primordials who favor Edar are referred to as Dissidents. If they're caught circulating any undesirable propaganda against Aros Cavalian in Cavale, they're sentenced to a lifetime in Terminus. You may meet a Dissident during your time here and never know it. It's not something you broadcast in Cavale unless you'd like to be tortured for the rest of your existence." Josefyn's lips pulled up at the corners. "If I were you, I'd ask Kellen to explain the story to you. He teaches History of the Gods, so he would do it justice far better than I ever could."

"Thanks, but if that's my only option, I'd rather search for the story myself." Ella turned back to the students. "Which one is Jamie?" She lowered her voice to maintain discretion.

"Middle row. Third pair from the left." Ella's eyes followed Josefyn's directions, landing on a blue-haired, average-height female. She was dressed in an oversized Delmarth Academy crewneck sweatshirt and black leggings that flared out at the ends, finishing off at her ankle, only a ghost of the fabric grazing her white sneakers. Josefyn had been correct in describing Jamie as clean—not a single blemish or spot of dirt scarred the surface of her shoes, her ponytail pristine and yanked high above her head so the strands couldn't drip down her back. Jamie awkwardly passed the sword from one hand to the other, as if weighing the damage a real sword could do and struggling to picture herself brandishing one. Where one might have walked into the room and only noticed the students swinging their rapiers wildly and using the exercise as an excuse to exert their aggression, Ella paid close attention to Jamie's body language and her facial contortions.

The class began practicing the eight different angles of attack, directed by Mr. Armstrong to strike at the air first before attempting to run the drills with each other. It didn't take long before the class erupted into a frenzy of frothing energy and dangerous excitement, jamming their wooden blades into the cushioned floor. Jamie remained reserved with her blade, only half-heartedly attempting the different movements. She kept clutching her chest, her fingers clawing at the material of her sweatshirt.

With every cry of excitement, Jamie flinched, her body folding inward, her hand jerking to her chest.

"Do Cerebri emotion-manipulators feel other people's emotions in their minds or their hearts?" Ella asked Jo.

"I'm not sure. That's an Akio question. I'm not that intimate with Cerebri sensations."

"Come on, Jamie," Mr. Armstrong shouted to her from the front of the room, clanging his hands together. "Look around you. Everyone else is doing the drill. Pick it up." Jamie's eyes narrowed into slits.

"*No,*" she snarled, chucking the wooden sword at Mr. Armstrong's head. The rapier instead crashed into the head of the student in front of Jamie. The female whipped around with a strident cry, cupping the back of her now throbbing skull, and grabbed her own sword from off the ground, lunging at Jamie.

"Shit!" Josefyn hissed before she and Ella dove off the bench to sprint across the room. "Rain, stop!"

Rain crawled on top of Jamie, a curtain of her magenta-pink hair showering down over their intertwined bodies, and flattened the even surface of the wooden blade into Jamie's trachea to cut off her air supply. Jamie writhed beneath Rain's weight, spluttering choked wheezes as her fingers slapped the mattress in vain, searching for something she could use in retaliation to defend herself. Mr. Armstrong reached Rain first, wrenching her off Jamie by lifting her around her waist and dragging her away. Rain's legs flailed in their quest to stretch back towards Jamie and make contact with the side of her head. Ella lowered to the ground beside Jamie, proffering her hand.

"Are you okay?" she asked in a soft, subdued voice to preserve some semblance of privacy in a room filled with students whose undivided attentions were latched onto them. Jamie raised topaz-shaded yellow eyes, glazed over in a sheet of tears, and subtly shook her head. Ella nodded her head in answer. She pulled Jamie to her feet, then turned to Josefyn and said, "We're going to talk outside."

Ella draped her arm over Jamie's shoulders to lead her outside. Rain bellowed nonsense behind them, lobbing insults at Jamie's back.

"If you ever come close to me again, I will fucking destroy you, Jamila Finley!" Ella tightened her embrace around Jamie when she felt a tremor ricochet through the Varmin's tense muscles.

"Let's sit here," Ella suggested, guiding Jamie out the front door and directing her to squat on the asphalt. Jamie hunkered down and curled up in a crushed ball against the metal dome, burying her face between her knees to shroud her face. She expelled a sob that sounded as though it had been trapped inside her imploring to be released, the kind of scream that escaped in a throttled, vicious cadence, so nasty that it scraped against her throat. Ella settled on her knees in front of Jamie, gifting her a moment to *feel* before laying her hand on Jamie's shoulder. She whispered, "Jamie, I want you to breathe. Inhale for four seconds, exhale for six. Can you do that?" At first, the only response Jamie granted Ella was a strangulated, hoarse wail. Jamie shook, then squeezed her knees inward to dig them deeper into her temples. "Jamie, please don't do that. It'll give you a headache."

"It…it *hurts*," Jamie whimpered, tears escaping down her cheeks in hurried, unbridled streams.

"What hurts?"

"*Everything!*" She finally lifted her head out from between her legs to yell at Ella. Jamie's yellow eyes now appeared as rounded pupils surrounded by vertically elongated irises, the gaze of a serpent blinking back at her.

"Can you tell me *where* you feel it hurt?" Jamie rocked forward, her fingers tearing at the soil, mashing the pulverized dirt within her fist. Her hand then released the loam and trembled on its journey to splay over her chest.

"H…Here. And…" Quivering fingers danced over her temples, her cheeks drenched in pools of sadness. "Here."

"What is it you're feeling that hurts so much?" Jamie sunk her teeth into her bottom lip, a string of blood trickling down her chin. Ella used the sleeve of her jacket to smudge the crimson droplets off Jamie's face. "Do you know who I am, Jamie?"

"You're the human everyone hates." Ella's lips twitched in a small smile.

"Well, yes, but I also have a name. It's Ms. Rose. I'm your school counselor. Do you know what a school counselor does?" Jamie shook her head. "I'm here to be academic, social, and emotional support for you. That feeling that you have right now? That pain? It's my job to try and help you deal with that."

"H…How?" Ella crawled around Jamie to position herself against the steel dome, flanking Jamie's side.

"Talking helps, unburdening that feeling so you're not carrying it alone. Sometimes there are truths inside you that burn longer when you keep them contained. By sharing with me, you pass some of that burden to me, so you're not burning alone." Jamie licked the flood of tears off her lips.

"It's heavy," Jamie mumbled. "Too heavy. I don't know if you can handle it."

"Trust me. I'm stronger than I look." Jamie rested the back of her head against the metal dome and exhaled a trembling breath.

"Sometimes I fantasize about taking my own heart out." The words rushed off Jamie's tongue like she was afraid that if she didn't spit them out, they would remain stuck inside her, burning her from the inside out. She quickly added, "I wouldn't ever do it, though. It's not a serious thought. It's not that I want to die. I just…don't want to feel anymore. I walk around this campus and am bombarded with what everyone else is feeling. I can't escape it. It's just too much. And *Rain*—" Her voice ensnarled with a sob before her eyes fluttered shut to squeeze out more tears.

"What happened with Rain?" Jamie hugged her knees to her chest.

"Rain is my girlfriend. *Was* my girlfriend." The word *was* sounded like it ached to produce. "I broke up with her at the start of the year. I…I didn't want to." Jamie buried her face in her palms, sobbing into her fingers.

Ella waited a second, then asked gently, "Why did you?"

"Because! I…I didn't want to feel anymore." Her fingers slipped off her face, drooping to her sides. "Loving someone hurts enough. Try loving someone and also feeling the pain of how much they love you at the same time. It's not as magical as it sounds. It's fucking exhausting to always feel what your partner feels. I couldn't shut it off. I had to sit with that feeling all the time. It just got to be too much, so I ended it. Now all I feel when I'm around her is how much she *hates* me. She *hates* me, Ms. Rose, and I have to *feel* it all the time, every second of every day because we're in all the same classes. Hate hurts even more than love does. I don't want to *feel* anymore."

Jamie arranged her elbows to rest on her arched knees. She dropped her head into her hands to stare down at the ground.

"What would it look like for you not to feel anything?" Jamie twisted her head to look at Ella.

"I can't stop feeling," she protested with an edge to her tone. "That's impossible."

"I know. I'm saying, in a hypothetical situation, what would it look like to not feel anything?"

"I…I don't know." Jamie itched her nails down the length of her thighs, straightening up against the wall. "I'd feel lighter? Less heavy? I would finally be able to breathe. I wouldn't be in pain anymore."

"What would you do if you didn't feel that pain?"

"I…I don't know." She tipped her chin at Ella. "What do you do, Ms. Rose? How do you not feel pain?" Ella smiled wistfully.

"We all feel that pain, Jamie. Maybe not to the same extent that you do, maybe not as strongly as you do, but we all feel it. It's uncomfortable and tragic and beautiful. It's a consequence of living."

Jamie choked on a sob. "But it hurts so *much*. Every second. It never ends."

"It shouldn't end. That pain lets you know you're alive, and there's so much beauty in being alive. I know you think there will be freedom if you can't feel it, but there's only one thing worse than the pain of love. It's the pain of loneliness. The only way to stop feeling is complete isolation from the world, and that is the farthest thing from healing. You are idealizing feeling empty when that loss of feeling would be the most painful experience of all." Jamie turned her face into the metal wall, pressing her forehead against the cold, smooth surface, tears rolling onto her chin.

"I don't know how much more of this I can take," she wept, her fingers skulking across the asphalt in search of something to clutch. Ella extended her hand as an option. Jamie took it, crushing Ella's fingers in her grip—not enough to truly hurt her, just enough for Jamie to unpack a tiny drop of the burden weighing her down, passing some of her pain to Ella. "I'm so tired all the time, Ms. Rose. I feel so fucking weak."

"What does being weak mean to you?"

"I can't do anything with all these emotions. I can't use them to defend Cavale against Lantari. You saw me in there. I was fucking pathetic. I couldn't focus cause everyone was getting so riled up and all their emotions started flooding me at once. Imagine if that was an actual battle with the Sireres. I'd be fucking toast. I can't do anything productive with emotions. All they do is bring me down." Ella squeezed Jamie's hand, bidding Jamie's serpent eyes to elevate from off the floor.

"So you think being strong means you have to have powers that can be useful in a fight?"

"I think being strong means you have to be able to provide something that can be of real help to the Gods," Jamie replied, then added tersely, "You're not from here, so you might not get that."

"You're right. I'm not from here, so it's hard for me at times to understand that way of thinking. I understand that this is what you've been taught to believe, but Jamie, there are infinite ways to be strong. Being able to fight or having powers useful in a fight is just one of them. Another is being able to use that ability of yours, to empathize deeply with others, to help people learn how to manage their own emotions, which in its own way *can* be useful in this war, if you're able to help others to regulate their feelings in battle. That *is* real help, Jamie, or it could be if you learn how to separate your feelings from others so it doesn't overwhelm you like this." Jamie rested her head on Ella's shoulder, dissolving into tears. Ella pulled Jamie closer, then said, "Feeling intensely does not make you weak. You of all people should know that. You walk around this school every single day, carrying not just your emotions, but everyone else's inside you. It should be considered an accomplishment that you're able to stand at all, let alone that you're able to be in a classroom and complete all your work. You think feeling emotions makes you weak because you're attributing strength to something physical or tangible. Feeling intensely makes you stronger than every person who wastes their breath telling you not to feel at all."

Jamie and Ella sat against the dome for another five minutes in silence. Jamie cried into Ella's shoulder. Ella became a soundless pillar of support, wordlessly encouraging Jamie to drown in her emotions, to welcome that pain of feeling rather than shove it away, one step closer to learning how to manage it. When Jamie was ready, she began inhaling for four seconds and exhaling for six to abate her tears, emulating what Ella demonstrated.

"On a scale of one being *Terminus is looking mightily attractive* and ten being *I could burst from happiness*, how're you feeling right now?"

"A six?" Jamie answered uncertainly through a slight chuckle, not quite understanding Ella's system of measurement.

"We can work with a six. I think we can get you to a higher number, though." Ella used the wall to help rise off the ground, then pulled Jamie up to stand. "Let's start meeting together once a week. I'll look at your schedule and figure out a time that works. Do you have any preference for a time?"

"Um…can we meet during lunch? It'll be less obvious that I'm going to *counseling* if it's during a period when everyone's in different places on campus." Jamie spat the word *counseling* like it tasted vile.

"Let's meet on Thursdays during lunch, starting this week." Jamie departed for the dome, but Ella called out before she made it to the door, "Jamie?" The Varmin rotated around, the ends of her blue hair whacking her cheek. "There is no shame in going to counseling. There is no shame in needing or asking for help. Anyone who tries to shame you for it probably needs the same help."

For the first time since they'd been sitting together, Jamie's lips settled into a smile—a tiny one, a barely sturdy one hanging on by a thread, but a sweet, beautiful smile, nonetheless.

"You're not so bad for a human, Ms. Rose." Her fingers gripped the door handle before she tossed over her shoulder, "See you on Thursday," and headed back inside the dome to rejoin her class.

## CHAPTER 10

# ELLA

A KNOCK on her office door yanked Ella away from the notes she'd been scribbling about her encounter with Jamie. She'd only had three minutes of peace before the next crisis arose, though that was standard procedure in the life of a school counselor.

"Come in," she shouted, then closed her leather notebook and tucked it safely inside her desk drawer.

Headmistress Dyer peeked into Ella's office, adjusting the red spectacles on the bridge of her nose. She only poked her head through the small opening she'd made in the doorway, the rest of her body remaining hidden in the hallway.

"I have a student here who needs to speak with someone," Headmistress Dyer explained, a strange twinge of tenseness in her tone, conveying emotion Ella didn't know the Headmistress was capable of expressing or feeling. "This kind of thing is *way* past my level of expertise, so I brought him to you."

"Sure." *What the hell does that mean?* "Bring him in."

Headmistress Dyer shoved the door the full way open, gesticulating with her hand for the student to go to Ella. A gangly young male who appeared no older than twelve inched his way inside her office. There was something oddly familiar about him, though they'd not been formally acquainted. The young boy slid the red beanie off his head, raking his fingers through his short, black curls, and yanked at the tendrils, then lowered onto Ella's couch and proceeded to stare blankly at her wall.

Headmistress Dyer locked Ella's door. Ella rose from her chair, circling her desk to meet them by the couch.

"This is Jarion Ates," Headmistress Dyer introduced, then lightly kicked Jarion's calf and mumbled, "Can you say hello to Ms. Rose, Jarion?" Jarion said nothing. Just continued staring vacuously at the wall. Headmistress Dyer huffed at the lack of response, then turned back to Ella. "Mr. Park, the middle school dragon-shifter instructor, brought him to my office this afternoon. Jarion, would you like to tell Ms. Rose why?"

"I'd rather not," he spat in a flat, emotionless voice, still refusing to look at them.

"In what universe do you think it's acceptable to take that tone with me, Mr. Ates?" Headmistress Dyer barked, her volume making even Ella jump. Jarion peeled his smoldering green eyes off the wall and pinned them on Headmistress Dyer, the pupils thinning into the slender slits of a dragon.

"You asked me if I'd *like* to tell Ms. Rose what happened. I answered the question. You should choose your words more wisely next time." Ella should not have found his insolence amusing, but instead struggled to suppress a smile. A furious flush raged through Headmistress Dyer's cheeks.

"Just like your brother," she hissed in a way that implied she didn't mean it as a compliment.

"Don't fucking mention my brother." Plumes of steam puffed from Jarion's flared nostrils.

"Alright," Ella interrupted, stepping between them. She'd been around enough dragon-shifters now to recognize those eyes and that steam as indicators of flames brewing in their throat. If she didn't intervene, her office would soon drown in dragon fire. "Someone tell me what happened."

When Jarion steered his frown back to the wall, Headmistress Dyer explained, "During Power Practice, Mr. Park noticed that there was blood on the back of Jarion's shirt. He made Jarion lift it so he could see what was there. Then, he called me."

She wrenched Jarion to his feet by fisting the back of his shirt and spun him around so his spine faced Ella. Then, she tugged down on the material around his collar, exposing Jarion's upper back.

Ella sucked in a harsh breath.

Along his trapezius muscles were a series of staples nailed into his dark brown flesh with dried blood crested on the metal legs. There were empty holes around the same area that suggested other staples had been there and fell out, now replaced with a new set. Mixed in with the tiny marks were faded scars with a squared-off edge, the welts in the shape of neat, thin triangles, the kind left from the point of a knife's blade.

Images flickered across Ella's eyes, choppy and incoherent, blurred through the eyes and memory of a terrified child.

*Her mother. A hanger. Pain. Darkness. Her back splitting open. Her mother. A belt. The crack of her cheekbone shattering. More pain. The taste of metal in her mouth. More pain. Oblivion beckoning her forward.*

*Shut it down, Ella. Not here. Not now.*

Jarion shook Headmistress Dyer off, fixing his shirt to conceal the staples, and plopped back down on the couch. Once Ella no longer looked at the injuries, she was freed from the clutches of her cruel memory, regaining the ability to breathe. Headmistress Dyer swung her eyes to Ella, silently pleading for some assistance.

"Jarion," Ella started, taking a seat on the couch beside him. "You're not in trouble here. Headmistress Dyer and I only want to understand so we can help you." Jarion flung a glower at her from the corner of his eye.

"I'm not saying shit to you," he growled.

"Alright then," Headmistress Dyer said, a threat fermenting in her tone of voice as she entwined her arms across her chest. "If you don't want to speak to us, I'll call your brother down here and you'll speak to him. Those are your two options. Either you speak to Ms. Rose, or you speak to Kellen."

*Kellen? This is Kellen Kilic's brother?*

Ella forced herself not to flinch or verbally react. She glanced at Jarion again, really drinking him in this time. *Now* she understood why he seemed so oddly familiar. So many of his features were copied and pasted from Kellen, starting with his burnished complexion, to the hue of his eyes, to the sharp bone structure and those same heated glares she was all too intimate with at this point.

Jarion's eyes widened at the mention of Kellen.

"*NO,*" he exclaimed, finally some emotion leaching into his speech. "Please, don't. Kellen can't know about this."

"Why not?" Ella asked gently. Jarion finally looked at her, pain wrought in his emerald stare.

"It will break his heart," Jarion whispered, his throat vibrating in conjuncture with his swallow.

"Whether you tell us exactly what happened or not, Kellen has to know what we saw," Headmistress Dyer said. "It will be better for you if when we tell him, we have all the information."

"I am *begging* you not to tell Kellen." Jarion's voice cracked in the middle of his plea. "*Please,* Headmistress Dyer. I'll…I'll tell Ms. Rose why I did it. Just please don't tell Kellen. Please."

Headmistress Dyer let loose a heavy breath. Ella prayed that the law in Cavale was the same as it was on the Earthly Plane, that they were legally obligated to share this with Kellen. No matter how she felt about Kellen personally or professionally, it was wrong to with-hold something of this magnitude from him, especially since it appeared he was Jarion's legal guardian, information she'd gleaned from the fact that no one had mentioned a parental figure besides him.

"Alright," Headmistress Dyer relented much to Ella's horror. "I won't tell him, as long as you explain the staples to us right now. So start talking, mister."

Jarion squinted his eyes at her. "*Only* Ms. Rose," he asserted. "I will only share it with Ms. Rose."

Headmistress Dyer's mouth opened to argue.

"It's okay," Ella insisted before another quarrel supervened. "We can talk alone. Headmistress Dyer, can you step outside for a moment? I'll call you back in when we're finished."

Headmistress Dyer scoffed in surprise at Ella giving out a direc-tive, but didn't argue. She stomped out of Ella's office with a distinct grunt, slamming the door behind her. Whether or not she remained in the hallway or headed back to her own office was unclear.

Once they were alone, Jarion shut his eyes so he didn't have to face Ella's possible judgment and exhaled a tattered, unsteady breath. Then, he confessed, "My wings are starting to emerge."

That was the extent of his explanation.

Ella waited for more, but nothing else came. She paused for a moment to devise a response.

"And you don't want them to," she extrapolated from what little information he gave. Jarion opened one eye to look at her and bobbed his head in a stiff nod. "Why?"

"You asked me to tell you why I stapled my back," he snapped. "That's why. What else do you want from me?"

"I want to understand *why* you don't want them to emerge." Jarion clenched his fists at his sides, seeing that Ella wouldn't just fold over and let him walk out that door without revealing some hard truths. "So you stapled your back to keep your wings from emerging. Have the staples been working?"

"No," he grumbled, his nails biting into his palms. "My wings keep budging them out, so I have to reapply."

"I saw there were also marks that look like knife cuts." Jarion cringed.

"Those weren't from me," he whispered in a barely audible voice, just loud enough for Ella to catch.

"So all you've done is staple your back." She didn't need to address that comment right now. They could circle back to it after she earned Jarion's trust. "Does anyone else know you've been doing this?"

"No. I didn't tell anyone, not even my twin sister, though she knows now. She was in the class when Mr. Park saw the blood." Jarion's shoulders deflated before he sunk back against the cushions.

"How do you think she felt seeing that?" Jarion's cheeks depleted of color. His bottom lip trembled.

"Sad," he answered, his voice growing hoarser. "I would feel that way if it was the other way around."

"You mean, if it was your sister who had stapled her own back?" Jarion nodded. *He just gave me an in.* "If it was your sister who had done this and you found out, what would you say to her?"

Jarion stuffed his fist into his mouth to impede either a sob or fire from toppling off his tongue. Tears rolled down his cheeks as he bit down on his fingers, imprisoning a scream in his throat. Without saying a word, Ella crossed the room, grabbed the tissue box on her desk, and set it down next to Jarion before reclaiming her spot on the couch. Jarion wordlessly leaned forward and grabbed a tissue.

"I would tell her…that I wouldn't want her to suffer," he whimpered, smudging the tears on his cheeks with the napkin.

"Don't you think you deserve the same?" He hesitated, then shook his head. "Why not, Jarion?"

"It's complicated, Ms. Rose I don't want to get into everything right now."

"That's okay. You don't have to say anything you don't want to, Jarion. I'm not here to force you into speaking if you're not ready. If and when you choose to share these details with me is up to you. I'll be here for you regardless." Ella rested her cheek in her palm, positioning her elbow on the back of the couch so she could twist her whole body to face him. "Look, I'll be honest with you, Jarion. If we were on the Earthly Plane right now, I would be legally obligated to tell your guardian that you've been self-harming."

"I'm not self-harming," he growled, rolling his eyes.

"You are stapling your back to keep your wings from emerging, which is literally fighting against your being. I can only imagine that not releasing your wings hurts you in some way, but even if it doesn't, you are injecting staples into your own back. That is, by definition, causing harm to yourself."

"Are you going to tell my brother?"

Ella sensed that if she said yes, Jarion would march out that door and never come into her office again.

"Since it doesn't appear to be a rule in Cavale that I need to share self-injury with your legal guardian, no, I won't tell your brother. All I can do is encourage you to either talk to me or talk to your sister or brother yourself. Again, I will not force you to speak to me if you don't want to. I don't feel comfortable, however, allowing you to leave this office if you continue to use the staples on yourself. Even if you don't want to talk to me about what's going on with you, we need to establish a plan together to ensure that you stop these behaviors." Jarion vibrated with the intensification of his tears.

"I can't release my wings, Ms. Rose. I can't."

"One thing at a time. We can discuss that more later, but right now, my biggest concern is getting you to stop using the staples on yourself. Here's what I propose. We will have daily check-ins. You report to my office first thing in the morning and show me your back so I know you haven't stapled yourself and I can keep you accountable."

"Seriously?" he groaned.

"*Seriously*," she asserted, narrowing her eyes at his tone. While she'd taken a gentler approach with him, he needed to remember that she was an authority figure here at Delmarth and deserved to be treated with the same respect he should be granting all his instructors. "You are more than welcome to come to my office at any time during the day if you ever wish to discuss anything with me further, or if you ever need a place to just sit and be alone for a moment. If you're not ready for any of that yet, for right now, we'll start with this. Please trust me when I tell you that this is not a punishment, Jarion. You're not in trouble. This is meant to help you. Okay?"

"Fine. Can I go now?" Ella sighed.

"Yes. You can go." Jarion grabbed his beanie, slipped it back over his curls, and headed for the door. "I'll see you first thing tomorrow, Jarion," she called out to him when he crossed over the threshold, not turning back to look at her.

Ella raked her fingers through her hair with a wearied sigh just as Headmistress Dyer stepped back into the room.

"How did it go?" she asked Ella.

"Okay, I think. He doesn't trust me yet, so it'll take some time for him to warm up to me, but I'll keep working at it."

"Great. What did he tell you?" Ella dithered.

To support her students' rights to privacy, she needed to maintain confidentiality with her students even against the wishes of her principal and fellow educators. She already knew this would not go over well with the Headmistress, but she was determined to continue to act in this role as she'd been taught, even with all the different rule changes in Cavale and her needing to adapt so much of this job to their customs.

"If there is anything shared in our sessions together that I believe is pertinent for you to know, I will share it with you. Otherwise, I must maintain confidentiality with my students." Before Headmistress Dyer could object, the fight building in her eyes, Ella added, "What I *can* say is that Jarion agreed to come to my office at the start of each day and show me his back so we can be sure the behavior doesn't continue. If he does this again, I will immediately update both you and Kellen, if it's a behavior Jarion can't stop doing on his own. I encouraged him to tell Kellen what happened today, though I don't think he will."

"I bet Laya already told him." *Laya must be the sister,* Ella thought to herself. "Thank you for speaking to him, Noella. I feel for Jarion. He and his sister have been through so much. Their mother and father are dreadful people."

*You should not be telling me this right now. It should be Jarion who tells me if and when he wants to.*

"I will keep a close eye on him and make sure he's alright," Ella promised, hoping to terminate this discussion before she learned anything more about Jarion and his family without their consent.

"Perfect." Before she left, Ella took advantage of having the Headmistress there to ask a question.

"Just so I know for the future…do I need parental consent before beginning counseling with a student?"

"No," Headmistress Dyer replied. "If you ask any parent, they'll automatically say no, since you're a human. We have no rule that states you need it, since we have no rules attached to having a school counselor in general, so don't bother trying to get consent. Just start counseling with the students you need to see."

"Alright." This was one rule change she was pleased with. "Thank you, Headmistress Dyer."

"Keep me informed on any changes with Jarion."

"Of course." Ella watched the Headmistress exit her office.

The minute the door clicked shut, she blew out a sigh of relief, then dropped her cheek onto the cold surface of her desk.

*I need a fucking nap.*

126

"Markus Loewe," Kellen bellowed when he spotted the Cerebri passing by his office. "I need to speak to you."

Markus came to a halt, staring down at the floor as if weighing the choice to defy Kellen's order and keep walking. When he determined the end result of disobedience would be ugly, a correct supposition, Markus turned back around and scampered to where Kellen leaned against the doorframe of his classroom, gesturing for the Cerebri to enter. Once Markus plopped down at his desk, Kellen shut the door, then took his sweet time crossing the room to take a seat on his own desk, purposefully dragging the moment out to promote unease in the student. He positioned himself so he towered over the seventeen-year-old, his shadow dousing Markus's face in murky disappointment, not that the Cerebri seemed to care, his amber eyes filled with boredom.

"You haven't handed in a single reading log since the start of the semester," Kellen began. "In case you didn't know, you're supposed to read the assigned myths in *Chronicles of the Cavalian Gods* and write a paragraph with your thoughts and questions about each lore. You've made it to your senior year, so I imagine that means you possess some scrap of intelligence that you can use to manage your workload." Markus gulped, fidgeting in his chair, but provided no verbal response.

*Soften your tone, Kilic. Don't be so harsh with him.* The voice in his head who uttered this didn't sound like him—it sounded like the female he despised, the human who haunted him in his waking hours and in slumber.

"Why haven't you handed in any of your assignments?" Markus shrugged his shoulders.

"I don't know. I forgot."

"You *forgot?*" Kellen bit his tongue to try to hamper the flow of vitriol that threatened to spill out of his mouth. In the end, he lost the battle of wills against the venom. "You do realize that's an unacceptable answer, right? You're a senior. You're supposed to be graduating in June. Do you need to have your hand held through every assignment like a fucking three-year-old? Should I send you back to Kindergarten?" Markus flinched. Kellen felt it in his gut, as though Markus had punted him.

*Don't be a dick,* Noella's voice hissed in his head.

*Get out of my head, Rose,* he hissed back at her, but found himself heeding her warning by taking a different approach.

"I don't understand, Markus." It pained him to speak in a gentler manner. "You've always been a good kid. You've never been top of your class, but you've never struggled to keep up with coursework like this before. I see you in the hallway with your friends, and you seem fine. Is something going on that I should be concerned about?"

"No," Markus insisted, now appearing chagrinned, unable to meet Kellen's eye. *Maybe I should bring him to Ms. Rose.*

*Terrible idea, Kellen. We're trying to limit our contact with that woman, not increase it.*

"Look, I wouldn't normally do this, but I'm giving you a chance to make up the missing logs. You won't get full credit for them, but you can receive partial credit if you get them to me by Wednesday. Think you can handle that?" Markus bobbed his head *yes.* "Good. Get them to me by Wednesday."

"Okay." Markus rose from his chair. "Thanks, Mr. Kilic." Kellen waved his hand in response, his eyes glued to the screen of his phone as he read the message waiting there from his sister.

**Laylie:** *I need to talk to you. Are you in class right now?*

**Kellen:** *I just finished speaking with a student. Are you okay?* His mind ran rampant with possible reasons for her urgency.

**Laylie:** *I'm fine. It's about Jare.* Kellen called her immediately.

"What happened?" he spluttered, fumbling to pack his briefcase in case he needed to sprint over to them.

"Please try, and I really mean *try,* not to freak out about this, Kellen. I'm only telling you this because Jare won't and I think you should know, but he will *kill* me if he knows I'm talking to you about this right now. I need you to promise you're not going to storm our room and hunt him down or anything. I'm serious."

That did nothing to assuage his anxiety. "You know I can't promise that. Just tell me what happened, Laya."

Laya sighed, her heavy breath vibrating through his ear, before she finally confessed, "Jare has been stapling his back to keep his wings from emerging. Mr. Park saw blood on the back of his shirt and made him lift it in front of the whole class. Everyone saw." Kellen's blood ran cold.

He felt it freeze in his veins. An avalanche of shudders surged down his back, coating his flesh in tiny bumps of horror. Oxygen was unattainable, refusing to make a home in his lungs, his ribcage tight.

"Kell?" Laya squeaked when he hadn't spoken in several minutes. "Are you—" He hung up the phone.

Kellen dashed through the hallway and lunged out the open window as his wings split past his back, ripping through his flesh and razing the flimsy material of his button-down shirt. He beat his wings against the pressure of the wind, shredding the current apart so nothing could hinder his flight, and flew across the Varmin quarter to student housing, locating his siblings' shared dorm on the third floor. Then, with no preamble or warning, he burst through their window.

Glass spewed everywhere.

Laya screamed from where she'd sprawled out on her bed, scrambling to sit up and flatten herself against her wall, shielding her eyes from shards of glass by covering her face with her hands. Jarion toppled out of his chair, ripping his headphones off and darting to stand in front of his sister, in case the intruder was a dangerous threat.

When he realized it was just Kellen, Jarion groaned and skulked back to his desk, sinking into his chair.

"Kell," Laya gasped, jumping off her bed. "Don't—"

"Show me your back." Kellen hovered over Jarion, letting his shadow swallow Jarion's scrawny figure. When Jarion didn't move, he snarled, "Show me your back right fucking now, Jarion."

Jarion turned to stone. His cheeks paled. "Who told you? Was it Ms. Rose?"

*"Ms. Rose?"* If Kellen was angry before, he was *furious* now. "You spoke to *Ms. Rose* about this before me?!"

Jarion didn't acknowledge that. "Who fucking told you, Kellen?!"

"I DID!" Laya squeaked, threading her fingers in her hair. At the look of utter betrayal devouring Jarion's features, at the way his shoulders wilted, she cried, "I'm sorry, Jare, but Kellen needed to know."

"How could you do that to me?" he snarled. Laya fragmented into tears.

"Don't be angry at Laya, Jare," Kellen interjected. "Don't be angry at either of us right now. We're trying to be here for you, but you won't let us!" Kellen paused when he felt a sob grind inside his throat. In a grief-stricken tone, weighed down by love and devastation, he whispered, "You've been *stapling* your back? *Why?* Why are you fighting against what you are, Jare?"

"I don't want to talk about this with you," Jarion stammered in a voice so divergent from the strong, charismatic boy Kellen knew and loved. The kid in front of him now sounded fragile, lost, terrified and angry at both himself and the world.

"Do you know what will happen to you if you don't release your wings? Have they explained it to you in Power Practice yet?" Jarion's lips knit shut to show they had, but Kellen still recapped it for him. "Your dragon will eat you alive from the inside out. Your flesh will be consumed by fire. You could *die*, Jare. This is really fucking serious, way beyond you injecting staples into your back, which is a whole other issue."

"I really don't feel like being judged by you, Kellen," Jarion snapped, causing Kellen to double back.

"Judged?" Kellen gasped. "I'm not judging you, Jare. I'm *concerned* about you. I *love* you. I'm *scared* for you. But I'm not judging you." Jarion scowled at Kellen, giving him nothing back.

*Come on, Jare. Fucking talk to me!*

Kellen exhaled in defeat, then chose a different tactic. "I need to know what you said to Ms. Rose."

"I didn't say anything to Ms. Rose," Jarion insisted. "She mostly talked *at* me and tried to get me to tell you." *Interesting. She was on my side?* "She now wants me to stop by her office first thing every morning."

Kellen jerked his head back. "Why the fuck does she want that?"

"She wants to check my back every morning to make sure I'm not stapling myself anymore. Something about *keeping me accountable* or what the fuck ever." Kellen fought the feeling of gratitude he felt swell inside him at hearing how Noella handled Jarion, reminding himself of what would happen if their mother caught wind of Jarion sparking a relationship with Ms. Rose.

"You will not begin counseling with her in any capacity."

"I don't *want* to begin counseling with her in any capacity," Jarion spat out, while Laya took a step forward in protest.

"Good," Kellen said. "Keep it that way."

"Why?" Laya asked. "Ms. Rose seems nice. My friend, Claudia went to speak to her the other day about an issue she's been having with a kid in our grade, and she said Ms. Rose was really helpful."

"I don't care if she's the nicest, most helpful individual who's ever graced the fucking universe. She's a *human*. There's nothing either of you can say to her that you can't say to me, that you *should* be saying to me. Neither of you will speak to her in a counseling capacity or in general. If you see her, you will walk the other way. Stay away from her."

"*Why?*" Laya pressed, her volume rising. "If Ms. Rose could possibly *help*—"

"You will not speak to her because I asked you not to, Eulaylia. Do not make me repeat myself."

Laya stumbled back from Kellen as if he'd struck her. She blinked at him before she schooled her features into a mask of dispassion, aligning her posture to disguise the hurt he saw resonate in her eyes.

"Whatever you say, *Mr. Kilic*," she hissed, then took a seat on her bed.

"Laya—" His words faded into mist when Jarion began trekking to the door. "Where the fuck do you think *you're* going right now?"

"*Out*," Jarion hissed.

"We're not done speaking, Jarion."

"I'm done speaking to you, Kellen. You said your piece, and now, I'm done listening to you."

"*Jarion Ates*—" Jarion slammed the door shut behind him.

Kellen had never had such a difficult time grasping for words, but none came to mind after that performance.

"You deserved that," Laya tossed at Kellen, folding her legs into a pretzel on her bedspread.

"Why are *you* mad at me now?" Kellen groaned.

"Because you shouldn't be banning us, especially Jarion right now, from talking to someone who could possibly be of help to him. The big brother I love, the one I look up to more than anyone in this world, he wouldn't care that Ms. Rose is a human. He would recognize that she's the only person in Cavale who has a chance of getting through to our brother and helping him to stop hurting himself. You really think he's going to stop, Kell? That he's going to open up to either of us about whatever the fuck he's going through? He won't. She's the only person he might talk to, and you just stopped him from doing that. No matter how angry he seems right now, he idolizes you. If you tell him not to speak to her, he will listen to you, even if it's the worst thing for him. If something horrible happens to Jarion, Kellen, I'm going to hold you personally responsible."

Kellen felt all the oxygen in the room being cleaved from his lungs, knocking the wind out of him. The blow reverberated down to his knees, almost clouting him to the floor, fire stinging his throat.

"Laya," he whispered, then tentatively treaded towards her and took a seat at the foot of her bed. She didn't cringe away from him, but she didn't welcome him either. She stayed frozen by her pillows. "I want to help Jarion. I'm trying to help him in the only ways I know how. I may do or say things you don't agree with, but I need you to know that I'm always acting in both of your best interests. I promise, my love."

"How is prohibiting us from speaking to the school counselor acting in our best interests?"

"Do you know what our mother would do if she found out you're speaking to the *human* about our family issues?" he blurted, losing control over his filter. Laya's eyes almost fell out of their sockets at the mention of their mother. "You know why she came to campus at the start of the year? It was because she tried to have the two of you removed from Delmarth when she found out a human was joining the faculty. Imagine what she'll do if she finds out either of you are seeing her. I...I may lose you both." Laya's expression softened, the anger dissolving from her gaze, replaced by a film of tears glazing over the green hue. "I know Ms. Rose can help him. I've seen her with other students. I hate to admit it, but she's damn good at her job, which is why it kills me to say this to you guys. I would never ask this of you if it wasn't necessary. I would never normally tell you this, but I'm scared, Laylie. I'm scared of what Mom will do if she finds out. I'm scared she'll try to take you away from me, and I'm scared she'll win. Please, Laylie. Trust me."

Laya stretched forward and slipped her fingers through the empty slots between Kellen's. She said nothing to assure Kellen that she understood his position. She gave him no promises that she would stay away from Ms. Rose. She simply squeezed his fingers and offered her version of a conciliatory smile.

"I wish you would have told me that sooner," she whimpered through tears, yanking at the strings of his heart.

"I wish I never needed to tell you," he replied, smudging her tears with his thumb.

"You should probably go," Laya whispered contritely. "Jarion will be pissed if you're still here when he gets back. Give him some space, Kell. I'll keep an eye on him. I won't let him hurt himself anymore. I promise."

*That,* she could promise him.

"Your soul is too old for a twelve-year-old," Kellen quipped, stroking her cheek. He leaned forward and pressed a kiss to her forehead. "I love you, Laylie."

"I love you more, Kellings." He glided off the bed, heading to the door this time rather than use the window to exit.

Only one thought resounded in his brain: *I need to find Noella Rose.*

CHAPTER II

# ELLA

"WHAT DOES IT SAY?" Rylee prodded Ella, holding the phone so close to her face that Ella could see inside her sister's nostrils.

"I'm still finding it," Ella said, skimming through the pages of the text for the section on dragon-shifters.

After Jarion left Ella's office, she couldn't stop thinking about him and decided to make the trek to Delmarth's library to find a textbook on the process of Varmin shifters coming into their forms. She wanted to understand the consequences of Jarion denying his wings from emerging, if the refusal to release them could cause permanent damage in any way to his being. Rylee had called Ella on her way to the library for their daily check-in, so she'd taken her sister along with her on the journey; through searching the shelves and procuring the book, to hiking back to her dormitory to begin her investigation. After explaining the situation to Rylee—leaving out names and details to preserve Jarion's privacy—Rylee was now almost as invested in finding the answer as Ella.

Freya curled up between Ella's legs, which were extended on the coffee table and submerged beneath a thick blanket. She rested her chin on Ella's calf and settled one of her paws on Ella's ankle, as if staking a claim over Ella's legs as *her* bed. It was moments like this that Ella wondered if Freya thought of her as her personal climbing structure and mattress, nothing more.

"I found it!" she announced, her exclamation rousing Freya temporarily from her slumber. The dog lifted her head to fling a glance at her owner, then let her head droop back onto Ella's leg after confirming Ella wasn't in trouble.

"Tell me what it says." Rylee hunkered down on her own couch, shaking her brunette bob out of her eyes.

"It says here that for dragon-shifters, they experience two indications that their dragons are emerging," she read off the page. "They either feel pain in their backs where their wings will come in, or they start tasting fire."

"What do you think fire tastes like?"

"I've been told it tastes like burnt firewood and cigarettes."

"Can you imagine having that taste in your mouth all the time?" Rylee gagged. "Just thinking about it makes me want to hurl."

"Please don't," Ella begged. "You know every time I see someone throw up, it makes me throw up."

Rylee cackled, "That's because you have the weakest disposition ever, Ells."

"Only when it comes to vomit." Ella traced her finger over the sentences. "More information here about what wings feel like… where is the section on what happens if you *don't* release your wings?" Her eyes scraped across the page, searching the sea of tiny black letters for something useful. "Aha! Got it." She brought the book closer to her face. "It says here that if you don't release your wings, they will turn inward."

"What does that mean?" Ella skimmed the image depicted on the next page, her eyes bulging out.

"It means your wings literally will turn inward and try to open inside you rather than break free from you. They cut through your organs and break your bones. Same thing with fire. If you don't release it, it will burn you from the inside out."

"So it will kill him?" Ella looked at Rylee, gulping down a harsh breath, and nodded. "*Shit.*"

"Shit is right," Ella mumbled.

"Do you think he already knows this?"

"There's no way he doesn't, with the amount they try to prepare the students." There was no way this hadn't been communicated to the Primordials during Power Practice. If age twelve was when Varmin forms typically emerged, then Jarion's class needed to be discussing this in extensive detail in preparation. The thought made Ella's lunch churn in her stomach. "He comes from a family of dragon-shifters. If the instructors haven't drilled this into him, his parents must have."

*Or his brother.* Ella shoved that thought from her mind. She didn't want to think about Kellen right now.

"So he's trying to die?" Rylee's grey eyes frowned along with her wilting lips.

"I don't know. Maybe. Or there's some other reason he doesn't want to release them and he just doesn't understand the magnitude of that decision. Either way, if he doesn't release them soon, he's looking at maybe two or three months max before his dragon kills him."

"It'll happen that fast?!"

"That's what it says here." Ella rubbed her temples with the tips of her fingers to keep a migraine at bay.

"You need to get him to release his wings, then."

"How?! I can't reach inside his back and pull them out myself. His body, his choice." Ella pinched the bridge of her nose, the corners of her eyes throbbing. "I can't do this, Ry. Five months ago, I was still in grad school learning how to do this job, and now the fate of a child's *life* may be in my hands? I can't do this!"

"Take a second and breathe." Rylee breathed in through her nose and let out a loud gush through her mouth, cajoling Ella into joining her. "It's not going to help anyone if you start spiraling right now."

"I can't be responsible for a student dying, Ry," Ella squeaked, a tear escaping down her cheek.

"You wouldn't be responsible, Ells. Not if you do everything in your power to try and help him. The only way you're liable here is if you do nothing at all, but you've already begun to do something by speaking with him. If in the end, he makes the choice not to release his wings, that's his choice, Ella. It would fucking suck, *and* it's not your fault if that happens. You of all people know that."

Freya took notice of Ella's tears and fully roused from slumber, then shifted her body so she was now facing Ella. She placed her paws on Ella's shoulders and proceeded to lick away her tears. Ella giggled, like she always did when Freya did this, which was exactly why Freya licked her face every time Ella cried.

"Freya's got her emotional support role on lock," Rylee admired with a smile.

"She's the best." Ella kissed the top of Freya's head, then said to Rylee, "So are you, Ryles."

"So are *you*, Ells. You'll find a way to help that kid. I have no doubt." A sob clogged Ella's throat.

"I miss you so much." Rylee's gaze glimmered.

"I miss you more, Ella. We'll be reunited soon. Remember to ask Headmistress Dyer if she'll give you a pass to return to New York for winter break. If she says yes, then it'll only be nine weeks before we see each other again. We can do nine weeks. And if she says no, we can make it nine months. That's such a small blip in the grand scheme of our lives. We'll have forever together after that."

"Promise?" Ella whimpered.

"I promise we'll have as much time as all the Gods in this universe will grant us, my honey. And even after that, I will never leave you." They were both crying now, faces smeared with devotion.

"You're my favorite person ever, Rylee Hart."

"And you're mine, Noella Rose. Always and forever."

Rylee sat silently on the other end as Ella released all her pent-up emotion, sobbing a river of longing and love and loneliness and grief and exhaustion, all that feeling gushing out of her like a starved torrent. Freya licked away her tears, only for more buckets to spill down her cheeks. She spent so much of the day compartmentalizing her own emotions for the sake of her students, for the sake of needing to be present in *their* emotions, that sometimes she forgot she had her own feelings that needed to be tended to. In moments like this, she only needed Freya and Rylee.

They were the most secure safety net she could ever ask for.

When she got off the phone with Rylee, she guided Freya off her lap so she could stand, then grabbed Freya's leash, hitched it to her harness, and shepherded her outside. Ella balked at the chill in the air, a stark difference from October in New York and a nasty glimpse of what she could expect from a Cavale winter. The breeze tickled the dry patches of tears caked on her cheeks. Leaves rustled to create a symphony of susurrous sounds, whispers dancing between the trees, snaking through the grass. With each stride, her mind became clearer, more resolute, as if the distance she'd placed between herself and her worries had now become a gaping chasm. Pausing to close her eyes and take in a deep breath of dewy, glacial air, she gifted herself an hour—just an hour—to be mindful of her surroundings, to separate herself from her work, to not wear the hat of a school counselor for just a short while. She left Ms. Rose behind and slipped back into the skin of Ella, permitting herself to be the flawed, imperfect human who was just doing her best. Just an hour to rest, before she would return to contemplating the best ways to help Jarion.

Unexpected movement flashed in her peripheral vision.

Kellen emerged from within the depths of a tree's shadow. What appeared like plumes of white smoke wafted out from his parted lips, but was really the cold air capturing his breath. Freya began barking the moment he came into view—not her threatening bark when she sensed danger, but the same excited squeal she let out whenever she saw Rylee, which made no sense to Ella since Freya had never met Kellen before.

Ella yanked Freya's leash back when she tried to dive towards Kellen, maneuvering the dog to stand behind her legs.

"Look who decided to grow some balls and leave her dormitory for a change," Kellen taunted, tucking his hands in his pockets.

Ella raised her chin in defiance. "I prefer to think of it as embracing my vagina. Balls are far less sturdy." Kellen choked on a laugh before he could stop himself, then immediately fixed his facial features into a frown. "Did you just *laugh?*" she gasped. "I didn't even know you knew how to do that."

The longer he scowled at her, the larger her smile grew.

"I need to talk to you," he said, eyeing Freya nervously before he dared to take a step forward.

"Alright. But you'll have to *walk* and talk, because she hasn't gone to the bathroom yet and I'm freezing."

Kellen's jaw fell open. "You're kidding."

"Do I look like I'm joking?" The two glared each other down before eventually, Ella burst out, "Figure out if whatever you have to say is worth joining my walk. It's far too cold for a stare-down."

Ella stomped over the cracked branches and pulled Freya along with her. Kellen huffed, then traipsed after her.

"You met a twelve-year-old dragon-shifter today," he stated. His shoulder brushed against her temple due to their height difference.

"I did," she confirmed. "Jarion." Silence stretched between them before she admitted, "I know he's your brother."

"Good. That will make this quicker." Kellen cut into her path, forcing her to stop. "You should know that I'm Jarion's legal guardian, and I do not consent for him to begin counseling with you."

Ella braced herself for the argument that was about to ensue. "Good thing I learned today that in Cavale, I don't need parental consent to counsel someone. I just need the student's consent."

"ROSE—"

"How much do you know about what happened today?" She didn't want to say anything to Kellen that he hadn't already been told, so as not to break confidentiality and her promise to Jarion.

"My sister filled me in. Apparently, he's been stapling his back to stop his wings from coming in."

*Good,* she thought to herself.

Ella was privately thrilled his sister filled him in. He deserved to know what was happening with his brother, even if the truth came from his sister and not from his brother's mouth directly.

"Your brother is suffering greatly. I saw it today. I know you know what will happen if he doesn't release his wings. He needs someone to talk to, Kilic. Don't prevent him from using me as a resource."

"He talks to me," Kellen argued. "He doesn't need you."

"Does he talk to you about his anxiety?" Nothing about her voice was accusatory or judgmental. She worked very hard in this moment to treat Kellen like she would any parent of a student, not allowing her personal sentiments to bleed into how she handled this conversation. "There are therapeutic techniques I can use to get him to open up, to share what's causing him to reject his Varmin form so he can join the other dragon-shifters and release his wings. Give me a chance to—"

"Absolutely the fuck not." Ella jumped back at his volume. He lowered his face so it was an inch apart from hers and snarled, "You will go nowhere near Jarion, do you understand me? If I see you near him again, I swear to you, I will rip you apart, limb from limb, and happily walk to Terminus on my own accord."

Ella's lashes fluttered. Where normally, she would have fought back at the aggression in his tone, something stopped her from rivaling his antagonism—the fact that beneath his vehemence, she sensed panic there.

"Why don't you want me speaking to Jarion?" she asked with gentle curiosity.

"Don't you dare speak to me like I'm one of your students, earthborn. It's fucking insulting."

"I'm not. I'm speaking to you as a person with feelings to another person with feelings, who's sensing that there's more to this than you're letting on." Kellen clicked his teeth, looking away. Thoughtlessly, Ella reached for his hand, yanking on his arm to intreat his eyes to meet hers. "Forget for a second that I'm me, and you're you. Pretend I'm someone you can shed your walls with. Talk to me, Kellen, and maybe, I'll listen."

She wasn't sure what got through to him—the soft tone of voice, the proposition to forget that she was someone he was supposed to despise, his hand still held in hers, or maybe the fact that she called him *Kellen* for the first time—but he exhaled a sigh that resounded to her like he was conceding a victory.

"My mother has been working to regain custody of Jarion and Laya since she was released from Terminus. She tried to have Jarion and Laya removed from Delmarth when she heard a human had been hired to the faculty. If she finds out that I allowed him to work with *you*—" His words tapered off, melting into the wind, but the implication hung between them. "If my mother finds out, she will petition the courts to deem me an unfit parent. I will lose him and my sister."

Ella didn't know what to say. "They would really deem you an unfit parent for letting him *near* a human?"

"Yes," Kellen answered without hesitation. "You underestimate our kind's hatred for your kind."

"I certainly don't underestimate that, Kilic. The phantom of many broken bones in my body reminds me every single day." The corner of his mouth twitched in his effort to repress a smile, as if the thought of her broken bones thrilled him. "You don't think the Gods would be on your side? They've allowed me to be here, after all."

"I'm not willing to take the risk that they won't be, or that they won't care enough to meddle in the court proceedings to rule in my favor. Not where the twins' lives are concerned." Ella's heart stung.

This version of Kellen fractured the picture of him she'd painted in her head, a hard-hearted man incapable of human emotion. The man standing before her now was almost a mirror image of the person she loved most in this world, the person who'd saved her life the way it seemed Kellen had saved Jarion's—her big sister, Rylee. Through this light, he was someone she could almost respect.

Kellen grew tired of her resistance and barked impatiently, "I'm asking nicely here, Rose."

"I haven't heard you ask for anything nicely, Kilic," she objected, folding her arms across her chest.

Kellen sighed, then stunned her and actually *begged*, in a broken voice, "I'm asking you, as nicely as I'm capable of asking, to *please* not speak to him anymore. *Please*, Noella."

*Noella.*

No one called her Noella. Only Rylee on rare, rare occasions, usually when she was scolding her. Ella had always preferred to go by her nickname, since *Noella* was a variation of her mother's middle name, Noelle, and she wanted no association with that woman. On Kellen's tongue, the name sounded like poetry. She could almost rework the name to remove the previous meaning, letting his voice recreate it into something she would feel comfortable claiming as her own.

"Alright," Ella conceded, the shock apparent in Kellen's widened eyes. "Here's what I'll promise you. Apart from his daily check-ins with me so I can keep him accountable about the staples, I will stay away from him. I'll have Mr. Park keep a close eye on him in class and report back to me. I'll trust that you will be doing everything in your power to independently encourage him to release his wings, but the *second* he starts to show signs of internal or outward damage, which I now know is inevitable if his wings are not released, I will not only *not* stay away, but I *will* insist he begins formal counseling with me. This is not to punish you or Jarion. This is to help *him.*"

Kellen's eyes traced the way her lips pinched, then spat out, "Fine."

"Fine," she retorted on instinct.

"Good."

"Good!" They both shifted on the balls of their feet in unison. Kellen scratched the back of his neck.

"I don't like agreeing with you," he mumbled.

"I know," she agreed. "It feels wrong."

"Then stop agreeing with me."

"I'll stop agreeing with you when you stop making sense and go back to saying stupid shit. It's bound to happen eventually." Kellen's dimples made their highly anticipated appearance in his cheeks.

"There's the Ms. Rose I know and loathe," he crooned in a way that almost sounded like a compliment.

Ella twisted Freya's leash around her hand, unsure why she felt such a strong urge to stay here with him, why the thought of walking away right now made the corners of her eyes burn with some unidentified emotion.

"You called me Noella," she blurted out weakly in the end, searching for anything to say to keep him here longer.

"You called me Kellen," he replied as his explanation.

"Would you rather I didn't?" Kellen sucked in a large gulp of frigid air, trapping it in his chest.

When he released it in an exhale, spirals of white fog blowing in her face, he confessed, "No," then shoved his hands into his jacket pockets and began his trek back to the faculty housing.

## CHAPTER 12

# KELLEN

WHEN KELLEN RETURNED HOME after his conversation with Noella, Oliviana was waiting for him, completely naked, in his bed.

"How the fuck did you get in here?" he snapped at her, grabbing her clothes off the floor and chucking them at her.

"I'm an earth-bender, dummy," she laughed. "I can pick a lock with vines."

"I need you to leave. Right now." Oliviana slid off the mattress, prolonging her movements in an attempt to be seductive, but all it did was initiate a surge of flames to spark in his throat from anger.

"You seem stressed." She sidled her way over to him and reached up on her tiptoes to press a kiss to the hollow of his throat. Kellen yanked his body away from her before her lips made contact and held his hands up in defense of himself, in case she tried to invade his personal space again.

"I mean it. I'm done, Oliviana. I don't want to do this anymore."

"Are you fucking kidding me?" The gold flecks in her amber eyes blazed as they squinted in a sharp glower. Inside her irises, however, joined with the yellowish-brown hue, a twinge of hurt sliced through the enraged mask she'd coated her features in. "I spend three days in Terminus, and you're ready to toss me aside? You're that fucking worried about your reputation?"

"This has quite literally nothing to do with my reputation." Only someone consumed with their own reputation would immediately go to that place. "I don't have the time, energy, or frankly the feeling to give you what you clearly want. I'm sorry I didn't end this sooner. I should have, and that's on me. I respect you as a person, but we're just not compatible. It was fun while it lasted, but it's over now."

"What if I don't want it to be over?" Kellen's mouth opened and closed. What response could he give to delusion like that? "Didn't you miss me at all when I was in Terminus?" She took a step forward.

He took three large steps back.

"No. I'm sorry to be an asshole, Oliviana, but I need to be honest. I didn't. You deserve someone who would miss you if you were gone. Like Daniel. He went out of his mind, batshit crazy when you were in Terminus. You should be with someone like Daniel. You deserve to find that."

"I don't want Daniel," she groaned as she *finally* began to redress herself. "I want *you*, Kell."

"I *don't* want you, Oliviana. I don't."

"You're not the only one with feelings in this, Kellen. You're not the only one whose desires matter."

"I never said I was." *I wish I was anywhere else right now than having this conversation.* "But why would you want to be with someone who is telling you they don't want to be with you?"

"Because I don't believe you mean it." *What planet is she living on? Are we having the same conversation?* "You're all I thought about when I was in Terminus. The thought of you got me through the torture. Do you know what they do to you in Terminus? They take the worst thing that's ever happened to you and make you relive it, over and over again, with no breaks, no end. It's *maddening.* The only thing that kept me connected to life was the thought of you, of being with you again. I'm not going to give that up so easily, not when you saved me at my worst moment."

*Fuck, this is infuriating.*

Jare was right. Kellen never should have started this with her, or let it continue after the first time.

"Oliviana." He spoke slowly and with clear enunciation to make sure she heard every word. "*I* didn't save you. The *thought* of me saved you. Those are not the same things. You are clinging to an idea of me, not the real me. The real me is not compatible with you. The real me cannot give you what you want. You're putting the idea of me on a pedestal, and the real me can't live up to that image. Stop torturing yourself. Go find someone who can give you that, but it's not going to be me."

Oliviana stared at him with a look that insinuated there were no real thoughts bobbing around in her brain. Her mind wasn't present in the room. It existed in the conversation she'd rehearsed having with Kellen and was trying to keep on course, even though the real him wasn't playing the part right.

"You didn't treat me like this last week. Did something happen? Did you fuck someone else? Oh, Gods." She gasped. "Did you fuck *her* while I was gone?" Kellen knew immediately who she was talking about.

"This has nothing to do with Noella."

Oliviana's eyes bugged out. "You're calling her *Noella* now?" *Oh shit.*

He usually only called her that in his head. A private place where he could appreciate the beauty of such a name without ever attaching any real meaning to it. So what if he liked the way the name rolled on his tongue? So what if sometimes, her name slipped out when he was pleasuring himself?

It didn't mean anything. Not in privacy, at least.

But he'd called her that out loud now. He called her Noella to her *face,* after she called him *Kellen* for the first time and it fucked with his head. So now, her name fell off his tongue as easily as breathing.

"That's her name," he said like Oliviana was being ridiculous for trying to twist this into something strange. "What else should I call her?"

"How about *the human scum who doesn't belong here?* Since when does she deserve the respect of being called *Noella?*"

"Don't make it a big fucking deal when it's not. It's just a name."

"Do you think about her?" *What the literal fuck?*

He'd tried to handle this in a nice manner. He'd tried to be the gentleman in this situation, but he didn't know how else to get Oliviana to leave other than to be the bastard everyone expected him to be.

Kellen grabbed her elbow—not harshly, but not gently either—and began dragging her to the door, telling her on the way there, "I'm not entertaining this shit anymore. Hear my words and believe them when I say this. *I. Don't. Want. To. Do. This. With. You.* I'm not fucking anyone else. This has nothing to do with the human. I don't need a fucking reason. I'm just *done.*"

At the exact moment Kellen opened the door to toss Oliviana into the hallway, he found Noella frozen outside her door, her keys gripped between her ashen fingers, with the gremlin plastered to her side. Her big grey eyes swung to him, resembling a deer trapped in headlights, a child caught with their hand in the cookie jar.

*"YOU,"* Oliviana hissed, about to lunge for Noella. Kellen grabbed the back of Oliviana's blouse and wrenched her away.

"You don't want to do this," he cautioned her, unsure if he was trying to help Oliviana here or Noella. "You just spent three days in Terminus. You really want to make it a permanent stay just because you're angry at me? I'm not worth it."

Oliviana's gaze oscillated between Kellen and Noella, debating which of the two she wanted to kill more. In the end, she relented with a rough growl, shaking Kellen's hand off her, and marched down the hallway, a blur of crimson tendrils dissolving in the wind, wretched sobs following in her wake. He found no pleasure in her tears the way Oliviana had found pleasure in Noella's.

Kellen turned back to Noella. The two stared at each other with equal uncertainty of how to proceed.

"That wasn't about you," he blurted out, not sure why the fuck she needed to know that or how much she'd actually heard before he opened the door. Noella looked as confused as he felt.

"I didn't think it was," she replied. The corners of her lips lifted before she taunted, "*Now,* I do."

Heat rushed to his cheeks, blasting across his whole chest,

scalding him from the inside out. His throat scorched from a flurry of emergent flames. He wanted to rip off his enflamed skin and slap her with it.

"Leave. Right now, Rose." *Before I vomit fire all over you and burn this building to the ground.*

"I'm going. I'm going." Noella snickered to herself as she jammed her key into the lock, needling the fire in his throat so it nipped his tongue. Kellen unintentionally made eye contact with the gremlin.

*I heard everything,* the dog sung, flashing him an absurdly large—frankly frighteningly large—smile.

*Great for fucking you,* he hissed. *Too bad you can't tell her about it, since you can't fucking talk.*

*Don't worry about me. I'll find a way to tell her somehow.*

"Goodnight, Kilic," Noella threw over her shoulder with a grin, shepherding the dog inside her dormitory.

*It will be a good night,* he decided, his mind set as he headed back inside his apartment. *Because if you think I'm going to let you stay on your high horse, you're fucking wrong.* He wouldn't let this interaction end with him the embarrassed loser and her the smug victor. In the cold dark of night, he let his lips form a cruel, malevolent smile. *I'm about to fuck with your evening, Rose.*

———

Sleep evaded Ella.

She tossed her body across the mattress, contorting into different shapes to try and obtain some semblance of comfort, but no matter how hard she tried, her limbs refused to rest, her mind refused to slow down, her heart refused to stop thrashing. Her thoughts belonged across the hall, with the irritating dragon-shifter who uttered her name and she didn't know why. She'd only caught the backend of Oliviana and Kellen's argument, so all she heard him say was, *"This has nothing to do with Noella."*

She hadn't heard what question prompted him to give this response, why her name had been brought up at all.

Here's what she did know: he didn't call her the human scum, or Ms. Rose, or even just *Rose*, like he usually hurled at her in a frigid manner. He'd called her *Noella*—for the second time that night.

And it was driving her *insane*.

Her questions tripped over one another and stumbled through the pathways in her mind, blurring together to create an incoherent echo chamber overflowing with curiosity. She fought every urge she had to scramble out of bed and storm across the hall to ask him herself. She made eye contact with Freya in the dark, the cavachon watching her like a hawk through the bars of her crate, assessing Ella's mental state.

"I shouldn't. Right?" she asked Freya, as if her dog could respond. "I don't know why I care. He sucks. He's the worst. He hates me. So why do I care that my name came up in his conversation with his fuck buddy?" Freya blinked at her, providing no guidance or recommendation. All she did was swing her eyes to the door, as if encouraging Ella to go seek answers to her questions. "You know what?" she decided aloud, yanking her comforter off and sliding out of bed. "He doesn't get to take up this much space in my brain. No fucking way. I'm ending this right now."

Ella stomped out of her bedroom, leaving Freya curled up in her crate. She marched out the front door in nothing but her light blue matching pajama set with little white stars speckled across the soft fabric. She came to a halt when she landed in front of Kellen's door. She had no plan. No reason for being there. She'd simply lost control of her feet, and they'd carried her there at their own accord, with their own mission in mind. Now that she was here, she didn't know what the fuck to do.

*Go back inside your own apartment,* she tried to counsel herself. *You don't need to know why he said that. Just because he showed you a softer side tonight and he saved his little siblings the way Rylee saved you does NOT make him worthy of your time or energy. Remember, he tried to drown you in a pool. This is a bad idea, Ella.*

Against her better judgement, Ella pounded her fist against his door.

That minute of waiting elapsed at such a slow pace that it felt like hours before Kellen finally opened the door. Words shriveled up on Ella's tongue as she drank in the Varmin in nothing but black sweatpants, hanging so low that it should have been considered illegal on his waist, allowing her to glimpse his well-defined lower obliques and the fact that he wore nothing beneath the trousers. Soft brown flesh pulled tight across an immaculately chiseled chest, carved from raw power with a web of demarcated sinew snaking down his midsection. Eight abs—yes, she *counted* his abs—were accompanied by bulging muscles ringing up his arms, which pulsated when he twisted them across that delicious chest.

"What do you want, Rose?" he spat, leaning against the doorframe.

"I…" She didn't know anymore. Her purpose was lost to the wind, lost within the ridges of his beautiful physique. She liked to think of herself as someone who wouldn't be blinded by physical attraction, who could retain control of her faculties and remember that what lived on the inside of him wasn't nearly as flawless as what was portrayed externally. That viewpoint felt so far away when her mouth literally watered at the sight of him, her body heating up to a degree it had never warmed to before, almost dangerously hot, making it uncomfortable for her to exist in her skin.

Kellen either sensed the change in her body temperature or scented something in the air. His posture straightened against the doorframe, his arms falling away from his chest to make it impossible for her to avoid his magnificence. A flicker of a smile played with his full lips as his eyes haunted her body, perusing her pajama shirt and matching pants, then examining her face, the swish of color no doubt staining her cheeks.

"If you want it, sweetheart," he said, his voice like gravel as his pupils overshadowed the green of his eyes, "you're going to have to beg for it."

*Want it? No! We hate him!* her subconscious roared. *Ella, step away from that man right now!*

Ella's body was no longer connected to her brain.

It now belonged to some invisible presence that took control of her limbs and forced her feet to move closer to Kellen in spite of her deafening thoughts. One second, she stood before him, vibrating with the need to touch him, to run her tongue down the length of his chest and feel those glorious abs against her tongue, and the next, she found herself lunging at him. Her fingers dove into his short, black curls and wrenched him down to her, her lips crushing his. Ella tasted Kellen's shock, swallowing the gasp he spluttered, before his body collapsed into her and she found herself pinned beneath him against the wall. There was nothing gentle or romantic about this kiss—it was pure hatred mixed with lust passing between them, fueled by determination to see who could dominate the other. When Ella's fingernails scraped down his chest, Kellen nipped at her bottom lip, yanking down on her hair to stretch her neck and expose her throat to his lips, which lithered down the slender column, sucking at the skin there to no doubt leave a pathway of marks in his wake.

"I hate you," she groaned, sinking her nails into his ribs, wishing she possessed claws of her own to make it hurt.

"Hate me while I have my hand between your legs," he hissed into her mouth, prompting an ache so painful in her core that she felt like sobbing. "And I'll hate you when I replace my fingers with my tongue."

"You—" His fingers ghosted across the hem of her pajama pants. In a shocking turn of events, he didn't just skate his hand inside her pants, but loitered there as if waiting for permission to enter, forcing Ella to act on her desire rather than have him submit to his, another tactic in their battle of wills.

*Fuck*, Ella hated herself more than she hated Kellen when she grabbed his hand and slid it inside her pajama pants, helping him to make contact with her clit. Ella extended her fingers out towards his own sweatpants, hoping to return the sentiment in retaliation, but Kellen snatched both her wrists before she reached him and pulled them above her head, trapping them against the wall.

A grunt heaved out of her that bled into a moan when his fingers pressed down on her clit and began massaging the nub of flesh in a slow, circular motion. Ella's hips rose to meet the heel of his palm, desperate for more friction.

"Be a good girl, and I'll let you come," he ordered, which

provoked Ella to thrust her knee upward, hoping to collide with his dick. Kellen ripped his hand out of her pants to obstruct her knee's journey, her wrists still gathered in his other hand. He made a disapproving *tsk* sound with his tongue before he used the knee of hers now in his grasp to spread her legs wider. Kellen sunk down to a crouch on the floor, using his height to his advantage so he never had to release her wrists, which were still in his confinement. With no preamble this time or an offering of choice, Kellen pressed his nose between her legs, then kissed her through her pajama pants, sliding his free hand up the back of her thigh to hold her steady. She felt his tongue move through the cotton fabric and loosed a sound that was more of a whimper than a moan, her hips betraying her and jerking closer to meet what his mouth was doing. "That's it," he growled, tugging at her clit through her pants with his teeth. "Give in to me, Noella. Gods, you're breathtaking when you surrender."

"I will never surrender to you," she panted, her skin on fire. His fingers dug into the back of her thigh.

Raising the end of her pajama shirt, he whispered into her stomach, "What do you call this then, Ms. Rose, if not the ultimate surrender?" He lay a succession of kisses and tiny nips along her waistline.

Ella bit her lip to destroy the moan on her tongue.

"You're the one on your knees, Mr. Kilic," she challenged, arching a goading brow. "Seems to me that *you're* the one who's surrendered, and I'm reaping the benefits." Kellen dropped the bottom of her shirt to recover her stomach.

"Is that what you crave, Ms. Rose? My surrender, or my tongue?" Ella tugged at her wrists. To her surprise, Kellen's fingers eased off her, freeing her hands. Her own fingers flew down and twisted in his hair.

"Why not both?" she responded, pushing his face back between her legs…before the thunderous screech of an alarm shredded the image of Kellen on his knees before her, yanking Ella out of her dream and dumping her back in reality.

Ella jolted awake with a scream.

She was lying on her stomach—she *never* slept on her stomach—and drool dribbled down from the side of her mouth to slather her pillowcase, her hair in chaotic disarray, a tangled nest of blonde atop her head. It took her a second to get her bearings, to realize that what she'd experienced wasn't real, that she'd never left her apartment to confront Kellen and hadn't jumped him in the hallway. She pulled herself into a sitting position, rubbing the sleep out of her eyes, unable to shake the feeling of Kellen off her, her wrists burning with the impression of his touch. She pressed her thighs together to bring some reprieve to her tender clit, feeling how damp her panties were.

Her eyes swung to Freya.

The dog remained curled up in her crate, staring back at her with no judgment, just pure love and a tiny sliver of concern in the way she cocked her head at Ella, silently asking *are you okay?*

"I'm not sure," she answered the question in Freya's eyes, then crawled out of bed and headed for the bathroom.

She dressed for the day, sweeping a brush through the tangles in her hair, then ultimately braided the tousled tendrils to keep them from swinging in her eyes. She grabbed Freya's leash, retrieved Freya from her crate, and began leading her dog out the door, coming to a standstill at the threshold.

Kellen leaned against the doorframe to his own apartment, exactly as she'd seen him in her dream.

A roguish smile sprawled out across the bottom half of his face.

"Hello, Ms. Rose," Kellen drawled. "Have any good dreams last night?" The air was ripped from her lungs.

"You fucking bastard," she roared, his licentious grin enlarging. No part of her now was distracted by his physical beauty, no urges to jump his bones. Whatever magic he'd wielded through the dream had no claim on her anymore. She saw him for exactly what he was, what he'd always been.

"Do you usually have such erotic dreams? Do I make frequent appearances in your fantasies, Rose?"

"STAY OUT OF MY HEAD, KILIC," she threatened, getting right in his face. "If you *ever* fuck with my dreams like that again, I'll tell the Cavalian Gods' envoy that you sexually harassed me."

"What makes you think *I* was responsible for your dream?" Ella stared at him like he'd grown a third arm out of his head.

"You're an image-manipulator."

"It's true that I can project images and speak into people's minds, but all I did was drop myself in your head. I wanted to search through your memories for something embarrassing to use against you, but I got pulled into your dream instead. You manufactured that vision all on your own based on my presence in your head. I didn't do anything to influence it." Ella sensed that he was being truthful, but it was a truth she refused to accept, that her mind was capable of fabricating a fantasy of that nature, with *Kellen Kilic* the star of her pleasure, of all fucking people.

She wrinkled her nose and snarled, "I don't believe you."

"You don't have to believe me, but I'm actually telling the truth. You can blame me all you want, but that dream was all you, sweetheart." Ella gritted her teeth and wrapped Freya's leash tightly around her palm.

Freya nuzzled up against her calf as a show of comfort.

"I need to walk my dog," she huffed, shoving her shoulder into Kellen's as she turned to leave. She paused a moment, a thought occurring to her, and slowly spun back around to face where Kellen was still leaning against the wall. "Why did you stay?"

"Huh?" he snapped at her, split away from whatever far-off place his own thoughts had drifted off to.

"You said you didn't manufacture the dream. You could've left as soon as you realized you were in my dream and went looking through my memories like you planned to, yet you stayed to watch the dream instead." Kellen sucked in a harsh breath that brought a winning smile to Ella's face. He hadn't anticipated her calling him out, but he should have known by now that she wouldn't go quietly. "I'm glad you enjoyed the show, Kilic," she tossed over her shoulder on her way down the hallway, then raised her middle finger high in the air. "It's the last one you'll ever get."

# CHAPTER 13

# KELLEN

After Noella left, Kellen sat in his shower for an hour, letting the frigid water pelt his chest, to cool off from Noella's dream and their confrontation, trying to deal with his unwanted erection. He hadn't lied to her—he'd played no part in contributing to her erotic fantasy of them in the hallway. He'd been sucked into the reverie against his will, though she was right that he could have easily left the dream if he wanted to, which he didn't. He felt every single moment of that fantasy as if it were truly happening, every touch, every graze of her nails on his flesh. He devoured every moan of hers that tasted like the sweetest honey. The flavor of her lingered in his mouth and became a permanent stain, a savor he hadn't been able to remove even with toothpaste, though his toothbrush scrubbed his tongue raw. As much as he tried to pretend the vision hadn't affected him, his body insisted on remaining connected to the parts of her left within him.

She'd been right in the dream. Noella hadn't surrendered. Kellen had been the one to submit to her, to drop to his knees and worship her as though she were the only Goddess he would ever believe in. It left him with a feeling like he'd been cursed by the Gods, that he would forever find himself in this cycle of fighting and yielding to her, that her existence would continue to plague him and fester inside him until he rotted from the inside out. He couldn't tell anymore if she was meant to be his savior or his executioner.

Finally, somehow, Kellen found the strength to drag himself out of the shower, making peace with the fact that he might never be able to wash the feel of Noella off him. He reached for one of his crisp white button downs—he'd laughed in his head when Noella asked him the night of The Dow if he wore the same shirt everyday—then found himself deserting the shirt he would normally wear to work, reaching instead for a reddish-purple crewneck sweater. He'd just buttoned his grey slacks and was slipping his feet into loafers when a knock pounded against his door.

*Noella?* was where his brain flew first.

*She left for work thirty minutes ago. You heard her lock her door. Weak. You're fucking weak,* he chastised himself, yet found his hands wiping against his slacks to sluice the sweat accumulating there. He may have even checked his hair in the mirror before approaching the door.

The face he met was not the human who'd been occupying his thoughts—it was Daniel Madix.

"What are you—"

Kellen wasn't allotted time to finish his sentence before Daniel's fist came barreling into Kellen's face.

Kellen's shock prevented him from dodging the blow, so the ball of crunched fingers slammed into his eye and clouted him to the ground, the blow reverberating through his skull where it collided with the wooden floorboards. He was just about to stand when Daniel's shoe swung between his legs, directly into his already sensitive dick. It felt like a muscle spasm combined with having the wind knocked out of his gut combined with a million broken bones shattering at once.

"*Dude,*" Kellen groaned in agony, rolling onto his side. He squeezed his thighs together to prevent Daniel from repeating the gesture. "What the fuck?"

"How could you do that to Oliviana?" Daniel growled, face flushed with ire.

"You're going to have to be specific about what it is *you* think I did, so I know exactly what she told you."

"You dumped her after she came back from Terminus! Do you have any idea how fucked up that is? She spent three days being tortured beyond compare by the Gods, only to come home and be dumped by you. You're a fucking asshole, Kellen."

"*That's* what you're so upset about?" Once the crippling pain between his legs subsided, Kellen could finally press up off the floor and rise, his legs a little shaky. "What? Would you have rather me continue seeing her even when my heart wasn't in it? How would that have been fair to Oliviana?"

"Maybe you shouldn't have fucked her *at all*," Daniel snarled.

"You're right. I shouldn't have. I own that. And alright, maybe my timing wasn't stellar, but I couldn't keep pretending with her, Dan. She deserves better. She deserves to be with someone who wants to be with her, like *you*. I did you a favor, so I don't know why the fuck you're coming in here, gun's blazing."

"Because you're supposed to be my friend, and this whole time, you've been *fucking* her!"

"You *knew* I was fucking her! This isn't news to you!" This is why Kellen rejected friendship. This is why he was content to spend all his time with Jarion and Laya and never work to develop any connections beyond that. The act of caring about someone was too fucking dramatic for his limited patience.

*Don't be an asshole,* Noella's voice warned in his thoughts.

*Will you ever leave my head?* he asked the voice. Kellen exhaled a conceding breath after receiving no response.

"I'm sorry for hurting her, Dan. I'm sorry for hurting you. I fucked up, and I'll admit that. Don't waste your time fighting *me*. Go be there for her. I've given you a chance here, so don't blow it."

"Fuck you," Daniel spat, a clump of spittle soaring into Kellen's now damaged eye. "Don't act like a fucking martyr or like you did any of this to help me. I don't need you, Kellen. I don't *want* you. As far as I'm concerned, you and I are no longer friends. You're fucking dead to me."

Kellen opened his mouth to respond, but Daniel spun on his heel and stormed out of the apartment.

He left Kellen's door ajar just to fuck with him.

Kellen shouldn't have cared. He'd never cared before. He'd

always thought he simply tolerated Daniel for the sake of getting through the day, but maybe, somewhere deeply submerged in his subconscious, there was some genuine affection there. Maybe, when he'd stopped Daniel from attacking Noella, he really had acted in defense of a friend, not just a colleague. Daniel and Kellen grew up together, stuck by each other through their studies at Delmarth, attended Nosrerry together and climbed the ranks of Delmarth as instructors to become department heads together. That history wasn't entirely insignificant, despite what Kellen told himself most days. This was a rude reminder that he wasn't completely unfeeling, which became impossible to deny with the way his heart was squirming in his chest, stinging from the loss of someone he may've actually cared for.

*Tuck it away,* he told himself, catching a glimpse of his swollen eye in the mirror, his blood settling near the wound in preparation for a bruise to mar his brown skin. *He doesn't matter. This feeling will pass. Focus on Jarion and Laya. They're all that matters.*

For some reason, Kellen's eyes wandered to the still open door, landing on Noella's door across the hall.

He shook off whatever feeling twitched in his gut and headed out for the day.

**Ella:** *I need your help with something. Can you come to my office?*

**Akio:** *On my way.*

Five minutes later, Akio sauntered into Ella's office, blue-black hair gelled off his forehead. The lack of hair framing his features somehow made him appear more harsh, the lines of his face resembling razor blades.

His smile, however, was pure sugar and kindness.

"Good morning, Rosie," he crooned in a cheerful melody, employing the nickname he'd taken to calling her.

"Too loud," she groaned, rubbing her temples with the tips of her fingers. "I haven't fully woken up yet."

"Awe, did someone wake up on the wrong side of the bed this morning?"

"You have no idea," Ella muttered, her words fractured in the middle by a yawn. She leaned her backside against the edge of her desk. "How do you always have such a good attitude in the morning?"

"It helps to have a wife who insists on being thoroughly fucked before she leaves for work in the morning."

"Damn. I feel bad for your neighbors." Akio laughed.

"What did you call me down for?"

Ella toyed with a loose thread at the end of her cream white sweater. "I need you to put up a mental shield in my mind so Kellen Kilic can't peek around in my head anymore." The smile vanished from Akio's face.

"What did he do?" he growled, brown eyes clouded with indignation. "Did he do something to you?" Ella twisted the strand of cashmere between her fingers so she didn't have to make eye contact with Akio.

"Yes. And no. It's…I don't really know how to explain what happened." Akio looked her over, searching for signs of external and internal wounds. "He didn't hurt me. I just don't want him to have the ability to enter my head anymore. Can you do that?"

"I can try, though that's not really what my powers are."

Ella was curious about the details of Akio's Cerebri gifts, but she didn't know if he'd share them. Akio surprised and delighted her by going on to say, "My Cerebri abilities manifest as extrasensory perception, essentially perceiving information without gaining it through physical senses. Could be through telepathy and reading thoughts, but mostly I receive information in the form of a vision, either about future events or events at remote locations."

"So you're clairvoyant?" Akio nodded. "Do you receive visions at random?"

"No. I receive them if I concentrate on a certain person or place. I need to be seeking that information out, but even then, the answers I receive are never a full picture, probably the Gods intercepting in some form."

"So no one can gain enough power to rival them," Ella extrapolated, remembering their conversation about the Gods from The Dow. Ella's nose wrinkled. "You already know what I think about that."

"Yes, you've been very vocal about your disdain for the Gods, Rosie. Subtlety is not your strong suit."

She stuck her tongue out at him.

"Could you use your extrasensory perception to see if there's any way to shut Kellen out of my head permanently?"

"I can definitely try." Akio slid his hands out of his pockets and stepped towards her, his fingers hovering near her face, silently asking for permission to touch her. Ella smiled at the respectful gesture, then bobbed her head in agreement. Akio pressed the pads of his fingers into her temples and shut his eyes, his features scrunching up in deep contemplation. He then winced. "That's weird," Akio muttered to himself.

"What's weird?" Ella squeaked.

"I sense Kellen inside your head. Curdles of his magical imprint are entrenched within the tissue of your brain. It's like he's left a trace of his power to leave the doorway to your mind open."

Ella shuddered. "That is not a comforting mental image."

"He shouldn't be able to do that when he's not in your direct vicinity. His Cerebri abilities must be far more potent then he lets on." Akio sounded like he was analyzing evidence before coming to a conclusion about something.

"Can you remove whatever trace of him is there?" Akio's lips twisted in an odd shape.

"No. I'm sorry, Ella, but his powers are different than mine. I can try to gain a vision about *how* you might be able to remove it, but I can't remove it myself. Would you like me to try that?"

"Yes, please. Thank you for doing this."

"Of course. I want my friend to be protected." Ella's chest warmed as she watched Akio's eyes flutter shut, his lashes dancing across his cheeks and sending soft shadows over his creamy complexion. He was silent for a long moment, wrinkles crinkling his flesh from the way his brows pulled together, rippling with concentration.

All of a sudden, Akio gasped, yanking his hands away from her forehead and stumbling back from her. His expression was wild, a maelstrom of surprise and fear as he stared at Ella like he didn't recognize her.

"Akio? What's wrong? What did you see?"

"I…I'm sorry. I need to go." Akio turned on his heel and stalked to the door, throwing sloppily over his shoulder, "I'll catch you later, El."

Ella was left alone in her office with her hands extended towards her friend, who was no longer there.

"O…Okay?" she spoke to the nothingness now filling her office. *What the fuck just happened?*

The door to her office creaked open before Jarion poked his head through the crack. She quickly schooled her facial features into one of welcoming warmth, shoving her confusion over Akio's actions into a box she could reopen later. She beckoned Jarion into her office with a wave of her hand. A female straggled in after him, long black hair embracing small shoulders, those same emerald eyes that belonged to both Jarion and Kellen twinkling at her as the young Primordial lifted her hand in a tiny wave at Ella. Jarion tossed his backpack onto Ella's couch, then shed his jacket.

He swiveled so his back faced her and pulled the collar of his t-shirt down, allowing Ella to see his spotless back—well, unblemished of staples. It was certainly not an untarnished back, with a constellation of faded scars sketching a swirled pattern across the fragile brown flesh, disappearing into the parts of his back still concealed by his shirt. Once she'd gotten a good look, he fixed his shirt to cover himself.

"Can I go now?" Jarion spat.

"How're you feeling today, Jarion?" Ella knew her promise to Kellen, but that wouldn't stop her from asking a probing question masqueraded as a polite pleasantry. If Jarion deigned to answer her and it sparked an actual conversation about what was troubling him, Kellen couldn't blame her for that.

"Like I'm walking on a fucking cloud." Jarion flashed a sardonic, toothy smile that revealed a hint of fangs, then let the artificial grin fade into the gloomy frown he perpetually wore. "Can I go now?" Ella sighed. She'd get through to him eventually. She wouldn't give up that easily.

"Yes, you can go. Be back here first thing tomorrow."

Jarion started for the door, then paused when he realized his sister hadn't moved with him.

"Laya?" he asked, signaling with his head for them to exit. Laya dithered, her eyes swinging between Jarion and Ella.

"I'm going to stay a moment," she decided, receiving a wide-eyed look from her brother.

"Are you sure?" he whispered. Laya nodded, then shooed him away with a swipe of her hand through the air. "Alright. Your funeral, Laylie," Jarion shot at her, then shut the door behind him.

Once alone, Laya rotated to face Ella. "You must be Ms. Rose."

"And you must be Laya. Would you like to sit down?" Laya hesitated, then nodded, sinking onto the mustard yellow cushions of Ella's couch. Ella hauled her office chair around the circumference of her desk, positioned it across from Laya, and took a seat in the plush leather, arranging her legs off to the side. "What can I do for you?" Laya stared down at her tangled fingers in her lap.

"I don't know what my brother told you…my big brother. Well, both my brothers, actually." Laya loosed a shaky laugh, pulling at her fingers. She must've felt Ella's eyes on her because she raised her head, cautious green meeting hospitable grey, their gazes clashing in the center of the room. "My brother would kill me if he knew I was here…well, not really. It's Kell. He wouldn't hurt anyone."

*Yeah right!* Ella screamed in her head. Externally, her expression was one of serene empathy.

"He told us not to talk to you." Ella worked overtime to control her reaction. *Don't let your anger show on your face, Ella.* "I would trust Kellen with my life…I *have* trusted him with my life, but I just don't think he's right about this one. I'm watching the person I love most in the world disappear before my eyes, and there's nothing I can do to help him. The only person who possibly could is *you.*" Laya's eyes overflowed with tears. "*Please,* Ms. Rose. Please. I need you to help my brother. I need you to help Jarion. I don't care what Kellen said to you. I need you to help him."

"I have every intention of helping your brother," Ella assured

Laya, the young Primordial choking on a sob, dissolving into a river of tears on Ella's couch. Ella extended to Laya a box of tissues, which the female grabbed with eager fingers. Ella inclined her head to the side, then said gently, "I'd like to help you too, Laya."

"I'm fine," Laya insisted, smudging her tears with the tissue. "I don't need anything."

"I hear you say that, but I'm seeing something different in front of me. There are a lot of emotions in your eyes."

Laya gulped. "What do you see when you look at me?" Ella took a moment to craft her words with care.

"A lot of pain you're holding in." Laya's bottom lip trembled, a tiny whimper leaking free along with a stream of tears. "Your dragon is beginning to emerge too, right? What have you experienced so far?"

"I think I'm starting to taste fire." Laya sniffled, blowing her nose into the tissue. "It's been making me sick. I can't eat anything without throwing it up. The only thing that works is liquids, but not so much."

"I can imagine you'd feel very weak if you're not taking in enough nutrients." Laya crumpled her tissue into a ball as she nodded.

"There's not really much I can do about that, though. Once my fire fully emerges, I'll be able to control it so it won't affect the taste of food, but while it's sparking, I've got to get used to the soot in my mouth. I just miss food. I miss chocolate. I miss mashed potatoes. I could eat mashed potatoes for every meal."

"Me too," Ella agreed, earning a tiny smile from Laya. "Is it just when you eat that you taste the fire, or have there been any other indications of your fire emerging?"

"I felt flames in the back of my throat last night." Laya swallowed at the memory, then fidgeted on the couch.

"Tell me what happened last night."

"Kellen barged into our dorm room to confront Jarion about the staples. I haven't seen him that upset in *years*. Not since the night he got me and Jare away from our parents." A haunted look annexed her face, but she shook it off, literally shook her shoulders to shake off the memory, then continued speaking. "He told Jarion that he didn't want him speaking to you. I felt this rush of something hot shoot up my throat. It felt like heartburn, but in my mouth, if that makes sense." Laya snickered at her own description. Very quickly, Laya tempered the laughter and returned to her original thought. "I had to clamp my teeth together to keep the fire from coming out."

"What were you feeling when that fire sparked?" Laya's fingers squeezed into a fist, shredding the tissue in her grip.

"Angry," she answered. "It didn't make sense to me why he was cutting Jarion off from speaking to someone who could help him. Jarion may be going through some shit, but he idolizes Kellen. If Kellen told him to jump, he'd ask how high, even if he hates himself for it. Kellen has devoted his entire life to ensuring mine and Jarion's safety, even at his own expense. He doesn't talk about it, but I know what he's given up to be there for us, to raise us. The way he was acting last night was so different from my big brother. He was so… unsympathetic. But after Jarion left, I talked to him more, so I understand now. He's scared. He's scared our mother will try to take us from him if either of us work with you in any capacity. He knows you're the only person who could help Jarion. He said it last night. He knows you're great at your job. He's just so scared of our mom that it's blinding him from seeing what could be best for Jare."

*He said I was great at my job?*

*Ella, that's the least important thing she just said. You're being ridiculous. Snap out of it and focus.*

"How did it feel for you to see your brother scared like that?" Laya pouted.

"It made me sad. Kellen has always been the pillar of strength for me and Jare. When I was younger, I thought Kell was a God. He was so perfect. So loving. So strong. He's been my savior all my life, even before he was my literal savior. It never occurred to me that he has his own feelings under all that strength and power."

"Seeing him scared brought him closer to your level," Ella para-phrased. Laya's eyes twinkled in agreement.

"Yeah! It reminded me that he's not a God. He's not perfect."

"Does that change the way you view him?" Laya considered the question carefully before answering.

"Yes and no. No in the sense that it doesn't make me love him less. Yes in the sense that it makes me question now if his way of doing things is the right way. Before this, I've always just followed his lead. I've always trusted that he knew best. Now…now, I don't know." Laya squirmed as if the thought made her uneasy.

"You're entering a time in your life that's meant for you to discover your identity," Ella said, leaning back in her chair. "You're coming into your own, in both an emotional sense and in a literal sense, through your Varmin form emerging. That should come with a certain amount of independence and exploration. This questioning of right and wrong that you're experiencing is normal at your age."

"I don't like it. I want to go back." Ella smiled at the diminutive, playful smirk curling up the corner of Laya's mouth.

"What is it you want to go back to?" Ella questioned.

"The protection of having someone take care of everything and always trusting that they know best." Laya fidgeted. "My parents never provided that for me. It was always Kellen. I don't like sitting with the thought that he might not be able to provide that either, cause then who does? How do you feel safe in the world?"

"It doesn't mean he can't provide that. It doesn't mean he's *always* wrong. You're just beginning to see that you can participate in your own protection."

"Huh." Laya leaned back on the couch. She beamed, her beautiful visage illuminated in a wide grin. "I like that! I can be my *own* protection. I never thought of it that way." Ella gifted Laya a moment to let the thought marinade inside her before propelling the conversation in a different direction.

"You said Kellen is afraid your mother will try to take you and Jarion away from him. Are *you* scared of that happening?"

"Until last night, I didn't even know that was possible. I knew she tried to come on campus at the start of the year, but Kellen never told us why, just that security didn't allow her access and he'd been working with an attorney to issue a restraining order against her. She finished her probation last year, so technically, there's nothing barring her from coming for us now, though Kellen won't let that happen. I know if I ask him to tell me more, he won't. He tries so hard to protect us, to his own detriment." It was hard for

Ella to remember that the girl in front of her was only twelve-years-old. She spoke way beyond her years, with a maturity that Ella knew far too intimately, the kind that accompanies unparalleled hardship. "Jare doesn't know what Kellen told me last night. He was so angry at Kellen that if he even heard a mention of our mother, it would've been his final straw. I've been trying to keep Jarion's environment as calm as possible to help encourage him to release his wings. Maybe if he feels safe enough, he won't hold back."

"That's a lot of responsibility for you to take on." Laya shrugged.

"It's what we do," she said with finality. "It's what we've always done. We learned it from Kellen. Kellen gave his life for us. He surrendered his dream future to take on the mantle of being our legal guardian. I can't let that sacrifice be in vain. We owe each other the same devotion in return."

Ella's thoughts temporarily wandered to Rylee. That same feeling drenched her bones. She would spend her entire life attempting to recompense Rylee for all she did to save her, and it would never be enough.

"I think there's a universe where you can hold all of what your brothers feel, while *also* making space for what *you* need," Ella encouraged. "It doesn't mean abandoning your family. It doesn't mean you need to lose that empathetic side of you that makes you such a good sister. There is nothing wrong with being there for your brother, for both your brothers. It just means holding room for yourself too, giving yourself the same love and attention that you give to your brothers. That may mean following your instincts and going against what your big brother says if you believe that's the right thing to do. That may mean figuring out who you and accepting it may differ from what you've always thought you wanted. It means making space to listen to your needs just as much as you attend to theirs."

Laya frowned. "That sounds so selfish."

"Selfishness is defined as concentrating on one's own advantage, pleasure, or well-being without regard for others. Taking care of yourself is different than putting yourself above someone else. It doesn't mean you don't care for others to care for yourself. In both our dimensions, apparently, we have all been conditioned to think that prioritizing our needs or setting boundaries is a selfish thing to do, but it's not. Putting yourself first is not selfish, Laya. It's necessary, and it can help you be more selfless to others." Laya's eyes glimmered before she let her lips form a small smile.

"I want to keep seeing you," Laya said in a nervous voice, as if she feared being rejected by Ella.

"You are absolutely welcome to begin counseling with me, Laya. I would love to work with you."

Laya's smile was outlined by tears. "My brother will hate it."

"We have confidentiality here. Everything you say here stays here. He doesn't have to know if you don't want him to."

"Good." The two females simpered at each other, their secret stretching between them.

Ella and Laya discussed a time to meet for counseling. They agreed to meet on Fridays during lunch so the Varmin department head – her *brother* – wouldn't have to sanction a change in her schedule.

"Kellen can't know," Laya said on her way to the exit, Ella following her there. "No one can know."

Ella opened the door for Laya before she swore, in a muffled, gentle voice, "Then no one will know."

## CHAPTER 14

# ELLA

AFTER LAYA LEFT HER OFFICE, Ella spent the morning preparing for her first counseling session with Connor. She scrubbed the office from head to toe, sluicing the surface of her mahogany desk until a watery reflection of herself flickered over the polished wood. She sprayed her favorite perfume over the couch, the woodsy notes melting over the sofa, which Ella hoped would help create an environment conducive to self-disclosure. She opened a new packet of tissues, resting it on the coffee table. Ella then settled herself in her office chair, which was still arranged in front of the couch after her conversation with Laya. She stared at the door, waiting for him to arrive.

She waited.

And waited.

And waited.

He never came.

After thirty minutes of staring aimlessly at her door, hoping for him to materialize, she rose from her chair and strode out of her office, journeying to the Varmin sector to track him down. Her mind went rampant contemplating his absence: *did he forget? Did someone prevent him from coming?*

She braced herself outside Kellen's classroom door, gulping

down precious mouthfuls of oxygen to relieve the strange acceleration of her heart rate at the thought of seeing Kellen after this
morning. Once the pounding in her ears died down, she twisted the
doorknob and pushed the door open.

Her eyes swept over the rows of seventh-grade Primordials, her
intent to search for Connor, but against her will, her gaze sought out
the dragon-shifter at the front of the room. His back faced the class
as he scrawled something on the whiteboard. His grey slacks clung
to the contour of his ass, perfectly emphasizing its desirable shape,
blending into the same wiry legs that Ella watched bend in her
dream before he sunk to the ground in a kneeling position before
her. Those fingers of his she'd felt pressed against the most sensitive
part of her now wrapped around his marker, long and nimble and
oozing masculinity, even while he scribbled the words *What is a
Cavalisha?* on the board in surprisingly neat handwriting. When
she'd pictured his handwriting—not that she had, of course—she'd
expected it to be large, messy, and harsh, like the rest of him.

The words were written with careful consideration, like every
letter deserved sweet dedication. He added a swirled flare to the way
he wrote the letter *t*, with the tail end sweeping up to the right in a
tiny curve. Kellen Kilic did not seem like the type of person who
would add flare to anything he did, let alone to the way he fashioned letters. So many elements of this man contradicted themselves. If Ella didn't catch herself, she could spend the whole day
analyzing his micro-movements.

Kellen whirled around to face the class, opening his mouth to
either begin or continue his lecture when his eyes snagged over Ella.
Ella's own gaze trickled down to his sweater—the hue of a raspberry, hugging his physique like the material was a disciple vener-
ating its favored god. The images and sensations from her dream
twisted together to engulf her senses, a phantom of his lips coasting
over her body, the sandalwood aroma of his cologne surging
through her veins, overpowering her ability to recognize what was
real and what was fantasy. She was so engrossed in those memories
that she nearly missed the fact that his right eye appeared as if
someone had smushed the organ under a wrecking ball. It was
disgustingly engorged and besmirched with purplish-black under-

tones, some dried blood crusting along the periphery of the eye socket. His eye hadn't looked like that this morning. This had to have happened after their conversation in the hallway.

His gaze had darkened over her the moment she appeared in the doorway, his pupils transmogrifying into the slits of a dragon. The entire class shifted their heads back to look at her, sensing the powerful tension choking the air between Ella and Kellen. Neither educator took note of the students' watchful eyes, completely absorbed in each other.

*Why are you here?* he spoke into her brain. His voice resembled crumbled stone in her ears.

*Connor missed his session with me,* she answered mind-to-mind. *I came to check if he was here today.*

*He's right by the door.* Ella's attention dropped down to the young Primordial whose desk flanked the entrance to the classroom. He was deftly avoiding her line of vision, drawing the hood of his sweatshirt over his face to escape her eyesight. Ella's focus diverted back to Kellen when he asked, *Can you please wait to pull him until I'm finished?*

*Sure.* Ella didn't mind waiting. With a twitch of her lips, she said softly, *thank you for saying please for a change.*

Kellen didn't answer back. He broke their eye contact to address the class.

"You've heard this myth countless times since your Kindergarten year, so I'm expecting the entire class to raise their hands at my next question. Who can tell me the creation story of the Lantari empire?"

Fifteen hands shot up into the air—including Connor.

Kellen swooped his pointer finger to the right, landing on Atlas Ehann, a Meteoro water-bender.

"It formed when Edar Lantarian broke away from the Cavalian Gods," Atlas supplied as an answer.

"That is the bare minimum of an answer," Kellen said in a flat, dissatisfied tone of voice. "No candy for you."

Atlas slumped in his chair.

*He gives them candy when they get an answer right?* Ella bit her lip to keep from smirking. *Don't find this cute, Ella.*

Kellen's eyes flew to Ella, her thought having leapt out of her brain and landed inside his ears.

*You think I'm cute, Ms. Rose?* he asked with a goading cock of his head. Ella narrowed her eyes in a scowl.

*Don't you have a class to teach, Mr. Kilic?*

*Believe me, earthborn, I'm trying, but you're making it increasingly difficult to concentrate.* Ella didn't respond. She shut her brain down to avoid him eavesdropping on her internal monologue and to prevent him from having a real reason to blame her for disturbing his class.

"Who can tell me *why* Edar broke away from the Cavalian Gods to create the empire of Lantari?" He called on Anastasia Branwen, the same female he'd made stand at the front of the room last week when she attempted to cheat on her test.

"Edar fell in love with Aros Cavalian's Cavalisha, Tala Milov. Edar stole Tala in the middle of the night and crossed the Middledeen waters to an unoccupied island that he claimed and named Lantari."

Kellen reached his hand into the red velvet sack on his desk, procuring a tiny piece of candy encased in gold wrapping, and threw it to her. Anastasia snatched the reward with a squeal before unwrapping the chocolate square and popping it into her mouth.

"That's the story that's been passed down through generations for the last thousand years," Kellen continued, leaning back against his desk. "Edar is depicted as the malicious abductor who stole Aros's heart in a living form. But what if Tala wasn't actually kidnapped? What if she'd willingly gone with him? How does that perspective challenge what we know about Cavalishas?"

"But that's not how the story went," another student near the front of the room blurted out.

"How do you know?" Kellen challenged her. "Were you there when it happened, Dalia? Did you see with your own eyes Edar steal Tala?" Dalia slid down in her chair, dipping her chin onto her chest.

*You could've said that nicer,* Ella criticized.

*Get out of my head, Rose,* he snarled back, though when Kellen spoke again, she noted that his voice rang softer.

"All Primordials are given a Cavalisha. A perfect match. A piece of our being we can't live without, whether we accept the bond with an offering to Mara or not. Yet Aros Cavalian has lived a thousand years now without his Cavalisha, if we are to believe the story that Tala, whether she was kidnapped or left willingly, is no longer with him and now belongs to Edar. How do you think it's possible for Aros to live without his Cavalisha if we're taught that once we find our Cavalishas, we cannot live without them?"

"Maybe he can live without her because he's a God?" Anastasia offered. "Gods have the power of immortality, so maybe it doesn't affect him the same way it would regular Primordials to be separated from their Cavalishas, since his lifespan is eternal." Kellen tossed her another piece of candy.

"Possibly." He countered, "Or maybe a Cavalisha isn't what we think it is. Maybe it's not that we *can't* live without them, but that we don't *want* to, that we *choose* not to. Maybe that's more meaningful than being unable to separate from someone because divine intervention demands you stay together." Kellen's eyes glassed over. Just like his sister, he literally shook off whatever unpleasant thought had plagued him and continued his lecture. "The Gods give us a Cavalisha, but we have the choice to either accept or reject that bond. Why do you think we're given an option of rejecting the bond if supposedly, once we find our Cavalisha, we're destined to never part?"

Silence swelled through the room. Kellen waited, then inevitably answered his own question.

"The Gods can select who they deem to be a perfect partner for us. They can entice us with the promise that accepting the bond means we will experience a power proliferation, but they can't force love upon us. Love isn't surefire just because the Gods manufacture for us a soulmate, throw them in our path at some point in our life, and say, 'Here's your perfect match. They are the only person in the entire universe you are predetermined to love.'" Kellen demonstrated cupping something precious between his hands and shoving it forward to emphasize his point. "Yes, in all cases of having a Cavalisha, love has been proven to develop through time spent together, but that's because these two people happen upon each other in the world and *choose* to take that time to develop that love. Love isn't just a feeling. It's a deliberate action we take. Love is something we may be gifted, perhaps something we fall into with no control, but it requires work to remain solid. It's not a structure that can continue standing without support, without nurture. It's a choice made every single day, to look at the person you love and say, 'This union may have been predestined, I may have fallen into love with you, but I am *choosing* to *walk* into love with you too.' Our Cavalishas may've been fated for us by the Gods, but perhaps the Gods fated us to be together because it's something we would've independently chosen anyway, because they know our souls that well. They toss us this person, this other half of our heart, and give us the space to come to that realization all on our own, so it feels like an organic decision we made for ourselves. Maybe that's why the bond can't awaken until the first time those feelings are articulated into the ether, because it needs to be ignited by the choice to walk willingly into love."

No words.

Absolutely nothing graced Ella's head or tongue.

Kellen had been looking at Ella the whole time he'd been speaking, like he couldn't stop his eyes from falling onto her, falling *into* her, when he spoke about the concept of love. Ella forgot the proper measures required to breathe. If she wasn't leaning against the doorcase, she would have toppled over.

Someone in the room squawking a strangled sound shattered the trance Ella and Kellen had tumbled into. Their eyes ripped apart as they were thrust back to Cavale and recklessly dropped back in the classroom.

Kellen cleared his throat, then said, "Take out your journals. I want each of you to write a three-page essay answering this question. If Tala had left Aros willingly despite their bond as Cavalishas, how does that challenge what we know about Cavalishas? I expect all three pages completed by the end of the class. You have thirty minutes, starting now." Kellen peeked back at Ella.

*Take Connor now,* he told her, then turned on his heel before she had a chance to respond, busying himself with cleaning the board, which Ella sensed was an excuse not to remain in her line of vision.

"Connor," she whispered, keeping her voice low to not draw attention. "Can we speak in the hall?"

"I need to write this paper," he argued, glancing nervously at Kellen.

"It'll only take a moment." Connor sighed, then laid his pencil down between the pages of his notebook and followed her out into the hallway. "You missed our session today. I just wanted to make sure everything was okay."

"I'm sorry, Ms. Rose, but I can't see or speak to you anymore." Fear drenched the outer surface of those words.

"Why not?" Connor twisted the sleeve of his sweatshirt around his fingers.

"I made the mistake of telling my parents I'd agreed to begin counseling with you. They told me that if I associate myself in any way with the human, they will disown me." Ella couldn't contain her horror.

"I'm so sorry, Connor," she expressed, her voice trembling under the weight of her own emerging tears. "Please know that no matter what, my door is always open. Anything you say to me will stay confidential between us, but I understand if you don't want to take that risk. I will always be here if you need anything."

"Thanks, Ms. Rose." Connor lingered there a moment, leaving her with the impression that he *wanted* to speak to her, but familial responsibility crushed that desire into powdered dust beneath his hoodie. He awkwardly retreated back into the classroom, gathering his pencil to begin writing.

Ella made eye contact with Kellen through the still-open door. She had no doubt that he'd heard every word Connor said to her, whether that be through his heightened Varmin hearing or with the looking glass he'd implanted for himself in her head. He wasn't looking at her now like he hated her.

He was looking at her like he was trying to see inside the depths of her psyche, like the clod of his power he'd left to nettle in her brain wasn't enough and he needed to invade the rest of her.

It was too much for Ella to bear. She hurried down the hall without a further glance.

"They told him they would *disown* him for speaking to you?" Josefyn gasped. The females had commandeered a bench on campus close to Ella's office to meet for lunch. Ella enjoyed her kale salad with parmesan croutons and apples, courtesy of her special fridge, while Josefyn picked at a bird carcass that Ella worked *very* hard to dodge looking directly in the eyes while she ate.

"I can try to understand that Primordials are raised to hate humans, even though, to be honest, I *don't* understand, but what I *can't* understand or accept is that they hate humans so much that they would seriously *disown* their child for speaking to one." Ella rammed a parcel of kale into her mouth.

"The hatred of humans comes from the myth of Aros and Tala." Josefyn tore a chunk of fat off the quail with her teeth, the streaked and stripped upper part of the bird hulling from the side of the bone. "Tala is Aros's Cava—"

"I know the myth. Tala was Aros's Cavalisha who Edar stole in the middle of the night that started this war between the Primordials and the Sireres." Josefyn flung Ella a curious look, grinning around the quail bone.

"So you finally got Kellen to tell you the story." *Not exactly,* Ella thought to herself. After swallowing her last mouthful and chucking the bone into the grass, Josefyn wiped her mouth off on a napkin provided by Ella and said, "What I doubt Kellen added is that Tala isn't a Primordial. She's a human."

"*Human?*" Ella sputtered. "There are humans in Cavale?"

"Not for the last thousand years. After Tala vanished, Aros eliminated the existence of humans in Cavale. Since her disappearance, she's been condemned for causing the Primordial and Sireres war."

"For *causing* the war? What did *she* do?"

"People seem to think that if she wasn't a human, she would have been able to fend Edar off. They blame her weakness for the war."

"That is unbelievably sexist," Ella burst out, finding this so outrageous that she couldn't breathe. "She was *stolen* by Edar! And everyone turned around and decided to blame *her* for the actions of a *man?*" The thought made the kale in her mouth turn stale and tasteless. "It's just like Helen of Troy."

"Who's that?"

"It's a Greek myth on the Earthly Plane." Ella closed her salad and rested her fork on top of the plastic covering, swinging her legs onto the bench. She balanced her chin between her knees. "Helen was the daughter of the Greek God Zeus and a mortal woman. She was best known for her beauty. She had countless suitors pinning after her and ultimately married a man named Menelaus from Sparta. Helen ended up leaving Menelaus for Paris, who was a prince of Troy, sparking a war between Sparta and Troy. In different versions of the story, it's questioned whether or not she went willingly or was abducted. Like Tala, Helen was denounced for her part in causing the Trojan War. It's fucking ridiculous that these women are falling on the sword in the place of the men whose actions caused all this strife. It further perpetuates the belief that female lust pollutes male intellect and all women are toxins and long-live-the-patriarchy bullshit. It's *bullshit,* Jo!"

"Tell us how you really feel, girl." Ella playfully kicked at Josefyn. Jo jerked back to circumvent the swing of Ella's foot, which resulted in Josefyn losing command of her balance and tumbling off the bench. The females disintegrated into laughter before Ella proffered a hand to pull Josefyn back onto the pew.

"Have you spoken to Akio since this morning?" Ella asked before picking her salad back up.

"I know what you're really asking," Josefyn laughed. "Did he tell me whatever vision he saw when he entered your head this morning?"

"He told you about that?" Hope burgeoned in her chest.

"He didn't tell me what he saw, and if he didn't tell *me*, there's no way he's telling you." Ella's hope staggered off a cliff and plunged to a painful death.

As if their conversation had pulled on an invisible rope to summon him, Akio's silhouette split apart the horizon. He veered off the path he'd been following to traipse across the asphalt and sunk to the ground in front of Ella and Josefyn, folding his legs into a pretzel amongst the long stalks of grass.

"Quail?" Akio quipped to his wife when his leg jostled the bird bone discarded in the sward.

"You know me so well," Josefyn crooned, beaming at him. Akio's brown eyes floated over to Ella.

"Hey, Rosie." He flicked the end of her braid so it thwacked her cheek. Ella squinted at him.

"Don't act all sweet now. Are you going to tell me what the fuck happened this morning?" Akio grimaced, flinging a quick look at Josefyn that Ella wasn't given enough time to decipher.

"I can't," he eventually said.

"Can't," Ella disputed, "or *won't?*"

"Can't *and* won't. I legitimately cannot tell you. I would if I could, El, but I was told—" He cut himself off from finishing. He swallowed a desperate breath before spluttering it out in a heavy sigh. "I was given a directive from the Gods—"

"The *Gods?!*" Ella squeaked, her heart leaping into her throat.

"Yes, the *Gods,*" he confirmed, urgency powering his words now. "From Aros Cavalian's lips to my little, insignificant ears, I was told not to tell you what I saw until you were ready to hear it."

*What the fuck?* "How will you know I'm ready?"

"You're going to have to trust me, Ella." How the fuck was Ella supposed to sit with that information without begging for more detail? He'd given her an ocean of knowledge, and yet at the same time, a measly pond.

"You shouldn't have told her that," Josefyn reproached with a shake of her head. "Now she's going to want to know even more."

"Would you have rather I'd said nothing at all?" Akio posed to Ella.

"Yes and no. I would have kept asking if you hadn't." Her concern had centered around wondering if he'd been handed a vision of something from her past that had caused him such distress that he couldn't handle being in the same room as her. The little information he shared with her, that the vision had been a message from the Gods and not some extract of her life on the Earthly

Plane, had assuaged that concern enough that she could let her fact-finding mission go—for now.

Akio's gaze raised above Ella's head, his eyes brightening. "Kellen!"

"Kellen?" Ella repeated in a gasp, her head whipping around. Her eyes engulfed Kellen's figure as he strolled down the path to her office building, most likely on his way to the teacher's lounge to grab lunch.

Kellen ceased movement when he heard his name called. His gaze descended instantly over Ella, as though he had no choice but to meet her stare, as though there was no world in which he could possibly keep walking without returning the look. Confusion splashed over his features when he realized the voice that had shouted for him wasn't her soft, feminine cadence, but a male's tenor.

His gaze passed onto Akio—apparently with some reluctance, displayed in the way he had to jerk his head to the side to peel his eyes off Ella.

"Come sit with us," Akio called out, both Josefyn and Ella gaping at him with barefaced bemusement.

"What are you doing?" Ella hissed, Josefyn smacking Akio's arm. "We hate him!"

"Trust me, Rosie," was all Akio said when much to Ella's surprise, Kellen began advancing towards them.

Kellen mumbled a clipped, yet warm greeting to Josefyn before lowering down into the grass next to Akio, keeping three feet of space between them. Inevitably, the person he ended up sitting closest to was Ella, with the way he'd angled his body away from Akio. Kellen looked between the three of them like he was trying to search inside their eyes for the reason why he'd felt inclined to sit down, while the three of them looked back at him wondering the exact same thing.

"What happened to your eye?" Josefyn gestured to the enflamed, puffed-up flesh surrounding his eye socket.

"Daniel Madix punched me in the face," Kellen answered with a grim frown.

"I thought you two were friends," Akio said. If it was possible for Kellen's frown to droop lower down his face, it did, like his mouth was melting.

"I deserved it," was all he supplied as an answer, his tone not inviting further inquiry into the matter. His focus latched onto the salad resting at Ella's feet. "Are you going to finish that?" he asked, not looking at her as he addressed her, keeping his eyes pinned on the salad.

"No. Take it." Ella tendered to him the salad and her fork, their fingers brushing in the middle when he accepted the plastic container. They sprung apart at the first graze of skin. Ella tucked her hands underneath her ass on the bench to calm the outlandish outbreak of electricity effervescing through her fingers.

"How's your day going, Kellen?" Akio asked with sincere interest, in his thoughtful, inimitable way.

"It's been uneventful." Kellen smirked with a mouth full of kale. "Nothing could be more eventful, which includes getting punched in the face, than what I experienced last night." Ella rolled her eyes.

"What happened last night?" Josefyn questioned Ella with a smirk and a nudge.

"Ms. Rose had a sex dream about me," Kellen revealed with a grin that rivaled the luster of the stars.

"I hate you so much," Ella growled at the same moment Josefyn and Akio gasped in unison, "She *did?*"

"Why don't you ask him *how* he knows that," she snapped. Kellen met the challenge in her eyes.

"Would you like me to go into excruciating detail for your friends about how you pushed my head between your——"

"I had an idea I wanted to float by you guys," Ella exclaimed to change the subject, then flung begrudgingly at Kellen, "I guess you can hear it too." She swung her braid off her shoulder and sat up against the arm of the bench, resting her forearms on her arched knees. "I've been trying to think of creative ways to teach the students behavioral and coping skills, since the majority of them don't want to work one-on-one with me. I thought, for the elementary school students, we could start giving out character awards each month. I'll pick a word for the month, like integrity or resilience or kindness, and the teachers will dedicate their morning circle lessons to teaching skills associated with that word. The students in each class who exemplify the word the most by the end of the month will be chosen by their teachers to receive a character award. If the students respond well to it, we can implement it within the middle and high school too, though they may need something more concretely rewarding than a paper prize to be motivated to participate."

"I *love* that idea, Ella," Josefyn approved. "I can definitely see the little ones wanting to win so badly that they actually try to learn the skills."

"It's like drowning vegetables in cheese to trick children into eating something healthy," Ella said. Josefyn barked out a laugh at the analogy.

"Using the natural competitiveness ingrained in all Primordials to get them to change their behavior is a great idea, El," Akio prided, giving her hand a friendly squeeze. Kellen's gaze tracked Akio's hand to where it grasped Ella's, plumes of smoke raging from his flared nostrils. Akio's fingers quickly slipped off Ella's when billows of Kellen's soot glided along the wind to abrade his knuckles.

"It's a cute idea, Rose," Kellen said, taking Ella by surprise with the fact that his answer was supportive and not disparaging…until he added, "Except no teacher will agree to supply you with a new student name each month, because that would require them to actually speak to you." Ella's mouth thinned.

"Maybe I'll just have the department heads give me the names for each class," she seethed. "How does that sound, *Varmin chair?*" From the corner of her eye, she caught Akio stifling a grin behind his index finger.

Kellen tossed a parmesan crouton into his mouth and grumbled, "That sounds like a shitload of work I have no interest in doing. Stick to asking the teachers. Just be prepared to plan your own funeral."

*Is that your twisted idea of a warning?* she asked through the conduit connecting their minds.

*Whatever helps you sleep at night, sweetheart,* Kellen replied, a smile laced through his words despite the fact that his lips outwardly remained in a flat line. *Other than fantasizing about my tongue between your legs.*

Ella was about to snap back, but just as an argument stained her tongue, her amulet vibrated between her collarbones, sending rays of purple light to scatter across her chest and lick up her throat.

A frisson of something cold and spikey scraped through her back. Somehow, she knew who this was about.

*Jarion.*

"Rose," Kellen yelled, having heard his brother's name appear in her head. Ella scrambled to her feet.

"Don't follow," she ordered, gathering her things. "I'll find you later." She sprinted off before he could respond.

## CHAPTER 15

# ELLA

Ella ran to the Varmin sector with the force of the wind driving her to a degree of speed she didn't know she could reach with her human legs. Her breath heaved hysterically with every urgent stride. Wheezes burned her throat as she tore through the shredded asphalt of the Varmin sector, sketching anxious footprints on the unpaved path in her wake. Her pace faltered, abating to a jog that bled into an abrupt freeze of movement when she yanked open the door to the dragon-shifter dome and discovered it cleared of people.

All that remained was the aftermath of what the walls and floor implied had been a nasty, violent breakdown.

Blackened spots speckled what once was a spotless surface of pewter. The steel structure still sparkled with flames that had yet to be extinguished, the metal walls caving in, denting the dome so it was no longer spherical in shape but, rather, jagged and sunken in. Not just the vestiges of fire injured the interior make-up. A pathway comprised of crimson mosaics, which were really droplets of seething blood strung together in a potholed line, spilled across the terrain. Ella followed the trail, trepidation cloying her senses, filling her mouth with the sour taste of fear.

The stream of blood and flaked embers—some of which were dragon scales, the texture fried, charred leather—ran into the

Canterna Thicket. The branches twisted and gnarled like grasping fingers above her head. Her pace quickened once more, breaking out into a full sprint when she recognized Laya's silhouette amongst the flock of slender tree trunks, the young Primordial's cries saturating the land.

"JARE!" Laya cried from her spot in the circle of Varmin children. "Please, stop!"

"Jarion!" Ella shouted, causing Laya to twirl around and stagger back, permitting Ella to see what the rest of the class of Primordials had gathered around. Jarion lay in the middle of the circle, a thrashing shell of a person, twigs minced and scorched beneath where he'd collapsed. Spasms quaked through his frail, lanky body. When he rolled onto his stomach, Ella could see that the material of his t-shirt had been ruptured down the middle due to the sharp edge of a dragon wing shattering through his flesh, striving to stretch towards the sun. When Jarion clenched the earth between desperate fingers and buried his face in the soil, expelling a monstrous scream while mustering all his strength to keep the wing from fully extending outward, instead of sound traveling out of his mouth, a cascade of flames escaped his parted lips and set the earth aflame.

"MOVE!" their instructor, Mr. Park, hollered to one of the students named Rubie Sullivan, who was in the direct line of fire.

Without a second thought, Ella raced between the terrified children and pounced on Rubie, thrusting the Varmin out of the way before the flames engulfed her. However, Ella's own ankle didn't make it out in time before the flames charged forward and wrapped around her calf, the sensation of her skin melting off reminiscent of what she imagined it felt like to have a bucket of acid thrown on top of her. The scream that left her body was a brutal outpouring that she felt dribble down through her veins to her toes, down to the leg that no longer possessed any sensation, the pain of dragon fire so ghastly that her body decided to slip into numbness to protect her mind against the horrific feeling.

"Ms. Rose!" Laya shrieked.

"I'm okay, Laya," Ella croaked, crawling to Jarion on her elbows. Maybe approaching him was a dumb decision, given the display of power he'd just exhibited, but laying on the forest floor and drifting into her pain while this child descended towards the clutches of death was an even dumber choice in her eyes. "Jarion," she whimpered, the young Primordial raising grief-stricken eyes, so engulfed by anguish that she couldn't even see the green hue of his irises, the color blocked by a film of agony.

"Help me," he cried, his voice cracking. Tiny cinders leaked down his chin along with his tears.

"I want to help you. Tell me how I can help you, Jarion."

"Push my wing back in." Ella hesitated. She glanced down at the embryonic wing working tirelessly to be birthed from Jarion's back, staring up at her as if pleading with her to tug it the full way out. Ella wondered momentarily if Jarion's dragon had emotions and thoughts of its own, if all Varmin shifter-forms did, and the dragon was experiencing its own layer of sorrow on top of Jarion's.

"Jarion…" Ella tried to carefully construct her words to not further agitate him. "That isn't going to help you. Resisting this is only going to make everything a million times worse. If your wing is begging to come out, you need to let it out, right now."

"I *CAN'T!*" he roared up at the sky, the sound mixing with Laya's sobbing in the distance. Along with the declaration came another upwelling of flames from deep within his chest, and this time, Ella wasn't fast enough to ensure everyone got out of dodge. Fire rippled through the ether, drizzling enraged sparks over all the children's heads. Screams seemed to echo from both the children and the forest itself. The Varmin class dropped to their knees and covered their heads with their arms, crawling through the soil with their faces burrowed inside the loam, seeking protection from the blazing rain.

One unlucky classmate hadn't yet moved to protect her face, the embers landing in the child's eyes.

"Ariana!" Mr. Park yelled as the young Varmin girl's nails clawed at her face in an attempt to clean the cinders off her eyes. "Ariana, don't touch it. You'll make it worse!"

"I CAN'T SEE!" she bawled.

Mr. Park finally reached her at the same moment the pain became too much for her body to withstand and she collapsed. Mr.

Park caught her limp body before it hit the ground, scooping her up into his arms.

"Ari!" Jarion yelled when he realized what he'd done. "Ari, I'm sorry! I can't…I can't control it."

"Get everyone out of here," Ella ordered. Mr. Park actually heeded her instruction the first time and gathered all the students to leave. Ella glanced at Laya, the Varmin's face smeared in tears. "That includes you."

"I'm not leaving him!" she refused.

"I need you to go get Kellen right now." The objection vanished from Laya's eyes, replaced with something far more potent: a determination to fulfill this command, anything for her to feel useful.

Ella waited until she knew everyone had departed the Canterna Thicket safely before she focused once more on Jarion, who was currently stuffing soil into his mouth to keep his fire down.

"Jarion, *please*," she begged, not sure what else she could do except beg. She refused to grab his wing and pull it out herself, refused to make such a monumental choice for him, even if that was possibly the only thing that could save him. It needed to be his choice to free his wings. "Please don't do this to yourself."

"I hurt her," he mumbled to himself over and over, leading Ella to wonder if he was even able to hear her right now, if he even knew she was sitting right next to him. "I hurt her, I hurt her, I hurt her!"

"Jarion—" The hand she reached out towards him rear-ended with a paroxysm of flames that erupted from his flesh, the force of the explosion launching Ella through the air into a nearby tree, her back smashing into the bulky timber. Ella plummeted to the ground, her muscles screaming from the collision with the tree, her body still anesthetized to deter her from really feeling the impact of the trauma.

She lifted her head at the exact moment Jarion rose off the ground, coated in fire from head to toe, the flames metamorphosing the pupils of his eyes into diminutive sparks, superseding the humanity within him. When he set his focus on Ella, it wasn't the young Varmin looking back at her.

It was a blood-thirsty dragon who needed to sink its teeth into something. And it had just found a perfect meal in her.

*Oh, fuck.*

---

Kellen had been watching, thanks to the conduit connecting his mind and Noella's, as Noella raced across campus to the Canterna Thicket. He'd viewed through her eyes as she found Jarion in the forest, had seen his brother writhing in the soil, throwing what little energy he had left towards fighting against the wing desperate to be unfettered from confinement. He'd seen his little sister begging Jarion to stop resisting, had seen his brother vomit a river of flames that would have killed that girl, had Noella not jumped on the student to knock the child out of the way, endangering herself in the process.

When Jarion's fire struck Noella, the conduit Kellen had been looking through in her mind flooded with unbearable heat, prompting a partition of opaque red to build over his vision. The air within the channel grew too humid for him to stand without suffocating on wheezes. He was kicked out of her head.

When he tried to push through the haze to reenter, he met a wall of fire on the other side that refused him entry.

He tried speaking into her mind, hoping that even if he could no longer see through her eyes, his voice could still travel to her ears.

*What's happening? Is he okay?*

*I'm going to need you to answer me right fucking now, earthborn, or I'm coming to find you.*

*ROSE. Is he okay? Just tell me he's okay.*

*Fuck it. Tell me YOU'RE okay.*

*Noella. Please. Answer me.*

If she wasn't answering, she either couldn't hear him, or she *couldn't* answer at all, for a multitude of conceivable reasons that made Kellen wish he could rip his skin off.

He knew he should get off his ass and go there, but for some reason he couldn't begin to fathom, his legs refused to move. Noella's demand to not follow her soaked his bones, keeping him restrained in his classroom. She'd given him an order, and while his mind revolted, his body refused to break the unconscious promise it had made her to listen.

A ghastly thought stained his heart: *What if Jarion killed her?*

Kellen couldn't allow that thought to permeate his being because it made breathing impossible. If Jarion killed her, Kellen could do nothing to save him, not from Terminus or from himself. Jarion would be lost forever, whether he lived to see tomorrow or not, which depended on his dragon not killing him first.

Knowing his brother as well as he did, Kellen knew Jarion wouldn't *want* to see tomorrow if he seriously hurt her.

*She's alive. She has to be. She has to be.*

He found himself praying to Aros Cavalian, not just for the life of his brother, but for the life of the courageous human who'd leapt on that child, saving both Rubie and his brother from the guilt of her death.

Suddenly, Laya appeared in the entryway to his classroom. She choked on gasps, her cheeks sullied with dirt and tears, drawing strips of brown sludge down her face. She spoke no words, but she didn't need to.

The horror in her eyes spoke volumes for her.

Kellen strode across the room and grabbed her hand. When they'd cleared the exit and were kissed by the wind outside, his wings broke free from his back, a mind of their own taking control of his body for him while his brain descended into panic. He hefted Laya into his arms and flew them to the Canterna Thicket, skimming the trees for a sign of Jarion and Noella. Through the clefts in the canopy of helical branches, he spotted a flash of yellow light, tinged blue at the edges, and bounded towards it, vaulting himself and Laya through the knotted twigs, splitting the boughs apart to make space for them to land. Laya squirmed out of his arms once they'd alit on the forest floor.

The sight before Kellen caused his jaw to drop.

First, his eyes drank in his brother. Jarion's brown flesh had been consumed in flames, varnished in a crimson inferno that twisted in his hair and curled around his ears, appearing to not harm him. The ground around him had been scorched and razed apart, the charred soil reeking of smoke, coated in a blanket of crumbled ash. Across from him, withered on her knees, lay a crumpled version of Noella, her white sweater tarnished by blots of soot and smudges of her own blood, which spilled down from the gaping gash rending through her shoulder, the skin flayed from what must have been a pellet of fire chucked at her. The fact that she was still conscious, with the burn in her shoulder and the burn on her leg, was either due to adrenaline, the amulet around her neck from Headmistress Dyer, or sheer willpower that Kellen couldn't help but be in awe of.

"Jare," Kellen gasped, about to take a step forward before Noella threw out her hand to stop him.

"DON'T!" she cried, Kellen and Laya reeling back. "You'll make it worse. I've got this."

Laya wrapped her arms around Kellen's arm, offering support while she equally sought support from him.

"Jarion," Noella cooed in a cadence reminiscent of what he imagined velvet sounded like. "Take a step towards me. That's all I'm asking. You don't have to release your wings. I just need you to take a step forward. Okay? Can you do that for me?"

Jarion vibrated, flames lapping up to his chin, tickling the lips of his that were trembling. Laya squeezed Kellen's arm as they watched their brother take a minuscule step forward, barely a full step, but the movement had Noella gasping with relief, her grey eyes shining with emergent tears.

"That's good," she prided, beckoning him closer with her hands. "Can you take another?"

The fire adorning him lashed out at the request, striking through the ether towards Noella. Kellen nearly shouted at her to move, but Noella dropped to her knees before the flames could swallow her. The inferno arrested over the tree behind her, lacerating through the bark to make the trunk teeter precariously.

"He's going to hurt her," Laya squeaked at Kellen's side, chewing on her thumbnail. "We have to do something, Kell."

"If we touch him right now," Kellen murmured, "we might make it worse." *Especially me*, Kellen thought to himself.

"I don't want to hurt him," Noella avowed. It took Kellen a minute to realize she was speaking to Jarion's dragon, not to Jarion. Jarion's upper lip lifted in a snarl, smoke billowing from the sides of his mouth. "I know you want to be free. I want that for you too. I want to help *both* of you."

"I've given him time," a voice that didn't sound like his brother—it was older, throatier, colder—boomed.

*What the fuck?*

Primordials were taught to believe that their Varmin forms emerged from within their souls, that their forms sharpened when they reached puberty and their own identities began to solidify. Kellen had never known a dragon to take on its own essence beyond the Varmin, but was it possible that his dragon had a spirit separate from him too, and he'd just never resisted it enough to find out? If he hadn't accepted it so easily when his dragon first emerged, if he'd fought against the two becoming one, would his dragon have taken over in this way, becoming its own person?

"I've been patient," Jarion's dragon said. "I've waited for him to feel ready to combine us. He has wasted my gift of time."

"You know him better than anyone," Noella persuaded. "You know what he's suffered. You know what he's feeling inside. Don't you want to help him? Don't you want to see him free of that burden, not just for you, but for himself?"

Jarion—or rather, Jarion's dragon—grimaced. "I did when I believed he would come to the right decision."

"He still can. He's not hopeless. If you give me a chance, I can help him sort through those emotions. I can help him come to a place where he can finally accept you." The dragon shook his head.

"He has wasted the chance for us to be united."

"*Please!*" Laya screeched, drawing the dragon's focus over to where she and Kellen stood. "Please don't take my brother from me," she wept. "He's my best friend. I need him. Please."

"I am truly sorry for your loss," the dragon expressed, as if Jarion had already passed within him. The thought made Kellen nearly keel over. "It's time for me to let him go and move on to another host."

"Host?" Kellen spluttered. "What the fuck do you mean *host?*"

"Did you believe that your Varmin form was a piece of *you?*" Jarion's dragon chuckled. "Your dragon is not *you.* Your Varmin form chose to live inside you for your limited time in this universe. Varmin are centuries old. Older than your Gods. We don't originally hail from Cavale. We come from the kingdom of Varminia, which no longer exists due to Aros Cavalian. Our king crossed him, so Aros cursed us to be dependent on the Primordials to survive. We must slip between the bones of different hosts or we're unable to exist. Your brother is not my first host, and he certainly won't be my last. It will not be difficult for me to find another. I'm sorry, but this is the way it has to be."

"Kellen," Laya wept, turning to her brother for guidance, for *something.*

Was there a way for Kellen to communicate with his dragon, if it could possibly help Jarion?

He didn't know how, but he'd try.

Kellen leapt into the depths of his mind, searching for the link between himself and his dragon, an ever-present rope that tethered his brain to his core, where his dragon lay dormant. He'd never tried it before, but he spoke through the cord, sending a message down the line to his dragon.

*Tell me what to do to help my brother.*

At first, there was nothing. No answer. Kellen descended into despair, his throat congested with sobs, before all of a sudden, a guttural, masculine voice echoed through the chambers of his mind.

*Trust Noella Rose,* his dragon instructed. *She's the only one who will get through to him.*

"Please, don't do this," Noella begged, threading her fingers together and raising them to stress her entreaty. "He's so young. He has so much life ahead of him. You see how he's wielded your fire. You chose him for a reason. He's a strong host."

"He could have been," the dragon said, Kellen's heart dropping into his stomach. "I wanted him to be."

"He still could be," Kellen growled, the chains over his impa-

190

tience snapping in half. "If you decide to give up on him now, that's *your* choice, and a dumb one at that. You won't find a better host than him."

*Kilic, watch your tone,* Noella hissed in his head. *We don't know what the fuck we're dealing with right now. If you provoke him, he might do irreparable damage to Jarion. Control yourself.*

*Listen to her, Kellen,* his dragon reproached him.

*So NOW you decide to have an opinion,* Kellen snapped at his dragon. *Where the fuck have you been all this time?*

Silence distended down the line. Then, pervading his ears, his dragon responded, *I was waiting. For her.*

"Let Jarion take control so I can talk to him," Noella implored. "So I can help him. So I can help *you.* "

His brother's eyes, devoured in flames and unrecognizable, scrutinized Noella with fervent wariness. Her gaze was soft in comparison to his hardness, a supple ocean of warmth and gentleness. Kellen had to give her credit where she deserved it, and she'd earned respect at the way she didn't balk under the intense appraisal of a dragon who could end her life with a flick of his brother's wrist.

"What can you, a *human,* offer him that would be useful?" the dragon questioned her.

"I can offer him acceptance," she answered. "I can offer him a safe space for him to explore what he's feeling without judgment. I can offer him support as he processes his past and comes to terms with what's holding him back. I can teach him skills to help him regulate his emotions when they try to overwhelm him. What I can offer may seem insignificant to beings who value strength and power, but there is nothing trivial about kindness. There's nothing small about empathy. I can promise you that I will use every tool in my arsenal to help him. To help *both* of you."

Kellen and Laya stopped breathing as they waited for Jarion's dragon to determine if her answer was satisfactory.

Noella appeared to have stopped breathing too.

Jarion's dragon looked at Noella. "Do you really believe that *you* are the right person to help him?"

"I'm all there is," she countered with a slight tremor heaving through the words, some of her resolve wavering.

The dragon narrowed its eyes in a scowl. "That's not what I asked."

"Regardless of what everyone else here thinks about me, I'm good at my job. I know I am." Assurance once more powered her speech. "I know what I'm doing. Yes, I can help him. I can help *you*. Please, give me the chance to. Let me talk to him." Jarion's dragon scraped his eyes across Noella's face.

"Very well," he *finally* relented, Kellen exhaling the breath he'd been stashing in anticipation. The dragon tossed in, "Let's see what you can do, earthborn," before suddenly, the fire disappeared off Jarion's flesh.

Jarion spluttered a gasp and fell to his knees, his soul unencumbered from wherever his  dragon had stored it inside his own body.

"Jarion?" Noella called out. "Is that you?"

"What happened?" Jarion's voice had returned to normal, to the young, guileless cadence of a twelve-year-old. Laya yelped a sob, then covered her hand over her mouth to keep the rest of her tears imprisoned. Jarion took note of Kellen and Laya's presence, then looked back at Noella, the only person he remembered being there before he blacked out. "I don't know what happened."

"Your dragon took control of your body," she explained. "You're okay now. Everyone is okay."

Jarion's eyes widened in horror. "Did he release my wings?!"

"No. He didn't." Jarion's hand flew to his chest, to where his heart was thrashing. His eyes then drifted over to the burn mark cleaved through Noella's shoulder, which Kellen had completely forgotten about until Jarion brought attention to it.

"Did I do that?" Noella hesitated before she nodded, covering the wound with her hand to hide it from him. "I'm so sorry, Ms. Rose. I didn't mean to," he whimpered, fire filtering down his chin along with tears. The flames knew not to harm him, though, rolling off his flesh like beads of water.

"I know you didn't," Noella assured, "but if you don't release your wings, Jarion, this will happen again. You will lose control of your dragon again, and not just with other people, but with yourself.

You will *die.* You will die, Jarion, and I cannot let that happen. None of us here can let that happen. Please, *please,* release your wings. I will help you. *We* will help you, the people who care about you. Whatever you're struggling with right now, we can manage it together, but you need to be here still for us to do that." Kellen waited with bated breath for Jarion's response.

He felt every mangled shard of his fractured heart when Jarion shook his head. "I can't, Ms. Rose."

"Then at least tell me why," she pleaded, not yielding. "Tell us why. Help us understand so we can help you."

"Please, Jare," Laya interjected, her twin's eyes swinging to meet her. "Please let us help you."

"*Please,* my love," Kellen beseeched, and when Jarion looked at Kellen, he erupted into sobs. "Talk to us. Don't hold this in. Please." Jarion's restraint shattered under Kellen's loving gaze.

"I don't want to do this anymore," he declared at no one in particular, threading his fingers in his hair.

"Do *what?*" Noella asked, taking a step closer to Jarion, sensing something Kellen couldn't.

"Live like this. *Live.*" The universe emptied of all sound. Time came to a standstill and held its breath.

"Is that why you don't want to release your wings?" Noella whispered. "Because you don't want to live?"

Kellen smothered his hand over his mouth to keep the rush of bile mixed with fire from leaking off his tongue, clinging harder to Laya to stop himself from collapsing under the weight of his dismay.

He thought Jarion wouldn't say anything else, but then, Jarion murmured, his bottom lip quivering so much that the words shook, "It *hurts.* To be in my head. To exist in my body. I can never…I can never be free of him, anywhere I go." Kellen knew exactly who Jarion was talking about, but Noella didn't.

"Who?" she asked. "Who can't you be free of?" Jarion sucked in an unstable breath.

"The person who gave me those scars," he answered, providing no further intel, not that Kellen or Laya needed it.

Not a day went by where the image of that man didn't creep

over Kellen's eyes, forcing him to remember that disgusting piece of shit's existence and what he did to the two most important people in his life. Not a day went by where Kellen didn't work his fucking ass off to ensure that Ciaran Ates would never see the light of day outside a prison cell, a feat he hadn't been able to accomplish with his own mother due to her status. While Ciaran was sentenced to six years in Terminus—not *nearly* enough time for what he'd done to the twins—Miya had only been sentenced two years. Kellen would give up his place in the afterlife and accept a lifetime in Terminus after his death if it prevented the twins' father from ever being released, if the Gods would allow it.

Kellen's fingers ached to wrap around Ciaran's throat, an urge that scratched his fingers often, but stronger now than it had ever been before when watching his brother crumble before his very eyes.

"So it's not that you want to escape your life, but just escape the *feeling* of being alive?" Noella asked to clarify.

Jarion weighed the question before he responded.

"What other escape is there?" he asked in the smallest voice, breaking the rest of Kellen's sanity.

Laya buried her face in Kellen's shoulder, wracked with sobs.

He wished he could offer her more than just a body to lean against, but in that moment, Kellen had nothing left to give her that his own misery hadn't devoured inside him. There was nothing for either of them to do except stand there and listen to the hardship their brother had been bottling up inside him, gifting him that space to finally release it, no matter how painful it was for them to hear.

"Death would not be an escape, Jarion." Noella's voice sounded calm and patient. He didn't know how she managed to control her own emotions. Kellen could barely hold himself together right now listening to this, trying to be a pillar of strength for his sister when everything inside him was disintegrating. Noella paused, then took another step towards Jarion. "Death would not be an escape, Jarion. It would just be an end. You want to escape these feelings because you want to experience something better than what you're feeling right now. Death wouldn't grant you that. Death would be a perma-nent solution to a temporary problem, and I don't say temporary to

194

undermine your experience and how long you've suffered. I only mean that it *is* possible for you to feel something else. I know it doesn't feel like it, but it is possible. Death would prevent you from finding out what that is."

The forest wept along with them, the wind rumbling a moan as Noella's words dripped across the earth. Jarion dropped his head, shudders quaking through his shoulders in accompaniment of his tears, of the abject screams torrenting out of him like a waterfall of pent-up emotion.

Noella closed the remaining distance between them and lowered onto her knees in front of Jarion.

"Everything you're holding in right now feels so much bigger because you're keeping it *in,*" she told him, placing her hand on Jarion's shoulder. "When you leave these feelings inside you with no outlet, they start to rot. They get infected over time. They take on a life of their own and plague every part of your being. You don't have to live like this, Jarion. Death doesn't have to be your only option. You deserve to experience more. The only way to do that though is to release your wings. Don't give up now. Give yourself the chance to find out what else is out there."

Noella lifted her hands to sluice the tears off Jarion's face with her thumbs.

"I'm so scared," Jarion croaked. "I've been pushing my wings down for so long. I don't even think I can do it."

"Start with the one that tried to break out today. Don't worry about the other right now. Just release one wing."

Jarion spun around to glance at Kellen, then squeaked, "Kell? Can you help me?" Kellen lost it.

"Of course I will, Jare," he bawled. Laya disentangled her arms from around him so Kellen could cross the forest and sink to his knees beside their brother, across from where Noella still kneeled.

He couldn't fit all his gratitude for what Noella had done for Jarion into his eyes, into one measly expression. Noella simply nodded in acknowledgment of what she saw in Kellen's face, then refocused on Jarion, on what was more important right now than accepting his appreciation. It forced him to do the same.

"Tell me what you want me to do, Jare," Kellen requested his brother.

"I want you to pull the wing out," Jarion entreated, fisting the soil with both hands. "I don't think I can do it myself."

"Do you want to hold my hand while Kellen pulls your wing out?" Noella asked him, proffering her hand.

Kellen's whole world tilted when he heard her say *Kellen* and not *Kilic*. It felt like invisible hands shoved at the earth to slant the entire formation of Cavale, so the ecosphere mirrored the way his heart swayed almost drunkenly in his chest.

"Please," Jarion agreed, looping his fingers through Noella's, yanking Kellen out of the rose-colored daze she'd just put him in. Jarion peeked up at Kellen, then forced out, "Do it now," squeezing his eyes shut.

Kellen plucked the tip of Jarion's wing still poking out of his back and yanked on it with all his might, funneling the wing past Jarion's human casing to meet the world beyond. Jarion crushed Noella's hand while hollering an anguished cry, his tears fusing with the fire and smoke jetting down his face.

"You're doing great, Jare," Laya cheered as she hovered above them. Noella beamed at her with approval.

"It's almost out," Kellen assured him. "Just a little more." He studied the design of Jarion's wing, similar to his own in shape, but a different color. Where Kellen's wings were black glazed in a golden sheen, outlined by wrinkled orange membrane that wrapped around the pointed bones comprising the edges, Jarion's wing was completely red, with sharp talons at each tip. When Kellen felt resistance, he knew he'd drawn the wing out to its full breadth and released the end, scooting back in the soil to give Jarion room to adjust to the sensation.

"How does it feel to have the wing out?" Noella asked him.

"It hurts," Jarion mewled, squeezing his eyes shut.

"Can you flex the wing?" Kellen asked. Jarion quickly shook his head. "That's okay, buddy. You don't have to move it right now. Just get used to what it feels like outside of your body. What you did today was amazing." Noella nodded at Kellen with a tiny smirk, like that was the right thing to say.

196

Why did that simple gesture make Kellen's legs feel like jelly?

"If you want to push it back in, go for it," Noella allowed, which Jarion immediately heeded by swinging his right arm forward, demonstrating for the wing the direction he wanted it to move in. The wing rustled between the gust of wind prodding at the fragile membrane before it melted into Jarion's back, disappearing beneath his brown flesh, the open wound stitching so there was no leftover remnant of the wing's advent. Jarion sighed with relief when the wing was finally gone.

"You did so good, Jare," Laya applauded tearfully.

"Well done, buddy," Kellen decreed, resting his chin on his clasped hands, his fingers drenched in tears.

"I don't want to do that again," Jarion groaned, peeking over at Noella.

"I know," she said, then added, "but you have to. We will do this together. You're not alone in this, Jarion. Everyone here will help you through this." Noella gave his shoulder a squeeze. "Hey. Guess what?"

Jarion blinked at her. "What?"

Noella grinned a kind smile, steeped in pure goodness, that cracked Kellen's chest in half.

"You just took your first step towards something better. I'm so proud of you." Tears gleaned on Jarion's lashes, on Laya's and Kellen's, on the entire universe listening to Noella Rose.

*There is a queen beneath that fragile flesh,* Kellen's dragon told him as Kellen watched Jarion choke out a strangled, pained, hysterical laugh, resting his cheek on Noella's shoulder. *It's time for you to start treating her like one.*

## CHAPTER 16

# ELLA

KELLEN OFFERED to walk Laya and Jarion back to the dorms so Ella could clean herself off. Before they left, Laya threw her arms around Ella's waist, burying her face in Ella's sweater, and sobbed a river of gratitude into the cashmere.

Kellen tried to guide Laya back to give Ella space. Ella shook her head at him, wrapping Laya in an even tighter embrace. Only when Laya softened against her did she feel comfortable releasing the young Varmin.

"I'll see you in my office first thing tomorrow," Ella said to Jarion, giving his hand a squeeze.

"Thank you, Ms. Rose." His hand slid away from her, opting to lace his fingers through Laya's before the twins bounded towards the exit of the Canterna Thicket, their limbs intertwined.

Only Kellen and Ella remained in the forest.

So many emotions swirled in the depths of Kellen's green irises that Ella couldn't decipher them fast enough to give names to each individual feeling she saw flicker there. She wondered what her own face showed, if he was able to interpret whatever emotions she couldn't withhold.

"Get those burns looked at," was all he said, the only suggestion of appreciation he could present to her. Ella was beginning to understand that for Kellen, tendering even that, what would be considered trivial or the bare minimum to others, was a big deal for him. A sign that he was trying amidst his own struggles.

"Look after Jarion tonight," she extended in return, understanding that beneath his statement, he'd been saying *thank you,* and beneath her statement, she'd replied *you're welcome.* He nodded in acknowledgment of the hidden message before stalking out of the forest, abandoning her to the wreckage of cauterized branches and corroded earth, the stench of smoke littering the ether.

Ella limped back to the academic sector. Even after she'd had Headmistress Dyer heal her burns through the amulet, her leg refused to catch up to the fact that it was no longer injured, clinging to the numbness for safety. She hauled herself first to the school's infirmary to check on Ariana, the student who'd been incapacitated by Jarion's fire. The infirmary was located down the hall from her office, which was why so many students confused her office for the nurse's station. Rows of cots strung together like teeth unfurled across the gargantuan space, this wing of the infirmary empty, apart from the woman behind the front desk.

"Hi there," Ella greeted the grizzled Primordial, who drummed her crimson-painted claws on the marble countertop in a manner that suggested she was trying to drown out the sound of Ella's voice. "I'm looking for a student who I believe was admitted here in the past hour. Her name is Ariana."

"Seek your answers elsewhere, earthborn," the female spat, starting to rotate her chair to give Ella her back.

Ella's hand lashed out to grab the back of the woman's chair before she could complete a full swivel.

"Just what do you think you're doing?" the woman hissed.

"I've had it with everyone here refusing to give me answers when I ask for them," Ella snapped, her adrenaline from the last hour heightening her courage, crashing into the woman's brashness. "I may be a human, but I'm also an educator at this school and am asking you to tell me if this student is okay or not. If you give me five fucking seconds of your time, I will be out of your hair before you know it, but if you drag this out, I will stand here for the rest of the day until I get an answer."

The nurse studied Ella's face for any sign of capitulation, any hint of weakness she could latch onto to fracture the foundation of Ella's nerve. Ella narrowed her eyes in opposition and pointed at the woman's computer.

"Has anyone ever told you you're a pain in the ass?" the woman grumbled, but finally began typing the child's name into the database, her claws clicking against the keys of her computer.

"Not until I arrived in Cavale," she muttered, "but now it's a daily occurrence."

"Here it is. Ariana Sarkis, admitted thirty-two minutes ago." Ella stretched her abdomen over the counter to review the computer screen with the nurse. "It says here that she was seen by a nurse who attempted to heal the damage in her eyes. They were…" The nurse grimaced, her lips twisting into a frown. "Shit."

"What is it? What's wrong?"

"They were unsuccessful."

"Unsuccessful?" Ella stammered, her heart lunging into her throat. Her blood no longer felt warm in her veins, converting to glacial ice. "Is she dead?"

"Not dead. But she is blind now."

"Blind?!" *Oh, fuck. Oh fucking, fucking hell.* Ella gripped the edge of the counter so hard that her knuckles turned white. "She'll never see again? That couldn't be healed by a Herculea mender?"

"Dragon fire is quite potent. They might have been able to heal her if she'd gotten to the infirmary faster, but dragon fire having contact with the eyes is substantial. If it's deeply submerged, not even magic can repair that."

Ella dropped her face into her hands, groaning between her fingers. How the fuck was she supposed to tell Jarion that he'd inadvertently been responsible for blinding a fellow student? How would this impact his motivation to accept his dragon when he learned that his dragon was capable of causing this kind of impairment?

"Has Headmistress Dyer been informed?" Ella asked, not lifting her face out of her hands yet, wanting to hide from the world for a little while longer.

"I've told you what I know. Now it's time to hold up your end of the bargain." The nurse gestured to the door.

"It was unpleasant speaking to you," Ella sneered, then marched out of the infirmary and stomped down the hall, busting the door to her office open with an unruly groan. She froze at the threshold when she found her office cluttered by Headmistress Dyer and the Cavalian Gods' envoy.

"What happened to you that you needed to be healed?" Headmistress Dyer's statement didn't communicate as a question, but rather a demand for an answer with an undercurrent of genuine care.

"Jarion's dragon took over his body," Ella explained, sinking onto her couch beside Headmistress Dyer. The envoy leaned against the wall across the way. If their arms didn't shift to fold over their chest, Ella would have thought Headmistress Dyer had dragged a metal statue into her office, the envoy so still that one could be mistaken in believing it to be inanimate. "He wasn't in control of his dragon fire, but thankfully, in the end, I got him—"

"What did he do to you?" a masculine voice dripping authority questioned from inside the envoy's titanium helmet.

"He didn't *do* anything to me," she argued, not sure where to look when she couldn't see the envoy's eyes through the armor. "He wasn't in control of himself." She felt the envoy glare at her through the titanium shielding his face.

"That is not a suitable answer to my question. Headmistress Dyer said she needed to heal you in two places. Tell me where, and the extent of the injuries." Ella blinked. She stayed silent a moment so she could formulate a response that was compassionate towards Jarion, but the envoy didn't give her a chance to execute that kindness. "There's a tear in the material of your sweater over your left shoulder, and the ends of your pant leg on your right side are frayed like the material was burned. Would I be correct in assuming that you underwent injuries in those two locations?"

Ella frowned. "If Headmistress Dyer told you I'd been injured in two spots, she surely told you the extent of the injuries and their nature. Why do you need me to repeat it for you?" The envoy cocked his head, the metal armor squeaking as his helmet and breastplate brushed against each other.

"Because my boss demands to hear the words from your lips before proper sentencing can be administered."

"Whoa! Who said anything about *sentencing?*" Ella whirled around to look at Headmistress Dyer. She could only interpret the Headmistress's expression as one of anguished submission.

"The Gods made a judgment," Headmistress Dyer said, heavy with sadness. "Anyone who brings harm to you will spend three days in Terminus. Unfortunately, Jarion cannot be omitted from that."

"So you're going to send him to *Terminus?*" She looked back at the envoy. "He's twelve!"

"The decree states that *anyone* who lays a hand on Noella Rose that she didn't want there will be sentenced to three days in Terminus," the envoy recited. "A distinction was never made between students and faculty."

"There fucking should have been!" Ella yelled, speaking recklessly without a single care about exhibiting proper etiquette when speaking to the Cavalian Gods' representative. "What Oliviana did to me deserved to be punished. She wanted to hurt me. Jarion didn't mean to hurt *anyone* today, not me or Ariana."

"What happened to Ariana?" Headmistress Dyer asked. Ella winced.

"Some of Jarion's dragon fire got into her eyes. They couldn't fully heal her. She's blind now."

"Oh, *fuck,*" Headmistress Dyer seethed, removing her glasses to pinch the bridge of her nose.

"You still have yet to tell me what he did to *you,*" the envoy pushed Ella.

"Do you have a name?" she asked rather than answer his inquiry. The envoy fell silent for a long stretch of time before she received a response.

"Eyal," he answered in an averse tone. "Eyal Drury."

"Don't you care about Jarion at all, Eyal Drury? About the young boy who lost control today and hurt his friend?"

She wished she could see what Eyal's expression was when he said, "I'm only here to care about you, Ms. Rose."

"Well, the only reason *I'm* here is to care about these kids, so there's no universe in which I'm allowing a *student,* who had no control over his actions, to be punished for an *accident* by spending any amount of time being *tortured.*" Eyal only huffed at Ella's powerful glare.

"I hear you, Ms. Rose, but this is out of my hands."

"Get me on the phone with Aros Cavalian then." Headmistress Dyer gasped at Ella's request. "I'm fucking serious. I'm not afraid of your Gods."

"You do understand that speaking to a God directly is not as simple as just calling them up on a phone?" Eyal spoke with humor, treating her assertion as if it were a joke. "When a God wants to speak to you, they send an envoy in their place. I belong to Aros Cavalian. By speaking to me, you are speaking to him."

"Then tell your king that if it's a choice between Jarion or me, choose him. If I'm telling you right now that I was not harmed, not in the way you're suggesting, then that should be enough for Aros." A dangerous idea graced her tongue, escaping before she had a chance to stop herself. "Maybe throw in there that I learned some shit about Aros today, shit he doesn't want getting out there, so if he tries to take that boy to Terminus, maybe I'll share what I know with the entire school."

"Noella," Headmistress Dyer cautioned, but it was too late to warn her off this path.

"What do you think you know about Aros Cavalian that would frighten him enough to listen to you?" Eyal challenged.

Ella's lips splayed in a scathing smile. "Does the name Varminia mean anything to you?"

That piqued Eyal's interest enough that he leapt off the wall, striding closer to hover over Ella.

"How did you learn about Varminia?" he barked. Ella's spine straightened.

"A certain dragon was very forthcoming today. The Varmin in my company were very surprised to hear the dragon call the young boy his *host.* I take it Aros doesn't want the Primordials knowing that their Varmin forms are individual beings separate from them, creatures he cursed to be dependent on the Primordials for survival after destroying their land. I wonder how the kingdom of Cavale would react, knowing their precious God wiped out an entire civilization over a single mistake. If he's kept that a secret for over a thousand years, maybe he knows that truth won't be well received. How would that influence the Primordial's decision to back him in the war against Lantari?"

*Stop talking,* a male voice—a voice that sounded like Kellen, but throatier, older—admonished in her head. *You're going too far.* Ella felt Eyal's rage radiate off the heated metal of his armor.

"You have no idea who you're threatening, Noella Rose."

"I know who I'm threatening. I don't *want* to be threatening the King of the Gods, so help me make him understand that punishing Jarion Ates with a sentence in Terminus is not an option. Give him an in-school suspension if you must punish him somehow, but please don't send a twelve-year-old to be tortured. *Please,* Eyal."

If only she had access to Eyal's face for any indication that she was winning this argument.

Finally, after what had felt like hours elapsing into wasted space, Eyal exhaled a surrendering sigh.

"*Fine,*" he relented with a groan. Ella forced her lips not to cave into a smile. "I shall speak to Aros Cavalian and see that the boy not be sentenced to Terminus for his actions today. However, I accept the punishment of an in-school suspension, effective immediately, for the span of three days. I will supervise his suspension. I'll have his teachers give me his work and will administer the lessons to him so he remains in isolation from the rest of the student body as punishment." Eyal didn't sound thrilled about having to supervise Jarion's suspension. He started heading towards the exit.

"Thank you, Eyal," Ella gushed, holding back tears.

Eyal paused where his fingers enfolded around the doorknob, turning back to look at Ella through his helmet.

"I sense your aversion for the Cavalian Gods," he said. "I would withhold your judgments until you hear from Aros himself what truly happened. There is so much in our history that you don't understand."

"I'll never get the chance to ask him."

"You will," Eyal proclaimed. "When you're ready." Ella jerked her head back.

"That's the second time I've been told to wait to hear a message from the Gods until I'm *ready.* You tell your king that if Aros has something to say to me, he can say it to my face. Stop with the vague, cryptic messages. When *he's* ready, he knows where I'll be." She heard the smile in Eyal's voice.

"You will thrive in Cavale, Noella Rose." He left that declaration dangling between them as he departed the office.

"I need to go call Ariana's parents," Headmistress Dyer spluttered through a wearied sigh, rising from the couch. Ella echoed Headmistress Dyer's exhaustion in every aching crevice of her body, the impact of the day finally catching up to her. Headmistress Dyer placed her hand on Ella's shoulder. "Are you okay?"

"I am now that I know Jarion won't be sent to Terminus." There was something she needed to do before she could call it a day and go home to Freya. "I'm going to go find Mr. Kilic and let him know about the suspension."

"Okay." Headmistress Dyer lingered a moment, then declared, "I made the right choice in hiring you, Noella."

She squeezed Ella's shoulder, then glided her hand away and left the room.

———

Each step Ella took back to the Varmin sector was weighed down by the bulk of exhaustion burdening her muscles, wrapping talons around her bones and requiring her limbs to work twice as hard to propel her forward for her next step. By the time she reached Kellen's office, she'd spent the journey smothering yawns into her palm and felt another vibrate through her jaw.

She clamped her mouth shut when she heard Oliviana's voice whine from inside the classroom.

"I saw you with her today," she accused him, her shrill, high-pitched lilt grating against Ella's ears. "You were sitting with her and her stupid friends, sharing her *salad.* You used her fork without blinking. You shared her *germs,* Kellen."

"So you're stalking me now?" Kellen growled. Ella could hear his eyes roll toward the ceiling.

"I need to know if something's going on between you two. Is she the reason you dumped me?"

"I did not *dump* you, Oliviana, because dumping you would imply that we were actually together. You knew what you and I were. It was always meant to be casual sex, no strings attached. I am not going to stand here and beat myself up any longer for the fact that your feelings got hurt when you've known since the start what I could offer you. As for Noella Rose, lay the fuck off her."

"Lay the fuck *off* her?" Oliviana repeated in a snarl. "She's a *human!*"

"She may be a human, but today she risked her life saving two students from potential death. She may be a human, but she deserves some fucking respect for how much she gives to protect these students every single day. This school would be better off if we all just took a step back from our egos and let her do her fucking job. These kids and this whole kingdom would be better for it."

"I cannot believe you're saying this right now." Oliviana's voice became artificially sweet with concern, so sickeningly syrupy that it made Ella want to gag. "Did something happen to you, Kell? Are you unwell?"

"I feel better than I have in a long fucking time," he announced. "Stop concerning yourself with what I do, Oliviana. Move on. Fucking *move on* and let me go, because it's not servicing either of us to keep having this same conversation. And if I hear that either you or Daniel do anything to make Noella Rose's life more difficult in Cavale, I will offer you up to the Cavalian Gods' envoy myself."

Ella was just as shocked as Oliviana. "You're choosing *her,*" Oliviana cried. "You're choosing *her?*"

"You need me to make a choice?" Kellen exclaimed in a desperate cry. Without even looking at him, she knew he threw his hands up in the air when he roared, "*Fine!* I'm choosing *her.*"

Ella yawned quite loudly, which alerted the two Primordials of a presence in the hallway.

"Who's there?" Oliviana shouted, her heels scratching against the composition tile as she quickly dove in front of Kellen, blocking him from a potential intruder. Ella smacked her own forehead, then sucked in a preparing breath and stepped into the classroom, revealing herself to them.

Kellen's cheeks paled at the realization that Ella had been there the whole time they'd been speaking. He recovered quickly, schooling his features into a mask of disinterest, one Ella now knew not to believe.

"You're not dead yet?" Oliviana spat, then crashed her shoulder into Ella's clavicle, sending her toppling into the wall.

Ella rubbed her collarbone, loosing a startled, sinister laugh. She chortled, "It's been a minute since you've thrown me into a wall." She met Oliviana's glower head-on, then sneered, "I almost missed it."

"Fuck you," Oliviana screamed, receiving only a callous smile in return from Ella. She marched out of the classroom, slamming the door shut behind her. Ella straightened up, cinching her eyes with where Kellen was stroking his index finger over his bottom lip, studying her carefully.

"You need something, Rose?" he asked her huskily. Something about the question left Ella wondering if he meant that in more than one way.

"I came to talk to you about something, but if this is a bad time, I can come back later."

"No, it's fine. Come." He gestured to her with his index finger, summoning her forward. Ella leaned her backside on one of the student desks, grappling the edge with her fingers to balance herself.

"That sounded heated," she muttered under her breath, her way of admitting she'd listened to their conversation.

Kellen tilted his head, then mused, "Is that why you came in here? To discuss me and Oliviana?"

"Gods, no," Ella denied, the corner of Kellen's mouth twitching as though he were repressing a smile. She exhaled a deep breath, then mustered the courage to tell him, "I came in here…to give you the respect of hearing from me first." Kellen took a seat atop his desk similarly to how she was situated. Their knees almost kissed from the close proximity. "I just had a meeting with Headmistress Dyer and the Cavalian Gods' envoy. They wanted to send Jarion to Terminus for harming me." Kellen's eyes grew close to falling from their sockets with how wide they expanded.

"*What?*" he gasped, his voice raising above a whisper.

"I convinced them not to," she rushed, waving her hands in front of her before he tumbled into a panic spiral.

"You convinced them not to? How?" Ella's lips lifted.

"I told the envoy that if he didn't stop Jarion from being sentenced, I'd tell the entire school about what Jarion's dragon told us about Varminia and the Varmin." Kellen blinked at her.

"You blackmailed the King of the Gods?" he said in disbelief.

"He's not *my* king," she said with a shrug, like that excused her insubordination.

"You're crazy," Kellen laughed, and once he started, it amplified into a full on, hysterical cackle, so infectious that Ella found herself snickering too, joining his mirth. "You're fucking crazy!"

"Hey! It worked, didn't it?"

They both tried to stop laughing, but Ella ended up snorting in her struggle to swallow her giggles, which prompted them both to spiral into gales of laughter once more. Kellen regained control over his chortles before Ella did, so for a time, only the sound of her cackles pervaded the room.

"Your laugh is exquisite," he sighed in a dreamy voice that insinuated he didn't mean to speak this aloud. It triggered her laugh to bleed into a gasp, her saliva getting caught in her throat.

"And your laugh," she said, converting her voice into a deep, menacing monotonic accent to mock him, feeling uncomfortable with the sudden affection and wanting to bring them back to a place she was more used to,  "is average in sound."

"Is that the best you could give me, Rose?" He pressed his hand to his chest, pretending to be wounded.

Ella braced herself to return to the topic of Jarion.

"I was able to keep Jarion from being sentenced to Terminus. However…he did seriously injure another student. His punishment is a three day in-school suspension. The Cavalian Gods' envoy will supervise him. He'll still be expected to do all his coursework, just in isolation from the rest of the student body."

The ghost of a smile that had been toying with Kellen's lips vanished, along with the appearance of his dimples.

"What do you mean he seriously injured another student?" Ella gulped.

"His dragon fire blinded Ariana Sarkis." Kellen's mouth popped open, then sealed shut, unable to form words.

"I don't…I don't even…" He framed his cheeks with both hands. "He's never going to forgive himself for this."

"We will help him through this," she assured, then said again, with an emphasis on the word *we*, "*We* will help him through this.*" Ella paced her breathing in preparation for whatever reaction she expected to receive from Kellen with her next words. "I know the promise I made you to stay away and not force counseling on him, but I can't do that anymore. I think you even know that. I came here to ask you if it would be alright if I begin formally counseling Jarion, starting tomorrow."

Kellen's brows pulled together. "I thought you didn't need my consent," he said, not angrily, much to her surprise.

"I don't, but I'm asking for it anyway. I know what's at stake for you if your mother finds out I'm speaking to your siblings." She didn't mention that she'd already spoken to Laya. That was hers and Laya's secret to keep. "I don't want to do anything that's going to jeopardize your custody over the twins, but your brother needs help, and he needs it *now*, before he hurts someone else or himself."

Ella rose off the desk she'd been occupying and took a step towards Kellen. She dared herself to rest her hand on his shoulder, a simple graze of her fingers against his sweater. Kellen jolted at the contact.

However, he didn't recoil from her or shove her away.

When he raised his eyes to hers, startled green hurtling into compassionate grey, she whispered, "I know I'm not one of you. I can't possibly understand, truly, what Jarion is going through. But I know depression. I know how it moves. I know how it operates. I know how it takes hold, and I know how it can destroy. Please, Kellen. Let me try to help him. I can't promise I know exactly what to do, but I can promise I will try every tool in my arsenal to help him. Just let me try."

Kellen expelled a gasp that sounded animalistic and throttled, then raised his hand to lay it atop hers. His long fingers hugged her hand, the warmth of his touch seeping past her feeble flesh, staining her bones in a way that left Ella certain that she'd never be able to wash off his touch.

"Why is it," he mumbled, leaning towards her a fraction of an inch closer, "that when you say my name, I forget how to breathe?" At that same moment, Ella forgot the mechanisms of breathing too.

What were words again? She couldn't recall.

Kellen's eyes dropped to her lips before the two of them realized where they were and who they were with, springing apart. Ella found herself stumbling away from him, knocking over the desk she'd been leaning against. She quickly helped fix the table back into an upright position, stammering out a pathetic apology to the desk, as if the table had feelings she'd just wounded.

"I'm going," she declared, hurrying for the door.

"Noella?" he called out before she made it to the exit.

At the usage of her full name, her feet no longer belonged to her, but to the dragon-shifter who'd made *Noella* sound like a benediction on his tongue. Ella slowly turned her body to face him.

"Yeah?" she squeaked.

"You can begin counseling with Jarion." Her heartbeat screeched in her ears.

"What about your mother?" Kellen swallowed, sliding his hands into the pockets of his trousers.

"Let me figure that out," he said, adding, "You focus on helping my brother. That's far more important."

A lump pressed against the walls of Ella's throat.

"Your siblings are lucky to have you," she said, then ran from the room before Kellen could respond.

## CHAPTER 17

# KELLEN

AFTER NOELLA LEFT HIS CLASSROOM, Kellen slumped in his leather chair. His body and mind were at war with one another, his body wishing to rest and his mind begging to move, his eyelids pulling shut against his brain's will. All he wanted was to steal a quick nap, though he felt like, after the insanity and heavy emotion the past hour had leached from him, he could have slept for a hundred years.

The sound of his phone beating on the desk with an incoming call compelled him to open his eyes and prop his chin on his hand so his head didn't descend back towards the desk. His fingers crawled sluggishly across the mahogany surface and slid the phone over to him, spinning the device around so he could read the caller ID. There wasn't a name written on the screen, just the image of a pitchfork.

*Oh, fuck, not now,* he groaned to himself, considering for a half second letting the call go to voicemail.

*Answer it,* his dragon ordered in his head.

*You're awfully opinionated for someone who hasn't spoken to me once in the last twenty-eight years.* When Kellen received no response from the dragon, he exhaled a huff and begrudgingly answered the call.

"Mother," he spat in greeting.

"Kellen." Gods, her voice was infuriating, each word she spoke honed by a sultry rasp, like she endeavored to seduce the world. "I saw you tried to have a restraining order placed against me. It's adorable you thought that would work, considering you had no proof of any wrongdoing, aside from me trying to walk onto a school campus."

"A campus you've been banned from," he reminded her, adding, "And I thought your history of being a sadistic cunt would've been enough for the court. It slipped my mind that you've sucked off the whole Cavalian law enforcement team, so they'll do whatever you say." She laughed as though he'd just told a hilarious joke.

Kellen drew the phone away from his ear so he didn't have to torture his brain with the grating sound.

"Darling, I finished my parole. I'm a free woman. I can go wherever I please in Cavale. You cannot keep me from the school."

"Yes, I fucking can, and I fucking will. You may be a free woman, but you have no parental claim to the twins anymore. And need I remind you that if you lay a finger on them, as per the court ruling, I will meet no resistance in shipping you off to Terminus for a permanent stay."

"Yeah…about that court ruling." He heard her shift on what he imagined was her bed on the other end. "I've been speaking with the judge who made the original declaration, and he said the order may be subject to change if the other party, being you, my sweet boy," Kellen pretended to stick his finger down his throat and mock-hurl, rolling his eyes, "hasn't complied with the order."

"What the fuck are you talking about?" he growled, nearly crushing his phone. "I have complied with the order. *You're* the one who tried to come on campus when you've been banned from the school."

"A stipulation in the agreement was that Jarion and Laya be raised in an environment conducive to the enrichment of their power. Allowing them to remain in a school where a *human* litters the grounds is not in keeping with that stipulation."

"That is the most outrageous thing I've ever fucking heard." *Watch your tone, Kellen,* his dragon cautioned.

*I can't watch my fucking tone,* he barked back. *She's being ridiculous!*

212

*Doesn't mean you have to be. Control yourself.* Kellen sighed, smothering his hand over his eyes to block out the overhead light.

"What you're suggesting is false. There has been nothing unfavorable about having Noella Rose at Delmarth. There have been no negative effects of her presence here on the student's powers."

"Really?" Miya sounded strangely thrilled, leading Kellen to wonder if he'd just stepped unknowingly into a trap. "Then how do you explain what happened today with your brother?" Kellen's blood froze in his veins.

"What...how..." How did she know what happened today? How many moles had she sent to infiltrate the school to keep tabs on the twins? Did she know about the staples? Could this really be used against him?

*Take a second to gather your thoughts,* his dragon advised.

Kellen heeded the warning, sweat forming rivulets across his body. His breaths came in shallow gasps, chest rising and falling rapidly as his fear threatened to pulverize what little remained of his sanity.

"I can assure you," Kellen said as calmly as he could muster, "whatever you *think* you know about what happened today, you *don't.*"

"Jarion's dragon took over his body and injured a fellow student." *How the fuck does she know this?* he wondered to both himself and his dragon. Miya continued, "Jarion blinded that girl, and guess who was right there with him? Noella Rose."

"Noella was *helping* him," Kellen asserted. "Noella Rose *saved* him. His dragon would've killed him if not for her intervention."

"How did it get to the point where she *needed* to intervene, Kellen?" At that, Kellen flinched.

*I did the best I could,* he thought to himself, not quite believing that to be true.

*You've done everything right,* his dragon reassured him. *Now shut this bitch down so we can go grab something to eat. I'm craving meat.*

"I am not discussing Jarion with you. You have no rights to him anymore. He is *mine.* Mine to love and to care for and help, which is exactly what I'm doing by letting him speak to Noella Rose. I dare you to try and prove that Noella's influence is harmful to the school, because I have all the confidence in the world that you won't find anything to corroborate that claim. She is a blessing to these kids, and you'll be making a fucking ass of yourself trying to declare otherwise. I welcome any excuse for the world to see you for exactly what you are." When Miya replied, she sounded skeptical.

"Sounds like personal feelings might be clouding your judgment, son." *What a stupid thing to say.*

"This conversation is over. Next time you want to chat, reach out to my lawyer. I'm blocking your number."

*"Kellen—"*

"Fuck off all the way to Terminus, Mother." Kellen hung up the phone, tossing it onto the desk.

*Good job, Kellen,* his dragon prided. *You handled that beautifully.*

*Do you have a name?* Kellen asked the voice, gathering his things to shove into his briefcase. His plan for the evening was to check on the twins, then get the fuck into bed and sleep that conversation away.

*Cozzeos,* the gravelly voice declared. *But you can call me Coz.*

*Are you going to explain to me why you said you've been waiting for Noella Rose to make yourself known to me, Coz?* Silence echoed down the line. *Great. Fucking great. So your help is conditional?*

*The answer to your question is one you must come to on your own,* Coz replied as Kellen trekked through the Varmin sector to student housing. *You are my host and I will protect you for as long as the Gods allow us to remain united, but I will not steal from fate in order to help you. That is where my help is conditional.*

*Then why the fuck did you say that to me if you're not allowed to speak on it?* Kellen grumbled aloud and in his head.

*A slip of the tongue. I will work to be more careful.*

*Yeah, try only sharing things with me that I can ask follow-up questions about.* Kellen shut down the line of communication between him and Coz so he could pound his fist against Laya and Jarion's door.

The dainty pitter-patter of feet advancing on the other side of the door alerted him that it was Laya before her face appeared in the doorway. Her normally bright eyes lacked their peerless glisten and looked bloodshot, from either hours of crying, fatigue, or a combination of the two. Her head tilted to the side to rest on the

214

doorframe, too heavy to keep lifted. She scrubbed her eyes with her knuckles.

"Hey, Kellings," she yawned into the back of her arm.

"Hey, Laylie. I won't stay long. I can't imagine how tired you both are." His own limbs wept for sleep. "Where's Jare?"

"Lying down. I got him to eat something, though, so that feels like progress."

Love filled every hollow in Kellen's body with abounding light. Gods, he loved this beautiful, kind girl with his whole fucking being, loved her beautiful, stubborn twin with just as much devotion. He would give anything to take away their pain, would trade his own happiness to safeguard theirs a million times over. If it stole every last breath from him to keep them safe from their mother, he'd give it all up, the rest of his life, whatever comes after that, he'd give it all up for them.

Kellen cupped Laya's face, pressing a kiss to her forehead. "What an angel you are, my perfect Eulaylia."

Laya beamed, then stepped to the side so Kellen could enter their dorm, shutting the door behind them.

A bulky duvet covered Jarion's lanky frame, only a glimpse of his curly black hair peeking out from behind the comforter. Jarion raised his head, then twisted his body around when he saw it was Kellen.

"I don't want to speak to anyone right now," Jarion murmured through a yawn.

"You don't have to say anything. Let me speak *to* you. To both of you." Kellen situated himself on Laya's bed across from Jarion. Laya stood in the middle of her brothers, prepared to intercede if need be. Kellen rested his elbows on his knees, leaning forward. "I want to start by apologizing to you, Jare. I never should have told you not to speak to Ms. Rose. Both of you. I was scared about what our mother might do if she found out and was putting my own feelings above yours, which *never* should have happened. Your feelings come first. What you *need* comes first. I failed you both, and for that, I'm so sorry. I love you both so fucking much. I only want what's best for you."

Laya touched her chest to echo the sentiment, her gaze glazed over in tears. Jarion just blinked at him. Kellen wasn't sure if Jarion's deadpan expression was due to exhaustion or simply having nothing left to give.

"This next part is going to be harder to get out." Kellen swallowed a valuable mouthful of air, releasing it in a rough exhale. "I wanted you to hear this from me. Ariana Sarkis is blind now."

Jarion lurched upright, ripping off the duvet. "Ari's *blind?*" Laya yelled, Jarion's cheeks now ashen.

"Yes, she's blind. I'm sorry, Jare." Jarion's bottom lip quivered before he flopped back onto the bed, buried his face in his pillow, and *screamed,* so severely that embers leaked out with the cry and singed the cotton pillow casing, dribbling ash off the sides of the bed. Kellen lunged forward, taking a seat next to his brother, and hugged his shoulders. "She's blind, but she's *alive,* Jare. She's alive, and she'll be okay. You can feel this sadness. You can feel whatever you need to feel about what happened, but what we need to focus on right now is making sure *you're* okay, too."

Jarion's body heaved deeper into his mattress along with the intensification of his sobs.

Kellen didn't know what to do. He looked at Laya helplessly, hoping she had the answers he needed.

Laya crawled onto the bed, then tucked herself into Jarion's body, modifying her shape to fit against him. Kellen eased his hands off Jarion when he cuddled closer to Laya. Laya threw her leg over Jarion's to further entangle their bodies, like this sort of embrace was routine for them.

"This wasn't your fault, Jare," she whispered. Jarion lifted his face out of the pillow with a mewl.

"I *blinded* her!" he shrieked. "Because I didn't release my dragon, I lost control and *blinded* her!"

"We're going to make sure that doesn't happen again," Kellen assured him. "Starting tomorrow, you're going to begin working with Ms. Rose in counseling." Laya's eyes widened before her face illuminated with a smile, while Jarion's jaw fell open. "You will work together to get you to a place where you feel ready to accept your dragon."

Jarion immediately shook his head, protesting, "But—"

"No buts, Jare. This is what's going to happen. Accepting your dragon is the safest thing for you, for everyone, and letting you die is *not* an option. Ms. Rose will help you, and Laya and I will support you in whatever ways we can. How we can help is for you to decide and tell us, Jare. No more telling you what *we* think you should do. It's your turn to tell *us* what you need, okay? Can we commit to that for now?"

"You're telling me what to do right now," Jarion snarled, his pupils transmogrifying into tiny flames. "Don't you see the hypocrisy? You're telling me you won't tell me what to do, while telling me I have to go to counseling. I take it you're about to say this isn't up for discussion, right? *Mr. Kilic?*"

"Jare," Kellen cried, desperate at this point, "*Please—*"

"I want you to leave. Right now." Kellen sighed. He couldn't fight him. He'd just told Jarion to express his needs, and if he fought against what Jarion requested now, then he really would be a hypocrite.

"Okay. I'm leaving." He rose from the bed, his eyes flicking over to Laya, her expression one of sympathy.

"I'll talk to him," she mouthed, snuggling closer to Jarion.

"I'll go, but first, listen to me, Jare." Kellen cradled the side of Jarion's face, threading his fingers in Jarion's hair so he couldn't pull his head back, so he couldn't avoid Kellen's insistence and undeniable love. "I love you. I fucking *love* you, Jarion Ates. You can yell at me and hate me all you want, but it's not going to make me love you less. It's not going to get me to leave you. I'm not going anywhere. I don't want to see you in pain anymore. I agree with everything Ms. Rose said today. There is more out there for you, my love, and I want you to find out what that is."

He dropped a kiss on the top of Jarion's head. Jarion extended a tender look, hinting at words and sentiments he didn't know how to start formulating, for now letting them rest in his eyes.

Kellen released him, squeezed Laya's hand, and departed the room.

## CHAPTER 18

# ELLA

UNDER A SKY of perfect midnight silk, Ella dreamt about her father, as she did almost every single night since she'd arrived in Cavale.

Tonight's dream was one of her favorite, and last, memories of him. A five-year-old Ella curled her little legs around Alec's waist, her arms wound tightly around his neck as he carried her up their building's fire escape. His long legs and bulk caused the black metal to shudder and squeak under his weight. Ella removed one hand off him, the fingers on her other hand digging into his shoulder so she didn't slip, and lifted her ponytail away from her neck so the wind could kiss her sweat sodden flesh on the journey up. Their air conditioning had expired last night, forcing them to rely on gawky fans that were unstable and kept sputtering out in the middle of the night.

It was too hot for Ella to sleep, so Alec suggested they head to their building's roof for some reprieve from the claustrophobic humidity of their apartment. They'd left Rylee and Ella's mother to their slumber and snuck out the window into the night.

"Almost there, my beauty," Alec promised, climbing the rungs with an effortless flair that Ella couldn't help but admire. She nuzzled her face in the crook of his neck, humming softly against his shoulder.

Finally, they reached the top. Alec dipped his head forward so Ella could crawl over his shoulders, clamber above his skull, and jump onto the cement, landing swiftly on her feet. Once she'd alit successfully, he climbed the rest of the way up the ladder, staying on his knees so he could maintain eye level with her. Alec's gaze shadowed where Ella's eyes had wandered, pinning over the night sky, the moon hanging low and casting a soft, silver glow onto Ella's tiny body.

"You looking for stars, little one?" he asked her. When she nodded, he beckoned her over to him. She situated herself in the cocoon of his legs, his arms a more comforting embrace than any blanket would have been.

"Why can't we see stars here?" Ella asked, leaning back against her father.

"Because we live in New York. The city's lights conceal the stars." He kissed the top of her head, descending into the depths of his thoughts. He then said dreamily, his voice sounding faraway, "Where I come from, you can see every single individual star in the sky. Their patterns are fixed and yet ever-changing. We have nights of the richest blues that become the purest black, hugging heaven's eyes so sweetly. The stars are brilliant pearls of nighttime that sit as if cushioned upon black velvet. They come to greet our eyes and lift our heads and hearts heavenward."

Ella rested her cheek on her father's chest, captivated by the vision he'd painted. "I want to go to there," she whispered through a yawn.

Alec kissed her hair. "You will one day, my beauty. I just wish I could be there when you see it."

"Where will you be?" she squeaked, clinging harder to him. His arms tightened around her.

"With you," he answered in a grim, strangled voice, stroking her hair. Ella raised her eyes to find tears besmirching her father's cheeks. "Even when I'm not, even when my arms can't hold you, I will always be with you, in here." He pointed to her chest, to her heart, to where the memory of him would be safe.

"Daddy? Why do you sound like you're saying goodbye?"

Alec choked on a sob, "Oh, my beautiful Noella. I love you so much. You know that, don't you?" He cupped her face, golden eyes crashing into her grey irises. "My heart beats for you and you alone. The degree of love I feel for you shouldn't be physically possible. I have no room left inside me for anything else."

"You can make room, Daddy." Ella leaned back in his arms, then started bouncing on her knees.

"What're you doing?" Alec laughed.

"I'm stacking!" she answered in a squeal. "I'm making more room for my love for you." Alec's eyes softened like a cloudless dawn before he choked out an anguished moan and dragged her back into his arms, squeezing her so hard that she coughed up a wheeze. "Daddy, I can't breathe!"

"One more second, my beauty," he whispered into a cloud of her hair. "Give me this memory. Give me this moment so I can live inside it forever." Ella didn't understand, but she didn't need to for her to relax in his arms, snuggling closer despite the mugginess. They'd fallen asleep like that, Ella tangled around him, Alec holding her like she was the air he needed to breathe.

When Ella awoke in the morning, her father had vanished: both from the roof and from her life.

She never saw him again.

Ella roused from her slumber with patches of dried tears rubbed over her cheeks, cracking the rough flesh, her pillow damp from crying. Until she came to Cavale, she hardly ever thought about her dad, but since the second she'd arrived here, he'd made an appearance in all her dreams, apart from the one the other night about Kellen. Freya poked her snout through the bars of her crate, keening softly as she tried to reach Ella, rattling the cage. Ella crawled across the floor, unclasping Freya's crate, and swung the door open. Freya skittered out and climbed into Ella's lap, assuming position to lick the tears off Ella's face. Freya's love removed the sensation of loneliness that had expanded inside Ella's chest, mending the heart that ached for a man she hadn't seen in twenty-one years.

With each lick, Freya said, *you're not alone, Mommy. I'm here.*

"You're perfect," Ella cooed, caressing the fur around Freya's jaw, the tips of their noses kissing as their heads came together.

Ella and Freya exited their bedroom for their morning walk and came to an abrupt halt when Ella discovered a wrapped package on her kitchen counter that hadn't been there at the time she'd went to sleep. She approached it with tentative steps, holding her hand out to communicate to Freya to stay behind her. She extended her leg to block Freya's path when the cavachon attempted the lunge forward to shield Ella.

"I'm trying to protect *you,*" Ella rebuked. "That doesn't work when you're trying to protect me."

Ella finally reached the counter. The package looked inconspicuous, small and spherical in shape, the casing composed of wrinkled grey paper that reminded Ella of her eye color, messily taped together.

There was a card beside it, with *Rose* adorned on the front.

From just the usage of her last name, she knew who'd left the gift. She decided to wait to open the card until after she'd unwrapped the present. She shredded the paper apart with her fingernails, revealing underneath a metal orb with an indent in the center that resembled the shape of a finger. Ella rolled the globe between her fingers, searching for any engravings that could explain what this was, but found nothing etched into the smooth metal surface. She set the globe aside and shimmied the card out of the envelope.

*This contraption is called an astral projector. Astral projection is an out-of-body experience that allows your consciousness to function separately, for a short time, from your physical body and travel through the astral plane to wherever you wish to go in the universe. All you have to do is place your finger in the indentation and think about where you want to be projected to. You can stay in that place for up to an hour before the astral projector will bring you back to Cavale.*

*I've imbued it with my power. Use this to visit your sister whenever you want. No one should have to go months without being in their sibling's presence.*

*You gave me  another day with my brother, so now, I give you your sister.*

Ella's tears dripped onto the card.

She quickly pulled her face away before the beads of water smudged the beautifully scribbled words. Freya leaned against Ella's leg, licking Ella's hand to signal her support. Ella scratched the top of Freya's head in assurance that she was fine, then slid the card back into the envelope, bringing her face down to inhale the paper. The scent of sandalwood and masculinity emanated from the page, streaking across the ether to stain her nose, to saturate the world in his odor. The familiarity of that scent made her wish she could curl herself inside the note and live within these words, within this gift of kindness. Ella dropped the note, then stumbled a step backwards away from the counter.

Was she…starting to *like* Kellen Kilic?

She placed her hand over her forehead to check her temperature. She *felt* normal, normal in the sense that no delirium clouded her vision, no fever clambered through her limbs, nothing that could be responsible for such a startling thought. Physically, she felt the same as she always had.

*Emotionally…*

Ella couldn't put words to the change. Those words didn't exist. When she thought about Kellen now, none of the usual surges of vitriol filled her mouth. No upwelling of rage tautened her limbs so her muscles ached with the urge to strangle him. Her body felt lighter at the thought of him, not heavy with rage.

Within her heart, a section had been numbed all this time awoke, a piece of her she didn't even know she possessed.

Filling her ears, someone sighed, *finally, you're seeing him.* The voice that spoke those words in her head was similar, yet different from Noella's own voice, coarser and yet soprano and sharp at the same time.

*Who are you?* Ella asked the voice. She received no response. *I'm crazy. I'm going crazy.*

Ella slapped the side of her head, shaking her hair out of her face, and grabbed Freya's leash to rush out the door, running away from the strange voice and the strange feelings about Kellen that she didn't want to understand.

222

Before the school day began, Ella enlisted Josefyn and Akio's help with preparing for her first session with Jarion. In order to maintain confidentiality, it wasn't explained in full what they were helping with. All she told them was that she needed them to meet her at the art department in the academic sector to help her steal balloons and paint. Akio guarded the door as Josefyn and Ella snuck into the building and pilfered six large bottles of paint, a ball of rubber bands, and twelve balloons tinted each color of the rainbow, the three of them bolting back to Ella's office once they'd acquired the contraband, the wind embraced by their laughter. Now, they were tucked safely in her office, pouring paint inside the balloons to fill them to capacity and using the rubber bands to tie them at the top. Ella was thankful she'd thought ahead to get six extra balloons.

Filling balloons with paint was a lot harder, and messier, than she anticipated.

While they worked, Ella decided to share with her friends the gift Kellen left her. She didn't anticipate the reaction she'd get.

"He got you a *what?*" Akio gasped, spilling some blue paint onto her rug.

"Watch it, Kio!" she cried, guiding Akio's hands to right the bottle so no more paint fell out and blemished her carpet. "If you ruin my rug, you're paying for a new one." *Maybe we should've done this outside,* she thought to herself, preparing for an afternoon of scrubbing the paint off the floor.

"He got you an *astral projector?*" Josefyn repeated, using her forearm to swipe flowing strands of violet hair out of her eyes. "And he told you to use it whenever you wanted?" Ella nodded. "El, that's *huge.*"

"Why is that such a big deal?" She felt like she was missing something obvious.

"Because in order for an astral projector to work, it needs to be imbued with a shitload of power," Akio answered, the rubber band he was trying to tie around the end of the balloon flicking his fingers. Josefyn giggled when Akio's hand flinched, then gathered his fingers and kissed the tips of each digit, washing away the sting.

"Astral projectors typically can only be used once, given the amount of power that's required to make them work," Josefyn explained, reaching for a rubber band to tie the end of the full yellow balloon in her lap. "Kellen told you to use it whenever you wanted, which means he knows there's enough power in the object to fuel it for everyday usage. He's linked the object to his entire volume of power, which is the *biggest* fucking deal I can think of. No Primordial would ever do something like that."

Ella frowned. "Why not?"

"Because if he can power an astral projector whenever he wants, that man is more powerful than he lets people realize." Josefyn set the yellow balloon aside in the basket on Ella's desk after she knotted the end. "That is *God*-level power, El. The kind of power the Gods would take notice of if it was regularly displayed. It's safest for someone like him not to use grand sweeping gestures to show how much power he has, but he did so. For *you*. So yeah, it's a big fucking deal that he did that."

Ella fiddled with the end of the red balloon in her lap.

"I'm not sure what to make of that," she muttered. Ella peeked at Akio. "Will it hurt him for me to use the astral projector?"

"With the amount of power I suspect he has, I doubt you using the projector will leave a dent. Depends on how frequently you use it, but I doubt it." Akio smirked wickedly at her. "You sound worried about hurting Kilic, Rosie. One might be mistaken into thinking you care about our Varmin department head."

"Hey, Kio? I have a present for you." Ella raised her middle finger and shoved it in his face.

"Gods, I've never received a prettier present!" He wrapped his fingers around her middle finger and pretended to yank it off her hand, cradling his balled up fist to his chest. "I'll cherish it for all my days."

Ella rolled her eyes.

A knock on the door fractured their jovial bubble and launched them back to reality. Ella gestured for the remaining balloons to be placed in the basket as Josefyn and Akio gathered the paint bottles.

"Lunch today?" she asked them.

"Always," Josefyn replied, blowing her a kiss before pulling on Akio's arm to drag him to the door.

Ella used her water bottle to wash away the smears of color on her paint-soaked hands, wiping the water droplets off on the skirt of her navy blue dress before she scampered to the door to meet Jarion.

Her smile faded, however, when she found Eyal waiting in the hallway instead of the dragon-shifter.

"What do you want?" she snapped without a care in the world for repercussions. "I have a session in five minutes."

"I've been assigned to shadow you from here on out," Eyal spoke through the opaque titanium helmet.

"*Shadow* me?" she spluttered. "Who ordered you to do that?"

"Who do you think?" Ella groaned, bumping her head against the doorframe when she rocked to the side.

"Tell your *king* that I don't need a babysitter."

"After what happened yesterday with the dragon boy, Aros is concerned that a lack of protection detail will invite other Primordials to bring harm to you, whether that harm be intentional or not. I'm not inclined to disagree with him."

Ella's annoyance didn't stem from the fact that she found this order pointless. A part of her recognized that it was actually a very kind gesture on the King of the Gods' part to provide her personal protection.

What she didn't understand, what pissed her off, was why Aros Cavalian was providing this protection *now*, after leaving her vulnerable for the past six weeks. He'd suddenly awoken from his daze to take an interest in her safety, yet not enough to deliver the message himself, sending this poor imbecile in his place to face her wrath. She shouldn't have been special enough to attract the attention of the Cavalian Gods in the first place, but since she'd already gotten it, why wasn't she being given the respect of direct communication, if Aros Cavalian was taking it upon himself to force a bodyguard on her?

"Your presence will hinder any therapeutic alliances I try to form with students. No one will feel safe opening up to me if you're standing two feet away. When I'm in a session, you keep your distance. When the school day is over, you do not bother me at home. That is the only way I will agree to having a shadow stalk my every breath." Ella arched a brow. "Do you accept these terms?"

"Not sure I have a choice," Eyal quipped. She wished she knew what his face looked like, so she could envision his frown.

Jarion emerged around the corner of the hall.

He halted when he saw Eyal, then asked, "Should I come back?" ready to bolt if given the opportunity.

"No. He was just going." Ella jerked her head to the right to signal the envoy to take his leave.

Eyal shook his head at her, grumbling, "Aros, spare me," then marched down the hall, disappearing around the bend. Once Eyal was gone, she turned to Jarion and proffered a sunny smile that was met with a morose frown in response.

"How're you feeling today?" Jarion swayed his head from side to side, then shrugged his shoulders.

"I don't know how I feel." She nodded in understanding.

"Well, what I have planned for us to do today is going to help with that." She asked Jarion to hold the door open for her so she could scurry back into her office, gathering the basket with all the balloons.

"What the fuck are those?" Jarion asked, rising onto his tiptoes to see into the basket.

"You'll find out soon." Ella locked her door, then beckoned for Jarion to follow her to the elevator.

***

Ella led Jarion to the Canterna Thicket, purposefully avoiding the scorched earth from yesterday by finding a vacant patch of land within the forest for them to use. She set the basket down, then lined up each of the balloons in their color order, starting with red and ending with purple. Jarion lingered a few paces behind her, shifting

226

on the balls of his feet, his hands stuffed into the wide pockets of his sweatshirt.

"Okay," Ella pronounced when she was done, staggering back to create a wide berth for Jarion. "Here's the activity. I'm going to name an emotion, and I want you to pick what color you would associate the emotion with."

"How is this going to help me accept my dragon?" he grumbled, kicking at the soil.

"You said you didn't know what you were feeling. This exercise is going to challenge you to describe how different emotions manifest for you, so you can start to put names to the sensations in your body." Ella took a moment to formulate an explanation that Jarion would be able to understand, working to speak his language. "Think of emotions like your power, like your dragon. Emotions are a form of energy, forever seeking expression. Sharing what we're feeling helps us to better contain and manage it. By naming emotions, we are effectively taking responsibility for them, which is the same as you releasing your dragon to accept it. Noticing and naming emotions gives us the chance to take a step back and make choices about what to do with them that will best suit us, so those emotions don't then turn on us and harm us. Does that make sense?" Jarion slowly nodded. "Are you ready to start?"

"Do I have a choice?" Jarion spat. Ella sighed.

"You always have a choice, Jarion. I won't force you to do or say anything. That's not what this space is for. Counseling is for you to explore what you're feeling and what you *need*, without judgment. Everything you say here stays between us. You are in charge of this process." His green eyes sparkled with something she couldn't decipher fast enough before it dissolved into the emerald hue.

"Okay. I'm ready." He cracked his knuckles in anticipation.

"Pick a color to represent anger." Jarion surveyed the six colored balloons sprawled out on the loam. He then lurched down to pick up the red balloon, holding it up for Ella to see. "Why did you pick red?"

"Because of the saying, 'when you're angry, you see red.'" Jarion shrugged. "I don't know if that's right or not."

"There are no wrong answers here, Jare." Jarion's cheeks flushed when she used his nickname. "What does anger feel like for you? In your body?"

"It feels…hot. Like fire. But a kind of fire I'm used to, I guess. It doesn't hurt me." Jarion looked to her for confirmation that this was an acceptable answer. She gave him an encouraging nod and a smile.

"Can you think of a time when you felt anger?"

"Gods, there are so many." He loosed a bitter laugh, then scratched the back of his head. "I don't know how to choose."

"Pick the first one that comes to mind." Jarion nodded, his eyes glassing over as he dove into his subconscious.

"Um…when we were ten," he began, his eyes closed, holding the memory in the forefront of his mind, "about a month before shit hit the fan and Kellen saved us, my mother bought Laya a dress for a banquet we were supposed to attend. The dress was fucking ugly. It had all these stupid ruffles and sparkles. Laya *hated* it. She said it made her skin itchy, but Mom didn't care about that. The dress didn't fit Laya the way it was supposed to. It never occurred to my mother that perhaps the dress was supposed to be made to fit *Laya*, not the other way around." Jarion's eyes squeezed tighter, his throat bobbing when he swallowed. "My mother made Laya strip, then stand on a dais as she drew circles around all the parts of Laya's body that she deemed imperfect." Jarion's hand not holding the balloon crunched into a taut fist. "Yeah. I was pretty fucking angry."

Ella took a moment for her own disgust to mitigate in her veins, so when she spoke again, she sounded warm and neutral.

"What did you want to do in that moment?"

"Kill her?" Jarion opened one eye to look at Ella, smirking slightly. "I mean it. I wanted to cut out her tongue so she could never say such horrible things to my sister ever again. I wanted to rip her heart out of her chest and show her what an ugly thing it was, what a flawed, *disgusting* thing it was, show her that the thing she feared most, us being imperfect, was exactly what *she* was."

Ella surprised Jarion and beamed. "That's good, Jarion."

"How is that good?" he snorted. "I just said I wanted to kill someone."

"What's good is that you're associating emotions and actions.

228

The point of this exercise is for you to identify what different emotions feel like in your body and what they urge you to do. That will help us design a plan for you to control those urges so they don't overwhelm you. Does that make sense?"

"Yeah. It does."

"Good." Ella then gestured to the trees. "Throw the balloon." Jarion's eyes lit up like the sun.

"Is there something inside it?"

"You'll find out when you throw it." Jarion raised the balloon over his head, then hurled it across the forest with all his might, watching the crimson sphere trundle through the ether and slam into the tree trunk. A flurry of red paint detonated in a savage explosion of color when the balloon rear-ended with the tree and the latex split apart. Jarion spluttered an astounded laugh, whipping his head back to look at Ella.

"Have you done this before?" he asked her.

"No, actually," she laughed. "I came up with this idea for you. I thought you'd enjoy throwing things."

"I feel *so* special," he taunted, but there was some truth in the underbelly of the joke.

"Okay. Now pick a color to represent sadness." Jarion didn't hesitate before diving for the blue balloon. "Why blue?"

"It's the color of tears." He moved the balloon from one hand to the other, as if the concept of sadness was an uncomfortable burden for him to hold. Ella noted that he seemed far more open to holding something that symbolized his anger than something resembling his sadness. She chose to probe into that further.

"Do you cry when you're sad?" she inquired. Jarion winced.

"I think I used to cry, when I was younger. Laya was allowed to cry, but my father couldn't tolerate my tears. He said real men didn't cry and my sensitivity was a detriment to our family's power. Sometimes, I feel the corners of my eyes sting, like they want to shed tears, but I haven't cried in years. Not until this week." He shuddered. "I don't want to talk about what happened yesterday."

"We don't have to." Ella took a small step closer to him. "When was the last time you cried? Before this week?"

Jarion exhaled a trembling breath.

"I haven't cried since the night Kellen saved us." Jarion refused to look at her, focusing on the blue balloon.

"You don't have to talk about anything you don't want to, Jare."

"I know." His stance softened. "I want to. I want to tell you." Jarion hugged the balloon to his chest. "Kellen had suspected for a while that our parents were abusing us. Laya and I have a different father than Kell. Kellen's father died the same week our mother met my father. Kell's believed for a long time that my mother was involved somehow in his father's death, not that he's ever been able to prove it. My father *hated* Kellen, from the moment they met. My brother's…not the easiest person to get along with." Ella stopped herself from smiling in agreement, though from the way Jarion's lips twitched, he sensed her concurrence woven into her silence. "Kellen is someone who can't be controlled, unlike Laya and I."

"You were so young," Ella started to say. Jarion waved his hand for her not to finish her sentiment.

"Kellen was sixteen when we were born. He graduated from Delmarth two years later and went straight to Nosrerry University to study teaching. He'd had an offer to join the King of the Gods' personal cadre and fight for Cavale against Lantari, but he turned it down to become a professor. He did that for us, because he knew how terrible our parents were and wanted to finish his studies by the time we started at Delmarth for Kindergarten, so he could be an extra pair of eyes on us."

Ella's heart thundered in her chest. She placed her hand over the pulsing spot to soothe the writhing.

"Kellen spent years trying to gather evidence of our parents hurting us. He begged our teachers to pay attention. He begged law enforcement to look into our family, but no one listened. No one wanted to cross Miya Kilic. Even though he already knew, Laya and I were so scared that we couldn't outright tell him what was happening. We wanted to, but we'd been so brainwashed by our parents that we didn't trust Kellen to help us. They kept us isolated from Kellen. In the months leading up to that night, Laya and I were husks of who we once were. They were starving us, giving us just enough to survive but not nearly enough to live. That final night, Laya was so deeply malnourished that she couldn't move. I begged my mother to take her to the hospital, but she refused, claiming that she couldn't get Laya help because it would open questions into how she'd gotten like that. She'd made her peace with Laya dying. She'd made her peace with her *daughter* dying, her only daughter, just to protect the secret of what vile people she and her husband were." Jarion vibrated with rage. "I will never understand or forgive that.

"Kellen never told me how he knew something was wrong, but somehow, he'd sensed what was happening that night, how close to death Laya was, and flew to Avatia, where the Gods live. He wasn't allowed entry into the holy city, but according to the story he always tells, he slammed his dragon tail into the gates until the Gods sent an envoy down to speak to him. He claims he threatened the envoy to send aid to us, and they listened. The Gods sent the Avatia militia to our home in Yorkdill and arrested my parents on sight. They found Laya in the basement and healed her enough that they could transport her to the hospital to have nutrients injected into her system. My brother was with them."

Jarion's eyes shone with love, love he might not have been aware was so palpable in his gaze.

"I'll never forget the way he ran to me, the way he gripped me in his arms, the way he sobbed into my hair. Kellen didn't say anything for several minutes, just holding me. Then, he pulled back, holding my face," Jarion framed his cheeks with his hands, emulating what Kellen had done, "and said, 'You're safe now, Jare. I've got you, my love. You're safe.'" Jarion's hands slid off his cheeks, falling to his sides. "I fell into his arms and burst into tears." Ella choked back her own emotion.

She was temporarily brought back to the night Rylee saved her, her history possessing some outlandish parallels to the Ates/Kilic family. Her mother, unsurprisingly wasted, had reached for the belt she kept hanging on her nightstand for Ella and without thought grabbed the broom instead, too inebriated to realize what she was using. Annalise hit Ella so hard in the head that she cracked her skull. Ella suffered internal bleeding and would have died, had Rylee not chosen *that* night, of all nights, to visit them from college. Rylee and Mason, who was just her boyfriend at the time, had walked into the apartment to discover Annalise folding Ella's unconscious body into a large cardboard box to toss in the dumpster, having thought she'd killed Ella.

When Ella woke up, she'd been in a hospital bed with Rylee by her side, who promised that she would never have to suffer at the hands of their mother again. What she'd said to Ella was frighteningly similar to what Kellen had said to Jarion, her sister's voice deluging her ears now with the memory.

*"You're safe now, my honey," Rylee decreed with tears gleaned on her lashes, her hands cupping Ella's battered face. "I've got you."*

That was the last night Ella ever saw her mother. After Annalise had been sentenced to thirty years in prison for nearly killing Ella, on her first night in custody, she'd taken her own life. What relief Ella might have felt from her mother's existence no longer tainting the universe was overshadowed by rage at how she'd evaded the justice Ella felt she deserved. Ella spent her life trying to shove that rage down in order for her to keep living, because that was the only justice she could claim now, in living her life and finding happiness while her mother no longer could.

She'd gotten to the point now where most days, she didn't even think about her mother, not unless she encountered something that triggered the memories to come rushing back to her, like right now with Jarion.

*Isn't that strange?* she thought to herself, that hers, Jarion, and Laya's circumstances were that similar, down to the words their siblings said when they saved them?

"Do you remember what you were thinking in that moment?" Ella asked Jarion, pushing away the memories of her mother and sister, for they had no place here right now. "What you were feeling?"

"I don't know," he answered, his voice strangled by the invisible tears yearning to spill down his face. They remained trapped inside him, imprisoned in the box where Jarion's father had forced him to lock them. "I remember thinking, *'Thank the Gods. Thank the Gods.'* But I don't remember *feeling* anything. I was so hungry. So tired. I could've slept forever. I don't think I had space to feel anything else beyond my hunger and exhaustion. But I know I must've been grateful. I must've felt love."

"Why do you say you *must've* felt love?" Jarion considered the question.

"I don't know. Because shouldn't I have felt love? I mean, my brother stormed Avatia and threatened the Gods to save my life. I *had* to have felt love for him in that moment, right?" Jarion searched for the answer in her eyes, frustrated when he couldn't find anything. "I know I'm capable of feeing love," he asserted, as if Ella had expressed she didn't believe him and he needed to prove it somehow.

"I fully believe that," she affirmed. Jarion exhaled. "What does love feel like for you? Can you pick a color for it?"

His eyes skimmed the balloons. "Can I throw the blue one first?" Ella smiled.

"Not yet. Go grab a color for love first." Jarion lay the blue balloon on a pillow of tangled branches, then scuttled forward and collected the yellow balloon in his hands, stepping back. "Why yellow?"

"Because when I feel love, I feel lighter, and when I think of light, I think of yellow." Jarion concentrated on the yellow balloon, his fingernails scraping across the latex, tracing the rubber casing.

"What does love feel like in your body?"

"Love frees up room in my chest. When I look at someone I love, like Laya, it helps me to breathe."

"So focusing on love helps you to feel less heavy?" A smile fiddled with Jarion's lips as he nodded. Ella smiled back. "Throw the balloon." Jarion reeled his arm back before he launched the balloon, rivulets of yellow paint flecking across the tints of red on the tree bark. When Jarion turned back around, Ella stated, "Love is an anchor for you."

"Yeah. It is." He looked bewildered by his own ability to recognize his feelings. "It keeps me from getting lost in my head."

"It's a feeling that grounds you rather than overwhelms you," she rephrased. Jarion's posture straightened.

"Yeah. Exactly." He seemed surprised by her ability to give voice to feelings he'd never been able to attach words to.

"What emotions overwhelm you?"

"Anger, for sure." He deliberated for a moment if there were any others, then added, "Sadness, I guess."

"Does sadness overwhelm you?" Jarion peeked down at the blue balloon for sadness.

"I don't feel sadness," he said, looking at her with uncertainty. "I can recognize anger. I can recognize love. I can recognize fear. But I can't tell you what sadness feels like, even though I think I'm sad all the time."

She cocked her head. "What makes you think you're sad when you say you don't feel sadness?"

"Because I think about death all the time, so that must mean I'm sad, right?" Ella crossed her arms over her chest.

"Have you ever heard of depression?" Jarion shook his head. She wasn't surprised to hear him say no, knowing what she did about how Cavale, as a kingdom, pointedly ignored mental health issues. "Depression is different from sadness. Feeling sad sometimes is a normal reaction. You can feel sad for a short period of time and those feelings will more easily go away. Feeling *depressed* affects how a person feels, thinks, acts, for a much longer duration of time. It impacts your mood, the way you understand yourself, and the way you understand and relate to things around you. Sadness and depression have similar symptoms. Lack of motivation. Loss of interest in pleasurable activities. A need to isolate from others. Exhaustion. Irritability, restlessness, fretfulness. Hopelessness. But sadness doesn't take hold the way depression does. It doesn't embed itself in your bones in the same way depression does."

Jarion pinched the flab of skin on his forearm, a nervous gesture, she assumed. "So you're saying I'm depressed?"

"Did anything I just said resonate with how you've been feeling?" Jarion sucked on his bottom lip.

"Lack of motivation. Need to isolate from others. Irritability. Hopelessness." Ella tipped her chin towards the balloon at his feet.

"You can throw the blue balloon now." Jarion sunk to the ground, grabbed the blue balloon, and chucked it towards the deluge of red and yellow, strips of blue dividing the bright colors.

He spun back to face her. "Why didn't you let me throw it before?"

"Because you didn't name the feeling and how it manifests for you. Now, you did." Jarion's lips formed an impressed smile.

"Damn. You're good at this, Ms. Rose."

"It's what they pay me for, so I better be." Jarion spluttered out a surprised chortle, not having expected Ella to have a sense of humor. "You said earlier that you can recognize when you feel fear. Can you pick a color for fear?" Jarion skimmed the remaining three options. He reached for the green balloon. "Why did you pick green?"

"Cause green is the color of vomit." They both snickered. Jarion's smile enlarged when he heard Ella laugh too.

"What does fear feel like for you?"

"It feels like someone has their hand around my throat and is strangling me. It feels like my heart is trying to break free from my chest. I get nauseous when I'm scared. I tend to throw up." Jarion wrinkled his nose at the thought.

"Can you think of a time when you felt afraid?" His cheeks depleted of color.

"I used to have a pet Fueco, a tiny bird with fire for feathers. I named her Jade. Whenever I disobeyed my father, he would pin me down to his workout bench, take Jade out from inside her crate, and use her claws to carve lines across my back." Jarion cringed, flexing his muscles like he was trying to expel the prickly sensation rippling through his spine. "He knew to only mark my back because Kellen couldn't see it. It got to a point where I couldn't take it anymore. Not the abuse of me…of Jade. So I tried to free her one night. I stole her cage and carried her to the edge of our property. I was about to open the cage door when my father found us." Jarion gulped, sweat percolating on his brow at the memory. "I have never felt fear like that. I could've passed out from how dizzy I got. My father took Jade out of the cage, snapped her leg off, and incinerated her right before my eyes. He kept the foot so he could continue to scar me with her claws. To scar me with the reminder of what a failure I was."

Ella knew there was evil in the universe. She'd tasted it before, at the hands of her mother, but the extent of evil that had beleaguered Jarion and Laya was a degree she'd never been exposed to before. It sickened her to her core, made it difficult for her to maintain her sympathetic expression and not scream her outrage for how the universe could be so cruel to such sweet, innocent children. It could have been so easy to forfeit to the danger of the world, to the monsters that had plagued them, but as Ella worked every day to push past the burden she carried, to seek out goodness where it lingered in the gaps of pain, she would now work to help Jarion do the same.

"Throw away your fear, Jarion," she directed, resting her chin on her clasped hands.

Jarion's lashes fluttered at her phrasing, then heaved the green balloon, watching it tumble diagonally through the wind and collide with the variegated timber, dripping dews of green onto the gulley of pigments.

"Now pick a color for happiness." Jarion's fingers hovered over the last two options—orange and purple—before he chose orange, plucking the balloon off the soil by pinching the bottom. "Why orange?"

"Orange reminds me of the sun." The balloon dangled from between his fingers, slapping against his thigh.

"What does happiness feel like for you?" He tensed.

"I really don't know." His shoulders sunk.

"What do you think happiness would feel like?" Jarion raised wet eyes to her, but the tears never flowed.

"Like freedom," he whispered, his voice barely audible.

"Freedom from the pain?" He nodded his head. "Does being with your siblings make you happy?"

"Being with them makes me feel safe. I don't know if I'd say it makes me feel *happy*. Especially with Kellen recently." Jarion frowned, shaking his head. "I don't know why I've been so angry with him. He's doing the best he can to be here for me, but every time he talks, I want to rip his head off."

*I know the feeling,* she thought to herself.

"When you feel yourself getting angry with him, can you identify what causes you to have that urge?"

Jarion pulled at his red beanie, adjusting it on his head.

"It's usually when he's telling me what he thinks I should do. He

236

disguises it like it's my choice, but it's never my choice. Like coming here. He first tells me I *can't* speak to you, then turns around and tells me I *have* to speak to you. Like, make up your fucking mind and stop dicking me around, for fuck's sake."

"Damn. Tell me how you really feel, Jare." Jarion laughed, a beautiful, free, youthful sound. "How does it make you feel when Kellen tells you what to do?"

Jarion hesitated. "Can I be super honest here?"

"As honest as you want. Everything you say here is completely confidential and stays between us."

*Kilic, if you're in my head right now, get the fuck out of here,* she threatened, just in case Kellen was watching their session—if he was, they would be having words, and not so kind words at that.

*Is Jarion okay?* Kellen answered immediately, which didn't diminish her worry that he'd been listening this whole time.

*He's fine. I just want to make sure he has privacy to share freely with me.*

*I haven't been watching your session. I'm about to head into a meeting with Headmistress Dyer.*

Ella sagged with relief. *Promise me you won't ever watch our sessions.*

*I wouldn't do that to Jare.* Silence swelled down the line before she heard him say, *You never thanked me for my present.*

*If you gave me a present just for the hope that you'd be thanked for it, it kind of cheapens the present. Now, go away. I need to focus.* The sound of husky laughter scuffed the walls of her brain, sending shivers down her spine. A second passed before she added, *Thank you for the astral projector, Kellen.*

She held her breath waiting for a reply.

It took a minute before she received a soft, *You're welcome, Noella.* Her breath stuttered when he called her *Noella.*

She returned her focus to Jarion just as he declared, "It feels like he's trying to control me. Like I traded one evil for another. I know Kellen's not evil, nowhere close to my parents, but I feel like I have no space to breathe or figure out what it is that *I* want separate from someone else's desires for me."

"Is that something you'd want to express to him?" Jarion winced, then shook his head. "Why not?"

"I don't want him to be mad at me."

"If you don't tell him how you feel, then he won't know what he's doing is hurting you." Ella leaned against a neighboring tree. "There's a quote I learned during grad school that's stuck with me ever since I heard it. If you're silent about your pain, they'll kill you and say you enjoyed it."

"Oof." Jarion pounded his fist against his chest. "That hit hard, Ms. Rose. Who said that?"

"A human from the Earthly Plane named Zora Neale Hurston. She was a writer and anthropologist."

"You should have that quote framed in your office." Ella grinned at the idea.

"You know what? I might just do that." She took three steps closer to Jarion, now standing right next to him. "You've spent a large portion of your life suffering in silence because you had to in order to survive. It's only been two years since you've been removed from your parents. It may take your body and mind a while to recognize that you're no longer in that place, so you don't have to rely on those old coping strategies anymore. The only person who can break that cycle is you. It's in your power to make that change, Jarion, and that can be through starting small, like telling your brother how he makes you feel. That's a great first step towards gaining agency over yourself and your needs." Jarion flashed a small, but genuine smile, laced with indebtedness that the young Primordial didn't yet have the vocabulary to articulate. "You can throw the orange balloon."

"Why? I didn't identify how happiness makes me feel."

"That's okay. You'll be able to answer that question eventually." Jarion glanced at the balloon, then handed it to Ella.

"You throw it," he said, sliding his hands into his pockets.

Ella cradled the bottom of the orange balloon, then lobbed it with all her might. The balloon stuttered before it descended to the ground a few feet away from the tree, bowling in the opposite direction.

Jarion snorted as Ella burst out, "I'm not as strong as you Primordials are!"

"That was pathetic, Ms. Rose," he chuckled. She was so grateful to hear such a joyous sound leave him that she didn't reprimand him for making fun of her. She grumbled on her way to the balloon, picking it up from where it had ceased movement, and too aggressively shoved the sphere at the tree trunk. The orange paint exploded onto her face, hair, and dress, lodging itself in the snarled wisps of her blonde hair. Jarion's laughter escalated into a strident cackle, the forest echoing the merriment and joining the chorus with its own rendition of the jubilant melody, the world laughing with him. "Fuck, I wish I'd filmed that," he roared, wiping laughter-induced tears from the corners of his eyes.

"Alright. Let's finish the last balloon so I can go clean this off." Ella's inability to tolerate being dirty was in overdrive, threatening to overtake her senses, her legs close to crumbling to the ground. She wiped her orange-stained hands on her dress, accepting the fact that it would need to be cleaned anyway, and pointed to the purple balloon. "Pick up that balloon." Jarion heeded the order.

"What emotion will this one be?" he asked, the question making Ella smile.

"Hope," she answered. Jarion's eyes glistened. "Tell me what you're hoping for, for your future."

"Um…I hope…" He struggled with his answer. Eventually, after taking the time to thoughtfully consider, he declared, "I hope I can come to a place where I accept who I am, so living in my body doesn't hurt so much. So I don't hurt other people." Ella squeezed his shoulder.

"I hope so too, Jare," she said, then took a step back so Jarion could throw the last remaining balloon at the tree.

## CHAPTER 19

# KELLEN

KELLEN KNOCKED his fist against Headmistress Dyer's door, waited two seconds, wondered why the fuck he was knocking and not just entering, then smashed his elbow into the door, barging in.

"Your manners lasted all of two seconds," Headmistress Dyer reprimanded from where she sat behind her elaborate desk, her red glasses slipping down the bridge of her nose when she dipped her head and narrowed her eyes in a scowl. "I feel like you broke a record somewhere in the world."

"I expect my trophy hand delivered at dawn." Headmistress Dyer rolled her eyes, but couldn't completely contain a smile.

Valerie Dyer was Headmistress of Delmarth when Kellen was a student here. He spent much of his time in her office as a kid—mostly for disciplinary reasons, starting fights, never following directions and being an all-around shithead, though sometimes he would come to her office to have lunch, just because he didn't have anywhere else to go. He never thought they would get to a place of being quiet acquaintances with a gulf of mutual respect between them, but fate has a funny way of giving you what you need when you least expect it. She'd been a massive support to Laya and Jarion, the only person who believed his concerns about what their parents were doing and who worked alongside him to instigate the Cavalian law enforcement to take action. She'd gone above and beyond providing resources to them when Kellen first became their legal guardian, setting them up with lodgings near the school that were protected by wards so his mother couldn't find the location when she was released from Terminus. He would be forever grateful to her for that.

"How's Jarion?" Headmistress Dyer asked, closing the lid of her laptop to give him her undivided attention.

"Physically fine, thanks to Ms. Rose." Headmistress Dyer leaned back in her ornate seat, which was really more of a throne than an office chair, framed by gold spikes that jutted out from the backrest.

"Oh? So maybe hiring Ms. Rose wasn't the colossal mistake you accused me of making?"

"*Maybe,*" he conceded. Headmistress Dyer tossed her head back with a triumphant laugh.

"I believe you told me that by hiring Ms. Rose, I would be sinking the entire school into an early retirement. For Kellen Kilic to actually admit he was wrong, she must be better than even I realize."

"I didn't come here to listen to myself be quoted, though I do enjoy hearing my words repeated back to me." Kellen crossed his legs, resting his ankle on his thigh. "I have a student who's failing my class. Markus Loewe. I've given him multiple chances to make up the work he's missed, but he's failed to hold up his end of the bargain. He's received zeroes on all his chapter quizzes and the first two exams. At this point in the semester, I'm not sure how he could possibly catch up enough to pass my class. I've never dealt with this before, so I wasn't sure of the proper protocol."

"Bring it to Ms. Rose. See if she can talk some sense into him before you give up." Kellen groaned. "You just said she wasn't that bad," Headmistress Dyer reproached. "Why are you groaning at the thought of needing to speak to her?"

"I said it *maybe* wasn't a mistake to hire her. Not that I enjoy speaking to her." *Liar,* Coz crooned in his ears.

*Crawl back into your hole,* he snarled at Coz.

*I am quaking with fear.* Sarcasm dripped down the walls of his mind.

"We're halfway through the semester," Headmistress Dyer reminded him. "If there's a chance Markus can be guided down a different path, let Ms. Rose try. He just needs enough at this point to simply *pass* the class. We're not gunning for an A, just enough to scrape by for a D. Worst case scenario, we bring his parents in and have a more serious discussion about what the rest of the year looks like."

"Fine. I'll go talk to Ms. Rose." Headmistress Dyer lifted the lid of her laptop—her subtle indication that his time with her had finished. Kellen chuckled at the passive-aggressive gesture. "And you lecture *me* about manners," he spat at her, hefting from his chair and storming to the door.

"Still lasted longer than you," Headmistress Dyer jested.

"The bar is set extremely low, then." She lifted her fingers in a dismissive wave without looking away from her laptop screen.

After dropping Jarion at his next class, Ella reentered her office with the intention of scrubbing the orange paint off her body. She almost tripped over her desk, which Kellen had hauled across the room and positioned in front of the couch so he could prop his feet up, thus blocking her doorway.

"Kilic!" she yelled, smothering her eyes with her hand to prevent a headache from stretching into its full form across her skull. "What did I say about breaking into my office when I'm not in here?!"

"Do it more?" he mocked, resting his intertwined fingers on his stomach and wielding those disgustingly handsome dimples against her.

"Why did you feel the need to drag my desk over here? There was a coffee table already in front of the couch." She gestured to the tiny table hidden beneath the arch of her large desk, the glass rectangle submerged in shadows.

242

"I wanted to elevate my legs, and your coffee table wasn't tall enough. You should really think about redecorating in here, Rose. It's not a conducive environment to relaxation." Ella's cheeks boiled.

"Fix my office right now and then get out."

"But I need to talk to you."

"Do I look like I'm in the mood?" she barked, gesturing down to her sullied dress.

"Do I look like I care?" he shot back, not glancing away from her face to take in the blemishes of orange she was referring to. Ella's mouth fell open, then sealed shut. Why did she think she liked him again?

"You know what I don't understand? You claim to hate me, yet you spend more time in my office than I do."

Kellen blinked at her, then shrugged. "It smells nice in here."

Ella shook her head. "Get out of my office right now."

"No. I came here to talk to you about a student." Kellen adjusted the desk, shifting it to the right a marginal distance so Ella could squeeze through the small opening and successfully slip into her office.

"I already told you that I can't speak to you about your brother." She looped around the desk and dove for the drawer that contained her hand sanitizer, squirting a dollop onto her palm and rubbing her hands together to spread the translucent liquid, scrubbing off the orange paint cresting in the creases of her hands.

"I'm not here to talk about my brother. It's about someone else." Ella froze.

She set the hand sanitizer on the desk and turned to him slowly, drawing out the moment for dramatic effect, savoring the place on her metaphorical high horse that she was about to officially claim.

"Wait a second," she said, a flicker of a smile toying with her lips. "Did you actually come here to talk to me about a student?" Kellen offered nothing but a blink of his eyes. Ella's face illuminated with a wide smile, her hands coming together in a thrilled clap. "You did! Oh, this is HUGE. This might be the greatest thing that's happened in the history of all universes, the Earthly Plane and Cavale combined!"

The corner of Kellen's mouth quirked up. "Conceit isn't a good look for you, sweetheart."

"I think I wear it well, thank you very much." Ella swung her hair off her shoulder. "In fact, I wear it *so* well that if you want my help, I'm going to need to hear you ask for it. The whole sentence."

"Really?" he groused.

"Would you not request the same from me, if it was *I* surrendering to *you?*" Kellen  cocked a brow, leading Ella to fear she might've just stumbled into a trap where her precious victory would be robbed from her.

"How would you like me to surrender to you, Ms. Rose? With words on my tongue, or my tongue between your legs?"

Heat bloomed across Ella's cheeks.

She dared herself to goad, "And if I chose the latter and not the former? Would you get on your knees, Kilic?"

One second, Kellen was seated on the couch.

In the next breath, he'd crossed the span of the office until he was crowding Ella, his proximity and that intoxicating, sandalwood scent causing her to stagger back, her spine colliding with the wall. Kellen's hips pinioned her beneath him before he caught her chin and lifted it, his breath stippling over her lips. His eyes burned into her, dancing with roguish intensity and a glint of his own arousal, the blinding vehemence of it ripping the life out of Ella's legs, her knees buckling in their strain to remain upright.

Kellen skimmed his mouth across her cheek in his journey to reach her ear. He barely touched her, the contact not sufficient to be considered a kiss, yet she felt like he was kissing her everywhere, like his lips were becoming a part of her skin, embedded in her bones, coalescing with her blood, so the very things that fueled her, that permitted her to live, were now his lips, his embrace, *him.*

He then brought his lips to her ear and whispered against the shell, "Noella Rose, I need your help," before his teeth tugged down on the lobe. Her eyes fluttered shut as the oxygen in her lungs escaped through a heaving wheeze.

Her fingers begged to fist his black sweater, to yank him into her, to eliminate the useless space between them. Would pulling her face back and lifting her chin high enough for her lips to find his be so bad?

She found her hand raising, not to gather the material of his sweater to pull him closer, but to delicately traipse her fingers over his face. The digits moved with a mind of their own, up the scales on his neck to where the flesh around his eye was still bruised. Kellen flinched, not because the wound still hurt, but in surprise of her actions. He didn't withdraw from her, though he had turned to stone under her careful examination. She skimmed the injury, her touch akin to a feather sweeping over his brow, wanting to streak his flesh with her existence the way his lips had just tinged hers.

His own hands slid down her waist, gripping her hips, mirroring the possessive nature of her own appraisal, their battle of wills extending into who could mark the other deeper with their touch.

His fingers burrowed into her torso when her index finger brushed curiously atop his lips. His mouth opened on instinct, his teeth lashing out to gently, playfully, seize the tip of her finger and bite down.

His tepid breath puffed around her finger when they both gasped.

Neither of them could deny the electric pull they felt towards one another, the undeniable rope tethering their minds and bodies, like the invisible hands of the universe were shoving them together, screaming *this is where you're supposed to be.* In that moment, Ella didn't want to deny it. She didn't want to fight with him or fight against him. She wanted to yield, just for a transitory moment, to explore this strange, burning thing between them, even if it was a taste of something she couldn't keep.

Ella was about to succumb to the combustible chemistry when the door to her office banged into the desk still blocking the entry. Ella thrust Kellen away from her just as Eyal poked his helmet into the office.

"Did you put this here to keep me out?" Eyal growled at her.

"No, actually, but now I might just leave it there." There was nothing friendly about her smile.

"Do you mind?" Kellen snarled at the envoy, either not realizing who this was or simply not caring about the consequences. "We were having a private conversation."

"I heard no talking, so I assumed Ms. Rose was in here alone." Ella directed her face at the floor, just in case her cheeks were as red as they felt. "I can come back when you're finished."

Kellen barked, "Yes," at the same moment Ella insisted, "No," the two of them glaring at each other.

"Mr. Kilic was just about to speak to me regarding a student." She'd come to the conclusion that the moment had passed, the tension fizzled into the ether. Disappointment lingered in its wake, though whether it was one-sided or shared between them was unclear. Eyal pushed the desk forward to make more space for himself to enter the room, then arranged the desk back where it was supposed to be, towards the backend of the room. Kellen watched Eyal move around her office to come stand at Ella's side, glaring at the envoy like Eyal's breaths were offensive to him.

"His name is Markus Loewe," Kellen explained, peeling his eyes off the envoy to gaze at Ella.

*Can he leave?* Kellen asked her privately.

*Aros Cavalian has assigned him to be my protection detail,* she answered, sending him an image of her rolling her eyes. Kellen coughed out a laugh, then bit his lip to silence it when he received a quizzical look from Eyal.

*Wait. Aros Cavalian?* he suddenly spluttered when he thought deeper about what she'd just said.

*Stop getting distracted and tell me about the student.*

"He's a Cerebri student in my History of the Gods class. He's a senior. I've had him in class before. He's never been the best student, mostly because he doesn't apply himself, but he's always been able to at least scrape by to pass his classes. He's currently failing my class." Ella slid her laptop towards her, lifting the lid, and typed in the password to the official Delmarth database to access his report card, taking a seat in her office chair.

"How badly is he failing?" she asked while she typed in the name, needing Kellen to spell it for her.

"He hasn't handed in a single assignment all semester. He's failed all his chapter quizzes and the first two exams."

Ella ripped her eyes off the screen to look at him.

"He hasn't handed in a single assignment *all year?!*" Kellen nodded. "Did you speak to him about it?"

"Of course I did," Kellen snapped, then softened his tone when her eyes thinned into slits. "I spoke to him on Monday. I gave him an opportunity to make up the work. I told him he wouldn't get full credit for the assignments, but if he got the missing reading logs to me by today, by Wednesday, I would give him partial credit for them. He didn't even show up for class today. I later saw him with his little friends on the quad, and he literally ran away from me when I tried to talk to him." The corners of Ella's lips twitched. Kellen growled, "This isn't funny, Rose."

"I know. I'm sorry. I was just imagining a kid running away from you." He glared at her until she got her silly smile under control. "Why did you wait until now to bring this to my attention?"

"I wanted to give him a chance to fix his behavior, something I've never done and won't ever do again. I went to Headmistress Dyer this morning about what to do, since I've never dealt with something like this, and she told me this was your jurisdiction, for some reason." Ella's glowered sharpened at the *for some reason.* "I didn't know you dealt with this kind of thing. I thought you were only a therapist."

"I'm not a therapist," she reminded him.

"Then what the fuck *do* you do?" Ella's brows soared up to her hairline. Kellen winced, then rushed, "That came out more aggressive than I meant it to, but it was a genuine question." Ella shook her head.

"I don't know what to make of you, Kilic."

"If it helps," he drawled, sliding his hands into his trouser pockets, "neither do I."

"It does a tiny bit." Her muscles relaxed when his expression softened. "To answer your question, I provide social, emotional, and *academic* support to all students, so *yes,* a student failing a class absolutely falls under my jurisdiction." She focused back on her computer screen when Markus's current report card loaded. Her eyes scanned the data. "He's passing his other courses. Barely, but he's passing."

"So it's just *my* class, then?" Kellen leaned over her shoulder to look at the screen. His chin hovered near her neck. She had the strangest urge to nuzzle her cheek against his, but stifled it by gripping the edges of her computer screen.

"We should get him in here and talk to him together." Ella glanced at Eyal. "Would you go grab Markus Loewe and bring him to my office, please? He's currently in…" She pulled up his schedule. "He's currently in mathematics with Mr. Anesh in the Cerebri sector, room three forty."

"I'm not a delivery boy," Eyal barked at her. Ella felt Kellen's scowl mug the air around her, her expression far more gentle and pleading then she knew Kellen's was without even looking at it.

"Please?" she entreated.

Eyal sighed, grumbling, "I don't get paid enough for this," then exited the room, slamming her door shut.

"He seems lovely," Kellen quipped.

"It says on Markus's schedule that Mr. Takeshi is his advisor," Ella read off the screen. "We should loop him into this conversation after we speak to Markus. Also Daniel Madix."

"Why the fuck do we need Daniel Madix?" Kellen's still swollen eye convulsed at the mention of Daniel.

"Because he's the Cerebri department head. He should know that one of his students is failing a class."

"I'll let Headmistress Dyer tell him." Kellen took a seat on her desk, folding his arms across his chest, the material of his black sweater pulling around his biceps. Ella forced her eyes to move to his face, wandering to his black-and-blue eye.

"What happened with you two?" She had no business asking, but her own curiosity got the better of her.

"He's pissed at me for hurting Oliviana. For sleeping with Oliviana. For everything really."

"And why did you? End things with Oliviana?" Her voice was barely above a whisper.

"I couldn't give her what she wanted," he answered after a minute of quietly considering the question. He grew silent, then added, "and she couldn't give me what I wanted." Ella spoke with vigilance and tender consideration of each word.

"What is it that you want, Kellen?" Kellen sucked in a breath when she called him by his first name.

"I don't know anymore," he murmured through an aggrieved sigh. He suddenly reeled his head back, seeming to truly look at her for the first time, and laughed, "Why are you covered in orange paint?"

"An activity I didn't anticipate being as messy as it was." Ella pinched the dirty fabric of her dress and moaned, "When I tell you I am craving a bath so badly right now that I want to scream, I mean it."

"I believe it." Kellen lifted a strand of her hair brittle with orange paint, rolling the crunchy wisp between his fingers. It was such a casual invasion of her space, as though he believed it was entitled to him, that the act stole the air from her lungs. He murmured distractedly, "I hear you do laundry every night, some-times twice in a night if your clothes get dirty after your walk with your dog. You carry a brush with you at all times to make sure your hair stays untangled. The pencils on your desk are always arranged in color order. Any time I move your couch or your chair even an inch to the side, just to see if you'll notice, you always move it back, without fail."

"I didn't know you noticed all of that about me," she whispered breathlessly.

His gaze pierced her lips when it lifted from her hair to her mouth. "I notice everything you do, Noella."

Any response Ella could have given died a merciless death when Eyal returned with Markus. Kellen released her hair, fixing his features to remove the dark glint of need that had flashed within his irises, slipping on the mask of the strict professor. Ella threaded her fingers together on her desk, offering Markus a smile that was *not* returned, then gestured for him to take a seat on the couch.

"We haven't formally met," she said, rising from her chair and circling around the desk to stand closer to Markus. Kellen shadowed her movement. "I'm Ms. Rose. I'm the school counselor."

"You mean the *human*," Markus corrected with disgust, wrinkling his nose at her. She sensed where the tone of this discussion was headed.

"Yes. The human." Ella rested her backside against the edge of her desk. "Mr. Kilic came to me with some concerns about your grade in his class. He said you haven't handed in a single assignment all semester and you've been failing all your assessments."

"You *told* on me?" Markus yapped at Kellen, who, to his credit, was succeeding in keeping a rein on his temper.

"I'm concerned that at this point in the semester, you're too far gone to be able to pass my class." He spoke with a gentleness Ella wouldn't have expected from him. "I'm trying to help you, Markus."

"So I'll take the class again next semester. No big deal." Kellen's jaw ticked.

"This is your last semester of History of the Gods. Next semester, you're supposed to move on to War Strategy. If you don't pass this semester, then you don't get to take War Strategy. You won't graduate in June."

"Fine. So I won't graduate in June. Whatever." Ella's heartrate spiked. Kellen tensed next to her.

*I don't know what to do if he truly doesn't care,* Kellen said mind-to-mind.

*Let me try to dig a little deeper,* Ella proposed. *There may be something else going on. I doubt he actually doesn't care, but if he really doesn't, then we will all need to accept the consequences of that choice.*

"You seem to be managing the coursework in your others classes, considering you have no other missing assignments," she probed. "What about Mr. Kilic's class has been so difficult for you?"

Markus twisted the sleeve of his sweatshirt around his hand. "I don't know," he replied, refusing to look at her, like he couldn't stand the sight of her. "I really don't want to be here right now."

"Well, you have to be here right now," Kellen barked, not as aggressive as he could have been, which alerted Ella that he was *really* trying to contain his rage. "We're here because you refuse to do the work and accept the help I've offered. I gave you an opportunity to make up the work, and you missed it."

Markus started to roll his eyes, but Kellen's glower stopped him in his tracks. He then began to form a sloppy explanation, starting with, "I forgot—"

250

"Not the *I forgot* excuse again," Kellen hissed with his own eye roll. Ella could feel his anger as though it were a tangible object being hurled at Markus's head. He rose from where he'd positioned himself at her side to incline closer to Markus. "Did you *forget* to come to my class today? Did you *forget* that you have a responsibility to show up and do the work, like every other fucking student here? Did you forget that your parents are paying an exorbitant amount of money for you to attend the best school in Cavale? I don't think you realize what a privilege it is for you to be attending Delmarth, and you're *wasting* it, in your last year, when you're so fucking close to the end. *Now* you decide to waste it?" Kellen shook his head. "It's sad, Markus. It's really sad."

*Damn,* Ella thought to herself, awe-struck by that performance. She was tempted to clap.

"Did something happen over the summer when you weren't at school?" Markus laughed like what she'd said was intended to be funny.

"What a dumb question," he chuckled to himself.

"It's not a dumb question," Kellen argued in her defense, taking her off guard for a moment.

"I'm trying to understand if there's something outside of school that's preventing you from being able to focus on your work." She tried another approach. "Do you have an issue with Mr. Kilic specifically?"

"No," Markus answered, then threw in, "I mean, he's a dick, but no." Kellen's lips wrestled with a smile. "I just don't like the class. We've been reading this same book since *Kindergarten.* It's boring."

"There are a lot of myths to go through," Kellen contended, though beneath the statement, she sensed he agreed with Markus. "The Gods want us to be steeped in their full history before we enlist in the army."

"*Fuck the Gods!*" Markus exclaimed. Eyal flinched in the corner of the room. "Who fucking cares? I don't need to know their whole fucking history. I don't want to fight in their bogus war, so what's the fucking point? What has Aros done to actually earn my support, huh? So he lost his mate a thousand years ago. Now every Primordial is expected to give their life to his cause? To do what exactly? What are we even fighting for? Are we trying to get Tala back? *No.* We're essentially fighting our own people, just because our stupid kings hate each other and refuse to coexist. It's ridiculous!"

*Well, that was very telling,* Kellen marveled.

*What if he's a Dissident?* Ella speculated. *Maybe he supports Edar and that's why he doesn't want to read about the Gods.*

*Not much we can do about that,* Kellen replied. *He either puts his head down and plays the part of loyal subject, even if he hates it, or he risks the Gods tossing him into Terminus.* Ella had her own personal feelings about that talk track that she didn't have time to delve into right now.

"I understand the work being tedious," she said, validating his feelings, "and at the same time, we sometimes have to do things that are tedious because that's what's required of us. If there are accommodations we can make to help you, we can discuss that together. If the material is too dense and you're having trouble understanding it, Mr. Kilic or myself can work with you one-on-one after hours to go over the chapters. *I* want you to be successful. *Mr. Kilic* wants you to be successful. We want to put you in the best position to be able to graduate in June, but in order to do that, we need you to work with us."

"I have no interest in working with *you,*" Markus snarled at her, launching his saliva through the air right in her direction. When the spit struck her face, Eyal came to life from the corner of the room, rushing forward. The envoy lunged at Markus like he was about to tackle the Primordial to the ground.

"Don't!" Ella cried, swatting at Eyal to make him back away from the boy.

"You do not spit on a teacher," Kellen reprimanded, flames sparking around the pupils of his eyes. "That is completely unacceptable, especially someone who is only trying to help you. Ms. Rose is your school mom. Exercise some self-control and give her the same respect you'd give your actual mom. What is wrong—"

"It's fine, Kilic," she interjected, wiping the spit off her cheek. Lashing out with cruel words wouldn't help Markus take this seriously. Ella lowered her focus back over Markus, the breath she released wearied and desperate. "You say you don't care if you graduate. What *do* you care about? What do you see for your future?"

Markus blinked vacuously at her, no evidence that there was a soul within those lifeless amber eyes.

"Nothing," he answered in a way that left her certain he only said that to spite her, not because he actually didn't care about his future. "Can I go now?" He had the audacity to sound bored with this conversation.

"The fuck you thin—" Kellen started to shout, but Ella raised her hand to fetter the flow of outrage.

"Do you understand the consequences of the choice you're making?" she asked Markus, her tone more stern then she'd typically use with students. "Do you understand that if you fail this class, you will not graduate? You won't get to take War Strategy next semester, so you will have to repeat both classes next year, when all your friends have graduated and started their lives. Not taking this class isn't an option, so if you put it off now, you will eventually have to take it again, because that's what's required in Cavale. Do you understand?" Markus's only response was a blink of his lashes. Ella sighed. "Fine. You can go."

*What're you doing?* Kellen asked her as Markus rose from the couch and gathered his backpack.

*We can't force him to care,* she said. *If this is how he's choosing to make his bed, then it's time to help him prepare to lie in it.*

"This discussion isn't over," Kellen called out. Markus raised his middle finger over his head before he slammed the door shut. "What a little *bitch,*" he grunted, spinning towards Ella.

"Did you just call me his *school mom*?" she laughed when Markus shut the door. "What does that make *you* then?" Kellen's lips sprawled out in a brilliant, mischievous grin, unveiling those dangerous dimples.

"I think you know what I'd call myself, sweetheart."

"Ew!" she cried when the meaning clicked in place. She steered her finger at his face, specifically his impish grin. "EW! That is so inappropriate! Do I need to do the sexual harassment training with you again?"

"Again? When did you do it the first time?" Ella's jaw dropped.

"The second week of school. I did it for the whole faculty. I did sexual harassment and suicide prevention. Was no one paying attention?!"

"Everyone hated you back then," was his only response. She deflated in her chair.

"That was such important information." Ella suddenly rethought what he just inadvertently admitted. "You said everyone hated me *back then*. Does that mean you don't hate me anymore?"

"I never said that." She knew he was lying. "I just think we've found a common enemy."

"Markus is not an enemy. He's a lost kid who's having a crisis of faith in a country that won't allow him to question what's being taught to him, not without the threat of being tortured for the rest of his life if he expresses any kind of dissent. Honestly, I understand his frustrations with the Gods."

"I would be careful with what you say," Eyal warned, pointing up at the ceiling—not the ceiling, but to the heavens.

"I am not a Primordial," she objected, "so I will not be cut off from my right to freedom of speech."

"As long as you remain in Cavale, Ms. Rose, you must abide by the same laws as all Primordials."

"So I'm not allowed to have an opinion? No one is, without the threat of being tossed into Terminus? It's *wrong.*"

When Kellen lightly grazed her knee with his hand, his fingers crawling up to squeeze her thigh in an act of disapproval, for a brief moment, Ella thought she saw stars pepper over her vision.

*You're entering dangerous territory, Noella,* the same male voice that both sounded like Kellen, and yet didn't, cautioned her. *Do not overestimate the protection the Gods have given you. Even Aros.*

*Who are you?* Ella asked the voice.

*Coz. My dragon,* Kellen explained, adding, *he doesn't shut the fuck up, but he's right this time.*

*Your insolence is uncalled for,* Coz spat at Kellen, then directed at Ella, *Apologize to the envoy for your disrespect, then ask him to leave us alone a moment.*

"I'm sorry," Ella stammered, contorting her voice to sound deferential and conciliatory. "That was unfair of me to say. You've done nothing but follow the orders given by your king, and I've been such a bitch to you. You don't deserve for me to give you such a hard time. I'm sorry."

Even though she couldn't see his face beneath the helmet, she heard the smile in Eyal's voice.

"I appreciate that, Noella." She tasted genuine guilt on her tongue for the way she'd been treating him. Everything she'd said had been true—he didn't deserve her anger, not when it was directed elsewhere.

*Can you please ask him to call you Ella?* Kellen requested.

*Why?* she asked.

*Because if it's alright with you, I'd like to be the only one to call you Noella.* Ella's face burned.

"Please, call me Ella," she extended to the envoy with a sincere, agreeable smile. Then, she intreated, "Would it be alright if Mr. Kilic and I had a moment alone to discuss our plan for Markus?"

"Of course. I'll wait in the hall." Eyal dipped his head in his version of a bow, then stepped outside.

*Why did you make me send him away?* she asked Coz.

*The sound of his voice was irritating me,* the dragon replied.

"Like I said," Kellen grumbled aloud, tapping his index finger against his temple, "He never shuts the fuck up."

"So he's just like you, then." Ella flashed an artificially sweet smile. Kellen didn't bother to dignify that with a response.

"What are our next steps with Markus?" The smile faded from her face, replaced with a disheartened frown.

"We call in his parents and explain that he won't graduate if he doesn't get his grade up in your class. Maybe he'll care more if his parents are involved, or maybe he won't, but either way, his parents should know what's happening. Headmistress Dyer, Mr. Takeshi, and Mr. Madix should be included in that meeting."

"Let me make the call to his parents," Kellen suggested. "If you call, they'll hang up. They'll come if I ask them to."

"Fine. You call, but I'll still be at that meeting."

"It might be better if you're not." Ella pulled her head back to glare at him. "Didn't you see how he just reacted to being in the same room as you? That anger comes from somewhere. It's entirely possible his parents will react the same way to you."

"I don't give a shit," Ella burst out, Kellen's brows raising along with his widening eyes. "It's my job to be a support for the students, even the students who hate me. If a decision is made about a plan to help him, I want to be part of that discussion. I will absolutely be at that meeting, and his parents will have to suck it the fuck up. If I can tolerate being around people who hate me and literally fantasize about *killing* me, then they can tolerate being around me for an hour."

Reverence spilled out of the heated look he threw her. Did he know how much emotion he revealed in his eyes? Did he know the way it caused her heart to thrash wildly in her chest, caused the blood in her cheeks to simmer, caused every muscle in her body to ache with the need to be close to him?

"You make it so fucking hard," he mumbled on his stroll to the door.

"Make what hard?" she asked, bringing him to a halt just when he'd enfolded his fingers around the doorknob.

Kellen spun around, green eyes shimmering, then answered, "For me to hate you." Ella's heart leapt into her throat.

"Good," she whispered, then watched Kellen swallow a harsh breath and quickly flee the room.

## CHAPTER 20

# ELLA

"THIS IS STUPID," Jarion grumbled.

"No, it's not," Laya protested, smacking Jarion's arm. "Don't be rude to Ms. Rose."

"What about the idea of giving yourself a compliment is stupid to you, Jare?" Ella asked patiently.

Laya had shown up for her session with Ella on Friday during lunch with Jarion in toe, begging Ella to let him join. Ella decided to take advantage of having both twins here and use the session to make them craft positive affirmations for themselves, which felt in keeping with each of their counseling goals, for Jarion to accept his dragon and for Laya to become empowered to take control of her life.

Not surprisingly, Laya found the concept of this activity delightful, whereas Jarion resisted.

"It feels pointless," Jarion groaned, slipping the red beanie off his head to readjust it. "What's the point in sitting here saying good things about myself if I don't even mean it? How is this supposed to help me?"

"Because we're trying to change your mindset about yourself," Laya replied for Ella.

"Affirmations gain power through repetition," Ella explained, sending Laya an approving smile. Laya's cheeks flushed in reception of the esteem. "Yes, if you give yourself a compliment one time, it may not hold any meaning or change anything, but saying good things to yourself every day helps put positive thoughts in your mind and push out the bad ones. Part of what's holding you back from accepting your dragon is that you see yourself, and your dragon, as the enemy."

"My dragon *blinded* someone," Jarion reminded her forcefully, a flash of a flame flickering in his eyes.

"Because your dragon felt rejected by you, not because your dragon, or you, are inherently bad. It may sound silly, but the best way forward for you is to essentially befriend yourself. Identifying things you like about yourself is a good start." Ella glanced at Laya. "This is good for you too, Laya, not just Jarion."

"In what way?" Ella adored how Laya genuinely seemed interested in what counseling could bring her.

"You spend so much time worrying about everyone around you. Your compassion is a beautiful thing, and at the same time, we need to work on you giving yourself that same care that you give everyone else."

"True," Jarion piped up. Laya stuck her tongue out at him.

"Who wants to go first?" Laya's hand shot up towards the ceiling. Jarion chuckled at his sister's eagerness.

"I'm a good person," she declared, tucking the front strands of her long black hair behind her ears.

"How do you define being a good person?" Ella asked as she leaned back in her office chair.

"Um…" Laya began chewing on the end of her hair. Jarion's hand lashed out to gather the tendrils stuck between her teeth, sliding them out of her mouth and holding the strands hostage in his fist so she couldn't gnaw on them. "Thanks, Jare." She fidgeted, her nails sketching lines down her jeans. "I guess I would say being a good person is someone who thinks about others. Who cares about others. Well…maybe not *everyone*." Ella found that distinction interesting.

"Why not everyone?" she probed.

"Not everyone deserves it." Jarion nodded in agreement, bobbing his head with extra emphasis.

Ella could concede to that stance. She had an itemized list in her head of people who didn't deserve her kindness, though she'd recently amended that list to no longer include Kellen's name.

"How do you maintain being a good person even with people who may not deserve it?"

"I guess you stay open to the possibility that there's more to them?" Laya supplied as an answer, shrugging her shoulders. "Or stay open to the possibility that they can change and become better people?"

"That's a hard belief to hold for everyone," Ella said.

"Like I said," Laya continued, "I don't think everyone deserves it. I think some people use up all their chances for your kindness. But I'd like to think that most people deserve several chances to prove who they are. Not unlimited chances, but enough to make it fair."

"How do you determine what is a fair amount of chances to give someone?" Laya's eyes lifted to the ceiling in contemplation.

"I don't know," she eventually answered. "I feel like you just know when you've had enough."

"You know yourself better than anyone," Ella confirmed. "You know how much you can tolerate. And you're right. Kindness is a gift that isn't always deserved. It's also okay to give compassion to someone and then take it away because it's too much for *you*. That's what valuing yourself sometimes looks like, putting up boundaries when you need to in order to protect your peace."

"But isn't that selfish?" Laya pouted.

"Remember what I said. Taking care of yourself isn't selfish. Sometimes your peace is more important than assuring the comfort of others. There will always be time for you to take care of those around you, but making space for you to take care of yourself is a deliberate choice you need to make every single day." Ella demonstrated with her hands cradling a vessel. "Think of kindness like a battery. It needs to be charged to remain strong. How do you think you charge that battery?"

Laya dropped her chin into her palm. "I don't know. How?"

"You take time to focus on yourself. You can't be expected to have enough kindness to give to others if you don't take time to nourish that kindness for yourself, if you don't take time to understand yourself and your own needs."

Laya's fingers dove for her pencil, scribbling down Ella's words into her pink notebook for safekeeping. Ella peeked over at Jarion, who appeared to be distracted by twisting Laya's hair between his fingers.

"What do you think being a good person to people who may not deserve it looks like, Jare?"

"Why are you asking me?" Jarion spat when his attention was reluctantly pulled back into reality. "It was Laya's comment."

Laya jabbed her elbow into Jarion's ribs.

"I'm curious to hear what you think," Ella explained. Jarion blew a ring of smoke out of his mouth.

"Um…I guess you can give them the benefit of the doubt and try not to hold them to one bad thing they did."

Ella sat up in her chair. "Can you give a little more detail on what you mean by that?"

"No one should be defined by one single moment, or even a collection of singular moments," Jarion said. Laya's smile stretched up to her ears as she scrawled his words on her paper, under where she'd written in bold letters **Jarion quotes**. "We're made up of our complete history, not one particular moment in time. When we focus on one bad thing someone did, we lose the rest of who they are."

Ella leaned closer, her tone of voice gentle. "The same applies for you too, Jarion."

"That's not…" He sighed heavily, the exhale bleeding into a laugh. "How do you do that?"

Ella smirked. "Do what?"

"Get me to say shit I wouldn't normally say."

"These things exist somewhere inside you. I'm just using techniques to draw them out." Laya beamed at her brother, grabbing his arm and shaking it with a gleeful squeal. Jarion sunk his teeth into his bottom lip to keep his mouth from submitting to a smile, but in the end lost the battle, the corners quirking up. "It's your turn, Jarion. Come up with one positive affirmation for yourself."

"Can you give me an example of a positive affirmation?" Ella narrowed her eyes at the wayward twinkle she found woven into his smile.

"If I do that, you can't use what I come up with. You need to come up with your own positive affirmation."

"Fine. Whatever." Ella and Laya simpered at him and then each other.

"I choose myself," Ella declared. Laya quickly jotted the phrase down in her notebook. "Your turn, Jare."

Jarion's knee bounced, slapping against Laya's thigh. "I really don't want to do this," he groused.

"I know it's uncomfortable, but the more you do it, the less uncomfortable it will feel. The more you do it, the less those statements will feel like a lie." Jarion exhaled a surrendering breath, tinged with smoke.

"I am doing the best I can," he finally answered, throwing his hands up as if to say *that's all I've got.*

"I *love* that, Jare," Ella prided. A crimson blush kissed Jarion's cheeks. "Can you give each other a positive affirmation?" Jarion was far more willing to proffer a kind word to his sister than he was willing to gift it to himself.

"It's okay to put yourself first," Jarion told her. Laya's eyes became iridescent with love.

"You are worthy of being alive," she whispered in response. Jarion reached for her hand to squeeze.

"I have one for both of you." The twins swung their eyes to Ella. "We can do hard things."

"We can do hard things," Laya repeated, staining her notebook with the idiom. Jarion swallowed.

"We can do hard things," he repeated in a low voice, testing to see how the phrase tasted on his tongue. When he determined he didn't mind the flavor, he repeated it again, more loudly. "We can do hard things."

Ella's office door suddenly budged open.

Kellen waltzed across the threshold, then froze when he discovered his siblings sitting on her couch.

"Oh," he gasped, staggering back. "I didn't know you guys would be in here." He glanced between Laya and Jarion, carefully studying their faces for any signs of injury. "Are you okay?"

"We're fine," Jarion hissed, reaching for his backpack.

"What're you doing here?" Ella stammered, a slight tremor limning the edges of her words.

She'd spent the last two days consumed by thoughts of their encounter in her office. She'd obsessed over the feeling of Kellen's body pressed against hers, overanalyzed the way his voice embraced her name like it was an honor to have any part of her grace his tongue. She'd fixated on how badly her lips ached to trace the scales on his neck, her fingers weeping to feel every flawless sinew of his vibrate with need for her, confirmation that she'd pilfered as much of his attention as he'd stolen from her. All her energy had been depleted from forcing herself to keep away from Kellen, to not slam her fist into his door like she did in her dream and concede her victory in their battle of wills.

Even if she acknowledged she felt *something* for Kellen—she wasn't entirely sure *what* that was, though it was definitely more than lust because whatever she felt was so potent that when she gave herself permission to focus on it, it knocked her breathless—she couldn't act on it. Regardless of whether or not her feelings were reciprocated—she didn't let herself consider if they were because she would spiral with those thoughts and never climb out of the abyss of wonder—what was the point in starting something that would have to finish when the school year came to a close and she returned to the Earthly Plane? She wasn't staying in Cavale, so why would she place herself in a position where she'd inevitably be left mourning something if she didn't have to?

So, Ella had made the decision to keep her distance from Kellen.

She'd lasted a full day without purposefully seeking him out, avoiding the Varmin sector in case she bumped into him. She'd been dreading their meeting with Markus's parents, for more than one reason, but mostly because she knew she'd have to see him again. She'd mentally coped ahead to see Kellen at one o'clock in Headmistress Dyer's office—not at twelve-fifty in her office, with his siblings sitting right there. He was ten minutes ahead of schedule, and she wasn't prepared to deal with him yet.

"We have a meeting with Markus's parents in ten minutes," Kellen reminded her, pointing at the clock.

"I know. That's still ten minutes away. You didn't have to come get me." Kellen shifted on the balls of his feet.

What he neglected to say in front of the twins, what hung palpably in the air between them, was that he wanted to. He wanted to come get her. To bring her to the meeting. To walk in with her at his side.

He wanted to.

And what Ella refused to say, which was equally felt in her soft tone of voice, was that she'd been hoping he would. She'd been eyeing the door, her subconscious praying that he'd appear.

Laya watched the two of them stare at each other intently, a smile fiddling with the corners of her lips, sensing something between them that neither of them were ready to give voice to yet.

"Let's go," Jarion barked at Laya, dodging the hand Kellen extended out to him, swatting it away.

"Jare—" Kellen tried.

"Later, Ms. Rose," Jarion tossed over his shoulder, brushing right past Kellen.

"Remember to go to room two for your in-school suspension!" Ella called out to him, but he'd already vanished.

Kellen focused on Laya. She stepped around the coffee table and embraced her big brother's waist.

"Hi, Kellings," she murmured.

"Hi, Laylie," he whispered affectionately into her hair. Ella's heart yelled at the doting nicknames. "Is Jare okay?" Laya's shoulders tensed before she raised her head out of Kellen's chest.

"I know you mean well, but I can't keep telling you how Jarion is doing," Laya rushed out like she couldn't keep the words inside her anymore. "I can't take on the responsibility of being your messenger. I love you, and I love Jarion. I want to be there for you guys, but it's too much pressure for me to take on what everyone else is feeling and keep feeding everything he tells me to you. You guys need to talk to each other, and I need to put my own emotions first. Do you understand?"

Ella was so proud of Laya that she nearly burst into tears. Kellen's lashes fluttered, his mouth opening, then closing.

"I'm sorry, Laya," he mumbled, pain wrought in his eyes. "I never meant to put pressure on you. I'm floundering with what to do to help Jare, but that's not a burden I want you to carry. Please know, I never meant to add any stress to your life. I never meant to take advantage of your compassion. It's my favorite thing about you, but I don't want it to become something that's at your expense. Put yourself first, my love. I'll be okay. Jarion will be okay. It's important that you're okay, too."

Laya choked on a sob. "I love you, Kell."

Kellen cupped her face, then gushed, "I love you so much, my beautiful girl," and kissed the tip of her nose. The corners of Ella's eyes stung. She had to look away from them before she dissolved into embarrassing tears. "Now go to class." Laya took a step back, peeking over at Ella.

"So proud of you," Ella mouthed to her with a subtle thumb raised.

"Thank you," Laya mouthed back, then blew her brother a kiss and scurried out of the room.

"So you're speaking to my sister too," Kellen stated once they were alone.

"I'm not at liberty to confirm or deny that," Ella responded with her hand pointedly placed on her hip.

Kellen's gaze warmed. "Good," was all he said, then started for the exit, holding her door open for her.

*I don't know what to do with Jare,* he whispered into her mind on their way to Headmistress Dyer's office. *Jarion is really fucking mad at me. I don't know what to do to make it right.*

*He's not actually mad at YOU,* she disputed, possibly saying too much, too comfortable in his company to filter herself. *He's mad at the world, and you just happen to be the person closest to him that he's chosen to project the world onto.*

Kellen stopped walking. He stared at her like he'd never seen her before, like he'd never truly taken the time to memorize her features. *Sometimes you say things that take my breath away, Noella Rose.*

Ella's breath stuttered. Heat flooded her cheeks. She paused, her brain clashing with her heart, before she ended up confessing, not strong enough to fight the truth, *Sometimes you do too, Kellen Kilic.*

"Rosie!" a male voice shattered through the intense eye contact Kellen and Noella were sharing.

Noella's eyes tore off his. Kellen wanted to slam his fist into the face of the person responsible for ripping Noella's focus away from him, fracturing the sweet, adoring way she'd been looking at him, a look he was certain he would never get back. He raised his eyes to find Akio Takeshi running towards them, the Cerebri's soft features illuminating like a cloudless dawn over Noella.

"Hey, Kio," Noella greeted him with a dazzling smile that made Kellen's chest ache with longing—for what, he wasn't entirely sure, but for a moment, he pondered what it would be like, *feel* like, to be warmed by that smile, for every breath from those lips to be directed at him, every word, every sound, every smile, every laugh.

*Wait a second. Did he just call her Rosie?* Kellen wanted to gag.

What a stupid fucking nickname. There was no meaning behind it, no intimacy, just a silly variant of her last name that sounded like something a child would say. A name as magnificent as hers—a name he couldn't understand why she chose to truncate, those first two letters she cut off from the rest of her name adding so much splendor and individuality—deserved to be embossed into the ether, deserved to be stitched into the earth and used to illuminate the universe.

*What the fuck is wrong with my thoughts today?*

It must have been seeing Noella with his siblings, seeing how whatever she'd said to Laya had empowered his sister to choose herself for the first time in her life. He'd been so fucking proud of Laya for saying that to him, so indebted to Noella for the influence she had on Laya that it was clearly clouding his judgment, making him confuse gratefulness for desire. That had to be it.

When Akio draped his arm around her shoulders in a welcoming hug, Coz's hoarse voice invaded Kellen's ears.

*Who is this bastard putting his arm around our Noella?*

*Since when is she OUR Noella?* Kellen contended. *She's not even MY Noella, let alone OURS.*

*She could be, if you got over your ego for five fucking minutes.* Kellen huffed out a growl.

Akio finally acknowledged Kellen standing there, his arm *still* dangling off her shoulder. "Hey, Kellen."

Kellen replied outwardly with a curt nod of his head.

Into Akio's mind, he snarled, *If I see your hand on her again, I will cut it off.* Akio's lashes beat against his eyebrows in surprise before his arm slid off Noella, falling limp at his side.

*I am not a threat to you, Kellen,* Akio assured, then said more forcefully, *but Ella is my friend, so if you've gotten your head out of your ass and finally realized that you want her, then you have to earn her. No more fucking with her head or heart.*

*Fuck off,* Kellen rumbled, then quietly considered Akio's threat.

Or was it his misguided way of giving advice, of being supportive? Was Kellen actually angry at Akio, or was he just pissed at how Akio was allowed to touch her so casually when he couldn't?

"How did the lesson go?" Noella questioned Akio, completely unaware of the silent standoff they'd been engaging in.

"It went great," Akio sung in a jovial tone. "The kids loved it. You did good, El."

"What lesson?" Kellen barked, not enjoying being the only person in the hallway not clued into their conversation.

"Remember the other day, I had that idea to pick a word for the month and tailor lessons for the elementary school students around teaching skills related to that concept?" While she was talking, Kellen admired the periwinkle hue of her blouse, how it complimented the amber undertones in her hair, emphasizing the golden highlights. Something about Noella in any shade of purple or blue fucked with his head. "Today was the first day we implemented the social emotional learning lessons into their morning circle time. Kio, show him." Akio rummaged through his briefcase, pulling out his laptop, and rallied the screen, tipping it towards Kellen so he could see the presentation Noella had made for the teachers to use for the month of October. Each day, she'd created a new, ten minute activity that centered around the word she'd picked for the month, this month's being resilience.

The activity they'd done today was making a mistake art, to embrace making mistakes as a part of building resilience. The activity provided the students a safe space to practice making mistakes and turning that into something beautiful, rather than abandoning it because it wasn't perfect.

*Fuck, this is really good, Rose,* he spoke into her brain, so she could feel how sincere he was in privacy.

*Thanks, Kilic.* Kellen considered for a second what the blush on her cheek would taste like to his lips.

"Did any of the other teachers use this today?" she asked with hope. Akio grimaced.

"Not that I know of. No one else in the Cerebri department did. I'm sorry, Ella." Noella's shoulders sunk.

"I figured," she murmured tightly, the verve in her eyes vanishing.

Noella was famous for wearing a brave face so well that it was impossible to believe it wasn't real, but Kellen knew it had to get to her, the way the teachers dismissed her, the way none of them used any of her ideas in their classrooms, the way none of the students trusted her enough to let her help them. From the careful consideration and colorful design of the entire presentation, Kellen knew that must have taken her hours to complete, all that hard work tossed aside just because she was a human. It never occurred to him before, though it absolutely should have, how unfair and cruel that was. She'd done nothing to warrant this disgusting treatment besides existing, and her existence was not the blemish on their world he'd originally thought it was.

Kellen glanced at Akio, who'd noticed the dip in Noella's mood alongside him, then said mind-to-mind, *Send that presentation to me.* Akio nodded in answer, closing the laptop and stuffing it back in his briefcase.

"Should we go in?" Akio pointed at Headmistress Dyer's door.

"Shouldn't we wait for Mr. Madix?" Noella wondered. Both Akio and Kellen groaned at the mention of Daniel.

"Fuck, I forgot he was going to be here," Kellen grumbled.

"Should Akio and I plan to run interference if you two start throwing fists?" Noella mockingly waved her tiny fists under Kellen's nose. Kellen's hands lashed out at their own accord, grabbing Noella's balled up fingers, and pulled her fists behind her back, cuffing her wrists just above her backside. The imprisonment of her hands behind her back compelled her spine to arch, her chest brushing against him as she unintentionally fell into his body, her nose skimming his chin due to their height difference.

"Not sure you'd be able to do enough damage with those fists to stop me, Rose, but I'd love to see you try," Kellen breathed against her cheek. Noella's pupils obscured the grey of her eyes when they expanded.

"Tempting," she shot back, aiming to be sarcastic, but the words emerged in a stutter, showing Kellen she wasn't unaffected by him. She leaned in a touch closer, and for a precious second, time screeched to a stop as Kellen thought she was about to kiss him, the world shifting its focus onto Kellen and Noella's embrace. Then, her lips sprawled out in a puckish grin, full of gorgeous trouble, and she drawled, "Try your luck with Akio," before sliding her wrists out of his hands and making her way inside Headmistress Dyer's office, her long hair swaying behind her.

"Um, I'm not touching him like that," Akio interjected. Kellen stifled a laugh as he and Akio followed her inside.

"I was wondering why you three were lingering out there," Headmistress Dyer quipped when they entered. The vibrant red dress she wore, clinging to her gaunt figure, possessed an asymmetrical draped neckline, three-quarter length sleeves, and a banded waist with a leather belt surrounding her thin torso.

"I've never seen you this dressed up," Kellen said in greeting, claiming a spot on Dyer's red couch, propping his feet on her table.

"I have an important meeting to get to," she answered elusively, grabbing a black purse off her desk before fixing her glasses back on the bridge of her nose and shaking her untamed ringlets out of her face.

"Wait. You *have* an important meeting?" Noella spluttered. "You're not joining us for this one?"

"I planned to," Dyer replied, "but I've been called to Avatia to speak with Aros Cavalian."

That certainly piqued Kellen's attention.

"To speak about what?" he probed, already prepared for his fact finding mission to be unsuccessful.

"Nice try," Headmistress Dyer laughed, though Kellen noticed her fleetingly glance over at Noella. "I trust the four of you will be able to carry on without me. If you need anything, call for the envoy. I won't be able to answer my phone while I'm in Avatia." She threw over her shoulder, "Good luck!" and rushed out the door, leaving Akio, Noella, and Kellen alone in her office.

"Where the fuck is Daniel?" Akio griped, glimpsing his watch for the time. "The parents will be here any minute."

"We can start the meeting without him," Noella said, drifting across the room to seize Headmistress Dyer's office chair, settling right into place with an adorable sigh. Kellen couldn't help himself from admiring the look of her in a throne, how right it felt, a queen missing a crown. "Is Markus joining this meeting?"

"No," Akio answered with a shake of his head. "He's at Power Practice now. I didn't want to pull him."

"Daniel knows he's supposed to be here, right?" Kellen asked Akio just as Daniel emerged in the doorway.

The fingers of his that were raking through his blonde, greasy hair crunched into a fist when he saw Noella in Headmistress Dyer's chair.

"What the fuck is *she* doing here?!" he hollered, advancing towards her with horrifically fast strides. Kellen was off the couch and had leapt in front of Noella before he realized his legs had made the choice to move.

"She's the school counselor," he explained, "so she has to be at this meeting."

"There is no reason to have the filthy human here," Daniel argued, every inch of his face flushed with ire. "She doesn't even know the kid. She will just incite anger in the parents and get them to blame the school for Markus failing."

"That's not true," Noella interjected, rising from the throne with imperial grace and stepping around Kellen to face Daniel herself. "I have met this kid, and I do have every reason to be here. This is a meeting to make a plan for this child to finish the school year, and I'm part of that plan, whether you like it or not."

"No one wants you here," Daniel hissed at her, hatred drugging his eyes. Kellen was about to step between them when Noella dared to bring herself even closer, getting right in Daniel's face without shame.

"Did you ever stop to think that maybe Mr. Takeshi wants me at this meeting? Or Mr. Kilic?" Noella gestured to both men, then yelled, "No, of course not, because that would suggest that you *thought* at all."

"Um, guys? I think I hear them coming down the hall," Akio squeaked, but no one heard him.

"If you can't handle me being here, then feel free to leave." Noella motioned to the door. Daniel's jaw dropped.

"*I'm* essential here," Daniel asserted. "*I'm* the Cerebri department head."

"We have the teacher whose class he's failing, his advisor, and the school counselor," Noella counted off, swinging her index finger between Kellen, Akio, and herself. She steered the finger back at Daniel. "Your presence here is superfluous." *Gods, she's fucking stunning,* Kellen marveled to himself.

Daniel's face turned red before he started to roar, "You little bi—"

"This arguing is getting us nowhere," Kellen intervened, receiving a ruthless glare from Daniel and an even more dangerous one from Noella.

"Was I speaking to you?" Noella snarled, turning to Kellen like a seething hellcat. "No? Then maybe you should shut the fuck up. For once in your life, Gods forbid." Kellen shouldn't have found her snapping at him attractive, but *fuck*, when she got going, she was a glorious sight to behold.

"Guys, I hear people in the hallway," Akio proclaimed more vigorously this time, retrieving everyone's attention.

"Have fun dealing with this mess yourselves," Daniel declared, heading to the door. "I'm out of here."

"Wait, you're actually leaving?" Akio exclaimed.

"Daniel, come on," Kellen groaned. "You don't have to leave. You're needed here. Just stay."

"Don't *come on* me, Kell," Daniel roared. "Just because you liked what you found between her legs and suddenly you're on her side doesn't mean I have to fall for her little innocent act. They couldn't pay me all the gold pieces in Cavale to sit in a room with that disgusting cunt of a whore." The beautiful color Kellen relished to see departed Noella's face as Daniel stormed out the door. From inside the hallway, they heard Daniel hiss, "There's a human in there if you want to bail now."

Kellen couldn't stop looking at Noella.

He wasn't sure what had upset her so much—possibly what Daniel said about Kellen and her, possibly the words *cunt* and *whore* amalgamated together and lobbed at her in such a callous assault— but she was slower to fix her face then she usually was, her eyes glistening with embryonic tears.

*Ignore him,* Kellen said in an attempt to console her. Noella fired daggers at him through her eyes instead of accepting the solace, but at least she no longer looked like she was about to cry.

*You should've stayed out of that,* she growled at him. *I don't need you to fight my battles for me, Kilic.*

*Trust me, sweetheart, I know.* Just as he'd hoped, rosy color returned to bless her cheeks when he called her *sweetheart,* one of his favored names to wield against her, second only to *Noella.*

"Please try not to fight in front of the parents," Akio pleaded them on his journey to the door to welcome the parents in. "We're about to tell them their son isn't graduating. A gentle touch would be nice here."

"Of course," Noella assured her friend, then arched a brow at Kellen. "I can control myself. Can *you?*"

"Of course I can," Kellen snipped back. "I have self-restraint."

"Oh, do you? I haven't seen you use it once since I've known you." Kellen dipped his head so he brought his lips to her ear.

Noella turned to stone at the close proximity, swallowing a large gulp of oxygen and trapping it in her chest.

"It's been forty-eight days that I haven't killed you, Ms. Rose." His lips tickled her cheek, her breath hitching at the evanescent contact. Kellen could smell her arousal, so pungent that he nearly groaned and fell to the ground, nearly begged her to let him worship her. "Trust me," he spoke in a gruff voice, his mouth tingling from how badly he wanted her. "I have self-restraint."

"I'm opening the door now," Akio warned them.

Noella stumbled back from Kellen just as Markus's parents—or, rather, parent—entered the room.

CHAPTER 21

# KELLEN

MARKUS LOEWE's father looked exactly like him, down to the amber eyes, severely sharp features, and undeviating frown that seemed far too comfortable on his face. The glower deepened, if it was even possible for the scowl to darken more than it already was, over Noella. The Cerebri came to a screeching halt at the doorway, debating if he was going to step inside the office or not.

"Get her out of here," Markus Loewe's father snarled at Kellen and Akio, pointing at Noella.

"This is Ms. Rose," Akio introduced, gesturing to Noella. "Our school co—"

"I know who she is, and I don't want her here." Mr. Loewe focused his glare on Kellen. "You didn't tell me *she* would be here. If I'd known, I wouldn't have come." Noella's lashes fluttered.

*Maybe I should go,* she whispered sadly in secret to Kellen, her eyes flitting to the door.

*You're not going anywhere,* Kellen declared, ready to throw his arm out and block her path if she tried to make a break for the exit. *To quote your eloquent words back to you, he needs to suck it the fuck up.*

Noella's lips combatted the urge to smile.

"Ms. Rose is our school counselor and has been a great help to many of our students," Kellen pronounced in defense of her,

273

speaking words he never thought he'd say, let alone believe to be true. "She's offered her services to Markus, and as someone who has spent considerable time with your son and witnessed his decline this year, you should take the offer."

"There is nothing a human can offer that would be of value to me or my son," Mr. Loewe decreed, his fingers burrowing into the doorframe, threatening to penetrate the wall. "Nothing but poison and destruction."

"What is your problem with her?" Akio snapped, taking Kellen by surprise. In all the time he'd known Akio, he'd never seen the Cerebri lose control of his precious decorum. "Why is a human so bad?"

"Do you not know what she *is?*" Mr. Loewe hissed at Noella, spittle flying out with every stressed word. "She is a reminder of what this kingdom lost, what threw our world into one of war and devastation. She's revolting. Aros rid this kingdom of humans for a reason. She doesn't belong here."

Kellen opened his mouth to argue, preparing to carve his message into the shape of blades and cut Mr. Loewe down to the size of his puny heart, but before he could, Noella stepped forward.

"This is just a conversation about Markus's progress," she said conciliatorily, presenting the Cerebri father with a warm, tender gaze the bastard didn't deserve. "I am not here to be a nuisance to you or your son. I'm here to help. I care about helping your son be successful and figuring out the best course of action to help him make it through the year. If you really can't stand the sight of me, I will leave, but I would like to stay and help make a plan for Markus." Mr. Loewe blinked at her.

Even the Cerebri couldn't deny the sincerity of her declaration, the earnestness of her gentle smile, the courage and strength it took for her to continue maintaining that kindness in the face of his disrespect and nasty insults. Noella held Mr. Loewe's gaze, pleading with her expressive eyes for him to stay, to not give in to his hatred of her and let it overshadow the need to help his son.

That might've been what Kellen admired most about her. She never let ill-treatment of her dominate the needs of their students.

She never stopped fighting for them, even when everyone around her worked untiringly to shut her down, remaining a fierce, faithful advocate for the students of Delmarth.

How could no one else see how important she was? How did it take him this long to see it for himself?

Mr. Loewe didn't dignify her with a response, but he did finally tread over the threshold and move into the office to claim a spot to sit. Noella breathed a sigh of relief when he chose to stay.

Mr. Loewe plopped down on the couch. Akio lowered down next to him. Kellen gestured with his hand for Noella to take the empty chair next to the couch, but she rejected the offer, electing to stand near Headmistress Dyer's desk. Kellen hesitated, gifting her a moment to change her mind, then eventually dropped his ass into the chair and crossed his legs, his fingers folding around the wooden arms.

"I know you've been in contact with Mr. Takeshi and Mr. Kilic about Markus's progress." Mr. Loewe scowled openly at Noella from across the room, but she refused to let that dissuade her from carrying this meeting. "Markus's grades haven't improved. His average right now in History of the Gods is a ten, which is far below the line of passing. With the fall term coming to an end in a few weeks, we're concerned that Markus won't be able to make up the work enough to pass the class. Without the credit from this term, he won't be eligible to graduate in June."

"What would that look like?" Mr. Loewe addressed Kellen, completely ignoring the fact that Noella had been the one speaking. Kellen's gaze swung back to Noella, tilting his head in her direction, a signal for her to continue.

"He would need to repeat the school year," she answered for him.

"What about his classes next semester?" Mr. Loewe pushed. "If he passes those, can't you just change his credits to say he passed the full year?"

"They're different classes," Akio interjected. "He's not taking the same subjects next semester as he is this semester. Those credits can't transfer. If he doesn't pass History of the Gods, he can't move on to War Strategy, so he will have to retake both classes next year." Mr. Loewe balled his hands into fists in his lap.

"Well, can't you just fudge it in the system?" the father demanded.

"We can't," Noella started to say, but Mr. Loewe wouldn't let her finish the thought.

"I'm not speaking to *you*," he sneered at her. "I'm speaking to the competent Primordials whose opinions I actually respect." Mr. Loewe ripped his eyes off Noella and glued them to Kellen, finding respite in no longer needing to regard the human. "What do *you* think, Mr. Kilic?"

Kellen gripped the arms of his chair. Fire burnt the back of his throat.

"I echo Ms. Rose's sentiment," he said in a cold tone of voice. "We cannot give allowances to some students that we wouldn't give to all students. That is not an option."

"Fine," the father relented. Noella turned her head to the side to roll her eyes at how he yielded to a man over her.

Kellen covered his hand over his mouth to stifle a cackle. Noella caught the corner of his mouth lift behind his fingers and bit her lip to subdue her own smile, clearing phlegm from her throat to keep from laughing too.

"Did anything change for Markus this summer?" she questioned Mr. Loewe, bringing Kellen reluctantly back to the meeting. "How have things been at home? Has his demeanor seemed different to you in any way?"

"He's the exact same kid he's always been. Nothing's changed in our family or his life. The only difference in his world is the human littering his school." Noella gulped. The taste of fire in Kellen's mouth grew stronger.

"Has Markus shared with you any goals that he has for himself and his future?" Mr. Loewe choked out a bitter laugh at her query.

"What kind of ridiculous question is that?" he mocked.

"I'm trying to gain a better understanding of Markus, of things he likes or cares about, so I can use that to help motivate him to care about school," she explained. The way she upheld her patience was venerable.

"I know my son," Mr. Loewe asserted. "I promise you, you're the *last* thing in this universe that will help motivate him." This cycle of bringing the conversation back to slighting Noella wasn't getting them anywhere.

"Has your son expressed any Dissident beliefs at home?" Kellen piped up. Noella's eyes bugged out of her skull before she shook her head in warning. It was too late though to backtrack what he'd said.

*"Excuse me?"* Mr. Loewe seethed, amber eyes blazing. Despite Noella's attempt to save him from shoving his foot in his mouth, Kellen pressed on.

"He seems to have very strong opinions about the Gods, which is making it difficult for him to engage with the course material. I was just wondering if that was something he's spoken about at home."

"What you're suggesting is offensive and dangerous, Mr. Kilic," Mr. Loewe snarled, stretching himself across Akio's lap to get as close to Kellen as he could. Akio flung himself back against the cushions to separate his personal space from Mr. Loewe's incense. "My son is a good person. He would never betray the Gods by undertaking any Dissident values. That accusation is outrageous."

"It wasn't an accusation," Kellen objected. "I simply asked a question."

"A question that implies our family holds those same beliefs, which I can assure you, we do *not*. We are loyal followers of Aros. We would never debase ourselves and choose to follow Edar."

"There's no judgement here," Noella said, not quite recognizing the gravity of this discussion. "To us, it doesn't matter what his personal beliefs are, as long as he understands that he has to still do the assigned work."

"You're not from Cavale, earthborn," Mr. Loewe roared, "so you don't understand the severity of such an allegation. An accusation like that could land my son in Terminus."

"It *wasn't* an accusation," Kellen repeated in a grumble. "It was a question based off things I've heard from your son's *mouth*. Like Ms. Rose said, I don't care what he personally believes, as long as he follows through on his duty to be a student and does the work like everyone else."

"The only thing I can think of that would make my son question his loyalty to Aros is *you*," Mr. Loewe accused Noella. From her wearied sigh, Kellen suspected she'd been expecting him to blame this on her somehow. "Your human presence here must be fucking with his head."

"In what way would Ms. Rose's presence make him side with Edar?" Akio asked furiously.

"Perhaps she's taken to the defense of her people and made my son believe those bogus claims that Aros was abusive to Tala and that's why the girl defected with Edar." Noella's quiet gasp exhibited that she didn't know this other perspective to the Aros and Tala myth. She had no reason to. It wasn't a standpoint taught to Primordials, the entertainment of such a theory cause for immediate sentencing to Terminus, which did nothing to absolve Aros of the suspicion that it could possibly be true.

That was a thought Kellen kept private in his head, a thought that would stay there permanently.

"I can assure you, Mr. Loewe, I've had no conversations with your son where I've indoctrinated any support of Edar into his head," Noella tried, she *really* tried, to promise. "I have no stake in whether he supports Aros or Edar. I just want to help your son get to the end of the year. That's all I care about."

"Your word means nothing, earthborn." Mr. Loewe faced Kellen. "What will the plan be moving forward for Markus?"

"We will—" Noella began, but once again wasn't permitted to finish.

"I'm going to need you to shut your fucking mouth for the remainder of this meeting," Mr. Loewe hissed.

"*ENOUGH.*" Everyone in the room shifted in unison to where Kellen's eyes had transformed into the slits of a dragon, plumes of smoke wafting from his flared nostrils, flames drenching the fingers of his crushing the arms of his chair. With everyone's attention on him, he growled, "This needs to stop. Ms. Rose is not the issue here. Ms. Rose is not responsible for your son failing my class. Your son is. We can offer all the support we have. We can offer to work privately with him after class hours to help him keep up. I can keep making allowances for him, but if your son doesn't apply himself, if he doesn't fucking care, then there's nothing we can do. This is not Ms. Rose's fault. If she were to leave tomorrow, this would still be an issue, because the issue lies with *your son*. Neither I nor Mr. Takeshi will tolerate this constant attack of Ms. Rose's character when she's done nothing but try to support Markus, just as we all have. If you refuse to have an adult conversation with us, then this meeting should just be adjourned, because we're not getting anywhere going in circles like this."

Noella's gaze scraped across Kellen's face. Her incendiary appraisal burned every section of his skin that it skimmed over, scorching his lips when she zeroed in on his mouth. He might've purposefully licked his lips just to see how she'd react. He received a sharp intake of breath in response, her eyes scattering away from him. If he'd known that would get her to look away, he never would have done it.

"If there's anything you think we can do for Markus, please, let us know," Noella entreated softly. "Anything you think would help him. Any style of learning you know he prefers. You know your son best. We just want to help him." Mr. Loewe was silent for several moments, focusing on his breathing.

"Try working with him one-on-one," Mr. Loewe requested of Kellen. "I'll have my own separate conversation with him. If he fails the class and has to repeat a year, it's not the end of the world. I'm more concerned at the moment that he's expressing Dissident opinions then I am about him passing a dumb class."

*He cares more about Markus's beliefs then about his son graduating?* Noella scoffed mind-to-mind.

*Try to remember what's at stake for people who side with Edar before you judge,* Kellen reminded her.

*I'm trying really hard not to judge,* she said, *but I find it difficult not to when what's more important is pressuring a child into submission than the child's actual wants or wishes. Faith is a personal thing that should never be forced upon anyone.*

Kellen deliberated her words thoroughly, then admitted, *You're not alone in holding that opinion, Rose. There just isn't a time or place to voice it in Cavale.* Noella frowned at the sentiment.

"I will set up meetings with him after class to go over the material together," Kellen vowed to Mr. Loewe. He refused to commit to trying to change the boy's mind about his opinions on the Gods, but he would commit, even if it stole pieces of his precious free time, to working with Markus to complete the assignments he'd missed. "If I can work with him separately to finish assignments and get him to at least a fifty in the class, maybe we can squeeze in a passing grade. *Maybe.* But your son will need to work his fucking ass off to pass the chapter quizzes and tests. I can't do that for him. If he doesn't pass those, then the grade is out of my hands."

"I can also begin meeting with him weekly to make sure he's keeping up with his coursework," Noella suggested, not appearing surprised when that was quickly shot down by Mr. Loewe.

"*NO,*" Mr. Loewe declined. "Not *you.* Anyone but *you.*"

"I can meet with him weekly," Akio intervened, the Cerebri father's stance brightening with relief.

"Thank you, Mr. Takeshi. That would be preferred." Akio nodded, then flung a sympathetic look at Noella. It was the first time Akio winked at her and Noella smiled back that Kellen didn't want to kill him.

"I will talk to my son tonight." Mr. Loewe rose from the couch, signaling to the rest of them that he'd reached his quota of being in Noella's presence. "Thank you for doing everything you can to help my son, and for speaking to me today, Mr. Kilic and Mr. Takeshi." Mr. Loewe brushed over Noella to shake both of the men's hands. She didn't even try to proffer her hand for a shake, faltering back a step to give the men room.

"You should be thanking Ms. Rose for this meeting." Kellen squeezed Mr. Loewe's hand a bit too hard. "This was her idea." Mr. Loewe's nostrils flared before he yanked his hand out of Kellen's.

"You've always been a revered member of this institution, Mr. Kilic. It's sad to see who you've chosen to align yourself with." Mr. Loewe knocked his shoulder into Noella's, shunting her backwards.

"It's been a pleasure," Noella jeered, lifting her chin to show she didn't fear him.

"I hope someone self-sacrifices and kills you before the end of the year," Mr. Loewe snapped in her face, the closest he'd dared to get to her since he entered this meeting. When he finally cleared the threshold, Noella released all the oxygen that had been entombed in her chest in a spluttering, fatigued gasp.

"Thank the fucking Gods that's over," she exclaimed, leaping onto the couch and fanning herself with her hand.

"Are you okay?" Akio asked her.

"Me? I'm fine." Kellen didn't believe her casual shrug. He'd seen in her eyes that Mr. Loewe's maltreatment impacted her, but if she wanted to maintain the charade that nothing touched her, he wouldn't give her away. "If he doesn't want me near his son, I won't insert myself. I'm going to rely on the two of you to keep me up to date on Markus's progress. Any suggestions I have for you to try with him, I'll share."

"That would be great." Akio gave her hand a squeeze. "I've got to head back. You'll be okay, Rosie?"

"I'm fine, Kio. Really." Just like Kellen, Akio didn't seem convinced.

"Kellen," Akio said in goodbye with a brisk nod. Kellen nodded back in a much more friendly manner than he had previously. *I'm rooting for you,* Akio declared in confidence on his way to the door, Kellen's eyes widening.

He had no time to respond before Akio crossed the threshold and disappeared down the hall.

Kellen finally dropped his gaze onto Noella, over the only place his eyes ever seemed inclined to wander to anymore. She looked up immediately, as if she'd been watching him from the corner of her eye, waiting for him to look at her. He wanted to tell her she never had to worry, that his eyes would always find their way back to her, but he didn't have access to that sort of vocabulary.

"That was a shitshow," was all that came out of his mouth in the end.

"It was a shitshow that needed to happen," she replied, rubbing her eyes to try to keep them open.

Kellen found himself lifting Noella's legs to make space for himself to sit on the couch with her. Instead of swinging her legs to the side to lay her feet on the floor, he unfurled them across his lap. Noella might've been astonished by the intimate gesture, but she didn't recoil or make any attempts to withdraw her legs from his grasp. She sunk into the cushions when Kellen's fingers began kneading her calf muscles, working with a mind of their own to please her.

"You shouldn't have brought up the Dissident comment," Noella chastised him, even as she flexed her legs deeper into his palms, her body beseeching for him in a way her mouth never would. "Markus told us that stuff in confidence. You just set him up to be confronted by his father. Who knows how that conversation will go."

"You're right. I shouldn't have said it, but I felt like I had to so we could gain come clarity on the family." Noella sat up suddenly, edging closer to him on the couch, and splayed her fingers atop his forehead, her brows cutely furrowing in concentration. "What the fuck are you doing?"

"Checking to see if you have a temperature," she answered.

"Why?"

"Because you just said I was *right*, so surely you must be ill." Kellen chuckled, snaking his fingers around her tiny wrist to pry her hand off his face. Her fingers trickled down from his temple, sliding over his cheek.

Her eyes up close were like storm clouds congealed in two orbs. Lightning crackled through the hue, representing the fire in her he felt enticed to kindle rather than lessen. He wasn't afraid of her fire. She didn't seem afraid of his. She may have been the only person he'd ever known who didn't shy away from telling him exactly what she thought, from putting him in his place.

It was what he needed, what he'd been missing all this time, someone worthy of being an actual partner.

*Fuck*, she smelled so good. Like the woods, mixed with berries and flowers. Was that her perfume, or just her, her natural odor, her natural perfection? How had he ever existed without that scent?

On that couch, with Noella's legs draped across his lap, her wrist ensnarled in his fist, her face so close to him that he could taste her breath as it puffed in his face, it hit Kellen like a tidal wave just how much he wanted her.

He wanted Noella Rose. The human girl who'd come to invade his world and somehow invaded his mind and heart instead. The human girl who pounced on that student to save his brother from his dragon and cared about his siblings in a way he never would have expected. He wanted her so much he couldn't breathe. The way he wanted her wasn't just a physical need, not a mere desire to satisfy his lust, but a deep, emotional need for her, a need to know all of her, her mind, her heart, her soul, *everything.*

When did this need for her suddenly arise?

Had it always been there, lurking under the surface, gathering strength to consume him from the inside out?

He felt a tug from within his fingers. He'd been so absorbed in his thoughts, in his stunning epiphany, that he hadn't even noticed Noella trying to retract her arm, trying to separate herself from him.

*Don't go,* he found himself imploring.

*I need to walk Freya.* The voice in his head sounded less confident, more resigned, then the Noella he'd come to know and respect, the Noella he'd just determined he wanted more than his next breath.

*Why are you fighting this, Noella?*

She gasped, her grey eyes growing big with shock, with desire she didn't seem to realize he could see, could smell, could *feel* radiate off her. While her next words were harsh, Kellen knew better than to trust them.

*There's nothing to fight here, Kellen.*

*If you really mean that, then say it to my face.* Noella's breathing escalated, heaving through her chest. *Come on, Noella,* he pushed. *Use those pretty lips and tell me you don't want this.*

"You haven't done anything to show me *you* want this," she snarled aloud. Kellen delighted in the fact that she didn't use her first opportunity to tell him no outright. "You think you can joke around with me a few times and that just excuses all the shit you did? The names you've called me? The fact that you tried to *drown* me in a pool?" Kellen huffed, arming himself for a fight.

"I didn't try to——"

"Don't even finish that sentence because that is not an answer I will accept." Kellen's lips knit shut. Coz was right. This was a queen in his arms, and there was nothing for him to do besides obey her. "You tell me to use my lips to tell you I want you? Why don't you use *yours* to actually apologize for treating me like crap the last six weeks?"

She waited.

She waited for him to say it, and fuck, he *tried,* but the words wouldn't come.

Why couldn't he give her what she wanted? He felt remorse for his actions, yet for some reason, he couldn't say it aloud. Was his ego really so large? Was he so broken inside that he couldn't chip off a morsel of the wall he'd built around himself to truly let her in? He'd never expected to feel this way, not just for her specifically, but for anyone. He'd only trained his heart to hold two people inside it, and the possibility of letting someone else share that space was unfathomable, unthinkable, impossible. His body revolted against the concept, the fear of falling for her and subsequently losing her too strong to tolerate. He didn't know how to do it. How anyone did it.

Maybe that's all he needed to tell her.

The truth. Maybe that would be enough. But just as the words finally came to him, he'd run out of time.

Noella wriggled within in his arms until he finally let her go, allowing her to crawl off the couch.

"Until you do that, Kilic…until you take some accountability for the way you've hurt me, there's no conversation to be had here. You and I are not friends. We're *nothing.* It's better if you just stay away from me."

"Gods, why do you have to be so fucking difficult?" he blurted, instantly regretting it.

*Shit. That was the wrong thing to say.* Her eyes widened before she fumed a horrified laugh.

"I believe I once said that to you, and you told me to fuck off. It brings me great pleasure to return the sentiment." She tilted over him, her perfume attacking his senses, infecting his ability to breathe. She snarled, "FUCK OFF, Mr. Kilic," then strutted to the door and left it hanging wide open behind her.

*You fucking idiot,* Coz rebuked.

*I don't need you to rub salt in the wound, Coz. I know I fucked up.* Kellen dropped his head into his hands. *Fuck. I fucked that up so badly.* She had every reason to hate him, every reason to shut him out, yet she hadn't. None of what she just said was a complete no. All she wanted was for him to acknowledge how he'd hurt her, for him to acknowledge what a dick he'd been and take ownership of his shit decisions. If he did that, and meant it, maybe he'd have a chance to turn this around.

*I can turn this around,* he announced as he rose from the couch and stormed out of Headmistress Dyer's office, declaring this to Coz, to himself, to the universe waiting with bated breath.

He could put his ego aside. He could make this right. He had to try. The chance of something with her, even if all she gave him was friendship at this point, far outweighed the risk of having his heart crushed further. He'd gotten clarity on that couch from fate itself that he could no longer ignore.

Kellen sprinted across campus, first running to his office to grab his briefcase, then bolting to the faculty housing. He'd just made it to the entrance of their building, about to dash inside and race right to Noella's door, when he saw an incoming phone call from Headmistress Dyer.

She never called him. Only in cases of emergency.

Kellen's heart dropped into his stomach. Somehow, when he answered the phone, he knew what she would say.

"I thought you couldn't make calls in Avatia?"

She didn't even acknowledge that. "Security just alerted me that your mother is approaching campus."

## CHAPTER 22

# ELLA

ELLA HAD MISSED Rylee's apartment. She'd missed Rylee's plush, velvet teal couch. She'd missed the gorgeous splashes of pink and blue and white that fused together to create the painting that hung above the sofa. She'd missed the marble coffee table and the blue, gold, and cream stripped carpet. She'd missed the way the atmosphere always smelled a tiny bit like chocolate.

Most of all, she had missed her big sister who now sat beside her, her heroine, an angel without wings, the only deity she believed in. Even if she couldn't truly feel her through the astral projection, sitting in Rylee's company, even as a ghost in her world, was more than Ella had felt in so long.

"Damn." Rylee whistled through her teeth. Ella had just finished telling her about her final conversation with Kellen. Rylee raised her hand for a high-five, shouting, "I'm so fucking proud of you!"

Ella laughed, trying to return the gesture, but her fingers went through Rylee's hand.

"I don't know what to do now," she grumbled, resting her cheek in her palm. "Every fiber of my being is begging me to go to him, but how is that right? He's been a massive dickhead and made the first four weeks of my time in Cavale absolute hell, yet now that *he's* decided he doesn't hate me, I'm supposed to just spread my legs and act like nothing happened? Fuck that!"

"Fuck *that!*" Mason, Rylee's husband, echoed from the kitchen. "You deserve better, El. I'm proud of you for sticking up for yourself."

"Thanks, Mase." Mason finally emerged from the kitchen with a mug of hot chocolate for his wife, cheeks flushed from the steam blowing up from the heated beverage, his black hair pulled back in a messy bun.

"Thank you, baby." Rylee accepted the mug, then pouted at Ella. "I wish you could have some with us."

"Don't worry about it. I'm fine." Watching her siblings enjoy their drinks and exist in front of her, not through a phone screen but *really* in front of her, even as a hologram, was enough to complete her joy.

Rylee sipped her drink, then asked, "If Kellen comes back to you and apologizes for what he's done, what will you do then?" Ella threw her head back against the couch pillows and groaned up at the ceiling.

"I don't fucking know!" she cried, Rylee and Mason laughing at her dramatics. "It doesn't make sense for me to start anything with him, with anyone in Cavale. I'm not staying. The second the school year is up, I'm getting the fuck out of there. Why put myself in a position to lose something if I don't have to?"

"Because you *want* to, El." Rylee nudged her. "You want him, and there's nothing wrong with that."

"How can I want him, though?" She lurched into an upright position. "He's been a terrible person for the majority of the time I've known him. What does that say about my morals?"

"He hasn't been a terrible person for the majority of the time you've known him." Ella squinted her eyes at Rylee.

"He tried to *drown* me, Ry."

"Weeks ago, because the Primordials are conditioned to hate humans and he didn't know yet how amazing you are. Look, I'm not excusing what he did. If we ever meet, he'll need to kneel at my feet and beg for forgiveness if he wants my approval, but I don't think you can entirely blame him for his treatment of you at the beginning, given the way the Primordials are taught to view humans. You know him far better than I do, and for you to have any interest in him, when you're the pickiest person I know, tells me he's worth *something.*" Rylee scooted closer to her. "He hasn't been all bad to you, El. He's defended you multiple times against Daniel, Oliviana, and with that rude father today. In his own limited way, he's actually been trying to make an effort with you. It's not the words you want to hear or *deserve* to hear, but I don't think that's nothing."

"You're such a lawyer," Mason laughed at her. While Rylee flipped him her middle finger, Ella chewed her bottom lip.

"Do you think I was too hard on him?"

"Absolutely not," Mason asserted. "You had every right to say those things, and he needs to apologize."

"If he doesn't apologize," Rylee continued, "then you have your answer and you're better off for it. If he *does* apologize, and he really means it, I hope you don't shut it down completely. Let yourself explore it a little. There would be no harm done, and you might get something great out of it, even for a short while. You owe it to yourself to see."

Ella wasn't ready to capitulate. "I'm counseling his siblings," she reminded them. "It's a *huge* ethical dilemma."

"A forbidden romance? Oof!" Rylee squealed, fanning herself. "Even sexier." Ella rolled her eyes.

The sound of a fist pounding into a door—followed by a strangled holler that sounded like a garbled rendition of her name—pierced the ether, hacking through this beautifully crafted illusion and raining an anguished ballad down onto their heads.

"*Noella, open up!*" the distressed voice yelled.

"Is that Kellen?' Rylee began hitting Mason's arm and kicking her feet at the cushion, shrieking, "Oh, it's so *on!*"

"I'll check in later," Ella promised, then yanked her finger out of the astral projector, demolishing the illusion so she abruptly returned to her apartment in Cavale, where she'd been squatting on the couch, Freya licking the bottom of her feet. She set the astral projector aside and scrambled off the sofa, hurrying to meet the voice.

Ella was not prepared for the Kellen she found when she opened the door.

Kellen's face was not a man who'd come to grovel for her forgiveness. It was a man who was experiencing, piece by piece, the disintegration of his sanity, panic blistering in his emerald eyes.

"What's wrong?" she gasped, left winded by his haunted expression.

He gushed out in a frenzied breath, "My mother's here for the twins."

Ella didn't think. She didn't hesitate. She ran into her apartment, poured some water and dry food into Freya's bowls, grabbed her jacket, slipped her feet into her shoes, and scurried to meet him at the door.

"Are Jare and Laya waiting outside?" she asked him, locking her door behind her and zipping her coat.

"I don't know where they are." Ella whipped around to face him.

"You don't know?" she spluttered. "You didn't get them yet?"

"No. Dyer just called me. I was on..." He tripped over his words. "I was on my...my way...to talk to you."

The implication of that struck her in the heart. She felt the impact of it crash into her as if he'd thrown a physical object at her chest. He was coming to speak to her. To apologize. To give her what she needed.

He rushed on, "I was coming to talk to you, and I got the call, and I didn't...the first thing...I just...I just needed to...you... I...I..."

"Hey," Ella whispered, framing his face with her hands, stroking her thumbs across his cheeks. "It's okay. We're going to go get them now. They'll be fine. Everything is going to be fine, okay?"

"I need you," he groaned, like it was essential for her to hear him say that at least once, in case he never got the chance to say it again. Ella swallowed the lump digging into the walls of her throat.

"I'm here," she breathed, her thumb tracing his trembling bottom lip. "Let's go get them together."

"Don't leave."

"I'm not going anywhere, Kellen." There was so much for them to still discuss, but right now, none of that mattered. "Let's go get them together, okay?" She wrapped her arms around one of his, shepherding him down the hall, her pace quickening once Kellen seemed able to keep up with her.

They began sprinting through campus—then, when Kellen determined Ella was lagging too far behind and wasn't running fast enough, he grabbed her waist and tossed her over his shoulder, racing across Delmarth with her dangling from his back and his hands cradling her hips to keep her from slipping off.

"Is this really necessary?" she hissed, bobbing on his shoulder.

"It's necessary to me," he answered, though that could have meant a million different things that Ella didn't have time to carefully analyze.

Kellen lifted her off his shoulder and set her down on her feet once they were in front of the Varmin student housing.

"Go get Jare and Laya," he directed her, shedding his jacket. "They're in room three-seventy, third floor. I'll be fucking shocked if they're not in there, but if they're not, we'll scour the whole campus until we find them."

"What're you going to be doing?" she fretted.

"Shifting into my Varmin form so we can get the fuck out of here the minute you come downstairs."

Ella paused a moment. "I've never seen your dragon form before." She couldn't hide her excitement.

"Go, Rose," he demanded, shooing her towards the door, then threw in a clipped, but sincere, "Please," at the slow raise of her eyebrows.

Ella rushed inside, taking the stairs two at a time and springing herself forward with the help of the railing. She skimmed the tiny numbers on the doors, finally landing in front of room three-seventy, where she proceeded to bang her fist into the door in a synchronized succession, not relenting until Laya answered.

"Ms. Rose?" Laya squeaked, sounding a mixture of confused and thrilled.

"Is Jarion here?" Ella asked, peeking over Laya's head to see into the room. Jarion lounged on his bed, bulky headphones shrouding both ears, his head bumping to the tinny music blasting from the

290

speakers. Ella slid past Laya into the room, slapping her hand at the end of Jarion's bed to rip his attention off his phone.

"Ms. Rose," he spluttered, yanking the headphones off. "You scared me."

"Sorry. Grab some clothes to sleep in and toiletries," she ordered both twins. "We need to go. Now."

"What's happening?" Laya demanded, her voice cracking. Ella's heartbeat hammered in her ears. She didn't want to tell them, aware of the emotions she'd be engendering in them, but they deserved to know.

"Your mother is here." Nothing could've set the twins moving faster.

Laya's movements were quick and erratic, stuffing random clothes and anything possibly essential into her backpack. Jarion's breathing grew labored, his pace more slow, fumbling his items as he hurried to pack them away. Ella ended up taking over for him, directing him to sit in a chair and quietly asking where certain things were located so he wouldn't need to fuss over anything.

"Where's Kell?" Laya asked, her tone of voice strong with determination, like she'd given herself a task and couldn't see beyond that into her own feelings, wouldn't allow herself to go there yet.

"Outside. Shifting."

"He sent you to come get us?" Ella nodded. Laya's eyes glimmered with the emotion she was expending energy compartmentalizing. "I'm glad," she whimpered. Ella squeezed Laya's shoulder.

"Is that everything?" Ella asked Jarion, whose breaths were so tortured that they sounded like they were corroding his lungs. Ella dropped to her knees in front of him. "Jare, look at me." She cupped his face, guiding his eyes to meet hers. "We've got you. Okay? Kellen and I have you guys. Nothing is going to happen to you. We won't let her touch you."

Jarion choked on a sob. "Promise me?" Ella stretched up on her knees to plant a kiss on his head.

"I promise with every fiber of my being, Jare, your brother and I will do everything in our power not to let her touch you," Ella swore against his forehead. Jarion squeezed her so tight that she coughed out a wheeze. "Shall we go?" Jarion nodded, gripping her wrists like he needed her hands on his face, like he needed the extra warmth to remember how the function. "Let's go meet Kellen downstairs."

Laya, ever the sweetheart, offered to take Jarion's backpack for him so Ella could keep her arms around him.

When they cleared the stairs and shoved past the front door, they met the humungous, glorious dragon sitting on the lawn. His massive form was cloaked in glossy, obsidian scales, imbued with a resplendent gold sheen. Enormous, pearly eyes sat high within Kellen's horned, bony skull, one gargantuan central tusk jutting out of his forehead, just above thick, rounded ears. A string of small crystal growths trickled across the jawline, several rows of sharp teeth leaking out from the sides of his mouth. Four powerful limbs carried his cumbersome body and ended in huge nails resembling onyx. His wings, which at their full breadth were the same width of the entire Varmin sector, were scythe-shaped, sharp hooks growing from the endings of each bone, almost giving it a feathered look, the sheath framing his wings tinted orange, glowing as if fashioned from fire.

Where one might have been overcome by fear from beholding a creature with such an imposing presence, Ella felt nothing but reverence, in awe of the unfathomable power emanating from the regal beast.

Familiar, molten emerald eyes landed on her, over where her arm surrounded his shaking brother.

*Is he okay?* Kellen's voice saturated her mind, his eyes soft despite the rest of his appearance being so gruesome.

*He's terrified,* she replied, not wishing to lie to him.

Kellen tucked in one of his wings while he unfurled the other towards the asphalt, creating a gradient for Jarion and Laya to climb. Ella would have offered to help them mount their brother, but the twins seemed to know what to do, how to carefully ascend his wing without hurting the delicate membrane that composed the center of it, which under the spotlight of the sun almost resembled the texture of gossamer.

She lingered close to Kellen, her eyes keenly tracking the twins' trajectory up the bulky figure.

Something leathery kissed her cheek.

Ella twisted her head to the side and found Kellen's face right there. The world seemed to collectively suck in an anticipating breath as the monstrous dragon sloped his head and nuzzled her neck in a manner one could only describe as loving, the corners of Ella's eyes burning at the romantic gesture.

*Is this Kellen, or Coz?* she asked, then raised a hand to caress the curved scales, trailing her fingernails along the growths.

*Both,* Coz's gravelly voice answered before the dragon sighed a heady moan at her amorous touch.

*Where does Kellen go when you take over his body?*

*I'm here, sweetheart,* Kellen purred in her mind, heat flooding through her veins at the sound of his voice, pooling in her cheeks. *When I'm in my humanoid form, Coz stays curled up inside my chest. When I shift, we switch places, though I always maintain control of our mind, even when Coz takes over.*

*So you're sitting inside your own chest right now?* The dragon cuddled closer to her in answer. Ella wondered what that felt like for Kellen, to be essentially imprisoned inside himself, what that felt like for Coz to be caged inside a body that didn't belong to him. *How do you maintain control of your body if Coz takes over?*

*It's part of the Varminia curse from Aros,* Coz explained. *If we possessed the ability to take complete control of our hosts, it would be too obvious that their Varmin forms are separate beings. It's why we're prohibited from engaging in any behavior that could reveal our identities to our hosts. We're supposed to stay inactive so our hosts always believe their Varmin forms are a part of them. We will always be subservient to our host's desires, as it is the only thing that can breathe life into us.*

*That's so sad,* Ella mused. The dragon licked her affectionately beneath her ear. It reminded her of Freya. *If you're prohibited from making yourselves known to your hosts, why did Jarion's dragon make himself known to us? Why did you?*

*Nivrun made himself known because he was growing impatient.* Nivrun must have been Jarion's dragon. *And I...* Coz's voice trailed off before he declared, his tone whetted by silk, *I made myself known for you, Noella Rose.*

The words slithered down to Ella's heart, yanking at the strings, tattooing over the soft tissue.

*Don't ask him to explain what that means because he won't,* Kellen grumbled, which led Ella to suspect they'd had this conversation before and Kellen came up empty-handed of any real answers.

Ella elevated her eyes to Kellen—Coz's back, searching the reptilian skin for signs of Jarion and Laya. She found a wink of their coloring between Kellen's wings, a small smear of brown amidst the black scales, with specks of pink and green mixed in for Jarion and Laya's backpacks. Ella braced herself for the climb, her legs buckling at the thought of being suspended a thousand feet in the air without the protection of a roof that accompanied flying on an airplane. There was no shelter available on the back of a dragon, no access to any anti-anxiety medication to calm her nerves.

She focused on Jarion and Laya, on the need to get them to safety, to combat the overwhelming flurry of panic kindling in her chest, forcing her feet to move towards the wing to begin her own ascent.

Suddenly, the wing lifted off the ground before she could step on or even jump to grab it, pulling back to meet where his other wing had begun hoisting off the ground in preparation for take-off.

*What're you doing?* Ella asked Kellen, watching her only chance of joining Jarion and Laya on Kellen's back swing away from her. *I can't climb on now.*

*You're not sitting up there,* Kellen replied.

*Then where am I—*

Suddenly, a clawed hand seized Ella around her waist, enclosing her in his fist before Kellen leapt off his hind legs and launched them all towards the heavens, his wings beating with a thunderous roar that echoed from all corners of the sky. The ground fell away beneath them, shrinking into a diminutive structure before dissolving into the horizon. Then, all Ella could see were billows of vapor, a backcloth of blue sky with sinking sunlight fracturing through the hue, and a blur of trees flitting below her feet, crowned with yellow, rotting leaves and crooked branches.

Ella had no time to react apart from screaming. She quickly grabbed onto Kellen's thumb to stop herself from losing her balance and plummeting to her death, careful to avoid the jagged talon at the end of the digit.

*I'm going to kill you, Kilic,* she snarled at him, tunneling her nails into his claw, not that she could actually pierce him hard enough for him to truly feel it. *You don't deserve quick. It's going to be slow and agonizing.*

Kellen's voice was outlined by roguish charm. *Why does it sound like you're flirting with me, Rose?*

*Because you're a fucking asshole who hears what he wants to hear and not what's actually being said to him!*

*Oh, I hear you, sweetheart. You want to take your time with me. Trust me, I want the same with you.* Ella raked her fingernails over the leathery scales, seeking to draw blood, but she barely left a scratch. Kellen's laughter permeated her ears, hugging her bones. *Are you trying to tickle me, baby?*

*I hate you, Kellen Kilic,* she growled, repeating it over and over again, willing it to be true even as her heart jolted at the way he called her *baby* for the first time. *I hate you. I hate you. I hate you.*

*I love the way you say my name, Noella.* His voice left her mind to refocus on their voyage. Ella didn't want to admit to herself that she missed his voice the moment it no longer cluttered her ears, how the absence of him left her with a gaping hole in her chest where he should have been.

The wind whipped through her hair, tugging at her clothes. Ella dared herself to peer over the edge of Kellen's fist and watch the kingdom of Cavale undulate beneath them. She admired the tiny villages dotting the landscape, the rivers snaking through the countryside, glimmering like silver ribbons, the forest resembling a verdant carpet in the way it stretched out, treetops swaying in a choreographed dance with the wind. If Ella wasn't so enraged with Kellen for not giving her the respect of a warning before he grabbed her and took off, she might've found the experience enjoyable.

Kellen's wings thrashed within the powerful stream of wind, creating blustery gusts that rattled the earth beneath her feet. From behind them, Ella heard a menacing screech, jarring the peaceful scenery into a turbulent state that compelled her to turn within Kellen's firm grip and search the clouds for an intruder. In the distance, gaining on them, she found a silver adversary to rival

Kellen's gold, the dragon sleek and agile, clearly feminine. Eyes of piercing ice, baring no humanity within them, scrutinized Kellen's moves, plotting her path forward with calculated precision.

*Is that—* Ella started, but Kellen cut her off before she could finish the question.

*My mother,* he confirmed, his tone thick with worry. *I need to get us to our house. The wards around the house are spelled to keep her out.*

*How close are we?*

*Not close enough.* Ella hugged one of Kellen's claws, this time not angrily, but to offer her support.

His mother's massive chest expanded, as if drawing from the very essence of the kingdom. Flames flickered inside her maw like stars in a celestial ballet. Roars erupted from deep within her throat, a primal symphony of fury before the tempest released. A torrent of searing flames cascaded forth, the air crackling with the intensity of the inferno, the very fabric of reality itself igniting as the upwelling of fire rushed for them. Kellen banked to the right and twisted his body away from the flames, performing a series of aerial acrobatics that defied the limits of Ella's imagination to keep the fire from touching them. His fingers nearly crushed Ella's waist from the tautness of his grip, ensuring she couldn't fall out when they rotated upside down. Ella's hair spun in random directions around her before plopping back messily over her shoulders.

*Jare and Laya!* she gasped when they were once again upright.

*They're holding on,* he assured her. Kellen's powerful muscles flexed beneath her. *I need to do something.*

*Do what?* She didn't like the tone he'd used when he said that. She disliked the tone he used to utter his next words even more.

*Please don't hate me for this, Noella.*

*Kellen, what're you—*

Kellen swung his massive body around so he now faced his mother, then proceeded to let go of Ella.

Ella plunged towards the earth, the wind belting her cheeks from the velocity in which she plummeted at so she couldn't find the ground beneath her, couldn't see anything beyond the tears blearing her vision. She only fell for a total of five seconds before Kellen's back foot caught her, but those five seconds felt like an eternity.

Once Kellen had his front hands free, his claws extended like razor-sharp billhooks and clashed with his mother's in the middle of the ether, the two massive dragons crashing into one another and releasing a cacophony of metallic, belligerent clangs. The collision of their bodies sent ripples through the wind that created seismic tremors in the earth below. Sparks spewed with each strike, illuminating the clouds with fleeting bursts of light.

His mother's tail thrust in the direction of Kellen's side, aiming to sink the sharp talon at the end into his stomach.

*KELLEN!* Ella yelled in warning, unsure if he could see his mother's tail heading right for him, his focus absorbed in trying to shunt her backwards. *Watch out for her tail! She's about to stab you!*

Kellen's tail whipped through the air like a whirling cyclone and snatched her tail before the talon succeeded in impaling his side. He wrenched down with all his might to pull her body away from them, his mother shrieking a startled cry as she nosedived for the earth, giving him enough time to flap his wings harder and renew their journey to the house, propelling them at a swifter speed.

Kellen flung Ella through the air like she was a ragdoll, passing her back to his front hand.

*Thanks for the warning, Rose,* he expressed. *I owe you one.*

*WHAT THE FUCK, KILIC?!* she bellowed, slamming her weak fists into the back of his hand. *YOU DROPPED ME!*

*I'm sorry.* At least the apology sounded genuine. *I needed to move you to free my hands.*

*I GOT THAT, BUT A LITTLE WARNING WOULD'VE BEEN NICE!* Ella's breath hadn't returned to her.

Concern graced his voice. *Noella, are you afraid of heights?*

*YES! NOT THAT YOU FUCKING ASKED BEFORE YOU GRABBED ME AND TOOK OFF!*

She couldn't stop panting. She couldn't see through her tears. Sobs clogged her throat. Bile tickled the back of her mouth. She clamped her lips shut before she spewed vomit onto the clouds, then shut their line of communication down because the process of producing words was making her more nauseous.

*Hold on, baby,* Kellen assured, sensing her nausea. *We're almost there.*

Her heart betrayed her by reacting to the way he again called her *baby*, fluttering against her ribcage.

*Calm down, stupid heart,* she reproached herself. *We hate him.*

*I heard that,* Kellen drawled, an invisible smile coloring his voice.

He gracefully maneuvered through the open sky, avoiding clouds as though they were corporeal obstacles blocking his path to freedom. The landscape below became a blur of vibrant color smothered in a gilded sheet of descending sunlight. Ella could almost feel the adrenaline course through Kellen's muscles, emitting a sharp, blistering heat from the inside out, like his blood had transformed into a liquid fire in his veins. The air grew thinner at their escalating height, his wings straining against the resistance of the wind. She heard Kellen's mother's wings hacking through the breeze behind them, using the airstream to claw her way back to them. Kellen pitched forward, vibrating from the surge of energy he expended sustaining the distance he'd placed between himself and his mother.

Sparks dripped from his mother's serrated teeth before a cataclysmic explosion of fire gushed out of her open mouth, warping the clouds from the intensity of the unfettered wrath. Kellen's tail coiled into a ball to avoid the flaming deluge, the heavens seeming to recoil along with him from the sheer force of his mother's fiery breath.

*Noella, cover your face with your arms,* he ordered.

She quickly folded her arms around her eyes, crinkling herself into a ball inside Kellen's fist just as he swerved his head to the side and released his own outburst of fire. She watched through the cracks in his fingers as his flames twisted and writhed across the ether like serpents ablaze, streaking crimson with an undercurrent of blue, so the flames appeared almost violet. They snaked out to meet his mother's flames, the infernos blasting into one another. Kellen's firestorm was the more potent of the two and extinguished his mother's fire the moment his converged with hers.

"KELLEN!" Ella heard Jarion yell, the first she'd heard from the twins the entire flight. "I see it!"

Ella squirmed out from the protection of Kellen's fist, peeking over the side to glimpse the grounds underneath. Nestled amidst a variegated meadow, a quaint cottage stood as a time-worn sanctuary, its weathered exterior exuding an undeniable charm. The thatched roof, adorned with patches of vibrant wildflowers, added a touch of whimsy to the humble façade. A winding cobblestone pathway sprawled out from the opulent gate guarding the property to the entrance of the cottage, veering off in the middle to create a different path that led to a lively garden bursting with an array of blossoms, containing garish red roses that climbed the lattice pergola arching above the garden.

Ella marveled at the beauty of the home, felt her heart called down to the estate below. This was the kind of home she used to dream of living in, the kind she thought only existed in fantasy books.

"SHE'S GETTING CLOSER!" Laya shrieked from above. "GO, KELL! GO!"

Kellen flew towards the cottage at a breathtaking speed, allowing the current to pilot his course to give his wings a rest.

*Noella, I'm going to enclose you in my fist so you can get through the wards,* he told her in advance.

*Oh, so NOW you decide to warn me,* she hissed, but welcomed his fingers bowing above her head to secure her inside his hand, protected on all sides by his leathery scales and soothing warmth.

When Kellen made contact with the invisible wards protecting the property, she couldn't see it, but she felt it in the atmosphere, felt the impact of his large body breaking through the forcefield, vacuuming the wind into the electromagnetic shield so when they passed through the wards, the world fell silent. The moment Kellen's tail successfully entered the shelter, all sound and oxygen returned. The wind breathed a sigh of relief along with them. Ella watched Kellen's mother smash her body into the wards, unrelenting, thumping against the forcefield that refused her entry.

*She can't see us anymore,* Kellen explained to Ella. *She can't see the house. We're safe now, sweetheart.*

Ella burst into tears, wilting against Kellen's hand. She watched his mother concede with a defeated roar and push off the forcefield with her back feet, finally flying away in the opposite direction.

## CHAPTER 23

# KELLEN

With a final descent, Kellen landed on the property, his massive claws sinking into the soft earth, grinding the flowers beneath his cumbrous feet. The dust settled around his folded wings, the beating of his heart gradually slowing with the reduction of his adrenaline and fear. Everyone was safe. Against all odds, he'd gotten all four of them to the cottage. He didn't allow himself any room right now to think about his mother, to think about the fact that his own flesh and blood had just tried to kill him—all he had space for was Jarion, Laya, and Noella. He expanded his right wing on a slanted angle so Jarion and Laya could dismount from his back, then lowered Noella slowly to the ground.

The second Noella's feet touched the earth and he'd slipped his fingers off her, she retched into the sward, her body bucking violently with every painful heave, like she was trying to expel a demon from her chest.

*Time to switch back,* Coz said, stepping away from the forefront of their mind and reaching out a hand to where Kellen sat inside his own chest, wrenching Kellen to his feet so he could reclaim the mantle.

Kellen's dragon form began to shrink, his wings retreating into his spine, his limbs stretching back into their humanoid form, smooth brown flesh replacing the obsidian scales. Once he'd fully returned to his humanoid self, no trace of Coz left besides the scales lining the column of his throat on either side, he rushed over to Noella and gathered her hair in one hand so the tendrils were saved from the vomit.

Noella lifted her eyes to him, realizing that he was fully naked behind her, then turned back to the ground to puke even more.

*Did she just vomit at the sight of my penis?*

"Do either of you have a towel in your backpacks?" Kellen requested his siblings. Both twins dove into their packs, procuring a towel each, one red and one black, and handed them to Kellen. He passed the red one to Noella to wipe her mouth, while he used the black one to wrap around his waist to cover himself. The towel barely contained his dick, but it would have to be enough for now, until he found some clothes inside the house to slip on. "Is everyone okay?" Kellen asked the group.

"Is everyone OKAY?" Noella repeated after cleaning her face, her blonde hair a tumultuous, knotted jumble atop her head. She'd never looked more beautiful. "No, I am not O-K. You put me in your little dragon claw, with no warning, and just took off into the sky, and then you fucking *dropped me*. You *dropped* me, Kilic!"

Kellen didn't have time to react to her calling his dragon claw *little* before the twins erupted.

"You *dropped* her?" Laya gasped in horror.

"Kell!" Jarion cried, the twins coming to stand at Noella's sides, their allegiance resting with her in this instance.

"I did *not* drop her," Kellen objected, using all his strength not to roll his eyes. "I intentionally passed her from my hand to my foot. I didn't warn her before I did it, which I apologize for, but I don't apologize for doing it. I needed both my hands."

"What if you hadn't caught me, Kilic?" Noella pushed, setting her hands on her hips and raising her chin.

"I knew I would," he maintained. He'd go to his grave asserting this. He trusted his instincts and knew he was capable of catching her, knew there was no universe in which he would have let her fall.

She didn't trust that, though. She couldn't see into his mind the way he could see into hers.

"WHAT IF YOU HADN'T, KILIC?!"

"I KNEW I WOULD, NOELLA!" He carelessly used her first name in the presence of the twins. Laya's brows lifted to show she'd caught the slip of his tongue. Noella shook her head in refusal.

"Why wasn't I allowed to sit on top with Jarion and Laya?" she demanded, gesturing to the twins.

"Because you don't know how to seat a dragon," Kellen growled, losing control of his temper. "You would've slid off, and I didn't have enough time to explain to you how to sit correctly."

"Oh." The anger vanished from Noella's eyes. She was quiet for a moment, a first for her, then mumbled, her tone nicer, "I couldn't have just sat behind them and held onto one of their waists?"

"It's more dangerous if you try to hold onto someone than if you're seated properly," Laya said. "If the wind is too harsh, it will blow your arms off the person you're holding. You need to be properly seated and gripping onto the spikes in the dragon's back. That's the only way to keep your seat on a dragon."

Noella frowned at Kellen. "You weren't trying to kill me?"

"No! I was *not* trying to kill you." He'd told her he needed her. He begged her to not leave him, for fuck's sake, words he'd never uttered in his life, and she actually thought he was trying to *kill* her? While his thoughts spiraled, Noella nodded in acceptance of his answer. "Next time, I'll give you a warning," he promised.

"Next time?" Noella scoffed. "Gods, no! Not happening. That was the first, and last time, that I will ever ride you, Kellen Kilic." Kellen's lips sprawled out in a thrilled grin, concocting a comeback on his tongue. "WITH you," she quickly added, catching her phrasing. "Ride WITH you. UGH! I'm going inside."

She marched past the twins and stomped her way into the house, slamming the door behind her.

Laya beamed at Noella's shadow. "I love her," she announced.

"Go inside," Kellen directed, noting the grin that remained pasted to Laya's lips as she skipped towards the cottage. He turned his focus to Jarion, who was still staring at the gate like he was waiting for the wards to shatter and their mother to appear. "You okay, Jare?" Jarion raised his eyes, then answered with a curt nod.

"Be nicer to Ms. Rose," he pleaded. "She's actually pretty cool." Jarion then started for the house.

*Be nicer to Ms. Rose,* Kellen repeated in his head with a scoff. *What the fuck else am I trying to do?*

*You're doing a terrible job at it,* Coz reprimanded him.

Kellen flicked his temple to send the blow down to Coz, then headed to meet his siblings and Noella inside.

As he stepped across the threshold, a sense of warmth and tranquility enveloped his senses. The interior of the cottage, ornamented with rustic wooden beams and polished stone floors, exuded an old-world allure. Soft, natural light filtered through the small, leaded glass windows, casting playful shadows on the burnished wooden furniture and cozy nooks. The heart of the cottage was the living room, bathed in sweet, heated air from the crackling fireplace, spelled by a Meteoro fire-bender to always keep a flame even when strong winds wafted into the space. An overstuffed armchair, its cushions worn and appealing, beckoned Kellen to sink into its embrace, his limbs aching for rest from that flight.

This house belonged to Valerie Dyer. She'd gifted it to Kellen after he gained custody of the twins. It had become his favorite place in all of Cavale, the only place that ever felt like home, for his roots with the twins were implanted here, freed from the burden of their trauma, no trace of their mother polluting these halls.

Kellen's eyes flew to where Noella stood at the fireplace, like finding her was the only thing that mattered. He discovered her phone pressed to her ear and a pissed-off look blighting her beauty.

"I'm with Kellen Kilic and his siblings," she told whoever was on the other end tersely. Kellen's eyes squeezed shut while he stifled a groan. *Fuck, the way she says my name.* Kellen used his heightened sense of hearing to listen to her conversation, catching the clanging male voice reply to her.

"You can't just leave campus without alerting me," Aros Cavalian's envoy snapped at her.

"There wasn't time to alert you," she protested. "We needed to get Jarion and Laya to safety as soon as possible. That's all that mattered." Noella wasn't aware that Laya and Jarion were seated on the couch, listening to her conversation as intently as Kellen was, since her back was facing them.

"I understand that's what mattered to *you*," the envoy tried to reason, his friendly tone not convincing enough to be credible, "but I've been given an order to protect you, which I cannot do if you run off without any notice. I end up getting a screaming message from my boss about how you're in danger and I should have been there. I know you don't want me around. I know you hate that I'm watching over you, but I need you to work with me here a little, Ella, for both our sakes."

Noella's expression sharpened with ire. Her back straightened. Kellen watched her arm herself with an invisible breastplate, watched her deftly craft her next words, watched her steel herself to go to war for him and his siblings.

"You know what I got from what you just said?" She spoke with a regal sense of conviction, like she was the queen and the envoy was a worthless commoner, rather than the spokesperson for the King of the Gods. "Aros Cavalian knew we were in danger and did nothing to help Kellen or the kids. He knew their mother was trying to *kill* them and just let it happen. That is all I need to know about him and his morals. I'm sorry you have to be the messenger here, Eyal, but you tell your stupid, rubbish king that he can keep his lousy protection, because I don't want it if it's coming from him. I want nothing from him or any of the Gods. Not if they refuse to do anything of value, like save three deserving people from being attacked by their own mother. Aros does absolutely nothing to stop it, but he'll go whine to you about how no one protected me when he easily could have if he really wanted to, if he already knew we were in trouble. Besides that, who gives a shit about *me* here? I'm fine. What about *them? His* people? Why isn't he protecting *them?*" Kellen's heartbeat rumbled in his ears.

The envoy—Eyal, apparently. *How the fuck does she know his name? Why is she using it so casually, like they're friends?*—didn't acknowledge anything she'd said. He acted as though she hadn't uttered a word when he demanded, "I need you to tell me where you are right now so I can come get you."

304

"Well, tough shit, cause not only do I not know where we are, but even if I did, I wouldn't tell you, or your king," Noella snarled.

Eyal yelled, "Ella, *please!* This isn't a game."

"I have *never* thought this was a game." The glow from the fire cast yellow beams onto Noella's face. She clutched her phone so hard that Kellen heard the screen start to crack in her grip. "I'm taking this more seriously than your king is! If he won't protect these people, if he won't protect *children* from the woman who abused them, then I fucking will, because someone has to. As I've said before, but no one seems to listen to me around here, if Aros genuinely cared about ensuring my safety, he'd get off his fucking ass and do it himself. I'm done being told I have to wait for answers until *he* deems me ready to hear them. I'm done accepting protection from him if he refuses to extend that protection to the people who need it most. I'm done with anything having to do with Aros Cavalian."

"*Ella—*"

"You go back to Avatia, Eyal. Your services are no longer needed at Delmarth." Noella hung up the phone with a shrill *ugh*, blowing her hair out of her face, then pinched the bridge of her nose like she was trying to keep a migraine at bay. She spun around and gasped when Jarion and Laya began applauding her.

"That was fucking awesome," Jarion laughed. The corners of Kellen's eyes stung, his throat bunged with emotion. Kellen couldn't remember the last time he'd heard his brother laugh.

Noella blushed, then gathered the ends of her black coat and spread them out like a cape, bowing before his siblings with the purest giggle to ever grace this universe. She then glanced over at Kellen.

"You know his name?" Kellen seethed, though that was the last thing he wanted to say to her. He wanted to fall to his knees before her, pledge his undying fidelity to her, tell her how sorry he was for everything, *everything*, and beg her for forgiveness. But he needed to wait until the twins went to sleep before he unraveled.

"Yeah," she replied, her tone tinged with confusion. "Why is that a big deal?"

"Envoys never share their names with subjects. With anyone.

They always maintain the title of emissary and never reveal personal information about themselves." Kellen folded his arms across his chest, fighting a smile at the way Noella's eyes tracked the movement. "He must be fond of you."

"Ew," Noella spat, her unchecked reaction causing him to lose the battle against a grin. "I just asked him for his name, and he gave it to me. It meant nothing."

"And I'm telling *you*, that's not a small thing for an envoy of Aros Cavalian. That is *not* nothing." Noella shrugged her shoulders to indicate that even if that was true, it didn't concern her.

"Do we have any food here?" Laya asked, rubbing her stomach.

"Let me check." Kellen passed by Noella, his shoulder accidentally brushing against her back on his journey to the kitchen. Copper pots and pans hung from hooks above the stove, an oak table positioned off to the side with a colorful, hand-woven tablecloth draped across the surface, surrounded by mismatched chairs. The kitchen counters were made of smooth, aged marble, displaying an array of carefully organized jars filled with homemade preserves and pickles. The shelves were lined with cookbooks, their pages stained with splatters of various ingredients. Kellen strode to the fridge, pulled at the door, and discovered it empty. He grabbed the jar of pickles off the counter and walked back to the living room, holding it up over his head. "We have pickles."

"That's it?" Laya's shoulders deflated.

"Sorry I didn't have time to go shopping," he quipped, tossing her the jar. "I can go fly into town and grab something real if you want."

"No, don't leave!" Laya screeched, waving her hands frantically at Kellen before hugging the jar to her chest. "It's not safe. Pickles are fine. I love pickles. Pickles are the best. Just don't leave."

Noella and Kellen exchanged a quick, worried look.

"You're safe here, Laya," Noella swore, lowering down to the couch to sit beside Laya and Jarion.

"I know…" Laya started, then prattled in a frenzied rush, "But what if Kellen leaves and she finds him and follows him here? What if she's still in the sky, waiting for him to think the cost is clear, and she attacks him? It's too risky for anyone to leave."

"My love," Kellen sighed. "Mom's not going to find us here. There's no way for her to retrace our path. She could be flying all over Cavale forever and she won't find us. This place is protected, so if you really want some actual food and not just pickles in a jar, I can fly to the city of Sleka and get stuff. Even if she follows me, she won't get through the wards. She can't get in here."

"I don't want you to leave, Kellen." Laya's voice resounded with fervor. The emotion she'd bottled up to focus on getting here safely was bleeding through the lid of the vessel inside her, threatening to pop the top and explode. Everyone in the room sensed how close she was to detonating and chose to handle her current state with delicacy.

"Okay. Then no one leaves." Kellen's eyes wandered to Noella. "No one leaves," he repeated to her directly.

*I can't spend the night,* Noella refused into his mind. *I wish I could, but I have Freya to take care of.*

*Then ask Josefyn if she can watch your dog for the night. I'm not flying you back to campus and leaving them here without supervision. Besides, you and I need to talk. REALLY talk.*

Noella gulped. Color stole across her cheeks. Color Kellen desperately wanted to feel under his lips.

"Is there coffee in the kitchen?" she asked, her pledge to stay lying in the underbelly of the question.

"Not sure. I can go check."

"I'll come with you," she said, gently fondling Laya's hair before rising from the sofa to follow Kellen. Noella rotated to face the twins, inquiring, "Jare? Laya? Do you guys want some coffee?"

"I'll take a cup," Jarion replied, lifting his index finger before his eyes dropped to where Laya was chewing her hair.

"Laylie?" Noella crooned, her voice extra kind, employing the nickname Kellen always called her. "You want some coffee, love?" Laya bobbed her head in a tiny nod, folding into herself deeper, hiding her face between her knees. Jarion's mouth twisted to the side, his gaze flitting to Noella, a message passing between them that Kellen didn't understand. Kellen tried to step forward, but Noella threw out her arm to hinder his route. "Give them a second," she whispered, motioning with her head for the two of them to move into the kitchen, leaving the twins alone in the living room.

Noella made a beeline for the pot of coffee on the stove.

Kellen claimed one of the stools at the counter and studied Noella drifting around the kitchen, procuring four mugs for herself, Kellen, Laya, and Jarion. He rested his chin in his palm, content to sit back and observe her existence, fully aware of what an honor it was to be in her presence after everything he'd done to her.

"Thank all the Gods in existence that you have coffee in Cavale," she said, portioning the steaming brown liquid into each mug. "I would have been devastated to have to part with caffeine for ten months."

"Most of the foods in Cavale are the same as the Earthly Plane, no?"

"Mostly the same. You guys don't have artificial flavoring, though." She lifted her right and left hands, as if weighing two heavy options. "Traded one evil for the Primordials." Kellen couldn't stop himself from laughing.

"We're not all bad," he drawled, her grey eyes burning into him.

"Not all the time," she admitted, sliding his coffee mug across the counter to him. His fingers closed around hers before she could withdraw, keeping her hand trapped beneath his on the wall of the mug. She waited for him to say something. When he didn't, when he just continued staring at her, she croaked, "What? Is there something on my face?" touching her cheek with her free hand.

"You look pretty in this lighting." Noella's mouth popped open, then sealed shut.

"I don't understand you," she muttered with a shake of her head, trying to retract her fingers from the mug, but he clamped down harder, not ready to lose the precious contact. "Kellen," she warned. "Let go."

"It feels impossible," he professed, a dark confession wrenched from his soul.

"My fingers are burning from the coffee." At that, he reluctantly slid his hand away, allowing her space to detach her fingers from the seething mug. Once her hand was free, she sighed, then decided to unroll across the counter and flip his hand over so she could begin tracing the lines etched into his palm with her index finger. With her eyes glued on the map she sketched on his hand, she murmured, "Are *you* okay? That wasn't just the twins' mother who was after us."

Kellen swallowed. *Am I okay?* he asked himself. *What does okay even mean?*

"I stopped thinking of her as my mother a long time ago." Noella's finger stroked his pulse.

"I can relate to that," she whispered. He was about to request more detail, but she quickly changed the subject by bantering, "Are you going to put some clothes on at some point?" Kellen smirked.

"I kind of need my hand for that," he told her, having no plan to ask for his hand back anytime soon.

She didn't seem inclined to give it back either. "I didn't remember you lose your clothes when you shift."

"Would you like to watch?" Noella pinned a glower over his wolfish grin. Now that he'd managed to obtain her gaze as well as her hand, he continued, "I would have liked the first time you saw me naked to not be in front of my siblings. And for you not to puke at the sight of my dick."

"I didn't puke at the sight of your dick!" she squeaked, an adorable flush bombarding her cheeks, sprinting up to consume the tips of her ears. "I was nauseous! I honestly didn't even look."

*Thank the fucking Gods for that.* "My ego appreciates your honesty. It was quite wounded back there."

"Fuck, I shouldn't have said anything then." She joked, humor and light dancing in her eyes, "I should have let you continue thinking your dick made me vomit. You need to be knocked down a few pegs."

"Too late now, sweetheart. Can't take it back." Noella wrinkled her nose at him. If it was possible, his grin grew even wider, overwhelming the entire bottom half of his face, broadening up to his ears. How was it that ten minutes ago, he'd been barreling through the sky to circumvent his mother trying to *murder* him to get to his siblings, and right now, he was gripped by sheer happiness to the point where it made his limbs feel buoyant, like they'd disintegrated into clouds?

"Guys?" Jarion called from the living room, splintering their beautiful, rare moment of peace. "How long does it take to get coffee?"

"We're coming!" Noella shouted, pulling her hand away from Kellen to wrap her fingers around the cup handles, then carried two of the mugs to the living room, leaving him stranded at the counter.

He gathered the two mugs left behind, hissing down at his erection *control yourself,* then headed back to the living room.

Noella had passed off her mugs to the twins, so Kellen had the pleasure of handing her one of his mugs, gliding his fingers across her knuckles at a slow, coquettish pace as he relinquished the cup to her. Noella curled up in the armchair that had been calling Kellen's name since he'd walked into the house, but seeing her get comfortable in his space, making herself at home when she kicked off her boots and tucked her sock-clad feet under the cushion, was more satisfying than if it was his ass in that chair.

"I'm going to run and put some clothes on," he told the twins, noting the tears and snot smearing Laya's features and Jarion's arm swathed tightly around her shoulders, their entwined fingers resting on Laya's knee. "Laylie? Jare?"

"Go change," Jarion told him, giving their sister's hand a squeeze. "We'll talk when you get back."

"Okay…?" Kellen peeked over at Noella, who looked equally as perplexed. Why did that sound so ominous? What had the two of them discussed when Noella and him were in the kitchen? "I'll be right back."

Kellen dashed into the bedroom on the lower level, which had been appointed his bedroom when they first moved in. He maneuvered around the large bed, adorned with hand-stitched quilts and plump white pillows, and grabbed the first clothes he saw in the armoire; black sweatpants and a navy blue t-shirt. He threw them on, then rushed back to the living room, where it seemed like no one had moved an inch since he'd left, the twins resembling inanimate statues on the couch.

"Someone want to tell me what the fuck's going on?" Kellen blurted too forcefully, his own concern shadowing his ability to be gentle. Laya sniffled and cleaned the snot from under her nose with the sleeve of her sweater.

"We've come to a decision about something," Jarion declared, speaking for the both of them.

"Want to clue us in on what that is?" Noella fired at Kellen a look that hissed *soften your tone.*

"We don't want to go back to Delmarth." Both Noella and Kellen's eyes widened.

"Why not?" Noella asked gently, tilting closer to them on her armchair and setting her coffee mug down on the floor.

"It's not safe!" Laya wept at the top of her lungs. Every wretched, desolate sob she exorcized pelted Kellen in the chest and ripped more air from his lungs, clogging the channel so no new oxygen could travel into him. "She can come for us so easily there. There's nothing stopping her."

"There is an entire security squad in place at the school who knows what she's done and will not allow her entry," Kellen reminded her. "You have a Headmistress there who has alarms set up on her phone to alert her if our mother is approaching campus, so she can call for me immediately. In addition to all that, you also have a big brother who would take a permanent sentencing in Terminus before he let that bitch get her hands on you. I will always be there, Laylie, and I will always get you out in time."

"It's not enough!" Laya screamed, slamming her fists into the couch pillows. "*You're* not enough!"

Laya's nails clawed at her temples like she was trying to pry the terrified thoughts out of her brain. Kellen was so used to seeing this kind of panic gush out of Jarion that it felt extra jarring to see Laya in the throes of anxiety, to see his sweet little sister's lucidity dissolve before his very eyes. He tried not to take what she said personally, repeating to himself that this was her fear speaking, not her heart.

"She will find a way anyway!" Laya continued, bawling, "She always does, and what if, next time, you can't get to us fast enough? You can't guarantee that you'll always be there, Kell. You just can't. This isn't sustainable. Please, don't make us go back there."

"I'm sorry, Laya." Kellen glanced at Noella for guidance. All she could offer was a small, tight smile of encouragement, because this was a battle he needed to fight himself. He turned back to Laya and said, with tender consideration of her turbulent state, "I'm sorry, my love, but leaving Delmarth isn't an option. You need to be in school."

"Homeschool us, then," Jarion proposed, a bite to his words as he prepared to square off with Kellen. "You're a teacher."

"And deprive you of the chance to be with kids your own age? To be *kids?*" Kellen shook his head. "No. I can't do that."

"This is you once again making choices for us rather than hearing what we're telling you," Jarion growled, flames arriving in his eyes to battle the fire Kellen knew raged within his own irises.

"I am hearing what you're saying, Jare, but I get to make these choices because *I'm* your guardian. You can hate me for it, but being at Delmarth is the best thing for you. You deserve to have the best education possible. You are safer on that campus than you would be anywhere else."

"It's safe *here.*" Laya oscillated her hand around the living room, gesticulating to all corners of the cottage. "This is the only place in Cavale that she can't enter. We're protected here. We shouldn't leave."

"So what's the plan, guys?" Kellen was struggling to keep a damper on his rage. "For the two of you to hide here for the rest of your lives? In what fucking universe do you think that I would allow you to give up living an actual life because you're so scared of what she might do?" He pressed his hand to his heart, vowing, "I've got you. I've got you guys. Why can't you trust that?"

"Why *should* we trust that?" Jarion snarled. "You couldn't stop Mom from coming for us today. She never should've been able to get that close to us. We trusted you to prevent that at least, and you failed us."

*Fuck,* that hurt his heart. Kellen's throat ached from the lump burrowing into the walls of his esophagus.

"I will live with that regret for the rest of my life, Jare, but don't for a second think I didn't do anything to try and prevent this. I've been working tirelessly with my lawyer the past few weeks since she first tried to come on campus, fighting a system that is wrapped around Miya Kilic's finger. I don't think you understand what a big fucking deal it was that I even got custody of you two. That is only thanks to the Gods' intervention, because if that decision was in the hands of the court alone, Miya would've won, with her reputation in Cavale. My every request for a restraining order has been denied. I keep requesting them, even with all the refusals. I've fucking *tried*, Jarion. I've done everything I am capable of doing. I had her officially banned from campus. Headmistress Dyer set us up with this safehouse. And when I found out she was approaching campus today, I got off my fucking ass and got you two to safety. I'm sorry what I've done isn't enough for you guys. I know you want more, but my loves, sometimes more just isn't possible."

"*Please,* Kell," Laya begged, slobbering tears onto her clasped hands. "*Please!*"

"No, Eulaylia." His tone was more stern with her than it had ever been before. The twins kept accusing him of not listening to them and their needs, but neither of them were listening to him right now. "I'm sorry, but no. You have to go back to school. You have to live your life. I will not let you stop living because you're afraid."

"Ms. Rose!" Laya turned to Noella in vain, begging, "Please, help us!" Kellen peeked over at Noella, her expression giving nothing away.

*Unless you're going to take my side here, please stay out of this,* he pleaded with her mind-to-mind.

*Can you fucking trust me, Kilic?* she snapped back, though none of the ire in her tone was evident in her facial features.

"What's the worst thing that can happen if you stay at Delmarth?" Noella asked the twins.

"She'll come for us," Jarion replied automatically.

"She's already come for you. Now, you know what will happen if she does. The security squad, Headmistress Dyer, your brother, and *I,*" she added with emphasis, pointing at Kellen and herself, "won't let any harm come to you both."

"It's not safe there!" Laya screeched.

"Safety is not something that can be guaranteed anywhere," Noella argued. "Even here. Your brother has done everything in his power to make that campus safe for you both. He's set up so many precautions to protect you from her. I understand being upset with his answer. I understand why you don't want to go back to school, and at the same time, don't minimize all the work Kellen has done to keep you safe." The acknowledgement of his sacrifices made Kellen's eyes burn. His shallow breaths scorched his chest. "Try to hear what your brother is saying to you," she continued. "He's not trying to punish you. He wants you to *live*, and you deserve to live. Both of you."

"What life is this, though?" Jarion fought back. "Picking up and running away every time she comes near us? Watching the door, waiting for Kellen to appear and tell us we need to leave at any moment's notice? It was easier to put that fear aside when she was in Terminus, but now that she's free, we carry fear with us everywhere we go that she'll come back for us. We're not truly living right now, Ms. Rose. Why would leaving school be worse then what we're already experiencing?"

"So there's nothing at school you like?" she questioned. "No friends you've made in your classes? No activities you enjoy?" Jarion and Laya fell silent, neither one of them wishing to betray their position by admitting she had a point. Noella nodded in acceptance of their silence, as though their muteness was the verbal confirmation she'd been seeking. "Your mother did terrible things to you both. No one can deny that. She and your father robbed so much from you, and she deserves to rot in Terminus for the rest of her life for it...but she doesn't get to take your life from you, too. She doesn't deserve to hold that much power over you. There is so much about what you've been through that hasn't been a choice, but both of you can choose now to acknowledge your fear, to accept that it's there, and to keep living inspite of it. I know that's not easy to do. *Believe me*, I understand."

"You don't understand, Ms. Rose," Jarion barked. "You couldn't possibly understand what we've been through."

Noella blinked at Jarion, the light Kellen was so used to seeing blaze through her eyes extinguished. She sucked in a harsh breath that whistled through her teeth, then shut her eyes so she didn't have to look at anyone. She was quiet for so long that the air crackled with tension in anticipation.

"One time, I walked into the kitchen while my mother was boiling water to make pasta," she began, squeezing her eyes shut, either to keep from giving into the temptation of looking at them, or to keep the image of whatever memory she'd dredged up in front of her. "I accidentally knocked into her, and some of the pasta spilled on the floor. She got so mad…that she proceeded to shove my face into the boiling water."

Kellen's blood ran cold. Laya's cheeks paled. Jarion's mouth fell open. Noella flinched as though she'd felt the change in their demeanor, even though she hadn't seen it with her eyes closed. She kept talking.

"Half my face was melted off. She kept me from school for a week so no one would see. The only reason she eventually took me to the doctor was because a neighbor of ours saw me and told my mother that if she didn't take me to see someone, she was going to report us." Noella opened her eyes finally to regard Jarion, whose green gaze overfilled with tears. In a sensitive, mellifluous voice, she said to him, sadness thick in her words, "I understand all too well, Jarion. I wish I didn't."

No one spoke for several minutes.

The world stopped moving. The wind perished into the quiet. The fire in the fireplace became as motionless as the rest of them. Kellen felt like his heart had been cleaved from his body and stomped on under the sadistic heel of the universe that had been so fucking cruel to the three purest people he'd ever known, the universe that had allowed them each to be touched by such ghastly trauma. He watched tears slide silently down Noella's cheeks, streams she did nothing to scrub off, letting them roll down to her chin as she held her breath, stared at the twins, and waited for someone to say something.

The first person who dared to break the silence was Jarion. "I never would have known," he whispered.

"Because I seem so put together?" Noella snorted. She blotted away the pools collecting beneath her eyes with her fingers. Staring down at the teardrops amassed on her hands, staring at them like she could see her past through each limpid droplet, she said, "I worked years to pick up every broken piece of myself and glue them back together. It took a shitload of therapy and the love of my beautiful big sister who saved my life." She peeked up at Kellen when she added softly, "Just like your brother saved yours." Kellen had to smother his hand over his mouth to fetter a sob. She then moved her gaze back to the twins. "It's been fourteen years since I've been free of my mother, and even now, I'm not completely fixed. You can have a scar on your face from your mother burning you cosmetically removed, so for anyone who doesn't know, you appear to have never been harmed. You can mend the physical reminders, but nothing can ever fully wash away the internal wounds. It's something you learn to live with. Sometimes, the broken pieces still chafe against each other, or one wiggles out of place to remind me that there's glue there, why I needed the glue to begin with. I'm not going to sit here and sell a dream to you where you'll never think about it or feel that pain again, because that's not real. That's not life. That's not what healing is."

"How do you do it?" Laya mewled, tears speeding down her face. "How do you live with it?"

"I made a choice a long time ago that I would put myself first," she answered, her strength carrying into her clear tone of voice, overpowering the sorrow that lingered under the surface. "I decided that my right to live, my right to happiness, mattered more than what she'd done to me or what she thought of me. I deserved more, and the only person who could give me that was myself."

Noella tipped forward and grabbed Laya and Jarion's hands. The twins gazed at her with the same heady veneration that Kellen regarded her with, the three of them hanging on to her every word.

"Healing isn't forgetting," she proclaimed, squeezing their hands. "Healing is being able to remember, to look back at what you've been through and see how far you've come. Your brother is right. The two of you have come too far to give up now. Go back to school. Live your lives. Accept your dragons. Figure out what happiness looks like for you. Yes, your mother's not going anywhere. Yes, you have every reason to fear her, and you also have every reason to trust your brother to keep you safe, as he's done numerous times before and especially today. You have every reason to trust that there's more life for you to experience that could be so much greater than what you've experienced before. We cannot allow the people who have hurt us, who have taken things from us, to take anything more. You mother has taken enough from you guys. Let the cycle end here, and let that be a choice you're making for no one's benefit but your own."

Laya fell off the couch and crawled across the floor to enter Noella's open arms, burying her face in Noella's shoulder while expelling raw, tortured sobs from deep in her soul. Noella swaddled Laya with one arm and extended the other to Jarion, cupping his cheek and cleaning his tears with her thumb.

Kellen gazed at her embracing his siblings with a face covered in tears. He couldn't look away. He didn't know how he had the willpower to ever not look at her. She wasn't looking back—her eyes remained locked on his brother, on the quiet, painful understanding they were sharing.

Noella twisted her head to the side, her gaze searching the furniture before landing, crashing, into Kellen.

In the depths of her eyes, in the warmth of her tiny smile, he discovered his purpose.

When Noella Rose first arrived in Cavale, Kellen was certain she'd been brought to Delmarth to be the living embodiment of Terminus for him. Her presence could only be described as a penalization for all the Primordials who failed to help that student last year who'd taken their life. Staring into her eyes now, he recognized that she was the complete opposite of that, at least for him.

She was no penalty.

She hadn't come here to punish or plague them. She'd come here to be a savior for these kids, for the twins, for *him*.

She'd come to Cavale to help them all heal, to show them how, to give them permission to let go.

What do you give to the person who sacrifices everything of themselves for everyone around them? Who doles out kindness like its candy? What do you give to the people who spent so many years being made to feel small and unimportant by the person who was supposed to champion them most?

You make it your personal mission to protect the heart they wear openly on their sleeve. You let no one touch them again, and anyone who tries doesn't make it to see tomorrow. You put them on your shoulders and make them feel so tall that they believe they tower over the whole world.

He'd been that for the twins. They might not have always recognized it, but that had been his most important role, which he'd taken on willingly and proudly. He felt it now, deep in his bones.

It was his destiny to be that for Noella too.

He couldn't explain it, but the certainty left him winded. He was meant to be that person for her. She was meant to be that person for him. Why else would the Gods have placed such a dazzling angel in his path, filled with sass and fire that reminded him of his own, but so much kinder, who'd lived through such similar trauma to his siblings? Someone so perfectly suited for him, even if he wasn't worthy of her?

If she was put in his life to be his refuge, if she was put in his life to help heal his siblings and heal him in turn, then he would make damned sure he gave her everything of him and then some to make up for what she'd given him. He'd make it worth it, because there was suddenly nothing more important than proving himself to her, proving to the Gods that they'd made the right choice in bringing her to him.

No more fucking around. No more fighting his feelings. No more pushing her away or treating her like crap.

Into her mind, not that she fully understood yet—but he would make sure she did—he whispered, *No more, Noella Rose.*

And even though she didn't comprehend what he meant by that, didn't grasp the full weight of that declaration, she said it back, making him even more confident in his epiphany that she was a blessing to him.

*No more, Kellen Kilic.*

318

# CHAPTER 24
# ELLA

Laya had requested that Ella tuck her and Jarion into bed. Before heading upstairs, Laya quietly scurried over to Kellen and folded her arms around his waist, burrowing her cheek in his stomach.

"I'm sorry, Kell," she whispered. Kellen enveloped her in a tight embrace.

"Nothing to apologize for, my love." He kissed the top of her head, then looked up to find Jarion slowly approaching.

"I'm sorry too," Jarion murmured, which was a far more necessary and meaningful declaration than the one Laya had uttered.

Kellen lifted one arm off Laya to yank Jarion into their hug. He buried his nose in Jarion's curls.

"I fucking love you both," he croaked, tears gleaned on his lashes. He crushed them together without even realizing, though neither of the twins seemed to mind, finding the closeness consoling after such a harrowing evening.

When he felt ready, Kellen relinquished them to Ella, literally passing his siblings into her arms, where he trusted they would be safe.

"I'll be down soon," she promised him, spinning around to escape the intense way he'd been gaping at her, like he was trying to strip her jacket off with his eyes so he could stare into her soul.

Ella loitered at the doorframe of their bedroom as Jarion and Laya got ready for bed. All Jare needed was to throw on a hoodie and a pair of sweats, but Laya spent intimate time washing her face in the bathroom, strutting out in a matching pink button down and pajama bottoms that had white polka dots speckled across the fabric. By the time Laya crawled into bed, Jarion had already fallen asleep.

Ella took a seat at the foot of Laya's bed and helped drape her comforter over her curled-up body.

"Thank you, Ms. Rose. Not just for this." Ella cocked her head.

"For what else?" Laya gulped.

"For telling us about your mom." Ella sucked in a harsh breath. She hadn't intended to tell the twins, especially Kellen, about her mother, but in the moment, it had felt like a vital instance for self-disclosure. That was further confirmed when Laya said, "It helped me…to hear that you really understood."

"Oh, sweet girl," Ella sobbed, cupping the side of Laya's face, smudging Laya's tears with her thumb. Choking back her own tears, she whispered, "I wish I didn't understand." Laya gave the hand Ella had on her cheek a squeeze.

"I wish you didn't either," she whimpered.

"Gods, you are so beyond your years. You have the heart and mind of a forty-year-old. I mean that as the biggest compliment." Laya giggled, resting her head on her pillow. She called out to Ella before she successfully exited the room.

"Ms. Rose?"

"Yeah, Lay?" Even in the dark, Ella felt Laya's adoration seep out from her soft stare, shelling her in the face.

"I know he makes it difficult sometimes…but Kellen is someone worth loving." Ella blinked in surprise. "Just some food for thought," Laya tossed over her shoulder before she rolled her body away from Ella.

She descended the staircase in a purposefully slow manner, dragging out the time between now and when she would reencounter Kellen. As she grew closer, Ella's heart started to race, drumming a brutal tempo in her ears, and her palms dripped with perspiration. To her surprise, he wasn't in the living room or the kitchen. She forced her feet to move to the bedroom, where she found him waiting on the bed, long limbs sprawled out atop the eiderdown quilt, back propped against the headboard. His eyes flew to her the moment the door creaked from her weight leaning against it.

"Hi," he said in greeting, in a voice analogous to silk.

"Hi," she answered in a more gawkish manner, her hands weirdly shaking. She busied them with removing her coat, folding it into a square to rest on the wardrobe. Kellen's eyes stalked her every movement.

"Do you want to talk about it?" he asked. For some reason she didn't understand, this made her irrationally angry.

"Talk about *what*, Kellen?" Ella snapped, turning on him. "Talk about how my mother used to beat me? How she was so drunk most nights that she didn't even know what she was hitting me with? That she once shoved me down the flight of stairs in our apartment building because I asked her why she didn't hug me like all the other moms with their children? That in a drunk stupor, she beat me with a broom so hard she cracked my skull open, and if my sister hadn't walked into our apartment at the exact moment my mother was folding me into a cardboard box to toss me in the trash, because she thought she killed me, she might've thrown me in the dumpster and I would've *died?* Is *that* what you want me to talk about?" Kellen, for the first time since Ella had known him, was stunned into silence.

"I meant talk about *us,*" he murmured. Horror bashed Ella in the gut, clouting her to her knees.

"Oh, *fuck*," she sobbed into her hands. Kellen crawled across the bed to meet her on the floor.

"Noella," he gasped, pulling her into his lap, burying his face in the crook of her shoulder, stroking the back of her head as her fingers curved around his biceps and she wept violently into his shoulder. "Oh, baby. I'm so fucking sorry. Fuck." Her cries bled into dry heaves, scraping painfully through her throat. He swept her hair to the side, his lips brushing her ear, and whispered, "It's okay to feel it. To not always have perfect words. You give so much of yourself to making sure others are okay. It's okay to not be okay sometimes. You can be not okay with me."

She clung to him harder.

His fingers threaded in her hair, framing her cheeks so he could gently guide her face back. Her eyes crawled up his chest to snag with his, green and grey crashing together in kaleidoscopic wonder.

"I have so many things I want to say to you." He kept his voice low in case the twins were straining to listen. "So many things, but I'll start with two words that hold a great deal of meaning. Two words I should've said a long time ago. I'm sorry." Ella heaved a gasp. "I'm sorry, Noella, for everything. For the way I've spoken to you. Spoken about you. All the times I threw you into walls. For threatening to kill you more the once. For the pool. For not warning you today when I took off or when I dropped you. For not recognizing sooner how essential, how kind, how wonderful you are. So sorry, sweetheart."

Ella could have kissed him.

She thought about it. She was close enough. His breath tasted like burned marshmallows. But there was so much more to say, to see, more to understand, before she felt ready for that, before she could fully lay down her arms. Receiving the words she'd longed to hear was refreshing, but once she had them, she realized they weren't enough—the words would mean nothing without action to follow.

"Thank you," she whispered, then retreated from his lap, scooting back on her knees to create distance between them.

"I should be the one thanking you," he said, not seeming to mind the fact that she'd separated herself, or privately minding a great deal and expunging all his efforts towards masking it for her benefit. "For what you said to the twins. For all you've done for them. For coming with me today. For tolerating me when I'm a fucking dickhead. The list could go on forever, really."

"You don't make it easy." His shoulders sunk with regret.

"I know. I'm sorry. I want to be better. I want to treat you the way you deserve to be treated. I will give everything to prove to you how much I want you, even if all you can give me in return is just a morsel of your time. If there's only a small space for me in your life,

I'll make myself small to fit. Even if all you can offer is friendship, I'll take it. Whatever allows me to be near you."

Ella sat stunned by the fervor of this declaration, by the groundswell of emotion that gushed out of him, almost palpably slapping her in the face. "Since when have you felt this way about me?"

"It's been brewing for a while now, but it solidified the last few days, since you saved Jarion from his dragon. I'm in awe of you, Noella Rose. I'm in complete fucking awe of you, of your mind, your heart, your courage, the way you are with my siblings, how you've gotten them to open up, fucking everything. I know I need to work for this. I don't expect you to hear all this and forgive me that easily. I don't want this to be easy, because nothing worth having is easy." Kellen sloped forward and set his hands on either side of her, his face hovering over hers. All Ella could do was lean back and bear the brunt of his ardor. "I want to *earn* you, Noella. I want to deserve the honor of calling you mine."

Kellen tipped down and gently, lovingly, devotedly, kissed away the tears gathered on her cheeks. He trailed kisses up from her temple to her forehead, and she didn't stop him, her fingers fisting his shirt.

"You would be okay with just being my friend for now, until I feel ready to trust in us being more?"

"Yes," he swore. "Whatever it takes. Whatever you want. Whatever you can give is more than enough. I'll give you anything if you just ask for it, Noella."

Ella blinked. "And if I ask for a star?" she quipped, not expecting a real answer.

"I'll shred the galaxies apart to find you the biggest one," he responded without hesitation.

Ella was knocked breathless. There wasn't a shadow of doubt in her mind that he meant every word, that if she genuinely asked, he would find a way to rip the sky in half and secure for her a chunk of the constellations.

"I have an easy capacity to love others," she found herself telling him. "Believing they love me in return doesn't come as easily." He didn't need to ask why—he now knew where that insecurity stemmed from.

"Let me prove myself to you, Noella Rose. Make me work for it. Give me your worst, so I can give you my best." Kellen extended his hand out to her, like this was a business proposition he'd tendered to her.

Ella sputtered a strangled laugh, then slipped her hand into his. When she tried to pull it back, he gripped her tighter with a naughty, handsome grin. She narrowed her eyes at the unfair brandishing of his dimples.

"Can I have my hand back, please?" Kellen's fingers fell away. "So he *does* know now to listen," she jested, rising off the floor and smearing her tears with the end of her sleeve. Kellen stood with her.

"You can say no…but it would make me the happiest bastard alive if you slept in here with me tonight."

Ella's eyes grew to the size of saucers. "In here?" she stammered. "With…you?"

"Platonically, of course." There was nothing platonic about the way he looked at her, about the way her heart somersaulted in her chest, vibrating against her ribcage while screaming at her to eliminate the space between them.

"I don't think you know what platonic means," she mocked, but surprised even herself when she climbed onto the bed and situated her back against the headboard. Kellen didn't rush to immediately follow her. "What're you doing?" she asked when he lingered a few feet away with a reverent glow in his eye.

"Taking a mental picture," he answered, Ella's cheeks burning.

"For your spank bank?" Kellen tipped his head back with a gorgeous laugh before he finally crawled onto the bed to meet her. Ella braced herself for him to climb on top of her, but instead, he maintained a respectful distance by simply sitting beside her, only their shoulders connected by touch.

"I have a question for you," he announced when he'd gotten comfortable.

"One I possibly have an answer to, depending on the question," she joked, beaming at his pretend scowl.

"What do you dream about?" The corners of his lips twitched before he tossed in, "Besides me."

"Besides you," she giggled with an eye roll, hugging her knees to her chest. "What do I dream about? My father, actually. Ever since I've been in Cavale, I dream about him every night. Aside from that one night with you."

Kellen lifted a lock of her hair to twist around his finger. "Tell me about him. Your dad." Ella gulped.

"I can't," she whispered. "I don't know anything about him, not really. He left when I was five. Just took off in the middle of the night. My mom never recovered from the loss of him. I have my mother's eyes, but the rest of my features are all my dad's. She couldn't separate me from him. She couldn't look at me without seeing him. She couldn't love me because she hated him so much for leaving. I was the closest thing she had to him, so she took all her anger at him out on me. I was the substitute, but I didn't play the part right, which only made her hate me more."

Kellen's expression darkened. "How old were you? The night…" He didn't finish the sentence.

"Twelve," she answered. "Rylee, my sister, was eighteen. A freshman in college. We didn't have any other family apart from our mom…Rylee has a different dad than me, but he died from cancer when she was a baby, so he wasn't in the picture…which left Rylee to become my legal guardian. She didn't even hesitate. Adopting me was never not an option for her. She gave up so much to take care of me. She's the only person I consider to be my parent. I've never considered Annalise to be my mom."

"She does not deserve the privilege of that title," Kellen proclaimed. Ella's lashes fluttered. "Neither does your father for abandoning you. They don't deserve any credit for the person you've become."

Ella found her body shifting to face him, keening to be closer. Her hand inched towards his, her fingers falling through the spaces between his fingers before she asked, "What about *your* dad?"

What she knew about Kellen's father, she'd learned second-hand from Jarion during one of their sessions. She wanted to learn everything from his mouth, delivered in his voice with his words, with his emotion attached to it.

"He died when I was sixteen," Kellen answered, his tone of voice bland, lacking any flavor. He sounded removed from the thought of his father, like he hadn't considered him in years. "He was quiet. Submissive. He had no issue letting Miya lead. A man of very few words, content to blend into the background. Quite unimpressive. He took Miya's last name because in Cavale, you claim the name of the stronger bloodline, and the Kilic line is the strongest dragon-shifter lineage in the kingdom. Miya never intended for the marriage to last. She was just biding her time with him until she found her Cavalisha."

"Why did she marry him if he wasn't her mate?"

"In the Kilic dynasty, they don't care about Cavalishas." Kellen unconsciously squeezed her hand at the word *Cavalisha*. "Miya's father wanted her to marry for profit, not love. My father, Nerian, may've been a dud, but he came from a Cerebri family with a shitload of wealth. He had three brothers, and Miya got to pick between them who she wished to wed. She chose my father. No one understood why, but it's always made sense to me. She married the safe option, someone who would never dare to outshine her. Someone without ambition of their own who would view marrying her as their greatest accomplishment. Someone no one would miss when they eventually disappeared."

Ella dissected his facial features for any hint of emotion.

All she could garner was long-standing disappointment and acceptance of his father's limitation.

"How did he die?" she dared herself to probe.

"In his sleep. They told me at the time it was a heart attack, but I was given no proof of that by any doctor. Miya killed him. I feel it in my bones. In my soul. She wanted Nerian out of the picture so she could marry Ciaran, her true Cavalisha." Kellen rested the back of his head against the wall. "I think the only reason she had me was to keep her ties to Nerian's family. Without me, if Nerian died, she would preserve no claim to any of their wealth. I'm supposed to inherit a large sum of money in two years, when I reach the age of thirty, but I suspect she has plans to ensure I never see a dime of it. I

326

don't give two shits if I do or don't. I don't care about the fucking money. She can have all of it if she promises to stay away from the twins forever." Warmth swarmed Ella's chest. His love and devotion to his siblings would never not leave her weak in the knees.

"That's very noble of you." Her thumb stroked his knuckles.

"Maybe I should offer it to her," he joked with a bitter laugh, which blended into a heavy sigh, followed by a soft, tormented groan.

"What're you thinking about?" she mumbled, noting the frown wilting the corners of his perfect mouth.

"The night I got Jarion and Laya out." Kellen's tone was teeming with anguish. "I'd been reading Jarion and Laya's thoughts. I typically try to stay out of their heads, but during that time, it was the only insight into the house I got. My mother wouldn't let me see them, so all I could do was hover above the estate, cloaking myself in the clouds, and read their thoughts from above to check on them. I heard Jarion..." Kellen swallowed. "I heard Jarion think to himself, *she's going to die. She's going to die if no one gets her help.*" His gaze glassed over, haunted by the memory, plagued by the sound of Jarion's voice echoing in his ears, thrusting him back to that night. "I couldn't..." He looked over at Ella, his fingers clawing at his chest. "There was nothing in here anymore," he told her, patting his chest, where his heart was. "Everything of me belongs to those two, so the thought of losing one of them...I didn't think. I flew with every ounce of my strength pushing me the fastest I've ever gone right to Avatia, where I slammed my tail into the gate until the Gods finally sent someone down to speak to me, intending to send me away. I told the envoy, 'If someone doesn't send aid to my mother's home and get my siblings out of there, I will rain fire down on the entirety of Cavale. I will rip this world to scraps and dance over the remains of your precious people, over the ashes of the golden empire you've placed above the welfare of your citizens. If you don't help me save my siblings, the Sireres and Edar Lantarian will be the least of your problems.'"

Kellen chuckled to himself, the sound infectious, making it hard for Ella to fight a smile in return.

"A fucking reckless idiot I was," he chortled, "but somehow, instead of landing myself in Terminus, I got through to them. They sent the Avatia army through the gate, and they followed me back to my mother's house in Yorkdill. They arrested my mother, and Ciaran, on sight. They saved my sister."

"*You* saved your sister," Ella corrected. "Don't give the Gods that credit. *You* protected them." She caught his chin when he tried to dip his head, then breathed, "I know they seem angry, but Jarion and Laya feel so lucky to have a brother like you. A brother who would go to war for them. You want to know how I know that?" Kellen bobbed his head in a nod. "Because I have a sister who would go to war for me. Who *did* go to war for me. Who rescued me from a terrible situation exactly like Jarion and Laya. So I know from personal experience that Jarion and Laya, whether they say it or not, are forever indebted to you. That's not a small thing, Kellen. That's the whole fucking world." Ella wondered if anyone had ever drowned in someone's gaze before.

"You're a beautiful person, Noella Rose," Kellen declared, cradling the side of her face in his palm.

"You think so?" she whispered in a barely audible voice. He nodded and began tracing her bottom lip with his thumb, sliding his finger back and forth over the plump skin. "Then why haven't you treated me like you think so?"

Kellen's finger skated off her face. He shut his eyes. Ella waited patiently for him to reopen them, to clue her in to the thoughts barreling through his head. She didn't know how to wield the connection between their minds to hear his thoughts, so she had to rely on him sharing them willingly.

"I don't have much experience with kindness," he told her when he finally opened his eyes and looked at her again, marshaling his thoughts into an order that made sense. "Kindness was nonexistent in the home I grew up in. Miya wasn't abusive to me the way she was to the twins, but she was neglectful. My father kept to himself, so I didn't have much guidance in my life. I was very isolated. When kindness did appear in my life, it was conditional and attached to a bunch of strings. I don't understand how someone can offer it unconditionally and mean it. When I don't understand something, it makes me angry. That's an emotion I'm more comfortable feeling, so I latch onto it."

Ella took a moment to process his meaning. "So you get angry with me because you don't understand me?"

"Exactly. I don't understand how you can be so *good* all the time. It doesn't make sense to me. I spend an inexorable amount of time trying to figure it out, and that makes me angrier, that so much space in my head is taken up by the thought of you. I've felt like I've been going mad the past few months."

"You think about me, Kilic?" she whispered, unsure if he even realized what he just admitted.

"All the time," he confessed, his gaze scorching through her skull, like he was trying to drill a hole into her forehead to mark her permanently. "It never ends. I don't want it to end." Ella's breaths turned labored. As Kellen trickled the tips of his fingers down her face, he whispered, "You remind me of a painted masterpiece that could drive the artist insane with the realization they will never accomplish anything as perfect as you again." Ella struggled to remember how to breathe.

"That doesn't sound very platonic," she blurted in a nervous rush. Kellen's lips settled into a subdued smile.

"I'm trying, sweetheart," he chuckled, his laugh more hoarse, garroted by the desire he'd been actively shoving down, "but now *you're* making things difficult with the way you're looking at me."

"How am I looking at you?"

"Like you want to rip my clothes off. Not that I would mind if you did," he added, bumping the tip of his nose against hers. "I'd frame the scraps of clothing on my wall." Ella squinted her eyes in an artificial glower.

"I'll leave if you can't control yourself."

"Don't go. I can be good." Kellen scooted away from her as further evidence, gliding under the duvet and pulling the comforter up to his chin to completely shroud himself, only his head poking out.

*Why are you fighting this?* the female voice that both sounded like her and also didn't chastised her.

*Yes, why ARE you fighting this, Noella?* Kellen agreed with the voice.

"I'm going to sleep," Ella announced, crimping her legs into her stomach and rolling onto her side so she was no longer facing him. She stretched across the mattress and flicked the lamp switch off, bathing the room in darkness.

"Goodnight, Rose," Kellen whispered affectionately into the ether. His eyes sketched lines down her back.

"Goodnight, Kilic," she murmured, then closed her eyes and drifted off into a heavy slumber.

Ella awoke in the middle on the night still coiled atop the comforter, though her body had rotated in her sleep so she now faced Kellen. His succulent lashes fanned out over soft cheeks, drawing strips of shadow onto the dark brown flesh. He looked so beautiful lost in slumber, so serene, so innocent.

How was this the same man who just a few weeks ago had tried to drown her in a pool? She'd clearly misplaced her morals, but for the time being, she didn't really care to go looking for them. Her mind had made peace with the fact that she'd been wrong about Kellen, now finally aligning with her heart's desire. She'd spent the past twenty-six years seeking a home, searching for a safety net beyond what her sister offered. Lying in this bed with him was the closest she'd ever gotten to the feeling she always envisioned finding. Maybe this right here was where she was always meant to be.

Did that feeling fucking terrify her?

Absolutely. Would she let that fear control her? She would try not to, for no one's sake but her own.

Ella sunk her teeth into her fingers to keep them from stretching out to touch him, then slid off the bed and scuttled to the bathroom. She stripped off her clothes, leaving them in a crumpled pile by the toilet, and climbed into the shower, closing the glass door behind her and twisting the valve to warm. She'd just stepped under the deluge when suddenly, the door to the bathroom opened.

"Rose, what're you—" Kellen froze at the threshold.

The glass door hadn't yet fogged up from the tepid water, so nothing of her naked frame was covered from his vision. She did nothing to conceal her body from him, squaring her shoulders instead. Fire erupted in his irises, replacing his pupils with diminutive, boiling flames. Neither of them moved for several minutes, the air moistening around them, spirals of humid mist twirling within the ether.

"Tell me to go," Kellen demanded, his voice akin to minced gravel from how rasping it sounded.

"What?" Ella spluttered in a wheezy gasp.

"Tell me to leave this room right now, and I will go. If you don't, I'm joining you in that shower, and you can't stop me. You have ten seconds, Noella."

Producing words took her longer than it usually did, her brain muddled by the heat and his penetrating stare.

"Ten," he began the countdown, his chest rising and falling at a rapid pace. "Nine. Eight. Seven—"

*Stop fighting this, Noella,* that older, feminine voice pleaded with her.

"Join me," Ella pronounced, cutting through his succession. Kellen's eyes almost fell out of his skull.

"You're sure?" He needed to hear her say it.

"Yes. I'm sure." He wasted no more time after that.

Kellen kept her gaze as he grabbed the back of his shirt and yanked it over his head, revealing his sharply demarcated network of abs. He moved slowly, watching her facial cues to determine if he should keep going or stop. Her breaths came out as deep, burning pants when she watched him pull his pants and boxers down to the floor, then straighten back up, revealing himself in full.

*Holy shit,* she gasped in her head.

"Wow," she blurted out, in a trance. He was perfect. Composed of taut sinew, immaculate brown skin, and an impressive cock, you couldn't find a single physical flaw on that man.

He was the Gods' gift to women. The Gods' gift to *her.*

"I'm worth a wow," Kellen taunted, but his grin was filled with affection more than humor.

Ella opened the door to the shower to welcome him in. It was quite cramped with the two of them inside, which had them pressing up against each other, his hands on either side of her head as she leaned against the wall, the downpour torrenting over both of them. It turned his black curls into sopping ringlets adorned across his forehead like tufts at the end of a blanket, his hand lifting to brush the tendrils back. A second later, Kellen's breath feathered over her face before he tipped her chin up and consumed her in a kiss, devouring her soul along with her mouth.

Ella never knew it was possible to make love to someone with just your mouth, but Kellen was proving her wrong. She coiled her fingers in his hair and stood on the tips of her toes to twist around him, wishing she could curl into him, could melt their skin together so they'd never disconnect. His hands slithered to her waist, then glided up her back, splaying out over her spine and wrenching her even closer. Desire thrummed aggressively through her veins, especially when he nipped at her lower lip, then soothed the ache he'd left in his wake with his tongue.

"Gods, your surrender tastes like heaven, sweetheart," he groaned into her mouth. His hand crawled its way up her thigh to reach the juncture of her thighs, where he slipped his middle and index finger inside her at once, his thumb applying individualized consideration to her clit.

"Who said I've surrendered anything?" Ella reached her hand out and grabbed his erection.

"*Fuck*," Kellen hissed, tipping his head back. "Noella. *Yes.* Please."

"What was that?" She began to stroke him from the base of his cock to the top, her grip light, careful not to squeeze too tightly. She dragged her tongue up the column of his throat to reach his ear. "That sounded awfully like surrender to me." When Kellen's thumb massaged her clit with more friction, the two fingers inside her sliding in and out at a devious tempo in answer to her challenge, her knees buckled.

"Fuck," Kellen growled, unable to maintain eye contact, his lashes trembling across his cheeks when he screwed his eyes shut. "You win. You win, Noella. I surrender everything to you. Every fucking piece of me."

"Oh yeah?" Ella tugged down on his earlobe. She enjoyed being in control like this, the dominance almost hallucinogenic. "Prove it." Kellen spluttered a strangled moan, then slammed his mouth into hers.

Drowning in his kiss, Ella accepted that she was no longer in control.

Their tongues wrestled for dominance, her hips propelling closer to his hand between her legs while his hips rocked forward so his cock thrust further into her palm, their movements frenzied and synchronized. Her orgasm slammed into her suddenly, annexing her entire being, her body quaking as she came again and again and again, the undulation never-ending. Ella swirled the pad of her thumb over the tip of his cock when she sensed him approaching an orgasm, drawing out his climax.

"Holy fucking shit, Noella," he gasped, then let go and yielded to her.

Kellen spasmed in her hand before he loosed a rasping cry, falling into the vortex of her orgasm.

*Noella?* a voice hummed from a remote plane.

It sounded like Kellen. It *was* Kellen, the real Kellen, not the Kellen in her dream who was kissing her neck.

*Noella, wake up.* Ella jolted upright with a startled gasp, nearly tumbling off the bed.

"Hey, it's okay," Kellen assured her, extending his hands to touch her shoulders, but she sprung away from him without thought. She could hear her heartbeat thundering, its frenetic beat echoing with his.

"You saw that?" she stammered, trying to get control of her stupid heart and the ache that lingered between her legs.

"Yeah. I did." Kellen's tone was tight, curbing his desire because ensuring her well-being was more important.

"Was that my dream, or yours?" she asked.

"I honestly have no clue. Could've been either one of us." He scratched the back of his neck. Ella's eyes descended over the balled-up quilt on the floor, where she found evidence of his arousal within the crumpled folds. She pressed her thighs together to soothe

the throbbing. "We need to get this mind connection under control," he declared.

"We?" Ella spluttered, then accused, "It's *your* fault! Just take back the power you left in my head, and we'll be good to go."

Kellen blanched. "What the fuck are you talking about?" he exclaimed. "What power in your head?"

"A couple of days ago, I asked Akio to put up a wall in my mind to block you from entering."

"You *what?*" he snarled, plumes of smoke dripping from the sides of his mouth.

"It was after the first dream. Akio said he found…tendrils of your power lingering in my head. That must be what's keeping our minds connected like this, why your dragon is able to speak to me. Akio assumed you left your power there so you could see into my head whenever you wanted."

"Absolutely not," Kellen refused. "Yeah, I might've peeked a few times into your thoughts when you first got here, but I never left any piece of my power in your head to create a permanent door." Kellen edged closer to her, squinting his eyes as if he were trying to see into her mind. Maybe he *was* seeing into her mind. "Akio said there were pieces of my power in your head? *Mine?*" Ella nodded. "That's fucking weird. It must be why I hear your voice in my head all the time."

"Wait." She moved back. "You hear my voice in your head even when I'm not speaking to you?" Kellen hesitated, leading her to believe he hadn't meant to admit that. "What does the voice sound like?"

"It sounds like you…" He paused a moment, then amended, "but also—"

"Doesn't?" she guessed. Kellen nodded. "I've heard that voice before too. Me, but older sounding." She'd heard it twice tonight, both times pushing her towards Kellen. "What do you think that voice is?"

"I don't know. Maybe your subconscious?"

"Do people usually have different voices for their subconscious?"

"How the fuck would I know? I don't usually go looking into

someone's mind and accidentally create a conduit between my brain and theirs." Ella dropped her chin between her knees.

"You've never heard of something like this happening?"

"No." Kellen crossed his arms. "Never." She sensed he had hypotheses brewing in his mind about what could be causing this.

"What do you *think* it means?"

"I really don't know, Rose." She didn't believe that. She wished she knew how to use their conduit to see into his mind. She wished she wasn't the human at the other end of this bargain, so she could manipulate this power and give him a taste of his own medicine by reading his thoughts for a change.

"Well, until we figure this out or until I feel ready, I don't think it's safe for us to share a bed."

Ella hopped off the side of the mattress. "Wait, you're leaving?" Kellen pleaded, "Don't go, Noella."

"I'm going to sleep on the couch."

"Rose——"

"Goodnight, Kilic." Ella shut the door to the sound of Kellen growling *fuck me* into his pillow.

## CHAPTER 25

# ELLA

OCTOBER FADED INTO NOVEMBER, bringing winter to the forefront of the kingdom. Ella had finally gotten into a structured groove with the three students she counseled regularly, Jarion, Laya, and Jamie. She wouldn't necessarily say the hatred of her had died down, since none of the Primordials were shy about flinging their negative opinions at her, but her colleagues had begun to call for her in moments of genuine need, learning to put their dislike of her aside because they recognized she was good at her job and the kids needed her. She spent all her free time, which was limited during the school day due to the amount of crises she managed, strengthening her bonds with Akio, Josefyn, and now Kellen.

Kellen and Ella had fallen into a strange limbo the last three weeks of being friends who were also more. Friends who did nothing to hide their yearning for one another, evident in every flirtatious barb exchanged, in every brush of their hands, in the way their bodies always seemed to incline closer to one another in a group. Every cell in her being pushed her towards him like an intoxicating flux of energy was shunting invisible hands into her back, too powerful to resist. He'd upheld his end of the bargain and had been a perfect gentleman towards her the past few weeks. Kellen came with her on all her morning and night walks with Freya, even though it was clear he couldn't stand her dog, for reasons she didn't entirely understand, but she recognized that this was his way of trying to ingratiate himself in her life, to push past his personal feelings to embrace hers.

He'd gotten in the habit at random points during the day of dropping facts about himself in her head, just to keep the line of communication between them alive, answering all the silent questions she had about him.

*My favorite color? Purple,* he casually told her while she was in the middle of helping Oken during another rage spiral. While she worked to calm the strength-wielder's breathing, Kellen prattled, *If you asked me three months ago, I would've said green. But it's been purple since the day you wore that sweater. My second favorite would be a caramel shade of blonde. The color of honey. The color of your hair.*

*I don't really have hobbies,* he shared another day, when she'd been at her desk working on a distress tolerance lesson for the elementary school students. *I guess flying could be considered a hobby. I love flying. I much prefer it to walking. There's no encumbrance from the people below in the sky, nothing to hinder your path or trample your thoughts. The only thing I have to worry about up there is following the pattern of the clouds laid before me. There's liberation in that too—in not having space to think about anything else. It's the only time when my mind truly quiets down.*

*Ever since I found out that my dragon form is a completely different person from myself, I don't know how to view my body,* he confessed one night when Kellen, Akio, and Josefyn had come to Ella's apartment for dinner. They were sitting around Ella's coffee table, sharing a pizza, and he'd just declared this in her head, while Josefyn had been telling a funny story about one of her students. Ella's eyes found his across the room as he vented, *Knowing what I know now about the Varminia curse, it's hard not to view my body as Coz's prison. My body doesn't feel like how I think a true form should feel. It doesn't feel like home in here. Whatever configuration I take, I never feel fully settled. When I'm in my dragon form, I long to stretch my legs. When I'm in my humanoid form, I ache for my wings. Both skins feel wrong around my bones. I'm not sure what to make of that.* Ella soaked up all the knowledge with reverence and care.

She folded every piece of information he'd willingly imparted, all the little details he'd never shared with anyone before her, and placed them with delicacy into a box in her head labeled *essential.* With every new thing she learned, it became harder and harder to battle the attraction towards him, to resist that weird female voice in her head, who'd grown so confident at this point that she screeched openly in Ella's ears about what an idiot she was for denying herself Kellen.

She'd given herself, and him—not that she'd shared this with him—a deadline: four weeks for him to prove himself to her, to prove how sorry he was for the way he'd behaved and change his behavior. As they were now encroaching the end of that deadline, she found it impossible to think about anything but what it would be like to fully surrender to her heart's desire.

"Ms. Rose. Why are we painting our nails?" Jamie asked Ella during their session. The Primordial's blue hair swayed at the top of her skull when she cocked her head to the side, the tendrils crumpled into a shambolic ball and held together by a weak hair tie.

"Tell me what A stands for in the ABC Please skill," Ella entreated, blowing on her fingernails to help dry the wine-red polish.

"Accumulate positive emotions by doing things that are pleasant," Jamie recited from her homework. Her eyebrows furrowed in concentration over the tiny brush she slid over her pinky nail to coat the surface in white gloss.

"Good." Ella's chest warmed with pride. "The ABC Please skill is about taking care of ourselves so we can take care of others. Finding activities that force us to focus on ourselves helps us to better understand what we feel and need. It's called self-care. This is what *I* like to do for self-care." Ella fluttered her painted fingers under Jamie's nose. Jamie giggled and swatted Ella's hand away, careful not to smudge any of Ella's handiwork. "After this session, I want you to try different self-care activities that are personal to you. Could be listening to music. Could be going on a walk. Could be shifting into your snake-form. Whatever gives you the space to focus on yourself for a little. I want you to keep a list of different activities you try and whether you find them helpful or not."

"Again with the homework assignments, Ms. Rose?" Jamie rolled her eyes, but the corners of her mouth were raised in a smile.

"Is that not a better homework assignment than reading forty pages in *Chronicles of the Gods?*"

"Oh, I'd take painting my nails over that shit any day of the week!" Ella laughed, claiming the bottle of translucent topcoat. Jamie's cheeks reddened before she asked, "Could I maybe try these with Rain?"

"Have you two been speaking again?" Jamie nodded shyly. Ella squealed, "Tell me everything!"

"It's still very fresh. We're not back together, but we've lifted the no-contact policy. I feel like we're both dipping our toe back in the pool to see what it feels like to be together before we fully commit. It's nice to talk to her again. It's nice to feel like I can be around her and not be overwhelmed by what she's feeling."

"That's amazing, Jamie. I know that's a relationship that mattered a great deal to you and you were sad to lose. I'm glad you're feeling like you're in a better place to accept it." Jamie's gaze sparkled.

"So, could I do some of these activities with her?"

"Yes, you can, but I also want you to make sure you're doing these activities alone. The point of this is for you to take care of yourself. When you fall into a pattern of needing someone else to comfort you, you make yourself vulnerable to falling back into that cycle of being so intertwined with someone else's feelings that you can't separate them from your own. We're trying to break that pattern. Does that make sense?"

"Yeah. It does." Jamie spread her fingers apart and flipped her hand around to show Ella. "What do you think?"

"I love it."

"Thanks, Ms. Rose." She paused for a moment, then added, "For everything." Suddenly, the amulet around Ella's neck vibrated, directing purple light to lick up her throat. "You're being summoned," Jamie said, tipping her chin towards Ella's necklace.

"I can feel it." They'd reached the end of their session anyway. "I'll walk you back to the Varmin sector."

Ella and Jamie broke apart once they approached the Varmin sector, Jamie veering in a separate direction to go find her friends. In the distance, Ella could hear the faint sound of children playing in the snow, their joyful screams rumbling across the campus. She followed the blissful melody, as that's where her amulet led her anyway, and marveled at the magnificence of Cavale's winter on her walk to the dragon-shifter dome, the crisp, unpolluted air, the unspoiled snow, the festive atmosphere all combining to create a scenery alive with bliss. This kind of heavenly backcloth tricked Ella for a moment into considering what it would be like for her to stay in Cavale, even after the school year was over. Maybe she could live at Akio and Josefyn's home during the summer break, or even with Kellen and the twins. She'd seen what good she'd been able to do here when the Primordials got over themselves and let her do her job, how much growth she'd already seen in Jamie, Laya, and Jarion through counseling. There was so much more left for her to do.

*You can't stay here,* she reminded herself, shoving those outlandish longings into the back of her mind. *You have Rylee and Mason waiting for you on the Earthly Plane. The Earthly Plane is your home. Not Cavale.*

Those thoughts shrank into nonexistence, descending so far down into her subconscious that she couldn't even remember what they were, the second she spotted Kellen's silhouette by the dragon-shifter dome.

She'd learned over the past few weeks that Kellen didn't need a jacket to stay warm. The dragon fire in his veins took care of that, so the only material clad over his chiseled muscularity was a red sweater—the same color of dark, wine red she'd just painted her nails—and black trousers, her favorite of his trousers due to the way they highlighted the shape of his ass. She lingered a few feet away for a moment, quietly enjoying the view of him surveying the horde of frolicking seven-year-olds in the snow. Ella once thought him to be a terrible teacher, from the way he'd treated Anastasia that day with the test. The more layers she peeled away from Kellen, the more she realized how wrong her first impression of him had been. There was so much complexity there beneath the surface, mixed with a sincere desire to help turn these kids into strong-minded warriors capable of handling themselves. His methods may have been harsh to her at first, but she understood them now, understood Cavale and *him* now, in a way that made sense to her.

Kellen turned like he'd sensed her behind him rather than heard her approach. The smile he presented her was filled with affection, outweighing even the desire that bordered the edges of his grin.

*There she is,* he sighed with relief, as if the sight of her gave him permission to finally catch his breath.

"Hey there," she greeted softly, bounding through the snow to stand beside him. He was a full head taller than her, the top of her skull skimming his shoulder. "Why'd you call me down? Who's the student in crisis?"

"There's no student in crisis."

Ella's forehead creased when her brows pulled together. "Oh. Then why'd you call me down here?"

"Headmistress Dyer roped me into supervising the first graders during recess, and I got bored."

She blinked at him.

"Let me get this straight. You called me down here, making me leave the comfort of my warm office, so I could, what…babysit you?" Ella crammed her hands into her jacket pockets. "You're unbelievable. I'm leaving."

"Wait." Kellen wrapped his fingers around the inside of her elbow, guiding her around to face him.

*Don't go, Noella,* he implored through their mind connection. *I'm sorry I used the amulet. I should have just told you I wanted to see you, that having to wait hours to spend time with you is fucking torture. If you have a session right now, you don't have to stay, but if you can, please, don't go.*

A million different emotions battled for dominance inside her, half the feelings fighting for her mind's desires and the other half representing her heart. In the end, her mind's inclination to return to the warmth of her office suffered a debilitating defeat at the hands of her heart, who just wanted to be close to him.

"If I stay," she eventually postulated, humor coloring her words, "what will you give me?"

Kellen couldn't contain a grin. "You'll have my undying respect."

"I already have that," she challenged, arching a brow with a proud smirk.

*Gods, you're glorious,* he gushed into her mind, heat fulminating between her legs before he said aloud, "If you stay, I'll make you dinner tomorrow night." Ella's mouth popped open, then sealed shut.

"You cook?" she spluttered, her chest fluttering.

"Why is that so surprising?" he laughed, the fabric of his red sweater cohering to his strapping chest when the wind pelted him.

"I can't really picture you doing anything domestic." That wasn't entirely true. Her heart had spent the past three weeks crafting fanciful fantasies about a life with Kellen, while her mind grew talons to claw those visions apart, spilling venom between the fissures to remind her that those stupid wishes weren't possible.

"I'm a very good cook," he assured, "if I'm to believe what my siblings have told me all these years."

"I'll believe it when I see it," she quipped, and his eyes lit up like glittery emeralds.

*Is that a yes?* he whispered into her mind. *You'll let me cook you dinner for our first date, Rose?*

*Is that what you're asking for, Kilic? A first date?*

*I mean, I'd rather ask for every night of the rest of your life, but I'll take a date for now if that's all you're offering.*

Ella was rendered speechless for a moment.

Instead of verbally answering him, she turned to face the children and bumped her hip flirtatiously into his. Kellen threw his head back with a delighted laugh, then repeated the gesture and bumped his hip against hers with little force, just a playful tap. She knocked hers into him a little harder, which prompted Kellen to give her the full range of his strength and slam into her side, launching her into a heap of snow.

"Shit, Rose!" he yelled, lunging to offer her his hand. "I'm sorry. I didn't mean—"

Ella pulled on his arm, wrenching him down into the pile, and crawled on top of him to shove his face into the snow, smearing the frigid sleet onto the back of his neck and entangling the slush in his black curls with a maniacal laugh.

Kellen choked on a gasp and a mouthful of snow. "I did not see that coming," he chuckled.

"Everyone!" Ella screamed to the children. "Get Mr. Kilic!"

All the Primordial children steered their focus onto Kellen, gathering snow in their tiny palms and bending the snow into the shape of spheres. They then hurled the snowballs at the Varmin department head in a synchronized succession of launched missiles, the ether filled with the sound of youthful mirth. Kellen, with supernatural swiftness, rolled both him and Ella to dodge the frigid bullets, so she now lay beneath him and his knees dug into the snow on either side of her hips, effectively trapping her under him. Ella's fingers collected as much snow as could fit in her hands and rammed it in his face, just as he returned the gesture and wiped a handful of sleet down her cheek, their laughter combining into one unique, beautiful noise of ample happiness.

*Make me a promise, Noella,* he entreated amidst of their hysterical laughter. *Promise me that, no matter what happens, you'll never stop laughing. It's the greatest sound in the universe.* Laya had told Ella that Kellen was worth loving.

As she gazed up at him and whispered into his mind, *I promise,* she suddenly wasn't afraid of heights anymore—not if it meant she could remain on top of the world, cradled by the promise of his devotion, for the rest of her life.

---

"You two need to fuck already," Josefyn declared.

"JO!" Ella shrieked, shushing her. They were in Delmarth's faculty gym, which was swarming with people, including Oliviana Bryan and Daniel Madix, occupying the treadmills in the back and shooting daggers at Ella over their shoulders. Akio and Josefyn had just run Ella through a series of drills. She asked them a few weeks ago to begin training her to fight, so she'd never end up in a position like she'd been in when she first arrived in Cavale where she couldn't defend herself. She'd been just as surprised as they were by how quickly she picked up the moves, how natural she'd been with a sword. She'd just finished what had become a daily ritual of practicing with one of the dragon-simulators to properly seat a dragon and was stretching her aching legs, her inner thighs burning. The machine consisted of two levers to hold onto, emulating the kind of spurs you'd find on a dragon, and a widespread bench that imitated the back of a dragon, coated in leathery scales. The machine mimicked what flight would feel like, rocking you in several directions to try to buck you off, but you had to cling to the handles and squeeze your thighs inward to keep your seat. She hadn't told Kellen she'd been practicing this, to keep his ego in check.

"No one's listening," Akio insisted despite Ella's panicked, wide eyes. "And you know it's true, Rosie."

"I swear, every time I leave after spending time with the two of you, I need a cold shower." Josefyn fanned herself, her violet hair spilling down to the floor when she tipped her head back.

"If she's taking cold showers, then you're not doing your job right," Ella taunted Akio, prompting him to flip her his middle finger.

"Oh, trust me, El. He's *great* at his job." Josefyn winked at Akio.

"Kellen's cooking me dinner tomorrow night." You'd think Ella just told them Kellen proposed to her from the way the two of them erupted into squeals and crowded around her to give her individual hugs.

"Fucking finally!" Akio burst, ruffling her ponytail.

"Our baby's growing up!" Josefyn shook Ella in her embrace before smacking a slobbery kiss onto her cheek.

"You two are insane," Ella reproached through a laugh. "It's just dinner. Doesn't mean anything is going to happen."

"Wear something hot," Josefyn recommended. Ella frowned.

"I don't own anything hot, other than that corset top I wore to The Dow."

"You want to borrow some of my clothes?" Ella's eyes scraped down Josefyn's willowy physique.

"If you have anything that would fit these," she touched her breasts, "then please, pass it my way."

"Why is Rose grabbing her breasts in a crowded room?" Kellen asked when he sauntered across the gym to join them. The moment he stepped into the room, Ella felt Oliviana's gaze stick to him. Ella's hands fell away from her chest, heat blasting through her veins to boil her cheeks. "Sorry I'm late," he added as he plopped down

344

on the ground next to Ella, his knee kissing hers. "I was meeting with Markus."

"How's that going?" Akio asked. Kellen's pinched lips said more than words could.

"Not great, but he shows up every day to our meetings even if he barely participates, so that's something."

"Is he doing enough work to pass the class?"

"He just passed his last exam with a sixty." Akio and Ella reacted to that as if Kellen had said Markus scored a one hundred.

"That's amazing!" Ella rejoiced, proffering her hand first for a high five to Akio, then to Kellen. Kellen's palm slammed into hers before his fingers curved around her fingers, refusing to liberate her hand from his grip.

"What were you doing that's got you so sweaty?" Kellen asked her, lowering their entwined fingers to the floor. Somewhere in the back of the room, Ella heard a shrill grunt that had to belong to Oliviana.

"Ran some practice drills, and then…" She decided to just tell him. "I've been practicing how to properly seat a dragon with the dragon-simulator." Ella was left winded by the volume of sheer delight oozing from Kellen's smile.

"This I've *got* to fucking see."

Kellen's eyes swung between her and the machine as a subtle implore for her to show him. Ella huffed, then willed her tired legs to rise from off the floor and head back to the dragon-simulator, crawling onto the gargantuan bench and spreading her legs to assume the correct position.

"*Fuck,*" Kellen growled as he approached the machine. "This is definitely going in the spank bank."

"Alright. I'm getting off now."

"Not before *I* get off, Rose." Ella whirled her head around to pin him down with a glare. His smile was pure sex and mischief. "Can I make some adjustments to your form?" She squinted her eyes.

"Is this to actually help me, or just to touch my ass?"

"A little bit of both?" Ella laughed, then waved her hand to grant him permission to touch her.

Kellen's long fingers bowed around her waist before he pushed her closer to the handles, straining her hamstrings from how wide this spread her legs. She hissed between her teeth at the acute discomfort.

"Are you hurt?" He immediately lifted his hands from her.

"I'm fine," she assured. "I'm just not super flexible, so my legs aren't used to being spread that wide."

"You were sitting too far back," he explained, walking around the machine to face her. Kellen, her friend, was no longer in the room, replaced by Mr. Kilic, the brilliant instructor who she found equally attractive. "The dragon-simulator is good for knowing what it feels like to sit on a dragon, but it doesn't account for the environmental factors you face during flight, like wind. If you sit too far back, your hands are more likely to slip off the spikes when the pressure of the wind picks up. If you're going to practice, get comfortable with the proper form."

"Got it. Thank you, Mr. Kilic." Her smile fluctuated from grateful to wicked. "Look at you! You didn't even touch my ass."

"Told you I had self-restraint, Rose." Similarly to her, but in the opposite direction, his smile switched from roguish to sincere. "When you're ready to try on the real thing, I'll be here." Ella beamed.

"El, show Kell how good you are with a sword," Josefyn urged. Something flickered in Kellen's eyes when Josefyn casually called him *Kell,* the sweet intimacy of it seeming to catch him off guard, the ghost of a smile fiddling with the corners of his lips. He recovered fast enough that only Ella noticed the change. "Kellen, you're going to be fucking amazed by how natural she is."

"I can't wait to see it." Kellen lowered down to the gym floor next to Akio.

"Who am I fighting first?" Ella asked, grabbing the slightly curved blade with a black hilt that she'd discarded on the floor after finishing the practice drills. Josefyn dove to the ground to retrieve the other sword.

"Me," Jo announced, skipping onto the matt across from Ella.

"My bestie? Fuck." Ella mockingly pouted. "I love your face. I'd hate to mess it up." Jo cackled.

346

"You're going to eat those words, Rose," Josefyn promised, her muscles primed for action.

Ella mirrored her stance, her own sword poised for attack. "Enjoy the taste of losing, Yilanci."

With a nod of agreement, the two females charged forward, their swords clashing in a shower of sparks. Ella's blade sliced through the air, while Josefyn's movements were graceful and fluid, lithe like a snake. They moved in a dance of steel and skill, their laughter ringing through the gym. Josefyn was skilled, no doubt, but Ella clung to determination, her need to win heightened by Kellen's eyes burning through her leggings and sports bra. With a swift and calculated strike, she parried Josefyn's attack and countered with a powerful blow of her own. Josefyn fought back fiercely, throwing her whole body into their fight. Ella met every attack with equal measures of power.

Neither of them were laughing anymore.

With each strike, Ella grew more confident, her movements becoming more effortless, the act of brandishing a sword as easy and undemanding as breathing. Silence bandaged the gym, every Primordial halting their own undertakings to watch the skirmish transpire, a crowd forming around their mat. The only eyes Ella cared about, the only ones she felt traipse after her, were Kellen's.

In a moment of perfect clarity, she saw her opening.

With a lightning-fast strike, she disarmed Josefyn, stealing her friend's sword, and swiveled around to hold the weapon up to her throat, the point of her blade hanging precariously close to the feeble skin of Josefyn's neck.

Her victory washed over her, settling around her bones. A triumphant smile splayed across Ella's face.

"How does losing taste?" she asked Josefyn.

"I fucking love you," Josefyn laughed, then extended her hand, silently asking for her sword back.

Ella received no applause from the crowd.

No one had been rooting for her—no one except the dragon-shifter still seated on the floor, whose gaze had darkened to a degree so extreme that she couldn't even see the green of his irises behind the film of his expanded pupils. Ella's chest heaved from exertion, savoring the pride flagrant in his smile, even as Oliviana's scowl from within the crowd drew boiling lines down her body.

"You've never done this before?" Kellen doubted when he'd regained the ability to speak.

"Alright. I *may* have taken a few sword fighting classes in college," Ella finally admitted.

"I fucking knew it!" Akio hollered, pointing accusingly at her. "I knew you were too good to be a beginner!"

"I only took three classes, though," she insisted. "And I haven't done it in years, so I'm rusty."

"That was not the performance of someone who's rusty," Kellen challenged, blood pumping aggressively through her veins. "I don't think you understand how fucking insane it is that you just won against a Primordial. I don't mean this offensively, but you shouldn't be able to do that." Kellen elevated off the floor, then pilfered the sword from between Josefyn's hands. "I want a turn."

"You want to fight me?" Ella stammered. She watched Kellen climb onto the mat to meet her.

He hovered over her, his face so close to her that she could taste his breath as it peppered over her face.

"I told you to give me your worst, sweetheart. Make me earn it." Ella simpered at his choice of words.

"What do I get if I win, Kilic?" She readied herself in a fighting stance.

"Me, Rose. You get all of me, whether you win or not." She was so magnetized by that declaration that when he began sprinting for her, she hadn't yet recovered, still standing there frozen, his words enveloping her heart.

She came to life just in time, deflecting his blade before it made contact with her cheek, spinning on her heel to dodge the next strike. Their blades sparkled when they collided, effervescent light sliding across the metal, a touch of Kellen's fire frothing from the point of his sword. She mustered all her strength to swing her blade down and apply enough pressure for Kellen's sword to fly out of his hand, elbowing him in the gut and shunting his back. Kellen nearly stumbled onto his ass.

"Don't let me win," she growled, clenching the hilt of her sword. "Give me your all, Kilic."

"Trust me, Rose," he grumbled, shaking his arms. "I am." He hadn't expected needing to work quite so hard to battle her.

"You've got this, Ella," Josefyn encouraged from the sidelines.

Kellen rolled his shoulders, cracking his bones to chase away the tension gathering there, and swept to the floor to recapture his sword. He rallied all his strength and came at her with brutal fortitude, the hard lines of his face rigid and drenched in firm resolve. Ella's heart pounded in her chest as their blades twirled between them, pushing against her ribcage like it was trying to escape her body.

She regarded this fight as her final chance to banish all the resentment she'd bottled up over the way he treated her when she first arrived in Cavale. This was her opportunity to leave it all behind and prove, not just to Kellen, not just to all the Primordials watching, but to *herself,* that she was worthy of being here.

Kellen took advantage of the close proximity to seize her wrist and yank her into him,  sliding his sword behind her back to keep her from tilting away from him. Her back arched to avoid the blade, her chest grinding against his. The fingers of his not around the hilt of his sword skated under her chin to raise it.

"Hello, gorgeous," he drawled, his warm breath staffing her lips. "How pretty you look when you want to kill me."

"You think you're real charming, don't you, Kilic?" she spoke in a breathless pant.

"Quoting the woman I most admire, who's going to back me if I don't back myself?" Kellen sloped his head closer. Ella's breath hitched in her throat as he floated his lips across her cheek to reach her ear. "My lips are lonely, Noella," he crooned, his teeth tickling her earlobe. "Please keep them company." Ella pulled her face back, dragging her nose down the sharp delineation of his cheekbone.

Kellen's breath stuttered in response. She had him.

"You look so pretty..." she whispered along the column of his throat, a heady groan echoing deep in Kellen's chest. He was so distracted by the gentle, innocent way her lips lithered over the scales on his neck that he didn't even notice her hand wrap around the hilt of the sword he still held against her back. "…when I'm about to win."

Using her grip around the hilt as leverage, she spun out of his arms, then tugged the blade out of his hand and swung the sword over her head to direct the sharp point at the center of his chest.

"YES ELLA!" Josefyn cheered, jumping to her feet and whooping without a care in the world for how loud she was. "That's my fucking girl!"

"Well done, Rosie," Akio prided at Josefyn's side.

Kellen gazed at Ella with such astounding awe that her legs buckled. They studied each other, breathing heavily but still smiling, feeling deep in their souls that their connection wasn't just a bond of the heart, but a partnership of equals.

The crowd began dispersing now that the fight had concluded. Oliviana was the last to linger there, tossing a wad of spit at Ella's feet before following Daniel to the exit, leaving the door to the gym swinging behind her.

"I don't know what you are, Rose," Kellen exhaled when everyone had left, "but I'm not convinced you're human."

"Searching for a reason to say I cheated? No one likes a sore loser, Kilic." Kellen strolled over to her and stole his sword back, then lightly tapped the end of the blade on the tip of her nose to make Ella giggle.

"Guys? Has anyone checked their emails?" Akio asked the group, his eyes pasted to his phone.

"We've kind of been busy," Kellen answered through a laugh, his tone of voice lighthearted.

"What're you looking at?" Josefyn peeked over Akio's shoulders. Her eyes bugged out at whatever she read on the screen. "Oh *fuck*."

"What is it, Jo?" Ella asked. Josefyn gulped.

"Bryara Cavalian is visiting Delmarth tomorrow." Kellen's sword clattered on the ground when it plummeted out of his hand.

"Are you fucking serious?" he exclaimed.

"Cavalian?" Ella repeated in surprise. "I take it she's a God, then."

"A *Goddess*," Josefyn corrected. "She's the Goddess of Penance and the original Cerebri image-manipulator. She runs Terminus. She's fucking ruthless."

"And she's coming to Delmarth?" Ella gasped. *To a place filled with children?* "Has a God ever come to Delmarth before?"

"No," Akio replied with a shake of his head. "Never." Ella's chest tightened.

"Why do I have a feeling this is going to be blamed on me?" she groaned, massaging her temples with the tips of her fingers.

"Cause it probably will." Kellen used the end of his blade to lift Ella's chin, forcing her eyes to cinch with his. "Keep this on you tomorrow," he advised her, "Cause I have a feeling you're going to need it."

## CHAPTER 26

# KELLEN

THE FACULTY of Delmarth had disintegrated into a hysterical frenzy over the impending arrival of Bryara Cavalian. Classrooms were scrubbed clean until they were sparkling, until hands were raw and cracking. Every desk was in order. Primordials were tripping over themselves to ensure that everything was up to par and worthy of the Goddess of Penance. The only person not bending themselves into knots to prepare for the Goddess's arrival was Kellen Kilic, for he didn't have space inside him to feel any anxiety about her visit. There was no room for any worry when he was so chock-full of bliss.

The last three weeks had been the best of Kellen's whole life.

Thanks to Noella's inspiring speech, the twins agreed to return to Delmarth, not allowing their fear of Miya to prevent them from living. Jarion was no longer icing Kellen out. The three siblings had taken to having dinner together every other night, and it was the most connected Kellen felt to the twins in months, the most they'd opened up to him about what was happening in their lives.

When he wasn't with the twins, he was glued to Noella Rose's side and, consequently, her friends.

At first, Kellen exhausted the majority of his energy in Akio and Josefyn's presence battling his jealousy and the desire to keep Noella locked away so only he could enjoy her beautiful smile. The more time he spent with Akio and Josefyn, though, the more he began to ease, the more his heart softened to them separate from the way he felt about Noella. Spending time with them was different than what it had felt like to be in Daniel and Oliviana's presence. It was filled with more light, more laughter, less pessimism and petty drama, or the pathetic need to judge everyone and everything. He'd realized in the last few weeks that he'd clung to Daniel and Oliviana because he didn't think he deserved this kind of friendship—he didn't think he deserved the light, the joy, the kindness that came from being around people who only wanted to lift other people up.

Noella had given him the gift of realizing that healing for him was determining for himself that he was worthy of this connection, that he didn't need to seclude himself in just Jarion and Laya. It was possible for him to hold enough space in his heart for the twins and anyone else who brought him peace.

And then, there was Noella Rose.

The last three weeks with her, getting to truly know her, spending intimate time with her in the absence of angry looks and words of hatred, was a fucking dream. He thought he'd reached the utmost extent of feeling for her, but the way he felt about her now, versus even a week ago, was exponentially higher and just kept ascending to new heights, new volumes, new potencies. Kellen had never allowed himself to experience the other side of a romance, building an emotional connection separate from physical attraction, and had discovered that nurturing an emotional connection was even more rewarding than if they were exploring their physical draw to one another.

He gave her so many shards of himself that he'd never shared with anyone else, every tiny or large thought he'd ever had, whether they were positive or negative, desperate for her to know him, to see him, to understand him.

With every piece of himself he shared with her, Noella offered him a piece of herself in return.

*The reason I've always gone by Ella instead of Noella is because I was named after my grandmother, Noelle, which was also my mother's middle name,* Noella revealed to him during one of their many confessionals. *I've never wanted to have any part of myself associated with her, so I truncated the name.*

*Do you mind that I call you Noella?* It would be difficult for him to stop, the name so addicting, his favorite drug. However, if it bothered her, if it brought her pain to hear it, he would stop calling her that.

*Not at all,* she answered, his chest easing with relief. *You've taken the name and made it mean something else. I no longer think about my mother when I hear that name. You've made it something I can feel comfortable claiming as my own.* Kellen might've felt like he was close to fainting when she said that.

Another evening, when they were in their respective apartments, but talking to one another as if they were sitting across from each other, he'd told her, *My birthday is the first day of April.*

*So you're an Aries,* she proclaimed, that word meaning nothing to him. She chuckled, *That makes sense.*

*I don't know what an Aries means.*

*It's your zodiac sign.* She explained, *It refers to one of the twelve specific constellations of the zodiac that the sun passes through. A person's zodiac sign is where the sun was when they were born. It's all part of astrology, which is a type of divination. It's believed that a person's personality can be predicted using their zodiac sign. A lot of people think astrology is bullshit, but I've always found it kind of fascinating.*

*What does my zodiac predict about me, Rose?* Noella's gorgeous laughter blessed his ears.

*Aries men are strong, bold, passionate, impulsive, short-tempered, and fiery. They're romantic and will commit to someone they love with no reservations—all traits I would attribute to you, Kilic.*

Kellen's chest was ablaze with adoration.

*You think I'm romantic, Rose?* Noella sent him the image of her rolling her eyes and flipping him her middle finger. A carefree laugh bubbled to the surface and rumbled through his body. *What sign are you?*

*Pisces. I was born on February twenty-ninth on a leap year. I don't know if you guys have that here or not, but on the Earthly Plane, every four years, we have an extra day added to the calendar in February as a corrective measure, because the Earth doesn't orbit the sun in three hundred and sixty-five days. In the years we don't have my actual birthday, I celebrate it on March first.*

*I knew you were special. Rose.* Warmth traveled through the conduit between their minds to alert Kellen that she was blushing. *Are our two signs compatible? Aries and Pisces?*

*Not typically, but they can be.* She explained, *Aries is a fire sign, and Pisces is a water sign, so they're naturally opposed. It just means they need to put some effort into understanding one another. If that's achieved, they can have a successful relationship where they'll be figures of inspiration for one another.*

*Do I inspire you, sweetheart?*

*You inspire me to want to put my head inside a meat grinder.* Kellen's laughter escalated in intensity and volume when Noella's laugh joined him from across the hall, padding his whole body with abounding light.

Of course, he thought about kissing her, pretty much every second of every day. Of course, he craved to know what it would really feel like to finally claim her body as well as her heart, not just through her dreams, but he wasn't rushing it. He didn't feel the need to rush anything because he was already with her. He had what mattered right now, her time, her interest, her friendship. There would be so much time in their future for all that other stuff, but this time now, this period of getting to know one another, they wouldn't be able to return to it in the same way they could return to physical sensation.

So he was happy to be her friend for now.

Her friend who they both knew was really more than a friend. He was happy to wait until she was ready to take that next step, because that waiting period consisted of inordinate ecstasy, enough to last him a lifetime.

Kellen first dropped his briefcase off in his office, then began his trek through the Varmin department to the academic sector. On his way to Noella's office, he bumped into Josefyn—literally barreled right into her because he'd been focusing so much on lengthening his strides to diminish the time between now and when he was back in Noella's presence that he wasn't looking where he was going.

"Someone's in a hurry," Jo joked, helping to balance him by placing her hands on his biceps and tipping him back to an upright position. Kellen got a whiff of her vanilla perfume that masked the odor of rotting animal carcasses still lingering on her tongue from breakfast. The mingled scents made him momentarily nauseous, but he'd spent enough time with Josefyn now that he was getting used to it.

"Just wanted to stop by the academic sector before my first class." Kellen dithered. "Were you with her this morning?"

"We always have breakfast together." Kellen adored Josefyn and Noella's friendship. When Kellen and Josefyn were in school together at Delmarth, Josefyn didn't have many female friends. She'd spent all her time with Akio. The females in their class didn't understand Josefyn, her soft nature so divergent from what Primordials considered strong that most people kept their distance from her. Noella was a perfect match for Josefyn, and watching their friendship develop, how much that relationship meant to both women, had made Kellen like Josefyn that much more. "I just left her in her office. Unless she was already summoned to one of the four sectors, she should still be there."

"Thanks, Jo." Kellen gave her hand a squeeze, then began heading for the academic sector.

"Hey, Kell?" Kellen swung around when she tossed that friendly nickname at him. "I heard you're cooking Ella dinner tonight. Good luck. I'm really rooting for you guys." Kellen's throat felt congested by a rock of emotion.

"I was planning everything last night," he found himself divulging to her, Josefyn's eyes softening. "I cleaned the whole apartment. I bought candles, Jo. *Me.* Kellen Kilic. I bought fucking *candles.* And roses, cause duh." Josefyn giggled as he sighed, "I just want it to be perfect for her."

"It already will be because you care enough to make it so." His heartbeat thundered in his ears.

"Thank you, Jo. That means a lot coming from you." Her smile was kindness personified.

"I always wondered why we weren't friends in school," she admitted, taking him off guard with her honesty. "I always quietly respected you. The way you cared for your younger siblings. The way you gave up being a member of Aros's cadre to take care of them. I used to wish we could be friends."

"You did?" The corners of his eyes stung. "Why didn't you say anything?"

"Because back then, you didn't seem receptive to any offers of friendship." She wasn't wrong. "And then, when we started working here, you were hanging out with Daniel and Oliviana all the time, and I've always made it a point to keep my distance from them, so I kind of made peace with the fact that we'd never be friends." Kellen didn't know what to say.

"I always wanted to be your friend too, Jo. I just didn't have space back then to ask for it or even welcome it."

"I know." He truly believed she understood that, that she didn't blame him for it. "I'm glad Ella has helped bridge the gap I've always wanted to. I always knew you were worth a friendship, Kellen."

She fluttered her fingers in a wave and turned to leave. Kellen stood there a moment just admiring her shadow, letting the warm feeling of amity wash over him, then recommenced his trek to the academic sector.

He found the object of his desires standing outside her office rather than inside it, with a basket of provisions resting on the floor at her feet and a roll of tape between her teeth. Inside the basket, there were at least thirty laminated photographs of the elementary school students chosen from each class to win character awards for the month of October, with a quote beneath the photo from their teacher explaining how that student had exemplified the character trait of resilience. Kellen had assisted Noella in getting every teacher to pick a student to receive a character award, even though none of them had wanted to give Noella anything, but under the threat of Kellen's dragon fire, they'd conceded. Noella had already taped up signs on the wall between her office and the infirmary for each grade level, ranging from kindergarten to fifth grade.

The pictures of the five kindergarten students who'd been chosen from each class were fastened to the wall under the *Kinder-garten* sign, arranged in an organized line where every photo lined up perfectly to feed Noella's need for consistency. She'd just slapped

Tyrell Morris's photo under the *First Grade* sign and was about to rip some tape off to stick it to the wall before the photo slipped out of her hand and tumbled to the floor.

"Shit," she hissed, just as Kellen sunk to his knees to catch the fallen photo.

"I've got you," he vowed, handing it back to her. His fingers purposefully slid against hers when she accepted the photo back.

"Hi," she greeted breathily, glorious color stealing across her face. The shade of her purple knitted sweater was less vibrant than the fushia one and more analogous to the color of a grape, but it had the same effect on her blonde hair as the last sweater did, emphasizing the golden undertones. "Where were you this morning?"

"Jare wanted to run together before school." Kellen normally joined Noella and the gremlin—okay, maybe he should start calling her Freya—on their morning walk, but when Jarion asked to go for a jog, the first time in months he'd asked to spend alone time with Kellen, he couldn't say no.

The brothers barely spoke while they ran, but they'd quietly engaged in a playful competition of who could run faster, thrusting their elbows into each other's stomachs to try and thwart the other's progress, the kind of thing they used to do when Jarion was younger. It had been the perfect start to Kellen's day.

"Oh!" Noella's demeanor brightened. "Amazing! I'm glad you guys spent some alone time together." She dropped her eyes to the laminated photograph in her hands, then whispered, "I missed you."

"I'm sorry, what was that?" Kellen angled his ear closer to her. "I'm not sure I heard you right. It sounded like you said you missed me." She flicked him on the side of his neck, her lips twitching in a smile.

"I missed you, Kellen," she repeated, her voice like melted honey.

"I missed you too, Noella." *So much,* he whispered into her mind, hoping to pierce her heart. He then lifted his eyes to the character awards. "These are really good, by the way…"

"No!" Noella swatted Kellen's hand away, her blonde hair

smacking his shoulder. "I worked on these all day yesterday, and you're not going to do your classic Kellen Kilic thing where you come in, and you graze over everything really slowly, and then, when someone asks who's responsible for all this, you take credit. I did this. ME." Kellen's eyes dropped down to her lips.

"This took you all day to do?" Noella's entire body was bombarded in a rageful flush.

"I hate you," she seethed at Kellen's grin, balling her hands into tiny, adorable fists. "I viscerally hate you in my bones."

"It was just a question." She punched his bicep. Kellen didn't admit when he faltered back a step that the blow actually hurt a little. He subtly rubbed the throbbing area on his arm and asked, "Why are you taping these to the wall?"

"Headmistress Dyer asked me to. She wants Bryara to see them." Noella's dispassionate shrug made him cock his head.

"You don't seem fazed by the Goddess of Penance coming to Delmarth."

"I guess I don't feel the impact of it as much as you because I'm not from here. To me, it's just a name."

"I've obviously never met her before, but from the stories we cover about her in History of the Gods, she's depicted as what nightmares are molded from. If Terminus is any indication of her personality, she sounds like a real peach." Noella's lips lifted like she was about to laugh before her eyes suddenly widened and she cleared her throat, raising her chin nervously at something over Kellen's shoulder.

When he spun around, he discovered Bryara Cavalian perched at the end of the hall, flanking Headmistress Dyer's side, a meticulously pruned brow arching at what she'd just overheard Kellen say about her.

The best way to describe Bryara Cavalian was a nightmare masquerading as a daydream. Silky, lilac locks spilled down her chest in long, velvety waves, emulating a river of mauve that complimented the crimson shade of her eyes and the succulent white lashes outlining the rim. Her full lips, painted a vibrant red, wilted into a scowl, her eyes forming small slits over Kellen and Noella. Her golden gown glimmered like molten sunshine, the fabric luxurious satin, draping elegantly over every curve and contour of her body. The bodice was intricately embellished with delicate embroidery and shimmering sequins, creating a dazzling display of light with every micromovement. The hem was adorned with a border of intricate lace, adding a touch of regal splendor to the already majestic ensemble. The skirt of her gown flowed like liquid gold behind her as she began treading over to them, cascading down to the floor in a graceful sweep of gilded fabric.

Noella's spine went rigid. She may not have felt the impact of Bryara's name, but she sure felt the impact of being in Bryara's presence as much as Kellen did. She stepped closer to Kellen's side, and Kellen naturally angled himself so he stood half in front of her in a protective, possessive stance.

The Goddess surveyed their closeness with faint fascination.

Behind the Goddess and the Headmistress stood an envoy. It was hard to gauge whether the envoy was Eyal due to the armor shrouding their face, but Kellen assumed it was, even though Eyal had left Delmarth three weeks ago at Noella's behest and no one had seen or heard from him since.

"Eyal?" Noella asked. "Is that you?"

She received no answer from the envoy, either because it wasn't Eyal, or because he was maintaining discretion in front of the Goddess, since he shouldn't have given Noella his name in the first place.

"Ms. Rose, Mr. Kilic, may I present Bryara Cavalian," Headmistress Dyer introduced the Goddess.

"It's a—" Noella started to say, but the Goddess cut her off.

"You haven't been shy about sharing your disdain for Aros Cavalian." Bryara's voice was cold thunder.

Kellen edged closer to Noella.

Noella read something in Bryara's eyes that had her suddenly blurting, "He hasn't been shy about being the worst."

*ROSE!* Kellen reproached, his head snapping angrily to her.

He sensed the horror in Noella's stiff posture before she stammered into their bond, *Why did I just say that?!*

*Why did you just say that?!* Coz joined the discussion.

*I don't know!* she squeaked, her cheeks paling. *It just came out! Maybe she'll have a sense of humor?*

*Does that look like a face that has a sense of humor?* Kellen grumbled, nudging her arm in warning. If the Goddess took a swing at Noella, he was ready to defend her, fire primed for launch in his veins.

Bryara's eyebrows soared up to her hairline. She was silent for a long stretch of time, leaving Kellen and Noella and even Headmistress Dyer vibrating with anxiety before the Goddess's mouth warped into a shit-eating grin and released a surprised, slightly frightening, delirious laugh.

"I knew I was going to like you," Bryara decreed. Noella exhaled a mixture of a relieved sigh and a strangled laugh. The smile slipped off Bryara's face when she glanced at Kellen. "And then there's *you.*" The Goddess's voice filled his head, shoving Noella out to make space for herself.

*You're not working hard enough,* she snarled at him, her voice grating down the walls of his mind.

*At what?* he asked her.

*The fact that you even have to ask shows how little you've been paying attention, Kellen Kilic.*

A shudder rasped down his spine.

*Please, tell me what I'm missing, Your Highness.* All Bryara had to do was smile at Kellen.

The feeling that erupted inside Kellen's head resembled a flurry of bats awakening from a deep slumber and unleashing well-rested, angry claws onto the thin tissue of his brain, shredding his nerves apart. With nothing left to do except yield to the sensation, his own power feeling very far away with her influence ensnaring him, Kellen screamed and plummeted to his knees, raking his fingernails over his forehead to tear through his skin and free his mind from her terrorizing power.

"Kellen!" Noella shrieked, yelling at the Goddess, "What're you doing to him?!"

"Delivering penance," Bryara replied, never breaking eye contact from Kellen. Amidst Kellen's agony, when he had a fleeting moment of coherent thought, it dawned on him that perhaps

Bryara's visit to Delmarth had nothing to do with Noella, and everything to do with this, with *him.*

The pain was so blinding that black blots smeared across his vision, threatening eternal sleep.

"STOP!" Noella didn't think before she slammed her body into Bryara, shattering the Goddess's concentration on Kellen and liberating him from her clutches. Kellen expelled a series of coughs dripping with blood, spitting the crimson saliva onto the floor as he worked to catch his breath.

"Interesting," Bryara laughed, her eyes now trained on Noella. "You throw yourself at a Goddess to defend him, yet you refuse to welcome him into your bed."

"Fuck you!" Noella roared. Kellen felt Coz flinch inside his chest.

"Did you just tell a Goddess *fuck you?*" Noella lifted her chin without a single iota of fear. She met Bryara's crimson gaze, stony and teeming with cruelty, but didn't balk, leveling it with her own unique willpower. A callous grin curled the corners of Bryara's lips up. "Would you like to experience the extent of my power, princess? I may lose my head for a day, but it will grow back."

If Bryara laid even a tendril of her power on Noella, Kellen would fucking lose it, consequences be damned. He grabbed Noella's hand before she gave in to the temptation to lunge at the Goddess.

*Breathe, sweetheart,* Kellen insisted, watching Noella's chest rise and fall at a tortured pace. *She's trying to rile you up. Don't let her.*

*She hurt you.* That was all Noella was capable of saying, the only thing she seemed to care about—not the fact that she'd just said *fuck you* to a Goddess, not the fact that she was the human in this equation.

Her own survival was secondary. All she cared about was the fact the Goddess had harmed him.

There was a name for the emotion Kellen felt swallow his heart whole. He couldn't remember it with his brain foggy from the residue of Bryara's power, but he felt it overwhelm him, pour into his entire being.

*I'm fine, baby,* he promised, the tenseness in Noella's muscles reducing. *I won't be if something happens to you, though, so try to control your urges. I'm not worth getting yourself tossed into Terminus.*

*Ironic that you're telling ME to control myself for a change.* Bryara's eyes swung between Noella and Kellen in a way that suggested she'd been listening to their internal dialogue.

"You're not necessary here anymore," Bryara told Kellen, signaling with her index finger for him to stand. "I'm with you today," she then informed Noella. Both Kellen and Noella's jaws fell open.

"The whole day?" Noella spluttered. Kellen was wrong when he thought Bryara was here for just him. He didn't like the thought of leaving his girl alone with the Goddess, but he had a feeling asking to join them today wouldn't be welcomed. Noella stammered, "I have a session with a student later. You can't be there for it."

"Yes, I can, and yes, I will." Bryara disregarded Noella and glanced back at Kellen. "You can go now, dragon boy."

*Work harder,* the Goddess ordered him, then added in a softer, almost encouraging tone, *You're so close.*

*To WHAT?* he demanded.

*You'll know when you get there, Mr. Kilic.* Kellen peeked at Noella, whose expression was pure terror.

*You can handle her,* he reassured at the anxious tremor echoing through her bottom lip. He sent a thread of his power down the conduit between them to stroke her mind, leaving it in her care so she'd have a piece of him with her. Then, he threw in, *I pity the fool who thinks they can trounce you, Noella Rose.*

Noella's eyes burned into him even as the doors to the elevator shut in his face.

---

Bryara Cavalian was sent to Delmarth to be a thorn in Ella's ass.

Ella had to finish hanging up all the character awards on the wall, so Bryara was forced to lean against the door to Ella's office and simply watch her struggle to get all the photographs up. A smile expanded across the Goddess's face every time Ella accidentally dropped one of the photos or the plastic-coated picture slid down the wall because the tape wasn't secure enough. After the tenth time of Bryara chuckling under her breath, the damper on Ella's temper, which was already weak to begin with, ruptured.

"Are you just going to stand there mocking me, or are you going to make yourself useful and help me?" Ella seethed.

"Trust me, princess," the Goddess purred. "That's exactly what I'm doing here." Ella grunted at that response.

"Are all you Gods purposefully elusive? And why do you keep calling me *princess?*"

"I prefer not to answer that. It would give too much away." Ella couldn't tell if the Goddess was trying to be funny, or if that was a serious response. She glanced over at the silent titanium statue flanking Bryara's side.

"Eyal?" she asked again, hoping to get a response this time from the envoy.

"He's not permitted to speak to you," Bryara snapped. Ella's lashes beat against her eyebrows.

"Why not?" Bryara clamped her mouth shut, then dragged her pinched fingers over the space where her two lips met, mimicking closing a zipper. "Is this because Eyal wasn't there when Kellen's mother attacked us?"

"Ella," a familiar male voice warned from inside the steel helmet.

"Eyal did nothing wrong that day," Ella asserted. "*Aros* did by not sending aid to Kellen and the twins."

"This conversation is finished," Bryara announced, her cadence reminding Ella of a jarring clap of thunder. "And I'd be more careful with how you speak about my brother, earthborn."

*Brother?* Ella should have put their familial link together sooner, with the corresponding last names.

Bryara continued, "Do not think for a second that you are invincible just because my brother offered you protection, protection you've since turned away. You don't get to stand there and judge us when you know nothing of our history, or the sacrifices Aros has made for this kingdom and his people."

364

"What sacrifice has he made?" Ella's foot was already in her mouth. Might as well shove it the whole way down her throat. "It seems to me that all the sacrifices have been his own people, fighting this war for him against Edar and the Sireres while not being allowed to have any of their own opinions."

*Noella,* Coz's voice boomed in her mind. *This is not the fight you want to pick right now.*

Watching Bryara swallow, Ella sensed the Goddess was actually perturbed by what Ella had said.

"When you learn the truth," Bryara spoke with fiery conviction, her crimson eyes blazing, "and trust me, princess, *you will,* you'll eat those words. Until you know the truth, you keep your mouth shut."

Jarion suddenly appeared at the end of the hall. His eyes grew to the size of saucers when he saw the Goddess.

"I…uh…I can come back," he stammered before lunging for the elevator.

"You're not getting away that easily!" Ella curled her index finger inward to gesture Jarion to come closer.

Jarion took tentative steps forward. "Your…uh…your highness." He bowed his head to Bryara, who nodded in acceptance of the respectful greeting, then swung his eyes to Ella, silently entreating to be moved far away from the Goddess. "If you're too busy, maybe today isn't the right day for this."

"Today is the *perfect* day for this." Ella placed her hands on his shoulders and gave his body a little shake. "I'll remind you that this was *your* idea."

"Before I knew we'd have an audience!" He peeked anxiously over at the Goddess.

"Pretend they're not there." *I certainly will,* she thought to herself, then watched Bryara smirk and wondered if the Goddess had heard her thought. "I know you're scared, but putting this off is only going to make everything so much worse." Ella proffered her hand, palm facing the ceiling, and declared, "It's time for you to release your wings, Jarion." Jarion eyed her extended hand.

He sighed, then placed his hand in hers. "Your energy is a lot for this early in the morning, Ms. Rose."

"You can't get me down, Ates. I'm excited!" She pulled him towards the elevator, Bryara and Eyal shadowing their pace.

Ella's breath formed clouds in the frigid air. Translucent billows spiraled from her parted lips as she inhaled a paced breath, demonstrating what she wanted Jarion to replicate, and held the breath inside her for four seconds, letting the breath go in an embellished manner for a total of six seconds. Jarion consumed a mouthful of frosty air, trapping it in his chest, then stuttered it out exactly as she had done, repeating this sequence several times until his features appeared softer and less agitated.

"What're you feeling right now as you're about to do this?" she asked him.

"Terrified." He'd gotten better over the last few weeks at identifying his feelings and expressing them to her.

"What are you most afraid of?"

"That it'll hurt." He gulped. "It really hurt last time when I released the first one. It reminded me…it reminded me of my dad. What he used to do." He was careful with his words in front of the Goddess, who was sitting against a tree a few paces away.

"Tell me what you see around you," Ella instructed. Jarion's brows pulled together before he gave her an answer.

"Um…you? The trees? The…the Goddess of Penance." Bryara waved her fingers in a jeering taunt.

"Who do you *not* see?"

Jarion's forehead smoothed away the crinkles. "My father," he answered, his green eyes shimmering.

Ella nodded her head.

"He's not here, Jare. When you get that feeling that reminds you of that pain, look around and use your surroundings to check the facts. Prove to your eyes that he's not here to hurt you anymore." Jarion's mouth pulled into a tight smile, but a smile, nonetheless. "Give me your positive affirmation before we get started."

"We can do hard things," he recited. Ella's hands came together in a proud clasp in front of her.

"You've got this, Jare. One wing at a time."

Jarion's hands balled into taut fists at his sides, his eyes squeezing shut. His back muscles flexed before one wing split through Jarion's sweater and stretched out to meet the world, the leathery membrane contracting along the current of the wind. The scarlet wing spanned outwards and netted the light of the sun, reflecting crimson beams onto the overlay of snow beneath his feet.

Jarion hissed a broken sound of agony between his teeth, his face scrunching up in pain.

"Take a second to feel it," Ella counseled him gently. "There's no rush here. Take your time, Jare."

"It hurts, Ms. Rose." He whimpered and raised wet eyes to her.

"I know, buddy. The more you do it, the less it will hurt. I promise." She rested her chin on top of her interwoven hands. "You can call time whenever you want, Jare. You've already made huge progress today."

"No. I have to do this. I have to." He stared down at the rays of red light refracting off his wing, painting a twirling bloodred design on the snow. "I can do hard things," he whispered to himself, a mantra, a promise to the universe. He strained his muscles so hard that a ferocious flush blitzed his face, trickling down his neck, where his veins were protruding from his tightly clenched jaw.

She heard the rip of his sweater on the other side, holding her breath in anticipation, and watched his second wing, the one he'd been keeping contained, wiggle free from the binds of his skin, shattering through his flesh and rolling out towards the sun. It extended slowly, as if testing the air before making a choice to fully accept the world, then decided the taste of the universe wasn't a terrible flavor and lengthened out to meet his other wing. Jarion screamed through the whole thing—not a scream of pain, but a cathartic release of the feelings that had been maiming him from the inside out for so many years.

When Jarion wobbled a bit, Ella called out, "You okay, Jare?"

"They're heavy," Jarion gasped, then laughed. He broke out into a hysterical attack of thrilled laughter, then shouted with glee, without abandon, with tears streaming down his face, "I did it! They're out!"

"They're out, Jare!" Ella cheered with him, tears falling from her eyes as well. "You did it! I'm so fucking proud of you! Excuse my cursing!"

"I won't tell anyone!" Their laughter wove together.

Even Bryara was smiling, though it was more subdued, hidden behind a curtain of her lilac hair.

"How does it feel to have them both out?" Ella asked. Jarion looked behind him to admire the two wings.

"They're kind of cool," he marveled, looking impressed with himself.

"They're *so* cool! Don't tell your brother, but yours are so much cooler than his." Jarion cackled up at the sky.

"Kell's got that weird orange around his wings and on his belly," he chortled.

"It makes him look like a Cheeto," Ella teased back.

"What's a Cheeto?"

"An addictive food from the Earthly Plane that you're lucky you don't know." Jarion laughed so hard he started coughing. "Okay, let's not make ourselves throw up," Ella snickered, stepping towards him. "What do you want to do now that they're out?"

"I want to put them back," he replied, his tone laced in guilt, like admitting that meant he failed. "They really hurt."

"Let's put them back. You did everything you were supposed to do today."

Jarion sighed with relief, then swung his arms forward to direct the wings back beneath his skin, the slit they'd created in his spine stitching up once they'd safety returned inside him. The moment they retracted, Jarion fell into Ella's arms, sobbing into her shoulder. Ella clung to him with all her might.

"Thank you," he wept, repeating this over and over again, his fingernails digging into her back. Those words weren't sufficient to encapsulate his gratitude for her, but they were more than enough for Ella.

She raised her eyes to Bryara. The Goddess just nodded her head, but respect tipped out of the simple act.

"I have to go tell Laya!" Jarion wriggled until Ella removed her arms from around him. "Can you tell my brother?"

"You don't want to tell him yourself?" Jarion hesitated.

"I think it'll mean more coming from you." Ella didn't know how to respond to that.

"Yes, I can tell your brother." Jarion simpered, then started for the exit of the Canterna Thicket. "Jare?"

"Yeah, Ms. Rose?" Tears splashed over her smile.

"Claim this victory. Claim the joy. Claim all the feelings. You've earned the right to feel it all."

Jarion laid his hand on his chest. His message was silent, but poignant. He patted his heart, where her words would be cherished and safe, then turned on his heel and ran out of the forest to find his sister.

Ella's eyes flew to Bryara when the Goddess began clapping.

"I'll admit, I'm impressed," the Goddess conceded, trekking through the snow to meet her, Eyal close on her tail. "What you did for that kid was pretty special." Ella's lips settled into a smile…but it only lasted a second before the Goddess sighed, "But you could be doing so much more."

"What is that supposed to mean?" Ella waited for an answer that would never come. "I'm getting really sick of being given half-messages from the Gods. What are you and Aros waiting for me to do?"

Bryara's hands lashed out and seized Ella's face, yanking her forward, their noses crashing into each other.

"For you to *wake up,*" Bryara hissed in her face, tepid air bathing Ella's cheeks. "You told that kid to pay attention to what he was feeling. What do *you* feel, Noella? What do you feel that *you're* fighting against?"

Ella blinked. "Is this about Kellen?" Bryara brought her lips to Ella's ear.

In a chilling voice that sent a shudder down Ella's spine and caused her lungs to lock up, Bryara whispered, "Only when the child of the crown binds to the child of the flame can the chains of solitude be released."

"What? What're you—" When Ella opened her eyes, the Goddess, and Eyal, had vanished.

CHAPTER 27

# ELLA

ELLA WALKED to Kellen's classroom in a daze. Bryara's words echoed in her ears, through her skull, reverberating down into her bloodstream. They rippled across her bones, making a home for themselves in every corner of her being.

The verse felt both vastly important and wildly irrelevant. Both a warning and a misdirection.

A prophecy and a falsehood.

The more she thought about it, the less sense it made, and the more enraged she felt to have been left with this strange foretelling and be the only person in all of Cavale without the background information to understand it.

So the first place she went after Bryara abandoned her in the Canterna Thicket was to Kellen's classroom—not just because he was the History of the Gods professor and he might supply her with some answers, not just because Jarion asked her to tell his brother about releasing his wings, but because Kellen was the only place she ever wanted to be anymore. That was a feeling she needed to stop fighting.

Ella cracked the door of the classroom open and poked one eye into the room. Kellen was just finishing up a lesson with a class of second graders. When she saw the bright blue background behind his head that read on it *the five senses exercise*, Ella covered her hand over her mouth to keep a sob from leaking out.

"Autumn, tell me four things you can feel and touch," Kellen requested of the girl sitting to his right. They'd pushed the desks against the wall so the whole class was sitting in a circle on the floor.

"The floor," the redhead answered, spaying her fingers out on the ground. "My skin. My hair. My clothes."

"Good. Maurin," he went to the female sitting beside Autumn, "what are three things you can hear?"

"You," the young Primordial quipped, the whole class fragmenting into laughter. "Everyone laughing," she added, "and the sound of the wind." Kellen swung his finger to the next student.

"Shanell, name two things you can smell."

"Chocolate!" she squealed, cupping her face. "And…uh… grass?" Her voice blended into a squeak of uncertainty.

"You can definitely smell grass," Kellen confirmed. He lowered his focus on the last student seated on his left. "Jarius. What's one thing you can taste?" The young boy rocked back and forth.

"Coffee?" When Kellen nodded, Jarius's demeanor illuminated with a sweet simper.

"Great job, guys. Who can remember why we did this exercise?" Six tiny hands shot up in the air.

He called on Madelaine, who answered, "So we can use our senses to help stay focused in class."

Kellen reached into his red sack and tossed a piece of candy to every student.

Tears streamed down Ella's face. He used her presentation. He used her lesson with his class.

Kellen's eyes raised to the door and snagged over Ella.

"Alright, guys," he announced with his eyes gliding across Ella's tear-stained cheeks, "Class dismissed. Fix the desks back into place before you leave." He rose off the floor and strode back to his desk.

Ella held the door open for all the students as they exited. Once the classroom had emptied of children, she slipped past the door and shut it behind her, lingering by the entrance for a moment to just gaze at Kellen, admiring his irrefutable beauty and questioning if it was possible for this man to have been created for her.

"Was that really the end of your class time," she asked, "or did you just kick all of those kids out of here early?"

"I'm not sure and don't even care," he answered with a husky laugh. "I saw you at the door, and my mind emptied of all thought beside the need to get everyone out of here so we could be alone."

Ella's cheeks warmed. She hugged her arms around herself because she suddenly felt very conscious of the fact that her sweater's neckline was V shaped and he could probably see how flushed her chest was.

Kellen cocked his head at her timid fidgeting. "You okay, sweetheart? Did Bryara do something to you?"

"No. I'm fine." She dared her feet to take a step closer to him. Once she'd gained that tiny victory, she goaded her feet to complete the whole distance until she was standing right in front of him. "I have two things to tell you," she said, clasping her wrists behind her back and squaring her shoulders.

"I can't wait to hear both of them." Ella presented him with a euphoric grin.

"Jarion released his wings today." Kellen's arms fell to his sides. His gaze grew big and animated.

"He did?" Ella nodded, framing her flaming cheeks with her hands.

Kellen blinked once before his hands dove forward, grabbed her waist, and lifted her off her feet, spinning her in exultant circles as her arms naturally tied around his neck and she yelped a surprised squeal.

"You beautiful, magical creature!" he sung as he twirled her.

He stopped whirling them eventually and pressed his face into her chest—not sexually, but adoringly, clutching at her back and heaving a sob into her sweater. Ella's fingers found their way into his hair before she dropped her face into his curls. She inhaled the citrus scent of his shampoo and felt more at home here, with her feet off the ground, than she'd ever felt with her feet touching the earth.

*Thanking you isn't enough,* he gushed into her mind. She began kneading his scalp with her fingernails, an impulse that felt as intrinsic to her as breathing. *No words will ever be enough to express my gratitude, Noella Rose, but I'll spend my life trying to find the perfect ones to give to you.*

Kellen began lowering her back to the ground, not separating from her though. The second Ella's feet were cradled by the floor once more, his face nuzzled her throat, sliding up the pillar of her neck so his lips could descend upon her cheek. It was a gentle press of his mouth to her burning skin, such an innocent gesture, but she felt the kiss everywhere, in her lips, her teeth, her hair, her bones, surging through her like a flaring tidal wave, igniting everything inside her that had previously been numb.

She felt alive with raw energy in a way she never had before, as though she'd never been truly alive until his lips graced her skin. She unconsciously tugged at his hair, and he ripped his face back to look at her.

"I'm sorry," he stammered, stroking his thumb down her cheek, over where his lips had just been. "I got swept up in the moment. I should've asked." He'd mistaken her pulling at his hair as a bad thing.

"I would've said yes if you'd asked," she told him, eyeing his lips, craving a taste of them for herself.

The sound of students outside brought them both back to reality. Kellen's arms fell off her, and Ella took a small step back, shyly twisting her hair because she didn't know what to do with her hands.

"What was the second thing you wanted to tell me?" Her head had been drained of coherent thought when he'd kissed her cheek, so it took her a second to reach into her subconscious and pull forward the necessary information, hauling it through a thick, iridescent fog of ecstasy.

"Bryara said something strange to me." At the worried crease in his forehead and the flicker of a flame in his eyes, she rushed, "She didn't hurt me, but she left me with a weird prophecy that I don't understand and was wondering if you could shed some light on, being the History professor and all."

The fire extinguished in his gaze, replaced with warm affection.

"I'm honored you thought of me first." There was no sarcasm. Only candor. "What did she tell you?"

Ella took a deep breath in, then recited, "Only when the child of the crown binds to the child of the flame can the chains of solitude be released."

"Huh." Kellen spread his index finger and thumb to stroke them along his jaw.

Ella took a seat in one of the chairs beside his desk, then asked, "Have you heard that prophecy before?"

"No. Never." Her shoulders sank. "When I hear child of *the crown*, I immediately think of Aros."

"Does Aros have a child?"

"Not one that's been accounted for in history, but it's not impossible that he and Tala had a child before she was kidnapped. They'd be over a thousand years old now, but with Godly blood in their system, they would age much slower and eventually stop aging like all Gods do." Kellen dragged his index finger across his bottom lip in thought. Ella tried to control her body's reaction to the unintentionally sensual act, disciplining her features to hide the change in her blood's temperature. "The part that's tripping me up is the child of the flame. I've never heard of anything in history like that."

"Flame could mean Meteoro," Ella guessed. "Or dragon."

"True, but it says child *of* the flame, not child *with* the flame. There's Neeyar Cavalian who's the God of Fire, but he's never had any children, so I don't think the flame is referring to him."

"You've never heard of Aros having a child," Ella pointed out. "Maybe Neeyar had one secretly too?"

"No. It's impossible. Neeyar doesn't have a humanoid form like most of the Gods do. He is completely made of flames. He doesn't have a face, let alone a penis. It would be impossible for him to procreate with anyone, Primordial or God." Ella watched in awe the wheels turn inside Kellen's head, his mind greedily latching onto the prophecy and evaluating every singular word inside the statement with extreme care. "Only when the child of the crown binds to the child of the flame...*binds*. Bind means to tie or fasten to something. Or two things cohering together to create something else. I'm thinking that line refers to power being shared in some way, if both these two entities need to come together to release something. The chains of solitude…that's stumping me. I've never heard of that." Kellen seemed displeased at his inability to figure this out fast enough.

"Maybe the chains of solitude are referring to the Varminian curse," Ella speculated.

"Oh. That's good, Rose." His voice squeaked from excitement. "Maybe Bryara gave you a prophecy on how to break the Varminian curse!"

*I hate to spoil your fun,* Coz piped up in both their heads, sounding faintly amused, *but no, that's not what the chains of solitude mean.*

*Would you like to tell us, then, what it means, since you clearly seem to know?* Kellen grumbled.

*You will find out eventually,* Coz guaranteed. *When it's time, and when—*

*If you say, 'When you're ready,' I'm going to scream,* Ella exclaimed. Kellen smirked at her.

Coz went silent after that.

"I have another question." Ella lifted her hand over her head like she was one of his students.

"Rose, you don't need to raise your hand to speak." Kellen laughed.

"I didn't want to interrupt your flow." He tipped over to wrap his fingers around one of the legs of her chair and tow it forward so she was sitting closer to him, the act so indisputably sensual that the air was cleaved from her lungs. "It's not really a question," she stammered, Kellen grinning at the aroused shake in her voice, "so much as a request. I want to know more about Aros Cavalian. Everyone keeps telling me I need to stop judging him and there's so much I don't know about him. What can you tell me about what he's sacrificed for the kingdom of Cavale?"

"I'm not sure I can give you a satisfying answer, aside from what I know about the myth of Tala—at least what's taught to the kids here." Kellen's knee brushed against hers when he leaned forward. "Aros used to be the kind of king who was never not interacting with his people. He was deeply involved in the innerworkings of the kingdom. Edar and Aros are not just brothers. They're twins, actually, the closest bond you can have apart from a Cavalisha. When Edar left with Tala, leaving Aros without his twin and his mate, Aros stopping leaving Avatia to visit the heart of Cavale. He stopped personally aiding the villagers and deferred to sending envoys in his place. He grew disconnected from the land and the people. In my lifetime, Aros has never been seen outside of Avatia. The Primordials who still venerate him, they feel pity for him and all he's lost. They fight for him against Edar with the hope of stealing their king's joy back, hoping to bring back the days when Aros didn't entomb himself in Avatia. Those who rebel and become Dissidents are typically the Primordials whose ancestors remember a time when Aros was more involved with Cavale and have built up resentment for his abandonment of his people. Those stories are passed down through the family to create a new generation of Dissidents to back Edar."

Ella took a moment to consider Kellen's response.

Was it possible that Aros didn't send aid that day to Kellen and the twins not because he didn't want to, but because he *couldn't?* Was that why everyone kept telling her not to judge him for his lack of assistance and refusal to give her a direct message? Because he was so consumed by grief that he couldn't pull himself away from the place where he'd intombed himself as a protective measure?

Ella found herself in the camp of people who felt sorrow for the God. Not pity, but sorrow. She'd seen what grief had done to her mother after her father abandoned them. Not that Annalise was particularly affectionate with her before Alec left, but grief had taken a woman who had the potential to be loving—which Ella saw in the way Annalise doted on Alec—and bent her into so many painful shapes that she no longer possessed the capacity to feel anything apart from that loss. Ella had come to a place, thanks to several rounds of intense therapy, where she recognized that maybe Annalise wasn't truly evil. Maybe her grief was so strong that it overpowered the person who lay beneath it. Maybe the same had befallen Aros, had taken someone once benevolent and turned them into someone intolerant, incapable of empathizing with anyone outside of himself.

Even a God wasn't immune to that kind of intense reaction to loss. Perhaps grief, when left unchecked, was a killer who murders the person you used to be so you can join the person you lost.

None of it excused what Annalise did to Ella. None of that excused Aros's lack of support for Kellen and the twins that day, or the way he refused to tolerate anyone holding a different opinion from his own. Thinking about it this way, giving her mother and the king the tiniest benefit of compassion, only created space for Ella to move on and not be weighed down by her own anger and grief.

"What about the rumors that he was abusive to Tala and she left willingly with Edar?" Ella asked, remembering what Markus Loewe's father had said during their meeting.

"Never been proven. Then again, none of these stories have been proven. Aros won't confirm or deny them, apart from tossing anyone into Terminus who makes their dissidence known."

"What do *you* think?" she pushed, curious to know Kellen's true feelings.

"I think people are immensely complicated," he answered, not a real answer, just to placate her with something.

Into her head, in the privacy of their bond, he said, *I wouldn't be surprised if those rumors were true, or if they aren't. Everything I know about Aros is from reading the myths designed to put him in a positive light and paint him as the victim. Who's to say any of that is true, but who's to say it's not? What someone considers to be their truth, even if it differs from someone else's truth, is still a valid truth. People can live the same experience and see it in completely different ways. That's what I love about studying history. There is never one way of looking at something.*

Ella didn't know if she'd ever felt this attracted to him.

*You're very smart, Kellen,* she told him, appreciating the way he blushed at the compliment.

*You're very beautiful, Noella.* Ella was about to leap out of her chair and pounce on him when his phone began ringing.

"Shit, it's my lawyer." From Kellen's tone of voice and the way his fingers plunged for the phone, she sensed he was experiencing a dreadful premonition of what was waiting for him on the other end of that call. "Brunner," he choked out when he answered. "What's wrong?" Ella rose from her chair to approach him.

She stretched her hand out to touch his shoulder when Kellen suddenly flung backwards and erupted.

"WHAT?" he screamed, stormy eyes of dismay raising to Ella. "When did you receive this?"

Kellen pulled his phone away from his ear and pressed the speakerphone button to give Ella an opening into the discussion.

"I just saw it in my inbox and called you immediately," a muffled, gruff male voice resounded on the other end.

"How is this even possible?" Kellen demanded.

"The parenting order has been decreed on the basis that a risk to Jarion and Laya's best interests has been identified," Brunner explained, his voice focused in a way that suggested he was reading this off a screen or paper. "The Court deemed it salutary for the children to begin supervised visits with their mother, spanning once every week for a two hour timeframe, starting tomorrow evening."

"Supervised visits?!" Ella exclaimed, interjecting to yell, "She tried to kill them all three weeks ago!"

"Who is that?" Brunner asked Kellen.

"Noella Rose," Kellen responded, then tacked on at the end, "My girlfriend." Ella tried not to descend into a puddle when he called her that, her breath cluttering her throat. Kellen continued, "Anything you say to me, you can say in front of her. And she's right. Miya tried to kill all of us, including the twins."

"There's no way to prove that if there weren't witnesses," Brunner replied.

"You've got a witness right here!" Ella hollered, pointing to herself, not that Brunner could see her.

*Witnesses they'd want to hear from, sweetheart,* Kellen whispered with an apology spiked through the statement.

"What about the twins?" Ella pushed. "They were there too."

"The Court isn't looking to ask the twins what they want," Brunner said, not meanly, but honestly. "They only care about determining for themselves what's best for them. If the twins say anything now, when none of you went to law enforcement immediately when it happened, it will just look like Kellen convinced them to fabricate a story to turn on their mother. The Court will rule in Miya's favor."

"Of course I didn't go to law enforcement when it happened," Kellen snapped, pinching the bridge of his nose. "Because what the fuck were they going to do? They're in Miya's back pocket too!"

"What about Aros Cavalian?" Ella chimed in again. "Aros is aware of what Miya did to us because he got angry with his envoy for not being there to protect me. Doesn't that count for anything?"

"No," Brunner pronounced, "because Aros Cavalian was the God who signed off on the order."

Every bit of sympathy she held for the King of the Gods moments ago vanished, replaced with incendiary hatred. In that moment, she'd never reviled anyone more, even including her own mother.

"How does this impact the custody agreement?" Kellen asked Brunner.

"It doesn't, not fully anyway. You still have full custody. That's not changing, but the twins now have to spend time with their mother, and you need to let them, Kellen. No taking them and running away. If you don't comply with this order, then your guardianship will be subject to change."

"*Fuck, fuck, fuck!*" Kellen buried his face in his hands. "*Fuck.* This can't be happening."

Ella wrapped her arm around Kellen's shoulders. He dropped his forehead onto her chest with a pained groan and twined his arms around her waist, drawing her out of her chair and into his lap.

"You said supervised visits," Ella said, taking over the line of questioning for Kellen. "Supervised by who?"

"It could be a person known to the twins, or an independent supervisor provided through a service."

"It'll be *me*," Kellen asserted, lifting his head out of Ella's chest. "Tell whoever the fuck sent you the order that I will be the one supervising the visit. There's no fucking way I will let the twins be anywhere near her and not be present."

"You can be there too, Kellen, but the court won't agree to just you supervising."

"What about Aros Cavalian's envoy?" Ella suggested, taking the phone out of Kellen's hand.

"That would work," Brunner agreed. Kellen squeezed Ella's hip. "You think you can get Aros's envoy to agree to go?"

"He won't have a choice when I'm done with him," Ella swore.

"Alright. I'll let the representative know what you've decided." Brunner paused, then threw in, "I'm sorry, Kellen," before he hung up the phone. Kellen chucked the device across the desk without a care for where it landed or the final state of the technology after it clattered to the floor.

"This is my worst fucking nightmare." He squashed his fingers into his eyes to keep the tears from spilling over. He finally looked at her when he cried, "How am I supposed to tell Jarion and Laya about this? How am I supposed to tell them that they need to spend time with the woman who abused them, and there's nothing I can do to stop it?" Ella had nothing in her to give him.

No encouraging words. No perfect sentiment for him to latch onto. Nothing. All she could think about was if it was her in place of the twins, being forced to spend time with her mother after everything she'd done. She was thrust back into a time of terror and pain and isolation, a time when love was such a foreign concept to her that she didn't believe it to be true, darkness invading her lungs.

"This is all my fault," Ella stammered, tears escaping down her cheeks. Once she started, she couldn't stop drowning in her guilt, panting unruly sobs that kept torrenting out of her like a broken faucet, missing a handle to mitigate them. "You told me this would happen if I kept speaking to the twins, and I did it anyway. I'm so sorry, Kellen. I should've listened to you. I should've stayed away."

"No, you absolutely should not have." Kellen gripped her chin and forced her eyes to slide back over his, to meet his green insistence, his emerald voracity. "I was wrong to ask you to stay away from them. If you had stayed away, Jarion wouldn't be here right now. Laya wouldn't have found her voice. Do not think for a second that this is your fault, Noella. Miya's been looking for something to pin me with for the last two years. You were just an easy target. I don't blame you for any of this. In every universe, even if we always landed at this same result, I would be forever grateful for you being so stubborn that you refused to listen to me." Kellen's lips brushed against her cheeks, kissing away the tears, which only made the tears strengthen, taking on a life of their own separate from her despondence, becoming a deluge of adoration. "You fucking saved their lives, Noella," he said, then swallowed his own emotion and added, "and you saved mine."

Ella leaned forward so her nose rested against his. Neither moved for several minutes. Neither spoke. Neither did anything but breathe each other in, gaining strength from the evidence that the other was alive beneath them.

"Will you come with us tomorrow?" Ella yanked her head back.

"To your mother's house?" she squeaked. Kellen nodded. "Kellen…I don't think that's a good idea."

"Her whole argument is that I'm a terrible parent for letting them near a human. She'll have no leg to stand on if she lets that human in her space too. Aros's envoy can vouch for us by being there. Maybe Eyal can get Aros to change the order."

"Kellen. That's a *huge* gamble. You're risking all of us getting arrested on sight if I'm with you guys!"

"Not with Eyal there," Kellen argued. "He wouldn't let anything like that happen to you." Kellen's fingers burrowed into Ella's thigh before he vowed, "Neither will I. Anyone who dares to lay a hand on you will risk that being the last thing they ever touch." Ella gasped. His hand glided higher up her leg, inching precariously close to the aching juncture of her thighs. "Please, Noella? Please, come. I can't do this without you."

Ella knew in this moment that no matter how hard she tried, she would never be able to resist Kellen Kilic. She could thrash and scream and feign indifference, she could tell herself how wrong it was to feel this way about the parent of the kids she counseled, but at the end of the day, her heart would always call his name.

Her heart would always crush her mind to give him whatever he asked for, because her heart no longer belonged to her.

It was all his. This was her destiny.

"I'll be there," Ella whispered, falling deeper into his embrace when his hands splayed across her back and tugged her closer. Her heart refused to settle in her chest. That older female voice returned to her ears.

*This is where you're supposed to be, Noella,* the voice insisted.

*I know,* Ella said back, then nuzzled her face in Kellen's neck and let herself drift into his tranquility.

When Kellen and Ella approached the faculty housing building where Laya and Jarion waited outside, it suddenly dawned on her that she was supposed to be having dinner with Kellen tonight. Their plan for a first date had slipped her mind between Bryara's visit, Jarion releasing his wings, and that phone call with Kellen's lawyer. Ella's heart sagged in her chest, mourning the loss of what could've been as they advanced towards the twins and the fantasy of their evening shattered.

"Ms. Rose!" Laya greeted in a squeal. "I breathed fire today!"

"You did?" Ella exclaimed with a large grin. She squeezed Laya's shoulder. "That's amazing!"

"Um, excuse me, miss," Kellen drawled. Laya smirked at him. "Why wasn't I the first person you told?"

"Jarion was the first person I told. Don't start thinking you're special now." Ella laughed at Kellen's frown.

"What did it feel like?" she asked Laya.

"I thought I was dying for a second, but it was so cool! It wasn't a huge amount. Mr. Park called them baby sparks, but he said they'll start getting stronger the more I let them out. I felt like a badass."

"That's my girl," Kellen esteemed as Laya slammed her palm first into Ella's hand, then Kellen's, which he used to pull her into him and kiss the top of her head. "So proud of you, Laylie."

"Thanks, Kellings." She stretched up on her tiptoes to press a kiss to the edge of his jaw, as that was all she could reach.

"Why'd you call us down here?" Jarion asked, tilting his body half into Kellen to accept his brother's hug.

"Let's…let's talk inside." Kellen stumbled on his words before he opened the door and gestured Laya and Jarion to head inside the building, firing an anxious look at Ella that she met with a small smile of encouragement.

"Why are there candles everywhere?" Jarion shouted the moment they stepped into Kellen's apartment.

Ella froze at the door. Every surface of the living room was illuminated in gilded flames, each of the tapers holding the fire shaded purple. Her eyes flew to Kellen, watching his brown skin turn red, and felt her heart preparing to leap out of her chest and melt into liquid love on the floor.

"Um…I was just going to have a quiet night alone," Kellen stammered weakly, itching the back of his neck.

"With candles?" Jarion doubted.

"And roses?" Laya lifted the bouquet of red roses resting on the coffee table. Ella tried to swallow her own lips to keep from laughing at the intensification of Kellen's flush, threatening to erode his skin.

"Can't a guy spoil himself every now and then?" he snapped, snatching the flowers from his sister.

"Hey, no one's judging," Jarion laughed while raising his hands over his head. Laya was peeking over at Ella from the corner of her eye, not buying Kellen's obvious lie that he'd set this up for himself.

*This is incredible,* Ella cooed to Kellen when the twins were busying themselves with getting comfortable on the couch. She hoped he could see her admiration and hear it clear in her voice. *I'm sorry we won't get to enjoy it tonight.*

*I plan to have many more nights like this with you, sweetheart. This isn't our last chance.* Ella turned her head away so Kellen couldn't see the tears arising in her eyes. She claimed a spot on the couch next to Jarion and mentally armed herself for this difficult discussion while Kellen cleaned up all the candles, dropping them in a cardboard box.

"What's going on, Kell?" Laya asked, reading the anxiety in every micromovement of her brother.

"I have…some not great news," he started, situating in the wingchair beside the couch and resting his elbows on his knees, leaning forward. He slumped his chin inside his palm and opened his mouth to speak. "I found out—" An unexpected sob bled out from between his lips. "I can't," he wept, his gaze collapsing into Ella's. Her posture adjusted with concern as she watched the man she'd come to adore begin trembling uncontrollably. "I can't do it. I can't say it. Please, help me."

Jarion and Laya turned to Ella in vain, expecting an answer Kellen was no longer capable of giving.

It was on Ella now to tell them.

"I'm sorry, guys," she began, squeezing Jarion's hand. As calmly as she could muster, as it was on her now to be the voice of reason for all three siblings, she told them, "Your brother found out today that the court has ordered for the two of you to begin having supervised visits with your mother."

"WHAT?!" Laya screamed. Jarion ripped his hand out of Ella's to spring to his feet.

"How?! How is this even possible?" Jarion demanded, adhering to his anger while Laya immediately clamped her hands over her eyes and burst into tears. Ella tried to shove away the nausea of guilt, but it surrounded her and pressed against her temples, making it difficult to see straight with her own emergent tears.

"Because Miya is a vindictive bitch who has the Court wrapped around her finger." Ella sensed Kellen said this to protect her so the twins wouldn't know her presence in their lives was to blame for this. Now that he'd regained the ability to talk, Kellen promised the twins, "I need you guys to know that this doesn't change anything. Just because she won a small victory does not mean she's won the war. You're still mine. She has no claim to you. You just need to spend two hours with her—"

"TWO HOURS?!" they both screamed.

"Two hours tomorrow night," he continued, the color depleting from Jarion's face, "but both I, Ms. Rose, and Aros Cavalian's envoy will be there. You will not be alone with her. We won't leave your side."

"NO!" Laya seized one of Kellen's pillows and hurled it at him. Jarion had completely frozen, solid ice to Laya's exacerbated fire. "NO! I won't do it! I won't go back there! I'd rather be tossed into Terminus!"

"Laylie," Kellen moaned. He crawled across the floor to sit in front of her. "My beautiful love."

"NO!" She pushed at his chest, but Kellen didn't budge. He

wouldn't move, even when she recklessly slapped him across the face and thrust her elbow into his chest. "Don't tell me I have to, Kellen! Please!"

"I'm sorry." Kellen's facial features were bleary from desolate submission. "I hate this just as much as you do…but if you guys don't go, they'll call into question my guardianship over you. In a permanent sense."

"No," Jarion gasped, finally coming back to life. His fingers dug into his temples. "No. No. No."

"Please," Laya bawled, her fingers easing off from trying to hurt him and instead choosing to gather the material of Kellen's sweater desperately. "Please don't let her take us from you, Kell."

"I promise, baby," he swore to his sister, swiping the loose strands of hair out of her face so they wouldn't glue to her damp cheeks. "I won't let anyone touch you or Jare. Never." Ella lost the battle against tears.

"You'll be there?" Jarion asked Kellen. He nodded. Jarion then looked at Ella. "You'll be there, too?"

"Yes," Ella confirmed with a nod. "We won't let anything happen to you guys."

Laya wiggled in Kellen's arms, begging to be released. Once she was unfettered, she bolted right into Ella's embrace, wrapping her small arms around Ella's waist and burying her face in Ella's stomach.

Ella didn't hesitate to return the hug. "Thank you, Ms. Rose," Laya whispered into Ella's shirt.

"Of course, Laya." She lifted one arm off Laya and extended it towards Jarion. Kellen relinquished his hold on his brother so Jarion could join his sister in Ella's arms. "You don't ever need to thank me. Ever." She swung her head to the side, sinking her teeth into her bottom lip to contain a sob. She then shook her hair out of her face and slipped her arms off the twins, only to kneel in front of them and proffer a warm smile that didn't hold any of the anguish mutilating her lungs. "What do I always tell you guys?"

"We can do hard things," Jarion repeated, eyes warm with reverence.

"We can do hard things," Ella repeated, squeezing Laya's hand.

"You want to know why? Because we're *warriors*. We can do hard things because we've survived worse. We've survived worse, and we still fight every day to find the light, to believe there is light out there for us to reach, even through all the darkness we've faced. What doesn't kill us should better know how to fucking run. Excuse my language."

"Cursing twice in one day, Ms. Rose? That's got to be a record," Jarion teased her, smudging the tears under his eyes with his fingers.

"I'm not setting a great example for you, am I?" Ella laughed.

"You set the *best* example," Laya asserted, creating a new batch of tears in Ella's tear ducts.

*I concur with that statement,* Kellen agreed. His gaze set her skin afire.

"I'm sorry I hit you, Kell," Laya said to her brother, heading back over to him to envelop his neck in a remorseful hug. "I know this isn't your fault. I know you've done everything you can to protect us."

"It's okay, Laylie." He squeezed her back. "All your anger, all your sadness, you give it all to me. I can take it." Kellen raised his eyes to Jarion. "Both of you." Jarion nodded in quiet understanding, appreciation swelling between them.

Kellen's eyes swung to Ella.

*You're going to be okay,* she promised him, even though she had no evidence to support that claim.

*I know,* he answered, his voice a warm caress in her mind. *Because we have you.*

CHAPTER 28

# KELLEN

KELLEN AND NOELLA spent what would have been their first date comforting the twins and devising a plan for their voyage to Miya Kilic's home. The four of them shared the meal Kellen had prepared for him and Noella, huddling around his small dining room table to discuss how they would ensure they got through those torturous two hours in their mother's house with as little pain as possible.

It was Kellen's idea for Noella to wear a mask over her face when they first arrived at the estate, to disguise her identity long enough to be admitted onto the grounds of the property before anyone realized she was the human. Kellen expected—because Miya didn't do anything without an audience—that the return of her children would become a colossal event where she'd invite everyone in her social circle. She would play the part of doting mother in front of her peers as her way of showing the world she hadn't lost her power and rubbing her victory in Kellen's face.

Noella would play the part of Kellen's pet for the evening, costuming herself as someone docile and nonthreatening to make it impossible for all the Primordials in the room to view her as anything but harmless.

It wasn't an ideal situation—Kellen hated asking her to do this —but she hadn't hesitated to agree.

Kellen sat on Noella's couch the following evening, the gremlin curled up on the cushion next to him, and waited for Noella to emerge from her bedroom for their journey to the town of Yorkdill.

During dinner the night before, Jarion had flicked his eyes down Noella's body and said, "You're gonna need to wear something nicer than that tomorrow night," before popping a string bean stalk into his mouth.

Noella pinched the fabric of her sweater. "What's wrong with my clothes?" she'd said with a cute pout.

"It won't be Miya Kilic approved," Laya answered with a scornful wrinkle to her nose, emulating their mother.

"I don't care to be Miya Kilic approved," Noella spat.

"You'll care if she refuses you entry onto the estate because you're not dressed fancy enough," Jarion argued.

Kellen nearly laughed at the horror written over her face. "How fancy are we talking here?"

"Black tie," Kellen replied. Noella's eyes popped out of her skull.

"I don't have anything black tie!"

"Borrow something of Jo's. Or go shopping tomorrow after school and bring Josefyn with you."

*If you go shopping, please feel free to send me mental images of the dresses you try on,* he requested in private.

*For your spank bank?* she hissed.

*It's already full of images of you, sweetheart.*

From her wide eyes and crimson cheeks, he could tell she didn't know whether to find that flattering or revolting.

He hadn't received any mental images during the day, so he assumed she borrowed something from Josefyn, since she didn't know how to block him out of her brain, being the human at the other end of their mind connection.

"You need help in there?" he called out to her.

"Not yet!" an adorable squeak resounded back.

Kellen rested his chin inside his palm, peeking down at the dog —*Freya.* He was working on calling her by her actual name, not the gremlin or little monster, and accepting that Freya would always be around, as she was basically Noella's child who she thought of as an extension of her soul. In his head, he'd conceded the fact that he would always have to share her with the dog, so if the two of them were able to form an alliance built on an understanding that their primary purpose was to protect this angelic human, then Kellen could come to a place of tolerance for the Earthly Plane creature.

*Have you seen the dress?* he asked the Cavachon.

*You're going to love it,* Freya's sugary, high-pitched cadence echoed through his mind.

*Give me a hint of what it looks like.*

*It's long.* He squinted his eyes at her. All she gave him back was that dumb smile that would trick anyone who didn't have the ability to read her mind into believing she had no thoughts bobbing around in there.

Kellen had come to learn that this dog was surprisingly inciteful, kept an extensive list of all the little traits about her owner that would alert her if Noella needed comfort, and didn't forget a single time someone had wronged her owner. It made sense that Noella called Freya her soulmate.

*That's the best you can give me?* he grumbled. *Not even a color?*

*That was a real hint!* Freya squawked, then tipped her head forward and tapped her nose against the back of his hand. Kellen sighed, then reluctantly flipped his hand over and let her nuzzle the top of her furry head into his palm. *You know how I like it,* she said, Kellen kneading the top of her scalp.

"Kilic!" Noella shouted from the bedroom. "I need your help with the zipper." Kellen lightly knocked Freya's head off his leg so he could stand. He came to an abrupt halt in the doorway of her bedroom.

Noella was the epitome of modern elegance in a full-length, off-the-shoulder gown composed of sleek satin twill, glimmering in the ambient light while cuffing at the neckline, blending down into a trumpet skirt with a side slit. She'd parted her blonde hair to the right and slid a bobby pin beneath her ear on the left side to keep the cascade of honey-golden waves on the right side of her body, leaving her left shoulder unadorned. A touch of makeup graced her face, not heavy enough to make it obvious that she was wearing anything, but Kellen had spent a disgusting amount of time studying every facet of her face, so he recognized the different areas that were highlighted by a sweep of blush or a soft golden shimmer. Kellen found it ironic that the dress was shaded a purplish red that was reminiscent of the color of wine because he instantly felt drunk the moment he looked at her.

Noella twisted her head around, her eyelashes darkened and lengthened to such an extent that they fluttered against her eyebrows. Her full lips split to permit gulps of oxygen to travel through the gap.

*Incredible,* he gushed into her mind.

He preferred the natural blush stealing across her cheeks to the simulated flush created by her blush shade.

*Right back at you,* she replied, drinking in the immaculate black suit and matching black button-down he sported underneath, missing a tie, the first three buttons unfastened to create a more roguish, carefree appearance.

"Can you zip the back, please?" she asked aloud, either unaware of the desire rampaging through his body, or fully aware and choosing to taunt him rather than acknowledge it. Kellen whistled through his teeth as he closed the distance between them.

"I'm going to need you to help me here a little, sweetheart, 'cause my fingers want to bring the zipper down, not up."

"If I feel the zipper go down, I will knee you in the dick, Kilic." Kellen laughed before he caught the zipper above her backside.

*Fuck,* her ass in this dress was something of a miracle. A once in a lifetime phenomenon. The appearance of a glowing comet that had decided to brave the sun's wrath so he could personally behold its splendor.

"I'm going to write Josefyn a personal note of thanks for lending you this dress," he said, then entreated, "Do you have to return it after tonight?"

"Take all the mental photos now, cause this dress is going right back to Josefyn Yilanci first thing tomorrow."

"I've got to make it count, then." Kellen gradually dragged the zipper up her spine, wishing to draw out the moment so his hands could cling to an excuse to keep touching her. "Was Akio there when you tried this on?" The thought made him irrationally angry.

"If I say yes, are you going to have a conniption?" She spoke with humor and genuine concern.

"I hate the way he looks at you," he found himself confessing in a growl. Her eyes softened at his vehemence. "I hate when he calls you *Rosie.* I hate the way he feels the need to touch you all the time. I hate that you let him."

Noella peeked at him through the mirror. She sighed, an internal battle playing out on her delicate features.

"If I tell you something, can you promise to keep it between us?"

"Of course," he swore. Her eyes fell shut, her lashes dripping shadows down from her cheeks to her chin.

Using their mind connection for added discretion, she revealed, *Josefyn and Akio are Cavalisha.*

Kellen's jaw virtually dislocated.

*THEM?!* he exclaimed, his voice in both their heads crackling. *They've performed the ritual for Mara and everything?* Noella bobbed her head in a nod. *DAMN. I'm shocked. They hide that so well.*

*That's why I let Akio be affectionate with me, because I know it doesn't mean anything. He is madly in love with his mate. Our friendship is STRICTLY platonic. There is no reason for you to be threatened.*

*I never said I was threatened,* he scoffed. Noella sucked on her bottom lip to keep from laughing.

"Do you feel better now that you know that?" she asked audibly.

"I do. Thank you, sweetheart." He lightly pecked the edge of her jaw, a mere browse of his lips on her skin, and relished the way her breath heaved out of her chest in a boisterous pant. "I know this might be hard for you," he mocked, and she squinted kohl-lined eyes at him in a scowl, "but you're going to have to stay quiet tonight."

"I know what my role is," she said in a way that slightly concerned Kellen as to what she meant.

"I'm sorry in advance…for the side of me you'll see tonight."

Noella adjusted herself so she now faced him and snaked her hand up his neck to cup his cheek.

"Don't apologize," she whispered, her eyes so kind. The way she looked at him made him feel like she had stripped the skin off his bones and was looking at all of him, all the darkness, all the hollow grooves of pain, and didn't fear any of it, fully prepared to embrace every broken part of him. "You do what you need to do to protect the twins. I'll be there with you every step of the way. I've got you, Kellen." Kellen swallowed at hearing his own words spoken back at him.

The same words he spoke to Jarion two years prior on that horrible night when he rescued them from Miya. Hearing that before he was forced to walk his siblings back into the lion's den was exactly what he needed. Somehow, he believed she knew that, which was exactly why she said it.

"We need to leave before I decide to stop waiting for you to make a move and take matters into my own hands," he groaned, proffering his elbow for her to curl her fingers around his bicep, letting him guide her to the door.

Jarion and Laya were waiting outside the faculty housing building with Eyal. When Noella called Eyal the previous night, she hadn't even needed to beg or coerce the envoy into agreeing to be their overseer for this supervised visit, which Kellen found strange, considering Aros Cavalian had been the God to sign off on the visit to begin with. All he'd said to her was *I will procure a car for us. I'm not flying on the dragon's back,* and hung up the phone. While Kellen couldn't see Eyal's face beneath the shield of his helmet, he felt the envoy's resolve in his posture and the way his hands lingered over the hilt of the sword sheathed to his side, primed for battle if called upon to fight. Laya's dress was a burnt orange resembling an amber sunset that complimented her dark skin, a one-shoulder dress made of light and airy lux chiffon flowing gracefully from a tied shoulder bow to a dreamy full circle skirt, her black hair balled up in a bun atop her head. Jarion looked like the suit he'd squeezed his lanky limbs into was strangling his bones.

"Don't you two clean up nice!" Noella squealed to the twins, her hand falling off Kellen's arm now that they were in a public space, her veneer of professionalism reattaching itself to her being.

"I love your dress," Laya gushed to Noella.

"It's on loan," Noella replied with a wink that made Laya break out into adorable giggles. "I love *your* dress! That color is so stunning on you." She laughed at Jarion's expression. "That suit looks painful, Jare."

"Not as painful as what we're about to do," Jarion spat.

Everyone descended into a chilled, heavy silence, the weight of that truth closing in around them.

"We can do hard things," Kellen proclaimed, giving Noella's shoulders a squeeze with each word he quoted from her. She unconsciously tipped back to lean against his chest, the top of her head tucking under his chin, and sunk into the feeling of his fingers massaging her shoulders—until she realized what she was doing in front of the twins and sprung away from him, scurrying to stand at Jarion's side because that was safer than staying in close proximity to Kellen.

"We should get on the road," Eyal rumbled from inside the helmet, stalking off for the parking lot without any further preamble, leaving the four of them to scurry to keep up with his long strides.

They approached a sleek silver car, large enough to fit all five of them, with curves and lines that flowed seamlessly from front to back, the chrome accents and shiny rims sparkling when the setting sunlight peppered over the glossy surface. Kellen snatched the keys right out of Eyal's hands without thought.

"I'm driving," he declared, refusing to let anyone else be in control of the vehicle apart from himself. He needed to throw his angst about the evening into feeling useful, and driving felt like the perfect outlet for his pent-up frustration.

"I was going to suggest you drive, if you'd given me the respect of speaking first before you stole my keys," the envoy snarled. "I'm not your enemy, Mr. Kilic. I'm not here to make any of your lives harder. I'm getting really sick of everyone treating me like a punching bag. What happened to not shooting the messenger? I have feelings too, not that anyone ever asks about them."

Kellen felt a twinge of guilt scratch his throat when he watched Eyal angrily crawl into the backseat.

*We should all be nicer to him,* Noella said.

*I didn't mean to be rude,* Kellen insisted. *I just can't stand being the passenger in a car.* Her mouth quirked up at the corner in a way that implied she wasn't surprised to learn this about his character.

*Next time, say that rather than grab his keys from him.* Only Noella could scold Kellen like a child, yet he'd take in every word and internalize it so he never made the same mistake twice.

Noella claimed shotgun while Jarion and Laya funneled into the backseat with Eyal, the three of them squished together due to Eyal's bulky armor. Kellen settled behind the wheel, the plush leather cushions enveloping his taut muscles, promising fleeting relief until they reached the Kilic estate.

"I'm sorry," Kellen said to Eyal before he switched the car on.

The envoy nodded his head in acceptance of the apology. The momentary delay in their voyage had been worth it from the way Noella's features illuminated with a dazzling, proud smile.

The soft, muted purrs of the engine rumbled through his veins before Kellen steered the car out of the parking lot and onto the winding path that led to the gates of Delmarth, hurling them in the direction of Yorkdill.

Not a single word pierced the ether.

Everyone's minds were flung in random, diverging directions, a communal anxiety splattered over the vehicle.

"Jare?" Noella broke the silence to meet Jarion's eye through the rearview mirror. "How's the wing flexing going?"

Kellen expected Jarion not to answer her in the company of others, but instead, his brother surprised him and replied, "It really hurts. My dragon is angry at me for denying him for so long. It feels like he's punishing me."

It hurt Kellen to hear Jarion say this. It hurt him more that he knew Jarion would never tell him that as easily as he told Noella.

"Remember what we talked about last week?" She turned her head around to look at him. "Think of your dragon as an extension of you. As long as you keep telling yourself that you deserve to be punished, your wings will continue to think of you as the torturer.

We need to replace the thoughts to change the action. We can all stand around and support and love you, but the love that matters most needs to come from inside you, directed at *you*. I know you can do it. I've seen you do it and succeed. I'll keep saying it until you can say it to yourself and believe it." Jarion's eyes glimmered.

"Thank you, Ms. Rose."

"Of course, Jarion." She gave his hand a squeeze, then spun back around in her seat, shaking her hair out of her face. Kellen was awestruck by what he just witnessed. "Sorry," she said through a nervous laugh. "I'm not here to be your school counselor tonight. I'm here for moral support."

"That's okay, Ms. Rose. I needed to hear that." Jarion's expression displayed his reverence for her.

Kellen leaned over and placed his hand on Noella's knee, beckoning her eyes to meet his, and whispered into her mind, *I'll never stop thanking you for being there for him. For both of them.*

*And I'll never stop being there for them,* she answered in her own delicate whisper, then added, *and for you.*

"Actually, Ms. Rose," Jarion piped up, splintering Kellen and Noella's intense eye contact and stopping him from lunging across the car to consume her in a kiss, "I was going to ask you…can I start seeing you twice a week for counseling instead of once?"

"Of COURSE! As long as it's okay with your department head." Her eyes flickered to Kellen. "Mr. Kilic? Would that be okay?"

Kellen swallowed the lump in his throat. "We will make that work for you, Jarion," he swore, his brother's face engulfed by a smile that made the corners of Kellen's eyes sting. How he missed his brother's smile.

"Thanks, Kell." Kellen nodded to his brother.

"Lay?" Noella peeked back at Laya. "How's the fire going?"

"Horrible," Laya gagged. "My mouth tastes like burnt matches every second of the day now."

"Yeah, I don't envy you guys," Noella laughed.

*Gods, her fucking laugh.* Kellen's favorite sound in existence. It both healed and crushed him. *Can someone please invent a device to bottle up a laugh, so I never have to exist without the sound of her near me?*

"What Varmin form would you want to be, if you could pick, Ms. Rose?" Laya asked.

"Oh, good question!" Noella rubbed her hands together in thought, resting her chin on top of the stack of fingers. "Hm…you guys are going to think this is bullshit, but I really would pick to be a dragon."

"Really?" Kellen spluttered, fucking thrilled. He would've been jealous of any Varmin form she picked besides his.

"Really! I was a huge fantasy buff when I was a kid…still am. And I always wanted a dragon. My second choice would be a Gryphon, but that's just because the Gryphon was my mascot in college." Kellen would forever hold an irrational grudge against Gryphon-shifters now. "If I'm being more realistic about what type of Primordial I'd be, based on my actual personality…I think I'd have some Cerebri in me. Maybe an emotion-manipulator. And I think I'd be a Meteoro water-bender."

"Water? Really?" Jarion exclaimed.

"She likes to swim," Kellen blurted, catching Noella's blush behind a curtain of her hair. He was grateful they'd come to a place where the mention of the pool incident didn't dredge up any negative feelings, where they could even laugh about it and appreciate how far they'd come in their relationship.

"What about you, Eyal?" Noella asked the envoy, having heard his entreaty to be treated like a person and not the empty vessel his armor made him appear to be. "What type of Primordial are you under there?"

"I'm not supposed to answer that." Noella and Kellen exchanged a quizzical look.

"No one's here to strike you down," she pointed out gently, waving around the surroundings of the car.

"There is always someone watching, Ms. Rose. You are never free from the surveillance of the Gods."

Kellen squirmed in his seat at the shudder rampaging down his spine. "I think that's unfair," Noella declared, frowning. "How are you supposed to feel like a person when Aros doesn't allow you to share any of yourself with other people?" Kellen felt Eyal's warm gaze penetrate through the steel of his helmet.

"Your concern for my well-being is sweet and appreciated, Ms. Rose. As was your defense of me with Bryara, as unnecessary as it was." Kellen glanced at Eyal through the rearview mirror.

*I apologize for my behavior earlier,* Kellen repeated before he hissed, *but I can feel the way you're looking at my girl right now, and if you don't take your eyes off her, I will reach back there, remove your stupid helmet, and gouge your eyes from your skull so you never look at anything ever again.*

Eyal's husky laughter curled around Kellen's ears. *You're protective of her. That's good. That's how it should be.*

*How it should—* he started to ask, but the sentence never escaped in full before Eyal cut him off.

*You have nothing to worry about, Mr. Kilic. You are mistaking my admiration for the girl as attraction. I revere her. I do not want her. She is all yours, if you would just get off your ass and be brave enough to claim her already.* Kellen's foot almost pressed down on the brake peddle out of sheer rage.

*Kellen?* Noella murmured, sensing the change in his deportment from just the way his mouth tightened at Eyal's patronization, the only signal of anger in his otherwise unmoving countenance. *What's wrong?*

*Tell me a joke. Tell me anything to keep me from tearing Eyal's throat out and landing myself in Terminus.* Noella didn't need to know why for her to understand the severity of his wrath and scramble to come up with something to distract him.

*Where do you find a dog with no legs?* she stammered in a rush. Kellen glanced at her from the corner of his eye.

*Where?* he inquired.

*Right where you left him.* She pressed her lips together to subjugate a snort. The tension diminished from Kellen's rigid muscles, not necessarily from her dumb joke, but from the way she was fighting not to laugh, the sight of her happiness more palliative to his anger than breathing. She fixed her hand over her mouth while internally, her chortles surged through his whole body, permeating his entire being, a sound he longed to trap inside him so he never had to be parted from it.

*Thank you, Rose. I needed that,* he chuckled, though to himself, he knew what he'd always needed was her.

Far too soon, the Kilic estate devastated the skyline, amplifying in size the closer they approached. The manner, which constituted a castle more than a house, stood upon a rock-strewn, corrugated cliff, its towering walls made of corundum stone that had weathered centuries of Kilic family dragons, bearing the besmears of fire splotches and claw marks with pride. Turrets stretched high into the sky, their pointed roofs reaching toward the heavens like the fingers of a giant seeking to touch the clouds.

Kellen had grown up in the same home as the twins, though their experiences inside those walls were vastly different. Where the twins saw that estate as their prison, Kellen viewed it as the only acquaintance he'd had growing up, before the twins blessed his life and he never had to endure a day in isolation again. With a mother more preoccupied with gaining the affection of her social circle than extending that affection to her son and a father who barely spoke a word apart from *listen to your mother,* Kellen suffered so many years alone in that house, going some days without speaking a word to anyone, with only the walls to keep him company.

He let these memories and thoughts flood his mental connection with Noella, letting her see through the crack in his armor so she walked into that estate knowing the private pain he carried in his heart, the one he'd never allowed the twins to see. The one he'd gotten so used to shouldering alone.

Noella placed her hand over his and squeezed.

Not with pity. It was a quiet show of understanding, laced with sweet sympathy. The kind someone could sincerely offer when they truly knew what it felt like to be utterly alone in the world.

"Everyone, remember your roles." Kellen passed his gaze between Jarion, Laya, and Noella.

For the twins, they were to act as if their dragons hadn't emerged. If their dragons tried to make themselves known, they planned to practice tempering the urge to let them out. They were to talk minimally or not at all. They would give Miya no information she could propagate to the kingdom to further her own standing or use against them later. The twins were required to give her two hours of their time, but nowhere in the order did it say they needed to actually engage with her.

As for him and Noella, their assignment was different.

Make them believe Noella Rose was pliable. Make them believe she'd yielded to the Primordials and posed no threat to their power. Undermine the impact she'd had on the children of Delmarth so no one would believe Miya's bogus claims that her presence was affecting the students' powers. Make them believe Kellen was in control, when it was absolutely the other way around.

Noella dipped to the floor, rummaging through her purse for the elaborate lace mask Josefyn had given her. She slipped it over her eyes and reached behind her to tie the ribbon behind her head. When she struggled with the silk strings, Laya leaned forward and offered to knot the back for her.

*How do I look?* Noella asked Kellen once the mask was secure over her eyes. The lace sprawled out to split the bottom and top half of her face, spanning up to her forehead so only her grey irises and a glimpse of her full lips at the bottom peeked through. She'd only need to wear the mask until they were safely inside the gate, so the look of it didn't matter, but with it on, she became something darker, more sensual, not just a queen without a crown, but an enigmatic goddess seeking a land to rule.

*Doesn't matter how you look, sweetheart. How do you FEEL?* Her eyes shimmered inside the mask.

*Like I'm ready to make a room of Primordials my bitch.* Kellen's answering grin was wolfish.

*That's my fucking girl,* he prided, then directed the car up the mountain to the Kilic estate.

CHAPTER 29

# KELLEN

THEIR CAR ADVANCED towards the golden gate hedging the Kilic estate, a majestic structure of unparalleled grandeur that rivaled the opulence of Avatia itself. Towering arches rocketed above them, engraved with intricate carvings and filigree work that replicated flames licking up the gilded bars. Beyond the gate, leading to the entrance of the manner, lush gardens bloomed with exotic flowers that withstood the swell of snow, their florid perfume saturating the air in a heady fragrance. Fountains of crystal-clear, limpid water danced in the sunlight, casting polychromatic sprays of spiraling light onto the few patches of snow that survived the spell placed on the gardens to persist even in the winter. Kellen saw Noella's eyes widen beneath her mask, drinking it all in.

When one of Miya's sentries approached their car, Kellen's hand slid onto Noella's leg. His fingers lazily settled between her legs, stroking the interior of her thigh through the satin of her gown, a casual display of possession. Noella adjusted her posture to appear smaller by curving her shoulders inward. Her lashes tickled her cheeks as she lowered her head and hunched over in her car seat.

The ugly face of Miya's sentry, composed of harsh, nasty lines, fogged up the window at Kellen's left.

Kellen rolled the window down, then hissed in a voice he reserved for dealing with these disgusting people, "I assume I don't need to introduce myself to you, Krystofer, considering this is *my* house."

"Your friend does," Krystofer sneered, tipping his chin towards Noella. "Who is she?"

"She's *mine*," Kellen asserted with a flash of his fangs, giving Noella's leg a sharp squeeze in conjuncture with his assertion. Noella's fingers flew to wrap around Kellen's forearm, dragging his hand back between her legs and grinding her ass against her car seat while loosing a breathy, deliberately loud moan, thrusting her hips closer to where his fingers pushed into her, greedy for more friction. Kellen glided his hand up her chest, fondling the path skyward with veneration, these selfish, fake actions differing from the way he wished to truly worship her. He then slipped his middle finger between her lips without breaking his eyes from Krystofer. Noella's mouth suctioned around the digit, her teeth sheathed behind her lips, and clamped down around his finger, a throaty purr traveling deep from the back of her throat and vibrating through his finger.

Krystofer was so horrified by their tasteless display that he delved no further into Noella's identity. He hurried them along with a wave of his hand and a lurid flush billowing up to the tips of his ears.

"You know where to park the car," the sentry bit out, then scuttled off into the night to tend to his flaming cheeks.

Once the sentry disappeared, Kellen's finger retreated from Noella's mouth. She fixed her posture with a stuttering gasp, and they both squirmed in their seats. Kellen's dick ached, not unaffected just because the demonstration was a farce.

"I'm sorry you had to see that, guys," he tossed over his shoulders at the twins and Eyal, who'd been defenseless witnesses in the backseat.

"Don't worry about it," Jarion assured him. "We're not babies. Also, I wasn't looking."

"We know the plan," Laya confirmed, her own disguise of detachment inhabiting her sweet features.

*Are you okay?* Kellen asked Noella as he wove the car through the gardens to the front of the estate. His assumptions about Miya making this evening a spectacle were confirmed by the sea of random faces plaguing the grounds, strewn through the garden in their most expensive, lavish garb.

*I'm fine,* she answered in an abrupt manner that Kellen had a difficult time trusting.

*I hated doing that to you.* His power caressed her mind as he whispered, *I promise not to kiss you tonight. I've told you I will wait until you're ready, and I won't take that control away from you. I want to earn that honor when you're ready to give it to me.* Noella's bottom lip trembled.

The entrance to the estate was guarded by a massive wooden door, reinforced with iron bands. Above the door, the castle's coat of arms, a grisly, gargantuan dragon rampant upon a field of gold, gleamed under the graceful rays of sunlight spilling across the fabric. Kellen parked the car and waited until Laya, Jarion, and Eyal had climbed out of the vehicle and were lingering on the path outside before he made any moves to reach for the door handle. He stole a precious moment to steel himself, swallowing large gulps of oxygen to brace for the evening ahead.

*Any words of encouragement before we do this?* he begged Noella.

*You're Kellen fucking Kilic,* she pronounced. *You are the Varmin department head of Delmarth Academy. You're the dragon whom Aros Cavalian wanted for himself in his personal cadre. You are better than her. You will walk away tonight with the twins at your side, and she will be left with nothing.*

Kellen's chest tightened.

With that ringing testimonial, he nudged open the car door and lifted out of his seat, slipping on his own invisible mask—the son of Miya Kilic, the heir to the Kilic empire, the most powerful dragon-shifter of this generation.

Noella had asked him the night before why he felt the need to play a cruel character in front of his mother and her social circle. He reminded her that what was valued in Cavale wasn't your ability to get people to like you. It was your ability to get people to respect you, through whatever avenues you needed to take. Cruelty was admired in Cavale if it led to the obtainment of more power.

Power was all that mattered, so for Kellen tonight, his power needed to shine through most of all.

The power he usually underplayed to keep from acquiring unwanted attention from the Gods rushed up to the surface of his veins. It streamed out from his pores, showering the world in unfettered crimson energy before his wings broke free from his back, tearing through the fabric of his button down and suit jacket. The blackish-gold, leathery membrane unfurled, flexing between gales of wind and hacking through the current from the ferocity of his power unleashed.

He felt Coz slacken inside him.

Every muscle in his body breathed a sigh of relief at no longer needing to contain the scope of his ability.

Every single eye of his mother's guests, all congregated out in the garden, was pinned on him. On the vehement power emanating off him in scarlet ripples. Even his siblings' eyes were round with shock.

Kellen buttoned his jacket and gave the avaricious onlookers a cocky nod of acknowledgement. He then began rounding the car, embellishing the arrogance of his gait, and reached Noella's door, which he opened slowly for her. Before she rose, his fingers skated under her chin, his thumb smearing across her lips, careful not to smudge her lipstick. Her eyes raised to him, pupils expanding and bleeding black into the grey hue.

*Beautiful,* he echoed in her mind, a promise to her separate from the performance they were about to put on.

Using his grip on her jaw, he tugged her into a standing position. Then, with his eyes sweeping across the crowd, he trailed the top of his tongue up the column of her neck and suckled at her throat, her skin tasting faintly of cherries. It took everything inside him not to groan and fall to his knees, because that would show the throng of spectators that he belonged to *her,* not the lie they intended to create, that Noella had submitted to the Primordials and was the obedient whore they all wanted her to be.

*Fuck, you taste good, Rose,* he crooned in her mind.

Noella's head tipped to the side as she rolled and elongated her neck, offering him more access to her throat.

*It's my moisturizer,* she answered, her voice in his head breaking apart through an aroused stutter.

His hand wandered down her back to settle over her ass. He pushed Noella's body into him while his teeth inspected her slender throat. He was momentarily distracted by how her every curve and contour fit perfectly against the nooks and valleys of his own figure, further confirmation, not that he needed it, that this woman had been fashioned for him, his counterpart in body, heart, and soul.

His eyes scanned the crowd before snagging over his mother.

The practically translucent material of Miya's royal blue gown left little to the imagination in terms of her physique, a sight Kellen could've lived his whole life not seeing and would have been happier for it. Her silver hair, spun like moonlight, torrented down her chest in voluminous waves, like lightning leaking across a pavement, alive with the same sort of crackling energy. Her own power radiated out of her the same way his did, though not as potent. Kellen took pride in knowing he was the stronger of the two of them, that by the time his powers fully came into their own, he was already out of her house and not in a close enough vicinity for her to try and squash them.

The truth of their power imbalance simmered beneath every interaction they had. It seethed in her green eyes now as she felt his power bandage the garden and shove against hers, the force of it making her falter back a step. She could have the entirety of Cavale at her beck and call, could have every law enforcement officer wrapped around her finger, but when it came down to physical strength, if it all came down to an actual fight for the twins, she knew her power came nowhere close to Kellen's—not when he fully unchecked it, as he did now, for the world to see.

Kellen pulled his lips away from Noella's neck. He flipped over his hand and extended it to her.

Noella slid her dainty fingers into his. He tucked her hand in the gorge of his elbow as he led her over to Jarion, Laya, and Eyal, the twins using Eyal's armor as a shield. Kellen nodded to his siblings, and they nodded back before stepping out from behind Eyal's armor and positioning themselves beside Kellen and Noella on either side. The four of them created an impenetrable wall that not even Miya could perforate.

As they approached Miya, Eyal following in their wake, Kellen drawled, "Were you waiting for us to begin eating?"

"Quite the show you're putting on, darling," Miya said with contempt beneath a feeble mask of enthusiasm, her red painted lips bending into a grin. To the outside world, the smile she presented him looked like a mother who hadn't seen their son in ages and was admiring sunlight for the first time. Miya simpered at Jarion and Laya, but the two of them were looking at the wall over her shoulder, so anyone around them could be tricked into thinking they were meeting her eyes, but they refused. "My babies. My sweet angels. It's been too long." Laya tensed. Neither of them spoke. Miya's jaw ticked. "Neither of you have anything to say to your mother after two years of separation?"

"They were required to be here," Kellen spoke for them, plumes of smoke smoldering from the sides of his mouth. "There was no prerequisite for them to speak to you if they don't wish to."

"Maybe you should let *them* decide that for themselves," Miya hissed, though her tone of voice remained artificially friendly with all the eyes glued to their conversation. She admired Laya's dress. "Laya, you look beautiful, my love." Laya's eyes coasted to meet their mother's before she raised her chin.

"I finally found a dress that fits," Laya barked. Miya's jaw dropped at Laya's belligerence. Through their mind connection, Kellen felt Noella's approval resonate, even as her expression remained blank.

*So proud of you, Laylie,* Kellen encouraged his sister in private. Laya's lips twitched in acknowledgement of the praise. *Now look away. Don't give her the satisfaction of an opening to respond.*

"Eulaylia—" Miya began, but Laya twisted her head to the side in dismissal of her mother.

Miya, as someone who didn't actually care to win her daughter's affection back, moved on from Laya and looked to Jarion next. Jarion's eyes were glassed over in disassociation, his mind—or possibly his dragon—protecting him from fully experiencing this moment. If Kellen had the time or space, he would pull Jarion into his arms and buffer him from this himself, would offer his body and soul as reinforcement.

Miya snarled at Kellen, "What did you do to them?" All Kellen gave her in response was a curl of his lips. Miya's eyes finally flitted to Noella. "Care to introduce us to your friend?" she spat.

Noella lifted her head to Kellen, giving him a doe-eyed, submissive look, the same kind of look Oliviana used to give him that did nothing for him. He missed her fire. He craved her pushback. He reveled in her tenacity and her ability to cut so deep with words that you feel them score your soul.

He hated putting a leash on her.

He hated painting a picture of her for Cavale that was so far from the woman he'd come to worship, but if this fake image helped his case in any way with the Court, if it showed that having a human around the twins hadn't weakened them in the way Miya had suggested it did, Kellen and Noella both knew it was worth a try.

Kellen shifted his body to face her, gliding the tips of his fingers up her checks. His fingers crawled to the ribbon tied behind her head and unraveled the bow Laya knotted to keep the mask in place.

He tossed the lace guise away, revealing the irrefutable beauty that was Noella Rose to the garden of Primordials.

Everyone lost their fucking minds.

Screams echoed from all corners of the garden, reverberating from the very earth itself as everyone, *everyone*, recoiled from Noella like she was an infection they were terrified of catching. Some of the guests fled the garden and sprinted to the gates to escape Noella's presence. Miya's silver wings ripped through the fabric at the back of her dress and expanded into the night along with a rush of fire now drenching her hands, prepared to launch at Noella. It took all of Kellen's strength not to leap in front of her himself, relying on Eyal to do the protecting for him to maintain their act. Eyal unsheathed his sword and lunged in front of Noella, which forced Miya to take a single step back in deference to Aros Cavalian's envoy, though the flames at her fingers didn't disappear.

"You brought that *thing* here?" Miya bellowed, spitting at Noella, who was so used to this type of treatment that she didn't bat an eye.

Kellen placed his hands on Noella's shoulders to move her in front of him.

"She goes wherever I go." Tendrils of his fire snaked out in the form of fingers to clasp Noella's jaw. He used the flames to raise her chin so she had no choice but to look directly at Miya. His fire wouldn't harm her—to Noella, it would feel like a gentle caress, like a feather tickling her skin. Against her ear, his teeth teasing the lobe, he murmured, "Isn't that right, my pet?"

*You are no one's pet, Noella Rose,* he told her mind-to-mind. *You are not a plague. You are a gift.*

Noella's body melted into his chest, surrendering to his will, to their act.

His hand—his actual hand, not the hand composed of fire still gripping her jaw—slithered down her stomach and splayed across the expanse of space between her hips to push her back against him. Her head tipped back onto his shoulder, his lips slithering up the lean column of her throat. He sucked at the skin of her neck hard enough to leave a swollen mound of flesh in his wake, a marker of his conquered territory to everyone watching. Noella let out a yelp when he pulled his teeth away.

*I'm sorry, sweetheart,* he apologized in her head.

*Stop apologizing, Kilic,* she snapped at him, wiggling her ass against his crotch as punishment. *I'm okay. Focus.*

"Speak," he ordered her aloud, nipping at her jaw. "Tell them who you belong to."

"Kellen Kilic," she stammered in a small, fragile voice—nothing like his Noella. Damn, she played her part well.

"You're not fooling anyone, Kellen," Miya roared. "You think we can't smell your desire for her?"

"Can you blame me?" His hand of fire licked up her chin, dragging a thumb composed of flames across her bottom lip. "Look at these pretty lips…they're even prettier when they're wrapped around my cock. Who wouldn't find pleasure in having a weak human submit to their will?"

"If you don't get her out of here right now, Kellen, I will tear her to pieces," Miya thundered, her eyes transmogrifying to the slits of a dragon.

"If any of you lay a hand on Noella Rose, I, or Aros Cavalian's envoy, will rip you to shreds and toss what remains of you into Terminus. As a matter of fact…" Kellen's lips sprawled out in a depraved, callous grin before he stepped to the side. "Go ahead." He gesticulated to Noella, even as every fiber of his being shrieked at him to go to her, to defend her by throwing his life at her feet. "Try and touch her," he goaded, his voice rasping in warning. "I will delight in separating your limbs from your body."

"I will not stand for this," Miya stressed.

"Fine," Kellen replied with a nonchalant shrug of his shoulders, skating one hand into the pocket of his trousers before he gestured to the house with his other hand. "Don't stand. Go find a chair to sit in instead."

Jarion didn't try to stifle his grin. Miya burst out, "You little—"

"Careful, mother," he cautioned with mock care. "You wouldn't want to make a scene now, would you?"

Miya became aware that everyone who still remained in the garden was carefully studying this interaction—more specifically, her infuriated outburst, where a tiny crack in her perfect façade revealed a glimmer of the darkness underneath. She smothered a bogus smile over the gash in her armor, even as the flames in her eyes fired inflammable hatred at Noella, whose gaze was stuck to Kellen so she didn't even notice.

"The food must be getting cold now," she shouted to all in the garden, a slight tremor honing her words. "Everyone, let's gather inside for dinner. The kids can only stay for two hours before they have to return to school."

Miya flicked her gaze away from Kellen and Noella with a huff, lifting the end of her dress to ascend the stairs that led into the manor. Kellen scanned his siblings' faces for how they were doing.

*My loves? Check-in,* he spoke into their minds.

*How long have we been here and when can we leave?* Jarion stammered, his voice breaking apart at the seams.

*Not long enough yet, buddy. You guys are doing great.*

*Is Ms. Rose okay?* Kellen adored how worried Laya sounded, how much his sister cared for Noella.

*Ms. Rose is strong. She can take care of herself. We all can.* Laya nodded her head in agreement.

*You're doing amazing,* Kellen hailed Noella as he shepherded her up the staircase and held the door for her to enter the estate.

*I've had practice at this,* she said with deep sadness in the underbelly of the response. He knew she meant more than just dealing with Primordials, but with what she experienced at her mother's hands.

*I'm sorry you ever had to.* Her eyes cinched with his. He found his sanity within the warmth of her gaze.

Stepping inside the massive wooden doors, a hushed veneration settled upon them, accompanied by the gentle echo of footsteps as the other guests made their way to the dining hall. Sunlight filtered through stained glass windows, casting a mosaic of piebald colors upon the polished marble floors. The entrance hall, vast and imposing in both height and width, boasted hundreds of tapestries that breathed life and memories, recounting all the different patriarchs and matriarchs of the Kilic family who graced these very halls. Candle sconces perched between the draperies, carrying lambent flames. An ornate chandelier hung like a crown above, its crystals capturing and dispersing the light, crafting a starlit illusion onto their heads when they passed under the configuration. Ascending a spiral staircase, Kellen escorted Noella into a spacious chamber with a high-vaulted ceiling, which was overlaid in a mural depicting the Cavalian Gods in their grandiose glory. Beneath the celestial panorama lay a long banquet table, ornamented with silver and crystal, with enough seats arranged around the rectangular counter for fifty people to dine.

Miya, of course, claimed the helm of the table.

She'd reserved the two seats next to her for Jarion and Laya, their names scrawled on place cards in immaculate script handwriting. Before Miya could argue, Kellen and Eyal grabbed the backs of the chairs on her left and right so neither of the twins would be forced to sit next to her.

"My pet," Kellen cooed to Noella, signaling her forward with a curl of his index finger. "Pull out my chair for me."

He stepped back so Noella could draw the chair out for him.

She stood a few paces behind, clasping her wrist behind her back, and waited to sit until Kellen was fully settled, occupying the chair on his right. Once she'd situated, his hand collapsed on top of her thigh, massaging the soft satin.

Jarion lowered into the chair next to Eyal, while Laya sat beside Noella. Laya's hand twitched near Noella like she was about to reach for her. Kellen subtly shook his head, so Laya's hand retreated. He watched his sister stare down at her fingers and then choose to slide them under her on the cushion, sitting on them to hold herself back from the temptation of seeking comfort in Noella.

*I'm sorry, Laylie,* Kellen said into her mind. *We're trying to undermine Ms. Rose's influence so they don't view her as a threat. It won't help anything to see how connected you are to her.*

*I hate this.* His sister's lips fought a frown.

*Me too.* He would tell her and only her, *I hate having to diminish her like this. All I want to do is lift her up and let the world see how amazing she is. I…I have very strong feelings for Ms. Rose.*

*Kellen,* Laya laughed, though in reality, her expression was plain, her mouth a flat line as she folded her napkin on her lap. *You've made that really fucking obvious. I'm just waiting for you to tell me you guys are officially together so I can scream it from the top of my lungs and make banners.*

*No banners,* he snarled. The corner of her mouth lifted slightly.

"Dinner can commence," Miya announced before a swarm of servers flocked the room. They whirled silver trays atop their heads, performing an orchestrated dance as the servers lowered platters in front of the guests with luscious meat and fillets of salmon and beds of steaming rice.

Noella's eyes narrowed over the rice before she licked her lips. *You like rice, Rose?* he asked her.

*I'm a carbs girl. Rice. Bread. Noodles. Potatoes. If it was healthy, I'd eat carbs and nothing else.*

Kellen reached for the bowl of rice and scooped several spoonfuls onto her plate, trying to ignore how fucking good she smelled this close to him. He then portioned for himself a mound of beef.

"Cut my food," Kellen demanded her, then willed his gaze to look away from her despite it being painful to separate his eyes from what they most desired to regard. He felt Noella reach for her fork and knife to begin slicing his steak into diced squares. While Miya's guests chattered down the line of the table, veering off to have their own side conversations, Miya watched Noella with boiling aversion.

"I'm curious, earthborn," Maya seethed at Noella, who remained focused on cutting Kellen's food despite being spoken to. "How do you like being in our lands?" Kellen scraped his eyes over Noella's face.

"Speak, pet," he commanded her. Noella's eyes elevated to Miya. She withdrew her fork and knife from his plate.

"I am humbled to be exposed to beings with such immense power and strength," she answered, highlighting the features of Primordials that they as a species valued most. "I am respectfully aware of my own shortcomings, as a human, and understand that I could never hope to find a place amongst your kind. I do not plan to make a home for myself in Cavale. I only wish to finish out my contract and survive the school year so I can return home to the Earthly Plane, where I belong."

Kellen's teeth ground together.

While the beginning of Noella's speech was a farce to placate his mother, he sensed that her end statement was true. They had yet to discuss what would happen at the end of the school year, and hearing her say now that she planned to return to the Earthly Plane threw him into a tizzy.

*You're not leaving Cavale,* he declared into her mind.

Noella's eyes recklessly crashed into his. She tore them away before she got lost in his fervor and entertained this discussion in front of all these people, cementing her focus back over his mother.

"And why is it that you can't return now?" Miya pushed.

"I signed a contract that's bound me to the school, and Cavale, for the entire school year."

"There's no way to break that contract?"

"No, I'm afraid there isn't."

"Hm. Pity." Miya stabbed her meat with her fork. "And what exactly are you being paid to do?"

Noella sipped some water to clear her throat. "My job is a school counselor," she answered after setting her glass down. "I provide social, emotional, and academic support to the students."

"Not that anyone actually lets her do her job," Kellen chimed in with an unkind laugh, though under the table, he squeezed her hand. "The students hate her. She's practically invisible."

Every lie wounded his heart to utter. Jarion, from the corner of Kellen's eye, balled his hand into a fist.

"What's your impression of Ms. Rose?" Miya asked the twins. Neither one of them offered a reply. Laya stuffed her mouth with salmon so she wouldn't have to lie. "You're really not going to speak a word to me?" she hissed.

Jarion's shoulders strained in a way that concerned Kellen that he was fighting his dragon off.

*Jare? You okay?* Kellen asked.

*Don't ask me if I'm fucking okay, Kellen,* Jarion growled at him. Jarion's fire—which Kellen was startled to learn was quite potent in its early development—flowed through the conduit between their minds to singe him with disapproval. *I have to sit here with our fucking mother trying to make cruel small talk and watch you belittle Ms. Rose and do nothing about it while fighting all mine and my dragon's urges to unleash myself on Miya. I'm not fucking okay. How can you treat Ms. Rose like this?*

*I hate this just as much as you do, Jare. I'm not doing this to hurt her. I'm trying to protect Noella.*

*That's bullshit. You're enjoying this. You're enjoying demeaning her. You've never liked Ms. Rose, and you used her kindness towards us to get her here so you can cut her down and make yourself look better. You're acting just like Mom.*

*JARION*—Jarion shut down their mental line of communication. Kellen's heart fractured in his chest.

"This charade you're playing is almost convincing," Miya said, dabbing her mouth with her napkin before leaning back in her chair. "I think you're forgetting, though, that I know certain things. Like the fact that Jarion's dragon took over his body and Noella Rose was there with him when it happened."

All four of them went stiff. You could've heard a pin drop from how deathly quiet the atmosphere grew.

*Shit,* Kellen gasped to Noella. *I forgot she knew about that.*

*You FORGOT?!* Noella screamed in his head. *How could you forget about that, Kellen? Her knowing that undermines the whole plan!*

A blanket of silence swathed the room as all Miya's guests awaited the answer to her next question.

"You told me," she looked at Kellen, her smile outlined by spite, fully aware that she'd trapped him in his own lie, "that Noella Rose *saved* him. That Jarion's dragon would've killed him without her intervention. Does someone want to explain that, if Noella Rose is seemingly so useless at Delmarth?"

Jarion's eyes flew to Kellen, pleading him to be honest, to stop their act, to defend his school counselor.

Kellen suddenly realized that Jarion was right. This was stupid. This charade made no sense. This wasn't helping his own image or Noella's. This wasn't proving that her presence in Cavale hadn't been an impediment to the twins' progress. The only thing that would prove that was being honest about her impact on them, to show the room, and his mother, that her influence had made them all stronger.

"Yes, it's true," Kellen finally declared, relinquishing his performance. Noella's eyes rounded in shock. "Noella Rose saved Jarion's life that day. If she hadn't been there, I don't know what would've happened. She is not useless. She is not an invisible presence at Delmarth. She has made a massive impact on the student body, in a *positive* way. Attendance rates are higher than ever. We've seen a reduction in students struggling to keep up with their coursework by fifteen percent, which may not seem like a lot, but that's fucking huge, considering that number hasn't budged in all the time I've worked at Delmarth. Our students are happier with her around. She's been a gods-send to our school and lives."

"Yet you said she was useless." Miya plunged the knife deeper. She repeated his words for the room to underscore his deceit, to shrink his authority and diminish his credibility. "You said the students hate her."

"Some do," he admitted. "Those who haven't gotten over their hatred of her to see how important she is. Same with the faculty. Those of us who have let her in, who've stopped judging her, see how amazing she is."

Kellen first looked at Jarion, trying to convey in that singular gaze all the emotion he carried in his heart for Noella, the emotion he hadn't found words for yet, but planned to spend his life searching for. Once he believed the message had been received, his eyes ascended over Noella.

"There is nothing useless about Noella Rose," he asserted, permeating her mind with an influx of his admiration, her grey eyes shimmering with emergent tears. "She is not useless. She is essential."

"What I'm failing to understand," Miya said, destroying the adoring way Noella had been looking at him, "is how this *human,* this *thing,* saved the life of my son when you weren't able to, Kellen. I think that says all I need to know about you as a parent." Kellen's heart plummeted into his stomach.

"Don't you fucking *dare* say that about my brother!" Laya roared, rising from her chair to bellow at her mother. Miya had never heard Laya assert herself like this, so the shock was apparent on her face. "Kellen has done nothing but love and support us. He's taken care of us in a way you never did. Allowing us to speak to Ms. Rose was the best thing he ever did for us. I will not tolerate hearing you diminish his character or try to paint him as a terrible parent when he is the best person, the best parent, the best *everything* I know. At least he's never laid a hand on us that we didn't want there. At least he's never told us how worthless and small we are. At least he knows what love actually is. He is not a terrible parent. The only bad parent in this room is *you.* "

Kellen's chest burst with pride. Noella's hand found Laya's under the table.

She then cinched her eyes with Jarion and mouthed, *we can do hard things.* Jarion's gaze softened.

"Um, excuse me," Miya fumed, slamming her fist into the table to break Jarion and Noella's quiet look of understanding. "What the fuck did you just mouth to my son, you repulsive cunt?"

"She was being *supportive,* you malicious bitch." Kellen, Noella, and Laya turned in unison to look at Jarion, who'd chosen this moment to speak for the first time all evening. Miya's jaw fell agape, but Jarion wasn't done, his fingers curling dangerously around the stem of his fork. "She was being the real Noella Rose, not the meek version of her you've been seeing all night. The real Ms. Rose is *kind.* She is *strong.* She fights for us, even when we can't fight for ourselves. She's been more of a mother to us the last few weeks than you have our entire lives. She is the best thing that's ever happened to Delmarth, the best thing that's ever happened to Cavale." Noella's eyes glimmered. Jarion looked at her, then said, "Stop hiding, Ms. Rose. Show them who you really are." Noella peeked up at Kellen, silently asking for permission to let go of her mask.

Kellen gave her an approving smile and nodded his head. *Go on, baby,* he encouraged her. *Rip them to shreds.*

"Well," Noella laughed, shaking her hair out of her face now that she was no longer playing the role of unassuming whore. "That was quite the endorsement, Jarion. I better make it count." Her eyes, their usual warm kindness superseded by cold fury, descended over Miya. *"You,"* she said almost curiously, leaning back in her chair and trailing her eyes down Miya's face in a sluggish, purposefully drawn-out manner that had Miya fidgeting in her seat. "I've been thinking all night of what the best word to describe you is, and all I can come up with is that you're so…unimpressive."

*"Excuse me?"* Flames ignited in Miya's eyes.

"I expected so much more from you, given your reputation, and what I saw the other week." Noella swept her eyes across the room, landing on each individual face whose attention she had enveloped around her finger. "For those of you who don't know," she said flippantly, "Miya Kilic tried to kill her children three weeks ago." Gasps resounded from all corners of the room.

"That is NOT—" Noella lifted her index finger in the air to silence Miya's counterblast. Her compliant mask had completely disintegrated. What took its place was a queen in complete control. Miya's jaw unhinged.

"I was there," Noella told the room. "I saw the whole thing. She tried to shoot them down in the sky when they fled Delmarth, which they had to do because she first attempted to walk onto a campus she is *banned* from and *steal* them. Do not let this woman trick you into thinking she's an involved mother. Do not let her trick you into thinking she cares about her children's welfare. Do not let her trick you into thinking she's worthy of your support. She's not." Smoke ballooned from Miya's flared nostrils.

"I'm going to enjoy killing you, Noella Rose," Miya snarled, flames clobbering the silver strands of her hair.

Eyal reached for his sword.

"Go ahead and try," Noella dared her, Miya falling back against her chair in surprise. "Maybe you enjoyed Terminus and want to make it a permanent stay. Your children won't miss you. Actually..." She propped her elbow on the table and rested her cheek against her palm. "I think no one in this room would miss you. I think they all secretly hate you. They only spend time with you because they fear you." Kellen felt every person in the room flinch at her words, at the resounding truth dangling in the ether. "You know what they say about tyrants who value fear over respect...those who love to be feared are more afraid than anyone else." Noella cocked her head. "What're *you* afraid of, Miya? Are you afraid everyone actually sees how weak you are behind your mask of violence? Are you afraid you're not as special as you've convinced yourself you are?"

Miya only scoffed, but something about the gruff sound told Kellen she wasn't unaffected by Noella's verbal assault of her character. "Where do you get off speaking to me like this, earthborn?"

"I'm actually getting off quite a bit," Noella quipped, standing with a seductive freedom to the slow rise from her chair. She drew her fingers affectionately across Kellen's back as she began striding over to Miya, staking a claim to everyone in the room, showing them that he belonged to *her*, not the other way around like they'd been pretending all evening. "I've waited *years* to tell off someone like you. A person who conflates love and cruelty. A person who doesn't view the role of mother for what an honor it is. Someone who would take three of the most pure people ever created and purposefully make them feel small just to feed your own ego. You're not special, Miya Kilic. There are actually a lot of people just like you, though this universe would be a far lighter place if there were *no* people like you. And your three kids? Who you've spent so many years shoving under your boot to make them feel worthless? They are more special than you will ever be. It has been my absolute pleasure getting to know them the past few months. Laya..." Noella spun around to smile at Laya. "Laya is kind. She's so in touch with the world around her. She is so full of light and joy. She deserves to feel the love and warmth she showers onto everyone else." Her eyes passed over to Jarion. "Jare…he's so funny. So intelligent. So strong. He deserves to be made to feel worthy of being part of this world, because this world would be so dark without him." The twins choked on sobs, their love for her overpowering the air.

Her eyes finally found Kellen.

"And Kellen…" Noella's voice was noticeably softer when she spoke his name. "Kellen is not the cold man you've seen tonight. He is so selfless. So warm. So brave. He deserves to have someone fight for him the way he fights for everyone else." Kellen's eyes burned. He felt the absence of her gaze when she swung around to look back at Miya. "You had nothing to do with the making of these three incredible people. You don't get credit for their successes. Their achievement doesn't make you special. They became this *in spite* of you, not because of you. You are nothing. *They* are everything."

The subsequent events transpired in such a rapid succession that Kellen's mind struggled to keep track of the current moment.

Miya's fire submerged her entire body, overpowering her humanoid flesh so none of the light brown coloring was visible beneath the flames before she lunged out of her chair and pounced on Noella. The entangled women toppled to the ground as everyone flung their chairs back and dove to get a good viewing of the skirmish. Kellen's own fire sprinted to the surface to envelop his fingers, but Eyal surprisingly held out a hand to halt Kellen from launching his own power in defense of Noella. The back of Noella's head crashed against the marble floor as Miya's bony fingers enfolded around her throat and burrowed into the tendons of her neck, scorching the delicate skin with her flames, corroding the soft tissue. Noella did nothing to fight against her, her fingers splaying out on the floor, her body limp beneath Miya's weight crushing her stomach.

Kellen started forward, but Eyal stepped in his path. *Wait*, Eyal snarled. *She needs to draw blood.*

*What're you—* The realization of what Noella was doing, what she was sacrificing right now to give the twins a life free of their mother, washed over Kellen. His heart exploded in his mouth. *DID YOU TWO PLAN THIS?* Kellen nearly hollered out loud.

*It was Ella's backup plan,* Eyal admitted. Kellen's stomach roiled in horror. *If the first part of the plan failed, she intended to provoke your mother into attacking her to give me a reason to arrest her. Once Miya draws blood, I will be shipping her off to Terminus, and you will never see her again.*

Kellen tasted relief on his tongue, but it was overshadowed by the piquant flavor of terror.

*DO NOT LET HER DIE, EYAL, OR I SWEAR TO AROS, I WILL KILL YOU BOTH MYSELF.*

*I would never,* Eyal promised, watching Miya and Noella closely. His hand curved over the hilt of his sword, waiting for the perfect moment for extraction. *It is in Cavale's best interest that Noella Rose does not die.*

Kellen could do nothing but stand there as his mother squeezed the life out of the woman he loved.

Oh *fuck.*

The woman he loved.

It hit him like a truck barreling into his stomach, his chest, his soul, watching Noella's cheeks drain of the color he worshipped, watching the verve empty from her eyes, the emotion he'd been struggling to name finally thwacking him in the gut, overpowering his lungs. He loved her. He fucking loved her. He loved everything about her, her stubbornness, her kindness, the fact that she even formulated this plan behind his back and would willingly flirt with death just to get his mother sent back to Terminus. All of it made him fully confront how deeply he'd fallen for her, how every morsel of his being had become beholden to her. The extent of his love created earthquakes through his whole body while his legs struggled to maintain their upright position.

In this moment, he understood that she hadn't been made for him. He'd been made for *her.*

His life was bound to her. Without her, there was no him.

The second Miya's fire slit through Noella's chin and sketched a gash down her jaw, a drop of her blood splattering on the floor, Eyal moved. A hand cloaked in silver titanium lashed out to grab the back of Miya's neck. He wrenched her off Noella and lifted the

Varmin in the air, as if Miya were a weightless doll rather than a being who could transform into a twenty thousand pound dragon. Once Miya no longer smothered Noella, Kellen ran forward and fell to his knees beside her, reaching out his hands to pull her into his arms, arranging her in his lap. Her arms wound around his neck, a strangled wheeze heaving off her tongue.

"Miya Kilic, I hereby sentence you to Terminus indefinitely for your attack on Noella Rose," Eyal announced before pulling Miya's arms back and slapping handcuffs onto her small wrists. Eyal turned to the audience congregated around them and said, "Take your leave. This shambolic excuse of a party is over." The twins laughed through tears as the iron cuffs girded around their mother's flesh.

"INDEFINITELY?!" Miya screamed, thrashing in Eyal's grip, kicking her legs out to try and reach where Noella and Kellen sat on the floor, yearning to get one more hit on Noella before she was lugged away. "NO! YOU CAN'T TAKE ME BACK THERE! YOU CA—" Gilded vapor bordered Miya and Eyal's feet, swimming up the length of their limbs before the haze consumed them whole and they disappeared from the room.

"Enjoy Terminus," Noella laughed, then collapsed against Kellen's chest with a groan.

"MS. ROSE!" Laya yelled, the twins' knees crashing onto the floor as they knelt beside Kellen. "Are you okay?"

"I will be in a second." Her hand floated up her chest and squeezed the amulet around her neck. Filaments of silver that Kellen recognized as Headmistress Dyer's power snaked out of the pendant to encircle Noella's neck in what resembled iridescent ribbons. When the threads retreated back into the safety of the amulet, her neck had returned to its spotless glory, healed of any scars from Miya's power, including the hickey Kellen left earlier. "There," Noella sighed. "Much better."

"I can't believe you just did that," Kellen spluttered, shaking his head. Into her mind, he asked, *Why didn't you tell me?*

*Because I knew you wouldn't let me,* she answered. *It took hours last night after I left your apartment convincing Eyal to agree to this. It would've taken twice as long to get you to agree.*

*Because I never would've agreed to you hurting yourself, Noella.* Still, he was overcome by gratitude, which she felt and acknowledged with a tired, beautiful smile, resting her head on his shoulder.

"She's gone," Jarion stammered, his laughter merging into sobs. "She's really gone."

"She's gone, buddy," Kellen cried, cupping the side of his face. "She will never bother you again."

Noella extended her wearied arms out to the twins.

Jarion and Laya fell into her embrace, burying their faces between the crook of Noella's neck and Kellen's chest. Kellen closed his arms around his three favorite people, around his whole fucking world, and sent a prayer of thanks to the King of the Gods for the gift of their liberation.

## CHAPTER 30

# ELLA

ELLA STOOD on the porch of Kellen's bedroom in his childhood home, her hand resting on her throat, where the ghost of Miya's blistering touch haunted her skin. She took deep breaths and gazed out into the rich twilight to remind her body that Miya was no longer there. Below her, the castle grounds were vast and sprawling, the manicured gardens dappled with streaks of silver moonlight sliding across the variegated blooms. Ella's gown billowed gently in the cool breeze, the fabric whispering against the stone beneath her feet. The stars twinkled above her, seeming to stare back at her as she stared up at them. Her face unconsciously lifted to meet the heavens, craving for her limbs to disintegrate into something ethereal and buoyant so she could stretch herself through the ether and touch the sky, feel the stars between her fingers, become one with the night.

As she stood there, she felt the weight of what she'd experienced tonight crash down over her.

Nothing about this evening had been easy for her. None of it had come as naturally as Ella wanted Kellen to believe it did, not that she trusted he'd bought her pretense that she was unaffected by their charade. Somehow, the hardest part of the evening wasn't Kellen's fake treatment of her, the nasty vilification of her impact on the school, or even Miya's assault at the end. It had been the speech she'd hurled at Miya to provoke her into attacking. Those words had emerged from a place deep inside Ella she didn't visit often, the vestiges of pain lingering in her core from the years of torment she endured at her mother's hands. Giving life to that pain, to the anger simmering under the surface that she worked constantly to subdue for the sake of living, left her winded from exhaustion, made her long to curl up in a ball and sleep her life away, if only to never experience that pain again.

But that pain was a part of her. Not the total sum of her being, but a crumb of her history that shouldn't be ignored. It didn't need to be something she feared or pushed away. Acknowledging it didn't make her any less strong or any less capable of helping others face their own pain.

Something she told the twins often that she needed to start repeating to herself.

Ella sensed movement behind her before seeing it and spun around to find Kellen approaching. He'd sent the twins into the house to collect whatever belongings of theirs they wished to keep before they returned to Delmarth. Now that Miya was gone, the house belonged to Kellen, not that he planned to do anything with it. He'd said that their home would remain the cottage, and he would leave this meaningless opulence that none of them felt an attachment towards to rot along with their mother's reputation. Ella agreed that there was no greater justice for the twins than that.

"I couldn't find you," Kellen said as he advanced towards her.

"Sorry. I just needed a moment alone." She'd drifted up the staircase and stumbled upon Kellen's room, at first not realizing that it belonged to him. The space was depressingly nondescript, no character lining the walls, lacking decoration or anything that would indicate a personality had graced this bedchamber. She felt everything he must have felt living here, the unrelenting isolation and darkness, and found comfort inside a room that seemed to understand the burden she carried inside. She wondered if maybe the reemergence of her own pain had been seduced by the misery saturating the furniture and drew her to the room before she knew it was Kellen's.

"Can I join you?" he asked with caution, sensing her mood. If she said no, she trusted him to leave her here to continue wallowing.

Ella nodded, beckoning him forward with a wave of her hand. Kellen shrugged off his suit jacket on his journey over to her and draped it around her shoulders. The heat of his dragon fire coated the fabric and warmed her fatigued muscles, a soft moan escaping her mouth before she had time to damper it.

"Thank you," she stammered, hugging the material closer. She inspected his expression and found it incomprehensible. "Are you okay?"

"More okay than I've felt in a long time," he answered, the light she searched his eyes for constantly returning to his emerald gaze, setting his whole body ablaze with joy. "Tonight could not have gone better once you took control. My plan was a disaster waiting to fail. I should've let you lead from the start."

Ella beamed. "I'm going to need to hear you say that a million more times, please." His eyes warmed.

"I think I can manage that," he quipped, the corner of his mouth curling up, revealing one dimple. "Maybe this is why Aros signed the order. Because he knew this would be the outcome." Ella frowned.

"I'm not giving him that credit," she grumbled under her breath.

"You're right," Kellen concurred. "The only person who deserves credit for tonight's success is you."

He stepped closer, careening behind her, and stretched out his arms on either side of her to grasp the railing, effectively trapping her beneath him, her back to his front. Kellen dropped his face into the crook of her neck and inhaled the scent of cherries scattered across her skin from her moisturizer.

"In one evening, you managed to do what I've struggled my whole life to accomplish," he whispered. Ella gasped when she felt his fingers tickle her sides, sliding up and down her curves in unhurried strokes. Kellen brushed his mouth against her cheek. "I am forever indebted to you, Noella Rose."

Ella closed her eyes, her breaths purling in hysterical pants, as he pressed a whisper of a kiss to her skin, to the heat besieging her flesh, setting her blood and bones aflame. Hunger and desire ravaged through her system, overpowering her senses, the need to feel his lips on hers too uncontrollable, her strength depleted from an evening of wearing a fake mask. All she wanted now was to stop fighting herself and succumb to her heart's truest desire. She was twisting in his arms before she could stop herself.

Her hands flew up, snaking into his hair, and yanked his head down, his mouth crashing into hers.

Kissing Kellen for the first time reminded Ella of how addicts describe their first fix of a drug, which hooks them for life. He tasted like relief and euphoria, if euphoria took the form of two plump lips, which cajoled hers to respond with equal fervor, inundating her with a rush of ecstasy and a beautiful escape. Ella's back arched to bring herself closer, desperate to eliminate the distance she'd placed between them, both in a physical and metaphorical sense, this kiss her ultimate surrender.

She swallowed the gasp Kellen loosed as though it were liquor being poured down her throat, greedy to imbibe more of his passion, eager for the feeling to fill her body to capacity, wanting to drown in his need for her.

"Noella," Kellen whispered into her mouth, a half-groan, half-sob.

Her fingers tugged at his curls, dragging her lips back to his, applying even more pressure than before.

Kellen claimed her mouth a second time, laying siege to every part of her. All her usual instincts veered towards yearning for *him* rather than oxygen to breathe, her top priority now acquiring her next fix of the intoxicating drug that was Kellen Kilic. Her back dug into the railing as his hips pinioned her beneath him, her blonde hair torrenting off the rim of the rail and floating along the current of the wind. She felt his fingernails scrape her scalp when he pulled at her hair, angling her head back so she had no option but to bear the brunt of his osculation, consumed by the intensity of his desire. His tongue nudged her lips, begging them to part. When she obliged, their tongues skirmished in the middle of the shared space between them, tangling together in a sensual dance. Kellen kissed her like a man starving, like he hadn't gotten essential nutrients in weeks and she was his last chance of survival. He *devoured* her, not just her mouth, but her soul as well.

He claimed her with just one kiss. She conceded everything to him in that moment, resigning from their battle of wills to create a new game of dominance—who could make the other moan louder.

"If I don't touch you, I think I might burst," he snarled before Kellen's fingers scraped down her dress to find the slit in the skirt, using the opening to hike the fabric up, revealing her lace, black thong to the night. He gave her throat special attention, nothing like how he'd kissed her there earlier in front of the crowd, the small licks and nips he crafted into a pathway up her neck composed of gentle care and devotion. Ella's head fell back. If it weren't for the railing behind her and Kellen's hand threaded in her hair, while his other hand brazenly explored the apex of her thighs, she would have plummeted off the edge of the patio. Her hips twitched forward when Kellen's finger made contact with her clit through the lace, discovering the evidence of her arousal.

"Kellen," she groaned. Stars bleared across her vision, both the stars hitched above and stars produced from the incredible experience of him touching her in reality, not just in her dreams. She didn't even know what she was asking for when she moaned, "Please."

"Oh no, baby," he laughed, kissing her jaw, ravishing her skin in everything he'd been holding back from giving her. "You took your sweet fucking time with me, and now it's my turn to deliver the same torment."

"Okay, we're ready—" The sound of Laya dropping something metal clattered behind them. "OH!"

Ella shoved Kellen back and fixed her dress. Horror struck her gut and nearly smashed her to her knees when she found Laya and Jarion both in the doorway of the bedroom. The twins analyzed the overlay of red that had consumed Ella's skin and the muddle of Kellen's hair, mature enough to put two pieces of data together and make sense of their meaning. It brought her some comfort, though it didn't eliminate her self-disgust, that Laya's face brightened at their entanglement, clearly thrilled.

"Sorry!" Laya squeaked with a wide grin, covering her hands over her eyes. "We didn't mean to interrupt."

"Do you guys have everything?" Kellen asked them, his voice huskier than usual. The twins nodded. "Great. Go wait in the car. We'll be down in a second." Kellen tossed Jarion the keys to open the car.

Laya gathered what she'd dropped and rushed out the door.

Jarion loitered there, face unreadable for a moment, then offered them a gleaming smile and said, "I approve," before he walked away.

Kellen swiveled around, a smile splitting his cheeks apart, to find Ella burying her face in her hands.

"I can't believe I just did that," she stammered, shaking her head over and over. "What am I *doing?*"

How could she have allowed this to happen?

She was their school counselor, and they'd just caught her making out aggressively with their brother, their *guardian*. She'd spent the entire night—the last several weeks, it suddenly occurred to her, dismay clogging her throat— blurring the professional boundaries between herself, the twins, and Kellen, boundaries that if she didn't cement in place now would make her therapeutic relationship with the kids ineffective due to her overlapping relationship with Kellen. She wasn't the twins' sister, or their mother. She wasn't their family, yet she'd blurred the lines so much that she now dangerously felt like she was, willing to sacrifice her own life for their freedom.

Allowing herself to feel this way about Kellen, no matter how right it had felt in the moment, was a violation of how she'd been trained to do this job, an encroachment on her morals that she couldn't allow to continue.

*Don't do this,* that female voice in her head warned, but Ella's mind was made up.

"What's wrong?" Kellen asked, reaching out a hand to touch her. She whipped around to dodge it.

"Your siblings just caught us," she whisper-shrieked, raising her face out of her hands. Kellen blinked at her.

"So?"

"SO?" she repeated, her eyes bugging out. "SO, I just broke so many ethical codes. Kissing the legal guardian of the students I counsel? That can *never* happen again."

"Oh, it absolutely *will* happen again." Kellen grabbed her shoulders and steered her body to face him. "Many, *many* more times."

"Kellen," she hissed.

"*Noella*," he hissed back.

"Not here." Kellen drew his head away from her.

"Oh." The panic dissolved inside his eyes. "So you're saying not *here*. But somewhere else—"

"Kellen, stop." She lay her hand on his chest, over the heart of his that was writhing.

"Promise me that wasn't the last time I will taste your lips, Noella Rose." A sob itched her throat.

"I can't promise you that," she whimpered, her heart screaming for her to stop while her mind took control of the moment. "I can't be kissing you one minute and counseling Jarion and Laya the next. It's wrong."

"Your human rules don't mean anything in Cavale."

"They mean something to ME, Kellen!" she cried. "They mean something to *me*. I was taught a certain way to do this job, and that certainly didn't include making out with the parent of the students I counsel. I'm sorry I've let this go on for so long. I'm sorry I entertained it in the first place. I know this is my fault. I take full responsibility for my part in this. I got caught up in your family, in wanting to be part of something—"

"You *are* part of it," he asserted.

"No, I'm not!" she shouted inspite of the way her heart wept at his declaration. "I'm not, Kellen. I'm not Jarion and Laya's mother. I'm their school counselor, and I need to go back to acting like I am. In order for me to do that, I need to put up the boundaries I should have put up between us a long time ago. I'm sorry, but I can't do this with you anymore. If we can't go back to being just friends, then I don't think we should see each other anymore."

"Stop trying to run from this." Kellen took two steps closer. "You've been pushing me away ever since I told you how I felt about you. What we have is real. It means more than any arbitrary ethical code you could throw at me. I won't let you put these stupid ethics above what we have."

"Stop invalidating what's important to me just because it doesn't matter in Cavale!" Ella bawled.

"Stop pretending that *we* aren't important too!" His hands began to shake. "I am *yours*, Noella Rose. Don't you see? I am completely enamored of you. I am lost in you, found *by* you. We belong to each other. No amount of distance you place between us will ever change the fact that I now own your heart, as you own every broken shard of mine. I don't ever plan on giving up ownership, just as I hope you never give up ownership of me." Ella melted when Kellen cupped her face and paused to see if she'd pull away, to give her the chance to say no, even if it killed him to separate from her.

Then, when she remained still and ever so slightly lifted her chin, he dove down and kissed her again. She started to move her mouth against his, nearly giving in before her right mind returned to her.

"No!" she hollered, shoving him back. "*No,*" she repeated sternly, wiping her mouth with her wrist. "You're not hearing me, Kellen. If you can't even acknowledge that my feelings matter just as much as yours, then there's no point entertaining this anymore." Ella shook his jacket off her shoulders.

She thrusted it into his hands, then strode out of his bedroom, covering her hand over her mouth to keep herself from weeping. She pushed the tears inward, refused to let them leak, refused to let him see how much it was killing her to place this distance back between them when they'd finally closed it.

Laya and Jarion flinched when Ella slid into the car and they sensed the change in her demeanor.

"Ms. Rose?" Laya squeaked, placing her hand on Ella's shoulder. "Is everything okay?"

"Everything's fine, Laya," she assured, plucking Laya's hand off her—not meaning to be cruel, but she needed to put those boundaries up even with the twins, even as she saw the hurt flash in Laya's eyes and felt the look puncture her soul.

Kellen climbed into the car a few minutes later, plumes of rage seething off his tense shoulders.

No one spoke a word the whole ride home.

Ella kept her body angled away from Kellen and stared out the window, not that she saw anything through the glass between the film of tears covering her eyes. Ella felt Kellen's eyes flit to her several times during the car ride, but she refused to rip her gaze off the window to acknowledge him. She kept her hands underneath her ass on the seat so she wouldn't be tempted to reach for him and seek forgiveness in the warmth of his body. She knew in spite of how she'd just eviscerated him with words and dismissed their connection that if she touched him right now, if she sought out that amnesty, he would give it to her immediately and forget everything that had just happened.

Kellen deserved better than that too. Kellen deserved someone who would stay, who could give him all of her. Kellen deserved someone who wasn't going to leave him at the end of the school year.

Maybe one day he would understand.

He'd think back on this time in his life, and he would thank her for setting him free, so he could find his own happiness, his Cavalisha, and she would be a distant memory of a fleeing dalliance. That thought made the threatened tears trickle down her cheeks, because in her heart, a truth even her mind couldn't deny, she knew she would spend the rest of her life mourning the loss of him, that no man, human or Primordial, would ever compare, even when he eventually moved on from her.

Jarion and Laya crawled out of the car silently when Kellen parked in front of the faculty housing. They didn't even say goodnight to Kellen or Ella before linking their arms and heading off for the Varmin sector.

Kellen's eyes burned into Ella, waiting, hoping, but she declined to meet them and reached for the door.

"I've got it," Kellen grumbled, holding it for her. In spite of everything, he still held the door for her. She didn't thank him because she knew, if she tried to speak, the words that would come out wouldn't be thank you, but *I'm sorry, please forgive me, I need you more than I need to breathe.*

Kellen and Ella wandered down the hallway together to their dorms. It took them both twice the amount of time it would normally take to complete the stretch of corridor. Both of their steps were small, dreading the moment they reached their apartments and would have to separate.

Ella exhaled a tattered breath, reaching for the door handle to her apartment. Suddenly, Kellen's fingers skated down her arm to enclose around the fingers of hers folded around the knob.

"You're really going to go into your apartment right now?" His voice tickled her ears.

"Yes," she answered, not looking at him. She felt him rather than saw him step closer, his warmth and bulk dangling over her shoulders.

His fingers hitched tendrils of her blonde hair behind her ear, tracing the shell. Ella's eyes fluttered to a close.

"Alone?" he whispered roughly. Ella finally mustered the strength to raise her head to look at him.

"Alone," she asserted in as strong a voice as she could create under the circumstances. Kellen's jaw clenched.

"Fine." His lips brushed her ear. "I'll leave you with one thought before I go." Ella held her breath waiting to hear what he would say. "Let me make myself abundantly clear, since you don't seem to be getting it. The moment you kissed me, the moment you began this insatiable obsession, you claimed every part of my being. My body, my soul, my heart, everything. There is not a single piece of me that doesn't belong to you. You can go into your apartment right now, but know you're taking my heart in there with you. It's not mine anymore. It's yours." His lips swept down to press a soft, aching kiss to the corner of her mouth. Ella mewled, squeezing her eyes shut. "This is not over between us, Noella. It never will be." All too soon, his lips vanished from her skin.

*You've made a horrible mistake,* the female voice in her head hissed at her. *Go to him. Make this right.*

By the time Ella spun around to react, to take it all back, Kellen was gone.

430

## CHAPTER 31

# KELLEN

"You need to do something to fix this, Kell," Laya insisted.

"What else can I do, Laylie?" Kellen's eyes were sore from constant rubbing and lack of sleep. "She won't fucking talk to me."

It had been a week since Miya Kilic had been permanently removed from their lives, and a week since he'd last spoken to Noella. She'd started leaving for work well before he awoke to avoid seeing him in the hall, and deferred to locking herself in her apartment the moment school was finished so she wouldn't risk running into him at night. He would have thought she really didn't care about him, but he kept in constant contact with Freya to check on her and knew from the dog that Noella was suffering from the absence of him just as much as he was from the absence of her.

It didn't bring him comfort to know she mourned him, to know she did care and was pushing those feelings aside.

It made it so much fucking worse.

He would do whatever she asked, so while he hated every minute of it, he kept his distance from her. However, he tried everything he could think of to get her to talk to him, apart from banging on the doors of her office or apartment and beseeching her to lift their separation. Kellen left notes and roses outside her door every night, the accumulation of which now piled up high enough to tickle her doorknob, the hallway littered with the stench of rotting flowers and broken hearts. He screamed down the line of their mental conduit at all hours of the day, only receiving an echo of himself reverberated back down the abyss. He implored Akio and Josefyn to reason with her, to make her see how ridiculous she was being and to convince her to let him back in.

He spent that week trying desperately to understand her position, to really hear her words, as she'd accused him of not doing. The only thing he'd been able to find a way to accept was that she was afraid their relationship would affect the work she was doing to help Jarion and Laya heal.

That only made him love her more. That only made the loss of her hurt more.

"We'll stop seeing her for counseling," Laya declared in her sweet attempt to make this easier for them, desperate to help Kellen come to a solution. He probably shouldn't have confided in the twins about this, given Noella's comments about blurred boundaries, but he had no one else he could talk to.

Jarion flinched, then shook his head. "I don't want to stop seeing her for counseling," he objected.

"I don't *want* you to stop seeing her for counseling," Kellen affirmed. "No one wants that. Especially Ms. Rose."

"You can't just give up, Kellen!" Laya smacked his arm. Kellen narrowed his eyes in a scowl.

"I have no plans to give up, Eulaylia. I've never felt this way about anyone before, but there's not much I can do if she refuses to hear me out. I will not force her into this. That's not how I want to earn her."

"What have you said to her in your notes?" Jarion asked. Kellen sighed.

"I'm sorry. Please forgive me. I miss you. I need you in my life. Tell me how to make this right."

He hadn't told her the words that stained his tongue, pleading to be unfettered: *I love you.* Kellen planned to reserve that potent truth for a time when she was receptive to hearing it, when he would possibly hear it back.

"That's where you're fucking up!" Jarion said, hitting Kellen's arm with his red beanie—actually, *Kellen's* beanie that Jarion had never given back to him. "You're asking her to tell you how to make it right, but she's asking you to hear her, Kellen. She wants to know you understand her feelings and can come to a compromise because you value her morals as much as your own. She's scared that a relationship with you will affect her professional relationship with us. Explain to her why she doesn't need to worry. Let us all have a conversation to discuss boundaries so we can make this work for everyone involved. You don't need to fully understand why she's concerned. You just need to accept she feels that way and not push it aside because it doesn't fall into line with how you feel."

Kellen blinked. Who was this stranger, this mature young man, who had taken the place of his brother?

"When did you get so fucking wise?" he quipped.

"Since I started seeing your girlfriend," Jarion joked. Kellen laughed, but the laugh bled into a sob and he shielded his eyes with his hands. Laya leaned over on the bed and wrapped her arms around Kellen's shoulders.

"We want you to be happy, Kell," she whispered against his cheek. Kellen squeezed her wrists with a moan. "Whatever we can do to help with that, we will. It's our turn to help you, okay? You've given so much of yourself for us. Let us surrender a little bit now for your happiness."

"I don't want you to give up anything," he whimpered, smearing his tears on Laya's arm.

"And we don't want *you* to give up anything either. You deserve to be happy, Kellen. Give yourself permission to be happy. It's not selfish. It doesn't make you a bad brother. It makes you a person with a heart who has every right to fill it with the love he deserves." Laya kissed his temple.

"I fucking love you guys," Kellen sobbed, then twisted his head to kiss Laya's cheek.

"Do you love her, Kell?" He raised his eyes to Jarion and nodded. He nodded so hard that a headache threatened to sunder his forehead. Jarion smiled. "Then stop telling her you need her. *Show* her."

Ella had spent the past week away from Kellen a sniveling shell of her former self, a ghoul haunting the campus of Delmarth. She avoided the Varmin sector at all costs. Jarion and Laya each had spent their sessions with her that week begging her to talk to Kellen, but she refused to open the discussion. She'd read every single one of Kellen's notes that he left at her doorstep, even though she'd left them out there in the hallway as a cruel symbol of her rejection. Each one, every beautifully shaped letter expressing his need for her, had perforated her heart, poking holes in the feeble tissue, her pain wringing into every part of her being so she walked around all the time now in agony, close to keeling over and crumbling into ash. She'd gotten in the habit at night of tying kitchen towels around her ankles and binding herself to the legs of her bed because that's what it took to keep herself from crawling across the floor like a possessed demon and hurling herself at Kellen's door. The female voice in her head was so loud with condemnation that it physically hurt her ears.

Ella knew the only way to free herself from this torment was to go to him and make this right, but in doing so, she would be sacrificing her own morals, and she just didn't feel like that was a fair ask of her. Maybe her resistance made her selfish, maybe that made her terrible, but why did she have to give up something when he didn't seem to be willing to give up something for her in return?

Ella curled up on the couch in her office. Josefyn and Akio sat across from her, joining her for lunch, not that she had the stomach to eat anything. She'd barely spoke a word to them the whole week, but they kept coming to see her, kept trying to get her to hear their concerns, though she hadn't made it easy, her obstinacy refusing to accept that they might have a point in their arguments.

"I'm sorry, El, but I don't understand why you're fighting this so hard." Ella turned to face Josefyn.

"Why is it so bad that I have morals I don't want to break?" she asked.

"Because you've already broken them," Josefyn argued, moving closer. "You've been basically seeing Kellen for the last few weeks. I don't know why a kiss has suddenly changed that."

"Because his siblings *saw us*, Jo. My *students* saw their brother with his hand between my legs. It was beyond inappropriate and unprofessional." Ella wilted with shame. "Kellen and I the last few weeks were in that strange friend limbo where nothing physical was happening, so I didn't feel the weight of it as much. Now that something physical happened, I realize how wrong it was to let it get this far."

"But it's not wrong," Akio pushed. "You guys have real feelings for each other. There's nothing wrong with that, Rosie."

"It is when I'm counseling his siblings! It's called a dual relationship and a huge conflict of interest."

"Look, I'm sorry to be the one to tell you this, El, but you've already done enough damage to make it a conflict of interest, if it was *actually* going to *be* a conflict of interest," Josefyn objected. "You were with Kellen and the twins when their mother attacked them. You stayed at their cottage with them for a whole weekend. You went with them to their mother's house for that supervised visit and let Kellen do Gods know what to you to put on a show for his mother. You've already crossed all those boundaries. As long as your relationship with Kellen doesn't impact Laya or Jarion's progress in counseling, which you know it hasn't, there's literally no reason to be clinging so hard to these ethics when you've already stepped all over them." Josefyn reached out to place her hand on top of Ella's. "I'm telling you like it is cause I love you and I want what's best for you. And I believe what's best for you is Kellen. I wouldn't be a real friend if I didn't call you out when you make choices that are harming your own happiness."

Ella huffed out a breath, a tear sliding down her cheek. "So you guys think I'm being ridiculous?"

"YES!" both of them screamed.

"But don't you think his reaction to my feelings is enough of a reason to be hesitant here?" She wasn't ready yet to let go of her anger. "He was so dismissive of my values. Why do only his feelings matter?"

"Let me ask you a question." Akio took a seat on her couch beside her. "Why are you so resistant to being happy?"

"Excuse me?" Ella seethed.

"Why are you fighting your feelings so much for Kellen? Jo's right. You've already done the damage. So why are you still resisting?"

"Why do you care so much about this?" Ella shot back, finding his insistence, *both* their insistences that she return to Kellen suspicious. "Does this have something to do with that vision you saw in my head weeks ago?"

"I told you I couldn't tell you what that was," Akio argued, but the tremor in his voice told her she was heading down the right path.

"It matters to you that Kellen and I get together. Why?" Jo and Akio exchanged a quick look, laced with worry. "It mattered to Bryara Cavalian too. Why does it matter so much that Kellen and I—"

"*ELLA.*" Akio's voice rumbled through the room. "*Ella.*" When he spoke again, he sounded calmer, more like himself, but somehow less genuine then when he'd snapped at her. "We can't talk about this. I'm your friend, okay? I wouldn't steer you down a bad path. Don't you trust me?"

"Don't ask me if I trust you when you're clearly keeping secrets from me," she barked.

"No one is trying to hurt you, El," Josefyn insisted. "We love you. We truly love you, Ella. You're our best friend, and we want what's best for you. Don't keep yourself from happiness. Give yourself the same amount of love you give everyone else. You deserve to be happy, too."

The amulet around Ella's neck pulsated against her chest.

She clamped her fingers around the pendant to hamper the vibration, beams of purple light leaking through the cracks between her fingers. The moment she saw purple, she knew it was Kellen calling for her.

"I need to go," she grumbled, reluctantly crawling off the couch.

436

"Ella, wait," Akio called out before he dove into her path and blocked her from the door. "Just think about what we said, okay?"

"Trust me, it's given me *a lot* to think about." She shoved past him and slammed the door behind her.

She lingered there in the hallway a moment, pressing her ear to the door.

She heard Josefyn snarl at her mate, "What is your problem? You shouldn't have pushed her so hard!"

"What was I supposed to do, Josefyn?"

"Take her feelings into consideration a little bit and not just dismiss her! She's allowed to feel hurt that Kellen invalidated her. She's allowed to be upset. The weight of the world doesn't have to be on your shoulders, Ace. Don't let what Aros told you blind you from having a fucking heart."

Ella was forced to scurry down the hall and flee when Josefyn's livid footsteps stomped closer to the door.

She made it safely inside the elevator before her cover was blown.

Ella obsessed over what Josefyn had said—*what Aros told you*—the whole trek to the Varmin department. She stumbled on her feet because she kept replaying the phrase in her head, trying to pry different meanings from those four words by repeating them in different tones, yet couldn't decipher a clear enough message to understand. She was so distracted that she barreled right into Kellen, who was waiting for her outside the building to his classroom. His hands caught her shoulders before she capsized.

"If I had thought to cover myself in superglue before you showed up, we would be stuck for life right now," Kellen drawled with a laugh. The sound of his gorgeous chuckle made Ella want to scream.

She'd missed him. *Fuck*, she'd missed him so much. She missed his friendship, his laughter, his smile, the sound of his voice in her head, their private conversations into the night, the way his eyes searched for her in a room, his hands and their addictive warmth and how they always reached for her in some capacity, as if he couldn't stand them not being connected through touch.

It took everything in her to take a step back, to not collapse into his chest and fist his black sweater and yank him into her and never let his lips out from under the imprisonment of her own mouth.

"Why did you call me down here, Kilic?" She molded her voice into a dispassionate groan, hiding the cornucopia of emotion building in her chest. "I have a job to do that doesn't involve bending to your every need."

Kellen frowned. "I know that."

"Do you? Because this is not the first time you've taken advantage of my amulet to summon me here for no reason."

"I do have a reason. My reason is that I need you, Noella." Ella opened her mouth, ready to fight, but Kellen didn't allot her time to respond. "I need you, Noella Rose. I need you to talk to me. I need to be around you. I need to be breathing the same air as you. My lungs forget how to work when you're not in the room. I went from my siblings being the only people I had the capacity to care for to losing my fucking mind when I have to wait an hour to see you. I've spent the last week in fucking agony because I haven't been able to talk to you or look at your face, which is the only thing that brings me peace anymore." Kellen took a step towards her. His index finger caught her chin and lifted it, his green eyes smashing into hers. "You want a reason, baby? Because I've completely forgotten how to live without you, and I'm not sure I'll ever remember."

Ella was knocked breathless. The corners of her eyes stung. A sob clogged her throat.

Her heart and her mind wrestled for control over the next words to come out of her mouth.

Eventually, she settled on, "Do you have a free period now?"

"I have the next period free before I need to be at Power Practice for the dragon-shifters." Ella stuffed her hands into her jacket pockets.

"Do you want to shadow me while I work?" Kellen's face illuminated like a cloudless dawn.

"Fuck yeah, I want to shadow you," he exclaimed like he just won the lottery.

Ella hid her smile behind her hair as she began her trek to the Herculea sector, Kellen close on her tail.

Kellen shadowed her for the next hour. He followed her to every sector and stood back to let her work. He watched her have her daily check-in with Oken about monitoring his rage. When they stumbled upon two first grade, Meteoro water-benders who were mid brawl over one of the kids calling the other stupid, he watched her mediate a restorative conversation between the two seven-year-olds and get them to apologize to one another. He didn't interject once, seeming content to stand to the side and watch her do what she was born to do, watch her shine in her own unique power.

"Is this what you do most of the day?" he asked as they headed back to the Varmin sector to drop him off at his office. "Walk between the different sectors in case you run into a student who needs help?"

"Pretty much," Ella confirmed, her shoulder accidentally brushing his chest. "When I stay in my office, I always feel like I should be doing more. There's always someone I happen upon when I'm on the grounds."

"The students are so lucky to have you." Such a divergence from the things he used to say to her, or about her. "I know your biggest reservation is about Jarion and Laya. We talked about it, and if you're up for it, we'd like to sit down with you and figure out a strategy to ensure that no boundaries get crossed."

Ella stopped walking. She turned to him slowly. "You spoke to Jarion and Laya about us?"

"Well, they sort of spoke to *me*." She narrowed her eyes. "None of us want to make your job harder…but none of us want to let you go, either. I heard you the other night. I really heard you. I know your ethical codes matter to you, so let's talk this through and make a plan that will protect all of us. I don't want you to stop seeing my siblings, Noella, but I'm selfish enough that I also don't want you to stop seeing me. Please, just agree to have a sit down with us and talk through this. Please don't shut this down. I will get on my knees and fucking beg you, Noella Rose. There isn't a shadow of a doubt in my mind that we can make this work if we want it bad enough, and trust me, sweetheart, I want this more than I thought it was possible to want something."

Ella squeezed her eyes shut, the battle of wills between her rational mind and her emotion mind coming to a head. She was so *tired* of fighting herself. What won in the end was what she hoped was her wise mind, a combination of both, a path forward where she could honor her duty and honor her desires.

"Okay," she whispered, finally looking at Kellen. Something deep inside her raised its head with burgeoning hope.

"Okay?" he repeated, his voice catching at the end in a squeak.

"Let's have a sit down with Jarion and Laya to discuss ground rules. We'll need to formulate a plan that separates church and state, where our professional lives never bleed into our personal lives. When I speak to you about Jarion or Laya in a counseling or school context, it will be Ms. Rose speaking, not Ella. You will never take advantage of our relationship to get information out of me about our sessions. The twins can't take advantage of our personal relationship either. If we do this, you have to promise to honor those ground rules."

"I swear," he vowed, and Ella truly believed him. "Whatever it takes to keep you, I will do it."

"Alright." Ella exhaled a heavy sigh, then let herself smile, let herself feel the joy. "Then I agree to your proposition, Mr. Kilic." Kellen threaded his fingers in her hair and rushed forward to kiss her. Ella pulled back before his lips made contact. "Not here!" she cried, shoving him away. "Another ground rule. No kissing me in front of students. We need to be professionals."

"Fine." He didn't sound happy about it, but he consented regardless.

"Tomorrow, we'll speak to Headmistress Dyer and report our relationship."

"Wait." Kellen drew his head back. "I thought you didn't want people to know we were together."

"I didn't say that. I just don't want to be unprofessional in front of our students. We need to follow the school guidelines if there are fraternization policies between staff, and I'll feel better if we're up front from the beginning. I'm fine with a public relationship, just not public displays of affection."

Kellen took a step closer to her, his chest nearly grazing hers. "So I can tell people you're mine, Noella Rose?"

Ella let a slow, sinister smile splay across her face. "You can tell people…that you're *mine*, Kellen Kilic."

Kellen loosed a thrilled chuckle, then looked to make sure no one was watching when he kissed her nose.

"What an honor it is to be yours, sweetheart."

CHAPTER 32

# KELLEN

KELLEN HAD NEVER RUN FASTER in his fucking life then when two soft knocks pounded against his door.

He lunged across his apartment, straining his hamstring in the process, and yanked the front door open to find the face he most admired, that was the living manifestation of his heart, smiling up at him. Noella had changed out of her work apparel, now donning an off-the-shoulder white sweater tucked into dark jeans that clung to her legs, adhering to her glorious ass, and flared out at the bottom, fraying along the hem. Kellen reached for her at the same moment she reached for him. She leapt into his open arms and tied her legs around his waist with a delicious squeal.

Kellen pressed his face into her neck, inhaling the intoxicating fragrance of her moisturizer and perfume, and felt every muscle in his body ease, felt his heart breathe a sigh of relief to finally be reunited with the other half of his soul. He was so overcome by the feeling of her against him that he burst into tears.

"Don't cry!" Noella exclaimed through an unsteady laugh, battling her own emotion.

"You're so fucking beautiful," he cried—Kellen fucking cried and couldn't stop the deluge of tears embarrassingly raining down his face. She slipped her fingers under his chin to raise his face out of her neck, smudging his tears with her thumbs, a soft, questioning, awed look overtaking her features.

"You're crying because you think I'm beautiful?" she whispered.

"I'm crying because my arms have lived in solitary my whole life and ached to hold you, before I even knew you existed. Now that you're here…now that I get to experience this…I feel overwhelmed by how full I feel when for so long I felt so empty." Noella loosed a moan from deep in her throat and bent down to press her velvety lips to his cheeks, kissing away every droplet, yearning to kiss away all his internal scars from loneliness, if only she could crawl inside him to mend them.

"You're not alone anymore," she mumbled against his lips, consuming his groan as his hand rose to cup her cheek and bring her even closer, their noses smushing together. He couldn't get enough of the taste of her, couldn't slow himself down to savor the flavor of her love because he'd been craving this so much this past week and he needed it right now, all at once, every part of her.

"Can you say it just once?" he requested, her nose nuzzling his. Noella knew what he meant.

"I'm yours, Kellen Kilic," she promised, sweeping her lips down the bridge of his nose to kiss the tip.

Noella jumped down from his embrace, not separating herself from him though. She knitted her arms around his waist and rested her cheek against his chest, pressing her ear to his heart like she needed to hear evidence of his existence too, something to prove that he wasn't a fantasy.

"Don't ever leave me, Noella," Kellen groaned into the top of her head, then felt her tense up in his arms.

"We should…we should really talk…about the end of the school year." Noella lifted her face out of his chest, her mouth twisting from left to right in odd shapes as she struggled to organize her thoughts. "I hadn't planned to renew a contract with Delmarth. I want to go back to the Earthly Plane."

Kellen took a moment to temper his first reaction—which was to fall to his knees and beg her not to go—and paced his breathing so when he spoke, his tone wouldn't come off dismissive or angry.

"What about your life here?" He was proud of himself for how calm he sounded. Noella sighed.

"Until two months ago, I didn't have a life here. I was utterly alone. I was miserable in Cavale. And now…after the past seven weeks with you…now I feel…very torn." Kellen caught her chin when she choked on a sob, bawling, "I miss my sister. I miss her so much, Kellen. She's been my everything my whole life, the savior for me the way you were for the twins, and it physically hurts to not be with her. Telling myself that I would reunite with her in June was what got me through those first four weeks here. When I think about leaving Cavale now…about separating from my life here, from Josefyn and Akio, from the twins…from *you*…that pain is magnified tenfold. It feels like, with either choice, I'd be choosing to forever give up a huge part of my heart. I don't know how someone makes that kind of choice and lives with the consequences."

"Maybe you wouldn't have to give up one for the other." He brushed a kiss over her brow, pulling her back against his chest. "You're here for seven more months. Let's try and find out if there are ways for you to pass between the two worlds. If you choose to stay in Cavale, maybe there's a way to get your sister to come here, or for you to go back there for a short time to visit her. Maybe there's a way for me to go back and forth so the twins and I can visit you there. There must be a way, since Headmistress Dyer was able to travel to the Earthly Plane to meet with you for your interview. It doesn't have to be one or the other, baby. We can find a way to make this work where we wouldn't need to separate and you wouldn't need to compromise anything."

"You…" Noella's bottom lip trembled. "You would really do that for me? You would go to the Earthly Plane to see me, even with how much you detest it?"

"I would do fucking anything for you, Noella Rose. And the Earthly Plane can't be too bad if it produced my favorite creature who's ever lived." Kellen laughed when Noella slammed her face in his chest and wept hysterically. "Sweetheart, don't cry," he chuckled, wrapping her ponytail around his hand to pull her head back, then leaned down and swept his lips across her cheeks, returning the gesture of kissing away her tears.

"I know I haven't made this easy for you," she sniveled, sniffling, "but I need you to know how much I care about you, Kellen. I need you to trust in that. I wasn't pushing you away because there weren't feelings here. I never meant to dismiss our connection and pretend it didn't mean something to me. It was a constant struggle between my head and my heart, what I wanted to do and what I *thought* I should do. I'm going to make up for all the time my hesitancy stole from us. I promise."

"Baby, you don't have to make up for anything." Her fingers clinched his biceps while his hands traveled down to cup her behind. "We're here now. Let's not go backwards and live in that regret. Let's go forwards and live in the joy."

Noella's eyes shimmered. "Who knew you could be so insightful?"

"Definitely not me." Kellen's lips attached to her throat when she threw her head back with a laugh. He groaned, "I need to check on dinner, but I really don't want to separate myself from you."

"Then don't. I want to come with you." Noella traipsed after him into the kitchen, squeezing her arms around his stomach so tightly that he coughed out a wheeze. "What're you making?"

"I think you'll like it." He opened the oven for her to peek inside. "It's—"

"BREAD!" she shrieked, reveling in the large loaf currently baking on the oven rack that had sundried tomatoes, garlic, and beef amalgamated into the dough. She bounced on her feet like a child and sprang off her toes to leap onto his shoulders, planting kiss after kiss on the back of his neck and swinging around to land them on his cheek. "You're the best. That smells so good. I'm so excited for dinner."

"I've never seen you like this," Kellen marveled, gripping her waist and lifting her up onto his counter.

"You've never seen me fully surrender to my heart's desire," Noella told him, her cheeks glowing.

He cocked a brow. "Oh, is that what this is? You surrendering to your heart's desire?"

"Mhm. And my heart's obsessed with you." Kellen's body felt buoyant from bliss as he spread her legs apart and stepped between them. Her fingers greedily crawled up his chest before emmeshing in his hair.

"Right back at you, gorgeous." Noella trailed a sequence of tiny, doting kisses down the line of his chin. Love consumed his entire being, his heart whelmed by the way her lips traveled down the expanse of scruff on his jaw with innocence, care, and curiosity. His limbs disintegrated into something ethereal from an influx of desire. His hands gripped the edge of the counter to maintain his balance. "After our talk, when the twins leave," Kellen whispered in her ear, his warm breath dripping down her neck, "I plan to *devour* you, Noella Rose. I want to explore every inch of your body with my tongue, my teeth, my soul. I want to consume every beautiful sound you make and get drunk off your need, for you are the most addictive drug." The moan Noella loosed prompted Kellen's jeans to become painfully tight. His fingers scraped up her thighs. "No more waiting. No more fighting this. You're finally mine, and I want your body to recognize that, to feel my adoration, as well as your heart."

"It does," she keened, breaths heaving out of her when his fingers slid up to her waist and untucked her sweater from inside her jeans to careen across her bare stomach, floating around to splay on her spine. He slid her forward on the counter so her crotch rear-ended with his. Her feet dug into his ass. "I wish you could feel the way I feel about you, Kellen. I wish you could experience it in your own body. It's like a river with no end. A freefall with no ground to cushion your fall. A sky with no limit."

"It sounds like how I feel every single day." Kellen's nose dragged down the side of her face, his lips haunting her flesh. She stretched her neck to angle her face closer to his mouth. He smiled against her throat, then burrowed his face deeper inside her neck, his tongue lapping her pulse.

"What're you doing?" she squeaked, her head unconsciously tipping back to give him more access.

"I want to taste the proof that you're alive," he murmured almost absentmindedly. He lavished the column of her neck in tiny nips, sucking at the skin of her throat. Her back arched at its own accord.

"What does my heartbeat taste like?" she whispered.

"Like love," he replied without thinking, lost in the moment, in her. Noella gasped at the word *love*. His hand meandered up to curve around her chin, tilting her head towards him so he could capture her gasp in a kiss.

"Kellen," she groaned, her fingers releasing his olive green henley shirt to tangle in his curls.

"The way you say my name is music." Kellen yanked her bottom lip between his teeth. "Sing for me again, baby."

"Kellen—" Her words were vanquished by a moan.

"Beautiful," he groaned, pulling back so the tip of his nose kissed the tip of hers. "What an exquisite opera you are, my sweet Noella." Of course the twins decided to arrive at that exact moment.

"Come on, guys!" Jarion shouted, covering his eyes, while Laya vibrated similarly to the way Noella had reacted to the bread in the oven, bouncing on her toes.

"I'm taking your keys away," Kellen declared before reluctantly pulling away from Noella.

She jumped down from the counter and roamed around the kitchen island to make her way into the living room, correctly sensing that Laya was about to bound forward. His little sister vaulted across the room to pounce on Noella, the force of her elation knocking them both onto the couch.

"FINALLY!" Laya squealed, Noella laughing without abandon.

"This is the best greeting ever!" She lifted one hand off Laya and extended it out to slap Jarion's proffered high-five.

"Do we get to call you Noella now?" Jarion teased. Noella's eyes squinted into mocking slits.

"No one calls her Noella but me," Kellen argued, then unfurled his arm so Jarion could fit himself against Kellen's body.

"You did good, Kell," Jarion murmured in his ear. He clapped Kellen on the back. "I'm happy for you."

A lump fouled Kellen's throat. He ruffled Jarion's hair, knocking the beanie off the top of his head.

"This hat is mine, in case you forgot," Kellen joshed. Jarion swung his fist playfully near Kellen's eye. He ducked in time before the crunched ball of fingers made contact with his cheekbone.

"How long until dinner? I'm starving." Laya rubbed her stomach.

"Two minutes. Why don't you guys set the table while Noell—er, Ms. Rose," he stumbled on his words, unsure what to call her in front of the twins, "helps me with dinner." Noella pushed herself off the couch.

"That's part of what we need to discuss tonight," she said, strutting across the living room to meet Kellen. *Fuck*, her gait was so unintentionally seductive, her curves the epitome of sex. "If you guys can promise not to slip up when we're at school…I'd be happy if, when we're in private, you call me Ella. I don't need to be Ms. Rose when we're at home." The corners of Kellen's eyes burned when she referred to being with them as *home*.

This was his home.

Not Delmarth. Not even the cottage. It was these three people. These three angels all smiling at each other.

Nothing else mattered beyond them.

While the twins set the table, Kellen switched the oven off and shuffled the loaf of bread onto a serving tray. Noella busied herself with pouring four glasses of water for the group before carrying them to the table in two separate journeys, kissing the air near Kellen's cheek on her way out of the kitchen the second time. As Kellen approached them with the master loaf, Noella, Jarion and Laya began leading a deafening chorus of slamming their fists into the table and yelling at the top of their lungs in anticipation of their meal.

"We're going to get a noise complaint," Kellen chuckled, the three of them fragmenting into stitches of laughter.

"Alright, Kilic-slash-Ates family. Let's dig in!" Noella cheered, accepting the knife from Kellen to portion herself a large chunk of bread.

Laya and Jarion exchanged a quick look.

"We actually wanted to talk to you about that, Kell," Jarion said, nodding to Laya to give her the floor.

"We've been talking…" Laya took over, "…and now that Mom is gone from our lives…we want you to officially adopt us." Noella placed her hand on Kellen's shoulder when his bottom lip began quivering. "Dad won't be out of Terminus for another four years, so I don't know how that would play into this, but we don't want our name to be Ates anymore. We want to be Laya and Jarion *Kilic*. Not because of Mom. Because of you." All thought emptied from his brain.

"I...I don't know what to say," Kellen whispered through a sob. Noella leaned over to kiss away the tear that escaped down his cheek. "Of course I will adopt you both. It would be my honor. I'm already your legal guardian, but I'll figure out with Brunner if it's even possible to adopt you while Ciaran is in Terminus, or if I have to wait until he's out. I can call him first thing tomorrow."

"Great." Laya and Jarion slipped their hands into Kellen's.

"I love you guys so much. I'm so fucking proud of you and proud to be your brother." He kissed both of their knuckles before releasing their hands.

"So how do we make this work between all of us?" Jarion asked Noella, ripping off a chunk of his bread and tossing it into his mouth.

"This is unchartered territory for me," she admitted, smoothing her napkin on her lap. "If we were on the Earthly Plane and I developed feelings for a parent of my students, I would stop seeing you for counseling and refer you to someone else. We don't have that luxury here, since I'm the only counselor in the entire kingdom, so I'm going to need to make adjustments as I go. When we're in a school setting, we need to be professional. I can't be Ella to you. I am Ms. Rose, and you are my students. When we're in sessions together, we can only discuss our counseling goals. No mention of anything personal. I've told Kellen that our confidentiality in our sessions extends into our relationship outside of school too. Things you tell me in confidence in our sessions will not be shared outside of my office unless you want them to be shared with Kellen. In school, I have to treat you guys like all the other students because I need to ensure I'm always acting equitably towards everyone. No special treatment because I'm dating your brother. When we're outside of school, we shouldn't speak about the contents of our sessions anymore. Let our counseling work remain within the school hours to create some distance between our professional and personal lives. This isn't meant to cut you off from telling me things when we're not in school. When I leave school at the end of the day, I put my counseling hat away so I can focus on Ella's needs. I need that boundary for myself so I don't drown in what everyone else is feeling, because so much of my day is being consumed by other people's emotions, if that makes sense."

"It does," Laya confirmed. Jarion nodded too.

"I need to maintain that boundary even with you guys outside of school," Noella continued. "I haven't been good with that, and I take full accountability for my own slip ups, when I've asked you about certain things we've spoken about in counseling in front of your brother. Even though we all knew what we'd spoken about, I shouldn't have done that. I won't do that anymore. I will be more careful with maintaining our boundaries. When I'm with you like this, I don't want to be Ms. Rose. I don't want that pressure. I just want the freedom to be Ella."

"We want that too," Jarion said.

"Whatever you need from us," Laya promised. Noella touched her hand to her heart in reception of their acceptance. "We love you, and we love you for our brother. We want you both to be happy."

"You two have stolen so much of my heart," Noella said, dabbing away tears. "I adore you both more than words could express. Thank you for being so understanding." Kellen drew circles on Noella's back.

"Feel better?" he asked her. She exhaled a relieved breath and nodded. "Isn't she so pretty?" Kellen admired, cradling her cheek. Noella turned her face into his palm to peck the center of his hand.

"Don't be gross," Jarion ribbed, pretending to gag.

"I love it." Laya settled her chin between her hands and grinned. "I've always wanted a big sister."

"I always wanted little siblings," Noella reciprocated. "I couldn't have asked for three better people to call my family."

A single tear dripped from Kellen's lashes. Followed by another. Followed by a rivulet of liquid joy.

All the isolation he'd endured, all the pain, it had been worth it to arrive at this moment. In this place.

With these people. His people. His whole heart. His home.

---

Ella couldn't remember the last time she'd felt an almost intimidating amount of happiness—scary in the sense that her heart was teetering on the edge of rupturing from the overpacked feeling, the universe chockfull of bliss. It felt daunting to believe it to be real, that the world was capable of holding this much feeling, that *she* was capable of holding that much joy inside her.

She'd spent time with Laya, Jarion and Kellen outside of school, but tonight felt different. Freer, less encumbered, her heart unfettered from the restraints of her mind telling her she wasn't allowed to experience this, her soul now fully able to participate in the moment. She drank up every story the twins told about Kellen, and the stories Kellen shared about them in retribution. Water squirted out of her nose from hysterical laughter when Kellen told her the story of a time when the twins were two and he'd been helping put Jarion and Laya's diapers on. Jarion had kicked Kellen so hard in the face that Kellen collapsed with a broken nose and was unconscious for several minutes. When liquid shot out of Ella's nostril and sprayed the table, Kellen started yelling at Laya to run to the bathroom so she wouldn't piss on Kellen's chair from laughing.

Ella luxuriated in bearing witness to the beautiful connection these three siblings had with one another. What an honor it was to bask in their respect and adoration. Their intense devotion and years of pain tethered them together in spite of their parents' ploy to keep them separate, those ropes attaching their souls to one another giving them strength. Ella prayed that one day, she could have Rylee and Mason here with them, or perhaps the twins and Kellen could join them on the Earthly Plane. She wanted the chance to relish having all her favorite people around one table, all these gorgeous souls who were tied together through similar experiences and clung to light to push out the dark.

As they were saying their goodbyes, Laya wrapped her arms

around Ella's stomach and whispered, "I've never seen my brother like this. Thank you."

"Seen him like what?" Laya moved back so Ella could see and feel her smile in every corner of her body.

"Not tormented." Ella's eyes stung. "He thinks he's hidden it from us better than he has. I've seen how haunted he is. How much what we went through tortures him. I know how guilty he feels for not having done something sooner to stop it. You've helped him start to let that go. When I look at him now, his guilt isn't the first thing I see. His eyes are so much lighter. I can see his soul again, and it's all thanks to you." Ella squeaked a sob as she pulled Laya back into her arms.

"You are a beautiful person, Eulaylia Kilic." Laya cried when Ella called her *Kilic* instead of *Ates.* "Don't ever lose that part of you that is so open to the world around you. The way you see people is such a gift."

"Thank you, Ms. Ro…*Ella.*" She kissed the side of Laya's head, then relinquished her so she could hug Jarion.

"I'm really happy you're going to be in our lives forever, Ella," Jarion whispered in her ear.

"Me too, Jare." She adjusted his beanie that she knocked out of place. "I'm proud of you."

"For what?" he stammered.

"For admitting you're happy." Jarion's eyes shimmered with the depth of that feeling like he couldn't fathom how it was possible for him to experience any sort of contentment, let alone be able to put words to it.

"Get a good night's rest, you two," Kellen said, slinking his arm around Ella's shoulders. "You know what starts tomorrow?"

"MACCABIAH!" the twin shouted in unison.

Ella had been looking forward to experiencing what everyone at Delmarth deemed the best week of the year. The last week of November, the school split into two competitive teams, a red team and a gold team based off the school colors, and hosted a series of events intended for the students to practice their powers and show off what they'd learned throughout the semester. Their participation in Maccabiah counted toward their final grades in Power Practice and was considered a midterm exam, though none of the students viewed it through that negative lens. From what Kellen had told her about the event, the totality of both the student body and the faculty gave themselves fully to the healthy competition. She was just as excited for the games to begin as the twins were.

"Do you know what team we're on yet?" Jarion asked his brother on their way to the door.

"We'll find out tomorrow morning," Kellen answered. Kellen and Ella had a staff meeting scheduled for before first period, where Headmistress Dyer intended to announce which faculty members were being disseminated to which teams. Siblings were always placed on the same teams to protect against familial rifts, so Jarion, Laya and Kellen were guaranteed to be put on the same team.

"Oh, I hope we're on the same team as Ella!" Laya cried, jostling Ella's arm sweetly. She blew the two of them a kiss before she shepherded Jarion out the front door, sensing how much Kellen and Ella wanted to be alone.

"*Finally,*" Kellen sighed, twisting his arms around Ella's shoulders from behind and pressing his lips to the corner of her mouth. "I have you all to myself." Ella hummed as she leaned back in his arms.

"Tonight was perfect," she sighed, her breath bleeding into a moan as Kellen drizzled soft, feather-light kisses over her eyes, nose, cheeks, and chin, saving her lips for last. By the time his mouth stroked against hers, she was desperate for it, hunger pumping furiously through her veins.

Kellen either sensed her need or smelled it, because he didn't hesitate to heft her into his arms in an effortless sweep, like she weighed nothing, and carry her to the back of the apartment to his bedroom, laying her flat on his duvet. Ella lifted her arms on instinct, allowing Kellen to peel her sweater off her body, revealing the black lace bra she wore underneath.

"Are you kidding?" he gasped, eyes drugged with desire crashing into hers. "You're not real. There's no fucking way." Kellen abruptly climbed off the bed, crossing the room to the full length mirror that was perched against his wall, and lifted it from its resting position to bring it over to his wardrobe, arranging the mirror against the cupboard so Ella could see herself on the bed. He then crawled back onto the mattress and reclaimed his spot on top of Ella, sitting on her stomach. "Look at yourself, Noella. Look how breathtaking you are." Ella turned her head and met her reflection in the mirror.

Her blonde hair had spilled out of the weak elastic holding it together in a ponytail and now torrented over the comforter like leaked honey. Lucid, crimson color swept across her cheeks and flowed down her chest to where her breasts were nearly tumbling out of her bra. She barely skimmed those details, only devoting a fleeting moment to their inspection, and chose to bestow all her focus onto her eyes, on how they glowed, how they smiled, on the rapture pouring out of them.

"What do you see?" Kellen asked her, tracing shapes on her cheek with the tip of his nose.

"I see…peace," she whispered, her back flying off the mattress when Kellen sucked at the skin of her throat.

"You want to know what I see?" She nodded. "I see my heart in a physical form. I see my salvation, my hero. I see perfection."

"I need you closer if you're going to say such sweet things." Ella hooked her ankles behind Kellen's back and wrenched him down into her.

"I'm scared…" Kellen's eyes suddenly filled with tears. "I'm scared I won't be perfect for you, Rose."

Ella captured Kellen's face between her palms, smudging away the streaks of tears on his cheeks.

"You don't have to be perfect, Kilic," she said, nuzzling her nose against his. "You just have to be mine."

"Easy. Done. I'm yours, Noella. Without a doubt fucking *yours*." She swallowed a sob.

Ella looked at Kellen and saw every version of him that he'd been for her. Her enemy. Her reluctant colleague. The fierce protector of his siblings. Her ally. Her best friend. Her guardian. Her lover.

The extent of her feeling—the extent of her *love* for him— suddenly engulfed her so forcefully that she couldn't breathe. This man who had spent her first four weeks in Cavale making her life a living hell, throwing her into walls and nearly drowning her in a pool, was not the man who hovered above her now with tears in his eyes, essentially declaring his love, yet somehow, someway, she even loved the man he'd been then, because it had led them to this moment, here on his bed. There wasn't a single thing about her life, no matter how tragic it had been at times, that she would take back or change, because everything she'd been through had brought her here. If she hadn't suffered abuse at the hands of her mother, if her own school counselor hadn't been such a colossal failure and never noticed the warning signs to help Ella, she never would have been inspired to become a figure of support for children that she'd lacked growing up. She never would have ended up going to grad school to become a school counselor. She never would have landed her job at Delmarth.

All of that pain, all of that agonizing uncertainty that made her look up at the sky and beg whatever God could hear her to help her understand why, why *this*, why *her*, had culminated in this.

In *him*. Her ending.

Her beginning.

The start of her life.

The start of her heart.

The love of her life.

It all was so clear to her now. How could she have ever wasted so much of their time denying this?

She would waste none of their time ever again.

"I cannot imagine ever feeling this way for anyone else," she swore in a hushed whisper, those words not sufficient to express the magnitude of her feelings, but they were a start as she came to terms with the depth of her love for him. "I know I never will. You have all of me, Kellen Kilic. No distance will ever come between that. That kind of feeling cannot be constrained by time or space or even the membrane of an interdimensional void. No matter where in the universe I am, you have all of me, forever." Kellen's fingers curved around the insides of her knees.

With no preamble, he proceeded to roll them on the bed and position her legs on either side of him so she now straddled his waist. Her hands flew out to steady herself and sunk into the duvet on either side of his head.

"Did you just whisper the most beautiful declaration?" He gripped her chin to guide her head down, then mumbled against her lips, "Say it one more time, sweetheart. Loud enough for the whole universe to hear."

"You have all of me, Kellen. Forever." Ella could've drowned in his loving gaze and died happy.

"A couple weeks ago, you asked me what I thought this mind connection thing between us was. I said I didn't have any theories."

"Which I knew was a lie," Ella said, tracing his mouth with her index finger. Kellen caught the tip of her finger between his teeth. The impression of the sharp edge of his tooth piercing the pad of her finger created an incendiary throb between her legs.

"I think the mind connection between us is a mating bond brewing." The oxygen in Ella's chest dribbled out of her lungs through a gasp. With his hands fondling her backside, he declared, with such a staggering amount of conviction that it left her breathless, "I think you're my Cavalisha, Noella Rose."

Ella couldn't speak for several minutes.

"Is that even possible?" she stammered when she could finally talk again, when her breath had returned to her and she no longer felt like she was going to faint. "I'm not from Cavale. I'm not a Primordial."

"Aros's mate is a human, not that I'm comparing myself to Aros Cavalian." Kellen tucked a strand of her hair behind her ear. "I think you were meant to come here, Noella. To heal our world. To heal *me*." He found himself blathering, a floodgate opened by the innocence of her gaze. "We're raised to believe the Gods will provide us with the guidance and support to reach our fullest potential. There are contingencies to that support, though. It rests on the expectation that we will extend our deepest veneration in return, that our undying love for them will be rewarded with prosperity. Believing in the Gods has never gifted me anything other than isolation and loneliness…until the day I met my siblings. And then, the day I met you." Kellen's eyes trickled up Ella's body, an achingly slow ascent before landing on her face. "Those are the only times I have ever felt I had a God on my side. The deeper I've fallen into you…and I say fallen *into* instead of *for* because it feels as though my heart tumbled out of my chest and landed inside you, and I will forever be searching for my soul within the depths of your being... I've begun to see that it was not the Gods who led me to you, for they are not the Gods I believe in most. It's you, Noella."

Kellen's hands framed her face, his thumbs smearing away the beads of tears collecting on her cheeks.

"You are my divinity," he proclaimed, planting a kiss between her brows. "You are my God, Noella. You are the only thing I will ever follow in life and death, the only being I will ever worship."

"Kellen," she sobbed, her fingernails scoring his back to drag him closer so she could curl around him. "You paint such beautiful portraits with your words." He kissed away her tears, one by one. "I only hope that someday I can offer you something as precious as the gifts you've given me."

"You already have, baby." Kellen's hand swept down Ella's back, pressing her closer into him so there wasn't a single point on their bodies that weren't connected somehow through touch. "The gift is you, right here in my arms. The way you're looking at me right now, like the amount of passion you feel for me could combust you, is more precious than anything you could ever paint for me with words. All I need is the promise of that look, on me, forever." He pressed a kiss to her forehead.

"I promise," she vowed, that pledge flooding her bloodstream, becoming the collagen that fashioned her bones.

Kellen reeled up so Ella was no longer hovering over him, but seated fully on his torso. Her fingers plunged into his hair, her head tipping back from the weight of desire as Kellen's lips traveled across her stomach, drifting up to her bra, where his tongue flicked over her nipple through the lace fabric before he replaced his tongue with his teeth, gathering the material into his mouth so he could suck at her breast.

"Kellen," she groaned, grinding her pelvis into his, eager for a spark of friction to relieve the burn there. "Take it off. I want to feel you."

"I want more time valuing you in this glorious ensemble." Ella groaned a sound of pure frustration. Kellen laughed, the sound skittering under her skin. "Getting impatient, are we, sweetheart?"

"I want you, Kellen," she snarled.

"And I want you, my beautiful, precious Noella." He licked up her throat to find her lips again. He pulled his head back to look at her as he said, "We only get this once. A first coming together of our bodies and hearts. We will have a lifetime of this kind of connection, but we only get one chance to first experience it. I don't want to rush any of it. I have relished the time we spent getting to know one another. I want to maintain that respectful pace. I want to savor every minute of your heart's surrender, because you deserve an unhurried worship, not a rushed adulation."

Kellen kissed away the tears building in the corners of her eyes. "You are so sweet," she croaked, not understanding how she got so lucky as to be loved this beautifully by someone this special.

"I have loved being your friend, Noella, but I'm going to love being your lover even more."

Kellen's mouth crashed into hers, and for a moment, they were simply a clutter of tongues and teeth and groans of need, the personification of lust in their creation of an entangled statue. Ella finally had the chance to gather the fabric of Kellen's shirt and drag it up over his head, chucking it across the room without a care for where it landed. Her hands couldn't touch all of him fast enough, forgetting his request for a slow pace as her fingers drifted across every burly, powerful sinew of muscle, her fingernails sketching lines down the hard ridges of his chest. Kellen's head fell back at the sensation of her marking him, a groan vibrating inside his throat. Ella seized his chin to lift his head.

"Mine," she declared, the corner of Kellen's mouth quirking up at the possessive edge to her tone.

"You have me body and soul, Noella Rose, in every lifetime we're blessed to exist in together." Ella tipped forward and traced her tongue over the stretch of his abs as a reward for his declaration.

"Mine," she asserted again, her teeth skimming the scales outlining the sides of his throat. Kellen answered that assertion by sliding his hand inside her jeans and giving her ass a sharp squeeze.

"*Mine,*" he growled back.

"Yours," she answered, prompting Kellen to finally put them both out of their misery and skate his hand around the inside to the front of her jeans, reaching the apex of her thighs. He slid his finger underneath the lace material of her panties.

"Does this match your bra?" Ella nodded. Kellen hissed, "Did you wear this for me, Noella?"

"Don't give yourself that much credit. I always like to match."

"If this has been existing under your clothes the entire time we've known each other, then I sincerely apologize for ever suggesting that you don't have a fashion sense." Ella pulled back when Kellen tried to kiss her jaw.

"When did you suggest that?" she asked with confusion, not recollecting them ever having that conversation.

"The night of The Dow."

"I don't remember you saying that." Kellen's eyes rounded, grasping his mistake. "What haven't you told me, Kilic?"

"Um…" He removed his hand from inside her pants. He took a deep breath, then said, "The night of The Dow, I came back to my apartment and found you in the hallway. You were wasted and leaning against my door because you thought it was yours. I helped you get back inside your own apartment."

"You put the trash bin next to my head," Ella realized. Kellen nodded. "I woke up wondering how I'd gotten inside my apartment. Why don't I remember any of that?"

"Because I took those memories away from you. I was trying to convince myself back then that I hated you, and it made it easier to swallow that lie when you hated me too. If you had remembered, I was afraid it would've made you soften to me, and that would make it harder for me to keep my distance from you. Not that I was ever able to." Ella glided her fingers out of his hair to cradle his face.

"It's always been our destiny to end up here," she murmured, her thumbs floating over his mouth.

"I couldn't agree more." Kellen pressed a kiss to her fingers.

"While I truly adore slow and sweet Kellen, I'm ready for you to fuck me now." Kellen coughed out a stunned cackle.

"Lift your hips so I can get these jeans off you. I need to see the matching set in full." Ella heeded the command and rose up on her knees so Kellen could unbutton her jeans and slide the denim down her thighs. "*Fuck,*" Kellen gasped when the denim fell away and he could see the black lace thong. He didn't hesitate to lurch upward and clamp his mouth over the bud of her clit through the lace, his hands slithering up the backs of her thighs to keep her from toppling over.

"Kell," she moaned, her fingers diving into his hair, making a home for herself in his curls.

Kellen's mouth disappeared from between her legs when he leaned back.

"You've never called me Kell before." His expression was wholesome awe. "Say it again." Ella smiled.

"Kell," she purred. Kellen rewarded her by yanking her panties down and returning his lips to her clit, this time with no barrier of lace hindering him from the connection of her skin and his teeth.

"Tell me how you want it," he begged her, sucking at the sensitive bud, his eyes locked on hers.

"You. On top. I want to be able to look at your face the whole time."

"Would you like to come for the first time with me inside you, or on my tongue right now?"

Ella's skin was no longer composed of human flesh, but of uninhibited fire. "Everything. I want everything with you, Kell."

"Thank you for gracing my ears with my new favorite words." Kellen's tongue flicked her clit, and she nearly yanked a handful of his hair out of his scalp. He worked her in tender strokes, upholding his promise to not rush a single gesture, even as her hips drove towards him in a silent entreat for more. When his tongue slid inside her and applied that extra force she'd been craving, she exploded almost instantly, her orgasm rampaging through her with unexpected potency, her thighs clenching from the pressure to remain upright. The scruff peppered over Kellen's jaw tickled her thighs as he drew his head back and presented her a gleaming smile, her arousal glossed over his lips.

"No more waiting," she demanded, repeating his words from earlier.

Kellen rotated them so she now lay beneath him. Ella clawed his jeans down his wiry legs, his erection springing free, and circled him with her fingers, leaning up to surround the crest of his cock with her lips.

"No," Kellen gasped, tugging her hair gently to jerk her head back. "If you do that, I will come right now, and I want to come for the first time inside you." Ella nodded and slipped her fingers off him.

Kellen replaced Ella's hands on his cock with his own.

He inclined forward and positioned himself at her entrance. It suddenly occurred to her that they needed protection.

"What about a condom?" Kellen laughed at her nervous squeak, kissing her on both cheeks.

"I take a magic-infused birth control pill with my morning coffee. We're good." Ella eased against the mattress.

"So men take birth control in Cavale, not women?" She grumbled, "I wish the Earthly Plane could catch up with that."

"Women take birth control on the Earthly Plane?" Kellen exclaimed, "That's fucking bullshit. Why should women have to suffer through that when they're the ones who end up carrying the child?"

Ella gushed, "You just reached a new level of perfect." He cackled, teasing the tip of her nose with his teeth. "I want to see your wings," she suddenly declared before he could slide himself inside her.

"Right now?" he spluttered. She nodded. "I…I've never done that before."

"I want all of you, Kellen Kilic. I want to feel and claim all of you." Kellen's eyes softened before he bestowed a kiss on her nose.

His muscles flexed before two brilliant dragon wings unfolded from his back, the golden sheen varnished over the black scales catching the ambient light and painting gilded beams onto the walls around them, orange sprinkled within the hue from the orange outlining the rims of his wings.

"Beautiful," she breathed, reaching up to trail her fingers across the leathery membrane.

"I was thinking the same thing looking at you," he said, dropping his forehead onto hers. "You ready to become mine, Noella Rose?"

"I've been waiting my whole life, Kellen Kilic," she answered before he sheathed himself fully inside her.

"*Holy fuck,*" Kellen roared. Ella's fingernails tunneled into his biceps as he reared over her.

"*Wow,*" she gasped, her breath palpitating out of her. She'd never experienced anything like this before. Her whole body was filled with frothing energy, a sensation she didn't have a name for surging through her bloodstream, rippling across her bones, becoming the petroleum that powered her body.

"Fuck," Kellen said again, this time through tears. "You were worth the fucking wait, sweetheart."

"So were you," Ella cried, understanding now what it felt like to be truly worshipped.

Kellen sobbed before he began thrusting inside of her, no rush to each piston of his hips, a slow, sweet glide of himself in and out of her. That energy under her skin kept amplifying, like it was trying to swell large enough to break free from the confinement of her flesh and stretch over to reach him, like it belonged with him some- how. Ella had no way of confirming for sure, but she wondered if that feeling was a mating bond between them, if Kellen was right about his hypothesis that they were Cavalisha.

He certainly felt like the other half of her soul, the missing piece of her she'd been searching for all her life.

They couldn't stop kissing. She could only breathe properly now when his mouth was fastened to hers. Any separation, and she lost her breath and forgot how to function without that connection.

*You're so close,* that female voice yelled in her head. *End this all now. Tell him you love him.*

Too many things were happening at once for Ella to have time to question the voice or listen to it. Those three words on Ella's tongue turned to molten lava before she could breathe life into them.

"Look at the mirror," Kellen commanded her, sucking at her earlobe. Ella's eyes flung to the mirror, examining their joined bodies and Kellen's wings arching above them like a shield to protect them from the rest of the world. "Do you see how perfectly your body fits with mine? We were made for each other, Noella. You are not just my friend. You are not just my lover, or my prized God. You are my perfect counterpart. The mate I choose for myself, whether there's a true bond between us or not."

Noella's climax ripped through her. Her eyes scrunched as she screamed, his name rolling of her tongue over and over again, a litany she sang to the Gods as thanks for giving her the gift of this beautiful man.

Kellen followed closely behind her with a thunderous bellow accompanying his own climax, going still inside of her as he emptied himself, all his love, all his pain, into the safekeeping of her body.

She took all of it in her with gratitude, and with her lips over his, she swore an oath to never let him feel that pain again.

## CHAPTER 33

# ELLA

ELLA'S FATHER used to take her on what he called their *ice cream dates* when he picked her up from Pre-K. He'd collect her from her class with a bag of provisions already in tow, and they would walk together to Central Park, claim a bench, and enjoy their ice cream. Alec always got the same flavor—he never deviated from plain vanilla—but Ella requested to be surprised each time with a different flavor, always a curious child who wanted to experience every part of life and determine for herself what she enjoyed or not.

For today's ice cream date, he'd gotten her something called space cake ice cream, flavored like cake batter with pieces of red velvet cupcake mixed in. Two scoops sagged within a waffle cone, strips of white and red drizzling down over her fingers as she licked the mound on top.

Ella's little legs were sprawled out on Alec's lap. He'd just finished his ice cream, the empty waste discarded on the bench next to him. His frigid fingers from cradling the bottom of the cup now folded around her calves.

Ella had just finished telling him about a kid in her class, Hunter, who earlier in the day had locked her in a box on the playground while the children were in recess. He'd shoved her inside the cupboard of toys and sealed her in by sliding a hockey stick through the door handles. It took her teacher an hour to notice she wasn't in class before they came searching for her and heard her screaming within the cupboard. When Alec heard the story from her flustering, apologetic teacher at pick-up, he'd turned a shade of red that shouldn't have been possible for anyone's skin to turn and threatened to have the school shut down before he whisked Ella into his arms and stormed away.

She'd never seen him get angry like that before, and while she'd never admit it, it scared her a little.

The ice cream had helped to calm her father's flush. So had her unfurling her legs across his thighs.

"Maybe he likes you," Alec wondered aloud, giving her ankle a squeeze.

"He locked me in a box!" Ella shrieked, ice cream dripping down her chin. "Is that how people who like each other act?"

"No," Alec refuted, wiping the ice cream off her chin with his knuckle, then licking away the liquid from his own finger. "That's not how they *should* act, but sometimes people have certain feelings and don't know what to do with them, so they do things they shouldn't because they're not sure how to express themselves."

"Like lock people in a box?" Ella shook her head. "I don't like that. I'd never do that."

"Because you're kind, my beauty." He tapped her nose to beget a giggle. "Your first instinct is to always treat people well. You embrace everything the world has to offer you. You don't hold back from what you're feeling, so you'll never experience the pain that comes with loving someone and not being able to express it the right way. It's the worst kind of pain anyone could ever feel."

Ella lapped at the ice cream teetering off the edge of the cone. Alec raised his eyes to the awning of contorted branches and bourgeoning leaves overhead.

"Do you love Mom?" She was too young to understand the haunted look that swam through his eyes.

"I love that she gave me the gift of you," he answered, each word he spoke chosen carefully. "I will be forever indebted to her for that." Ella at the time was satisfied with that answer.

"How do you know you love someone?" Alec beamed.

"Love is really, truly knowing someone and wanting a life that has them in it, not being able to imagine a world where they're not there. Love is being apart from someone and feeling like there's something missing, like you're not whole unless you're together. Love is thinking about attaching yourself forever to someone and the idea being inviting, not terrifying. Love is doing something you absolutely hate, with someone who absolutely loves it, and loving every second of it because you live to see them happy."

"Like eating ice cream with me?" Ella smirked at the slow rise of Alec's brows. She laughed, "I know you don't like ice cream, Daddy."

"Do you?" His yellowish-brown eyes radiated with devotion. "How did you figure that out?"

"You make faces the whole time you eat and finish it in two bites." Alec cackled up at the sky.

"You're too smart for your own good, my beauty." He kissed her hair. "I can't get anything past you, can I?"

"Nope!" Ella shook her head for further emphasis.

"I live to see you happy, Ella. You make my day by simply existing." She scooted closer to him on the bench to rest her head on his chest. "You want to know how I know I love you, my girl?"

"How, Daddy?"

"Because I spent my life before you so consumed with myself and my own needs. Everything and everyone else was secondary. The moment I met you, you became my center of gravity. The planet I orbit around. I don't matter anymore." Alec brushed a kiss between her brows. "You are all that matters, little one. Your needs. Your happiness. Your life. Nothing else."

"*Noella*," Kellen's voice shattered through her dream.

Ella jolted awake with a gasp, flinging back into Kellen's arms, which arched around her in a protective shield. She touched her cheek and found tracks of tears staining the rough, cracking flesh.

"Baby, you okay?" Kellen swept her hair onto the pillow to keep it from gluing to her face.

"I think so?" The statement echoed like a question, laced with doubt. Kellen kissed the corner of her mouth.

466

"I woke up to the sound of you whimpering. I got worried. What were you dreaming about?"

"My dad." A heavy breath hurled out of her. The corners of her eyes prickled. "Always my dad."

"Tell me about it." Ella rolled onto her back.

Kellen scooted to the side to give her room, though he didn't stop touching her, his fingers careening across her stomach like he needed to be connected to her through touch in order to assuage his own concern.

"I was four. He used to pick me up from school and bring me ice cream. There was this kid in my class, Hunter, who picked on me a lot. I always thought it was because I was the smallest in my class and an easy target. He locked me in a box on the playground that day. It took my teacher an hour to realize I wasn't in class with everyone else and come find me." Incense spiked Kellen's breath, smoke wafting from the upward curl of his lip. "Dad suggested that maybe it was because Hunter liked me. It sparked a conversation between us about love. I asked him if he loved my mother, and he said he loved that she gave him the gift of me. It never occurred to me at the time that he didn't fully answer the question." She frowned. "I asked him how you know you love someone."

"What did he say?" Ella twisted her head to meet Kellen's eyes.

"He had a whole long answer…but it honestly hurts me to think about it." Tears rolled down the sides of her face. "I don't understand how he could've said all those things and still left us. Left *me.* He said he loved me so much that nothing else mattered apart from me, that his own needs were secondary to mine, yet he abandoned me on a roof, all by myself, in the middle of the night? How is *that* love?"

"Noella." Kellen dragged her into him by hitching his hand around her hip and pulling her across the mattress. Ella shifted her body to snuggle closer to his warmth, throwing her leg over his.

"Don't get sick of me," she pleaded, holding him tighter.

"I will never get enough of you, Noella Rose." Kellen sketched a line of kisses down her forehead. "I'm not your father, sweetheart. I'm not going to leave you in the middle of the night with no explanation. I'm not dangling the carrot of my devotion in front of you just to take it away. Your father told you he loved you so much that his own needs were secondary to you. I'll tell you how I'm different from your father. I need you so much that my own selfish desire comes *before* any and everything. My existence is tied to the look on your face. To the breaths you exhale. To the laughs you produce. I cannot exist without you. My needs *are* your needs, and I fucking care about my needs, because I care about *you.* Your father fucked up when he thought one needed to outweigh the other, when he looked at those as two separate things." Ella mewled into his kiss.

"I never want to be parted from you, ever," she cried.

"Then you and I share the same wish." His lips wiped away the vestiges of sadness off her cheeks, scrubbing the loneliness from her soul, leaving a scarless surface in his wake. "I know you struggle to believe words. Let me show you with action. You still want a star? I will steal one from the night sky for you." Kellen wrapped her up in his arms before pressing a kiss to the corner of her jaw.

"No," she giggled. "Certain things belong in the heavens, and certain things belong down here."

"You belong everywhere, Noella, for you are divinity in human form." Ella's chest tightened. Through the dark, her eyes found Freya inside her crate, her sweet Cavachon having awoken at the sound of her tears. Freya's nose poked through the bars to check to make sure Ella was stable. "She's okay," Kellen assured Freya, holding Ella tighter. "I've got her." Freya pulled her face back to rest it once more on her bed inside the crate, seeming to find comfort in Kellen's pledge.

"I don't know how much Freya actually understands," Ella said. "When I speak to her, I sometimes feel like it goes in one ear and out the other. I love her to pieces, but she's not the smartest."

"You're wrong," Kellen argued, staring at Freya. "She's incredibly perceptive and very fucking smart. She pays attention to everything and keeps extensive notes in her head. Trust me, she remembers everything that's ever been said to her or in front of her." Ella yanked her head back.

"How the fuck do you know that?"

"Because I've spoken to her before. Mind-to-mind." Ella's eyes almost tumbled out of her skull.

"You've *spoken* to my dog?"

"Against my will most of the time, but yes. She's very persistent and very protective of you." Kellen bumped her nose with his own. "I know the feeling." Ella pressed a kiss to Kellen's jaw. "I hate knowing what you've been through, Noella. I hate knowing anyone had the pleasure of having you in their life and couldn't appreciate what a blessing that was. I hate knowing you weren't loved right."

"It's okay, Kellen." Her fingers trickled down his cheek. They floated over his lips, which puckered into a kiss under her touch. "I have not been without love in my life. I'm certainly not without it now."

"You never will be again," he swore. For the first time in her life, she had no trouble believing him.

Kellen fit his mouth over hers.

When she nipped his bottom lip, he rolled on top of her with a heady groan, and they lost themselves to love.

---

In all his twenty-eight years of life, Kellen had never lost Maccabiah.

Not when he was a student at Delmarth or as a faculty member. He knew this week was primarily for the kids, testing their abilities to the highest extent and seeing what skills still needed to be honed, but that didn't stop him from taking the competition as seriously as the students. Last year, Headmistress Dyer banned Kellen from attending one of the events because his heckling of the students on the other team took on a life of its own and he'd been accused of trying to manipulate the results. His students often taunted him for his obsession with Maccabiah, since he kept a tally on the whiteboard in his classroom year-round of how many days remained until the event.

If anything, he cared more now about winning than he did back when he was a student, because there was now the added pleasure of Jarion and Laya winning along with him. This was their first year, now that their dragons had finally emerged, that they would get to participate in some of the events. This was also the first year he'd get to experience Maccabiah with Noella, through the eyes of someone who'd never been exposed to anything of this magnitude before. It would be like getting to relive his first year all over again. Noella teased him all morning about his tangible excitement.

"You'll understand when you experience the first two events today," Kellen told her, swinging their interlocked fingers between them. He cherished their walk to the teacher's lounge, wished he could stretch it out into an eternity, because the moment they walked through the door to her office building and joined the rest of the faculty, Noella would drop his hand and fix her mask of professionalism over her face.

For now, her fingers squeezed his through their entanglement. "What events are today?" she asked.

"Chop and rope burn. Chop happens right after the students are assigned their teams and Maccabiah officially begins, or *breaks out* as we call it. Chop is for the seniors. The seniors on each team get in a long line and one by one must fight an illusion made to look like a statue of iron that's been brought to life. The only way to win your round is to chop through the metal of your opponent. First team to successfully chop through every iron opponent wins. Second event today will be rope burn. That event is for the Meteoro fire-benders and the dragon-shifters. The teams collect large and small pieces of wood from the Canterna Thicket. Each team designates two feeders, who are always Herculean speed and strength-wielders, and three pit crew members, made up of fire-benders and dragon-shifters, who are referred to as the matches. They're assigned a faculty member to act as rope burn coach, which I'll save you the trouble of guessing is *always* me, no matter what team I'm on." Noella smirked at his cocky tone. "The feeders pass the matches the wood, and the matches build the fire. Once the teepee of wood is strong enough, the matches ignite. They have to maintain the fire until it burns through a wet rope that has been soaking in water, water that's also been infused with Headmistress Dyer's mending abilities to make it harder to break, the entire semester. First team to burn through the rope, and who has the least penalties, wins."

"How do you get penalties?" Kellen adored how genuinely interested she seemed in the events.

"Penalties can be administered if the wood hits the rope, or if you bump into the poles on the side that keep the rope suspended above the wood."

"So that's an event specifically for fire-benders and dragon-shifters. There are events for every type of Primordial and their power?" Kellen nodded. "What was your favorite event as a student?"

"I loved rope burn. I thrived in rope burn as a student. I had the most potent fire out of anyone in the school, so I was always chosen to be a match. I hold the record at Delmarth for fastest time burning through the rope. My second favorite event is the Sword Hunt. Cerebri instructors turn the campus into a battleground illusion that matches the conditions of land in Lavalden, right beside the Middledeen waters where most of our army's battles against the Sireres occur. Each team is tasked with hiding a sword somewhere in the landscape. In several different rounds over the course of two days, so everyone gets a chance to participate, the teams send out a group with representation from every grade level, starting at sixth grade when the Primordial's powers begin truly developing and ending with the seniors, along with one instructor. They then go looking for the other team's sword. You must successfully find the other team's sword and bring it back to your side of the territory without being captured or imprisoned by the other team."

"Sounds like capture the flag, but a lot more violent." Noella rested her chin on his shoulder. His lips hunted for her temple, needing some form of contact with her, and fastened over the soft flesh, peppering kisses down to her cheek. "I love hearing you talk about this stuff. Your eyes light up."

"I used to look forward to Maccabiah all year. I spent all my time outside of school mastering my powers so I'd triumph over the other team come Maccabiah week. My mother thought I was honing my powers because I cared about being the best Kilic heir, but fuck *that*. I just cared about winning Maccabiah." Noella's gorgeous laughter painted goosebumps across his flesh. "Back then, I used to look at excelling at Maccabiah as the best way to get the

Gods' attention so I could be recruited for Aros's personal cadre. Ironic that I got exactly that and in the end, I turned it down to go into teaching, of all things."

Noella grew silent a moment. "Do you ever regret turning Aros down?" Kellen sucked in a deep breath.

"Sometimes I find myself wondering what my life would've been if I'd said yes, but I've come to really appreciate this job for more than just the opportunity it's given me to keep an eye on Jare and Laya. I might whine like a bitch sometimes about grading papers and make the odd threat about quitting, but I fucking love my students. I love this school. The work we do here is meaningful towards Aros's cause, in a different way than actively fighting, but it's still meaningful. I love being a small part of what shapes these kids into warriors." He inclined down so the tip of his nose pecked hers. "And if I'd said yes to Aros back then, I never would've been here when you came."

"I'm personally grateful for that," she said. When they reached the door, Noella began unweaving herself from around Kellen, her fingers slipping out from between his to smooth perspiring palms over her black trousers.

"Why do you seem nervous?" he asked, holding the door open for her. "It's just a staff meeting."

"I know," she mumbled, sinking her finger into the call button for the elevator. Her eyes were glued on her shoes when she prattled in a rush, "But it's the first one we're walking into *together*, actually *together*, in front of the whole staff."

"And that makes you nervous?" Noella's shoulders sunk.

"I know what everyone thinks of me," she whispered, wrenching at the strings of his heart.

"Sweetheart," Kellen moaned with sadness. He gave her hands a squeeze. "Those people in there who can't see how amazing you are? They are so small. Like how I was once small. Their opinions might seem loud, but the part of them that really counts is so fucking tiny. Where they're little, you're beautifully massive. Let that part of you fill the room, and they'll be forced to take a look at their own size."

"Kell." Noella touched her hand to her heart, her eyes watering. "You just took my breath away."

"Well, you take my breath away all the time. I had to return the favor." He gestured for her to enter the elevator first.

As she passed him, she nuzzled her shoulder against his, a coquettish smile playing with her lips.

The moment the doors closed, Kellen couldn't maintain the respectful distance between them and pressed her against the elevator wall. Her body automatically tilted closer, her hips raising to meet his. He slid his hand down her thigh, savoring the way his touch made her breath hitch, then hooked it around the inside of her knee and lifted her leg to fold around his waist. "I swear," Kellen groaned, admiring her silk, blueberry-shaded blouse that complimented the evergreen hue of his button-down, "every day my favorite color changes depending on the shirt you're wearing."

"Mine stays the same." Her thumbs swept over his eyelashes, then trickled down his shirt. "Green. Like emeralds."

The elevator doors heaved open on their floor. All too soon, before he could pin her against the wall and bruise her lips with a kiss, Noella squirmed out from under him and scuttled into the hallway.

*Remind me why we got out of bed this morning?* he groaned into her head.

*Because it's Maccabiah!* she sang back, reciprocating the gesture of holding the door open for him.

The entire room twisted their heads to Kellen and Noella when they stepped into the teacher's lounge. Kellen instinctively angled himself slightly in front of her, wishing he could shield her from their hatred with his body. He wasn't used to his colleagues firing those vile glares at him as well, but the moment they walked in and the Primordials could smell her all over him, and him all over her in return, their loathing of her transferred to him, glowers being pelted at his front and back like corporeal bullets. Kellen had the luxury, though at this moment, it didn't feel like it, to be able to read everyone in the room's thoughts, their disapproval slapping his mind.

He simply rolled his shoulders and draped his arm around Noella's waist in solidarity.

*Mine,* he echoed into everyone in the room's minds, including Noella, who sloped her body closer to him in confirmation. He led her over to the windowsill he normally sat by during staff meetings.

Headmistress Dyer breezed to the podium shortly after Kellen and Noella were seated. Her eyes found them first, dropping to Kellen's hand resting possessively on Noella's knee. Headmistress Dyer sent him a brief, but unmistakable nod of approval, then swung her focus back over the room.

"I'll be reading the names for the Gold Team first," she declared, snagging everyone's concentration away from Kellen and Noella the moment she began speaking. "Once I've read the teams, I'd like everyone to break up into their groups and figure out which staff members will be supervising which events. Everyone has to participate in something. *I repeat.* Everyone *has* to participate in something. No staff member will be allowed to sit out, just like no staff member will be allowed to take over everything."

*She's talking about you with that last one,* Noella teased. Kellen gave her leg a sharp squeeze.

His eyes then found Akio's across the room.

*Why are you guys sitting so far away?* Kellen asked, noting the way Akio and Josefyn were huddled in the corner. For the past two months, the four of them always banded together during staff meetings.

*Ella's pretty mad at us right now,* Akio told him, his tone of voice flat. *We wanted to give her space.*

*Mad about what?*

*You should ask her.* Akio paused, then added, *Congrats, man. I'm really happy for you guys.*

Kellen offered him a small smile of thanks.

As Headmistress Dyer read the names, Kellen asked Noella, *Why are you mad at Akio and Josefyn?*

*Did Akio tell you that?* She rolled her eyes. *I'm really more mad at him than I am Josefyn.*

*But WHY?* he pushed.

*Because Akio sticks his nose into my business and then tells me he can't tell me certain things. He's keeping something from me about a vision he had where Aros spoke to him about me. I think it has something to do with you and me. That's why he's been pushing me so hard to be with you, but he refuses to tell me what it is. I feel like I can't trust him.* Kellen's eyes soared back over to Akio, who'd been watching them closely in a way that suggested he was listening to their internal conversation.

*What're you keeping from my girlfriend?* Kellen growled at Akio, all traces of amiability vanished.

*If I can't tell her, I certainly can't tell you,* Akio snapped back, ripping his eyes off Kellen.

*Great, now he's mad at me too,* Kellen grumbled to Noella just as Headmistress Dyer read Josefyn's name for the Gold Team. Noella nuzzled her shoulder against Kellen's chest to be comforting while not taking her eyes off Headmistress Dyer's lips, waiting for her name to be called.

Kellen's gaze surveyed the room and landed on Daniel.

*What the fuck, Kell?* Daniel hissed. *You're fucking the earthborn? How can you stick your dick in such a disgusting cunt?*

*Watch what you fucking say, Madix.* Fire singed the back of Kellen's throat. *I will turn your tongue into ash so you not only can't speak another vile word about the woman I love, but you will never be able to SPEAK again.* Daniel's eyes widened to the point of nearing the edge of their sockets.

"Daniel Madix," Headmistress Dyer called out, then declared, "and that's the end of the Gold Team. Everyone else is on the Red Team."

*We're on the same team!* Noella squealed, pulling Kellen back into a reality he found much more tolerable than the inside of Daniel Madix's head. *How'd you manage to get us on the same team? I take it you had something to do with it.* Kellen smirked.

*I might've threatened Headmistress Dyer two weeks ago and said if she didn't put us on the same team, I'd quit.*

*Of course you did,* she laughed in his head while nudging his chest with her elbow.

"Get into your teams," Headmistress Dyer directed. "You have thirty minutes to decide who's supervising what events and make a list for me before Maccabiah officially breaks out." She waved her hand in the air to motion for everyone to move.

Kellen and Noella headed to the back of the room where the rest of the Red Team had begun congregating. They maintained their distance from Akio by electing to stand on the opposite side of the circle, which also kept them away from Oliviana, who unfortunately also happened to be on their team.

"I'm rope burn coach," Kellen decreed immediately, not even waiting for anyone to argue before he wrote his name down on the piece of paper next to the rope burn event. No one fought him.

"We should write all our names down for Sword Hunt, since we'll all be in charge of a group," Akio piped up. Noella recoiled at the sound of his voice like it hurt her somehow. She stepped closer to Kellen.

"Not all of us," Oliviana spat, glaring at Noella.

"I want to run a group for Sword Hunt," Noella protested, accepting the pen from Akio to write her name.

"You can't run a group for Sword Hunt," Oliviana objected as she snatched the pen out of Noella's hand. "You have no powers."

"She can wield a sword," Kellen piped up in her defense.

"No one fucking asked you, Kilic," Oliviana snarled, holding her hand up to block his face from her vision.

"No offense, Ella, but you probably shouldn't run a group alone," Akio interjected.

"Why not?" Noella barked back. Akio staggered at her aggressive tone. "Because I'm a human? I may not be one of you, but I can handle managing a group of children through a game, no matter how dangerous it might be, because at the end of the day, it's a *game*. It's a *game* where the students are supposed to be leading anyway. You heard Headmistress Dyer. *Everyone* participates."

"I didn't say you shouldn't run a group, Ella," Akio argued, matching her belligerence. "I said you shouldn't run it *alone*, because again, no offense, but most of the kids still don't trust you."

"Don't say *no offense* when you clearly mean offense, Akio. It's insulting." If Kellen didn't intervene, they'd go at it for the next hour and cause all of them to miss the beginning of Maccabiah.

"I'll lead the group with her," Kellen decided for them, writing both their names down under the first round of Sword Hunt. He dropped the pen on the chair so he could splay his fingers over Noella's back.

"You can't do that!" Oliviana squawked. Kellen was tempted to stick his fingers in his ears to protect his brain from the sound of her voice. He seriously questioned how he ever had sex with her. "One leader per group!"

"Give it a rest, Oliviana," Kellen snapped. "No one fucking cares if I lead the group with her but *you.*"

"It's against the rules," she asserted.

"So is having a human in Cavale, but Aros let that rule go, didn't he?" Noella's lips fought a smile.

"What're you smiling about?" Oliviana fumed at Noella. "You think you're hot shit just because you have a dragon who would shit himself to get inside your pants? You're not special, earthborn. He's been inside lots of girls' pants. Including mine." Noella's eyes sharpened into raging slits.

"Oh, I remember," she retorted with a lift of her chin. "I live across the hall. I remember your fight. He may have been fucking you, but it was *my* name on his tongue when he came." Every jaw around the circle dropped in unison.

*That's my fucking girl,* Kellen marveled to himself. He squeezed the back of Noella's neck with approval.

Oliviana was silent after that.

The rest of the faculty members claimed the other supervising positions for the various other events, all of which Kellen explained to Noella privately through their mental bond. He described to her what Bucket Brigade was, where the entire team across all grade levels line up in an order that helps the younger kids be surrounded by older students and staff, starting at the dining hall and leading to the Canterna Thicket. The Meteoro water-benders fill up giant buckets with water, and the entire team has to pass the buckets back to the last person at the Canterna Thicket, where the water is dumped into a glass vessel. At the end of the event, Headmistress Dyer measures the amount of water and calculates which team filled their vessel higher. Kellen then explained the Apache event to her, the last event of Maccabiah, where the whole team across all grade levels scatter around campus and are assigned different tasks to complete that exemplify their powers while passing a baton to one another once they've successfully completed the mission. The last person to go, always a senior, runs from one end of campus all the way to the gates of Delmarth holding a lit torch.

Whoever reaches the gates first not only wins that event, but wins the honor of being valedictorian.

*I take it you were valedictorian,* Noella said while the team finalized their list to give to Headmistress Dyer.

*You may be shocked to hear this, but no. I wasn't chosen to run the torch that year. It was Akio.*

*REALLY?* Her eyes swung over to her friend, forgetting her anger for a short moment. When he didn't meet her eye, her shoulders wilted, her lashes frowning across her cheeks as her gaze dipped to the floor.

"I'll give Headmistress Dyer the paper," Oliviana grumbled, stealing the paper with their names on it from off the chair. She trudged across the teacher's lounge to shove it in the Headmistress's hand before marching out of the room in a chaotic huff. Josefyn wandered to the back of the room from where the Gold Team had begun dispersing.

"Is everything okay over here?" she asked them, either sensing the tension or having heard their argument.

"Ella, I'm sorry," Akio said, turning to Noella. "I didn't mean to upset you. Yesterday and today. Really."

"I don't want to fight with you," Noella murmured with a wearied sigh. "Can we just let it go? Please?"

"I'd love nothing more." Akio opened his arms for her. Noella sighed, then stepped away from Kellen to enter the embrace. Kellen noted that Noella didn't fully reciprocate, Akio enveloping his arms around her shoulders and Noella's arms awkwardly hanging at her sides. When Akio whispered, "I missed you, Rosie," she finally raised her arms and wrapped them around his waist, giving him a small squeeze.

"Are we ready to battle, Red Team?" Josefyn taunted, waving mock fists under her mate's nose, then acted out flinging a punch at Noella in slow motion. Noella angled her cheek towards Jo's fist to join the charade, the cluster of Jo's fingers very gently brushing her cheek. Noella feigned a dramatic scream and pretended to collapse to the ground in pain, clutching her cheek, the two women erupting into laughter.

Akio and Kellen shared a quiet look of understanding, recognizing that they would forever be deadwood next to Josefyn and Noella's love. Josefyn offered Noella her hand to yank her back to her feet.

"It's Maccabiah time!" Noella squealed, lugging Kellen to the door, not that she needed to pull him —he'd follow her anywhere.

## CHAPTER 34

# ELLA

ELLA COULD TASTE the excitement stitching through the air as they approached the Canterna Thicket. Before any of the students arrived, all the Cerebri instructors worked together to paint an illusion over the forest that shoved the trees back to create a wide breadth of open space, the enclosure bordered by metal bleachers for the totality of the school to sit on. Once the illusion washed over you, it manipulated the color of your shirt so you matched the shade of your team, Ella's blouse transmogrifying from blue to red once she crossed over the entrance of the Canterna Thicket. Ella and Kellen assisted the other professors in marshaling the students, once they reached the forest and the illusion assigned them a team, onto the bleachers on their team's designated side of the arena, splitting the student body into two rippling seas of red and gold. When Laya passed over the threshold and saw her color matched Ella's, she squealed, yanking at Jarion's arm.

Ella sent her a private wink of acknowledgement as the twins passed them on their way to find seats.

*Who did you pick for rope burn?* Ella asked Kellen for the seventh time since they'd left the teacher's lounge. When she first asked him if he'd begun thinking about which students he would pick to be feeders and matches for rope burn, as rope burn coach, Kellen had replied that he already finalized his list of which students would be eligible in his eyes three weeks ago, not that he elected to tell her.

*You can ask a million times, sweetheart, but you'll get that answer with the rest of the school after Chop ends.*

Kellen then barked out loud to a sophomore Pegasus-shifter, "Liam Huxley! I don't care that she's your girlfriend. If I see your hand between Luna's legs one more time, I'm disuniting it from your body." The sixteen-year-old Varmin boy's hand retracted from under the female student's skirt.

"S-Sorry, Mr. Kilic," the boy stammered.

"You'll be sorry if I ever have to repeat myself again." Kellen pointed to the bleachers. "Go sit down with every other fucking student before I decide you don't deserve to keep your hand and I take it anyway."

As Liam scurried away with his head hanging, Kellen swung his eyes back to Ella and groaned, *You have no idea how many times a day I have to tell that boy to stop touching his girlfriend.*

Ella laughed, *You're one to talk, Mr. Kilic.* Kellen's eyes darkened.

*I starved to be inside you for twelve weeks, Ms. Rose.* His words were delineated by a ravenous growl. *You bet your perfect ass, now that I've tasted what it's like to be with you, I'm touching you every second I can.* Ella blushed when Kellen's hip lightly bumped hers for further emphasis.

She bumped his hip back just as Headmistress Dyer spilled into the center of the open space, the swarms of children flocking the bleachers on both sides springing to their feet with deafening roars.

"Who's ready for Maccabiah?!" Headmistress Dyer hollered. The bleaches rattled from the students pounding their fists against the metal benches, the ether shaking along with the entire forest. "What was that?" Headmistress Dyer cupped her hand around her ear. "I can't hear you. I said…who's ready for MACCABIAH?" Clouds split apart and scattered into the trees from the force of the crowd's cheers. Their energy was so infectious that Ella's face erupted in an automatic smile. "There we go!" Dyer roared. "That sounds more like a school ready for break out! Seniors, start lining up for Chop!"

The first row on the bleachers, reserved for seniors on either side, lifted from the metal bench to begin forming a line. Oken Bennet was first on the Red Team's side, decked out in titanium armor similar to what Eyal wore, though Oken's breastplate was stained red due to the illusion's influence.

Oken shifted on the balls of his feet, passing his sword from one hand to the other in a manner that told Ella he didn't feel comfortable brandishing it in either hand. He suddenly squeaked, "Ms. Rose? Can you come here a moment?"

"Of course." Ella hurried to stand at his side. "What do you need, Oken?"

"I'm scared." Ella was stunned into silence for a moment. In all the time she'd been having her daily check-ins with Oken, since he refused to begin formal counseling with her, he'd struggled to name any of his emotions. The fact that he put a label on what he was feeling and shared it with her was huge progress. "What if I choke? What if Amira beats me and chops her solider first? Going first sets a precedent for the whole team. If I fuck up, I'm basically damning the rest of the team."

"Let's check the facts here. You've spent your entire time at Delmarth training for this. You've passed every single Power Practice class. You're the most powerful strength-wielder in the school, and I'm not just saying that to stroke your ego. Don't worry about what anyone else is doing. Lean into your strength, Oken. It's gotten you this far and never failed you." Oken's brown eyes softened.

"Thanks, Ms. Rose." He paused, then added, "For always being here, even when I act like I don't appreciate it." He folded his fingers around the hilt of his sword and sucked in a deep breath, spluttering it out in a refreshing sigh. "I think I've got this."

"I think you do, too. Make us proud."

Ella patted his shoulder, then dashed back to where Kellen was waiting by the end of the bleachers.

*You're amazing,* Kellen gushed when she rejoined him.

In the center of the arena, two towering figures comprised of iron appeared on the asphalt, lacking any distinctive facial features apart from eyes glowing red with malice, flaunting gilded swords at their sides. Oken settled into a proper fighting stance, fingers curved around the hilt of his sword.

"Warriors, are you ready?" Headmistress Dyer called out from the sidelines. Amira, the female fighting for the Gold Team on the opposing side of the arena, bobbed her head in a nod. Oken followed shortly after. "Then I hereby decree that Maccabiah has officially broken out. Let Chop commence!"

Without any further hesitation, Oken charged towards the iron solider. The two legionnaires in the center of the arena separated from one another, one sprinting for Amira and the other heading for Oken. Ella's focus couldn't absorb both skirmishes at once, her attention latching onto Oken, Amira and her iron solider blearing into the backcloth. As Oken and the iron solider clashed, the sound of metal on metal reverberated through the forest, echoing off the trees, amalgamating with the hum of students screeching on the bleachers as they watched the two battles play out. Oken's armor gleamed in the sunlight as he swiped his sword around the circumference of his head and swung it towards the iron soldier's neck, a blow the solider deflected with smooth dexterity. Oken launched a second attack, gunning for the soldier's ankles, but the solider cut him off from making contact by bringing their own sword down, slicing through the asphalt. The iron warrior retaliated with equal force, their blows raining down upon Oken like seething thunder, but Oken held his own, refusing to falter, meeting every counterattack. The two of them danced around one another, neither of them willing to give an inch.

"Come on, Oken!" Ella cried, the heat of the battle feeding her anxiety.

Behind them, Amira, a Meteoro fire-bender, was still engaging her iron solider, flames encompassing the tendrils of her hair, saturating her clothes. However, she didn't seem to be using the fire at her fingertips, relying simply on the blade in her hand to strike at the iron solider.

*Why isn't she using the fire to melt the iron?* Ella asked Kellen.

*She'd get a penalty for melting the solider,* Kellen said, his eyes glued to Oken and Amira. *Power usage is prohibited during Chop. Amira and Oken need to cut the solider with their swords. Chop is a test of strength separate from powers, especially for the Primordials whose abilities don't include strength as an additional gift. Powers are useful in battle, but you need to be able to hold your own without them, should you, for whatever reason, end up in a battle where you can't access them.*

Ella knew Oken well enough at this point to feel his rage in the air like the emotion had been congealed into a tangible, flaming object mugging up the ether. His grip on the hilt of his blade tautened in accompaniment of the hardening of his facial features and the narrowing of his wrath-filled eyes. With a burst of energy, Oken mustered all his strength and delivered a powerful blow to the iron soldier's chest. A collective gasp resounded from behind Ella as everyone on the Red Team stood in unison to tip forward and get a closer look. Ella's hand flew to grab Kellen's arm.

*He's going to make contact!* Ella hoped.

*The blade's not deep enough,* Kellen hissed with a shake of his head. *He'll scratch the solider, but he needs to push harder to cut through.* Aloud, Kellen yelled, "Come on, Oken! More!"

The iron solider staggered back, red eyes flickering. Kellen's conjecture was corroborated when Oken's blade skimmed the surface of the iron soldier's chest but didn't sink deep enough to break through. However, Oken took advantage of the close proximity and the iron soldier's falter of movement to slam his elbow into the warrior's face, then spun on his heel and reeled his blade downward to plunge the dagger into the iron chest. Ella shrieked so loud it scratched her throat.

"YES!" she hollered, her fingers burrowing into Kellen's arm.

"He needs to make a full cut," Kellen muttered to himself, yelling, "DRAG THE BLADE TO THE SIDE, OKEN!"

Screams exploded from behind them. "CHOP! CHOP! CHOP!" a chant began, sweeping across the chain of students.

The iron solider didn't fold over with the blade embedded in his chest, but began writhing around the sword and clawing at Oken's forearm to dislodge the rapier. Oken either heard what Kellen said or came to that decision on his own and rallied all his strength to pull the sword to the side, lacerating through the metal and carving a line across the soldier's chest. When the sword successfully completed the stretch of the warrior's sternum and reunited with the world on the other side, the ripple effect of his weapon being

484

freed from inside the warrior flung Oken backward, sending him flying across the asphalt and landing him close to where Ella and Kellen were standing. Oken watched with the rest of the school as the iron warrior crumpled to the ground and melted into a puddle of gilded liquid. Ella's eyes rose to where Amira was still engaging her iron soldier.

The chime of a victorious bell rang from the earth itself. Above them, a flash of red light detonated over the heads of the students on the bleachers, signaling a win for the Red Team, the strings of students behind them bursting with triumphant screams to celebrate Oken's victory. Headmistress Dyer scribbled something on her clipboard, then signaled for Oken to retreat so the next student, Lorelai Bepton, could step forward.

"You did it!" Ella cried as Oken ran right to her, proffering a high five that he accepted with a laugh.

"Thank you," Oken said with tears in his eyes. "Thank you."

"Good job, Oak," Kellen prided, clapping Oken on the back before guiding him over to stand at Headmistress Dyer's side, where all the winners of each of the skirmishes were expected to stand for the remainder of Chop.

"This is so intense!" Ella yelled to Kellen, waving her hands under her armpits. "I'm sweating so much!"

"Wait until you get to rope burn," he said with a gleaming smile.

While Amira continued battling her iron soldier on the other side of the arena, the puddle that once comprised Oken's warrior began lengthening upward, reconfiguring itself back into the shape of arms and legs until it was coagulated once more into a sentient warrior. No time was wasted before Lorelei stampeded forward and began her combat with the iron soldier. Across the way, Amira successfully trounced her opponent, beheading her iron soldier in one fell swoop, flames trickling down her face like teardrops. The bell tolled to concede to her a victory, and she sprinted to flank Headmistress Dyer as the next student on the Gold Team stepped forward for their battle.

The pace of the battles began picking up speed after Amira

finished her clash. Ella understood now why Oken had said winning the first round set a precedent for the rest of the battles. One by one, the seniors on both teams devoured their rounds, the clang of the bell going off every two minutes with the acceleration of speed. The Red Team remained in the lead for the majority of Chop, a string of seniors garbed in crimson unfurling from Headmistress Dyer's left, almost grazing the end of the bleachers from how long the line extended. Thirty minutes into the event, the Gold Team began catching up to Red, their line outspreading on Dyer's right to match the length of Red on her left, so in the end, each team was on equal footing and down to their last senior—Renera Zavala, a Herculea mender, fighting for Red, and Francesco Darino, a Cerebri, fighting for Gold.

The battlefield was a chaotic symphony of quarreling metal and roaring outcries from both Renera and Francesco, as well as the crowds watching, their names molded into hymns that enveloped the teams on either side, becoming the wind itself. Francesco fought with unwavering determination on his end, his movements swift and precise, whereas Renera's blows were slightly less confident, though still fluid and graceful. Renera and the iron soldier were locked in a deadly dance of steel and fury, sweat mingled with dirt and blood smeared across Renera's brow, tracing streaks down the side of her face.

"COME ON, RENERA!" Ella screeched at the top of her lungs. She'd needed to tie her hair back in a bun because having her hair in her face had become too distracting. Kellen stood beside her, a clenched statue of rippling muscle with rivulets of anxiety rolling off his shoulders, chewing his thumbnail. Ella was careful not to touch him now because she was afraid she would be shocked by the current of visible electricity gathered over his brown flesh, remnants of his power seeping through and blanketing his body in a protective shield.

Renera grew wearied and lost her footing, toppling to the ground at the same time Francesco blocked the iron soldier's attack from across the way by spinning on his heel and hurling his body weight into the warrior from the side. Ella trapped a breath in her chest, her hand flying to her mouth while Kellen's finger fell away from his lips, his eyes enlarging to a degree where his lashes fanned out over his eyebrows. They watched as Francesco bowled himself and the iron soldier so he now towered over the warrior and drove his sword through the steel, slender throat, hacking through the metal with a clean cut. The moment the head divided from the neck, the soldier Renera was engaging dissolved into a pool of deliquesced gilt, marking the end of Chop.

"Gold Team wins!" Headmistress Dyer declared.

The Gold Team leapt with joy, their harmonious, enthused movements fashioning an undulating wavelet of golden bliss. The Red Team drooped in unison like a wilting rose, their petals withering to the floor along with their disappointment as the students dropped back onto the metal bench and hung their heads in defeat.

"NO!" Ella shrieked, smacking Kellen's arm because she needed to hit something and he was right there. "She was so close!"

"It's just the first event of Maccabiah," Kellen said as reassurance for both himself and Ella. "We've got the rest of the week to catch up." He saw the way Ella was vibrating and laughed, "I knew you'd get as invested in Maccabiah as I do. Try and remember this is for the kids, yeah?"

"Hypocrite," Ella spat while punching his bicep, a stunning laugh rumbling through his chest.

"Coming from the bastard who was biting off his own finger just now because he was so anxious," Akio chuckled when he came to stand with them. Ella painted a friendly smile on her face, fighting against the pit in her stomach that screamed she still couldn't fully trust Akio. "And the asshole who last year got banned from attending Apache because he landed three students in the infirmary during Sword Hunt."

"Kellen!" Ella cried. "You didn't tell me that!"

"I didn't mean to land them in the infirmary!" Kellen promised her, glaring at Akio. "I just…may've lost control of my dragon fire a tiny bit." Ella shook her head, but couldn't fully subdue a smile.

"Rope burn coaches," Headmistress Dyer hollered, raising a hand in the air to swaddle a blanket of silence over the rowdy crowds. "Come forward."

"That's my cue," Kellen sang with pride. He winked at Ella. *Watch me do what I do best, Rose.*

*Go win this for us, Kilic,* she cheered.

All Ella could think as she watched him swagger to take his place at Dyer's side was, *that's the love of my life right there.*

CHAPTER 35

# KELLEN

"DID you even give anyone else a chance to try and be rope burn coach?" Headmistress Dyer drawled to Kellen before handing him the uncoated groundwood paper needed for rope burn.

"Fuck no," Kellen proclaimed, accepting her offering. "This event is mine."

Headmistress Dyer scoffed but wasn't able to concoct a response denying his claim. The whole school knew rope burn belonged to Kellen Kilic and Kellen Kilic alone. The Gold Team would be required to go through the motions of participating in the event, but everyone mutually understood that the likelihood of defeating Kellen was next to nothing. Kellen's eyes swept over the rows of children on the Red Team, identifying the names on his list of eligible students who'd been blessed with being assigned to his team and would soon taste their first victory of Maccabiah as feeders and matches. He also surveyed the Gold Team's collection of windbenders across all grade levels, since he would need to pick two Meteoro students from the other team to play the part of the Red Team's breeze. Once breezers were chosen, they would stand next to his team's pit crew and blow wind at the conflagration to make it harder for the matches to maintain a flame.

His top contenders were all on the Red Team. The weakest wind-benders, in his opinion, were all on Gold.

An easy win ahead.

"You couldn't have made it a tiny bit harder for me, Valerie?" Kellen quipped to Dyer. "Just to keep it interesting?"

Dyer gave him her shoulder as a firm dismissal.

The Gold Team's rope burn coach was Aithne Hayes, a Meteoro fire-bender who'd been in the grade above Kellen at Delmarth. Twice when they were students, they'd been matches together during rope burn and had claimed two victories. Any time they were against each other on different teams, Kellen always beat her. Flames appeared inside Aithne's pupils as she fired a provocative grin at Kellen. His own fire entered his gaze, smoke ballooning from his flared nostrils while his arms twisted across his chest so every burly brawn of his was on full display, his power unavoidable.

"Your reign ends this year, Kilic," Aithne taunted. Kellen loosed a sinister laugh.

"Remember to have fun, Hayes." He gave her arm a condescending pat. "It's all about the kids, after all. And try not to cry when you lose. No one likes a sore loser." Fire leaked down the unfettered locks of her black hair.

"Gold Team," Headmistress Dyer announced. "Since you won Chop, you'll be first to pick your feeders, matches, and breezers." Aithne swept her amber eyes over the throng of students on her side.

"For feeders," Aithne decreed, "I choose Achira Fallti and Dahy Artak."

Achira Fallti, a senior, had been on Kellen's short list for strength-wielders. If Achira was on the Red Team, he most likely would have picked her, so that was a choice he understood. He was surprised by the selection of Dahy Artak, though, an eighth-grade speed-wielder to whom he'd had no exposure. The two students barreled down the steps on the side of the bleachers, the crowd approving the selection with raucous shouts and applause. Kellen narrowed his focus over Dahy as they sprinted to stand beside Aithne, cords of Kellen's Cerebri power splitting through the young boy's mind to give him a window into Dahy's head, not that the Herculea could see or feel Kellen invade his mind.

He used that opening to take in the totality of the boy's power. He found a surprising volume of glute power lingering around Dahy's limbs for someone so young. Aithne smiled at Kellen like she knew exactly what he was doing and sensing.

*You're not the only one who planned ahead for this, Kilic,* she sneered into his head.

Dahy was powerful, yes, but not more powerful than Kellen's selection of speed-wielders on Red. Still, he plastered on a perturbed mask, hunching his shoulders so Aithne would *think* he was concerned.

"For matches," Aithne continued, "I pick Jade Cadmus, Ryu Goldeel, and Kaida Long." Kellen was impressed—everyone she'd picked had been on his own list, showing she'd clearly been paying as much attention as he had. "For breezers," her eyes oscillated to the Red Team, her fire-steeped fingers tapping against her chin in contemplation. "I choose Esen Coro and Nasmia Avel."

Kellen almost laughed out loud.

She just shot her own team in the foot by picking Esen Coro, one of the strongest wind-benders in the school, known for creating colossal cyclones with a flick of his wrist and zero exertion.

*Did you forget that you're supposed to pick weak wind-benders for yourself?* Kellen taunted Aithne.

*Why give the kids an easier time when they're meant to be using this to improve their skills?* Aithne shot back.

He couldn't deny she had a point there in how choosing Esen was better for truly testing the children's abilities, what Maccabiah was actually intended for. However, for his own selfish reasons, he cared about winning more than giving them a true test of skill, so he'd give them the advantage with easier picks.

Now that Aithne's pit crew and breezers were solidified, Headmistress Dyer turned her attention onto Kellen.

"Red Team," she said, "pick your feeders, matches, and breezers."

"For feeders," he began, his voice resembling thunder in volume and clarity, "I choose Suri Chapel and Gatik Avran." Aithne sucked in a harsh breath as the two Herculea students, Gatik a strength-wielder freshman and Suri a speed-wielder junior, climbed down the bleachers and joined Kellen by Headmistress Dyer. Suri reached him first, presenting a lustrous smile as she flanked his other side. For the last three years, Suri had asked him every day to make her a feeder, and he'd promised her that when her time was right, she'd be his first pick. He kept his word. "For matches," Kellen continued with a smile outlining his words. He knew the reaction he was about to garner with this controversial choice. "I choose Eliane Azar, Adeen Brigid, and Eulaylia Kilic."

Gasps resounded from all corners of the arena.

In the history of Delmarth Academy, a sixth grader had never been chosen to be a match in rope burn. Kellen thought his brother would be thrilled by his choice, but smoke dribbled out of the sides of Jarion's mouth when his upper lip curled skyward in a growl. Laya and Noella's jaws both dropped in unison.

*Kellen, what the fuck are you doing?* Jarion barked at him. *She's too young. She's going to be so embarrassed if she's the reason we lose.*

*Have some fucking faith in our sister,* Kellen snapped, watching Laya rise from her spot on the bleachers, fiddling with the ends of her long hair, and make her way down the steps onto the asphalt, scuttling over to him.

He heard Noella's voice in his head stammer, *Are you sure she's ready for this, Kell? Her fire just emerged.*

*She can do this,* Kellen promised, smiling down at Laya.

"What're you doing, Kell?" Laya whispered to Kellen. Suri made space for Laya to stand next to her brother.

"I'm making sure we win rope burn," he answered. Laya's eyes glimmered at his clear faith in her.

Everyone doubting this choice didn't have the window into Laya's head that Kellen had. Mr. Park might've called her fire *baby sparks*—a description Kellen found insulting, considering Laya's dragon fire was already at the level of a ninth grader—but where she was just starting with her fire was already far ahead of dragon-shifters who'd been working to enrich their fire for years. She was just reining it in because she hadn't been given a proper outlet to release it. Rope burn was the perfect opportunity for Laya to fully

492

unleash her fire in a controlled environment and gain confidence in her release from securing them a win.

He ripped his eyes off Laya and pinned them over the Gold Team, declaring, "For breezers, I choose Haizea Enlil and Anila Makani." Aithne shook her head as the two wind-benders on Gold descended the bleachers.

*Cop out,* Aithne snarled with an eye roll. *You picked the easiest wind-benders and your fucking sister.*

*Say another word about my sister, Aithne, and I'll feed you to our winning fire when my kids dominate yours,* Kellen hissed.

*You better be ready to comfort your sister when she's the reason you lose.* Aithne tossed her flaming hair over her shoulder before she began leading her pit crew to the Gold Team's side.

A moment passed before two gigantic poles appeared in front of the Red Team, the same materializing across the arena in front of the Gold lineup. The metal posts burrowed into the soil, a wide range of space between them due to the massive, thick rope the poles buoyed twenty feet above their heads and spread out to its full width. The rope was sopping wet from being submerged in enchanted water for the last twelve weeks, sprinkling streams of droplets onto the terrain.

"Feeders, get into position," Headmistress Dyer commanded. Suri steered her body to face the forest behind them.

"Look for oak wood," Kellen directed them in the short period he was given to offer advice. "It's the best type of wood for maintaining a fire. Oak has a distinctive grain pattern. It tends to be more wavy with knots and unique markings. Gatik, focus on cutting the trees down and passing Suri the wood to run back here. Don't go back and forth with her. Stay in the forest. She will need to run back to get more."

"Got it, coach." Gatik leapt onto Suri's back, hugging his legs around her waist, his arms twisting over her shoulders. Kellen passed Gatik the axe with a red hilt that had been lying on the ground in anticipation of rope burn.

"We won't let you down, Mr. Kilic," Suri promised.

"I know you won't." Kellen touched the back of Suri's head, then stepped away from them.

"On your mark," Headmistress Dyer yelled. "Get set…GO!"

The crowds erupted in screams as Suri launched frontward and dissolved into the wind from her staggering velocity. Kellen didn't take a single moment to look at the Gold's side to see what Dahy and Achira were doing, shifting his focus to his remaining pit crew, his three matches awaiting their orders.

"Begin by stacking wood as if you were building a cabin," he explained to the pit crew. Laya's brows adorably furrowed. with intensity as she absorbed every bit of information he shared with them. "Place several pieces of wood parallel on the bottom, then stack the next row on top, perpendicular. Repeat this until your fire reaches the desired height, which should be about halfway up the length of the poles, then place the groundwood paper in the center square before you ignite." He passed Eliane, the oldest of the chosen matches, the groundwood paper Headmistress Dyer gave him. The senior fire-bender tucked the provisions into her sweater pocket and squared her slim shoulders. "Don't use all your paper at once. Ration it. If the wind-benders blow out your fire, you're going to need more, so make sure you're not using too much at one time."

"How do you suggest to best way to ignite?" Eliane asked.

"I want you to go first, Elie, and lay the base for the fire," he commanded Eliane. "Your fire is the oldest of the three of you, so I want you to create the foundation. Then Adeen," he turned to the sophomore fire-bender, "I want you to pile your fire on top of Eliane's. Laya, you're last. I want your fire at the top."

"Why?" Laya squeaked.

"Because while your fire is the newest, it's the most potent out of the three. You have the best shot of burning through the rope." The three girls nodded their heads in understanding of their various tasks.

Suri suddenly returned, carrying four gigantic logs in her nimble arms. From Kellen's quick inspection, he confirmed it was oak wood and gave her a thumbs up in approval. She let the logs topple to the ground before she disappeared, blinking from existence as she sprinted back to Gatik, returning a second later with more wood, creating a pile of cleanly trimmed firewood on the asphalt. Eliane, Adeen, and

Laya rushed forward, gathering the wood, and began stacking the logs in the same way Kellen told them to, first with a row of ten firewood, parallel with one another on the bottom, then the next row perpendicular on top, facing the opposite way, repeating this switch of direction with each new row. Suri kept appearing with more logs for them to use, the Canterna Thicket regenerating with magic every time a tree was cut down, gifting them an unlimited supply of wood.

Adeen suddenly looked up and croaked, "Shit, they started their fire already!" Kellen turned to look.

The Gold Team's groundwork of logs was a fucking mess. Just wood tossed into a jumbled heap of kindling with no order or security. Yes, they'd already ignited a flame, but those logs would fall eventually and yank their fire right down with them. Kellen could hear Aithne screaming at them to fix their logs, but her team didn't seem to respect her opinion as much as his team did.

"Don't worry about them," Kellen assured. "Keep with what you're doing. Don't get sloppy."

Sweat percolated over Suri's brow—not from running, but from carrying the logs. The speed-wielder threw her whole body into feeding them the wood they needed, not letting a little thing like exhaustion deter her.

"You can take a breather," Kellen told her when she returned from one of her rounds gasping.

"No breaks," she snapped, not at him, but at her own body for showing any sign of weakness. He'd chosen Suri as a feeder not just because she was the best runner in her grade, but because he'd never met a speed-wielder with such a fierce determination and hunger for victory. She'd been the smallest in her grade when she first arrived at Delmarth and had defied all the odds stacked against her, proved everyone who doubted her wrong when all her teachers —apart from Kellen, who had always seen her for exactly who she was—thought she wouldn't amount to anything.

"They need four more logs before they can start igniting," Kellen said. "Go get them and then take a break with me."

"Okay." Suri wiped her brow, then vanished. Three seconds later, which showed Kellen she was slowing down and desperately needed a second to rest, she returned, dropping the logs at Kellen's feet and expelling a harsh wheeze.

"Sit," he ordered. "*Now*, Suri." Suri slumped on the ground next to him with an overwhelmed moan that bled into a whimper. Noella suddenly appeared and passed Suri a bottle of water. Kellen gave Noella a tight smile, then sunk to his knees to whisper to Suri, "I may get intense about rope burn, but this event is supposed to be fun. It's not worth killing yourself for. You've already made me immensely proud. I'll be even more proud of you for taking a breather when you need one." Suri choked on a sob, giving the hand he'd placed on her shoulder a squeeze.

His eyes found Noella, his reason for existing. She nodded her head in approval.

Kellen's matches were working in a synchronized succession with one another to build the foundation. Neither of the older classmen talked down to Laya or pushed her to the side, viewing her as an asset rather than a hindrance because of her size and experience. From the way they worked together in harmony, Adeen lifting Laya on her shoulders so his little sister could reach the top of their configuration and position the groundwood paper in the middle, Kellen knew he'd chosen his girls well.

"FUCK!" Aithne shrieked as the Gold Team's fire sputtered out, the force of Esen's wind vanquishing their burgeoning flame. The logs at the bottom of their unsystematic mess of a pile began slipping, sending the wood trundling in various directions, some rolling under the bleachers.

"Elie! Start igniting!" Kellen screamed at Eliane the moment the Red Team's last log settled into place, their firm foundation stretching out to reach the middle point of the pole, a perfect starting position.

His three matches backed away from their well-founded base to form a defensive wall between their foundation and the two wind-benders from Gold. Eliane spread her fingers and steered them at the wood, a groundswell of flames gushing from the center of her palms, drenching the surface of their formation of logs. Haizea and Anila, the wind-benders from Gold, sent a torrent of wind at Eliane's kindled flames, but she tossed more fire in opposition, throwing everything she had at the logs, fighting against the current. Adeen waited to see if Eliane's fire would taper off from the impact of the wind before she raised her hands and hurled her own fire at Eliane's, the two conflagrations combining to create a vortex of crimson and orange, tinged with gilded light from the dappled sun. Haizea propelled more wind at them, the breeze susurrating in Kellen's ears, but the two female's united flames were too strong for her wind to break through. The current failed to make a dent.

The Gold Team's matches had reignited a flame, though they were struggling to maintain it with Esen's wind crashing into the inferno. Every time their fire stretched close enough to reach the rope, Esen's wind knocked the fire to the side and kept it off the cable. From Aithne's mouth agape in a silent scream and her fingers wrenching at her hair, Kellen knew she was regretting giving her matches such a difficult challenge by picking Esen as a breezer. Kellen peeked over at his sister, her eyes glued to Eliane and Adeen's fire, waiting for their flame to broaden high enough towards the rope for her to jump in. Her fingers stroked her throat where her fire was building.

*You can do this, Laylie,* Kellen assured her, her gaze flying to him.

*What if I can't and I slow us down?* she squeaked in the form of a mewl. *I'll be the laughingstock of the school.*

*You've already broken the record for the youngest match in Delmarth history. You've already kept up with Adeen and Eliane beautifully. No one could ever call you a laughingstock, Laya, and no one will after you win us rope burn.* Laya's eyes filled with tears. Her posture straightened in acceptance of his praise.

As Eliane and Adeen's fire approached the rope, Laya positioned herself in a half-lunge, her hands balling up into fists at her sides. Her eyes fluttered shut, a sequence of slow, paced breaths passing in and out of her chest. When Laya's eyes reopened into the world, the green hue superseded by the slits of a dragon, she unhinged her jaw and bellowed a vociferous scream that scythed through the ether, fire spurting off her tongue along with the earsplitting sound. The entire Red Team stood in unison, beholding the twelve-year-old girl and her undeniably potent fire with awe as her flames jetted up to meet Adeen's and Eliane's, slamming into their concoction and topping their conflagration in violet embers. Kellen could hear Jarion screaming amidst the uproar of the crowd.

"THAT'S MY GIRL!" Jarion roared. "YOU'VE GOT THIS, LAYLIE! KEEP GOING!"

"GO LAYA!" Noella shrieked beside Kellen, her face cracking with an enormous, gorgeous grin.

The wildfire Kellen's matches created finally reached the rope.

All three females pitched everything they had at the rope. Eliane and Adeen pushed Laya's fire further up so her violet flames wrapped around the thick cable. Haizea and Anila lobbed wind at them to try and drive their fire away, the way Esen did to the Gold Team, but Laya's fire snapped back at the weak attempt to shatter their progression. A small morsel of her flames peeled off the rope and turned on the wind with a mind of their own, shooting boiling embers at the breeze to shunt it backward and send their wind wheeling back to them. Haizea and Anila stumbled from Laya's force and their own wind slamming into their bodies, losing their balance.

"YES, LAYA!" Suri cheered, fully rested now and bouncing on her toes.

Laya didn't break her concentration from the rope once. Her forehead crinkled in annoyance when the rope wouldn't budge. It wasn't that Laya's fire wasn't strong enough, but she was working against a cable that had been soaking in water immersed with Headmistress Dyer's healing abilities for the entire semester, so forcing the rope to break was intended to be near impossible.

"More, Laya!" Kellen hollered.

*I don't know if I have more, Kell,* Laya sobbed, her exhaustion wringing her unsteady voice.

*You are Eulaylia Kilic. You've suffered through worse and come out on the other side the victor. You are always the one left standing. You can do hard things, my love, because you've never not had enough to give.*

Laya's body bucked forward as she spewed more fire and loosed another raw, pained scream, tears sullying her beautiful cheeks. Noella squeezed Kellen's bicep, her nails jabbing into his skin. From the corner of Kellen's eye, he saw that the Gold Team's fire had also reached their rope in spite of Esen's wind and were beginning to make headway towards breaking through their own cord. Laya's fire snaked around the rope, her flames licking hungrily at the cable until the once sturdy fibers began to unravel and blacken under the relentless heat, emitting an acrid scent of burning. The crackling of Laya's fire consuming its prey echoed through the air, integrating with the boisterous crowd.

They were chanting her name. Eulaylia Kilic. Not Ates, but *Kilic.* Fuck, he'd never been prouder.

Laya's glowing embers chewed through the remaining strands with a voracious appetite, crafting a fiery gateway that threatened to sever the bond holding it together. The rope, now weakened and frayed, began to sag under the weight of its own demise, the metal poles holding it up in the air trembling. Laya's flames continued to devour it with fervor, until finally, with a magnificent snap, the rope gave way and fell apart in a shower of violet, red, and orange sparks, peppered with ash.

"Red wins!" Headmistress Dyer declared the moment the rope broke. The Red Team jumped to their feet and bellowed a glorious hail for Eulaylia Kilic, who would go down in history as the first sixth grader to ever win rope burn.

"YES!" Noella cheered, grabbing Kellen's arm before jumping up and down. "WE WON!"

"THAT'S MY FUCKING GIRL!" Kellen bawled, tears flooding his face.

Laya's fire triumphantly roared in victory as the once unbreakable rope drooped defeatedly off the sides of the pole, reduced to a pile of smoldering ashes. The three matches took a step back from the pile of logs. Eliane and Adeen pulled their arms back to their sides and closed their fingers inside their fists to hamper the flow of fire. Laya swallowed a mouthful of oxygen and gulped down the rest of her flames, then spluttered a gasp that formed puffs of smoke off her tongue, her hand flattening over her chest. Kellen rushed forward at the same moment she turned and dashed for him, his arms open for her as she leapt off her feet and threw herself at him with a beautiful mix of a laugh and a sob.

"Did that really just happen?!" she cried, grabbing Noella's hand when Noella reached for her.

"You did so good," Noella wept. Jarion barreled down the steps of the bleachers and pounced on top of Laya and Kellen, nearly knocking all three of them to the ground from his force.

"That's my twin sister!" Jarion thundered, all three of them sharing warm laughter. Laya's tears slipped down Kellen's neck when she pressed her face into his shoulder and hugged him tighter.

"Are you proud of me, Kellings?" she whispered, cracking his chest wide open.

"I've been proud of you since the moment you were born," Kellen gushed, his fingers threading in her hair to cradle the back of her head as he kissed her temple. He moved to the side so he could cup her cheeks and look her in the eyes when he proclaimed, "You are an exquisite, raging fire that cannot be dimmed, my love." He removed one hand from Laya to clasp Jarion's cheek. "You both are. I'm proud every fucking day that the Gods chose me to be your brother. I'll never not be proud."

Kellen's eyes landed on Noella. *How'd I do, Rose?*

*You were perfect,* she answered with tears in her eyes. *You ARE perfect, Kellen Kilic. I'm so proud to be yours.*

With the sound of the crowds intoning Laya's name and the sunlight splashing over their entangled limbs, Kellen drew his siblings into his arms with the love of his life standing a foot away.

## CHAPTER 36
# ELLA

"There's no way this is appropriate to wear in front of children," Ella scoffed at her reflection in the mirror.

Since Ella didn't own any fighting gear to wear for Sword Hunt, she'd relied on Kellen to acquire her some battle apparel from the school's supply. What he procured for her was the antithesis of what she typically wore and was her living nightmare crafted in a form-fitting jumpsuit, her body clad in sleek leather that hugged her curves like a second layer of skin. The glossy material gleamed in the ambient light of the locker room, accentuating the dangerous, seductive allure of the garment. Elaborate straps and buckles adorned the jumpsuit, giving the illusion of cushioning, with a belt wrapped around her waist to sheathe a weapon, her blonde hair contrasting starkly against the matte black. While the ensemble molded to her body, resembling a suit of armor, Ella had a hard time understanding how this garb would provide her any protection during the game.

"It's not that bad," Akio said, sitting on the bench next to the lockers. He was decked out in the titanium armor she'd expected Kellen to grab for her, a masterpiece of metalwork that exuded both strength and elegance, his bluish-black hair gelled off his forehead to give his face room to breathe.

"Not that *bad?*" Ella pointed to her backside, which was virtually visible through the leather. "My ass is out!"

"No one's going to be staring at your ass during Sword Hunt other than Kellen."

"That doesn't make me feel better." Akio chuckled as Ella dropped her face into her hands and groaned. "This suit makes my skin crawl. I'm practically naked in this! Is this Kellen's way of bringing to life some perverted fantasy about me?"

"Give him some credit. He'd never let a fantasy of the two of you play out in front of other people." Ella had to laugh at that. "And trust me, you're going to be thankful for that suit being so tight during battle. It's way harder to fight when you've got bulky armor on than something light and airy."

She began dividing her hair into two braids with a huff. "I still think Kellen did this on purpose."

"Did what on purpose?" Kellen asked when he reentered the locker room. His mouth fell open at the exact same time as Ella's. Similarly to Akio, Kellen was clothed in traditional armor, his pauldrons broad and imposing, festooned with fierce spikes that jutted out from the metal shield, mimicking the horns on his back in dragon form. Spears framed his face in a menacing silhouette. The vambraces that encased his forearms were decorated in an engraved pattern reminiscent of flames, flowing down the armor to his greaves, which were thick and sturdy, promising to protect his muscular legs from harm. Kellen had two swords suspended on either side of his waist—on his left was his own sword, and on the right was a much larger weapon, manufactured from solid gold and varnished in red, the Red Team's sword that they would need to hide and protect during Sword Hunt. Kellen gulped down a harsh breath that hissed through his teeth as he beheld Ella, flames twirling in his eyes. He then glared at Akio. "You better not have been watching when she put this on."

"I'd never!" Akio insisted. "Who do you think I am?"

"Seriously, Kilic?" Ella grumbled when she'd recovered her equilibrium and stopped mooning over how gorgeous he looked in his armor. She waved her hand down her body. "This scrap of material was all you could get me?"

"All the women wear this in battle," Kellen explained, moving with fluid grace across the locker room to stand with her. "Just not all of them look as delicious in it as you do." He cupped her chin and lifted her head so his lips could scrape against hers. His fingers slid down to curve around her throat. "I don't know what I find more appealing," he whispered against her mouth. Ella shuddered at the surge of lightning effervescing through her body from his tongue gently lapping her bottom lip while he spoke. "The leather clinging to your curves, or your hair in those braids."

"You like braids?" she stammered.

"I like *you*, Noella Rose." She melted onto his chest, her fingers tracing the titanium breastplate. Into their kiss, he groaned, "So much it's sickening." Kellen grabbed the front zipper on her leather jumpsuit and yanked it up to below her chin while they kissed, cloaking her neck in leather, the metal zipper grating against her throat. "My eyes only," he murmured, nipping her bottom lip.

"And that's my cue to leave," Akio joshed, pretending to rise from the bench and sprint away in slow motion.

"Did you get a sword yet?" Kellen asked, searching the floor for a weapon. She shook her head. "I'll go get you one." He seized her chin to pilfer one last kiss from her lips. "You're fucking impossible to leave," he growled, then slipped his fingers off her and stalked out of the locker room.

"You look happy," Akio observed. Ella cupped her flaming cheeks.

"I feel happy," she whispered, her heart hewed apart by the look of pure joy washing over her friend's face—her friend who she'd been so cold to simply because he tried to guide her towards repairing things with Kellen, her friend who all this time had been looking out for her and protecting her and wanting to see her happy, and she'd made him out to be this vindictive, selfish bastard in her head, undeserving of trust. "I'm sorry for accusing you of pushing me towards Kellen for your own selfish reasons," she stammered, truly meaning her apology this time. Akio's cheeks paled the moment she began apologizing, eyes rounding with something akin to fear. "I know now that you were just being a good friend and looking out for me. I'm so grateful—"

"ELLA," Akio cut her off mid-sentence. He squeezed his eyes shut, groaning an aggrieved sound like he was experiencing pain somewhere in his body, and whispered, "You weren't...you weren't completely wrong."

Ella's breath hitched. "What do you mean?" Akio opened one eye to look at her.

"My vision," he told her, her heartbeat rumbling hysterically, scuffing her eardrums. "It was about you and Kellen. Aros...Aros asked me to make sure you two found your way to each other."

"Why?" She needed this answered finally. "Why does he care so much about me and Kellen? What else did he tell you?"

"He said..." Akio scanned the doorway to ensure no one was lingering there. He then spoke into her mind for extra precaution, *Only when the child of the crown—*

"Binds to the child of the flame can the chains of solitude be released," Ella finished for him, the gasp she loosed singeing her chest. "Bryara said that to me. Are you saying that...that prophecy is about—"

"All staff members, report to base for the start of Sword Hunt," Headmistress Dyer's voice boomed from the loudspeaker.

"We've got to go," Akio sighed, starting for the door.

"Akio!" Ella yelled. "What the fuck?!"

"We'll talk after. I promise." He spun around to look at her. "You are my friend, Ella. My best friend. I have always wanted what's best for you. Please believe that." He abandoned her in the locker room.

A second later, Kellen returned with a sword for Ella, gifting her no time to process or react to what just happened. She accepted the sword from Kellen, then sheathed it in the holster hanging at her waist and followed him out into the hallway.

"Did you see Akio leave on your way here?" she whispered.

"No. Why?" Ella surveyed the hallway on either side to verify no one was in listening distance.

"I need to talk to you about what he just told me." Kellen came to a halt and turned his body to face her.

"Did he finally tell you about the vision?" She nodded. He demanded, "Tell me what he said."

*"MOVE,"* Oliviana snapped from behind them, shoving her way through Kellen and Ella to force them apart. Kellen's promise that her Sword Hunt ensemble was custom for women in Cavale to wear was confirmed through Oliviana. The earth-bender's apparel mimicked Ella's, down to the ankle boots with rubberized soles. Her crimson tresses were folded into an intricate bun, a few wisps wiggled free from her elastic to spill down her neck. She whipped her head back, pinning them down with a stony glare, and sneered, "You two don't have time to talk. You're supervising the first round."

"Is this really going to be the rest of your life, Oliviana?" Ella asked her seriously. "Being obsessed with everything Kellen and I do? That's such a useless waste of your time. Find something else to be consumed by, something far more advantageous to your own happiness. I mean that sincerely."

"Oh, trust me, princess. I have. You'll find out soon." Ella jerked back as Oliviana strutted to the exit.

"Ignore her," Kellen grumbled under his breath. "I usually do."

"You didn't find that a little ominous? *You'll find out soon,"* Ella mocked Oliviana in a low tenor.

"Honestly, baby, I don't take anything that bitch says or does seriously. Not since she asked me to tell her in extensive detail how I almost drowned you in a pool so she could get off on the thought of you in pain."

"She *did?"* Bile soiled the inside of Ella's mouth. "What did you say?"

"I kicked her out of my apartment and told her to fuck off. That's why I ended things with her. I found it disgustingly unattractive. No part of me would entertain that, even when I tried to convince myself I hated you, because deep down, the thought of you seriously hurt was abhorrent to me. Still is." Ella reached for Kellen's hand, giving it a soft squeeze. He squeezed back. "I wasn't trying to drown you that day. I wanted to scare you into quitting, but I never would've actually hurt you."

"I know that. You wouldn't do anything that would leave Laya and Jarion in a position to have no guardian. It's taken me a long time to fully understand your motives, but I know you were scared about your mother and were acting out of fear for the twins. I let go of my anger at you a long time ago, Kellen."

Kellen's eyes shimmered. He stared at her for a long moment like he was truly seeing her for the first time.

"The fact that you understand that makes me even more certain that you're my Cavalisha." Ella giggled as Kellen captured her face and kissed her in a rapid sequence on every corner of her skin, playfully biting her cheek. "Gods," he groaned, "I'd do fucking anything for you, Noella."

"Even walk Freya for me?" Ella bat her eyelashes at Kellen's frown.

"Really, Rose?" he carped as they resumed walking, heading for the exit of the office building. "Why?"

"Because I want you two to be best friends."

"Sweetheart," he laughed at her pout. Kellen held the door open for her. "You can't guarantee that."

"She already likes you. When you're around, she forgets I exist. She only wants to sit on your lap."

"The feeling isn't reciprocated."

"Come on, Kellen." Ella turned on her heel and stopped walking, plastering on her best, big eyed, beseeching sweet look. "Please? Is it so bad for me to want the two most important beings in my life to mean as much to each other as they mean to me?" Kellen screwed his eyes shut with a grunt.

"Fuck. I miss the days when I could say no to you." Ella reached up on her tiptoes to tease his jawline with the tip of her nose, dragging it down the sharp demarcation cloaked in scruff.

"You could never say no to me, Kellen Kilic," she mumbled over his chin. "Don't kid yourself."

Before he could shift his head and dive down to close the distance between them, she rotated with a vicious laugh, her braids slapping his armor, and skipped off to meet the accumulation of students, all dressed in red, gathered on the great lawn in the academic sector. The rest of campus was blocked off by a forcefield that began at the boundary line of the academic sector and shot up to arch over the entirety of Delmarth, so all Ella could see when she stared at the iridescent partition was her own reflection, not the Varmin sector that typically fringed her office building. Inside the forcefield, which she would pass through in a manner of minutes, lay the arena for Sword Hunt, created by the Cerebri instructors who were standing off to the side with their eyes glazed in silver, absorbed in maintaining the illusion. The Gold Team was on the opposite end of the dome, beginning at the Herculea sector, so she couldn't see them past the forcefield. Ella searched the queue of Cerebri instructors for Akio, but before she had a chance to locate him, Kellen shepherded her through the sea of students to the front of the throng. He guided her gently by her elbow to where their assigned group of seven students for the first round of Sword Hunt was waiting for them, one student selected from every grade level, beginning with sixth grade and ending with twelfth. Jamie was amongst their group, the tension easing from her shoulders when she saw that Ella was one of the designated faculty supervising her round.

"Tell me what's going through your head," Ella entreated her. "You look troubled."

"I hate Maccabiah," Jamie spluttered, her fingers clawing at her chest. "Everyone's emotions get so heightened and I can feel everything that everyone is feeling and it's just too much. It's too much, Ms. Rose."

"Take a second. Breathe with me." Ella placed her hands on Jamie's shoulders, ensnaring a mouthful of oxygen in her chest along with Jamie, and counted to four in her head, then released the breath in a heavy, prolonged gale, counting six seconds aloud for Jamie as she released her own gasp. "I know this is hard for you. It's a lot of energy even for me, so I can't imagine what it feels like for you. That's why we coped ahead for this. Can you remember some of the suggestions we came up with for you to fall back on when you get overwhelmed during the event?"

Jamie's forehead crinkled along with the shutting of her eyes, recalling the cope ahead sheet she and Ella filled out last week in preparation for Maccabiah and specifically for Sword Hunt.

"Go to where there's water and splash my face," Jamie recited from the sheet. "Make sure I never stop breathing. Shift into my snake form. Put my hand to my heart and focus on what my heartbeat feels like under my hand to return to my own body."

"Good." Ella squeezed her shoulders. "What do you know about what the arena is going to look like?"

"It's made to look like Lavalden and the Middledeen waters." Jamie's eyes were still closed.

"Exactly. You know there's going to be water there, so when you need a second, you give me the signal we agreed on and go find water. Don't worry about anyone else. Once you're in a calmer state, you find your way back to the group. Okay?" Ella's fingers fell off Jamie's shoulders before she stepped back to give the serpent-shifter room. "You can do this," Ella assured her, gripping the hilt of her own sword.

"Okay," Jamie stammered not convincingly.

"I want to hear you say it." Jamie exhaled a dilapidated breath.

"I can do this," the Varmin repeated, falling into the line of students and focusing on the pace of her breaths.

Kellen and Ella settled into place in front of the group.

"Ms. Rose and I are here to supervise," Kellen told the group when he swiveled around, "but this is your fight. Your search. Once we get in there, talk amongst each other and figure out your strategy. No asking us for help. We're here to make sure no one gets too carried away. Remember this is supposed to be fun. Do not seriously injure your classmates, or there will be consequences."

"Red and Gold, get into position," Headmistress Dyer's voice echoed from a faraway plane inside the loudspeaker. "Sword Hunt will commence in thirty seconds when the bell tolls."

"Good luck," Ella threw over her shoulder at the row of students. "I have no doubt you will do great."

*I'm really glad we're doing this together,* Kellen told Ella. *I want to experience every first with you. I want to do the rest of my life with you, Noella Rose. No one else.* Ella swallowed down her tears.

*Me too, Kell.* Love screamed inside her, imploring to be freed. She couldn't keep it in anymore. *I lo—* Ella never got to finish the sentiment before the roar of a bell cleaved the ether in half.

They led their group through the forcefield into the arena.

508

The arena stretched out before them as Kellen and Noella cleared the barrier. A vast expanse of chaos and destruction crashed into the backcloth of a boundless sea, emulating the Middledeen waters that divided Cavale and Lantari. The salty scent of the ocean mingled with the sharp, harsh smell of smoke and blood, amalgamating together to create a surreal, haunting atmosphere heavy from devastation. Unruly waves banged against the rocky shore, a rugged and unforgiving landscape with jagged cliffs rising from the water, their weathered faces carved by the relentless force of the whitecaps that slammed against them. The sand beneath their boots was stained with blood, a macabre canvas of crimson and gold. In the distance, the sun dipped below the horizon, throwing lithe rays of fiery light across the water and painting the cerulean sky in flourishes of red and pink. On the grounds itself, the illusion crafted deceased bodies and scattered them over the battleground, the carcasses covered in weeping wounds and mottled flesh.

Noella gasped at the ghastly sight, stumbling back a step. Kellen reached out his hand to steady her.

*It's not real,* Kellen assured her.

*It's real somewhere,* she answered in a voice full of sadness. Kellen was knocked off guard by the truth of that statement. It bashed him in the gut. He felt it reverberate and scar every valley in his body.

Sometimes, he found it difficult to remember what was happening on the frontier lines of Cavale, despite how often they spoke about the war with the students and prepared them for the conditions of battle. Delmarth was such a beautiful bubble entombed on the other side of the kingdom, so far removed from the destruction that it sometimes felt like a myth they told the students, not something that was factually happening and continued to happen every single day while they all lived their lives, as if people weren't dying every second. The sun still shone and the wind still blew, but somewhere in Cavale, mothers and fathers, brothers and sisters, waited in vain, their lives completely halted, their hearts ripped from their chest and existing with their loved ones on that battlefield. Those soldiers who were once children, just like the children behind Kellen now, were reduced to meat for the birds. Their eyes and hearts were as immobile as their limbs. What was displayed before them now on the Sword Hunt arena was only a fraction of the horror occurring in this exact moment in the real Lavalden, the wounded draped over the wintry grounds, garish scarlet flowing over the frosted white sand, blanketing the earth in tragedy.

Noella had not been shy about expressing her extreme disapproval for Aros Cavalian and how he expected his people to fight for him when he barely fought for them. Kellen had never looked at it that way before, but now, he wasn't able to see it any other way, the unfair hypocrisy of it all. He thought about what Markus had said weeks ago and suddenly couldn't agree more. What were they even fighting for anyway?

Why did they spend so much time talking about the war, training for the war, mastering their powers to take on the Sireres, but never got to actually *see* the war or what was happening in Lavalden? What was the point in giving their lives for a king who couldn't give two shits about any of them? These were children who were being molded into warriors. Expected to forfeit their lives to Aros's cause against Edar. Forced to side with a king who'd never given them an actual reason to side with him because the threat of being tortured for the rest of their lives was too grave.

What was the fucking *point?*

*Kell,* an angel's voice ruptured through his downward spiral, reaching out a dainty hand to yank him back into reality.

*My love,* he sighed in his head, relief flooding through him to have her sweet voice replace his depressing, crushing thoughts. Noella's eyelashes fluttered when he called her that so casually, as if he'd always called her that, which, strangely, it felt like he had, like she'd always been his love.

Kellen returned his focus to the squabbling students before he started overthinking the fact that he just called her that for the first time.

"Altair should take Robin in the sky with him and survey the grounds for the other team's sword," Callum, a senior Herculea strength-wielder demanded, taking the helm of the group because no one else seemed eager to claim the reins. "Me and Evander will hide and guard the sword. The rest of you should go searching for their sword."

That left Jamie, a Meteoro earth-bender named Clovis, and a Cerebri named Blair as the group hunting for Gold's sword. Kellen agreed with this plan, not that he elected to share that with Callum.

*Should we split up too?* Noella asked Kellen. Neither seemed thrilled about the idea of separating. *Maybe one of us should stay with the kids guarding our sword while the other goes with the group searching for Gold's sword.*

*I really don't want to leave you.* Noella's lips drooped in a taunting pout, her eyes laughing at him. Kellen realized what a fucking sap he sounded like and snapped out of it. *Fine. I'll stay with the group guarding the sword. You should stay with Jamie.*

"Mr. Kilic will stay with Callum and Evander," Noella shared with the group. "I'll join the group searching for the sword."

"Robin," Kellen addressed the sixth grade Cerebri. "When you locate the Gold team overhead with Altair, let Callum know where you see them so I can communicate it to Ms. Rose's group."

Altair, a gryphon-shifter, took no time to spare before he transformed into his Varmin form, his body becoming a seamless blend of a regal lion and a powerful eagle, with a massive wingspan that shimmered in the sunlight like a tapestry of gold and silver. Feathers of dazzling blue and green garlanded his wings, casting an incredible array of colors across the ghoulish landscape. Robin crawled onto Altair's back, her fingers fisting his feathers for support before he leapt off his hind legs and hurled them into the sky, a wink of green and gold amidst the panorama of blue.

*You okay, sweetheart?* Noella whispered before her group left. *You looked like you were dissociating before.*

Kellen nearly fell to his knees before her when she called him that.

He couldn't stop his eyes from hungrily devouring her in her battle uniform and her adorable braids, the leather of her fighting suit adhering to her flawless figure, worshipping her curves the way he wished he could right now. He never knew it was possible to become jealous of cloth, but right now, he yearned to shred the material apart and replace the fabric on her body with his tongue.

*Got lost in my head for a second. You brought me back.* Noella's gaze warmed.

*I always will,* she promised. He felt so overwhelmed by her beauty and mere existence that he could barely catch his breath.

Kellen bit his tongue before he snapped at the students in Noella's group to take care of her, since that was supposed to be their jobs as supervisors to take care of the kids. He watched her drape an arm around Jamie's shoulders and turn to begin their hunt for Gold's sword, gifting him a moment to appreciate the shape of her ass before he was forced to will his eyes off her and onto Callum and Evander.

"Where are you thinking you want to hide the sword?" Kellen asked them.

"In the sand," Evander, a Meteoro water-bender, replied, his eyes locked on the impersonation of the Middledeen waters. "I think we should stay near the water."

"Not the sand," Callum denied, "though I agree we should stay near the water. If I can create an opening in the rock for us to hide the sword, even if Gold makes it over here, they'll never think to look inside the cliff."

*Great idea,* Kellen wanted to say, but instead, he schooled his features to hide his approval, allowing the students to lead the way to the ocean. The sound of the surf heaving under the callused breeze filled the air with a sonata of rolling waves and swirling currents circling around the crenelated cliff, ridged with deep grooves. Pools of water collected in the crevices of the rocks. Kellen carefully assessed Callum's progression up the cliff, the rock beneath his feet slick and treacherous, worn smooth by the illusion imitating a rock that had endured centuries of pounding waves and shifting tides. Once he reached the top, Callum mustered all his strength to stab his fingers into the rock, mincing through the aggregate minerals to create a large enough opening for himself to slide their team's sword inside. He then used the debris gathered around him of pulverized granite to coat the top and shroud the hilt of the sword. He inched his way down the cliff slowly, prudent of his footwork so he didn't slip off the edge, and hopped back onto the sand.

Evander steered his hands towards the ocean and guided the marine to the left. A wave of water obeyed his command and swept onto the cliff base, dousing it in glassy liquid that would ensure anyone who dared to attempt an ascent up the rock would slip right back onto the beach. The boys high-fived when Evander was finished.

"Good job, guys," Kellen offered them.

While they waited, Kellen dove into Noella's head, looking through her eyes to check on the other group's progress.

Noella's group had reached the illusion's version of the Lavalden forest. The sun filtered through the cracks in the canopy of trees, designing dappled patterns and throwing a gilded spotlight onto the leaf-strewn path Noella and the students followed. She remained at the back of the group, intently observing as the students navigated the winding trails on their hands and knees to search for the Gold sword, her footsteps light and sure on the soft forest floor, her hand hovering near the hilt of her sword.

Through his connection with her mind, he could feel how the earthy fragrance of damp soil, moss, and pine needles relaxed the thrashing of her heart, how she used the pungent assault on her senses to help calm her nervous system.

*Hi, baby,* Kellen cooed to her.

*Hi, sweetheart,* she answered in equally as tender a voice. He groaned out loud and didn't care if Callum or Evander heard him. Gods, he loved her so fucking much. *Where did the boys hide the sword?*

*We stayed by the ocean,* he told her. *Callum had an idea to hide the sword inside the cliff. Even if Gold comes this way, they won't be able to get to it or even see where it's located. It was a brilliant move.*

*Good idea,* she agreed. *I wouldn't have thought of that.*

Fallen leaves crunched under Noella's boots. A soothing rhythm followed in her wake as her group moved deeper into the forest. The distant call of simulated birds provided a peaceful soundtrack to their journey.

*How's your group doing?* he asked despite being able to see through her eyes.

*No luck yet finding any sword. We haven't encountered anyone from Gold. The kids are getting along well. I'm keeping a close eye on Jamie.*

*She's lucky to have you. We all are.* Kellen felt her lips lift in a smile through their bond. *I miss you.*

*Is it crazy that I miss you too?* she laughed in his head. *We saw each other five minutes ago!*

*If you stay in Cavale, we'll never have to part again.* Wrong moment to be broaching this conversation, he knew, but he couldn't help himself from dangling the temptation in front of her and seeing if she'd bite.

*I've been thinking about that the past few days.* Kellen's heartbeat stuttered in his chest. *Being a part of Maccabiah has been so special for me. I never went to summer camp like some of my peers in school who got to live a version of these types of games. Maybe it's making me look at Delmarth and Cavale through rose-colored glasses a bit, but I honestly can't imagine leaving and not getting to experience this with you ever again.*

Kellen stopped breathing. *Are you saying what I think you're saying, Rose?* He felt a blush steal across her cheeks.

*I'm saying…I think I want to stay here,* Noella declared, filling Kellen with abounding light, so much he was teeming with it, leaking it, pouring his delight out into the universe. Tears graced the corners of his eyes.

He laughed a mixture of a cackle and a sob, gushing, *We'll talk later about how your feelings for me weren't enough for you to stay, but FUCK, Noella. You just made me the happiest man alive.*

Noella was about to object when suddenly, there was a flash of movement in front of them before a burly figure pounced on her from the side and pummeled her to the ground, her head smacking the forest floor. Kellen felt the blow to the back of Noella's skull reverberate through his own cranium, as if it had been him trampled and not her. Noella didn't hesitate to slam her elbow into the face of her assailer, not even checking first to see if it was a student, though from the bulk and the blonde hair, she'd figured out before Kellen that it was Daniel Madix on top of her.

"Are you two good to guard the sword alone?" Kellen asked Callum and Evander.

514

He'd taken off running before the boys had even lifted their chins to bob their heads in nods.

Kellen watched Daniel, through Noella's eyes, splutter a callous laugh at the torrent of blood spouting out of his now mangled nose. He rose off the forest floor, staring down at the crimson smudges on the center of his palm as Noella extracted her sword from its sheath, her beauty overtaken by rancor. All around them, students from both teams engaged one another in battle, red-tinted armor fusing with gold.

"You've got a mean right hook, earthborn," Daniel chuckled, taunting, "Does Kellen enjoy that in bed?" before he flicked his fingers and sent her soaring into a tree with nothing but his mind, grinning at the sound of her spine smashing into the trunk with an excruciating snap. Kellen's wings unfolded from his back, shattering through his armor as both his and Coz's concern amalgamated into one and he let his dragon take over to get him to Noella faster, leaping off his feet.

Noella pulled herself up with a pained groan, then hauled herself into a standing position, soil sliding down the leather of her jumpsuit. "Careful there," she seethed. "It almost sounds like you're jealous."

"Jealous of who? Of *you?*" Noella mocked him with a condescending shrug. Daniel's features darkened.

"Maybe you've actually been in love with Kellen this whole time, not Oliviana. Yeah, that's right. I pay attention."

She lunged forward right when Daniel opened his mouth to respond and swiped her sword through the air, taking Daniel off guard with her swift advance so she was able to notch his cheek, carving a blood-spattered line down his face. She dipped under his arm and slammed the hilt of her sword into the back of his neck, lobbing him to his knees. Daniel reached behind her, grabbed her waist, and chucked her over his shoulder, sending her plummeting back into the tree.

Noella crumpled into a jumbled stack of limbs amongst the verdant, discarded leaves at the bottom of the tree trunk.

"Is throwing me into trees the new throwing me into walls?" she groaned between a bitter laugh, her fingers clawing through the soil to find her sword. Her eyes darted to Daniel, dripping hatred, and sneered, "How original."

"Everyone's been wondering what power you must possess for Kellen Kilic to have gone from ruler of Delmarth to submissive, lovestruck fool." Daniel loomed over her and blasted his foot into the side of her neck, pressing down on her throat and smushing her into the soil. When he diminished her to a hurricane of throttled wheezes, the skin of her face altered a startling shade of red, his foot glided away and sunk to the ground to meet her, fisting his fingers in her hair to bring her face close to his. Against her cheek, he muttered, "Maybe I need to find out for myself what's so special about human cunt." Kellen had never beat his wings harder in his fucking life.

*Fly faster,* Coz snarled.

*I'M FLYING AS FAST AS I CAN!* Kellen yelled back, scouring the forest from above to find them.

"Try to put your hands on me, Daniel, and you will lose them," Noella threatened, her voice resounding clear despite the hammering of her heart in her chest. "If not by me, then by Kellen or Aros Cavalian's envoy."

"I can do whatever I fucking want, Ms. Rose. I don't see either of your guard dogs around here."

"Look up, asshole," Kellen growled, landing right on Daniel and pitching him off Noella. Fire surged out from the tips of Kellen's fingers, drenching his hands, so when he snatched Daniel by the throat and shoved him into a tree trunk, his fingers crushing Daniel's windpipe scorched his flesh as well, turning the skin into charred membrane, burning through to the underlying tendons.

"K-Ke—" Daniel choked.

"What was that?" Kellen drawled. "Speak up. I *really* want to hear you beg for your life." Kellen gripped him harder.

*Kellen, stop,* Noella pleaded.

*Stop?!* Kellen repeated, his head whipping around to look at her. *He touched you. He fucking—*

*I know what he did.* Her gaze was wet and soft with love. *I know what he said, but you're better than him, Kell. If you kill him, if you actually kill him, it will haunt you for the rest of your life. He was once your friend. Don't put yourself in a position to carry that burden if you don't need to.*

Kellen drowned in her gaze.

His rage and his love battled for dominance of the hand still clutching Daniel's throat. In the end, they reached a satisfying compromise as Kellen contracted his fingers and permitted Daniel to nosedive to the ground. Kellen's foot came down on the back of Daniel's neck, keeping him pinned. He withdrew his sword from his holster and veered it downwards, slashing through Daniel's wrist to sever the hand from his arm that had been in Noella's hair. While Daniel buried his face in the soil and screamed a violent lament into the earth, blood jetting out from the open wound, Kellen wiped the blood off his sword with a leaf.

"I once told the love of my life that if anyone dared to touch her, it would be the last thing they ever touch," Kellen told Daniel, tossing the blood-tarnished leaf into Daniel's face. "I'm a man of my word, especially where she's concerned." He spun around to begin heading over to Noella.

Daniel, with what little strength he'd conserved, stretched out his fingers towards Noella before Kellen completed a full step in her direction. A second later, Noella fell to her knees and began shrieking at the top of her lungs, her fingernails abrading her temples as she rocked back and forth, vibrating.

"NOELLA!" Kellen yelled, then charged at Daniel. Daniel's eyes flitted to him before Kellen was sent sailing backward into the tree Daniel had thrown Noella into, his power keeping Kellen restrained there. He writhed in vain against the trunk, jerking forward to fight the invisible chain ensnaring him against the tree, but kept meeting resistance on the other side, the shackle squashing his spine into the timber.

He had no choice but to watch the love of his life dissolve into a puddle of pitiful sobs as she tried to claw her own brain out of her head to free herself from whatever torment Daniel was inflicting on her.

Daniel pushed off the ground with the hand he still retained and marched over to Noella, his intent to kill her clear in his stormy gaze. Kellen fired his own power at Daniel and sent a film of opaque black to bandage over his vision, blinding him before he could reach her. Daniel destroyed the screen from over his eyes with ease, the black dissolving into the normally blue hue, then wrenched Noella to her feet by pulling on one of her braids, spinning her around so she faced Kellen.

"You had a chance to kill me, and you choked," Daniel cackled, grabbing Noella by the throat.

Noella kept her eyes over Kellen's, her bottom lip trembling.

She mouthed to him *it's okay, my love,* even as tears fell down her cheeks in unchecked streams.

"Let her go," Kellen begged, choking on gasps and the taste of vomit. "*Please.* I'll give you whatever you want. You want to kill me, Daniel? I will take out my own heart and hand it to you."

"Kell," Noella sobbed.

"Your love for her has made you weak, Kellen," Daniel continued jeering. "You are not the same man who Aros Cavalian chose for his personal cadre. The King of the Gods would laugh at you now. You—"

A giant purple snake slithered out from the underbrush and took a chunk out of Daniel's cheek, moving with sinuous grace as she sprang off the forest floor and flattened him in the soil, forcing Daniel to release both Noella and Kellen from his influence. Noella toppled to the ground and crawled to where Kellen landed on his knees, the two of them lunging for each other. Kellen collected her in his arms and buried his face in her neck for one treasured moment of reunification.

*Sweetheart,* he gushed as he kissed the edge of her jaw. *Are you okay?*

*I'm fine,* she gasped back, her fingers easing off him. *I take back everything I said. Go end him.*

*Anything for you, my love,* Kellen swore.

He moved her off his lap so he could join where the snake, her body coiling and uncoiling, devoured Daniel's face, gouging his eyes and spitting them out onto the forest like she couldn't stand the taste of him.

"Let me finish him off, Jo," Kellen said, flashing a wicked smile. He knew it was Josefyn from the second he'd seen the deep, rich purple hue of her scales, with subtle hints of blue and silver that caught the sunlight and sparkled like precious gems. Josefyn raised her lavender eyes, glinting in recognition, then eased back, emitting a soft, rumbling hiss before she glided over to sit with Noella.

Kellen's face contorted with undiluted rage as he accosted Daniel. Josefyn had masticated his facial features, mauling his flesh with teeth marks and bloodied gashes, his eye sockets bursting with gore. Despite no longer having eyes, he knew it was Kellen hovering over him.

"Kellen, please," Daniel pleaded. "Don't do this."

"It's a little too late for begging." Kellen seized Daniel's chin and burrowed his fingers into the battered jawline. "You think my love for her has weakened me? How fucking wrong you are." Kellen's fingers slipped down to Daniel's chest, positioning over his flailing heart. "Let me show you the power my love for her has given me. Let that be the last thing you ever feel in this life."

Kellen's fire tore through Daniel's chest and scorched through the tissue of his heart, frying him from the inside out, flames surging up Daniel's throat and tumbling off his tongue when he suffocated on the inferno. Kellen extracted his fingers from inside Daniel once no life breathed through him anymore. He pivoted to face Noella, finding Josefyn wrapped around her neck, the snake nuzzling her cheek.

*Thank you,* Kellen communicated to Jo, struggling not to weep. *I am forever in your debt, Josefyn Yilanci.*

*No debt needed,* Josefyn replied. Noella stroked Jo's vertebrae with her index finger. *Ella is my best friend. So are you, Kell. I'll always protect the people I love.* Kellen placed his bloody fingers over his heart.

"We should probably go find our team, my beauty." Kellen said to Noella with a sad laugh, realizing that the battling students had dispersed and the three of them, plus Daniel's deceased body, were now alone in the forest. He didn't understand why Noella's eyes got so big when he said that. Was it because he called her *my beauty,* which he didn't normally say? Why would that make her face pale? "Noella? What's wro—" The sound of screaming cut through the ether like a serrated knife.

"Jamie," Noella gasped, recognizing the voice. She hefted to her feet and took off running through the forest without looking back, leaving Kellen and Josefyn to sprint after her. Josefyn curled around Kellen's leg so he could drag her with him. Jamie's cries led them back to the beach, the salty sea air blending with the tang of sweat on his tongue. Near the water's edge, beside where he'd left Callum and Evander, there was a figure hunched over, shoulders shaking with silent sobs. As they advanced, her features became more distinct, her long blue hair tangled and windswept, one hand clenched tightly in the sand while the other splayed out on her chest, over her heart. "JAMIE!" Noella yelled at the raw pain etched on the snake-shifter's face, the anguish in her eyes seeming to reach into the depths of her soul. She finally made it to Jamie and knelt at her side.

"I can *feel* it," Jamie wailed, sagging against Noella.

"Feel *what*, Jamie?" Jamie lifted her desolate gaze, red-rimmed and filled with unshed tears.

"*Death.*" Noella looked up at Kellen with guilt wrought in her wet eyes.

He was about to tell her that this wasn't their fault when a body came barreling through the forcefield, ripping a hole in the illusion and soaring over the replica of the Middledeen waters to collapse on the beach in a crumpled heap of broken limbs. Kellen recognized the student immediately from the hair and build.

All the oxygen in his chest divorced from his lungs and mashed into the mass that once was Connor Paight.

"Is that Connor?!" Noella spluttered as she pulled Jamie closer to her protectively. She glanced at Kellen. "Was that part of the game?" When Kellen swallowed, it was a great feat to get the saliva down his throat.

"No," Kellen exhaled in a raspy voice. "No, it's not."

Noella scampered across the sand and sunk to her knees next to Connor. She pressed her fingers to his pulse.

Kellen already knew what she'd find. He could hear the silence echo beneath Connor's skin.

She whirled to Kellen in horror. "He's dead, Kell."

An earsplitting alarm, nails sliding down a chalkboard epitomized, resounded from the clouds. Kellen's eardrums wept for relief while his heart dropped down to his stomach and rattled his intestines. Noella's hands covered her ears to protect her brain against the ghastly sound.

"What *is* that?" she screamed.

"*Fuck,*" Kellen hissed, reaching for the hilt of his sword. "It's the Sireres alarm." Noella's hands descended into her lap. The color of Jamie's face hinted she was two seconds away from puking.

"*Sireres?*" Noella repeated. "On campus?" Kellen offered her his hand to pull her up, then did the same for Jamie.

"It's not a game anymore, Rose." He tipped his chin towards her blade. "You ready for another fight?"

"I'm ready," she answered without hesitation, gliding her dagger out from the sheath at her waist.

"That's my girl." Kellen looked to Jamie, Callum, and Evander. "Go gather the rest of the students. Both teams. Take them over the forcefield back onto campus. Get ready to fight." Jamie's breath stuttered, but she nodded in acceptance of her orders along with Callum and Evander. The three students sprinted off to the forest as Kellen looked down at Josefyn, who was still enveloped around his calf. "Go, Jo. Find Akio. We'll meet you over the forcefield." Josefyn slunk down his leg.

He watched her glide past the sand and shatter through the forcefield, disappearing on the other side.

"You wanted to watch me shift, sweetheart," Kellen crooned to Noella as he handed her his sword. "Now's your chance."

Kellen took a step back from Noella. His muscles tensed, his skin beginning to gleam and ripple, Coz moving beneath the surface, preparing for emergence. With a sudden and violent burst, Kellen's body warped and expanded, his bones cracking and stretching as his form shifted. His skin darkened from ebony brown to obsidian black, scales erupting from his flesh in a riot of midnight. His hands twisted and elongated into razor-sharp claws, his feet morphing into powerful talons that dug into the sand below. His massive wings unfurled from his back, his face lengthening into a snout filled with rows of polished teeth. Inside him, Coz's claw slipped into Kellen's hand, pulling Kellen down into a crouched position inside his own chest so Coz could amble to the forefront of Kellen's mind, claiming the reins of their body. From where he towered over the beach in all his fearsome glory, Noella looked puny, like a diminutive bug compared to his immense height.

*Let me ride on your back, Kellen,* Noella said, no fear in her eyes.

*It would be my honor, Noella Rose.* Kellen inclined his wing, creating a slope for Noella to crawl up. He felt her scale his back, mounting the trenches by using the spikes as leverage in her ascension. She settled into the correct form, gripping two of his thorns and squeezing her thighs around the muscles in his upper back. The groan that loosed off his tongue was either him or Coz. *You ready, my love?*

*I'm ready,* she answered, giving his thorns a squeeze.

With a powerful beat of his wings, he launched them into the sky, leaving a trail of smoldering embers in his wake. They crashed through the forcefield, emerging on the other side of the illusion.

Kellen couldn't believe what his eyes witnessed.

Delmarth had become a brutal battlefield, a chaotic scene of blood and smoke and carnage, the grim and desolate landscape scarred by the ravages of war. Smoke swelled into the sky, obscuring the sun and casting a dark, melancholic shadow over the blood-bathed ground. The campus was besieged with figures cloaked head to toe in black—Dissidents—with a flood of Sireres streaming between them, their black armor and the kaleidoscopic shimmer suffused in their flesh differentiating them from the Primordials. The sound of Varmin-shifters, both Primordial and Sireres, tangling in the sky shook the ground with each explosive impact of their hefty bulks rear-ending with one another.

Mangled bodies lay strewn across the campus, so many of them young students that Kellen's heart recoiled in his chest, their lifeless eyes staring up at the sky in a soundless plea for mercy.

In the midst of the chaos, Kellen watched his students fight with desperate determination, their faces twisted in grimaces of pain and rage. The clashing of swords, the thunder of fire, and the screams of the wounded created a cacophony of sound that terrorized the solidity of the kingdom itself.

Delmarth.

His home.

His favorite place in the world, being reduced to rubble and bloodshed and a morbid graveyard.

Kellen's gaze swept to the now open gates of Delmarth.

What he found there almost caused him to lose his grip on their flight, nearly dropping both Coz and Noella to the ground.

*Coz? Kellen? What's wrong?* Noella squeaked when she felt them stumble.

The Dissident manning the gates, swathed in black, was a face he hadn't expected to see for another four years.

A face he'd hoped he'd never see again.

Ciaran Ates.

## CHAPTER 37

# ELLA

*THAT'S THE TWINS' father at the gates,* Kellen gasped.

*Their FATHER?!* Ella's human eyes couldn't distinctively characterize Ciaran's face, but from where they were suspended in the clouds, she could make out a small figure by the opulent gold gates of Delmarth—small because she was so high up, not that she wanted to remind herself of how elevated in the sky they were—wrapped in the garb of the Dissidents. *I thought he was in Terminus!*

*He's supposed to be,* Kellen snarled, his powerful body tensing beneath her.

*If he's here, then Miya is probably here too.* Fear soiled Ella's mouth. Adrenaline and desperation powered her limbs. *We need to find the twins. NOW.*

Ella tried not to make eye contact with the harrowing sight below, but her eyes kept sliding down to the devastation, her stomach twisting at every deceased child scattered across the campus, broken and lifeless, their blood staining the earth in dark pools. The metallic tang of blood and the acerbic stench of smoke sullied the air, a sickening combination that made Ella's head swim with dizziness. There would hopefully be time later to question how the Sireres broke through the wards protecting the school, how the prisoners in Terminus were released to join the Dissidents, why the fuck they were even attacking the school or how the Sireres had reached Delmarth from the other side of the kingdom, where Aros's army should have been blocking them. Right now, all her brain was capable of processing was that she needed to get Jarion and Laya to safety, latching onto this one task because taking in the totality of what was transpiring below her was too much.

As a human, she knew there was little she could do to protect *all* her students on that field, no matter how badly she wanted to. Focusing on the twins, on getting them far away from their parents, was something she felt capable of accomplishing.

Ella clutched Kellen's horns as he veered them to the right, her fingers white-knuckled around his bulky antlers. She relied on Coz and Kellen's heightened eyesight from above to survey the battleground in their search for Jarion and Laya. Beneath them, the Primordials fought the Sireres with unwavering courage, their battle cries blending with the roar of Varmin and the vociferous clash of steel. Everywhere she looked, there was destruction. Craters marred the once pristine landscape, buildings lay in ruins, and trees stood charred and blackened by fire. She watched students, young and old, throw themselves into battle, some running towards their enemies with reckless abandon, while others, primarily the youngest students, huddled behind whatever cover they could find.

It didn't hit her how much she'd grown to love Delmarth until she saw it reduced to vestiges. Until she saw the chests of children she'd grown to care for no longer moving. Ella had to cover her mouth to keep the sobs clogging her throat contained. Demoralizing grief threatened to crush her bones into powdered dust.

Seeing the Sireres next to the Primordials, it dawned on her how similar they really were, apart from the speckled, multicolored varnish dappling the flesh of the Sireres, an indicator that their powers were different in some fashion. She couldn't understand how these beings could inflict such pain and suffering on each other, on *children,* when seeing them side by side, it was so apparent how alike they were, if only they could overlook the conflict between their two kings to embrace that likeness.

*I found Laya,* Coz announced, dragging Ella's eyes back to the battlefield, where her gaze caught a flash of long black hair lunging at a Dissident, cheeks smeared in perspiration and dirt, but fortunately no blood.

*Lower me to the ground,* Ella directed both Coz and Kellen. *I'll pass her to you, then go find Jarion.*

*Noella—* Kellen started to argue, but she refused to let his disagreement escape into the universe.

*Do not* Noella *me right now, Kilic. We don't have time to argue this.*

*I am not leaving you down there defenseless, Rose,* he snarled, his clenched muscles vibrating beneath her.

*I can fight,* Ella asserted, then assured more gently, *I'll be fine, Kellen. All that matters is getting the two of them to safety. Let me do this. Please.* A mixture of Coz and Kellen rumbled an exasperated grumble, delineated by plumes of smoke.

*Fine,* Kellen spat before steering them downward and hurdling towards the battleground. Ella's braids slapped her cheeks, whipping the tusks she clung to so she wouldn't vault off Kellen's back.

Out of nowhere, a gargantuan phoenix crashed into Kellen's side and sent them tumbling into a cloud, the mist disintegrating from their immense volume. The phoenix's feathers were a brilliant mix of crimson, gold and orange, flickering like living flames, each feather dancing with its own inner fire. With each beat of its wings, embers and sparks scattered in its wake, its blazing plumage painting the air in hues of red and gold. The subtle glitter outlining the surface of its feathers alerted Ella that this was a Sireres who breathed a stream of flames at Kellen, its amber eyes glowing like molten gold, the air around them distorting from being touched by the heat of its flaring presence.

Kellen countered the phoenix's attack with a gust of icy breath that sizzled against the heat of his opponent. Their claws clashed and teeth gnashed as the two titans grappled each other, locked in a deadly dance of combat. Fire and ice collided in explosive bursts of fuming energy, creating dazzling displays of light and heat that ignited the ether like a raging inferno. The sky trembled from their massive forms, clouds splintering and evaporating under the force of their battle.

With one final, earth-shaking roar, Kellen unleashed a devastating blast of ice and engulfed the phoenix in a blinding flash of white light. As the smoke cleared and dissolved into the wind, only Kellen and Coz remained, the phoenix detonating in a savage explosion of crimson and smoldering ash.

*Where did that ice come from?!* Ella squeaked as Kellen directed them back towards the battlefield.

*There are many of my skills you have yet to see, sweetheart,* was all Kellen drawled before he alit on the ground and unfurled his wing for Ella to slide down, landing on her feet in the grass. She had a clear view of Laya from where they'd disembarked, still engaging a Sireres twice her size, though the twelve-year-old seemed to be holding her own, her sword drenched in violet flames. Ella took a single second to acknowledge her pride in Laya before she unsheathed her sword and sprinted across the field, winding between the various skirmishes. With the Sireres absorbed in combatting Laya, they didn't sense movement advancing from their left, providing them no time to react when Ella came barreling into their side and leapt on them. On the ground, her fingers fisted a handful of the Sireres' hair and yanked their head back so her sword could slice through the thick neck, sketching an angry, red line across the delicate throat. When the body slumped against her, their life dribbling out of the open wound, she let the limp carcass melt into the grass and rose to her feet.

"Your parents are here," Ella told Laya before she could say anything. Laya's eyes had never looked so big. "Go get on your brother's back over there. I'm going to find Jarion. Where did you last see him?"

"I...I lost him in...the crowd...he was..." Ella cupped Laya's cheeks when her voice fragmented into sobs.

"I'll find him," Ella swore, brushing a kiss on Laya's brow. "Go get on Kellen's back. Jare and I will be with you soon."

Laya didn't hesitate before dashing over to where Kellen—or Coz, it was hard for Ella to know who was doing what when Kellen was in his dragon form—snatched a Sireres off their feet and tossed the flailing body into his mouth, munching down on their bones before spitting the smashed limbs back onto the terrain. As Ella turned to go find Jarion, it suddenly occurred to her that she just killed someone.

*Fuck.*

She just killed someone.

Noella Rose. A girl who grew up in New York City in a one-bedroom apartment with a mother who never loved her and a big sister who swore her life to protect her, who'd chosen to dedicate her life to the protection of children, just took a life. Someone else's child. Someone who may have deserved it, who would have killed Laya if given the chance, but maybe they didn't. Maybe they were just like Ella and forced to fight for something that wasn't even their cause because the circumstances demanded it.

The sensation of horror annexing her body felt like a cold, clammy hand gripping her heart and squishing it into pounded clumps. Shudders thundered down her spine. Her sword released a strangled, clattered whimper as it jittered against her leg, her hand refusing the steady, her palms slick with cold sweat, goosebumps pimpling her flesh, struggling to control the rising panic close to overwhelming her.

*Ella?* a voice that normally didn't enter her head—Akio—croaked. *Ella, where are you? I see Kellen but not you.*

*I'm looking for Jarion,* Ella replied, his voice bringing her out of the distorted, twisted, nightmarish landscape of her dark and despairing thoughts. She didn't have time to focus on her fraying nerves or the guilt enveloping sharp talons around her heart. She needed to focus. *Did Jo find you?*

*Jo's with me. If I see Jarion, I'll let you know.*

*Thank you.* Ella gulped. *Take care of each other. Don't let anything happen to either of my best friends.*

She heard the love honing his words. *The same applies to you, Rosie.* His voice disappeared from her ears.

In the grip of battle, time seemed to slow to a crawl, each second stretching out like an eternity, resembling the feeling of being on the edge of a precipice, teetering on the brink of a yawning abyss. Ella scanned the smoke-crammed horizon, desperate to catch a glimpse of Jarion's familiar form. With every step she took, the ground beneath her quaked from Kellen following behind her, protecting her rear from anything attempting to harm her. Ella's hands were callused and bloodied, but she refused to look at them, refused to confront the evidence on her stained fingers that she'd been responsible for stealing someone's life, that the Sireres died at her hand, that their life was forever vanquished because of her. She did everything she could to ignore the pain of that truth and the exhaustion and fear that threatened to subjugate her limbs and liquefy her into the grass, focusing only on the single-minded goal of finding Jarion. She actively tried not to look down at the fallen students beleaguered at her feet, a grim reminder of the stakes at hand.

After what felt like hours of stepping over departed children in her search for Jarion, her cheeks caked in tears and blood, she finally found him. The air was ripped from her lungs when she saw who he was with.

Jarion stood at Ciaran Ates's side, his father's hand on the young Varmin's shoulder with a film of silver overriding Jarion's green eyes. Seeing Ciaran next to Jarion made her confront how many of her favorite physical features of Jarion's came from his father, like the volume of his curly black hair and the shape of his large, expressive eyes, though Ciaran's gaze lacked his sweetness. Jarion's wings were expanded behind him. He wasn't moving, didn't appear to be breathing as he flanked his father like an unresponsive statue, gauging his surroundings with no emotion.

*Kellen,* Ella gasped. *What's happening to him?*

*He's fucking with Jare's mind,* Kellen answered in a gravelly voice. *Ciaran has the power of Telekinesis. You see the silver in Jare's eyes? Jarion probably has no idea what's happening right now.*

*I need to get to him,* Ella declared, squeezing the hilt of her sword.

*Baby, you shouldn't approach him. In the state he's in, Jare could hurt you. Let me shift back and get him myself.*

*NO, KELLEN!* Both Kellen and Ella were stunned by the vigor of her plea. What overrode her senses now wasn't terror or horror —it was the rage of a mother whose child was in peril. *I'VE GOT THIS. You keep Laya up there with you and cover my back.* Kellen surprisingly didn't argue.

Before Ella could complete a step in Jarion's direction, Oliviana

Bryan dove into her path and sent a cascade of vines at Ella's face. Ella's reflexes kicked in fast enough that she deflected the attack with her sword slicing through the vines, the boughs wilting onto the ground. She took in the black shawl wrapped around Oliviana's shoulders, matching the fabric swathed around the other Dissidents, and coughed out a cold laugh that sounded nothing like her, raising her sword over her head.

"Not surprised in the slightest that you're a Dissident," Ella sneered.

"Not surprised in the slightest that you're a raging bitch," Oliviana snarled back, lunging at Ella.

Ella parried Oliviana's blow by whirling away from the knife's edge, then slammed the hilt of her sword into Oliviana's temple, thrusting her onto the ground. Oliviana's sword swung around and made contact with Ella's leg, wiggling the blade inside Ella's flesh to create a large, gaping gash. Ella bit her tongue through a yelp, then lifted her foot and jammed her heel into Oliviana's chin, propelling her backward and thus separating Oliviana's blade from Ella's calf muscle. From her peripheral vision, she caught Kellen engaging a Sireres dragon-shifter, their fire tangling between them.

Ella charged at Oliviana, undiluted rage bellying her deadly skill. Oliviana met every attack with fierce, wild strength, her strikes turbulent in their brute force and sloppy, whereas Ella's were precise and calculated, careful not to exert too much energy too fast, so as not to tire herself out. Oliviana threw everything at Ella all at once, and Ella let her, purposefully slowing herself down to give Oliviana the impression that she was fading, conserving her energy for when she started to see Oliviana's strikes falter, less power driving her forward, her limbs shaking. Ella monitored the distance between them in finding her opening, keeping close enough to reach Oliviana's sword, but not close enough to risk getting struck. At the first buckle of Oliviana's knees, she disarmed Oliviana by using her own sword to redirect Oliviana's weapon downward and moved in to grab the sword out of her hand, sending Oliviana's rapier clattering to the ground.

Ella grabbed Oliviana's arm when she tried to make a grab for

Ella's sword and rotated it in an upward arch, dislocating her shoulder. Oliviana fell to her knees in the grass with a strident cry.

"I don't want to kill you," Ella said, her eyes flitting between Oliviana and Jarion. "But I will if you don't promise that, when I let you go, you won't pounce on me again." Oliviana cackled through her tears.

"Your human heart is pathetic," Oliviana hissed, her smile bordered by encrusted blood. "Despite how badly I want to, Ella, and believe me, I *want* to, I never planned to kill you. You are the only person on this battlefield who our king told us to leave standing by the end of this assail."

Ella's brows furrowed together. "Your *king?*" she repeated.

"Edar Lantarian." Ella's hitched breath blocked her airway. Her blood froze in her veins and blanketed her bones in frost. Oliviana's sinister smile stretched up to her ears, accompanied by a deranged, delirious laugh.

"What does your king want with me?" Ella asked in a low voice.

"Don't think you're so special. He wants your heart outside your body. He just wants to be the one to do it."

Ella's gaze sharpened.

"Unfortunately for him," she growled, "he won't get the privilege." Ella shunted Oliviana into the grass and plunged her sword into Oliviana's shin to keep her down, then left her to her screaming puddle of blood and tears. She passed Akio on her way to Jarion and Ciaran, Josefyn encircled around his neck.

*I'll take care of her,* Akio promised Ella. *You don't need to shoulder her death.* Ella's eyes burned.

Ella could hear Oliviana's wretched weeps and hapless appeals for her life before a choked resonance cracked through the ether, followed by the thud of Oliviana's body hitting the earth.

The sound made Ella flinch, but she pressed onward.

Jarion's gaze swerved to her the moment she stepped into their vicinity, no humanity flickering back at her, no trace of the young boy she'd come to love as if he were her brother. Jarion, blinded by the order to protect his father, lunged on her, their entangled bodies bumping into the grass. Ella cushioned his fall, whereas her collision with the ground was harsh and painful, her back throbbing from the force of his weight, made bulkier by his wings being out. Jarion rocked his fist in her face, but she blocked him by catching his balled-up fingers. She wasn't fast enough to deflect his other fist before it blasted her cheekbone, her bone fracturing under the surface of her flesh, the sting reverberating through her whole body. Ella refused to fight him back, refused to land a single blow on the young dragon-shifter, simply matching his moves whenever she could and weathering the storm of his strength when she didn't move quick enough to parry.

She wouldn't hurt Jarion. Even if he killed her, she refused to lay a hand on him.

"Jare, it's me!" she cried, spluttering wheezes when his fingers swallowed her throat and crushed her windpipe. "JARE!" she yelled louder, tears undulating from her eyes. "JARE, IT'S ME! IT'S ELLA! *STOP!*"

Something strange happened when she bellowed that last word in vain.

What came out of her mouth wasn't a puff of condensed air, but a smog of silver wafting in the young boy's face, seeping into his pores and crawling through his veins to reach his head. A second later, the layer of silver overhauling his eyes deteriorated, replaced by their normal, sweet green color.

"Ella?" Jarion squeaked, looking down at his fingers wringing her neck in horror. "Ella, what is——"

"You're okay," Ella sobbed, stroking the side of his face. "You're okay, Jare."

"I hurt you." His face crumpled with tears. "I'm sorry. I'm so sorry." Jarion buried his face in the crook of her shoulder.

"I've got you," she whispered as she enveloped him in a tight, possessive hug, her eyes narrowed in a glower over Ciaran, her grip on the boy screaming *mine*. From the way Ciaran's upper lip curled in a snarl and he brandished his sword, Ella slowly eased Jarion off her and scrambled to stand, pulling him up with her. "Go to your brother," she commanded, settling into a fighting stance.

As Ciaran charged at Ella, Jarion hurried in the opposite direction and leapt through the air to land on the wing Kellen extended out for him to grab onto. Jarion chaotically swung his lanky body onto the wing before beginning his ascent up to reach where Laya sat on Kellen's back. Once Jarion was secure, Kellen reared his head back, eyes glowing with otherworldly intensity, and opened his jaw wide, revealing rows of razor-sharp teeth and a cavernous maw. He pinned his focus on Ciaran and unregulated a torrent of flames, which Ciaran dodged by crunching himself in a ball and rolling out of the way. He trundled right into Ella's legs and caused her to lose her balance, collapsing onto the ground beneath him. Kellen's flames clobbered the air above their heads, twirling and curling through the ether, devouring a Dissident who was engaging a student close by while missing the target of Ciaran, who now straddled Ella's waist.

"You think you can take my son away from me?" Ciaran snarled, wrapping Ella's braid around his hand and using it to bash her head into the ground. Black spots blemished Ella's vision. She twisted her head to the side and sunk her teeth into Ciaran's wrist. His hand retracted in surprise, giving her the perfect opening to whack her forehead into his and force him off her, punting him in the gut with her boot.

"He is not *yours*," she hissed, retrieving her blade from inside the stalks of grass. "You have never deserved that beautiful boy, or his beautiful sister. You lost the right to call them yours the moment you lay your hands on them." Ciaran came at her full force with unbridled brutality, but Ella sidestepped his attack and retaliated by thrusting the blunt edge of her sword's hilt into his face, finding the crackling noise that split through the air when his cheek fissured to be a satisfying sound.

Ciaran fell to his knees with a startled, callous laugh, stroking his fingers over the fractured bone.

"Do you not wonder how you're able to do this?" he asked her, rising to his feet. "How a little human is capable of breaking the bones of a Primordial? Has it not crossed your mind how strange that is?"

"Maybe I'm just better than you," she snarled, his own sword a lethal blur as he parried her attack with calculated ease. Ella dodged his counter-strike and wove herself around him to evade his next attack, placing her foot between his legs before prodding her heel straight into his dick. Ciaran doubled over with a garroted yelp.

From his position on his knees, he shoved his head into Ella's stomach and knocked her to the ground, thumping his fist into her chest in a cyclic sequence until he heard a snap from somewhere inside her. Gales of gasps heaved out of her throat, her ribs smashed, blood gliding down her chin.

Through her now foggy eyesight, tarnished by dangerous black spots encroaching on her vision and threatening to shadow the whole universe, she saw Kellen fighting his way to get to her, clawing through the scorched earth and devouring every Sireres and Dissident in his path, flinging them into his mouth and grinding them into milled dust, as if they were the candy he kept in his classroom.

*Kellen,* she mewled, her lips forming his name in a silent cry for help.

*I'm coming, baby,* he promised, though every time he tried to lunge forward, someone new obstructed his path, preventing him from reaching her in time. *I'm coming, sweetheart,* he rasped again, spirals of smoke spilling from the sides of his mouth.

With his love shining unashamed in his eyes, his menacing form had never looked more magnificent to her.

"I thought your king gave an order not to kill me," Ella spat out in a choked, unhinged laugh.

"Edar may have freed me from my prison, but I do not take orders from him. I am my own master." Ciaran seized her chin and clambered for his sword in the grass. "You are naïve, girl. You haven't been paying any attention to what's happening, and it'll be your naivety that kills you in the end."

Ella, in her vertiginous, wearied haze, saw an opening and took it, mustering all her strength to lurch her body upward and sink her teeth into the side of Ciaran's neck. His flesh tasted charbroiled from the residue of smoke smeared across his skin and like metal from the bitter flavor of blood. Ciaran shook on top of her, writhing to free himself from her entrapment, but she clamped down harder, keeping him restrained against her long enough for her fingers to reach her sword.

"And it'll be your hubris that kills you," she mumbled against his throat before she speared her sword through Ciaran's back, the tip of her blade peeking past his chest on the other side. His body floundered around the steel blade, fighting off the clutches of death, until finally, he folded over, whatever life remained pouring out of him, and buried her beneath his body weight.

*I did it,* she declared to Kellen, sinking into the pillow of grass beneath her head, giving in to the temptation to shut her eyes and drift far away from this gruesome wasteland that was once a school.

*Noella!* A male voice—Coz—hovered above her. *Noella, wake up!*

Ella opened her eyes when she felt hands slide under her back and wrench her into a standing position against her will. The hands were masculine, but smaller than Kellen's, less hardened, more innocent.

Jarion. It was Jarion holding her, Kellen looming above in dragon form.

"I want to sleep," she groaned, struggling to keep her eyes open now that she'd given them a taste of what it felt like to close. Jarion hugged her to his chest, keeping her from slipping back down to the ground like she wanted to.

"I've got *you* now," Jarion whispered, crying into her hair. "We're going to get you healed, Ella. Okay?"

"I just want to sleep," she repeated again, hoping someone would listen.

*You can sleep soon,* Kellen promised in a tear-soaked voice. *You've earned whatever the fuck you want, baby, from now until the end of time. You are a miracle. I'm so fucking proud of you.*

"Can you walk, or do you want me to carry you?" Jarion whispered.

"I…I can walk." She didn't add *I think,* though it tickled her tongue.

Jarion let her go slowly, making sure she was steady on her feet before he put distance between them. Kellen and Coz extended their wing on the terrain to create a hill for Ella and Jarion to climb up to his back. Ella let Jarion go first, needing a second to regain her equilibrium before attempting to mount Kellen.

Jarion was halfway up Kellen's wing when his eyes suddenly bugged out and he screamed, "MOM! NO!"

"Wha—"

Ella's breath perished on her tongue when a sword met the world on the other side of her chest.

CHAPTER 38

# KELLEN

WHEN MIYA KILIC's sword plunged into Noella's back, Kellen's world crumpled to ash at his feet.

Jarion and Laya were screaming Noella's name, but he couldn't hear them over the deafening buzz in his ears. Time came to a standstill, frozen in a perpetual state of anguish. The desperate heave of the wind matched the accelerated pace of his strangled breaths, every movement exaggerated, as if the universe itself was mourning with him. Miya hadn't even extracted her sword from Noella before Coz lunged, snatching her in his claws, and flung Kellen's mother's screaming frame into his mouth, taking great pleasure in the taste of her bones crunching between his teeth, the flavor of her blood one of sweet justice. Coz turned around from where he'd taken the helm of their body to reach a hand towards Kellen, offering him the reins back.

Kellen couldn't move, his limbs inoperable.

"Kell..." Noella tried to say his name, but what loosed instead was a damp gurgle, accompanied by a river of blood leaking off her tongue as she collapsed in the grass and rested her cheek on a cushion of soil.

"ELLA!" Laya sobbed.

Laya and Jarion crawled down Kellen's wing to get to Noella.

The twins knelt beside her, helping to roll her onto her side, debating whether or not to pull the sword out of her and choosing in the end to leave it.

Jarion shrieked, with a face smeared in tears and blood, "KELLEN! DO SOMETHING!" Kellen couldn't move.

He screamed at his body to move, to grab Coz's hand, to take back control, to go to her, but he was paralyzed by horror and heartbreak, the vehemence of his grief suffocating his ability to function.

*Now is not the time to shut down,* Coz told Kellen urgently. *She needs you, Kellen. We ALL need you to go to her. Tell her you love her. It's her only chance.* The last part piqued Kellen's interest enough for him to lift his head.

*Her only chance?* he repeated.

*Cavale's only chance,* Coz amended, stretching his hand out further. Somehow, Kellen found the strength to take Coz's hand.

His scales shimmered and twisted, morphing into smooth dark brown skin and sinew. His wings folded in on themselves, his claws retracting into hands and feet, gradually shrinking in size until Kellen was standing upright on two legs. Once back on his feet, Kellen tore through the field to reach Noella, falling to his knees with a gasp. He slid his hands under her skull and placed her head in his lap.

"Get Headmistress Dyer," he demanded the twins in a voice so unlike his own, so fragile, so dilapidated, the edges unraveling. "Get a mender. Get *someone*. Now." Jarion took off running into the clearing.

Laya refused to leave Noella's side.

"K...Kell..." Noella whimpered, her skin smirched by dripping gashes and ghastly bruises, but fuck, she was still the most beautiful thing he'd ever beheld in all his twenty-eight years in existence.

"I'm here, my love. I'm here." Her fingers found his in the grass.

"I need you...I need you to promise..." Her breaths grew more labored. "Promise me that you...that you'll take care of Freya. Please. I know...I know you don't...like her...but don't...don't give her up—"

"I would never," Kellen swore, then added with a sad smile, "And I don't hate her." Noella spluttered a pained laugh.

"You would…pick now on my death bed…to admit that." Kellen shook his head.

"This isn't your death bed, Rose. You're not dying. Jarion is getting help. He's sending a mender to us. You're going to be fine. You hear me? You're going to be FINE."

"Kell…Kellen." Her weak hand lifted to his cheek. Tears skidded down the sides of her face. "I wouldn't…" She mewled through a cough. "I wouldn't trade this time with you for anything in the world. I would endure all that torture from those first four weeks here over again if it meant I'd get to experience this happiness with you every time. I know in my heart….the reason I was sent here…was to find you. To have this time with you. To become yours, even for a short while."

"Stop talking to me like you're saying goodbye." Kellen's wheezes injured him. His whole body hurt from ravaged sobs. "You're not leaving me. You can't leave me. I can't live without you, do you understand? You're not allowed to leave me. You have my whole fucking heart, and if you die right now, you're taking it with you. You will take me with you. Do you understand what I'm saying?"

"Kellen…" Her eyes began to flutter shut.

"ELLA!" Laya yelled as she grabbed Noella's arm and dug her fingers into her soft, human flesh.

"NOELLA!" He shook her with desperation until she reopened her eyes back into the land of the living. "Don't you dare close your fucking eyes. Stay with me, baby. You can't leave me. You can't. I…"

The words finally came. How it had taken him this long to say them would forever haunt him.

"I love you." Noella choked on a mixture of a sob, a gasp, and a squeal, the tears flowing from her eyes at a faster pace. "I love you." The words grew comfortable on his tongue. He found the flavor of them satisfying. He kept saying them, over and over, began screaming them, scratching his throat. "I love you. I'm in love with you. I'm *so* in love with you. I've been in love with you forever. I love you with everything I am, Noella Rose, so you can't leave me, because I won't live without you. I won't."

"Kellen." Noella pulled his face down, brushing her lips against his, and whispered into their kiss, "I love you so much."

The moment those words left her tongue, a surge of energy began coursing through Kellen's veins, walloping him in the chest and knocking the wind out of him, the potent force igniting a wildfire within his soul that made breathing nearly impossible with no space in his lungs for oxygen. His muscles contracted, responding to an unseen command as the power within him swelled and grew, filling every fiber of his being with pulsating strength. A piece of his heart snapped back into a place, a piece that had been dangling off the side, waiting to be reunited with his soul. Golden light splashed over his brown flesh, radiating out from his core to illuminate the earth around them. He watched that same light wash over Noella, their still interlaced fingers melting into one another through the inundation of light, becoming one being rather than two separate entities.

"What's happening?" Laya squeaked. "What is that light?"

"It's our mating bond," Kellen replied, then began laughing hysterically, unable to stop the flow of cackles, smiling amidst the downpour of tears. Every suspicion he'd had about their mind connection was confirmed through that light, through the power binding their souls together.

This stunning, courageous human who'd fought for his kingdom and school, for his sister and brother, and fucking *won*, was not just the love of his life and the proprietor of his being. She was his destined complement, the other half of his soul, not just symbolically anymore, but literally.

Noella Rose.

His love.

His mate.

His Cavalisha.

Kellen couldn't rejoice at this feeling flooding through him because the very thing fueling his body, the very thing that would forever connect him to the woman he loved, was the very thing killing her now, the force of the bond settling into place too much for her to bear. Where Kellen laughed at the extreme influx of power, Noella *screamed*, thrashing in the grass, clawing at her weak chest in an effort to tunnel through her skin and reach inside her to yank this feeling out, her body vibrating.

Not just gilded light emitted from Noella's pores.

An outlandish outpouring of silver, frothing energy discharged from her open mouth, tangling with her screams, creating spirals of glittering mist in the ether that hung all around them like festooned ornaments. Kellen didn't understand where that power was coming from and why it was channeling through her, its configuration unrecognizable, beyond anything he'd ever seen before.

Noella vomited a river of that silver fog, clouding the atmosphere in sultry vapor that made his knees buckle. If Kellen was standing, he would have felt inclined to bow to that mist, something undeniably regal and demanding about the power, the feel of it in the air ancient and reeking of authority.

As the sky blackened and clouds swirled, a brilliant light shattered through the darkness overhead, bathing the destruction below in resplendent warmth. From the heart of the light emerged a figure, shimmering with unearthly splendor. Cascading waves of blonde hair caught the dimming sunlight, vacuuming the light into the soft tendrils and reflecting it back onto the earth despite the shadows congregating in ominous clusters around them. The figure descended from the heavens with imperial grace, each step leaving a trail of iridescent stardust in their wake. As the figure drew nearer to the ground, their features began sharpening, becoming more distinguishable—chiseled jawline, high cheekbones, eyes a piercing, ocher yellow, all fused together to create a commanding presence exuding regality, the universe drowning in their aura. Their skin glowed a golden hue, crafted from the light of the sun itself, and effervescent, divine energy gathered around their shoulders like a coronet of power, spilling down their back to create a seething cape.

When the figure landed on the earth a few feet away, Kellen found his body folding over in a curtsy against his will, his own power responding to the luster of theirs. Coz stirred in his chest, shrinking in response to the strong influence. Only one name registered in Kellen's head and heart.

Aros Cavalian.

The Sireres and Dissidents still left standing immediately disengaged from battling the Primordials and retreated from the campus at Aros's arrival. Aros refused to grant them escape and sent his power sweeping across the field to latch onto the insurgents, cremating them into ash the moment the gilded light smothered their limbs. Once every Sireres and Dissident crumpled in the grass and all that remained were the Primordials, Aros's eyes passed over the boneyard of deceased children, his shoulders shaking from the fervor of his wrath. His gaze eventually landed on Noella and stayed with her. The oxygen in his lungs coughed out in a horrified gasp at the sight of her withered on the ground, her head lolling in Kellen's lap, chin sopping blood.

Noella turned her head to the side, her eyes squinting before she spluttered out in a weak voice, "Dad?"

"DAD?" Kellen gasped, whipping his head to Aros.

Seeing their similarities, the honey-golden hair, the bone structure, suddenly everything about Noella that hadn't made sense to Kellen clicked into place in his head, completing the strange puzzle. Her ethereal beauty. How easily she'd mastered fighting techniques. Her ability to keep up with the Primordials and land blows that were equal to their own vigor. Why Aros had even allowed her into his kingdom when he'd been so adamant for a thousand years that humans weren't welcome in Cavale.

Because the woman in Kellen's lap, to whom his heart was forever tied, wasn't human at all.

Aros smiled down at Noella, then said, in a voice that sounded like velvet, "Hello, my beauty. It's been a long time. Thank you for freeing me." His eyes then dropped to the sword still speared through her chest. He looked murderously at Kellen, as though it was *he* who'd plunged that sword into her and not his mother. "Whose idea was it to leave that blade inside my daughter?"

"If we pull it out, it will kill her," Kellen growled, his love for his Cavalisha outweighing his devotion to his king, decorum lost to the wind of his grief.

"Take it out of her right now before I decide I don't care that you're her mate and I incinerate you too."

Kellen grabbed the hilt of the sword and slid it out of her chest. Noella's body spasmed, blood spewing off her tongue and snarling with a baying moan. Aros knelt on the grass on the other side of her, then cupped his hand over the open wound, hampering the flow of crimson liquid from leaking out of her chest. As her frail form trembled, he closed his eyes and began to focus the power residing within him on Noella, funneling it into her. Warm, golden light radiated from his hands, enveloping Noella in a tender embrace. Aros's light eddied around her, tracing gilded patterns on her flesh that sought out the source of her pain and worked to restore what had been broken, her chest heaving upward with the mending of her shattered ribs. When the light intensified, Noella's features relaxed, resigning to Aros's powers and soaking up the healing energy, her wounds beginning to suture shut. The suffering slowly melted away under the gentle touch of her father's power.

"Take it all, my beauty," Aros cooed to her. "I give you everything I have and more, Noella Rose Cavalian." Kellen gasped at hearing his mate's name—her true name—pierce the universe.

Laya sagged against Kellen and wept into his shoulder. Kellen squeezed her hand, unable to take his eyes off his Cavalisha and the warm flush being refurbished in her cheeks. Aros' light began to fade, his hands sliding off her chest and falling to his sides. Noella's body drooped against Kellen.

"Noella?" Kellen croaked, shaking her. She wouldn't open her eyes. "Noella?! Why isn't she opening her eyes?!"

"She's asleep," Aros told him, raising a hand both with reassurance and also as a silent signal for Kellen to simmer down. "Her body isn't used to being brimmed with power. It's been suppressed for so long. She needs to rest now."

"Are you going to tell us what the fuck is going on?" Kellen regretted phrasing the question that way when Aros's eyes became sharp slits, reminiscent of the pointed edge of a blade.

"Try that again," Aros hissed. Kellen gulped.

"Are you going to explain how all of this is possible?" Aros bobbed his head in acceptance of that rewording.

"Not here." The King of the Gods stretched over Noella and

grabbed Kellen's arm, then looked over at Laya. "Mind if I borrow your brother for a little?"

Aros didn't wait for Laya to respond before his power encircled Kellen and they vanished from Delmarth.

Pain soaked Ella's dream.

It started as a dull ache, a subtle throbbing in her core where Miya's sword had impaled her, gradually gaining strength. With every breath that tried to pass into her lungs and expel out of her mouth, the pain flared up like a rupture of fire, shooting through her nerves the way lightning bolts fissure the sky. Between the pain, she was aware of something augmenting inside her, something large and warm and teeming with energy, hidden within the chambers of her heart and breaking free from restraints, swamping her veins in that formidable deluge. Her muscles protested at the intense invasion, screaming for reprieve, but the energy refused to relinquish its hold on her, nestling beneath her bones and crafting a permanent home for itself there. It felt like her body was betraying her, every ache and twinge a cruel reminder of its fragility, hissing at her that her human container had been a feeble host.

The pain told her that the overwhelming infiltration was punishment for years of keeping this power hindered inside her.

None of it made sense. She'd have a thought, develop a theory about what this feeling could be, and lose it amidst another undulation of agony. She thought she saw stars. She thought she saw her father.

She ached for Kellen.

Her mate. Her Cavalisha. That much, she'd been able to comprehend through the jumbled fog clouding her ability to form coherent thoughts and keep them. She felt her heart bind to his, could feel his power etching his name into her soul now, even through the pain, claiming possession of the rest of her life.

544

*Noella,* that older female voice she'd heard time and time again whispered inside the fog. *Wake up.*

*I don't want to,* she groaned, beckoning sleep to return to her. *Everything hurts.*

*Your Cavalisha is waiting for you,* the female responded. *It's time, sweet girl. No more hiding. Rise.*

Ella's eyes fluttered open on command.

She discovered herself lying in a bed in an opulent bedroom. Crimson and gold adorned the rich, ornate wallpaper, replicating the warm ruddiness of the crystal chandelier hanging from the ceiling, tossing the soft, lambent light across the room. She looked down to see herself splayed out on top of a plush, velvet canopy bed, dominating the center of the room, its towering pillars draped in layers of silk and satin, stained hues of deep purple and red. The bedding was a masterwork of embroidery and delicate lace, the cloud-like embrace it offered impossible not to sink into. Gold-plated mirrors lined the walls, and a marble fireplace crackled and popped in the corner, bathing everything in its close vicinity in glorious heat. The rest of the furniture was a mixture of antiquated and modern pieces, with a mahogany writing desk, decked in a collection of silver inkwells and quill pens, and a scarlet chaise lounging beside it, its cushions plump and inviting.

Her eyes fell down to her body. The leather jumpsuit that had garbed her in battle was replaced now by an indigo robe, lined with gold string and padded on the inside with fur. Her flesh had been scrubbed clean of any splotches of blood and appeared unmarked, sluiced of scrapes and bruises, no trace of battle lingering on her skin. Her braids were undone, crimped blonde hair pouring down her chest.

Ella turned her head—a great achievement with how heavy it felt—and found Kellen drowsing beside her, half seated in a chair he'd dragged next to the bed and half lying on the bed with her, her hand trapped between his with his cheek slumbering on top of their stacked fingers. The black tunic he wore, delineated in swirls of gold similar to the needlework on her robe, clung to his burly figure.

The moment her eyes found him, everything that happened at Delmarth came crashing down on her shoulders.

Sword Hunt. Daniel attacking her. Kellen killing Daniel. Connor's death. The many faces of the now-deceased kids flashing before her eyes. Ella slitting the throat of that Sireres. Jarion lunging on her. Ella's sword plunging through Ciaran's back. Miya's sword goring through her chest.

It was too much. All of it was too much.

She couldn't hold the memories inside her. The space they took up in her head stung. Her eyes felt scorched by grief.

"Kellen?" Ella moaned, flexing her fingers between his hands. Kellen jolted awake at the sound of her voice and the subtle movement, grabbing her arm as though he needed to feel her to believe she was really awake.

"Noella!" he sobbed, his fingers crawling up her arms to trace her face, sweeping over her lips, which carved the shape of a kiss under his touch. "Fuck, I missed you so much. Don't ever fucking do that to me again."

"I'll try not to," she quipped, tears rolling down her cheeks. "How long have I been out for?"

"Only a couple of hours. I think. Time runs slower here. We could've been here for days and I wouldn't know."

Ella frowned. "Where are we?" Kellen swallowed.

"We're in Avatia. In Aros Cavalian's home." Ella's jaw fell open.

"*What?*" She had so many questions swimming through her mind, now that her mind seemed to be functioning again, but didn't know where to start, didn't know what was most important to focus on first.

"Does your head hurt?" Kellen asked when he noticed her forehead crease.

"A little," she admitted. He splayed his hand across her forehead and focused on sending wisps of his power into her skin, spreading a pleasant warmth across the aching membrane of her mind.

"Better?" he drawled with a smile when she hummed and sunk into the mattress.

"Much better." Her eyes returned to Kellen, taking in the exhaustion rippling through the wilted skin beneath his eyes and the swollen red rims surrounding the green hue, suggesting he'd spent hours by her bedside crying. She couldn't stomach the thought of him in pain. The bond inside her flamed wildly at the mere thought, rampant with rage at considering how her actions might have caused harm to the other half of their soul. She said the only thing she thought might alleviate that pain, giving life to their connection. "Hello, my mate." Kellen dissolved into tears instantly.

"Hello, my beautiful Cavalisha." He leaned over her to peck her lips gently, undertaking her fragile state despite how much she craved for him to bruise her lips with a kiss. "How're you feeling?"

"I feel…" She didn't know how to put it into words. She knew she was awake, but her body felt like it was still submerged in slumber. "My body feels strange. My blood, it feels…like it's—"

"Buzzing?" Kellen interrupted, supplying the word she couldn't quite locate.

"Yes. And my skin…" Ella pinched the flesh on her arm, then her cheek. "My skin….it feels—"

"Rubbery?" he offered again.

"*Yes!* Like it might peel off." Ella's heartbeat pounded in her ears. "Kellen, what's going on?"

Kellen exhaled a heavy sigh. "What do you remember from before you passed out?"

"Your mother stabbed me. I almost died. Or, maybe I did die. I thought…it's going to sound crazy, but I think I saw…my father." Kellen stiffened. She watched his throat wobble along with his gulp.

"You did see your father," he confirmed, bringing her hand to his lips and kissing her knuckles. Against the back of her hand, he said gently, "Your father is Aros Cavalian, King of the Cavalian Gods."

Ella blinked.

All she could remember how to do was blink. "No," she refuted. "My father's name is Alecsandar Rose."

"That was the name he went by on the Earthly Plane, but no. Your father is Aros Cavalian."

"That…that's…" Ella spat out a panicked, hysterical laugh. "You're fucking nuts, Kilic. You're nuts! No! No fucking way! My father is Alec Rose! My father is a *human!*"

"Your father is not human, Noella, and neither are you." Ella's breath depleted from her chest.

"What did you just say?" Kellen spoke his next words with careful consideration of her current state.

"You are not a human, Noella Rose Cavalian." Her heartbeat spiked at hearing *Cavalian* tacked on to the end of her name. "You never were. You're a Primordial."

**_To be continued..._**

# ACKNOWLEDGMENTS

I started writing Bleeding Rose during my last semester of graduate school. I wanted to take what I was learning about being a school counselor, the impact this role can have on children, and what I've learned in my own mental health journey, and channel it into something that could be entertaining and informative and inspiring. Noella developed into a real hero of mine. She became someone I worked to embody at my internship sites. She taught me how to advocate for myself and my students, to not be afraid to speak up, for my voice is necessary and my opinions matter. My confidence as a school counselor grew during the time I created her. For that, she will always hold the most special place in my heart, as will this entire book.

Molly Ahearn and Azala Press—the best publisher a girl could ever ask for. I've thanked you a million times and will continue to thank you forever. You are the most supportive publisher who has gone above and beyond for me and my book. Cheers to a long and prospering partnership together.

Ioana Cheldiu, my editor—thank you for checking my verbage for me and genuinely making this book so much better than it was before you stepped in.

Robin Adelson (aka. Mom)—the first editor. The first editor on all my books. I cannot begin to express to you how much that means to me, that with every book I write, you're the first person to read it. I'm so lucky to have you as a mom.

For my Alex, my tooie. The best beta reader. I hope you always see yourself in Noella, because you're just as strong and just as powerful as she is. I love you.

Elie—my honey. Thank you for being such an amazing big sister. You inspired Rylee.

Dad, Laura, and Juliet—thank you for always supporting me and loving me. Juju, I promise I'll let you read the book when you're older. For now, if you want to draw on the pages, you go for it. What's mine will always be yours.

Tippi- my baby girl. My favorite dog in the world. Freya is you through and through. I honor you with everything I do, angel. Mommy loves you so much.

Emily Bentinck-Smith—my first school counselor. Thank you for saving my life.

For all the school counselors of the world—this job is so important. Schools couldn't run without us. We wear so many different hats during the day that sometimes it's hard to keep track. Sometimes it's hard to remember that we have feelings too when we're so deeply immersed in our students' lives, but I'm here to tell you that your feelings matter. You are essential to these kids. You are real life superheroes. Thank you, and all educators, for your service.

If you're new here, I always acknowledge my younger selves at the end of my acknowledgments. In the Until the Last Drop duology, I wrote to seven year old Ky and seventeen year old Ky. For Bleeding Rose, I'm writing to twenty-three year old Ky. The one who changed the course of our life.

Before her, I always thought I wanted to be an English teacher. I knew, in addition to being an author, I wanted to work with kids and in education, but to me, being an English teacher made the most sense, because of my love of books and writing. It was twenty-three year old Ky who discovered a different path—school counseling.

Really, it was my mother who found the program, so she gets the main credit, but twenty-three year old Ky, after getting ghosted by NYU's teaching program, made the choice to apply to Fordham. Apart from writing, I have never felt more certain that I was put on this earth for a purpose than being a school counselor and working to help students the way my school counselor in high school saved me. So it's only fitting that I thank you, twenty-three year old Ky, for pursuing the path that led me to Fordham. Which led me to Noella and Kellen.

Past Ky, I'll forever be in your debt. Now let's go change the world together.